About the Author

Born in Alès, Gard Department, and raised mostly in nearby Toulouse, southern France, to Parisian father and Andalusian mother, Jacques Carrié ventured into the Amazon Rainforest (Venezuelan side) early in his teenage years before traveling to New York a decade later, this time seeking city life. He then flew to the Deep South and earned a BSEE from Texas A&M University. While there, an article he wrote for *The Texas A&M Engineer* was voted "Best of the Year." Back in New York, he took some literature and creative writing classes at Columbia University. Then he drove to Hollywood, where he drifted into Method Acting (trained by Lee Strasberg and Peggy Feury). This led to seven exciting years of stage performances here and abroad. In time he married a recording artist from the Philippines and established himself as a software technical writer with several major Los Angeles companies while churning out short stories of speculative fiction on the side. Such were the days...

Looking back today, he applauds his strange seduction toward fiction writing, which quickly escalated to groundbreaking postmodern crossover literary fiction, heavy on suspense, fantasy, sociological science fiction, psychological dystopias, and black-humored social satire, dealing mostly with anti-heroes, playful surrealism, hysterical realism, and the theater of the absurd. Not an easy mix, he nevertheless persisted in his obsession.

"Being an Indie writer," Carrié declares with confidence, "is one of the most exciting things in the world. Also one of the most difficult, especially when it comes to getting some recognition. There's always that 'Berlin wall' planted in front of you by the Establishment." He drinks some juice from a chopped young green coconut, the only warm liquid other than water he likes, reflecting on his life. "I've moved around a lot since childhood (one wrecked by Fascism, Nazism, and Communism—the three evils of the time)...across many countries, cities and villages, either hitchhiking or driving fast cars, if not flying third class or taking a slow train for a change...in search of non-political, non-ideological adventure and culture, only to plunge again into a world of tyranny and terror. You can imagine the hordes of people I've met along the way...all races and persuasions...some pretty darn famous or influential (including *belles lettres* and fine arts practitioners), mostly everyday hard-working people.

"They all read my stuff, mailed to them in big brown envelopes or handed out over a coffee table." His eyes follow the zigzag motion of a mosquito. "What they thought and wrote about my work is gold to me, and I will not hide it from you (prospect readers)...only the *quotation marks* holding those thoughts and the *names* of such cool individuals willing to make a difference...for it'd take me forever to reconnect with them to secure what publishers call 'proof of their permissions to quote them,' having long ago lost all traces of their whereabouts, except for the most recent one. Simply follow my harmless general code: F (Famous person), VI (Very Influential), and I (Influential) to enjoy the ride."

Current work (big novel):
Thank you again for letting me consider OCTIBLAST. It's wildly original and smart and fast and unlike anything I've ever read before. – VI (editor, major publishing house), New York

Previous works (collected short stories and slim novel—both soon to reappear on the scene in new editions as largely revised, expanded or restructured, and retitled e-books):
These are startling fictions! Wacky, off-base, yet appealing in an almost narcotic way—Carrié makes a whole new world which is very inviting and—here's the miracle—which is contextually convincing at the very same time the reader knows it is all made up. – VI (national book critic), Iowa

Unusual, iconoclastic, challenging and off-beat. Thank goodness there are individual thinkers like Jacques Carrié still alive and working in this hackneyed world of pablum-spiked mediocrity. – F (national book critic), New York

[Slim Novel] out-Kosinski's even Jerzy Kosinski. Carrié knows the signs and symbols of our culture as only a master satirist can. If you liked PASSION PLAY, you'll love [Slim Novel]. – VI (major book critic), New York

[Slim Novel] *A cross between THE DAY OF THE LOCUST and HOLLYWOOD BABYLON. Any writer can detect and admire the complex verbal energy of Carrié's presentation.* – F, New York

A captivating style and an original voice. – I, New York

These writings are very competent and so enjoyable to read. – I, California

One can only be impressed by Carrié's continually exploding imagination combined with flashes of sensitivity and insight. – I, Illinois

Carrié's writing is gorgeous—lush and interesting. Good energy! – I, New Mexico

Very strong in its complexity and richness of imagery. – VI, Wisconsin

Fun and wacky. – I, Washington, D.C.

I must admit my careful devotion to Carrié's material. There is so much to his stories to be enchanted by. – VI, New York

Superior science fiction and fantasy. Much more believable and intelligent than most of the science fiction and fantasy I read. – I, Connecticut

Entertaining and sensual. – I, Michigan

I feel Carrié has a strong talent (one of the most vigorous I've come across)…and his devotion to language as its own entity is remarkable. – F (major book critic), California

I truly enjoyed Carrié's stories. Satire is doubtless the plaything of the gods…so they're on his side. – I, Illinois

Absolutely wild! The parody is so terrific. . .I think a science fiction editor would gag with laughter or choke to death in their reading. – I, California

This is intriguing. Keep the satire aflame! – I, Ohio

Carrié writes with style and is an original. – I, New York

Striking situations and many strong images that will stay with me. – VI, Kansas

Those are great stories, and I read them a couple of times to savor them. – I, California

Lively stories. We believe that this volume should have a ready market as an original mass market paperback. – VI (noted publishing house), New Jersey

There's great wit and style contained in these stories. – I, Illinois

I admire Carrié's energy and wish him luck—keep after us all! – F (novelist), Arizona

Very inventive and interesting. Exhibits throughout instances of fine writing. We were impressed. –VI, Washington

I get so much dull, dead, depressing stuff, it's good to get some good funny stories. I like the effect Carrié got with the difference between the straight-laced Spanish and the English gloss, which had me in stitches. – VI, New Jersey

I suspect it will be a very necessary book [Collected Short Stories], for the very reason of its title: in an age when we suspect the farthest reaches of imagination have been exhausted, or –even worse—when people would rather not imagine (preferring to sink back into a more comfortable quotidian), Carrié's fiction proves that there is still something fresh and new to think about. These are amazing fictions! – VI(major book critic), Iowa

[Directly to Carrié, guest writer, and his translator, at a televised press conference, during the International Festival of Humor and Satire]...I am impressed by your involvement in noble causes here in Bulgaria and in the world, your courage and graceful charm as both a writer and a person [nominated and competing for the major prize with Slim Novel]. I'm personally inviting you to my home by the Black Sea in Russia...and to Moscow where I'll introduce you to my audience, colleagues and publishers. – F (novelist, grand prize winner), Gabrovo, Bulgaria

Vonnegut, Tiptree, Woody Allen and Harlan Ellison–Carrié is very close to the work of those four. – F (science fiction novelist), Arizona

A triumph. Truly innovative and funny. Without any doubt [Slim Novel] should become here in Venezuela both a literary and bookstore success for its phenomenal stylistic and conceptual projections. It must be read! – VI (national book critic), Caracas, Venezuela

A Mel Brooks type charm. – VI, New York

I have not been able to read a book in the last year, thanks to politics. But if I were to read a book, I'd read anything by Jacques Carrié. – F (novelist, then running for the U.S. Senate), California

I hope it sells a million copies! – VI (editor, national science fiction magazine), New York

Coming soon...

PAPELITOS (Slim Novel)

From the ghostly depths of the punitive New York's Actors Studio to the vomited passions of West Hollywood's unending follies to the most enraging aspects of East Caracas' coming of age, Method Acting, Peaceniking, and Bridge Religion keep a bizarre control on the lives of five genius characters...who soon will reunite...somewhere in the ultimate plan. One must laugh –harder and harder—to really feel the pain. And Jacques Carrié provides us with the perfect tools.

HARD CONTACTS (Collected Short Stories)

Wildly imaginative, hard-hitting allegorical fantasies by a master of these out-of-the-box goodies!

OCTISPIN (Book two of The Octidamned Trilogy)

While the Zoliseum's Directors plot against "time serving" octillion-aire Richard, each other, and the Lords of Zundo in the far future, under mythology-deity-Mipho's spying eyes, Gaston and his new girlfriend try to liberate Pierre from jail-infested revolutionaries in machete-swinging tyranny-ruled 1957 Caracas.

OCTIFATE (Book three of The Octidamned Trilogy)

Hollywood-struggling Indie filmmakers Gaston and Nikki learn the hard way to outwit one of America's most heinous serial killers, among other street roaming thugs, and straighten their fragile relationship during the turbulent 70s while Zundo-based Richard in the far future succeeds in finding both freedom from greed and the right soul mate via inter-millennium correspondence and dating no longer trapped in Gaston's 13th punishing reincarnation.

THE FRENCH VOLUNTEER (Epic war novel based on the author's father's true story)

Awaiting next morning's quick execution by a Republican firing squad for punching a non-Nazi German commander in the face between the battles of Brunete and Belchite during the raging Spanish Civil War (1936-1939), French volunteer Robert Dassin (now Lieutenant) reminisces about his exhaustive contribution to this war and to the broader anti-Fascist cause in Spain as a rising figure in the famous International Brigades and administrator of the also famous Benicàssim Medical Center, which served over 10,000 war people, including 8,500 wounded soldiers, large distinguished staff of doctors and nurses (one of them his newly wedded and pregnant wife), and many luminary guests such as Hemingway, Malraux, Dos Passos, and Carpentier.

OCTIBLAST

Book one of the
OCTIDAMNED TRILOGY

Jacques Carrié

Charleston, South Carolina

Octiblast

Book one of the Octidamned Trilogy

ISBN-13: 978-1463712532
ISBN-10: 1463712537

Library of Congress Control Number: 2011912225

CreateSpace is the imprint of record

Printed in the United States of America by:

CreateSpace
7290 B. Investment Drive
Charleston, SC 29418

First Edition: April 2012

*To my enchanting wife
Eva and fabulous daughter
Manon—my closest links
to reality, love, and joy.*

CONTENTS

BOOK 5: THE CULMINATION OF PUNISHMENT

PROLOGUE

Amboseli National Park, Kenya, February 1982

"No wonder my finger feels lighter," remarked Gaston with chagrin. "I lost my ring."

"Your ring?" Nikki seemed disturbed. "How could this happen?" All kinds of negative thoughts crossed her mind. "Maybe because you're so skinny lately—face, body, fingers. You just don't eat anymore."

Gaston ignored her. *She's really in a cranky mood today. The dry landscape, the scorching sun, the fucking mosquitoes–they all seem to piss her off.*

"Maybe it's meant to be." Nikki reconsidered.

Facing them trudged the big ones, their heavy feet brutally pounding the arid soil.

Leading the way, marched a massive gray wall of flesh and bones covered with folds of stone-hard skin baked and dried by the rough calmness of time. "Ushhh, ushhh, ushhh, ushhh."

Majestically, it crossed the vast plain in front of snow-capped Mount Kilimanjaro, this one rising ever higher, through a wide disk of silvery clouds, into the opulent blue sky above, some thirty miles away from where they stood in Kenya, near the Tanzanian border.

Neatly painted cursive words in green, turning to meaningful sentences, still fresh and quite readable to Gaston, covered one side of its voluminous body–the one, wrinkle-free, facing him.

> Zundo the Conspirator—a born-again barbarian—conquered the world at the turn of the fourth millennium. California was the last stronghold anywhere on earth to surrender to the Zongdrolls, Zundo's terrifying warriors.

read Gaston loud enough for Nikki to hear. She stood near, aware of the march of the elephants, but looking away now, rehearsing her lines.

Fucking eerie, thought Gaston in distress. *The ring didn't just slip off my bony finger. Something else intervened. Maybe during my sleep...or reverie....*

A second, robust, large elephant followed, also garbed with painted words that seemed to continue the reading. Two enormous grayish ears swayed like wind-whipped rugs, so did the latigo-flexible tail at the end of the animal's body.

> Soon the entire globe was renamed Zundo in honor of this great conqueror and elections were held across the nation to procure a dignifying substitute, which turned out to be not one but three popular teenagers, self-named Z1, Z2, and Z3. Or, as a team, the 3Zs.

❧

A much shorter and younger elephant marched behind the large matriarch, still in his juvenile frailty, his elongated, sensitive trunk-tip nearly brushing the ground. His body was also tinted across with green cursive words.

> Three weeks before he committed suicide, Zundo the Conspirator betrayed the Zongdrolls by diluting them into the system like simple citizens, without any reference to their glorious battle cries.

Clearly, a message was being transmitted.

> No medals for heroic barbarism or slithering cruelty. No mention of their creepy Z-day invasion in history books. Nothing like that.

continued the story on another Savannah elephant of medium corpulence, marching behind, his imposing white tusks shining under the sunlight.

Gaston watched the parade from the top of a nearby hill where his small crew of hopefuls had camped out. "History has a way of writing itself...even in this most unlikely way," he remarked to the group, zooming in closer with his Arriflex 35-B14 camera.

"It's a beautiful procession," said Nikki, now casting a fuller, steadier glance, leaning against a sturdy acacia tree. "Can we afford this movie venture another month?" She brushed some red hair off her eyes with a tired hand.

"We should. Our producers are pretty imaginative investors."

"Not exactly major studio investors."

"Better."

"C'mon—be real."

Gaston's eyes now focused on the next marching elephant, a bit shorter, also wearing painted words.

> **On the day of his death, Zundo's final words—"let there be Zs all over the place, let's make it fun for the whole human race"—completed his conspiracy.**

Then, lifting up the tip of his French beret—which had annoyingly slipped over his eyebrows—with his free hand, he focused on the next elephant, of about the same size.

> **No one expected such foolishness from a departing warlord. A list of his z-spiced words (including wild ones, displaying the letter "z" anywhere in them) was posthumously found in his diary, with a note that such words would always provide the latest in meaning, version, form, and use.**

Turning to Nikki, Gaston whispered, "You're next."

"I'm not ready yet."

"How long until you're ready?"

"Four—five minutes."

More elephants followed.

> **His plan almost immediately rendered the world all-peaceful, instead of all-hostile, all-creative, instead of all-stereotyped.**

read one's painted words.

Even the mockingbirds hovering over his burial blessed this gesture in their own peculiar language. Not so the subversive elements...those with strange backgrounds and omnipotent ambitions.

read another's.

⁓

Herds of wildebeests, gazelles, and zebras crossed the blazing Savannah grassland in the backdrop. They traversed part of the rose-tinted formed horizon under nascent cumulus cottons a few hundred meters away past a dried-up, forsaken lake-bed. Not a mirage this time. Gaston's camera monitored their migration for a short engrossing moment.

"I'm confused." Nikki pointed to the latest changes on Gaston's script. "You want me to look a bit cynical here? Raise my voice?"

"Yes and no," said Gaston, relaxing his camera and arm. "It's a balancing act."

He himself wasn't sure.

Suddenly becoming an independent feature film director from the struggling reigns of a captivating spec script he recently wrote wasn't his idea—only a workable solution, among few, to get his story produced. And signing his talented, but inexperienced girlfriend as the star of his debuting project wasn't either a great idea, only his.

Together, however, they could rise to the limelight and become recognized professionally for their individual work—if everything went well, crew effort and budget planning included. Granted, they were optimistic amateurs in the field...naively trying to break in with a satirical fantasy film.

But a couple of days ago a strange event took place...with a force, thrust, and history behind it capable of changing his life forever. In effect, a most unusual letter had reached him in the mail naming him the sole inheritor of Monsieur Marcel Douvier's estate in Saint-Jean-du-Gard, southern France.

The letter was sent by Monsieur Douvier's lawyer as the famous archeologist had been deceased for nearly twenty-five years.

The subject was so creepy Gaston wasn't sure he should even mention it to Nikki. It required a lot of thinking, soul searching, and courage. Especially courage. *Not now,* he begged it off his mind again, as the issue kept coming back without relief. *Twenty-five years ago I was only nine, Juliette's boyfriend. An accidental and incidental tool in her Cathar-inspired sacred mission. A mission rooted in the Mary Magdalene faith, plagued by a series of incredible events and heinous crimes.*

Gaston's eyes moistened abruptly. They veered to the next elephant in line, about the same size as the previous three, also displaying verdant cursive written messages.

గ∽ు

A new elephant trudged the arid land in front of Gaston. Cursive words in fresh green ink marked the heavy skin of his body, like his predecessor's:

> So open trials of spectacular nature, reminiscent of the ancient Roman Empire's gladiator games, suddenly emerged...
> in defense and entertainment of this great nation...

Tears rolled down Gaston's cheeks, remembering. *Twenty-five years ago not only did I witness this terrifying 700-year-old horse-riding kite-flying journey across the Languedoc, but I also wholly participated in it with Juliette—its latest assigned rider. The Languedoc...that legendary land of powerful feudal lords, fighting knights, and performing troubadours. The same terre where chivalry flourished in near paradise settings and persecuted heretics perished by the whims and fancies of omnipotent Popes and succeeding Kings of France.*

Some elephants in the herd had been left behind, creating a large gap. The leading one in this strayed group, marching a little faster now to catch up with the others, displayed its batch of painted words,

> Spying societies from other planets quickly began to learn the following about Zundo's way of life—

"I wonder what?" mumbled Gaston to himself with a mix of deep sadness and cynical flair, capturing the moment with his rolling Arriflex.

Zundonians only do useful tasks. Zundonians are trilingual— English, Undo-English (abused English), and Peace-English. Zundonians only practice ZUECAP democracy.

"I can't do it," suddenly erupted Nikki. "Not until the last frigging elephant marches on! Why are you doing this to me, Gaston?"

"Sorry, I just got carried away."

Nikki wanted to bring up a bigger issue. "And this reverse Hollywood story of yours about a man's climb 'from riches to rags' doesn't quite bowl me over. It sounds like a downfall to me, not a climb."

Gaston replied, "No. It's a climb because it'll bring him happiness. Before he had *none*, when he was rich." His eyes followed the contour of her face, settling on the pale blueness of her irises. "The one thing he most wanted with his zillions, he couldn't have."

"What was that?"

"A woman who could love him for his personality, not his money."

Nikki reflected, then asked, "Why did you call him Richard?"

"For the obvious reasons, plus..."

"Plus what?"

"*Momentum* from dreams."

"What do you mean?"

"A guy named Richard has been appearing in my dreams, recurrent dreams."

"Recently?"

"No. For a long time now."

"Just that? A guy?"

"Super rich and powerful."

Nikki remained pensive, staring at the marching elephants for a lingering moment. She'd never told Gaston about her own secret. A long held uncanny secret. It involved another Richard, also rich and lonely. But absolutely out of this world. And no dream connection.

A year or so ago, already dating Gaston, she'd received a letter from this stranger telling her how much he loved her.

Nothing wrong with that, except that the letter had come from the future, hand-delivered by a mailman called "Mudge" apparently also from the future. Now, how could she ever break this to Gaston? Or anybody?

~○

The last elephant—as big as the one in front of him, but sporting a bizarre mop of fluffy blond hair on top of his head, large ears flapping mosquitoes away—entered now the focus field in Gaston's filming camera, showing what seemed to be the remaining painted words of the procession across his body:

Furthermore, breaking the Z-code happily revealed to these spying societies that ZUECAP meant "Zundo's Useful Energy Consumption and Production." A good thing.

Staring at a neutral object—the barren texture of a tent—Gaston said, a bit puzzled, "How did this weird-looking pachyderm ever make it to my movie?" He took a deep breath. "Oh well..."

Nikki interrupted, "ZUECAP? Sounds fucking terrible. Too stiff and academic."

Gaston stared at her. "Okay, I'll shorten it to 'ZCAP'. How's that?"

"Better."

~○

From a distance, away from the filming crew, a lounging lioness with thoughtful eyes watched the procession.

A used precision-spray-gun laced with fresh threads of spilling green paint, sat on the ground by her paws beside two badly chewed-up brown leather boots.

Next to it trashed about thirteen discarded cans of Zaspholto—a product used for flattening elephant wrinkles. They all bore the same manufacturing year "3081" in fine print, on a light-blue label perhaps too plain and faded to stir any attention.

Further down the hill a little red notebook, torn and dirty, lay face up. Its singing pages, ruffled by the evening breeze, revealed a list of familiar words, all adapted to the letter "z":

zachines

zlass

zloning

zoasis

techzut

zoliseum

mediazoop

zaptop

zobot

And so on.

BOOK 1

THE PILLARS OF PUNISHMENT

PART 1

TIME TRAVEL JOURNEY RETURN TO ZUNDO JUNE 3081

THE TRIAL OF THE MILLENNIUM

Bermuda Revelation Park
(in former Florida region), Zundo

Spectators made no effort to hide their excitement.

They glided ever faster in festivity over the rolling hills and surged, out of breath, through the screw pine, cedar, and palmetto trees encircling the six Bisected Stadiums contained in the partly submerged Zoliseum. This one justifying, even glorifying, in spectacular ways— as centerpiece gladiatorial arena—the existence of the 10-square-mile Bermuda Revelation Park housing it. More importantly, producing now, in universal scale, the so-called "Trial of the Millennium."

Throngs of people pushed their way deeper into the colossal structures through herculean gates, now open.

Soon they left behind a curious old metallic plaque attached to a small, quaint wall that read:

> **Home of one of the eeriest places on earth—the legendary Bermuda Triangle. Here, east of the Florida coast, inexplicable disappearances of certain planes, ships, and other wandering vehicles took place over a thousand years ago.**

Not exactly a comforting message, the old plaque further spooked the view by pointing to a chilling 20th-century sculpture, by a French artist, at the gates of the Zoliseum. Historically incorrect but comically worthy, it depicted the guillotine beheading of Adolph Hitler—a familiar, timeless name to all.

Up in the sky flashing its powerful ocean-analyzing cameras, wandered a news media zurbdog, doing an assigned aerial scouting.

The zurbdog roamed slowly over something that resembled a gigantic blue flower sparkled with mildly agitated ants.

Around the flower, six equally distant hills came into view.

Only that they weren't hills. They were the elevated brainy divisions of the Zoliseum—named, clockwise, Medics, Techs, News Media, Security, Judges, and Royal Den or commonly known as "the snoop boobs."

The zurbdog, an amphibious type flying submarine, veered to the left. Inside, a mediazoop, in her late twenties, wearing a dark brown outfit, touched a series of buttons while communicating with a second mediazoop two levels down the frame.

"See anything in the Zoliseum?" asked the first mediazoop, her voice dutifully strong and assertive.

"Yeah...the blue petals...the green donut in the middle...and the small red pancake in the donut's middle..." said the second mediazoop, ending with laughter. "Just kidding." Dimples cracked on both his cheeks, revealing his youth–a teenager. "I also see the approaching Celestial Sphere."

"Are you high or something?" said the mediazoop-woman, amused.

"Couldn't be higher," replied the mediazoop-teenboy, squeezing his voice to a provocative falsetto. "Now seriously, I see everything, including the snoop boobs."

"What else?"

"Some cruising ivory-white longtail birds and...ahhhh—"

"—ahhhh what?"

"We'd better move out of the way! The big thing's coming down on us like a falling meteor—RIGHT ABOVE YOU!"

Swiftly, the zurbdog pulled away, barely missing being hit.

Thrilled, both mediazoops watched how the big shiny Sphere decelerated and eased itself down deeper onto the jolly crowd of people, ever so slightly, without touching anyone. Its graceful tentacular limbs oozed a soothing eeehhhhh-uuuhhhhh, like the velvety vacuuming release of a late-model food distribution chopper propelled by zhydron-b technology.

The Sphere's computerized four-speed silver spinning surface, featuring digital and astral screens, split into top, middle, and bottom viewing areas. Local and world news, game scores, mini films, sexual images, and other displays of interest scrolled left to right with strikingly beautiful and varied flashing colors and sounds.

"Hey, zoop, any idea where Walking Brain is today?" said the mediazoop-teenboy.

"Noop. Heard he's at the Alternative History Palace, but that's one zoop's opinion," said the mediazoop-woman, talking through a chewable piece of zum she's just slipped into her mouth. "Why?"

"Need to talk to him."

"Bout wha?"

"Volunteerin'."

"Fo wha?"

"Time conduction."

"I wouldn'."

"Why?"

"Can't trust im," said the mediazoop-woman. "Plus you're only foteen."

"Regardless. I'm fucking tired of this job. Wanna try somethin' new up there."

"Wha if you never om back? Or om back with ix heads?"

"Ha ha ha. Better than six asses," laughed the mediazoop-teenboy.

"I'm serious," said the woman, spitting her zum.

"Might come back with six dicks in a parallel universe!" persisted the mediazoop-teenboy.

"Parallel hopes. Let's cut the shit and watch your language—we're on air now!" snapped the mediazoop-woman. "Well...almost."

༄

White longtail seabirds hovered around.

Sporting sharp black markings on their heads or wings, they had opinions of their own concerning the environment, what they saw or failed to see.

Joined by other coastal birds now, they simply greeted each other by winking their eyes or wobbling their heads.

"Fuck my language, but do they ever fly these *astro-dorks*? Never seen them rising over the horizon," said one of the longtails graced with a luminous orange-red bill, referring to the manned space travels believed to occur in this area.

"Ain't talking," said a shy but lovely cahow, native of Nonsuch Island in Castle Harbor. "They say, if you do, you never see the light of day again."

"That's probably crap too," remarked a white-eyed vireo, chewing at the same time a black spider with his hooked upper mandible.

"Not necessarily," said his companion, a yellow-throated vireo, staring jealously at his handsome gray-olive head. "I kind of agree with the cahow that just spoke. This piece of sky, like the forever-disappearing-into-the-ocean ground under it, I might add, is haunted… or worse."

"Worse?" gasped a gray tern, awkwardly dropping his prey into the vast ocean below.

"At least three strangers from the east have told me so," replied the yellow-throated vireo. "And I don't take that lightly."

"Neither do I," said a ring-billed gull, feeling the smooth stretch of his webbed feet contract a little. Turning to the longtail, who now glided beside him, he added, "You might not see them fly—those space dudes—but they *do* travel, and farther than you can ever imagine. I know that for a fact."

Skeptical, a black skimmer intervened, "Fact? Explain."

"Won't talk beyond what I said."

"Chicken," snapped a belligerent bird, wearing yellow-green spectacles around imposing big eyes, his white underparts and pinkish flanks gracefully showing.

"That won't make me talk either," replied the gull, calmly.

One of the longtails in the group, closing his broad white wings, soared majestically downward to sea with aiming flair and dove straight into his prey—a little squid. "…eeeeeech…"

"Can you see the process down there?" now asked the mediazoop-woman from her element.

"Yeah, clearly," said the teen-boy, activating a tiny red light above his head in the zurbdog.

The mediazoop-woman responded by pressing a button in the gadget implanted in her arm.

They were circling the Zoliseum several hundred feet above the ground.

"I'm ready," said the mediazoop-teenboy. Sounding truly professional, he began to broadcast, "The Celestial Sphere's coming down nicely, slowly, positioning itself in the middle on the Astral Floor, deeper into the six Bisected Stadiums over the cheering crowd's heads."

"Is it also spinning?" asked the mediazoop-woman, joining in the broadcast.

"Yes, it is…slowly."

"Is the Time Travel Chamber ready underneath?"

"Totally."

"Has the countdown begun?"

"Not yet."

"Any zurbdogs in sight?"

"No. We're the only one."

He noticed something.

"Hey! The countdown is just about to begin! In five seconds…"

THE HAPPENING

Five seconds seemed awfully short a moment.

Just enough for a doctor, judge, or techzut to occupy a reserved seat in his or her elevated snoop boob. Or for just anybody in the surrounding Stadiums to lock eyes with a passing stingray, dolphin, or seahorse.

But not long enough to fully appreciate the red, round, functional Astral Floor–Zoliseum's innermost entertainment center and showcasing marvel responsible for all cosmic projects, where everything happened...from simple carnival festivities to full-blown outer space blast-offs.

Within a split second, appearing and disappearing platforms, holding entire cinematic-like sets, would begin to unfold their strangest secrets amid more of those underwater creatures allowed by the transparent elastic zhoenix shield.

The Time Travel Set, one of Astral Floor's dazzling highlights, rose to the surface. On it rested the Time Travel Chamber–a large zlass-walled room furnished with just a mahogany armchair. (Zlass had become the super glass product of space explorations and one of Zundo's most used words.)

Floating around the zlass room, like a Hollywood studio movie camera, loomed a Zabroski Space Scanning Eyemax Model 55 funbox, popularly known as ZSSE-55. Eva Zabroski, its inventor, a British citizen, had mysteriously disappeared after a long professional working relationship with Dr. Ufahh, followed by a rumored short romantic affair.

"What do you think?" asked a passing hammerhead shark in his Caribbean dialect, noticing a lazy curiosity in his companion manta's eyes.

"Bahhh–same shit..." replied the manta, swimming away from what he understood to be a man aquarium of sorts. "Although..." he added, swiftly swimming back to the submerged Time Travel Chamber. "Looks like something gonna happen here...soon..."

"You think?"

They both continued their journey, heading north for the coral reefs.

Fitting the pulsating concave bulk of stadium-seated spectators with almost surgical precision in its softly ending descent, the Celestial Sphere now occupied this awesomely spacious, half-eggshell shaped, human-to-ground curvature–Zoliseum's deepest–virtually sitting on it like a warmed up and ready to incubate gargantuan hen, while majestically displaying on its rounded top screen panel, in this peaceful idling manner, the final countdown, starting with number 10.

Its bottom panel also displayed, in red-flashing scrolling fashion, the current status:

ONGOING EVENT: TRIAL OPENING AND PUNISHMENT TIME TRAVEL RETURN SHOW

Such was the ambiance for the trial's launching. Not just any trial, but "The Trial of the Millennium," according to the news media.

Stunning images of cosmic radiation in motion appeared on the Sphere's screen middle panel, followed by huge magnifications of real-time glimpses at time travel departures (to the left) and arrivals (to the right) to and from *The Unknown*.

The Unknown was different for every punished traveler. Today's Time Traveler's was about to be revealed.

"TESTING...TESTING..."

"MAY I HAVE YOUR ATTENTION PLEASE."

Speakers were warming up all around the Zoliseum.

Surrounding the imposing Celestial Sphere loomed the abrasive Bisected Stadiums, the extravagant Promenade Corridor, and the imposing Astral Floor–all three virtually holding hands into one gigantic throbbing bowl.

As usual, the six Bisected Stadiums were filled to capacity. Two camps of spectators prevailed: the super large and diverse crowd of boisterous, vindictive, and even violent regulars and the sharply cool, cordial, and well-kept transitory crowd from the adjacent Promenade Corridor.

Traditionally, the red-necks, skin-heads, and pop-culturalists didn't read or play the zachines (found in the Corridor) and, vice versa, the zintellectuals didn't eat popcorn or hot dogs (found in the Stadiums).

So each group to its own and zone, so to speak.

~

The Stadiums crowd—half a million strong—began to shout in unison, "**10!...9!...8!...7!...6!...5!...4!...**"

Every shouted number in the countdown lit up in bright orange in the Sphere's top area.

~

"CAN YOU HEAR THE NOISE?!" bellowed the mediazoop-teenboy above the crowd's shouts to the overhead-circling zurbdog's mediazoop-woman.

"FUCK YA!" she bellowed back, both her ears and brains frazzled by her partner's deafening shouts.

"WE'RE STILL ON AIR—YOU IDIOT!" bellowed back again the teenager, disrespectfully, realizing the harrowing situation.

The nerve! she thought. She could punch him in the face. *No way Walking Brain's gonna hire him. He's just a spoiled brat without any experience! Time conduction? Working up there in outer space? Won't even qualify! Plus the 3Zs might not approve. Well, maybe Z2.*

~

The crowd went on shouting, magnetized, "**3!...2!...1!...**"

Suddenly they all sprang to their feet, their eyes riveted to the glittering Sphere, where the amplified news-breaking close-up was about to happen—all shouting in unison, "**GOOOOOOOOOOOOO!**"

Hordes of people recharged their lungs. "**BRAVVVVOOOOO!**" they roared. "**AWWWWESSSOMMMME!**"

The Happening was as follows:

On the left screen of the Sphere's middle panel they all could see the time travel's departure from Bermuda Revelation Park, dated *December 15, 3081*, specifically a black-jacketed man in his thirties, identified as the Time Traveler, resting on a comfortable mahogany armchair inside a large zlass chamber somewhere on the Astral Floor.

No time travel vehicle here.

Only the top of his black-haired head was visible as he'd chosen to sink his chin into his chest during this sequence...for reasons unknown to anyone.

Near the tenth row in Stadium #3 a school of snappers drifted by.

One of them said to a fat and sleek moray who wandered near him, in their shared region fish dialect, "This is getting weird. Now why would that freaking time traveler hide his face, huh?"

"Secret stuff, my friend. Pay no attention. We've got better things to do down here in our deep and beautiful ocean than memorizing these fucking quantum-leaped places and dates out there. Follow me."

And they both vanished in the submerged Zoliseum's depths.

On the right screen of the Sphere's middle panel all Zundonians could simultaneously see the time traveler's final arrival to Bermuda Revelation Park, dated *June 11, 3081* (today), specifically the same man but frozen in action—running in terror—inside a zlass chamber, near a mahogany armchair.

No time travel vehicle here either.

He wore what appeared to be a Batman face mask, but, in reality, quickly recognized as a simple bat-eared hood and thick blue paint circling his eyes and mouth.

Exactly the same magnified scene was developing right now in the Zoliseum's Time Travel Chamber before everybody's eyes. Such Chamber, also made of zlass, had been empty a split second earlier. Now, of course, it had an occupant.

"This is worse than oil spills here." remarked a lobster in Bermuda undersea language, miserably crawling up the scaffold under the toilets.

"What do you expect Red Face—we live under Walking Brain's rule here!" snapped a slimy octopus, troubled by his own family problems. "I used to work for him—the bastard!"

"You did? Then you must know why that time-traveling dude up there arrived six months *before* he actually left, right?"

"Let me see...left in December...and returned in June...same year. You're right. Something fishy here. I wouldn't bet on it. But again, you never know, this is Walking Brain's triangle...or park...whatever they wanna call it...not exactly a normal environment."

They both swam away, chatting, toward the Zoliseum gates.

෴

A sharp, violet-blue thunderclap suddenly flashed the Time Traveler's body. Next thing, he was trotting in circles, then just walking in circles, in the Chamber, ready to come out.

And he did so with a big smile.

The crowd went wild. Their agitated hands held banners that read what they shouted, "WELCOME BACK TO ZUNDO! ENJOY FREEDOM FROM RICHES, FREEDOM FROM GREED!"

Shouts grew even louder, making all the Park's security fences rattle with noise. "LONG LIVE THE NEW ONE! LONG LIVE THE RIGHT ONE!"

෴

The big silver Sphere wrapped up its stay by showing snips of the Time Traveler's mid-journey departures and arrivals from the far past before it began to rise, up and up, the same way it had come down before, but faster...until it cleared the way.

Only to remain parked up high in the sky above the Zoliseum. Slowly turning around an imaginary vertical axis, it displayed local and national news as well as scores from some on-going Park's games and clashes—all easily seen by the crowd's ZCAPs' built-in cosmic zinoculars.

෴

The Time Traveler waved to the surrounding cheering audience, standing on the red-carpeted Astral Floor.

He wore late 20th-century casual summer clothes. Except for the intriguing bat-eared hood and thick blue paint circling his eyes and mouth, which he chose not to remove, his demeanor looked positive and healthy.

A gigantic banner slowly rose behind him. Big black letters on white background said:

**WELCOME HOME TIME TRAVELER! GLORY TO YOU
EX-SEPTIDARE! YOU'RE NOW GREED-FREE FOR LIFE!**

Just as octidare had become a Zundonian short name for octillionaire—an extremely offensive word in this new, clean-minded society—septidare had become a short name for septillionaire—another extremely offensive word. Fortunately, these "so-categorized despised individuals" were weeded out of the system or converted to Zundoism as soon as discovered, tried, and sent away to *The Unknown*...if fated to survive.

∽

Massive applause erupted all around the Stadiums. Fervently, the crowd shouted, "WELL DONE TIME TRAVELER! YOU ROCK! YOU ROCK!"

What they meant with this praise and warm reception was their collective acceptance of a visibly changed man—from riches to rags (in his case, the rumor went, from several septillions to *nada*)—after time traveling in space to unknown lands for years as punishment for previous wrongdoings. Those, for sure, unmistakably related to extreme money greed and the pursuit of godlike powers.

Space journeys were mostly punitive journeys of unkind degrees of harshness, controlled by the very charismatic and popular Zoliseum's host, Master Judge. In turn, controlled by Zoliseum's chairman and Zundo's foremost scientist, Dr. Ufahh. Both referred to as the Sub-Lords of Zundo.

Popularly nicknamed Walking Brain, against his wishes, Dr. Ufahh thrived on personal outer space discoveries and secret experimentation beyond anybody's imagining. Such mystery had made him a most controversial and feared person in recent years—no longer the trusted icon he once was cracked out to be.

"Too bad!" he often said to himself, or to Dancer, his beloved cat, in the privacy of his Palace with a creepy smirk playing across his face, self-cementing his supreme powers and intellectual wisdom.

Indeed, something big had to happen for his reign of devious endeavors, if not criminal affronts, to crumble.

A USEFUL SKY-HIGH FLOATING STRUCTURE

Many zorkflies zipped by near the Fuel Service Station–a floating structure two hundred feet above ground, a few miles north of the Zoliseum.

One of them entered the station and parked.

Aware, the attendant pressed a button on her left arm, which flashed her name, "Serene Lady of the Seventies," followed by her signature profile.

"Laidback Infant from Ex-California," replied the driver in similar manner, staring at his implanted arm device.

Distant sounds and shouts from the Zoliseum kept droning on in the background.

Serene Lady smiled.

She connected high-pressure air hoses to the base-plate of the zorkfly.

"May I check your ZCAP meter?"

"It's all yours. Let me roll my sleeves up a little."

She beamed her zotta ray on the device.

"A new person's born...I mean reborn. Have you heard?" the driver said.

"Yeah, I have," said the attendant.

He remained seated in his vehicle, waiting. "That new person's two minutes old now–wow!" he said, elated.

"Actually, *ten minutes*–already interviewed and everything."

"How d'you know that? *The Happening*'s launching park is four miles away."

"I just know."

She approached his face by the window. "Close one of your eyes, please."

He did.

"Tight."

Suddenly Oxana took her place. She was wild, bitchy, and mysteriously sexy—only a teenager. Speaking with a piercingly high-pitched voice, she said, "Open it."

Laidback Infant saw the beautiful face, heard the strange voice. He was thrilled rather than annoyed.

But his mind wandered off, losing touch with Oxana. This was typical of him, immature, in spite of his approaching middle age. *Two minutes old...I wonder what it'd be like to be two minutes old*, he thought.

Then Oleg appeared next to Oxana–two heads and four arms issuing from one torso. "You could not say *unforgettable*, because you would completely forget the moment...an instant later...at that age..." Oleg said, casually, twiddling his own Adam's apple with his hairy fingers, only to be followed by Oxana's sensuous delivery, swollen full-lips pouting in *femme fatale* fashion, "And you could not say *incredible* either, because you would be too young to believe in anything...at that age... hummmm." to which both Oleg and Oxana added at the same time, in a different tone and manner, "but you could say *wonderful*–that's how it would feel to be two minutes old."

Fuck! thought Laidback Infant in shock, especially after hearing their last sentence together. *They just read my mind! I feel like I've been raped!* But he kept his cool.

"I'm still waiting," reminded the *femme fatale* again.

"Waiting?"

"I asked you to open your eye, remember?"

"Oh...which one?"

"Either one, hon."

"My left, then."

"Sure."

He tried to comply, but his suspicious mind now got in the way. His eye just quivered, like a slightly rustled dry leaf in the wind.

Oleg intervened, "Can't you be a bit more cooperative...*swifter* maybe?"

Unlike Oxana, he was ugly and boring. Worse, his baritone voice quickly slipped into Undo-English, when he spoke again, "Aster pleas. On't hav al ay! (Faster, please. Don't have all day!)"

Laidback Infant finally opened his left eye, but inadvertently closed it again.

"OPEN IT AND HOLD IT THERE, DAMN IT!" both Oleg and Oxana yelled simultaneously. "NEVER MIND WHAT WE READ IN YOUR HEAD!"

He did.

Their combined four working hands quickly busied themselves with the wiring system. Compartment solenoid valve hoses uncoiled, agile fingers moved inventively, sexily, gaining access to the several levitation push buttons.

Oxana asked, "When did you get your implant?"

"My ZCAP?"

"Yes, Laid. What else?"

"When I got my vaccine shots."

"Kindergarten age." She sighed. "Well, you must have messed up somewhere."

"Why?"

"Two of your zycrochips in row 63...column 891...are not zingling well." Oxana studied his surprised face. "Don't worry. I'll take care of that."

Oxana's luscious lips blew soft air onto Laidback Infant's iris as his pink eyelid folded back to show the zupia light, prettier by the moment.

Oxana cheered, "Done."

Suddenly Serene Lady took over. For a split second, three heads stared at Laidback Infant. Then both Oxana and Oleg disappeared.

"Close the eye," said Serene Lady.

Hypnotized, Laidback Infant complied.

৵

Serene Lady's beamed zupia light produced a very soft, short-lived rainbow inside Laidback Infant's closed left eye, still under the effect of hypnosis. Satisfied, she clapped her hands and stepped back.

She now addressed him with chilling authority–part in English and part in Undo-English, "ZCAP: SOL999ET64R7GREEN. Good work. You will go very far this week." She winked at him. "An iego, an uis bispo, an rancisco, and farth."

"Fart?" Laidback Infant said, coming back to his senses from his trance. "I don't feel like."

Serene Lady laughed. "You know better, silly driver. Have I asked you to do that?" She caressed her long, silky, black hair. "I said and meant 'farther'...as in 'away and away from Los Angeles'."

I'll be damned, pondered the traveler. *She intercepted not only my thoughts, but the plans I made five days ago for the weekend. San Diego? San Luis Obispo? San Francisco? Damn!–I live over 3000 miles away in the Atlantic coast, not the Pacific!*

Oxana suddenly replaced Serene Lady with a sexy smile.

Laidback Infant got intimate in Undo-English.

"weet art–d'u ind elling e extly hen te fession il egin oday? (Sweetheart–do you mind telling me exactly when the confession will begin today?)"

"After the noise. Within the hour," said Oxana.

◦◦◦

A beautiful cluster of soft clouds floated under and over the elevated Fuel Service Station.

Oxana unplugged the ZCAP meter, heard the persistent hissing sound underneath the vehicle. Other sounds, from the distant Bermuda Revelation Park, could be heard as she serviced the zorkfly.

"Which stadium should I–?" asked Laidback Infant.

Oleg took charge. He answered in his deep baritone rumble, using Peace-English, a variation of English, made popular by liberal youngsters like himself, he often enjoyed conversing in. "Peace. All taken." His voice rang deeper. "Unless you want to let go from a copter, peace."

"Not again, peace. I did that last year–got bruised all over. They didn't catch me properly, peace."

Laidback Infant regarded Oleg's face with curiosity, but all too soon it became Serene Lady's again.

"You can't blame them, can you? Peace."

"No, peace," said Laidback Infant. "By the way, your full name says that you're "of the seventies"?"

"Yeah. But not of this century." She smiled. "Think harder ex-Californian. Think BC. Think ancient Egyptian times. Peace."

Laidback Infant exploded with laughter. "You're real funny and fun to be with, I bet you. Peace."

Serene Lady gave him a stern look. "*Don't* try me." She saw a new zorkfly enter the station. "I've got to go now. Peace."

CELEBRATION TIME

Around the Bermuda Revelation Park, the crowd's thunderous cheering had generated vibrations in the water so strong and persistent ripples formed on the ocean surface above their heads—a big distraction to a roaming shark and several playful dolphins in the area.

Facing the frenzied spectators, the Time Traveler continued to bow in deep appreciation. He acknowledged the adulation with grateful hand gestures and smiles, his offbeat blue painted face and bat ears adding to the excitement. If anyone on earth could be called a mega star this very moment, he was it.

Hundreds of frantically stretched arms began to make choreographed waves over the row of seats before they broke into a rally of wild whistles and unending applause.

"YEAH SPACE DUDE! YEAH TIMEMAN!" they shouted over their lungs. "YEAH WOOOO HOOOO!"

He bowed incessantly standing on the red carpeted floor to the tune of even more deafening cheers.

Meanwhile a new platform rose to the surface as the Time Traveler Chamber disappeared underground. It carried colorful balloons, special effect gadgets, and other funky party type decorations.

And a live band!

Yells from the crowd ignited the atmosphere: "WAY TO GO ASTRONAUT!" Always in unison, as scripted on their ZCAP meters. "YOU'RE ONE OF US NOW!"

Two gorgeous girls in bikinis ran to a spot near the Time Traveler in a grandiose way. To everyone's delight, they blew kisses around and a cloud of violet thick fog bearing the gigantic white-colored words "SEPTIDARE #6 NO MORE" formed around him on the red carpeted floor.

The Stadiums' crowd bellowed, "THAT'S RIGHT, TIMEMAN. NO MORE RICH GODS! NO MORE ZILLIODARES!" Among them, someone actually shouted the outdated word, "NO MORE ZILLIONAIRES!"

Blasting musical sounds took the two girls to a wild dancing frenzy as the dense fog cleared. They were followed by an electrifying rendition from Zundo's reigning zunk-rock band and its three nerdie-nerdie zunkie singers.

Zunk-rock music filled the undersea air everywhere. It was celebration time.

FIRST ON-THE-FLY INTERVIEW

The Zoliseum thrived with excitement on Day 1 of the trial. Overhead, the circular all-zlass sliding roof remained deactivated. So far, no rain or falling debris from orbiting man-made objects raised any eyebrow or demanded preventive action. A good day for debris abounded daily. So did debris casualties.

Everywhere loudspeakers transmitted the latest news. Exciting announcements to the world blazed the airwaves every five minutes or so. News media reporters orchestrated every angle, every nuance of their deliveries, competing for the highest ratings possible.

A female journalist from the Planet Undersea News approached the Time Traveler, who had just emerged from the debriefing room.

"Hey, that was really cool. You arrived here *before* you even left!"

"Are you talking about the last stage or the whole trip?"

"The whole trip, of course. The only one we saw. Six months?"

The Time Traveler smiled. "Six months here, many years back there."

"Wow! Wow!"

"They didn't show *the last stage*?" questioned the Time Traveler. "Maybe they should show it now so people can better understand the totality of–"

"Your ordeal?"

"No, just the journey's limits…"

The newspaper journalist said, "I'll make a request right away." Searching his eyes, partly camouflaged by the thick blue paint he wore, she added, "How did you do it, anyway? Arrive *before* you left?"

He stared back at her, impassive.

"I mean…you left in December and returned in June of the same year…today. That's quite a feat." She squinted. "And exactly where is

Chizola in Spain? And *Koonzi Beach* in Australia? And *Maziteli* in Italy? And some other key visited places in your punishment journey to the 20th-century?"

He kept staring at her, finding nothing to say.

"I mean...according to those stunning visuals we all saw on the Celestial Sphere? The mapped regions?" Her eyes blinked ungraciously. "My own research couldn't locate any of those places and I busted my butt one entire weekend trying to find them!"

"Ask Walking Brain—he's behind all this," he finally replied.

With caution, she now said, "Of course, he is." Her skilled voice changed. "So...are you missing being extremely rich?"

"Not at all. It's not even a reference point for me anymore." The Time Traveler smiled. "I'm enjoying life, with anything and everything I have now—whatever that is."

"Zero...nada...rien...zilch..."

"Right."

"One last question. Where did you get those sexy bat ears and spooky, circular blue paint around your eyes?"

"I picked them up at a funky store along my journey."

"On the Left Bank...in Paris?"

"No, near Aprilov High School...in Gabrovo, Bulgaria. It's a long story."

Around them, cheers and roars of every kind and intensity filled the air. "YOU ROCK, SPACE TRAVELER! YOU ROCK!"

The newswoman asked, fighting the crowd, "Why are you wearing a mask?"

"I don't want to be recognized. I'd like to be able to get back home in peace. No paparazzi or news media reporters after me."

"Are you happy now?"

"Humbly so. I've learned a lot in my trip."

"Such as?"

"Being able to cross a street or an ocean without owning it."

SECOND ON-THE-FLY INTERVIEW

The Promenade Corridor sizzled with unrest and exhilaration, its green, donut-shaped, caterpillar-like structure standing between the six Bisected Stadiums and the Astral Floor.

From the Bermuda Revelation Park's outdoors thousands of spectators had pushed their way inside the half-transparent cavernous hallways, strolling along cool gardens with picaresque water fountains and placid cobbled walkways.

Hordes of youngsters were engaged in fourth-millennium activities. Zescapade blues serenading, zipolar wicked-moment guessing, and bleed-on-demand zirror watching dominated the aura. A z-plentiful aura!

Perched on a thick bamboo-cut bar, from which hung all sorts of thud and sting whipping tools, a colorful parrot the size of a rooster, argued with a group of curious adolescent bullies.

"Are you...are you talking to me?" said the parrot to one of them, blends of green and yellow feathers billowing up his head.

"Tell me why you're so full of it, shithead?" instigated the kid, eyeing one of the thick braided whips he might want to steal.

"Tell you this, zunk. Might not be your type but as sure as hell I can fly!"

"How far can you fly, zophead?!" shot another kid, half-staring at the snake-headed handle of a whip ending with nine tails.

"Farther than your mind can see, silly boy," said the parrot. "Walking Brain made me time-conductive once. Time-manipulated me to outer space, back and forth like a yo-yo, in chunks of hundreds of years."

"Liar! Liar!" shouted another kid, with intent on grabbing any of these whips and causing him immense damage. "Walking Brain wouldn't waste a second on you, fussy head!"

"Not anymore. But he did once." Raising one leg, he pointed to a peculiar mark. "Got his stamp on my foot—see it?"

They all glanced at it in horror and broke into a wild stampede, away from the parrot.

ᖇ

Few people noticed them, their petty quarrel. After all, this was a fun center. A great place for youngsters and seasoned people alike, especially cozy couples wearing fresh smiles and progressive minds. What else but enjoy the "cool cavernous promenade"...mingling with such array of debonair strollers along the chic boutiques, colorful booths, and bewitching joints?

Except that whatever they did couldn't escape the monitoring devices of the very capable snoop boobs. They were everywhere, sensing each and every move of every Zundonian—whether real or impersonated, earthling or alien, dead or alive.

ᖇ

An alluring siren reminded everyone now to stay put in expectation of a special announcement regarding *The Happening*.

Outdoors' roaring cheers and hearty applause, mainly from the Stadiums, began to quiet down. Diminishing levels of dark and white noise, filtering through partly opened windows and deep cracks in the old Corridor structures, still easily picked up by non-quitting indoor game players, likewise vanished. A final anemic shout welcoming back the Time Traveler from a group of youngsters cut through the air.

Only remained the ever-present but hidden sinister network of sophisticated spying devices, hard-wired gadgets, radio frequency scanners, and audio eavesdropping tools strategically spread out around the premises.

"ATTENTION ZUNDONIANS WHEREVER YOU ARE. ATTENTION BELOVED ZOLISEUM SPECTATORS," suddenly came a commanding female voice through the complex system of speakers. "WE HAVE A TREAT FOR YOU. A BIGGER ONE, IF YOU CAN BELIEVE THAT. WITHIN MINUTES YOU'LL BE ABLE TO SEE THE PART OF THE HAPPENING THAT DIDN'T MAKE IT TO OUR SCREENS BEFORE. IT'S THE VERY LAST STAGE OF THE TIME TRAVELER'S PUNISHMENT JOURNEY, SPECIFICALLY THE BULGARIAN-AMERICAN CONNECTION. THIS PRESENTATION HONORS A SPECIAL REQUEST THAT SHALL REMAIN ANONYMOUS. PLEASE MAKE YOURSELVES COMFORTABLE FOR THIS GREAT EVENT. THANK YOU."

And so they all succumbed to this part of *The Happening*.

On the left screen of the Celestial Sphere's middle panel they all could see now the journeyman's last stage's departure from Gabrovo, Bulgaria, dated *June 11, 1981*, specifically a man in his thirties, identified as the Time Traveler, running through the woods in terror, chased by a tiger.

He wore a bat-eared hood and thick blue paint circling his eyes and mouth.

Between the running man and tiger suddenly appeared a running three-headed lioness with powerful eyes and ferocious teeth. It attacked the tiger and tore it to pieces.

∽

On the right screen of the Celestial Sphere's middle panel, all Zundonians could see the journeyman's final arrival to Bermuda Revelation Park, dated *June 11, 3081* (today), specifically the same man, but frozen in "terror-running-action" inside a zlass chamber near a mahogany armchair.

No time traveling vehicle.

He wore a bat-eared hood and thick blue paint circling his eyes and mouth.

∽

A CMM reporter made eye contact with the Time Traveler on his way out.

"That was awesome! You certainly will be nominated this year for the 'Time Travel Enfant Terrible Award'! How long were you away?" she asked him with annoying self-assurance.

"Lost count."

"I'm guessing twenty-six years 20th-century time," said the reporter, "but only six months our time."

"Good for you," laughed the Time Traveler.

"I have no problem with you arriving *before* you left," she said, staring at the thick blue circles surrounding his eyes. "But what's really weird is that the last stage of your journey alone–the Bulgaria-America time travel return–seems to have taken you *a thousand years*... inter-millennium time. Now how can this be?"

"I have no idea how to answer you," said the Time Traveler, struggling to control his laughter. "I'm just a punished traveler."

"You must know something." A wrinkle showed to one side of her eye in spite of the heavy makeup. "*A thousand years*," she pressed again, "except *one hundred* that I can't figure out."

Those I know, thought the Time Traveler. *The ones I spent in deep-freeze sleep...before they forced me out of it to stand trial.*

"*A thousand years*," she repeated, seeking some explanation.

"Some people say it took me five years our time to complete my journey. Other people say it took me only four hours. Yet other people say I never came back. So you see? It's all nonsense. No offense."

"But there's got to be a correct answer."

"To tell you the truth, I don't really care how long I've been out there. All I care is that I've changed. I've lost my sickening insatiable greed for wealth and power. I'm finally free and happy."

"LONG LIVE THE REDEEMED SEPTILLIONAIRE!" bellowed someone near them, so loud they both turned to watch his face.

"This may be harder for you to answer," the CMM reporter then said, staring back at the traveler. "But weren't you one of the richest persons in the world before you left?"

"Not hard to answer at all. I was indeed. Glad I'm not anymore."

"*When* during your journey did you begin to change?"

"I experienced my first personality change when I became a teen-ager...thirteen years old." He pulled a handkerchief out of his pocket, started to fidget with it—a habit not lost in spite of his trip. "I stopped being selfish, cocky, impulsive." He scratched his chin reflectively.

"When did you stop being greedy?"

"Oh...that took longer," said the Time Traveler, staring at her impeccable hairdo. "Much longer...in my early twenties. Actually, longer still." Unrelated pressing thoughts crossed his mind. "I've got to go now, thank you."

"YOU ROCK SPACEMAN! YOU DID IT!" someone yelled.

Fighting the crowd, the CMM reporter asked bluntly, "Do you miss being revered as a god?" Hearing no answer, she tried to hit a different side of his character. "I like those ghostly dark blue circles in your face...and erotic bat ears."

But her voice didn't reach him as he'd already stepped out of sight. Questions from other persistent individuals however kept hovering around.

"Any girls in your journey?"

"Tell us about your deep-freeze-sleep secrets."

"Are you a vampire?"

KIDNAPPED AND ZLONED

Underwater traffic was heavy but methodical.

Passing school azuabuses loaded with boisterous students flashed their zigmok lights in salute. They were speeding over the uneven roofs of this hydro-community, like flying storks, moving along the elevated, quarter-mile long "BERMUDA REVELATION PARK" sign, already in the vicinity of their destination.

Left and right fish went on with their normal life.

The Time Traveler managed to scurry off the overly abrasive crowd into the Exit Tunnel, where a tightly secured, chauffeur-driven ziderot waited. "This way, my son, said a friendly, thick-accented voice with a dash of urgency, followed by a hand that opened the vehicle's back door.

In a jiffy, he jumped in—a mistake—for inside, he was swiftly rendered powerless by a striking magenta-colored beam that incapacitated his body to zilch as the vehicle flew away.

Then Scientist Ufahh—in his deceptive visual sixties, while really pushing one hundred ten years of age—undressed the man completely down to his bare buttocks and genitals. He also removed his bat-eared hood, wiped off the blue paint from his eyes and mouth with a sponge soaked in a cleaning solution, realizing how nicely the man's hidden mustache came into view.

I'll be damned. I almost forgot he had one. That's how good this frigging thick Bulgarian paint is! he marveled in thoughts, and took out from the man's finger, with more difficulty than expected, his peridot ring.

"Slow down a little, will ya!" he shouted to his chauffeur. "I'm bouncing all over!"

From a shiny leather case, tucked behind his legs, his very long arms pulled out a refined, hi-tech purple gun the size and shape of a violin.

In no time, he zlone-gunned the disabled and nude spaceman, bringing instant duplication to his physical, mental, and spiritual being. Such on-the-spot zloning adhered to the unmistakable "z" marking of excellence instituted by himself many years ago and so far only attainable by himself. Zloning was a one-hundred-percent effective type of cloning achieved through precise and aggressive experimentation with his Secret Tools—the ones responsible for manipulating the laws of physics and other scientific breakthroughs in his wicked Alternative History Palace.

However, he'd programmed the zlone gun to temporarily erase during the trial any recollection of his previous time travel journey, including today's spectacular arrival and subsequent news media interviews. Such was the sophistication of his zloning beam and the reality of his victim's memory.

૦ᴗᴐ

"Bless his soul," his mother used to say before the avalanche of cultural changes overtook the world many years ago, believing he would one day amount to something in the little town of Pinamar—about eighty miles north of Argentina's biggest seaside resort, Mar de Plata—where he grew up in South America.

Of Arabian descend, his father had simply vanished from view the day after a happy gathering at a local restaurant celebrating his elementary school completion. Such disappearance, believed to be political, was not unusual in Argentina.

Wearing manicured design nail inserts, chimpanzee-long arms, and a peaceful koala-looking face (except for his enlarged zapillon ears), he looked more like a circus clown in a darkly surreal movie than a fastidious, lost-in-thoughts Doctor of Philosophy in Quantum Physics (a degree he also had). And the rumor went that he had something to do with the way he was put together, not necessarily by birth.

He dressed impeccably Hollywoodish–year 3081. Flamboyant, meticulous, self-centered, and all-knowing. He often wore soft, adjustable cobra-skinned shoes, knee-length reversible Adolpho shorts for all seasons (matching his average height), and breakaway sundust-fortified shirts with patchable designs. What a character!

Lately, strands of blond hair had strangely begun to spurt upward from the top of his bald head in two separate places, like soft oasis flowers tanned by the sun. "I may be thinking too hard these days, obliquely nurturing the roots of my glacial constitution," he was rumored to have mumbled to himself one late summer night in a seafood joint's men's room near Tel Aviv.

"But I love my work," he usually told his associates, Master Judge in particular, the press, and his mother, who'd noticed the stunning koala resemblance in spite of herself.

She'd curiously picked this thing up long ago, during the secret years he'd lived like a hermit in the confines of the Alternative History Palace, at the heights of his scientific discoveries.

Was there anything wrong with him? Yes–his brain. Per pound, it was perhaps the brightest in the world. Per decision-making, the most dangerous. Evil caprices seemed to creep into his ways of thinking, despite the peaceful koala resemblance, and manipulating the universe–at least the properties of both "time travel" and "soul travel"– was one of his greatest ambitions. For he had others, too.

So, zloning the Time Traveler without his permission didn't bother him a bit. *Who knows, something good may come out of it!* he thought now, as he did early this morning when brushing his teeth after getting up from bed.

Dr. Ufahh, however, kept to himself the unfortunate incident that had forced him to replace the original Time Traveler (a septillionaire, among many) with this new Time Traveler (Richard, the only octillionaire) when scientific miscalculations, apparently, took the former traveler's life near the end of his journey. A horrible accident! Neither Master Judge nor any other judge in the Zoliseum nor the defendant, Richard, should ever know about it...for any leak to the news media could be disastrous.

Staring now at the sleepy faces of the Time Traveler and his zlone, both looking identical side by side, the distinguished old man proclaimed, in his colorful accent and priest-like solemn intonation, "Blessed by the mighty power of science, you two will remain forever perfect copymates, unless either one or both should morph, merge, or die."

He threw a little smirk. "I didn't zlone your cute bat ears and silly paint work around your eyes and mouths for the same reason I didn't zlone your pretty ring and dirty underwear—sorry about that. I just didn't think the zloning would've worked well on these items."

He bent down and picked up the underwear from the vehicle's floor and put it on the zlone's naked body. He also fit the ring on the zlone's finger.

Done with it, he covered the disabled Time Traveler with a blanket after pushing him out of view to a corner of the vehicle's rear end.

"*Voilà.*"

PART 2

SOUL TRAVEL JOURNEY DEPARTURE FROM ZUNDO JUNE 3081

BRAINWASHED WHILE RIDING IN A ZIDEROT TO THE ZOLISEUM FROM A SECLUDED VILLA

The ziderot stopped in front of a ground-anchored secluded villa, whereupon the chauffeur got out. Rather furtively, he dragged into the driveway a stocky, plastic package the length and shape of an adult crocodile.

Dr. Ufahh watched from his comfortable seat in the ziderot how he opened the villa's front door and pushed the package inside.

Reappearing a couple of minutes later, the chauffeur locked the villa's door with a master key and rushed back to the ziderot, breathing hard.

"Did you unwrap the top a little so he can get out of it when he wakes up?" asked the scientist.

"Yes...it all went well."

The ziderot flew back to the Zoliseum.

∽

Dr. Ufahh held a piece of cloth moistened with a dark-blue liquid to zlone-Richard's nose. The pungent smell, ammonia-like, made him jump off his feet.

"Where am I?" he burst out. "What am I doing here?"

"You fainted. Security couldn't control the mob, so we tried to help."

"Oh...I kind of remember."

"You'll be all right. Wear this long gray hooded robe to avoid being taken to jail."

"Taken to jail?"

"Well, yeah, Richard—you're all naked. Almost."

"What?" He stared down at his hairy chest, thighs, and jockey briefs. "Why am I like this?"

"Remember? Secret and classified project? You're no longer *the returning* Time Traveler. You're now Richard Flynn *the departing* Soul Traveler. Well, depending on the trial's outcome."

He patted his shoulder affectionately.

"You're no longer Septidare #6—that was an arbitrary name we used Zundo-wide to make you look different, less rich, with a different journey. You're the Octidare—our short name for Octillionaire. The only one. A fact."

He patted his shoulder again.

"And the trial code requires that you appear before our highest magistrate humble and without any clothes on, except your underwear."

"Oh...I didn't know that."

He vigorously shook his head sideways, like dogs often do to reset themselves, making his thick, tousled, and curly brown hair stand on ends for just a split second.

"I mean, I know about the classified project, the intricate coaching I underwent. So yes, I guess I'm ready," he then said, remembering, ending his sentence with an odd smile. "And I *do* have a lot of good information stored from my just completed time travel journey."

"Good, good," said Dr. Ufahh without much excitement in his voice. "I'm glad we're on the same page now." Meaning the opposite.

"Oh—wait! What am I saying?"

"Anything wrong Richard?"

"I've never...time traveled...before."

A tiny smile escaped Dr. Ufahh's lips. Zlone-Richard had begun to act strangely, exactly what was expected of him. The full effect of the zloning beam was finally degrading, temporarily erasing specific areas of his memory.

"So...so...where are we going now...?" he asked, lost in thoughts, feeling the motion of the vehicle.

"To your trial," said Dr. Ufahh.

 srw

The vehicle swam under water now, skipping the intricate system of caves and fissures, sidetracking tropical colonies of spotted eagle rays and friendly nurse sharks along squashy hills of rust-colored reefs.

Roaming a vertical structure of black corals and emerald sponges, the vehicle surfaced with a little splash. It left behind an awesome trail of gorgonians hanging off a deep-sided wall.

They had just entered the Zoliseum from the north, headed for the six Bisected Stadiums and the Astral Floor.

Zlone-Richard rolled the window down, his face aglow with joy. "This is huge! Such a big place filled with people! Amazing! I never imagined Zundonians could be so interested in my trial, my soul travel journey!"

"*Just* soul travel?"

"Of course. Who would want more? This is big time punishment, not a vacation."

Splendid answer, thought the scientist. *He's right on track*. Sighting a lateral entry to the Astral Floor, he gestured the driver to stop the vehicle and pushed the back door open for the zloned man to get out.

"Good luck, my friend. Just be yourself."

"You bet!"

๛

Wrapped from head to toe in the hooded robe, Zlone-Richard rushed inside the building.

He was however recognized by a uniformed liaison officer who knew him well just a dozen steps shy of the Staff Reception Room. She'd been his intermediary advisor for several months before the court order that ended his luck and brought him here in the most unusual way. That was the time between his "forced awakening" from deep-freeze sleep by government officials and his "negotiated Zoliseum appearance" for time travel punishment journey to *The Unknown*.

"Hi Richard!"

"Hi Juanita," he replied, a bit surprised.

Following trial rules, she did a quick voice, smell, vision, and finger print check, which confirmed his identity.

"Break a leg," she said to him, meaning actually "good luck," as if he was a struggling actor about to face a theatrical audition. Over a thousand years old, this custom was still in use.

"Thank you."

He marched on.

Not knowing he'd been zloned and not told his memory about his recent time travel journey had been specifically erased for the duration of the trial, he made his way to the Astral Floor proper the only way he knew—being himself, Richard. Which, incidentally, was the only way both the audience and the judges knew.

∽

As he stepped on the Astral Floor, the only person in the world who knew he was Zlone-Richard, not Richard, was Dr. Ufahh—his secret zloner. And thus he was destined to be incorrectly called "Richard" here and everywhere, for as long as the situation demanded, invariably at the mercy of Dr. Ufahh's wicked aims.

Those aims had been carefully planned. In fact, Zloning Richard was a measure Dr. Ufahh had conceived to keep *the original* intact and safe somewhere in case of a catastrophic accident, while exposing *the copy* to the harsh menace and frightening perils of time and soul traveling to *The Unknown*.

In time, when all the dust would settle, Dr. Ufahh would publicly unzlone Richard—a Richard loaded with new experiences, visions, and feelings acquired in his traveling journeys, if he was still around—to keep Zundonians at ease with the issue of *fairness* and *transparency*. This would in turn discourage annoying Zundonian extremists from targeting him—the undesirable zloner—for whatever indiscretions or wrongdoings they could find. Which were plenty, at both levels.

Ultimately, however, he would have to get rid of Richard—the original, now struggling to survive after being kidnapped, disabled, and dumped in a remote location—and Master Judge—his mistrustful, hated-behind-his-back right-hand man—as well as anyone or any group messing with his life and work.

That would ensure his total control on Richard's immense wealth... for it was well speculated all around that money would one day make a comeback.

One thing at a time.

◇

Deep in the woods, a bird chirped his favorite song.

Picking up an earthworm that crawled out of a dirt mound edging a pond, he flew to the veranda of a quiet house in the vicinity to feast on it, only to realize he had company. It was a tall armed guard patrolling the area.

Without hesitation, he took flight again.

"Oh lucky you, Blue Jay," said the guard, imagining the bird roasting slowly over hot coals.

He had been working here several hours now, protecting this property, which was the secluded villa Scientist Ufahh had chosen earlier to dump the mysterious package.

Occasionally, he could see the back of a man's head and shoulders, apparently sleeping on a couch, through one of the windows. Also, a bat-eared hood resting on a nearby table.

The guy has finally come to life. He's adapting, thought the guard, seeing slight movements of his limbs.

◇

All walls, ceilings, windows, and doors in the villa teamed with wireless surveillance devices. So did everything the man inside saw or touched. *How long will I have to put up with this seclusion?* he pondered.

Getting up from the couch, he felt pressure over his eyes and a certain heaviness in his ears. *My head's killing me...need an aspirin or something. Now!*

For a while, he walked around the room, stretching his torso, flexing both legs, making sure he had no injuries. *Fuck! I'm all naked!* He suddenly realized. *I don't mind being stuffed in a frigging plastic bag like a corpse...but at least they should've given me some clothes to die in!*

He glanced at his hands. *My ring's gone too!*

Avoiding stepping on the discarded plastic bag that had contained him before, he headed for the kitchen and the bathroom, where he found, among a bunch of things, a box of aspirins. He swallowed two with a glass of water, and peeked at the patio through a netted door.

Nothing. Nobody, he pondered.

Likewise all the bedrooms and bathrooms were empty.

"*He lied to me—that mother-fucking scientist! He said he would cut my extreme poverty journey...all thirteen years...in half! Both my sentence time and pain in half! But I got twice that instead!*"

Returning to the living room, he paced back and forth a small area of it, his blood pressure rising. "*I'll find a way to get him arrested and pay for his treachery—that despicable bastard!*"

His eyes veered to a ZV set, left turned on, but with hardly any volume coming out, and a bookshelf holding a few paperbacks.

He raised the ZV volume. A Zoliseum spokeswoman was answering questions from a newsman regarding some aspects of the trial: "It's made up of two parts—a traveler's return from *The Unknown* (Part 1) and a traveler's depart to *The Unknown* (Part 2). Part 2 is the big deal, the main attraction or trial proper, and the chief reason for all the news media's fuss: the richest man in history, Richard Flynn, will finally be tried, sentenced, and sent away on a harsh punishment voyage to *The Unknown*. He will journey via soul travel, not the customary time travel expected for such convicts. Unknown parameters will shroud the...expedition, shall we say...partially visible to Zundonians on gigantic, state-of-the-art screens, for the duration." The presenter paused to catch her breath. "A new attraction—consisting of 13 very daring, if not life-threatening, pre-travel Clashes between Richard and several panel judges—has been added only because the defendant also happens to be the greediest person mankind has ever known. As you may have guessed by now, 13 is the defendant's favorite number."

Annoyed, Richard shut the ZV off.

♒

Curled up on the couch an hour later with a detective novel that didn't quite hold his interest, he alternated watching bits of the evening news, particularly when words like "white crime," "home detention," and "formerly rich" kept popping out. Keeping the ZV on, he'd realized fairly quickly, was to his advantage.

Restless, he walked to the bathroom to pee.

Slouching back to the couch, he picked up a small handwritten note someone apparently had dropped on the floor before he'd awaken from his ordeal. His urge to read it was overwhelming.

> You're in mortal danger, Richard. Do nothing but relax inside the house until we contact you again. No phone calls, online chat, ZV interactive talk, ZSSE-55 astral gossip, or any form of communication. No exiting the house either. You must remain in total seclusion. This should last a few days. There's plenty of food in the refrigerator and the kitchen cabinets. Serve yourself.

DECONSTRUCTING RICHARD
(FROM THE STADIUMS)

Slowly climbing back to the sky, the spinning Celestial Sphere garnered new attention as its bottom area scrolled, in red flashing mode, the words,

JUST COMPLETED: TRIAL OPENING AND PUNISHMENT TIME TRAVEL RETURN SHOW • NEXT: DETENTION Q&A SHOW

∾

Surrounded by half-a-million spectators crowding the six undersea Bisected Stadiums, Richard Flynn—thirty-four years old, of average height, and wearing brown curly hair—stood stubbornly firm and poised on the Astral Floor facing the newly activated Detention Set. He was the only listed octidare and, by Dr. Ufahh's malice and secrecy, the only zloned person ever to face *The Unknown*.

He wore only coffee stained briefs and a barely visible ring, shining in yellow-green. Evidently, some portal official had already confiscated his long hooded robe.

He was the main attraction of this season's most publicized *confess and fight* public trial, hailed as the "Trial of the Millennium," soon to begin, leading to a spectacular, punitive but redeeming soul travel journey to unknown lands across time, should he survive.

In particular, he highlighted the second part of this show, the first part already executed by the successful return of the Time Traveler, just witnessed and celebrated. Such traveler, a famous septillionaire, known as Septidare #6 by all Zundonians, had confirmed once again the validity of reforming, if not redeeming, insatiably greedy people like himself through castigating time travel journeys, unlike Richard's soul travel, a prototype, deemed vastly more dangerous.

All septidares, of course, were less offensive–by a thousand times– than any octidare. Fortunately, only one octidare, bearing the name Richard Flynn, had been found. For there wasn't any other.

On cue the restless Zoliseum crowd began to sing:

> **You've gone too far, Mr. Filthy Rich!**
> **You've abused Humanity!**
> **You've become our Supreme King, you think.**
> **Tell us all about it, Mr. Flynn, without vanity.**

౭౨

On the Astral Floor, Richard heard the insults and felt the pain. Yet he was not about to crack. Elegantly mustached and medium-built, he looked physically fit, except for that baffling aura of absentminded folly he so strongly displayed half of the time.

Not now, though.

Richard staggered a little in front of the huge, insolent crowd. He was ready to enter the Detention Set, his mind fully engaged in thoughts, his hazel eyes steadily open.

Had this story happened a thousand years ago–say 2081–and let's say in what-used-to-be-the-United-States, he pondered, *nobody would've cared and I would've continued being the richest man on this planet, expecting to get even richer many times over by the minute....In fact, I was so rich, I could've bought the planet.*

Briefly he stared up in defiance, confronting for the last time the contemptuous crowd.

At the other end of the spectrum billions of jobless, penniless, and homeless sufferers would've continued roaming the streets totally ignored and hopeless, awaiting at best the merciful call of death.

He took a deep breath, then lowered his stare.

But it's happening now...where civilization is so much more advanced and wiser and fairer...and while it's okay to be rich by the current rules, it's not okay to be filthy rich by means of a wasted life that has little or no use to the planet, or by any means that turns you into a godlike, reverence-seeking figure of total supremacy. And so...I must now face the consequences.

The crowd's noise level chilled down to a minimum.

Million eyes from the Stadiums, work places, hospitals, and homes all over the world just watched. They all were connected either physically or through the ZCAP meter or ZSSE-55 funbox.

Richard raised his stare a bit.

To be honest, the latest I've been told to believe, since I've awaken from ten decades of deep-freeze sleep—and that's hard to swallow—is that it's not okay anymore to be rich...if rich means the first step toward reaching for the stars...while the rest of the world remains grounded in poverty. They've changed the rules. So go figure.

His eyes flickered twice.

But let me clarify here that I'm currently in the process of mental and spiritual rehabilitation, heading for redeeming cure, if that's possible at all, having just seen a gleam of light, so to speak, at the end of the tunnel. But not today. Not this week.

The Royal Den loomed high above the anxious Stadiums' crowd that surrounded the Astral Floor, somberly perched like an exotic bird's nest on a rising boob-shaped, balcony-carved structure caressed by sumptuous vines and leaves. It housed a revolutionary computer system, spectral costumes, two large wall pictures of a peculiar cat, a box of colorful blowable balloons, and several bizarre tools from other epochs.

From its elevated, strategic position, blessed with soft lights, Master Judge conducted the trial.

He was tall and robust like a general, in his forties (his own statement), sporting a long, pointed beard.

A veteran and charismatic judge, he looked quite omnipotent with his glossy bald head. His powerful voice accentuated his knack for intimidating people.

"Will you step forward, please, and sit down?" he ordered the defendant.

Richard complied.

༄

The Detention Cell, centerpiece of the Detention Set, where Richard now sat, featured a spotless clean, small, round, and daunting room walled with zlass.

"It's cold..." mumbled Richard.

Indeed. A wall thermometer indicated barely 65 degrees Fahrenheit, but no one seemed to care. The judge didn't bother to respond.

"Can I have a handkerchief for my hands?" said Richard raising his voice.

No response.

Suddenly Master Judge, wearing a black cape and matching black boots and gloves, popped up near Richard's face, inside a big floating pale-orange bubble.

"Hi, pal!"

Richard jumped off his chair, frightened.

Around them the crowd erupted with laughter.

Calmly, Master Judge burst the bubble open with one pointed finger, delivering himself out of it.

Cockily, he threw both his arms up in the air like a pop star or preacher craving for the ultimate attention, revealing a fiery red shirt underneath his black cape.

He then asked pompously, with his signature booming voice, knowing full well it was broadcast live to the entire world through thousands of speakers and the news media networks, "How much wealth did you own before the Zaza-Team took you?"

Surprisingly Richard's face now looked relaxed through the zlass wall, his speech dull but clear. Ordinary voice.

"About thirteen octillion dollars."

Master Judge walked toward the defendant with quiet, measured steps.

"That's about thirteen octillion too many, isn't it?"

"I'm afraid, yes."

The Stadiums crowd exploded with lofty uproars and banging noise in protest. They all yelled in unison what they read on their

ZCAP meters. "DOWN THE FILTHY RICH! DOWN THE OCTIDARE!"

࿓

Below the Astral Floor, through some cracks in the supporting structure, threads of daylight teased a pair of gliding blue angelfish.

"Oh dear, they're yelling again up there," said one of them, showcasing her greenish-blue body and the yellow details rimming its fins.

"Apparently," said a neon gobie, straying perhaps too far from his brain coral base, "they're in the early stages of forcing him to confess his sins."

"Is...trying to be God...a sin?" wondered a triggerfish, joining them.

"Trying and *succeeding* is!" snapped a horse-eye jack.

"Well this one must be near succeeding. Did you hear what he said when asked how much money he'd made so far?" remarked a trumpet fish commuting from a nearby cavern off the coral reef formations flanking the submerged island.

"Thirteen million," tried a spotted grouper.

"No."

"Thirteen billion," uttered a box fish.

"Not even close," challenged the trumpet fish.

"Thirteen quadrillion," expressed confidently a spying trunkfish, overhearing their conversation on his way to the Stadiums.

"Nope."

"Thirteen quintillion," voiced a tiny red hilo umiushi, clinging to a hard coral.

"You guys are so far away. You have no idea how monstrous his wealth is."

"We give up," they all agreed.

"*Thirteen octillion!*"

"Oh my..." gasped the tiny red hilo umiushi, almost fainting.

࿓

A security camera panned over hundreds of heads in Stadium #2. Many of them were mutants, androids, replicants, or cyborgs—both adults and teenagers.

Caught up in expressions of rage, some began to ritually sing out their guts in unison, reading from their ZCAP meters:

How dare you become an octillionaire!
How dare you humiliate the poor!
How dare you amass so much wealth, I swear!
How dare you act as if you're the Lord!

Clattering noises from the crowd mixed with the shouted lyrics around the Stadium. They rang louder in the middle and top rows.

Laidback Infant sat placidly in one of the lower rows. He texted Serene Lady on his ZCAP meter.

"Hi, it's me, Laid. Can we meet somewhere after the show today?"

૭౨

Inside the Detention Cell, Master Judge remained thoughtful. He paced the floor up and down near the small room, studying the defendant's face.

"Can you imagine how many poor people would have benefited from this wealth?" He cleared his throat. "How many suicides would have been prevented among the needed?"

"Yes, I do."

Master Judge touched the zlass that separated him from Richard with one gloved hand, then, bending his head, he squashed his right cheek on it, making himself interesting. "How did you feel about this a year ago?"

Richard looked at the flattened, disfigured cheek against the zlass. "Total disregard for the suffering, hunger, and suicides. Absolute neglect." He scratched one leg. "Complete selfishness, avarice, and utter greed." He intently met the judge's probing eyes, hard as steel, and heard the outcries from the Stadiums echoing around him, but continued unmoved, "With no verbal capacity to express it properly."

Master Judge felt nauseated inside. It showed on his face.

"Did you look at yourself as a criminal all these years?" Lingering on his heavy breath, he added, "as a result of your degenerate wealth?"

"Always."

"Would you do it again if you had to relive your life?"

"No question."

"So you're no different from all those zillionaires that came before you–all aiming at bigger and bigger wealth and power–all demanding, in quite clever and polite manners, godlike reverence?"

"Very much so."

That was too much for the crowd to hear. They exploded: "SEND HIM AWAY! HANG HIM HIGH! CRUSH HIS BRAIN! MAKE THE BASTARD BEG FOR MERCY!"

Defiantly, Richard raised one hand to the crowd. Putting a finger to his lips, he pronounced, soundless, the word "hush." Not exactly a winning gesture. To Master Judge now: "Are we...? Is this...the beginning of my confession...already?"

"Oh no. This is only a 'Questions and Answers' session." Smiling over his anger, he said, "Your confession will be different. Trust me."

Cynical laughter erupted in the Stadiums. It was sorely needed.

Frustrated with the defendant's defiance, Master Judge touched a button on his ZCAP meter, which caused a series of tiny blue sparks to begin to gyrate in the Cell just above Richard's eyes.

Then he grouchily slipped into Undo-English, the language he'd been trying to avoid: "Ou ay ook at e iraling lue ight ow and bink wice efor aying e ords ''m er to eak onl e ruth." ("You may look at the spiraling blue light now and blink twice before saying the words 'I'm here to speak only the truth'.")

Richard hardly understood the ongoing special effect, but he complied and said, "I'm here to speak only the truth."

Master Judge went on, "Allo e lue lush to ouch yor oul so ou an ontiue eaking othing ut e ruth." ("Allow the blue flush to touch your soul so you can continue speaking nothing but the truth.")

Richard complied. At least, he thought so. Something however was bothering him. Emotionally, he said, "May I ask you...Master Judge...Your Honor...to–"

"You may call me MJ."

"May I ask you MJ." He scratched and fidgeted with his hair. "To—"

"To what?"

"To please quit using Undo-English. It hurts my liver."

"I will." Master Judge rubbed his chin delicately. "You'll need to be strong to be able to stand the ordeal and pain that awaits you...when sentenced."

He extracted something from his cape in a suspicious manner. Showing his back to Richard, he blew on it real quick.

The next moment, he was floating inside an orange bubble, up and away to his Royal Den.

Past the balloon's popping sound, up there, just above his desk, and the soft landing of his legs and butt on his ruling leather chair, he jotted a few words down a piece of paper.

His index finger pressed a red button on his ZCAP meter. It rang twice before someone answered.

∞

"What's up?" Dr. Ufahh's heavily accented voice filled the line.

"Something wrong with the defendant's behavior. He was okay when he first chatted with our pre-trial head shrinker last winter, but he's become obstinate, cocky, harsh, and as greedy as hell...ever since you coached him. I don't understand."

The scientist's eyes spied on parts of the Stadiums' agitated crowd from his large window inside the Alternative History Palace, where he'd spent the last two hours wrapping up some work. He usually did that when talking over the phone or the ZCAP meter, like now.

"I do. I understand," said the distinguished man. "True. I miscoached the son-of-a-bitch."

He meant "his *bribing*, not coaching, of the defendant before the trial didn't bring the result he had expected." Richard seemed to sail too easily on some extraneous way lately. Of course, his secret plans and rewards regarding Richard's fortune, the one he expected to possess eventually, excluded Master Judge. That's why he'd never told the enigmatic judge what he'd actually done to Richard after the "bribing"—a far cry from *coaching* or anything of the sort. Talking about secrets, Dr. Ufahh, out of his own accord, had privately one moonless night ago sent away a brainwashed Richard time traveling from the roof of his Alternative History Palace in emergency operation (Plan B) to replace the original Time Traveler...violently squashed to death (his own words) in his journey to *The Unknown*...without anyone on earth knowing about it. That's how the current Time Traveler, to nobody's knowledge, happened to be Richard, the octillionaire, not the sixth septillionaire sent away, and how crucially important this secret was. In no way, however, could he ever feel one fleck of remorse.

"What do you propose?" asked the judge.

"I'll have to debug my methods and pin down the problem. I know what to look for. It just may take some time to fix the sucker."

"That's really bad," said the judge with alarm. "Richard's already on trial."

"Well–just the Detention Q&A Show, right?"

"Yeah...but."

"Just move on with the program. I'll get back to you later."

"Please hurry."

"Of course."

DECONSTRUCTING RICHARD
(FROM THE PROMENADE CORRIDOR)

Lots of people populated the cavernous hallways of the gigantic donut-shaped Promenade Corridor, home of the zintellectuals, to watch the trial.

They did so in multitude of ways. Scattered along its membranous labyrinth of gothic chambers and spidery cells, many of them used the lateral zhobra-mirage walls, where the ongoing Detention Q&A Show phase could be seen surrealistically. Others, mingling with the strolling tunnel crowd, simply toiled with their arm-implanted ZCAP meters, hoping for a perfect reception and cool zuctha-angle viewing. Among those were the family types, well-behaved children and pets included. They wandered around in groups of four or more, seeking special thrills, all much related to the current soul travel show.

Of interest was the infallible crowd of indiscreet road-roving lovers, popping up at every unexpected turn, not exactly quitters regarding the show. They both smooched and peeked at the same time from inside their loaded slow-cruising zendallions or convertible zolls-dogs. Occasional roars such as "GO RICHARD–MAKE THINGS HAPPEN! OR DROP DEAD WHEN YOU GET THERE, WORTHLESS OCTIDARE, IF YOU CAN'T!" could be heard from their vicious throats at every interactive opportunity.

❦

Sprawling cobblestone pathways lined with exotic Madagascar plants, in various shades of green, red, brown, and yellow–often crossed by harmless tiny dappled-gray gawk-eyed reptiles–opened up to all these *regulars* in lavish and enigmatic ways. So did the gorgeous ancient Greek sculpted statues and golden Byzantine water fountains ornamenting the hallways, themselves shrouded with sensuous wild flowers and lush greenery.

No longer did they shop around the chic boutiques, play table games, or crack a joke while eating out. The time had arrived to stop every activity and give themselves fully to *The Happening*. The wealthiest person on earth by at least a thousand times its predecessor was about to publicly be hurled away like a piece of garbage to *The Unknown*.

The rumor went at least one-fourth of the Corridor crowd would soon invade the six Bisected Stadiums to watch, in the closest proximity possible, Richard Flynn's departure to his punishing soul travel journey.

Laidback Infant wouldn't be one of them.

He preferred to stay at his solitary and quiet table in the north wing of the main gallery, browsing newspaper headlines from his comfortable chair. A hot story on Richard Flynn he'd started to read, while nursing himself a strawberry shake, presently consumed his mind.

Seeing the defendant's photograph plastered next to the news piece made him react irately. *That's the man on trial right here right now! The scumbag in the Detention Cell!* his mind accused explosively. *That sickening octillionaire!* Cooling off a bit, he tried to read on, but anger residues still clogged his mind. *The mother fucker looks good, still in his thirties, after sleeping away for ten decades."* He pounded the table, dealing with a new surge of rage. *Ten fucking deep-freeze decades in a fucking trillion dollar coffin. The bastard!*

He drank some juice.

That money-bloody-sucking vampire!

His troubled eyes refocused on the printed words. He read on,

During his sleep, as we all know, many mega events shook the planet...

༄

The attractive CMM reporter who'd interviewed the Time Traveler a while ago, now casually reclined against a door near the Corridor's entrance, happened to be reading the same line, which continued this way,

> **...including the surrender of the United States, his country, to the Zongdrolls in 3000, and the formation of a new world, our world, eventually called Zundo.**

She scratched her neck, paused, went on reading,

> **That occurred, strangely enough, later on that year, after the unprecedented "Handshake with God Day" event celebrated in Alice Springs, Australia, with a physical presence of 100 million believers from all over the world.**

She picked at her nose, self-conscious of its poorly reconstructed shape after a cheap plastic surgery job.

> **But, as we all know, and sadly so, this event became a total "no show" from God.**

The CMM reporter had no idea Walking Brain's sensitive spying antennas had already marked her for some kind of upcoming *biochemical transformation*. More strange incidents were also in the works regarding other targeted individuals—a very common thing in this uncommon place.

Mounting tension lined the faces of many pacing ZV news reporters in the Corridor's main gallery as they adjusted their mikes and typed updates into their zaptops. Blood pressure also rose in the vascular system of surveillance mediazoops now busily monitoring all technical details in their hovering zurbdogs above the Zoliseum.

Thrilled spectators could see ground crew members of these News Media snoop boobs carrying production cameras and sound equipment, the many and varied cables of which dragged annoyingly under their feet like slithering snakes. "Glad I'm up here in my cool z-dog— no bloody messing with those coiling and slippery fuckers," scoffed one of the low-flying mediazoops.

Outside the Corridor, armed Security guards clad in olive-green uniforms and other types of camouflage outfits occupied visible posts overlooking the Astral Floor's lateral winding passageways.

Three barracudas cruised through tenacious steel scaffolds supporting the Stadiums. They searched for smaller fish to eat, uncaring for what transpired on the surface. Lucky for them, a group of tasty fairy basslets and blackbar soldierfish entered their terrain.

A rumor had spread underwater that two previously missing local predators—a giant loggerhead turtle and a white spotted tiger shark—both greatly admired by Richard—had reappeared and were seen swimming minutes ago under the Astral Floor through the cracks of the lumber structure. The rumor matured into fact when it became known that the two predators had simply slipped away for a few hours to attend the birth celebration of a baby barracuda in a neighboring habitat.

Above, on grassy grounds, recently dispatched bands of Security snoop boobs, wearing mauve-tinted berets, took positions in the many unsuspected sections of the Zoliseum and back alleys of the Bermuda Revelation Park. Some scurried around armed with latest model zinja-nuclee assault rifles, others zylvester-9X9 bazooka machine guns.

Riot police units patrolled everywhere, keeping the peace, if only psychologically. Many of them scampered around loaded with flame-throwing hand-cannons, rolling guillotines, back-breaking iron clubs, and police wolves. A dozen horse-mounted saber-swinging officers covered specific areas, just in case.

These peace-keeping squads remembered darn well the riot disturbances of 3073, when a few hundred youngsters ended up burned alive forming a huge human torch in protest for "algae stuffing poisoning" in the Zoliseum-served sandwiches. By then, food supply rationing had hit such a low, no other form of nourishment could be found around the globe. And there were no scientific programs in sight capable of changing that—not even Walking Brain's always handy ingenious ones.

∽

Several nearby fireman stations, also forming part of the Security snoop boobs, were on alert. Five fold. Their brave men's hearts pounded harder and harder, restless for action. One fireman, however, had taken the newspaper he was reading to the station rest room. Attending to his bowel needs, he sat there and read what came to his tired eyes, same printed story, third paragraph:

> **...he was supposed to remain in this frozen, sleepy state for three more decades, past his first ten, in honor of his favorite number, 13, only that Zundo's highest court cut him short of his wishes by reason of "undeserved sleep."**

A corny little smile curled up his lips as he dropped his load.

                                       ᦀ

Mobile hospitals and emergency rooms filled with doctors, surgeons, and nurses were parked outside the Stadium gates. Orderlies stood near stretches. They all pertained to the distinguished Medics snoop boobs.

An ambulance driver seated at the wheel with the engine idling was finishing reading a newspaper story. The same one:

> **...by court order he's appearing here today, virtually naked from head to toe, to prevent any foolish act from his part.**

The remaining three snoop boobs–Techs, Judges, and Royal Den– were also currently functional, all engaged, and attracting one hell of attention from the huge, agitated Zoliseum's audience. Defendant Richard Flynn happened to be their most valued asset.

And so unfolded the so-called "Trial of the Millennium" on Day 1 of its season's grand opening.

PART 3

THIRTEEN PRE-DEPARTURE CLASHES
ZUNDO, JUNE 3081

WICKED ROAD TO THE ZOASIS

Master Judge heard a tiny *zrrrrrr* sound on his ZCAP meter and checked it out. "Rain in twenty hours, seventeen minutes," he read.

From his elevated post in the Royal Den, he stared down at the transparent Cell where Richard sat unhappily. He could see his sad, darkened eyes and tense lips through the circular caged wall that contained him like a dangerous animal.

Behind him he could also see through the protective zhoenix shield a moray eel and two nurse sharks roving the area. Other sea creatures drifted by in the far background amid jagged rocks, yellow coral reefs, and virgin fissures.

"So, Mr. Flynn, how did you ever get so rich? From humble beginnings?"

Richard heard the big, resonant voice, scratched one ear.

"Oh no no. I was already rich at birth—*48* million dollars strong!" A silly smirk escaped his lips. "Passed on to me by my father." His eyes twitched in a funny way. "It all started like that."

Master Judge floated down from the Royal Den inside a bubble, macabrely dressed. It popped open, delivering him onto the Detention Cell floor.

"Please go on."

Richard regarded the annoying magician-judge with apprehension. Something amiss in his waxy bald head and freaky dark eyes unnerved him. Uncomfortably, he veered his stare down to the gruesome pacing black boots which showed under his ghastly black cape.

"For some reason, I wasn't pleased with the ending "*8*"–you know–*48*. It sounded unnatural." He paused. "I had always thought savings should end with zeros–upper range."

"You bet."

"I couldn't comprehend why my father didn't procure this exacting number—50—being so close."

Master Judge circled the zlass cell with careful steps, gazing at the defendant methodically.

"You can say that."

Suddenly Richard saw another bubble, light blue, float by his face, carrying a sinister man inside, looking exactly like Master Judge. The man's lips curled into a teasing smile. One of his eyes blinked eerily. *Shit*, thought Richard, pulling back, *he's a zlone of Master Judge!"*

The bubble spun around and bounced in the air with a will of its own, carrying the strange person. It was a fun and silly moment to watch...almost unreal. At least, that's how the audience felt.

"RIGHT ON JUDGE! YOU ROCK!" howled the crowd.

"Hi pal! Dig my magic act?" cheered the new Master Judge.

Richard trembled. *"Two of you?!"*

The Stadiums crowd exploded with laughter. Belly laughter.

Before Richard regained his composure, the weird visitor had already cracked the bubble open with his index finger and spilled himself wholly onto the ground. "Y-E-S-S-S-S!" he pumped himself up showily a la Rafael Nadal (still revered in 3081 as the greatest ever red-clay tennis player), with the perfect fist-clenching, biceps-bulging, body-jerking bravado.

Next thing, both Master Judges—truly identical—were circling Richard's chair, sneering at him like freaking detectives.

Richard tried to forget them, but couldn't. "Can you please be only one?" he implored. "One judge...one person...?" Enraged, hysterical, he shouted, *"P-L-E-A-S-E!!!"*

Master Judge snapped two fingers, making his zlone vanish away in a dark blue bubble. He also gave Richard a handkerchief.

"Satisfied?"

Richard nodded, his fingers quickly fidgeting with the piece of cloth...its softness. It was the pacifier he craved for the most—not a secret anymore. "Thanks."

Collecting his thoughts, Richard said, "It took me several years to achieve this goal, raise my wealth to 50 million." He paused. "I was considerably dumb to start with." He plucked at his mustache. "I was *eleven* then, when my uncle–mother's side–allowed me to exercise my rights as the son of a—"

Master Judge interrupted by balancing himself forward with one hand sharply raised, like the Hitler's salute, aiming to stop Richard's next word. *"Hold it there!"* he yelled.

"–dead millionaire."

"Didn't I tell you to hold it there, damn it!!!"

Richard heard the thunderous voice, watched the cold malice in the judge's intense eyes.

"The words were coming out of my mouth already. I couldn't–"

"Something else's gonna come out of your mouth...and ears...pretty soon if you don't shape up!" Master Judge collected himself a little. "Please step out of the Cell and take a walk to the river."

"What river? Where?"

He saw the judge hop into an orange bubble and disappear with it.

☙

Master Judge was still cracking up with laughter from his heavenly post, both his cheeks flushed red, after emerging from the bubble like a magician, while Richard watched him from his modest place down the Astral Floor's Detention Cell. *How fast! How amazing! How did he do it?* he thought. *Or maybe it's me...who lost the sense of things...*

"Don't be impatient, my friend," said the judge, breaking into more laughter. His laughter got grosser and louder. "Go change first!" He sat stately at the control panel high above the Detention Set, his black gloved fingers flipping one switch after another.

Then he stood up. Folding his black cape back over his right shoulder, he lifted his pointed beard, slit-eyed, in a wicked manner reminiscent of Dracula.

"Take him to the Zoasis!" he commanded a young girl, who sported a ponytail and stylish outfit.

Graciously, she led Richard to a walk area bordering the Astral Floor just a few steps away and motioned him to stay put.

Together they observed technology in motion as the Detention Set got replaced by the Clashes Set, while a third set, the Zoasis, minuscule by comparison but enchanting in its own right, rose to a spot near the Clashes Set—all by virtue of a quick exchange of platforms.

The Zoasis was a little isolated retreat, as hinted by its name, featuring a couch, jacuzzi, change room, fresh water bar, snack bowl, and cute palm tree.

Perfect! thought Richard upon being briefed about it.

The young girl now handed him a set of clothes for the occasion and asked him to give her his ring, which he did with mixed emotions and the eerie notion that he might then on become as vulnerable as a park pigeon...if he had to believe in Uncle George's words.

"It's very pretty, sparkling yellowish-green hues." She stored the ring away in a safety box. "You'll have it back—I promise—if you survive the Clashes."

Worried, Richard watched her go away.

But she hurried back carrying a syringe.

"May I have your shoulder, please? This shot of zezoid will make you and MJ equally stronger and alert during competition. No side effects."

"How strong?"

"Very."

⁊

Meantime various species of fish—chiefly yellowtail snappers, garden eels, and blue tangs—penetrated the system of narrow passageways and arches to and from the Stadiums. Some of them filtered through the wooden floor fissures, already populated with terraced tube sponges and coral heads, within range of Richard's field of vision.

Further east a dramatic wall drop-off riddled with sea fans, strawberry sponges, and coral formations teased the view. It guarded the entrance to a cave below the Promenade Corridor and allowed friendly eagle rays and glassy sweepers to meet and mingle.

Often, like now, they swam to the linking Zoasis tunnel underneath the Astral Floor, within the bounds of the elastic zhoenix shield, thus surfacing at will and flirting with the man-made environment.

∽

Alone in the Zoasis now, Richard began to hear instructions from The Zoice—an invisible soothing male voice that offered guidance during hard moments, such as this one. It carried warmth and care in its recognizable effeminate delivery.

"No handkerchief here. Button your shorts, please. Avoid snacks now. Jacuzzi's only allowed when and if you win a Clash," it whispered. "If badly hurt, bleeding, or left unconscious, do not hesitate to contact me."

To his chagrin, the whispers soon waned away.

∽

"MAY THE TWO COMBATANTS PLEASE MEET BY THE RIVER AT ONCE!" then commanded another voice, recognizable by its castigating booming quality.

Richard began to march toward no-man's land, feeling fragile and stupid. He wore, as told, a dark T-shirt assigned for the first Clash of the day. Instinctively, he brushed a spread of snow-white dandruff specks off the top of his shoulders—a perpetual nuisance he was terribly self-conscious of.

Suddenly, he realized a very unwelcoming huge crowd surrounded him, ready to unleash a demon of sorts that might entertain them to ecstasy while crushing him to pieces.

BLACK FOREST RIVER
(CLASH #1—LOG FIGHTING)

Stately spinning above the Zoliseum over everybody's heads, the Celestial Sphere descended the last few feet to display the trial current status. Words began to scroll and red-flash in the message area at the bottom:

> JUST COMPLETED: DETENTION Q&A SHOW • NEXT: PUNISHMENT CLASHES SHOW, STARTING WITH CLASH #1—LOG FIGHTING

❧

From his elevated controls tower in the Royal Den, Master Judge flipped the fist of thirteen toggle switches lined up on his console.

A river and accompanying forest trees strangely hued in black materialized on the Clashes Set's platform, this one disappearing right off underground. Two enormous logs floated on the agitated water under a partially clouded sky.

The scenario was spiced up by a nearby pelican that plunged to catch a fish. By the shore, a small sign mounted on an old, decaying wood post said, "BLACK FOREST RIVER."

Richard stood both amazed and scared, watching.

"Move along spoiled child, embrace the challenge of confession and confrontation—two ungracious monsters!" Master Judge's excited eyes lit up the moment. "This is the real thing now!"

Speechless, Richard attempted a few steps on the wet soil that flanked the river, realizing it was cold and real. Warm pee began to leak through his khaki shorts and down his hairy legs, but he could not feel it...just now.

All of a sudden, Master Judge ran past him, yelling like a wild high school bully. He wore ordinary mountain shorts and a rolled-up long sleeve shirt. Recklessly, he slowed down to remove his shoes on the run and waded into the river like a maniac.

The surrounding Stadiums' crowd cheered and shouted all kinds of hell-raising remarks. They also hurled objects up in the air.

"GET HIM NOW! DROWN HIM NOW!" a loud round of angry roars went.

Waiving their fists in patriotic ardor, they also began to chant lines from a war song that made the seats tremble with shattering force.

Master Judge waited for the commotion to calm down a little, staring up and down, long and wide, at the multitude with pride, both his feet in the water.

He then addressed Richard, "Please, grab a stick. Take your position on either log...and *confess!* That is, *confess and fight!*"

Richard just stood immobile, confused.

Giving him a hard look, Master Judge picked up a heavy stick from the shore and hopped on the nearest log with great agility. The log spun dangerously. But the judge's skills overtook the thrust and he was in complete balance all too soon, waiting for his adversary.

Richard stood knee-deep in the water near the other log, unsure, not noticing a stream of black squirming things approaching his body.

"But..." he said, timidly.

"No buts here. Defend yourself and confess!"

Richard climbed on the log, luckily before the squirming things grabbed him. With poor balance and fear, he stared at Master Judge.

"Why this?"

Master Judge hit him in the stomach with the stout stick.

Richard stumbled in pain, the log spinning under his feet. Quickly, he regained his balance. Only to be hit again in one leg, which trembled miserably before it recovered enough to hold on.

Master Judge laughed crudely with his booming voice, causing roars of laughter exploding everywhere in the Bisected Stadiums, Promenade Corridor, and all around the Bermuda Revelation Park.

"It's to your advantage, stupid! This is the first of thirteen Clashes you will have with me...and perhaps other judges."

"Thirteen?"

"Yes. Your favorite number, remember?" He rolled his eyes. "After which you'll be on your own soul traveling to *The Unknown*."

"*The Unknown*?"

"Can you stop being so *fucking naive*!?" shouted the judge.

Without warning, he waved his stick again and poked Richard hard in the chest, making him shake like a sardine.

"Every win you score will reduce your sentence by *four* years. But every loss will add *one* year to it. Understood?"

Master Judge addressed the audience also, "All Park activities will be open from eight in the morning till midnight every day. Hope you have a great time." Turning to Richard, he thundered, "Begin your confession now!"

The crowd roared.

Some spectators stared around at the spooky black trees, out of fear and curiosity. Others stared down at the mysterious black river, seeing things moving.

They knew the river contained at least untold quantities of ghostly looking mollusks, crustaceans, and segmented worms that had crossed over from the nearby ocean. Even black leeches swirled around like wasted embryos of a defunct past screaming for a new life. Alas, a revolting one.

This was not a place to fall, Richard figured quickly.

There were more ugly things down there...like hundreds of crawling cave-dwelling remipedes, dead-plant-eating echiurans, and zooplankton-preying lophogastrids....

❧

Angrily, Richard swung his stick low, knocking the judge on one knee, but the man just laughed.

His next blow landed on Master Judge's hip. This time there was obvious pain, forcing the judge to bend, crouch, and moan, almost losing his balance.

On his knees, Master Judge stared up at the defendant with extreme hate. He panted, "You were saying...you became the son of a... dead millionaire?" Then he laughed miserably. "Help me out."

Facing the judge on his floating log, Richard let one of his slippery feet rest a little, then lounged at the mad man with furious force.

He missed and almost fell.

The Stadiums crowd yelled with passion: "CONFESS FILTHY RICH! CONFESS!"

Boos and whistles echoed all around. They hurled objects in the air.

Remembering his past, Richard declared, "All right...I had no skills, no vision, no initiative."

His thoughtful head got a sudden blow from the judge. The pretty curls on it frazzled. Lengthwise, his body swaggered like a duck.

"Neither did I," said Master Judge, "in the beginning."

Richard whacked the judge in one shoulder, then the other–really hard. He also said with difficulty, "I feared commitment."

Such words only inflated Master Judge's ego. "I didn't. Not then, not now," he said. He turned his body and swung his pole with great malice, hitting Richard in the chin and neck. Blood began to leak from his mouth. "I love getting involved with people. I really do," he added cynically.

Richard touched his spilling blood with one hand, stared at it, and revengefully slammed his stick against both of Master Judge's legs, causing a balance crisis for both of them.

Richard's log rolled as wildly as the judge's own under his feet. Curiously, neither man plunged into the river.

Out of breath, Richard said, "I wanted to live a simple life...spend a good portion of that wealth." He noticed a paramedic van slowing to a stop near the set. Two male orderlies in white rushed out, carrying first-aid kits. "Marry a beautiful girl."

"Bravo!" rejoiced the judge.

His heavy stick smacked Richard's forehead, causing blood to spill from one ear.

In pain, Richard continued, "...indulge in..."

"I wonder what?" interrupted the judge sarcastically.

The two orderlies sat ashore cross-legged, waiting for a signal.

"...perfect vacationing...with perfect people..." said Richard, his face lightening up a bit as if daydreaming.

"No such place in this world, no such people."

Richard snapped out of his reverie. "Well, the Nazis were working on that, over ten centuries ago."

Master Judge began to switch his stick from one hand to another, repeatedly, challenging the defendant with his vicious eyes–a new tactic. Underneath, the sinister black river seemed to rise and fall mid-course, and spiral into ever deeper holes near the shore, with the pulling force of its current.

"You mean *killing* millions of innocent people–elderly, women, children," said the judge. "Filtering down the population to create the perfect race?"

"Oh, I don't believe in that," replied Richard. "I don't believe the Holocaust actually happened. Are you kidding me? How could the Nazis or any invading army have done that? I mean–that's *insane!*"

Master Judge whipped Richard's shoulder with the stick.

"Exactly. But it *did* happen," he said.

They stared at each other with burning hate.

"It's your belief against mine," snapped Richard.

"I don't think your belief has any value today," snapped back the judge. "Sorry." His legs probed for better balance on the unstable log. "Plus..." he added, shifting his torso a bit to face him, "the world has produced tons and tons of documentation about it over the years. It's a proven fact."

"Proven fact my ass!"

"LOOK OUT!" suddenly yelled the judge, charging with devilish force, finally knocking Richard into the water and claiming victory.

The Stadiums audience went wild. Big cheers for the charismatic judge, endless boos for the crushed defendant. They repeated: "HURRAH MASTER JUDGE! DOWN THE FILTHY RICH!"

Above, the Celestial Sphere's bottom area showed the results of this confrontation:

JUST COMPLETED: CLASH #1—LOG FIGHTING • OVERALL SCORE: JUDGES 1 DEFENDANT 0 • NEXT: CLASH #2— MOUNTAIN CLIMBING

Richard stood still for a moment in the river, the cold water reaching up to his neck.

Master Judge approached him standing on his log. "Ever been in love, Mr. Filthy Rich?" he asked.

"Nope."

"Too bad. You've missed one of the greatest experiences life has to offer."

He turned to go.

"But wait–" he said facing him again, "didn't you say a while ago that you wanted to marry a beautiful girl...someday?"

"You bet!"

A genuine little smile cracked Richard's face. He began to drag his feet out of the water, narrowing the distance to the two orderlies, three seconds shy from being bitten by a nasty undulating dark-green moray.

While they took care of him, the proud judge disappeared in a pink bubble, far and far away....

THE WORST OF THREE LETHAL CHOICES
(CLASH #13—POLE VAULTING)

12 Clashes later...

Something triggered Master Judge's mind.

His fingers, under his black cape, reached out for a button on the instrument panel. Two platforms moved up, one down.

A "track and field" setting materialized on the Astral Floor to everybody's delight, particularly the spectators' seated in the surrounding Stadiums' nearest rows.

Above, the Celestial Sphere began to descend a dozen feet closer to the cheering crowd's heads to announce the current status:

JUST COMPLETED: CLASH #12—INK BEACH • OVERALL SCORE: JUDGES 9 DEFENDANT 3 • NEXT: CLASH #13— POLE VAULTING

Having the defendant already experienced twelve of the thirteen punishment Clashes, many of them lethal or mind damaging, only one remained to be endured—Pole Vaulting—before qualifying for the dreaded journey to *The Unknown*—a soul, not time, travel journey, in his case.

Not told, each of these Clashes had a life of its own, so to speak. Unless programmed otherwise, collectively they meant to travel in space across time indefinitely, without chronological order, like stalking balloons...full of their very special stored cinematic energy.

Highly restless, as usual, the crowd was still behaving in a disorderly manner, creating pockets of noise and chatter.

"POLE VAULTING IS ON. PLEASE REMAIN SEATED AND OBSERVE SILENCE," said a commanding voice from multiple speakers around the Stadiums.

Two athletes, properly dressed and ready for this competition, trotted to center field. They were Richard Zilch, the defendant, wearing a dark blue T-shirt, and Sentence Judge, a very agile and sleek black woman in her twenties, sporting a red outfit that did justice to her body.

From his elevated post, Master Judge addressed the defendant, "Welcome to Clash #13...your last Clash." Pointing at the female judge with pride, he added, "Your opponent is a truly wonderful pole vaulter. You might learn something here today."

They exchanged polite smiles before entering the competition zone.

Master Judge left the area floating up in a violet bubble.

The crowd began to get impatient. They howled and cheered for hard action.

Meanwhile Sentence Judge flexed her legs a little, warming up for her first jump. Grabbing the long fiberzlass pole with confidence, she prepared to run.

Before she did, she approached the defendant. "I hate to say this, but it's time for you to choose your sentence which will begin right after this competition," she announced straight out, with clarity and the precision of a drill sergeant. "You have *three* choices..." She realized she was there to compete, mainly. "Let me jump first and I'll explain them to you later."

She went, leaving Richard scratching his mustache.

Taking position at the runway end, she held the fiberzlass pole high at an angle, concentrating on her goal. Then she sprinted towards the plant box holding the pole level with the ground before she began to lower it in the last few strides. Bang! Perfect planting and take off.

Her body swung up, higher and higher, with a final twist over the crossbar, which she cleared nicely.

Afterwards, she approached Richard again.

"Three choices: the *thirty*-year poverty journey, the *twenty*-year medium poverty journey, and the *thirteen*-year extreme poverty journey," she informed. "Think about it while you jump. It's your turn."

Richard nodded. *Nice body, great lips. Too bad she's killing me with her words*, he pondered.

Around him, the crowd's noise subsided. Hardly a sound.

Richard began to walk slowly toward the runway end, dragging the pole behind him. It was a loaded walk, crammed with tension.

Somehow the present competition took priority in his mind, and he let himself go, running down the dirt track with increasing acceleration.

He was no expert, but the bar wasn't high either. So when he planted the pole tip into the box and his legs jerked up into the air, he knew it could go either way.

Fortunately, it went well, and his body cleared the bar.

Watching, Sentence Judge clapped her hands. She then approached Richard as casually as before. "These are actual years of misery you will spend living and learning the poverty issue first hand."

Side by side they walked toward the runway end, dragging their fiberzlass poles behind them, while an official in the field raised the bar a few notches.

She stopped, holding the pole tighter with both hands. Noticed Richard had pulled out a handkerchief from his shorts, which he began to fumble with his fingers. "To you, these will be thirty, twenty, or thirteen real years of madness. To us, they'll represent only four hours of our time. A fixed time."

"Only *four* hours?"

"It has to do with time manipulation, thanks to Dr. Ufahh's research."

She stared straight to the bar. "Excuse me..."

Sentence Judge started off the long run with the long pole.

It was a superb jump. The crowd applauded vigorously.

Tropical fish, turtles, and crabs drifting through shallow undersea canyons near Stadium #5 allowed by the elastic zhoenix shield didn't applaud, but they watched.

Curiosity was their element.

Also, a sense of belonging.

∾

Holding her fiberzlass pole, Sentence Judge joined Richard again.

"You won't get older than four hours either upon your return, but you will suffer like a mistreated dog for thirty, twenty, or thirteen years—whichever package you prefer."

It was Richard's turn to jump, but Sentence Judge's words had affected him. His hands were trembling, and his face looked very pale—like a terminal leukemia patient about to take a cold shower.

Fussing with his handkerchief, he stared at her.

"You mean I will actually endure this agonizing insanity during the so-many-years of my choice?"

"You will agonize as long or as deep as you wish, according to your choice made," said Sentence Judge.

"We're talking about soul travel, not time travel, right?"

"Right. ST works in mysterious ways, and not exactly alone or isolated. Only Walking Brain knows all the details."

"Walking Brain?"

"Oh, that's our affectionate way of calling Dr. Ufahh." She bent a little to tap repeatedly her thigh muscles. "Sometimes we just call him WB."

"Walking Brain...now I remember," exclaimed Richard, rubbing his chin. "I once heard a kid calling him that way—Walking Brain."

"You've met him before?"

"Just once."

"Interesting." Actually, she meant a lot more than that. *A pre-trial meeting with the Zoliseum's chairman?* she mused uncomfortably. *Very unusual.*

Again, they walked side by side to the runway end.

Richard prepared to sprint, staring up to the distant bar he intended to clear.

"Remember—a thirteen-year sentence might not be right for you!"

Richard waited a little, listening, staring straight ahead now.

"Your body and mind might not tolerate such...such incredibly devastating and thickly compact poverty...such concentration of misery and starvation."

She gave Richard a solemn grim look.

"You might perish in *five* years out there."

"My God."

Richard started off. He ran well, but his jump left much to be desired. With obvious struggle, he barely cleared the bar, and he almost missed the landing pad on his fall.

He trudged back to the runway end, where the judge busied herself flexing her legs and doing some sit-ups and hip twisting.

"Plus there might be other dangers, life-threatening dangers, thieves, thugs, and criminals—the scum of society."

Self-mockingly, Richard said, "Swell."

The black judge did some push-ups and sat down on the grass, noticing someone in uniform had raised the bar a few inches.

"I'd suggest you take the twenty year medium poverty journey, to make sure you can stand it."

"Grrrr..."

Richard fretted with his handkerchief again. He also brushed off with it a bunch of dandruff flakes he saw over his right shoulder.

The agile black athlete stood up, took a deep breath and exhaled slowly. She repeated it three times.

"Or the thirty year poverty journey, to suffer less."

"Less?"

"But longer."

"Oh my."

Staring at the distant bar with a firm grip on the pole, she darted off at full speed.

Again, it was a great jump. The crowd applauded and cheered.

For a moment, Richard's eyes veered toward passing schools of tropical fish east of the elastic zhoenix shield. Wrasse, jacks, and grunts swam over a reef covered with lush corals, beyond which thrived sponges and sea fans of many shapes and colors.

Further down gobies, damsels, and groupers paraded almost flirt-ingly through a swim-through coral passageway inside a large sun-lit grotto. Red incrusting algae and rare cryptic gorgonians visited by angel fish flanked the grotto entrance.

Hauling the long pole behind her, Sentence Judge returned to the runway end, where Richard stood, confused, or just daydreaming.

For a tiny moment, she just stared at him. Then cynically, with accusing eyes, she uttered, "*Mon vieux*–you didn't think you could be-come an octillionaire for so long and get away with it, did you?"

Richard surprised the judge and every soul in the watchful Stadiums and Corridors when he spoke, "I'll choose the *thirteen*-year extreme poverty journey."

"Mr. Zilch, don't do it just because you like that number! You might not–"

"I will survive."

He flexed his legs in preparation for his jump.

"You've been warned several times now. The contrast is so se-vere–from super octillionaire to super penniless–almost like fall-ing vertically from the Empire State Building–that, my friend, you'll never–"

Richard was set to go. He held the pole steady in front of him. Joyously, he just said, "I like vertical falls. Sky diving is a part of my life."

Whistling in disbelief, Sentence Judge said, "It'll be a part of your life all right," and rolled her eyes.

Richard started running. Faster and faster. He stuck the pole into the box and vaulted up with all his might, but knocked the bar down with the edge of his right foot just before clearing it.

In the next seconds Sentence Judge's ZCAP meter rang.

"Hello?"

"Hi. This is Dr. Ufahh."

"Oh hi..."

"We have a little problem with our time travel and soul travel projects."

"I'm listening."

"Just a moment–I have one of the 3Zs on another line," he said, lying.

Two fleeting worries had crossed his mind that needed immediate attention before he even engaged in conversation with Sentence Judge. *One*, he reflected, *why did it take four hours and three minutes Zundo time for the Time Traveler to complete his TT on a thirteen-year journey choice…the choice I convinced him to take in exchange for that big chunk of money he agreed to?*

He scratched one ear.

I gave Master Judge the tools–the halfzun patch–to cut his journey in half, suffering included. So he should've returned in four hours even, like any traveler with those choices. Something's wrong here.

His eyes drifted to his shoes, thinking.

Looks like he's been journeying out there in the 20th century for twice thirteen years, not half. Insane! He stared blankly at the wall.

Two, he re-engaged his thoughts again, *that smart-ass CMM reporter that interviewed him, telling him all that jazzy research crap and analytical stuff she did about his secret TT and personal history, must go. She knows too much!* He debated what to do with her, quickly narrowing his choices down. *I'll turn her into a geese!*

Now he reconnected with Sentence Judge. "I'm watching and hearing you, honey, through my special screen here in the Palace. What you're saying to Richard is correct, whatever choice he makes–thirty, twenty, or thirteen years of ST in the 20th century–will mean only four hours in 31st-century Zundo, provided–"

"He already selected *thirteen*, sir…"

"I know that."

"Oh…"

"Provided he's only doing ST."

"*Ajá…*"

"What you don't know–and nobody knows, except me–is that Richard is doing *both* TT and ST–one after the other–today."

"*Are you shitting me?*"

Turning to Richard who sat neglected on the ground, she said, "Here…put these earplugs in your ears for a moment, please…"

He complied.

"Are you fucking shitting me, Dr. Ufahh?"

"No. Now don't tell anybody—not even MJ—because this is a *breakthrough* project."

"Not even Master Judge?"

"Yes! Never before has a human being spent years on consecutive TT and ST package journeys to *The Unknown*. Never. And it's very possible that Richard, our first volunteer—well guinea pig—might not make it back. It's just experimental, you understand?"

"You mean the Time Traveler that just arrived—well, returned—a while ago...*was*...*is*...Richard?"

"Exactly. But I zloned him and erased parts of his memory. So your man, your pole vaulting dude, is Zlone-Richard, not Richard, and don't tell MJ about it either—got that?"

"Yes, sir." She coughed slightly. "But I'm confused...in so many ways." She checked on Richard, who remained quiet by her feet on the ground. "I thought you and Master Judge were close friends...buddies."

Dr. Ufahh laughed real loud.

"No. No no. We actually dislike each other like hell, only pretend to be friendly and cooperative. I don't even trust him."

"I had no idea, but—what's the big problem about Richard doing ST after finishing his TT?"

"It takes *four hours* Zundo time to do a TT on a 13-year journey package and a *six-month* separation between journeys, with the inconvenience of arriving before leaving, so Richard, having chosen a thirteen-year package—I know he did—would have to wait at least six months to do an ST." Dr. Ufahh pressed harder to keep his train of thoughts together. "If he leaves now, his ST might not connect with his TT, since, although finished, it hasn't left yet. See what I mean?"

"No."

"Well, you don't have to understand yet, just continue the way you know it, the way you've been doing it, and I'll work on making Richard TT-conductive full blast with my tools up here in my lab...so I can squeeze his six months into one hour or less without harmful effects."

"Why is it so important to punish our zillionaire defendants with both TT and ST? And keep both travels so close to each other?"

"So far only Richard will have that option, and fate. But, if it works, if he doesn't perish out there in *The Unknown*, it'll make his travel a complete experience. The ST will complement the TT. It will allow him to not only time travel physically and dryly but *feel* the emotions...the vibes...the spices...the soul in it." He scratched his left earlobe. "You see, soul travel gets you closer to God–don't tell Master Judge I believe in God. He will use it against me!"

"I won't."

"Good. But, why so close to each other–TT and ST–you asked?" recapped the scientist. "The closer the better. It's like love. Lovers need to be close to each other to max the experience. But the problem of arriving before leaving gets in the way." He rubbed his nose. "So, our goal is–as close to science as possible." He checked his ZCAP meter. "I have to go now, honey. I loved your jumps, by the way. You're a great athlete. And don't worry about ST for the moment, but keep your lips shut about everything we talked. Bye."

She heard the click and hung up too, feeling funny inside.

"Okay, pole vaulter," she then said, staring down at a very depressed Richard. "You can now remove your earplugs."

Realizing he couldn't hear, she gestured what she meant with her fingers. "And please get up, fill your lungs with fresh air, and take a walk to the Zoasis or something."

∽

Unhappily, Richard slumbered to a nearby bench and sat down.

He could feel the rumbling motion of the Pole Vaulting Set disappear underground. *It's over. Another loss*, he thought.

Sentence Judge, on the other hand, basked in her glory.

The crowd kept roaring.

People were dancing in the Stadiums aisles. They cheered and shouted all kinds of crazy words.

Sentence Judge stood proudly in the center of the Astral Floor, bowing all around and blowing kisses to the dazzled audience the way tennis star Andre Agassi used to do after winning a grand slam over a thousand years ago.

Above, results scrolled and flashed red on the Celestial Sphere's bottom area:

> **JUST COMPLETED: CLASH #13-POLE VAULTING • OVERALL SCORE: JUDGES 10 DEFENDANT 3 • NEXT: SENTENCE NEGOTIATION AND SENTENCE SONG AWARD SHOW**

A VERY TELLING WINNING SONG
(AND HANDLING OF THE CLASHES)

Holding a mike, Master Judge addressed the audience from the Royal Den, clad in his usual clownish gothic outfit.

"Any math major here?"

Thousands of hands from the Stadiums went up.

"I don't think we need one, after all," said the charismatic judge. "It's too simple. We all know the defendant has won three Clashes out of thirteen." He smiled. "We've won the rest."

He exchanged sweet glances with his colleagues sitting in the Judges Box.

"But overall calculations give the defendant a short edge…since his winning points are four times bigger than ours."

He ran one hand over his glossy bald head, thinking.

"Which boils down to the defendant getting a reduction of *two* years to his sentence." He raised both hands to the level of his bearded chin, conciliatorily. "Because those two years are negotiable, I will ask the defendant to stand up and reason with us."

Richard stood up from a bench. He was back to wearing only his coffee smeared underwear, by trial rules.

Master Judge asked, "Would you like to negotiate now or later, upon your soul travel return?"

"Later."

"That's very bold of you. You may sit down."

Staring at the crowd, the jovial judge spoke up with an unusual warm voice, "We have a treat for all of you Zundonians. The winner of our 'Fifteen Minute Fame Sentence Song Award' is going to sing her winning song." Swiftly, he bent forward ninety degrees, facing the audience, to show his glossy bald head. Painted on it in black were the big words "FAT TENTACLES." Then he said to the crowd, "Which she wrote just this morning. She's only nine."

The crowd applauded and cheered feverishly as a cute, pig-tailed blonde holding an acoustic guitar walked on with amazing charm to a newly appearing platform designed for this purpose.

All people quieted down when she began to sing. She had an adoring voice and two gorgeously innocent shinning blue eyes. Purposely staring at Richard, she let her fingers brush the guitar strings in a remarkable way.

> **One big reason to dethrone an octillionaire**
> **One great day to send him away**
> **Name the reason, Mr. Flynn**
> **Oh you know so well**
> **Is that treason, Mr. Zilch?**
> **Getting rich without restrain?**

Her fingers strum the guitar, going solo, she went on,

> **But why treason? You may wonder**
> **Wealth-sucking octopus of the world**
> **Treason to the poor, there's your answer**
> **Empty-pot beggar-maker of the world**
> **Please go away, Mr. Flynn**
> **Please take the train, Mr. Zilch**
> **Please fly away, Mr. Flynn**
> **Please disappear, Mr. Zilch**

The crowd roared and whistled and threw hats in the air as she ended with this daring note.

Applause also rang from the Judges Box and Royal Den. Macabrely wrapped in his black cape like a blood-sucking vampire, Master Judge raised both his arms, facing the audience.

"She couldn't have said it better—*disappear*." He stared at Richard strangely. "We're going to help you do that. "Suddenly, he shouted, "ON YOUR MARKS!" Only to follow with big bursts of laughter. "Just kidding. Well, almost..."

From his control desk, he grabbed a padded mallet and ritually banged it against a red rimmed metal disk set on a wall next to his framed picture.

"GONG-G-G-G-G-G-G–G-G-G!"

The crowd stood quiet in dead silence, paralyzed.

"Ladies, gentlemen, teenagers, gays, mutants, androids, cyborgs, and replicants of all walks of life...we must now proceed with the execution phase of the defendant's sentence." He snapped two fingers to a young girl in his vicinity. "Sweetie, please return the defendant's personal items in preparation for his...disappearance."

Richard watched a familiar young girl in sexy outfit strut up to him.

"See? I kept my promise. Here's your ring," she said warmly. "And some decent clothes for your journey."

"But they're *black*," said Richard with mistrust and fear.

"*Soul travel black*—best kind!"

"Can I have a handkerchief...for my hands?" asked Richard hesitantly.

The young girl handed him a black handkerchief. "Sure. Here."

"*Black*?" Puzzled, he nevertheless grabbed it with desperation, quickly letting his fingers fidget with its soft texture—a feeling he so badly needed.

"Best kind," repeated the girl, winking one eye.

Big swimming groupers and Jew fish were now feeding on schools of glassy sweepers and silverside minnows, which both the young girl and Richard noticed.

Many escaping silversides crossed a pool of diffused sunlight radiating against a cavernous wall lodged under the Promenade Corridor's archery shooting field, visible from both the Astral Floor and the Stadiums.

Down there a system of sandy reefs, fringing with hanging threads of sea fans and finger-like pillar corals, thrived with life. One of Master

Judge's pens had actually fallen and landed here during Richard's trial opening...a reason for Laidback Infant to deep-dive the area on his own one day, having noticed the minor accident, and come up with a bagful of unexpected treasures instead.

Among them, a white pearl with her mother sea shell.

♋

This deep underwater plateau, housing mostly long-tailed sting-rays and oval squids, happened to be experiencing at this time a procession of hundreds of spiny lobsters, marching single file as if going to war.

Such was the unpredictable nature of the Promenade Corridor's underwater abyss.

♋

Above, the Celestial Sphere began to display the latest trial status:

JUST COMPLETED: SENTENCE NEGOTIATION AND SENTENCE SONG AWARD SHOW • NEXT: REMEMBERING A VERY OLD SPOOKY MOVIE SHOW

PART 4

MIPHO'S ANCIENT EGYPT
WINTER 4003 BC

HIT BY THE ELEMENTS OF
A VERY OLD SPOOKY MOVIE

A ten minute break was announced, during which strange things happened.

First, the silver Celestial Sphere sneaked out of view faster than usual.

Then all sorts of psychedelic lights, creating striking colors, bizarre patterns, and altered states of awareness, splashed the vast space left vacant by the Sphere inside the Bisected Stadiums. They mysteriously mingled with a series of spooky sounds coming out of nowhere, similar to nothing heard before. Nothing to all but one spectator: Serene Lady.

Hordes of reef-munching animals with distorted faces began to surface from the depths of the very abyss, twiddling their freaky eyes, then plunging back into the deep underwater nether world.

"I've seen them before!" cried out a kid, holding a paper-made airplane.

He'd also seen worse things floating around...before their decomposition and transformation...things like thick black crude oil globs from coastal oil rigs, industrial waste from unchecked chemical companies, used condoms in disgusting filth and quantity, and discarded syringes from the depraved human world.

Added to this ecosystem's calamity were the effects of coral disease, algae overgrowth, unbalanced fishing practices, and global warming... all conspiring to destroy nature...in spite of supreme elastic efforts by the protective zhoenix shield to battle out the ailing process.

Meanwhile marine reef systems, drop-off walls, and blue holes seemed to want to talk to those willing to listen. But a rumor persisted in higher circles that Walking Brain's secret experiments had screwed up everything.

∽

All the seats in the sixth row of Stadium #4 became rapidly illuminated in red-orange, blue-green, yellow-black, and solid gold, tweaking people's perceptions of things around them. Many faces there looked disoriented and scared when a certain sequence of loud thumps and whisper-like sounds rocked the place.

∽

Someone was eating peanuts, head bent over his knees, in the thirty-fourth row of Stadium #2. Unlike other spectators, he was outright receptive to the trippy kaleidoscopic lights and weird sounds invading the Zoliseum, both above ground and underwater.

A closer look revealed he was Laidback Infant.

"I should've invited her at the fuel station," he was saying to himself, "We could be sharing this peanut bar together up here right now... this Lady of the 70s."

He checked his ZCAP meter for possible messages from Serene Lady. Nothing. Frustrated, he talked to it. "Are you there? It's me, Laid. Wanna go dancing?"

A cannonball jellyfish drifted by stealing only a whit of his attention.

∽

Someone, drinking apple juice in the middle rows of Stadium #5, felt seduced by the growing atmosphere of unnatural special effects. He picked up a crumpled, coffee-stained copy of the show's program from the floor, and read a part from a paragraph, "...a horror film, directed by Stanley Kubrick, over a thousand years ago..."

∽

A little girl in Stadium #1 closed her eyes, scared of the wildly changing colored lights and creepy sounds.

She didn't have a program to read from.

"Oh...oh..." she said.

Another girl, a bit older and taller, began to share her own program by holding it close to the little girl's eyes.

She read, "...Jack Nicholson played the mad man..."

A third girl, about the same age as the older girl but shorter, sitting next to her friends, joined in sharing the reading. "...and Shelley Duvall played the mad man's wife...a good woman..."

The little girl seemed to know something. Staring at his friends with big, quizzical, innocent eyes, she said, "And the little boy? What was his name?"

"Danny Lloyd. That's what it says here, in the program," replied the third girl.

"Isn't he cute?" giggled the little girl.

Her eyes veered to a passing school of spotted damsel fish...slithering through a formation of large vases sponges and star corals.

∽

Laidback Infant, seated in Stadium #2, pressed his lips, mesmerized by the psychedelic lights and scary sounds. From his jeans back pocket, he pulled out a folded paper with printed matter. The program.

He read, eyes focused on something, "...based on Stephen King's famous novel, *The Shining*–creepy tale of a sinister hotel in what-used-to-be-Colorado...over a thousand years ago..."

He was familiar with creepy moments, particularly the ones created by himself—in fact, his own history of running stark naked across crowded stadiums had landed him in jail every time.

So far he'd committed four streaking exposures this year, no question driving crowds to roaring laughter and euphoria every time. He'd been warned in court that a fifth strike would be punishable by time travel to *The Unknown*–no doubt, a life-threatening journey. So lately he'd been restraining himself from doing it again, from becoming a repeat offender. Not a good thing in Zundo.

Part of his restraining effort had to do with self-discipline–the art of focusing on a new endeavor.

His good swimming background and great love for adventure quickly led to a specific ocean sport–shipwreck diving.

So one day, as he swam toward the bottom of the ocean, he saw a familiar form loom like a large ghost. It was a wreck from another century–the graveyard of a French battleship.

To his fascination, fish life down there teemed with excitement. Within minutes he'd made friendship with a bottlenose dolphin, two baby octopuses, and a congregation of blue-stripped grunts.

Plus he'd taken an eyeful of the immense beauty emanating from the living sponges and coral heads housed inside the wreck. Their flirting shapes, virgin looks, and striking colors ignited his imagination. Nothing could compare! From then on his underwater destiny was marked for life.

Not surprisingly, he became very interested in the meaning of this happening. So he made a point whenever he came to watch an event in the Stadiums to always sit, if at all possible, on the spot directly above the French battleship, a few thousand feet deep under his ass. His research and calculations revealed a seat in the 34th row of Stadium #2, exactly where he sat now.

Today he felt like chanting his secret to anyone, especially Serene Lady. If she could only be by his side! Or by his ZCAP meter!

He checked the meter again for possible messages from her, the seventh time this afternoon. Nothing.

The ten minute break was only half consumed, he realized. Rubbing his chin, he muttered to himself, "Maybe I should go wreck diving tomorrow."

∞

Serene Lady applied mascara to her lashes facing the mirror in the ladies' room of Stadium #6.

She'd observed with crystal clarity her facial features for a couple of minutes, but the invading hallucinatory flashes and creepy sounds put her in a different state of mind, whereby she could actually recapture fond memories from her amazing past.

Seduced, she stopped what she was doing. *The Shining*, she thought, recalling the movie. *I remember those sharp, pulse-raising sounds in the film... over a thousand years ago....*

She remembered the summer of 1980...being in a theater...in the dark...sitting next to a romantic couple, whose names she knew were Gaston and Nikki—both San Fernando Valley locals, in Southern California.

They were holding hands, spooked out by a horrific scene crammed with atrocious visuals and evil-charged sounds...like the ones invading the Stadiums right now.

She decided to leave the theater a bit earlier (to avoid getting stuck in the exit doors' crowd) by squeezing her body between the couple's legs and the front row of seats...with only a polite "excuse me" since they didn't know her.

The current droning sounds took her farther back in time...very far...

I also remember this tiny island in the Red Sea...off the coast of Egypt... Ancient Egypt....

A VICIOUSLY INHABITED ISLAND IN THE RED SEA

A weather-beaten merchant ship approached the vestiges of a small island through thick fog.

Shadows from three pointed mountains suddenly blackened the tempestuous waters. Facing the crew stood huge limestone boulders rising to towering heights through sinister rings of clouds. Their haunting presence brought deep fear to the sailors, already scared and worn out by the storm. They saw no sign of vegetation or animal life ashore, except for a few mean-looking birds scouting the waters for fish.

Whipped by brutal winds, the large vessel bounced so erratically through the Red Sea waves—almost like a discarded piece of trash—that no one aboard dared to say a word.

Except the pepper-bearded captain. He was husky and rude to no end. More than anything, he wouldn't allow his ship to wreck in front of this island. Legend had it, many curses had cracked the sanity of those unfortunate sailors caught up in its entrails.

With maddening fury, he yelled to his crew, "HARDER! HARDER! DAMN YOU ALL—BASTARD! GET THE FUCKING SHIP CLOSER TO THE SHORE...OR PREPARE TO DIE!"

A devilish wave exploded on his face, getting him angrier. Before he yelled again, his eyes took a blow from the loose end of the dangling sail mast.

"HARDER! HARDER! HARDER!" he nevertheless commanded his men.

Keeping one hand clamped to one of the sail cords, he brushed some of the blood off his eyes with the back of his free hand, without much of a fuss.

His men just obeyed—pulling the ropes with mighty force, trying to control the nasty elements—sail, wind, waves, and now rain. It was like hell descending upon them.

Drawing back in a tug-of-war manner, robust legs acting like powerful pillars, they began to take the upper hand.

Rather swiftly, as if the gods of heaven and earth suddenly sided with them, the trembling boat made a strange pass between two gigantic, bracing waves, claiming both control and direction.

Just in time for the captain to growl in his fieriest yet voice, "DROP ANCHOR!"

Done, all sailors exchanged a long glance of relief, but the human thunder continued, "STAY PUT! NO RELAXING HERE—NOT EVEN FOR ONE SECOND!" Finally, he lowered his tone a bit. "We're surrounded by some of the meanest sharks you'll ever know! There are also vicious mantas down there!"

The punished vessel slowly came to a stop at the boulders edge. They were inside what looked like a lagoon, amid dense reefs of coral and darkly moving shadows underneath the surface.

"And once you set foot on the island, something far more dangerous yet awaits you," uttered the captain, keeping his voice reasonably down. "So on with your luck now!"

෧

The tempest subsided, revealing a strange, barren land of anemic dunes, red-hued rock sediments, and tiny green crystals. Nearby long-legged crabs moved erratically.

The fog began to clear.

෧

Shafts of faint sunlight, filtering through passing clouds of various designs, reminded Mipho that the late afternoon was ending. She'd been there in the ship all along. Her stately presence and intelligent eyes dominated her spot, but no one was watching. She was just a sailor among many.

Well, hardly...

Suspicious, the captain walked toward her.

He couldn't see the long hair tied into a bun under her crumpled hat because she dressed exactly like everyone else—clad in high seas menswear.

"Young man—haven't seen a trace of fear in your handsome face during the worst hours of our despair today. What are you made of, may I ask?"

"People call me many things for different reasons, sometimes similar reasons, but I call myself Serene Lady because serene I am when not mad, and a lady when not a man. Although, I'm really a lioness. Does that answer your question?"

A cold shiver suddenly ran through the captain's spine, spreading across his entire nervous system. Legend had it that such an apparition could happen, had happened, and might happen again. He was too afraid to think otherwise.

"Oh sure..." His tongue felt thick, uncooperative.

With trembling fingers, he pointed to the path leading to the sandy beach and the eerie mountains. "After you..."

Most crew members already trudged the slopes, rushing inland like avenging beasts of the high seas, oblivious of the harsh sailor's code they'd just outlived.

Behind them, with different aims and expectations, began to march Mipho and the fearful captain, this one intently lagging the mysterious goddess by at least fifty feet.

Only Mipho could hear the distant echoes of working slaves—the crying droning of thumping tools and chanting voices. Only she could smell the stench of over-sweating skins and debilitating bodies. Only she could see the significance of such an evolving night.

∽

Mipho saw the captain enter a cave and followed him inside.

From a safe distance, so not to be noticed, she watched the captain prepare for some kind of a ritual.

There was an intensely touching, never seen before, human side to him as he bent on his knees, alone, in solemn quietude.

Facing him stood, on a rock, the statuette of a lioness-headed deity clad in a long, green, close-fitting dress.

Mipho quickly recognized the personification of her sister, Bast, in the statuette—the powerful, chameleonic, and ageless Lioness Goddess of Ancient Egypt.

Standing with her legs together, she wore arm and ankle bracelets, a collar necklace, and earrings that sparkled vividly in the semi-dark. Black-haired and dark-eyed, with a tanned facial skin approaching nirvana, the illusory feline/woman head (as actually seen by Mipho) seemed to radiate a divine aura about herself, not the inanimate treated clay material she was made of.

Staring at her reverently, the captain prayed and asked for forgiveness.

∽

Out of the cave, Mipho now climbed the steeper side of the nearest mountain, headed west for the location of the working and chanting slaves, casting repeated glances to the surrounding distrustful sea.

Meanwhile the captain continued to pray, oblivious of the few poisonous serpents that had penetrated the cave after Mipho had left.

Quickly and mercilessly, one after another, they bit his flesh in the legs, butt, arms, back, neck, face...over and over as they moved into the cave. A dozen more approached his dying body. Such carnage he'd feared and expected all along, but could not bring himself to relay to his sailors, given its utter demoralizing nature. After all, Serpent Isle—as it was mostly known to the veteran warriors of the sea—had merely once again lived to its nefarious reputation.

∽

Mipho marched over the rocky terrain ridden with crystalline minerals next to a big, jagged boulder, which she knew had extraterrestrial properties.

She then crouched over a crisp yellow-green lump of rocks that persistently shone in the dark. Staring at a particular, vivid-green craggy slab incrusted in the boulder, she gently touched a portion of it with two fingers. "Welcome to Ancient Egypt precious meteorite," she said. "Welcome to me divine green stone."

She then solemnly kissed the mysterious, glowing mineral, creating her own ritual as she slowly raised her head, eyes fixed on the source.

"I am Mipho, Secret Sister of Bast, Lioness Goddess and Eye of Ra," she began. "I, too, possess cosmic powers and agelessness and will use them ferociously to protect each and every new Pharaoh of our land, whoever they might be."

Her dark eyes turned emerald-green.

"My servitude, loyalty, and devotion to every new ruler of Egypt, therefore, will be chameleonic, boundless, and unstoppable."

She paused, observing the lustrous piece of slab as if it were Ancient Egypt itself, then added, "Likewise, your cosmic beauty and powers will join forces with mine to ensure protection to our future Pharaohs."

Something amiss suddenly made her turn around with incredible agility and strength.

Three-headed now, her ferocious feline eyes overwhelmed the moment. With a swift swipe of her paw, at least a dozen snakes found revolting death in the ensuing seconds. Blood dripped from the pointed edges of her retracted claws when she confronted the next, yet bigger attack...with similar results.

Thrown on the rocks around her lay bleeding pieces of gnarled flesh and a chilly variety of chopped up snake heads.

Incoming serpents began to retreat at the sickening sight facing them. Others changed direction, slithering away from the excavation area, heading for the sea.

Alone, finally, Mipho became a full-woman again.

෴

Basaltic-like bluish rocks, seemingly spewed from volcano-rich western Arabia across the narrow, reddish-brown, algae-laden sea, littered the tiny island's landscape.

These rocks, however, had popped out from miles underground many years ago as a result of explosive pressures from the collision of Asiatic and African continental plates. Even parts of the Egyptian coast, across the same narrow sea, showed marks of this monumental event, responsible also for the birth and appearance of the island itself.

The misty, cinnamon sky above had turned eerily grayish-dark and only delicate veils of dust swiveled around.

Deeper inland, the sailors gathered at the foot of the mountain before they began to climb a bizarre, bleak path of slumped pits and shallow trenches.

Past a rubbish heap of human bones, skulls, and organic waste, one of the sailors pointed a finger to a small group of armed men in the distance, appearing barely visible high above a slope as the night stealthily enfolded them. "They wear uniforms," he said to his ship mates. "Should we trust them?" His ragged face showed fear.

"I think they're here to protect the miners," remarked another sailor with an ugly, infected cut to his chin.

"From what?" asked the sailor who spoke first, quite tall, even without his feathered brown hat.

"People like us," replied a muscular lad wearing a simple gray sweater made of cotton. "Thieves...crooks...hoodlums. What else?"

They continued trudging through nearly impassable clumps of deformed boulders, large and small. Then they plodded through a series of gaping and tangled ravines leading to a small clearing.

"Stop a minute. Did you hear that?" said a dark-skinned sailor with a raspy voice and two missing front teeth.

"What...?" gasped the youngest in the group, his tiny blue eyes on great alert now.

In complete silence of their own, they faintly heard echoes of distant clanking tools and humming voices...coated by the whistling breeze from the sea.

෴

Gathered atop a hill, moments later, they could see what clearly appeared to be a labor camp in full session—slaves hammering, picking, and shoveling the rocky ground under the flames of oil lamps.

Many wore ragged shirts or shabby coats and dark trousers with rat holes in them. Swollen toes stuck out from their worn out shoes.

A furious round of whipping gusts caused some of the slaves to crouch in agony, making the sight all the more pitiful.

"Evil shit," muttered the tall sailor, rubbing his hands to keep warm. "Bloody cruel and sad. Wouldn't want to be one of them!"

The toll of such harsh conditions peaked when one of the workers collapsed. A camel-mounted soldier wrapped in bulky metallic clothes ordered someone to remove the fallen man. He was right away dragged out of the area by the feet and dumped into a large trash bin. The uninterrupted labor buzz of working wheel barrows and water wells continued nearby.

"Did you hear that?" warned again the dark-tanned sailor, cupping one ear in front of his comrades.

They all stared at him with suspicious eyes. "Not again!" one of them snapped, coldly.

"It's something else...a different sound...I swear..." His husky voice started to trail. "...do you guys hear it...?"

"I think so..." offered another sailor, holding his breath, growing scared.

"It's a scurrying sound..." said a seasoned Hindu sporting a red bandanna, his upper lips covered with mustache hair.

"C'mon, you give me the creeps..." remarked the tall sailor. "*Where?*"

Too late. In a split second, hundreds of viciously squirming, ravenous snakes, with bulging eyes and dripping saliva, assaulted them.

A slaughter ensued. Chunks of bloody flesh, jumping eyeballs, and chewed-up gums with teeth hanging from them exploded in the air. Human screams of horror mixed with the butchery as more chopped body parts, detached limbs, and dripping fluids from vital organs cluttered the ground. These were not ordinary sea snakes. They seemed to be evil, devouring sea monsters of a strange prehistoric age.

Only one-third of the sailors managed to run away, and they did so in total hysteria, looking like raving maniacs, yelling in stark terror.

"SAVE ME LORD!!!" and derivatives from it cut through the mountain cliffs.

A few men tripped several times with themselves and the slippery granite soil under their feet, trying to dodge a nearby latrine's stinking spills and sticky buzzing flies.

Promptly, they grouped together.

Standing on the upper step of a terraced wall—where he'd fallen backward from higher grounds in his run over the slope, one shoulder bone broken—the lead sailor addressed the group, "I'm the second in command—now in charge of the ship." His face stood stern, but his agitated pumping heart approached failure. He managed to shout, "We're sailing out immediately!"

⚞

Mipho was back aboard.

None of the sailors had yet noticed she wasn't the young man she appeared to be. One of her pockets held a slab of precious meteorite.

I'll get a beautiful ring from it...at least, she thought facing the sea, her lips curled up into a naughty little smile.

PART 5

BLAST OFF
ZUNDO, JUNE 3081

AGAIN, AT THE GATES OF THE ZOLISEUM

Restless Zundonians crowded the Zoliseum gates, where a bottleneck type of entry slowed everyone down. The "Trial of the Millennium" geared for another day packed with events, surprises, music...and humanity.

If the world had stood for years glued to their five favorite z-communicators—ZV sets, zaptops, zell phones, ZCAP meters, and ZSSE-55 funboxes—watching with great awe the peculiar, capricious, annoying, arrogant, and ultimately revolting qualities of the zillionaires, now they would do so glued to the spiraling silvery Celestial Sphere. ("Celestial" was one of the few Zundo the Conspirator's Z-listed words that had successfully retained its original name—and dignity, according to many linguistic groups—despite police brutality against peaceful anti-Z-words marchers who opposed its brief "Zelestial" appearance in literature, school textbooks, and scientific journals.)

Common people, victimized by centuries-long abuses from zillionaires, could now not only see the collapse and disintegration of those money-suckers on-line and on-astro as they journeyed away to *The Unknown*, but actually interact with them in their public condemnation and castigation, using the new tools.

Their inauguration, however, had been delayed owing to the fact that they might be too dangerous and far too difficult to supervise in those urgent cases involving national security. So far *only* Walking Brain and Master Judge were allowed to use those tools, and they kept all associated information very much to themselves.

None of Zundo's 3Zs (the three ruling teen girls), on the other hand, was scientifically inclined—except perhaps Z3, with a mild and passing interest—to impose her techno wisdom and guidance, so beyond their great administrative talents and fair-mindedness, nothing unusual could be expected of them in this area.

What everybody talked about lately here in the Zoliseum was the transfer of funds from this gigantically wealthy man—renamed Richard Zilch (from Richard Flynn) by an angry judge during Clash #11—a man who had alone gobbled up from the world's sinking economy nearly eighty percent of its value.

The Empire State Building in former New York City had been suggested as the best place to store his immense fortune—the paper money part. Renaming the building "Bank of Worthlessness" was another suggestion, since money not only had zero value in 3081, but had been declared illegal and punishable by severe and lengthy jail time.

But opposing groups claimed that it would take a thousand such buildings to store Richard's entire wealth, most of it hidden and spread in many countries. "We have to start somewhere..." a leading organizer had said.

Notwithstanding all this commotion, Richard Zilch had agreed to relinquish it all in this stunning public event that had so far moved along significantly well—confession, physical pain, humiliation, and final sentencing to the dreaded "soul travel journey" to *The Unknown*.

All good for the audience, not so for Richard.

A QUICK CITIZEN'S WORTHLESSNESS TEST

Master Judge raised a platform with the touch of a button on the control panel.

Turning to Richard, now dressed in his "soul-travel-black" outfit, he addressed him as kindly as he could.

"Would you please enter the Soul Travel Chamber?"

"My pleasure."

Richard complied, hearing the snap of the zlass door eerily closing behind him. Facing him was an armchair and a ZSSE-55 funbox. Impulsively, he brushed off with two fingers some dandruff he saw on his left shoulder. Then he sat down on the armchair.

The magician-judge had already bundled himself up into a yellow bubble, which now slowly descended into view near the zlass Chamber from his Royal Den.

"Are you ready?"

Richard freaked out, seeing the judge's grotesque smile level with his eyes from inside the floating thing. "...I...I am..."

His body trembled as the entertained crowd from the Stadiums laughed.

All too quick, like in one of the previous Clashes, the judge was out of the bubble in a snap, ready for action.

The Celestial Sphere was coming down, slowly turning on its invisible axis, positioning itself just above the Astral Floor, encircled by the Stadiums' crowd.

JUST COMPLETED: REMEMBERING A VERY OLD SPOOKY MOVIE SHOW • NEXT: PUNISHMENT SOUL TRAVEL SHOW

Briefly, it stood idle then flew away to its parking space in the sky.

Master Judge stepped closer to the Chamber, noticing the black handkerchief Richard's fingers fidgeted with. He knocked on the transparent wall.

"D'you mind if I come in?"

"Be my guest."

Inside, Master Judge approached the defendant.

"I'd like to do a quick test before you depart," he said casually. "Since you have no ZCAP meter implanted in your arm, I'll use mine to check your 'useful energy consumption and production,' if any, at your valued thirteen-octillion wealth."

Richard squeezed his handkerchief nervously.

"Why bother now?" he said.

"To be fair, to justify your journey," said Master Judge. "To see with my own eyes the truth...so I can feel no regret, so Zundonians can feel no regret, so you yourself can feel no regret...about the execution of your sentence."

He connected a wire with tentacular plugs from his ZCAP meter to the defendant's neck.

"Close one of your eyes, please."

Richard closed his right eye.

"Open it."

Richard opened his right eye.

"Close the other eye."

Richard closed his right eye.

"No, the other one," corrected the judge.

Richard closed his left eye.

"But keep the other one open."

Richard opened his right eye.

"Do you want me to keep the other one open, too?" he said.

"No, keep it closed."

Richard complied.

"Here's your reading...'**0000000000000**'..." said the judge, voicing each zero slowly. "Oh...my..."

Gasps of anger exploded everywhere in the Stadiums.

"KILL THE SON OF A BITCH!" a Corridor crowd bellowed, all zintelectuals in it tapping the floor with their shoes.

"What does that mean?" Richard felt bad.

"*Thirteen zeros*, which is the most distressing reading I have ever registered in Zundo, which validates your obsession for the number *thirteen*, which validates your *thirteen-year-journey* to hell–I mean, to *The Unknown*, which validates without any doubt your total uselessness to Zundo."

"In spite of my *octillions*?"

"Because of them."

Master Judge stared down at the defendant.

"What a shame!"

Suddenly he kicked him in the butt.

"Ouchhhhhhhh!"

He kicked him a second time.

"Ouchhhhhhhhhhhhhhhhhh!"

He kicked him a third time.

"Ouchhhhhhhhhhhhhhhhhhhhhhhhhhhhhhh!"

The crowd roared, overjoyed.

Large groups of youngsters in each Stadium began to chant a moral-buster song that had recently made it to the top of the charts in Zundo's popularity.

> Thirteen reasons to unsuccessfully cheat a Zundonian
> One dead octillionaire to name a Zundonian bloody mortuary after
> Thirteen treasons to unmistakably lay on a Zundonian
> One dead octillionaire to write a Zundonian dirty obituary after
> No way Jose, Mr. Richard Zilch
> You got no place in eternity
> No way Jose, Mr. Richard Flynn
> You lost your name and integrity.

Being there alone in the Soul Travel Chamber hearing the crowd lynching him with their mean eyes and vocal outbursts could be a very daunting experience, but sharing the space with Master Judge in this awful moment was the ultimate misery.

Good thing Richard's eyes had the tendency to escape the pain by drifting around to refreshing places, like the coral reefs and their tropical fish dwellers, joyfully spotting, for instance, schools of grass eels, angel fish, seahorses, and frogfish through multicolored lush gardens of elkhorn, brain, and fire corals. Also, the naughty sweepers and silversides he enjoyed so much.

Amid clusters of sand chutes and azure vase sponges wandered hidden colonies of baby mantas and sea turtles. To Richard's surprise, the appearance of a human form, scouting the underwater, possibly wreck diving the area, came very clear to his mind. It was a man, a few years younger than him, vaguely familiar, without knowing his name, without ever having exchanged words or thoughts with him, either down here or above the surface, he couldn't tell, but—*what a welcome surprise*!. Gradually, the blurred man became more familiar to his eyes in his proximity. Now he debated—was he the crazy guy who often ran *naked* across the Stadiums? The notorious *cheer streaker*? Even better!

His body, he noticed, moved covertly like a moray along a reef covered with orange elephant ear sponges and lilac gorgonians. Good for him!

Further down the reef, he discerned, stalactites hung from two whimsical and deeply indented caverns along a wall that suddenly plunged into the abyss a few hundred feet, never compromising the zhoenix shield protection, which he totally envied.

Totally envied because none of his octillions had ever contributed to its research and development. A huge mistake, for had he had that vision and fortitude years ago, before his ten decades of deep-freeze sleep, instead of wasting time and money in trivial and self-serving things, it too would've been part of his glorious empire.

Hell, now everything was going downhill for him—up there on the surface. He might as well live under water, where beauty and tranquility reigned.

MASTER JUDGE ALLOWS
A LAST MINUTE CHANGE

"Are you ready?" asked Master Judge.

"I *was* ready before," said Richard.

"Are you ready *now*?"

"I am...I guess..."

Master Judge watched the nervous man fuss with his handkerchief, dry out the sweat from his fingers.

"You'll have to be ready *all the time* now."

"Got you."

The judge removed his right glove and took something from a hidden pocket inside his cape.

"Before you leave, I'd like to provide you with a special kind of power, something that will make you conductive to soul travel. I call it *absorption energy*."

"*Wait!* Can I make a last minute change before I begin my soul travel?" uttered Richard suddenly with deep emotions.

Loud boos of discontent resonated everywhere in the Stadiums. They cried: "HE DOESN'T DESERVE IT! HE'S A STINKING PIECE OF SHIT!"

"I normally wouldn't allow it," said the charismatic judge. "Punished travelers should have some discipline, stand by their choices and decisions. But since you're the fattest cat we've ever had here, I'll make an exception. Just *this one*."

Master Judge licked his lips, thinking. "So, what's your change?" he then asked.

"I'd like to negotiate now—*before* my journey—the two years the Zoliseum owes me. Remember? I won the Clashes...by points?"

"True. So...you don't want to wait until your return?"

"Right. I've changed my mind."

The eccentric judge slit his eyes. "Just out of curiosity, what made you change your mind?"

"Humm. Nothing. Just me."

He lied. During his last visit to the Zoasis, he was approached, as usual, by The Zoice, who, among many good pieces of advice, urged him to request, for his own sake, a reconsideration of these *two* earned negotiable years.

The Zoice explained that the Clashes were designed to persecute him to *The Unknown*, way deeper and meaner than he could possibly imagine, while thrilling crowds real-time here in the Zoliseum's arena. They were meant to drive him, or his substitute, crazy with their persistent non-chronological *fallout*–like time-warped, stalking cinematic scenes–and it would be better for him to "ground" as many as possible of the thirteen fought Clashes. His *substitute*, if it happened that way, The Zoice told him with disarming clarity, could be *any* of his reincarnations—the problematic ones.

The Zoice coached him thoroughly on the meaning of these and other related scientific terms, invented by Walking Brain, as usual. In the end, The Zoice asked for and got from Richard a thirteen trillion dollar bonus for his insightful tip, recognizing that it was a very brave move from his part because such under-the-table information violated Zoliseum's policies. The bonus, naturally, was on speculation that Richard would survive his journey and regain his fortune one hopeful day.

"And what would you like to change?"

"I'd like to ground two of my thirteen Clashes."

"Oh...that's very advanced stuff," exclaimed Master Judge. Turning to the audience, he said, "Let me explain a little here...so you understand what the defendant is talking about. Clashes *happen chronologically* in Zundo, but *travel non-chronologically* across time after becoming time-conductive, which is the way they're picked up by recipients. None of this will affect you, but it will affect a traveler's journey to *The Unknown* as Walking Brain can testify."

He turned back to Richard. "And *which two Clashes* do you want grounded?"

Before Richard could answer, he turned to the audience again. "A *grounded Clash*, by the way, is one that won't fly away, so to speak, or won't 'time travel' away, more precisely, because it will stay here in Zundo." Turning back to Richard, he beckoned him to continue.

"I'd like to ground Clash #1 and Clash #13."

"*First* and *last?*" He reviewed them mentally. "*Log Fighting* and *Pole Vaulting?*"

"Yes."

"May I ask why specifically these two…since you didn't win them?"

"Log Fighting did something to me. It reminded me that my wealth, drive, and everything have kept me away all these years from finding the right woman and falling in love—something missing in my life." He Paused. "Pole Vaulting wasn't entirely bad. Competing against such a terrific black athlete and bright mind gave me a new perspective on women. True, I lost both contests but gained wisdom and feel both Clashes—my favorites–should steer clear of any potential outer space's wicked entrapments...by staying here grounded."

Actually, his real reasons for choosing them was spare him or his substitute the tormenting onslaught of their wicked persecution deep into *The Unknown*, as warned by The Zoice. These two Clashes were particularly loaded with rules, blows, and infectious elements of the worst kind. Their *fallout* could be devastating.

"So be it."

He gestured for Richard to sit down, drop his handkerchief to the floor, and relax. "Ready now?"

"Ready."

THE IMMINENT DEPARTURE

Delicately, Master Judge put a tiny blue metallic patch–looking like a former American dime coin, only smaller and thinner–on Richard's forehead. It stayed there stuck to his skin.

"Stare straight into my eyes without blinking for as long as you can," he uttered in a strange tone, similar to those tones spoken by church Cardinals during solemn rituals. To his growing satisfaction, the defendant complied nicely. "You will feel a penetrating warmth quickly gathering heat on your forehead, your ears, and your head. Can you feel it?"

"I do. It's beginning to burn."

"Perfect!" Master Judge put his right glove back on. "Relax now. Close your eyes."

A solemn silence from the Stadiums' crowd gripped the moment.

∽

The moment was intercepted by a distant presence...

Hi Richard...it's me Mipho, Returning Secret Sister of Bast, Lioness Goddess of Ancient Egypt. I go by many names, looks, and personalities, including Mipho, Serene Lady of the Seventies, Oleg, and Oxana...

She was mind-talking from Calabria, a seacoast village in the toe part of what used to be Italy, over three-thousand miles away, unseen by mortals and unexpected by recipients. Overlooking the Mediterranean Sea, she stood by Byzantine ruins.

"...hi..." said Richard from the Soul Travel Chamber, nearly voiceless, immobile, yet aware, given his wretched state of mind...just a split-second before his public departure.

O Mighty Pharaoh of Ever Changing and Expanding Egypt...O Fallen King of swiftly declining times...allow me to interrupt this uncalled-for and damn rude brainwashing performed on you by the Directors of the Zoliseum (lately promoted to "Lords")...Dr. Ufahh, also known as Walking Brain, and his clownish partner Master Judge...this malicious, suffocating, and destructive manipulator of your soul at this crucial time, went on Mipho in her god-full, time-expanding manner. *Allow me this instant to offer you guidance and direction on your immediate soul travel journey blast-off to The Unknown.*

"...I hear you..."

O Mighty Pharaoh let me express once more my timeless, boundless, and limitless servitude, protection, and devotion to you and your Kingdom...

"...you have my gratitude..."

You've been kidnapped, zloned, brainwashed, insulted, and sentenced to twice your chosen punishment journey...without your consent. I had no choice but intervene...especially now that you find yourself in a state of complete helplessness, numbness, disorientation, and mental fatigue...unable to speak, shout, cry, or even beg in silence...on your behalf.

"...go on, my Lioness Goddess Bast..."

Lioness Goddess Mipho, corrected Mipho with a smile, *Lioness Goddess Bast's secret sister...but equally powerful.*

"...oh...I'm sorry...my thoughts are not good this moment..."

No problem...I understand. Anyway, it is my duty, honor, and joy to offer you immediate and absolute clarification of where you're going now on your soul travel journey...after safely returning to Zundo from your time travel journey...six months before you ever departed...Zundo time. Congrats on what the news media in Zundo refers to as Day 1 of the Trial of the Millennium!

"...in...trig...u...ing..."

The Lords of the Zoliseum—better known as the Sub-Lords of Zundo—have set your destination to 20th century post-WWII France.

"...20th...?"

Yes, My Pharaoh.

"...post...WWII...?"

Yes, My Pharaoh. Always wear the ancient peridot ring that your uncle gave you and be prepared for the harshest and longest of times...including life-threatening situations at every step of the way.

"...per...i...dot ring...?"

Yes, My Pharaoh. It used to belong to me.

Master Judge noticed that the blue round patch had totally been absorbed by Richard's head within seconds. No trace of it on his skin.

"...breathe deeply, Mr. Zilch...again...again...you're about to depart on your thirteen year extreme poverty soul travel journey to *The Unknown*."

Everybody's eyes were now riveted to the middle area of the quickly descending and turning Celestial Sphere where a huge magnification of what was happening in the Soul Travel Chamber, occupied by the judge and the defendant, was in progress in amazing tension, real time.

They all watched the judge's piercing eyes, the defendant's receptive face...through the Chamber's zlass.

Master Judge then raised both hands into a "V" high in the air, his black cape shining behind his back.

"Hasta luego, mon ami!"

All too soon he was floating up, some thirty feet in the air, to his royal post in a mauve colored bubble and quickly at work with his controls.

Anything he touched on his panel buttons became magnified a hundred times on the Celestial Sphere's surface.

The following flashed in distinctive colors, one by one:

-Poverty Scanner <u>activated</u>
-Hunger and Hardship Loop Manager <u>activated</u>
-Suffering Accelerator <u>activated</u>
-Humiliation Oscillator <u>activated</u>
-Misery Recall <u>activated</u>
-Shattered Illusions Controller <u>activated</u>

Then, the following began to scroll down, slowly:

ONLINE UNIVERSITY OF ZUNDO
SCHOOL OF GENERAL STUDIES • SUMMER 3081
Principles of Underground Life (WWII and after)

FDSV1	Fake Democracy Survival 1
FDSV2	Fake Democracy Survival 2
RTSV	Religion Terror Survival

TTSV	Tyranny Terror Survival
NTSV	Nazi Terror Survival
FTSV	Fascist Terror Survival
CTSV	Communist Terror Survival
AQTSV	Al Qaeda Terror Survival
SWTSV	Super Wealth Terror Survival
SPTSV	Super Poverty Terror Survival
BGTSV	Barrio Gangs Terror Survival
ISTSV	Insanity Terror Survival
ITSV	Internet Terror Survival

Master Judge highlighted and selected, in this order:

RTSV	*Religion Terror Survival*
NTSV	*Nazi Terror Survival*
TTSV	*Tyranny Terror Survival*
SPTSV	*Super Poverty Terror Survival*
BGTSV	*Barrio Gangs Terror Survival*
ISTSV	*Insanity Terror Survival*

His gloved fingers typed other information on the keyboard, mainly disturbing in nature and hidden from the watchful audience.

The ingenious judge grabbed his Japanese sword from a secret place behind his bookshelf and raised it sharply high above his head in total splendor, like a symphony conductor.

"NOW!" he roared.

༄

The immense crowd from all six Bisected Stadiums was ecstatic. They began to shout in unison: "**10!**....**9!**....**8!**....**7!**...." each succeeding number lighting up in bright orange on the idling Celestial Sphere.

༄

"...per...i...dot......r...i...n...g...?" said again Richard from the Soul Travel Chamber in his weakest, slowest voice yet, still picked-up by Mipho in Calabria, former Italy.

Yes, My Pharaoh. Always wear the ancient peridot ring, repeated the Egyptian deity, with more muscles in her mind-voice to make sure he understood. *Regarding your immediate soul travel departure, you'll be going exactly to the same destination and journey you've just returned from via time travel... precisely on Day 1 of this trial.*

"......" Richard stopped responding.

Your soul travel journey is immediate now...thanks to time-space-manipulator Dr. Ufahh...even though it scientifically must wait six months to allow for your return from your time travel journey, which, although happened on Day 1 of this trial...it's contingent upon the fact that you actually haven't left yet...and—can you hear me, My Pharaoh Richard?

"......"

—and...beware of that clown...Dr. Ufahh...Walking Brain. For some sickening personal reason, he wants you back in space right now on his terms!

"......"

❧

They all jumped to their feet in the Stadiums, their eyes aimed at the remaining flashing numbers in the countdown,

"6!....5!....4!....3!....2!....1!...GOOOOOOOOOOOOOOOOO!"

Master Judge's irises were glowing, his lips parted into a naughty smile.

Enthralled, the crowd shouted in unison: "**BON VOYAGE, MR. ZILCH! GET A LIFE!**"

❧

But, trust me, you'll be returning to Zundo in four hours, Zundo time, went on mind-voicing Mipho from former Italy.

"......"

Are you still with me? Mipho realized the obvious. "*He's gone. The Pharaoh's gone!*"

LEFTOVERS ON THE ASTRAL FLOOR

Richard remained seated on his armchair in the Soul Travel Chamber near the ZSSE-55 funbox, his handkerchief still piled up on the floor.

Head hanging backward, dead-like, eyes deeply closed, breathing almost non-responsive—he surely looked finished.

Physically, he was there.

Spiritually, he was gone.

Eventually, depending on his journey's outcome (a surviving changed person or a dead body), he'd regain his normal strength and go on with his new life or be cremated like his predecessors. Such was the outlook for the last wave of zillionaires ever to exist on this planet.

PART 6

DR. UFAHH'S ALTERNATIVE
HISTORY PALACE
ZUNDO, SUMMER – WINTER 3081

A RISE TO FAME, POWER AND MADNESS

Summer 3081

Dr. Ufahh, Zundonian foremost scientist and chairman of the Zoliseum, lived a complicated life of joys, passions, caprices, and horrors up there in his isolated research kingdom some one-hundred feet above ground. A height he could lower or raise at will by touching a button on a wall.

Born Ueh Ulah Ulevah Ufahh, he normally wore zaigoo object spectacles, buggazis mind-scanning contact lenses, and khorzos sound-debriefing earzotrons. The latter, camouflaged inside his funky zapillon ears. In essence, he could see through most objects, read active thoughts from nearby people, and hear sounds prohibited to humans.

Far from paranoid, he was quite loose and outgoing, sometimes overly friendly, and even bugsome. This showed pointedly when he ventured out into the real world, mostly at night. But encounter-phobia kept most citizens off the streets and squares in all cities and villages where he was suspected to appear.

So, yes, refined spying of a lesser kind also existed among Zundonians–against him and Master Judge, not the 3Zs–together with other rising underground activities...but so elementary, because of extreme fear and doubts, it could take another century for anything to be accomplished.

Second only to the 3Zs in rank and power, Dr. Ufahh could do virtually anything he wanted in Zundo and in the ever expansive and mysterious universe surrounding it. His achievements were of the highest order, hardly explicable but indisputably real. Real to his art, imagination, intellect, and well-being.

"Bravo!" he would compliment himself at every step of his discoveries—all of them enormously risky and spectacular.

He'd never considered overthrowing the ruling 3Zs—a nearly impossible feat—because they always showed a cool attitude toward him, allowing him all the freedom and ZCAP meter support he wanted for his research and experiments.

Likewise, he never messed around with their style of governing the planet and their sexual orientation. "Better to have three happy teen lesbians rule my world than two freaking dysfunctional straight parents ruin it!" so went the slogan that had gotten them elected in the year 3076.

The planet was "the nation"—just one, for a change—ruled by three teenagers, not two adults, for a change. So far everything had worked out fine. People usually were happy and loving, not greedy or ambitious. Life was simple and workable, thanks in great part to the philosophy behind the ZCAP meter technology.

Zundonians laughed when reading very old, crumpled, and coffee-stained library documents about the "rat race," or watching scratched and damaged Hollywood films of the same era about "world wars" and "nuclear confrontations." Such things made virtually no sense. Suicidal societies? How stupid! And why split the planet into one hundred belligerent countries filled with jealousy and hate when you can unite into one single, big, cohesive, loving country like Zundo? Duh!

Mankind had finally evolved, it seemed, into a super species of progressive, caring, and convivial citizens...undisturbed by internal revolutions or external attacks from other planets. As such, Zundonians led the way into the fourth millennium, unscathed and confident. Nothing like that since the beginning of time!

༄

Time was always on Dr. Ufahh's mind. In fact, he had made time his reason for living, his excuse for experimenting with it, and his passion for applying his findings to mankind. The latter an incredibly risky and dangerous mission capable of subverting the status quo.

Only God, he claimed, was left to judge his actions...for they were truly unsettling among Zundonians. Plus his close association with Master Judge—the eccentric czar of the Zoliseum's open trials everybody pretended to like but hated—had made every citizen awfully nervous in recent years. "What's going on?" seemed to be the secret question everyone feared to ask.

Thanks to Dr. Ufahh, punishing fugitive zillionaires in public had become the most exciting and educational show on earth. They were castigated for their sickening drive to posses all the goods of the world, leaving none to the poor. But sentencing decisions made behind closed doors by the chairman and judges, without apparent intervention from the 3Zs, provided ground for dark feelings beyond mistrust and apprehension.

It was in this state of mood that Zundo operated in the summer of 3081.

BRIBING THE OCTILLIONAIRE

Winter 3081

Dr. Ufahh and Richard walked side by side along the lamppost-tall metallic fence that separated the community of Zancha from his Palace up a hundred feet in the sky.

They strolled now under a complicated system of pipes, valves, and scaffolds. The scientist wore his favorite breakaway sundust-fortified shirt over Adolpho shorts, Richard his blue denim Zabala combination.

Gray-green algae hung in suspension like colossal cobwebs, barely allowing schools of spadefish to drift through.

Darkening clouds amassed overhead, blurring the view. They originated in the spewing networks of industrial waste from dirty machinery, pumping hydraulics, and gas-emitting towers.

A leak from an overheating hose above dripped on the edge of Richard's head, at once smearing his face. He stopped on his walk to wipe it off. It looked like sewage sludge, but it was probably worse. Vapors seemed to emanate from it.

"Sorry about that," said Dr. Ufahh. "This environment's not exactly kind. But it's potentially safe."

Richard nodded, a bit intimidated by his koala-like face, in particular his small, close-together, oddly shining black eyes behind his cool spectacles.

Black eyes because a spaced-out Dr. Ufahh had forgotten about two hours ago to put on his purple-tinted mind-scanning contact lenses. He always did before meeting new people, like news media reporters, professors, and other scientists, whom he amply distrusted. He needed to read their minds before they spoke or planned something

against him. Chatting with Richard, on the other hand, didn't raise any
red flags. The man seemed as docile as a cat.

They continued trudging down the quiet road from Aguadulce
Square, past the leaking scaffold, approaching a herd of lazy cows,
some of them lying down on the grassless ground.

"Watch your steps!" cautioned Dr. Ufahh, noticing a twisted chunk
of metal on their path.

Richard dodged the piece of debris. His stare, facing him again,
met in distraction the big down-turned sweet potato nose anchored
there—so unreal and gross.

"My dear octillionaire, if you plead guilty and shut up, I can
help you cheat the boots off your sentence by half," offered the distinguished scientist with excitement in his eyes, his diction heavily
Argentinian accented. "What'd you say?"

"Half is okay with me," said Richard, impressed. "What's your
deal?"

"Pick the toughest sentence of the lot and I'll make it the silliest to
you." He shot his dark gaze into the octidare's hazel eyes. "What's your
favorite number? I know it's thirteen—but tell me anyway."

"Thirteen."

"Offer me thirteen quadrillion dollars—which I will gladly accept—
and I'll cut thirteen in half. Do you trust me already?"

"I do."

Richard discerned a little smirk on Dr. Ufahh's face—his paper-
thin smiling lips somehow reigning over his naive and frail constitution.

❧

They proceeded to discuss the "blue wowzpin," skirting a big
magnolia tree, with distinctively large oblong-ovate leaves. Some of
them vaulted over the tall fence to Zancha's territory.

Dr. Ufahh stopped momentarily, holding a little round blue patch
on the tip of his index finger.

"See how tiny and thin this is?"

Richard nodded, noticing the manicured design on his long nails.

"This piece of nothing can do amazing things for you."

"Why blue?" asked Richard.

"Blue's the color of the future."

He extracted a blue pen from his summer jacket with the other hand and casually threw it to the tree. On impact, the pen exploded, whirling blue sparks in the air, like firecrackers on a celebration day. The tree was also gone, except for a charred mess of smoky branches.

"Blue electricity. Deadly," said the scientist.

He watched the look of wonder in Richard's eyes.

"Still a secret," said Dr. Ufahh, fondling one of his zapillon ears, where hidden earzotrons were at work.

"...wow..."

∽

Dr. Ufahh and Richard renewed the march.

"As I was saying...this tiny little thing can do incredible changes to your life," uttered Dr. Ufahh, showing the tiny blue wowzpin he held on the tip of his finger.

Richard bent, brought his eyes closer to it.

A woman and her kid walked opposite them. The kid waved a hand. "Hi, Walking Brain!"

It stirred a corny smile from the scientist. Playfully, he made a funny face, which brought cracking laughter to the kid as he continued to march with his mom, his happy little heart beating faster now.

What Richard had noticed before now stood out in this comical exchange which made Dr. Ufahh stoop down clumsily, thus revealing two distinct blond bushes crowning the top of his head.

"Shhhhhhhhhh..." The woman urged her son away from the scene, fearing he might ask Dr. Ufahh impertinent questions.

Dr. Ufahh turned to Richard. "Did anybody follow you...when you came here today?

"No."

"You're sure...nobody followed you?"

Richard affirmed with his head, perhaps not too convincingly. "Well, except for this hobo...or something. More like a caveman, sitting on the sidewalk. Very disgusting sight."

"With no clothes on?"

"Just rags covering his crotch," said Richard. "One big mole on one shoulder."

"He's one of those who's slipped through the cracks of time," said Dr. Ufahh, taking his zaigoo object spectacles off. "Anyway, I still have to figure out how to send him back to Cro Magnon times...with his consent. Apparently, he likes it up here."

Richard wasn't certain what to say, so he said nothing.

Dr. Ufahh looked at the blue wowzpin again.

"This thing's made up of a substance I created in the lab–well, right here," he said, pointing to the gilded building, "inside the Alternative History Palace where I work–a powerful substance." He stored it back in his pocket.

"Sounds scary."

Richard pulled out a handkerchief and began to fumble with it, realizing at the same time how awkwardly long and hairy Dr. Ufahh's arms were.

"It's not. It's futuristic," said the scientist.

"What does it do?"

Dr. Ufahh put back his zaigoo spectacles on and stared behind him and to both sides with great caution.

"It zadiates energy to double, if using doublezun, or cut by half, if using halfzun, the bad elements of someone's life. In your case, it would cut by half your punishment. I would use halfzun."

"Did you say...*zadiates*?"

"Yes. It's a different type of radiation. Extremely powerful, versatile, and peaceful, if used properly."

Richard smiled, his mind hung on thoughts.

"Cut by half–just like that?" he then said.

"Just like that."

Dr. Ufahh's bright black eyes twitched.

"Well, via 'time conduction.' The blue wowzpin will make you time conductive when placed on your forehead and–"

"Time conductive? For how long? Hours? Days?"

"Ha! Years! Thousands of years!"

"Are you kidding me?"

"No. Time conductive for ages!"

Richard observed how the scientist took a tiny silver bottle from his Adolpho shorts.

"Meaning what?...really..." he said.

"Becoming super-able to move through time, past and future."

"Time traveling?"

"Exactly."

Dr. Ufahh drank a little from the tiny bottle, which he quickly returned to his pocket.

"So this substance will cut in half my punishment?—whatever it is?"

"That's right."

"And make me time conductive...so I can time travel around?"

"You've got it! Two new powers added to your life—one stoppable, the other unstoppable."

"That's something."

He noticed dandruff on one of his shoulders and twisted his neck to brush it off with one hand.

"Misery, disgrace, humiliation, pain, sickness, fear, paranoia—all and everyone will be cut in half."

"Amazing."

"So will police harassment, vagrancy, hunger, street fights, poverty, shop lifting, prostitution, drug addiction, and suicide tendencies, among others, if they come to bear."

Richard brushed off some dandruff from the other shoulder, noticing it had distracted Dr. Ufahh's attention a little.

"What about my punishment time?"

"It'll be cut in half too," said the scientist.

A school of peppermint gobies scurried behind them, seeking the soft coral reefs above, where queen angelfish and eagle rays frequented.

Dr. Ufahh removed his zaigoo spectacles to wipe something off from one eye that was bugging him. "I've said that already, instead of *thirteen* years, you'll suffer only *six and a half* years, which is half of thirteen."

"How do you know thirteen years is an option?"

Dr. Ufahh put back his spectacles. "I have connections. Thirteen is the toughest, and shortest, trust me."

Sneakily, he gazed to both sides of the street and shook hands with the defendant.

"I must go now. Good luck."

"Wait! Didn't you say before...one of these powerful things you created...is stoppable? Which one and how?"

"Doubling or halving the duration and intensity of events is stoppable." He pulled something out from his pocket, held it high on the tip of one finger. "This little round yellow patch...endzpin...will do that, if needed."

"If needed?"

"Yeah. You must always have a 'Plan B.' We scientists always do."

"How will I use it?"

"Same way as the blue wowzpin. I'll tell you more next time...we'll be in touch."

Richard took a last look at the yellow endzpin before the scientist put it back in his pocket and walked away, quickly disappearing from view.

Such impression of the yellow substance kept stirring his mind in a strange way as it entered a new dimension...blurring his vision...and other senses.

THE BULGARIAN MASQUERADE PARTY CONNECTION

June 3081—A Couple of Hours Before and After the Time Traveler's Return

Dr. Ufahh had been working very hard on his latest project in the wee hours of the night in his Palace. Such overwhelming task had everything to do with the secret manipulation of media information on a global scale for his own personal gain.

He wanted to make sure that what Zundonians saw on the Celestial Sphere, with all its 31st-century splashing visuals, seductive sounds, and glorified narration, wasn't exactly what really happened in *The Unknown* concerning both travelers—the Time Traveler (Septidare #6) and the Soul Traveler (Richard or "The Octidare"). Two different travelers and two different journeys—the first, returning to Zundo, after wandering through the 17th century, the second, departing from Zundo, headed for the 20th century.

Septidare #6, a septillionaire, not Richard, had accidentally died in his journey, and not squashed against something in space as Dr. Ufahh had pretended so hard to believe, but eaten up by a ferocious tiger in Gabrovo, Bulgaria, near the end of his journey. To avoid bad publicity, which could ruin his outer space programs and reputation, not to say turn him into a desperate jailbird, Dr. Ufahh put into motion with amazing speed and skill a very elaborate but workable plan, offering a solution.

Right off, he changed all kinds of evidence in secrecy. He replaced *real-time* Septidare #6 with Richard, who was scheduled to depart on his soul travel journey a bit later, adding thus a new journey to his heavy schedule. Septidare #6's TT journey, launched earlier, highlighted the first part of the trial, when returning to Zundo, before a huge cheering audience. Richard's ST departure, highlighting the second part, was to follow after completion of 13 Clashes. Now Richard needed to endure two journeys back-to-back—first, this new, urgent one (via TT) and second, his trial's officially assigned one (via ST).

What seemed most critical was Richard's *real-time* replacement of Septidare #6 via time travel (TT), launched separately with aims at merging somewhere somehow, and clearly both journeys couldn't be equal or Richard would end up dead too.

Furthermore, each journey was fragmentably watchable *real-time* on the Celestial Sphere by millions of Zundonians (and possibly zillions of others from other planets).

So in order to preserve the needed equality of journeying and prevent Richard from accidentally dying in his journey, Dr. Ufahh discovered that Richard's journey needed *only to appear* visually equal as Septidare #6's on the Sphere. All scientific parameters being the same—except for the "century" thing–he came up with the idea of *halving* in secrecy his journey–both in time and suffering. Never done before, such difference (costing Richard a big chunk of his wealth, if he agreed, but making him smile widely) would both cut in half his punishment and solve the problem. A good deal for both Richard and Dr. Ufahh (who certainly would make good use of Richard's money).

He'd recently invented and tested in the Palace's lab two products beneficial to the ongoing "outer space punishment program for extremely greedy zillionaires"—doublezun, to double a traveler's punishment, and halfzun, to cut it in half. Now he was finally ready to use halfzun for the first time on Richard.

Zundonians would never notice that on the programmed Sphere. However, they could notice any abnormal change in the journey's mapping structure. So visually, he had to reprogram the historical, geopolitical, and socio-cultural landscape (shortened to "geo-changes" in his notes) of the targeted journey, and a tad of other things, to begin with. Basically, Dr. Ufahh had no choice but change the way people saw the whole world. As crazy as it sounded, he ended up doing just that.

೦ಌ

Some major problems emerged...

A glitch in the Celestial Sphere's presentation allowed Zundonians *only to hear* fragments of the real-time journey narration. They *could not see* those fragments. So Dr. Ufahh inserted Richard's TT journey's visuals instead, with all its associated bazaar of geo-changes, so Zundonians wouldn't tell the difference.

It helped that today's advanced 31st-century culture had made Zundonians totally ignorant of the targeted 17th-century culture—the one voyaged by the returning dead man, namely, his TT journey through Germany, Italy, Spain, Australia, America, and other nations forming part of his *Unknown* punishment package. Swamped with matters of the present, future, and far future, no high school or university in Zundo bothered to teach that anymore.

Amused, he not only distorted names and locations of many cities, towns, villages, and hamlets on his fabricated Sphere maps, he even invented new ones. Names for key rivers, lakes, waterfalls, bridges, mountains, beaches, and the likes, suffered a similar fate.

Once Richard's TT journey began (launched in secrecy in the darkness of night from the roof of his Palace), sharing the outer space with Septidare #6's defunct TT journey, he shoved into the non-operational journey elements of Richard's ongoing journey, namely, incidents he encountered through *The Unknown* (his particular *Unknown*'s locations, which included France, Venezuela, Bulgaria, and America).

For example, one of Richard's awful situations in Hollywood—acquired during the young adult years of his 13th reincarnation as a growing French boy named Gaston by the punishing winds of his chosen "thirteen-year extreme poverty" package journey (while chasing nebulous screenwriting breaks in risky independent filmmaking land and dating redhead starlet Nikki at the non-spoken urging of her mom's firm belief he was none other than Jesus Christ), now transferred to Septidare #6's disabled TT journey—showed on the Celestial Sphere as a homeless Gaston thrown on the carpet floor of a trendy four-star Berlin-based hotel instead, half unconscious, like a derelict, after puking around midnight someone's cheese and meatloaf leftovers. Not a pretty sight those vomited residues...containing also bits of ketchup,

French fries, bacon, and crackers. The latter extracted, through painful clenching of his infirmed front teeth, from inside hard-as-steel cellophane wrappers.

Another incident, rather scary—transpired in the dunes of Palavas-les-Flots, southern France, from Richard's journey (actually, Gaston's, at the tender age of nine)—appeared on the Sphere's screen as a nearly missed morgue-headed victim when a sun-bathing beachgoer in Spain was hit by a Nazi gunshot meant for Gaston. Dr. Ufahh was astute enough to make Gaston's face look distant or hard to see, if not blocked, fully or partially, by some object every time it appeared on the Septidare #6 journey.

A third example, involving a peaceful student protest march in a nondescript prominent boulevard in 20ᵗʰ-century Caracas, Venezuela (so no one could tell exactly where, when, and how it had happened, as bloody machetes from dictatorship militia death squads swung violently by Gaston's head), trickily showed on the Sphere on a 17ᵗʰ century setting instead. Again, Dr. Ufahh was wise enough to change any street signs, political inference, people's clothing, or anything raising questions or suggesting a contradiction.

∞

From the start, Zundonians had been persuaded to believe, through the news media, that the so-called Time Traveler was Septidare #6, a very greedy and arrogant septillionaire, his real name undisclosed. But Dr. Ufahh knew better. He was The Octidare, Richard Flynn (or Septidare #6's secret substitute after his accidental death).

So Zundonians, half-submerged, in the Stadiums, Astral Floor, Promenade Corridor, and other special Park's areas, simply couldn't tell the difference by watching the visuals on the Sphere, and wouldn't know the truth. Neither could nurses in hospitals, carpenters in construction sites, and zaptop users in schools watching the Sphere's visuals on ZV. The same happened globally—from former Canada to former Philippines to former Russia to former any country.

∞

Dr. Ufahh had indeed succeeded in confusing the geographical landscape as well as the substance, scope, depth, and chronology of all time-traveled moments by both punished extremely wealthy journey-men—one approaching his death and actually dying, the other steadily alive—all appearing in hypnotic ways on the gigantic Sphere before everyone's eyes.

He'd swapped, altered, renamed, or relocated, via self-serving manipulation, regions and metropolises, freeways and turnpikes, as well as airports and harbors. The whole bit!

It did cross his mind, however, that by halving Richard's back-to-back journeys (TT and ST), something could go wrong. Perhaps not in the scale of his predecessor. These two journeys worked in such a way—so close to each other, complementing each other...physically, mentally, and spiritually—as to appear traveling as one.

He needed a backup plan, or Plan B, to ensure success and safety of his subject and the project. It still bothered him the fact that Septidare #6 had been wandering in his ill-fated TT journey for *twice* 13 years, instead of *once*, as intended, making his bribery look ridiculous, considering the hefty fee he'd charged—a habit he nevertheless pursued for every wealthy man he sent away to *The Unknown*. His promise of halving both his journey and suffering had fallen flat. Nothing should've gone wrong. Yet it *did*.

Could money be the reason for the traveler's death? Could someone else be derailing his secret journey replacement plan? His overall goals? Very unlikely...for he was in full control of his doings. *Was* he?

He'd bribed Richard the same way as Septidare #6, although for a lot more money given his absurdly enormous fortune. The man had actually died by a tiger's attack in the middle of a street in a Bulgarian town, but his 26 years of mysterious wandering in the 17th-century without his permission bugged him greatly...in a twisted way. What did really happen? Why? How? Ironically, had Septidare #6 journeyed only half of 13 years, as programmed, no hungry tiger would've been around to eat him alive!

‿

One interesting thing about both travelers' journeys, Dr. Ufahh discovered, was that they merged in Gabrovo, Bulgaria. In fact, they merged in the middle of a masquerade party, for different reasons, each one coming from different centuries.

Although Richard reincarnated into Gaston from the onset and lived this person's life from 8 to 34 during his 26-year journey (which should've been half of 13—not double!—a fact that kept Dr. Ufahh sick worried with recurrent insomnia), Septidare #6 remained the same person, growing older too, though, during the same period. So Gaston and Septidare #6 (about twice Gaston's age) happened to be enjoying this masquerade party in a big building that tragic night without ever meeting. All this made possible by Dr. Ufahh's ingenious ideas and scientific manipulations so the so-called Time Traveler's journey would not look interrupted to Sphere's watchers in Zundo. Meaning Septidare #6 never died, in their eyes. Nor was he ever thought to be heading that way.

Working hard in his Palace late at night, Dr. Ufahh accomplished all of this in a most peculiar way, realizing Gaston (already 34) would be using a female Bulgarian-English translator during his stay in this Eastern Bloc Communist country. Gaston spoke French, Spanish, and English, but no Bulgarian.

Gaston's translator saw someone wearing a Batman mask as she wildly danced in one of the crowded upper floors of the building, a rock band playing about ten meters away. She told Gaston—who was in Gabrovo, invited by the officials of the Festival of Humor and Satire, to represent his nominated satirical film—it would be more exciting if he also wore a mask. "Let's walk to nearby Aprilov High School where I teach. There's a can of blue paint up there that I could use."

"Blue paint?"

"Yeah, I've got an idea."

Next thing he knew he was facing a mirror in a rest room. The young shapely teacher was finishing applying a very thick blue paint around his eyes and mouth, covering his mustache. Over his head loomed a tight-fitted homemade blue hood with a pair of cute rabbit ears sticking out.

෨

A most disturbing incident was about to happen.

At one point in the night, a Bengal tiger escaped from the zoo in the neighborhood and leaped its way to the main road.

At about the same time, the person wearing the Batman mask headed to his hotel room on this road.

The horrific scene that ensued made big news the next day in the local papers. What was left of the chewed-up man's body could not be recognized or identified. The news however also mentioned that, for the strangest reason on earth, chewed-up and barely recognizable remains of the attacking tiger were also found in the spot.

But to Dr. Ufahh's satisfaction, it had all worked perfectly well. At the same time the Batman mask wearer (Septidare #6) died, Gaston took his place. Dr. Ufahh *knew* it would happen—a lookalike person would stroll on that road at the same time, but be spared of becoming red meat for the tiger on his sudden and panicking running, as a three-headed even hungrier and more vicious animal, in the shape and roaring rage of a ferocious lioness, swiftly materialized to devour the tiger. It happened so quickly, Dr. Ufahh could swear he'd counted three heads. And he was right.

This traumatizing masquerade event, thus, provided the needed continuity to the so-called Time Traveler's journey, past the hiccup, so to speak, to go unnoticed by Zundo's Sphere's watchers.

෨

Before he could get back to playing with his cat, Dr. Ufahh pondered about Richard and his 13th reincarnation, Gaston, at the start of his journey in France at the tender age of 8—a long way from the 34-year-old intellectual he'd almost sacrificed in his lab while merging two journeys in Bulgaria…a couple of hours before and after (Zundo time) the spectacular so-called Time Traveler's return to Zundo all citizens witnessed in absolute joy and awe.

The masquerade connection had been crucial in helping solve this enigmatic Time Traveler journey's dilemma without jeopardizing the character and scope of Gaston's own TT-ST journey, whose sole aim was to harshly punish Richard—the richest and greediest man alive.

∽

Halving a horrific 13-year sentence such as Richard's was already a terrible option, Dr. Ufahh knew. But doubling it? as it mysteriously turned out to be–could be deadly. In fact, most likely. At times Dr. Ufahh crossed his fingers, even prayed, for Richard's safe return to Zundo. Bulgaria might be the last stop in his journey, but not the end of it. No matter how far into the future Dr. Ufahh could see, he could not see it all.

And there was always a Master Judge to worry about—his eccentric, arrogant, often clumsy and irritating right-hand man. The chap who hosted the Zoliseum.

CHASING THE NOBEL PRIZE FOR PHYSICS

June 3081

Dr. Ufahh had won many trophies regarding his cosmic discoveries and inventions. In fact, one of the largest rooms in the Alternative History Palace was full of them. Projects dealing with "arriving before leaving" filled one entire shelf in it. "Transforming and morphing" experiments took up seven shelves. So did high order tasks pinning down new principles of Modern Physics leading to "halving or doubling outer space travel punishment journeys for extremely greedy people."

Now he was all excited inside regarding his new breakthrough experiment, but calm in his facial expressions so as not to jinx it. Several trophies could come out of it. Every so often he'd have a scientific orgasm in his office by just imagining the successful return of Richard from his back-to-back TT-ST journey.

Not only he'd been waiting years for this great moment in his career, but preparations for it had worked "delightfully well" (his own words when talking to his cat). He was going to prove—to himself first, then to the world—that back-to-back time travel and soul travel to *The Unknown* by one human being, using the harshest punishment package, was perfectly possible and even achievable.

Evidently, Richard's ongoing journey to the 20th-century would fulfill this promise. All he could say right now (in his mind) was *break a leg Richard!*

Such were the tenets of his punishment campaign to those he thought deserved it and the legacy of his genius.

❧

Watching Stadium #5's agitated crowd from his huge Palace's window now, Dr. Ufahh brooded over a lot of things. No other place gave his mind so much comfort. Not his living room, not his bedroom, not his gym. Not the mall (where he bought his Adolpho shorts) and definitely not the circus (where he'd pursued an illicit affair and learned to talk to the animals). Those were high times for him—his dangerous experiments and risky projects finally paying off. A near-grab encounter to an unbelievable fortune suddenly lurked around the corner. *Uau!*

Very few things he regretted in his life, the most obvious one being not winning the Nobel Prize for Physics. But it still could happen... for if God was on his side, he for sure was on God's side.

Roaming barracudas and sharks flirted with a large turtle in front of his window, he could see, as he had capriciously lowered the structure of his sky-floating Palace down to Stadiums and Corridor's height to be closer to them.

To his right, a slithering moving squadron of eagle rays charmed his attention.

Below, vertical walls dripping with white algae, violet corals, and orange sponges, had created habitats for hundreds of tropical fish—yellowtail snappers, French angel fish, amber jack, and Nassau groupers, among them.

Watching bigger fish gobbling up smaller ones, Dr. Ufahh couldn't help missing Dancer, his British cat. Sentimentally, his amorous eyes turned to the picture on the wall—his own artistic portrait, only a year old, of the feline he so much adored.

"We'll brainstorm together tonight, my love...there's a strawberry field of things I want to tell you..." he said ardently with a curious inflection.

"Meee-ooo-ooo-ooo-www..."

BOOK 2

THE EVOLUTION OF PUNISHMENT

PART 1

TOULOUSE, FRANCE
FEBRUARY 1955

IT ALL BEGAN IN A LAKE
(FIRST ATTEMPT ON GASTON'S LIFE)

Cold water reached up to his neck. His jaw and head were in great pain. He cried.

He was being pulled hard out of a wrecked car through murky water by several strong arms, two men in white uniforms.

School articles floated by, several pencils, a notebook with the name "GASTON" handwritten on its cover. Emotional voices from these men were saying things about a car accident. Ambulance sirens wailed. Confusion and commotion filled the mid-afternoon air.

"He's still alive," said a voice in French.

"Can you talk?" asked another voice, directed to the child they were holding. "Is your name Gaston?"

"...y-e-s..." replied the child, weakly.

Horrified, his face broke into spasmodic crying.

"Voici, Virginie. Emmenez-le à l'ambulance."

The person receiving the crying child in her arms wore also a uniform, in her twenties, more calm in appearance than the others. Hurrying, she scrambled her way from the lake shore to the ambulance.

Rushing toward the vehicle's rear, where a doctor awaited, she acknowledged the small, curious crowd gathered across the road with a sweet nod. They seemed to notice her motherly instinct, carrying the injured child as if he was her own. But they failed to see what she was up to when she momentarily disappeared from view behind a lattice of overhanging foliage near the ambulance, taking advantage of an opportune background noise created by a passing commercial truck. "I could kill you, *crétin! Petit salaut!*" she shouted, repeatedly slapping the child's face.

A deafening crying filled the air. The child's weeping exploded into a terrifying spectacle when she passed his trembling body over to the unsuspecting doctor already inside the med vehicle. "Calm down now, kid...you're going to be all right..." nurtured the doctor with tenderness, immediately keeping him warm and cozy.

∾

Hovering about the site was Richard's invisible soul, quietly watching and learning. And talking to himself, *Nice to be here...in post-World War II France. Nice to be in the 20th century.* A bunch of thoughts had emerged ever since his arrival a little while ago, coinciding with the car accident, *So this kid is related to me...I'm thirteen reincarnations his senior...I can already feel some affinity...some kinship...but what a terrible way to get to know each other...*

∾

A film projector was rolling inside the local police station.

Two detectives were watching a replay of the car accident—a film shot by an amateur who happened to be filming a school project in the area when the horrible crash took place.

"Clearly, it was the drunk driver's fault," remarked the police chief. "Amazingly the kid didn't get killed, like his parents."

"His half-conscious body was hurled up in the air like a ragged doll and landed in the lake," said a detective.

"Too bad his parents didn't follow the same jumping path. They were crushed in their seats by colliding metals," expressed another detective.

∾

Gaston lay down in a hospital's bed moments later, white sheets and a pathetic gray blanket covering his body up to his chin.

Serene room. A big plastic bag and spaghetti-thin tube hung from a post at his bedside, feeding intravenous fluids to his left arm.

Three nurses were engaged in small chat outside the room.

"...the car plunged into the lake...both his parents died in the accident..." one nurse said, lowering her voice more and more.

"...he's badly hurt...suffering from amnesia...and two broken ribs..." whispered another nurse. "...he can't remember a thing..."

"...poor kid..." whispered the third nurse, chewing gum, "...he has this strange vacant expression on his face...."

Moments went by before a registered nurse stepped into the room.

Looking down at the sedated little patient, she asked with a soft voice, "How d'you feel, kid?"

Smiling, she swayed in the air a ring she held in her hand. "You want your toy ring back? It's very pretty."

"...ring?"

"It's too soon now. You'll have it back when your auntie takes you home. She called twice today."

"...auntie?"

Above hovered Richard's soul.

STROLLING DOWN THE BOULEVARD DE STRASBOURG

Doña Manola Sandoval, a nicely aging Spanish widow with a wretched past, ambled along the tree-lined boulevard next to her handsome twelve-year-old son, Pierre.

He'd been conceived in the ruins of Malaga in 1942 after his dad's brief escape from prison and reunion with Manola, before Franco's secret police re-arrested and executed him. The Nazis were already terrorizing every village in France with the notorious experience gained in Spain during the raging 1936-1939 Spanish Civil War. So it took years of painful hiding in remote mountain cabins past the French border to finally legalize the papers that would declare him one of France's own boys, while still upholding in the background his Spanish heritage.

"Pas vous, pas vous—c'est Perpignan, ma ville d'adoption!" he'd signal off-handedly in time, dismissing both countries, one after the other, with one sharp pointed finger, but praising his adoptive border town, like any grateful kid living in exile would.

The process of healing for both war refugees—mother and son– thus began in this friendly community, tucked in a bay by the warm Mediterranean Sea. A place regarded by many as the "pearl of the Pyrenees Orientales."

୧୬

Several days had gone by since Pierre's winning school presentation in front of a large audience, about 15th-century Jeanne d'Arc, when they were informed of the tragic car accident. Both Doña Manola's sister and her sister's husband were killed, while their badly injured son, Gaston, lay, memory-numb, in a hospital somewhere in Toulouse some two-hundred kilometers away.

Accustomed to tragedies, Doña Manola, now in her late thirties, regarded this as a new phase in her life, a new challenge, and, God willing–still a staunch believer in spite of what General Franco and his bloody army of Roman Catholic insurgents and priests had done to Democratic Spain–she would move forward with the same tenacity and vigor that had always characterized her. She would continue to ignore her terribly thick Spanish accent when speaking in French, and get her life in order in this foreign land, which, after all, spoke the language of freedom and democracy.

Not long ago she had protected dozens of Republicans (also known as Loyalists), mostly wounded soldiers and black listed intellectuals, keeping them hidden down in the basement of her Madrid home. Again and again she'd put her life on the line for one of the noblest causes of her time–the defense of Democratic Spain against Fascist invaders.

Led by maniacal General Franco and his even more maniacal German and Italian allies, they had crushed the whole country, literally burned it to ashes, before the General himself gave his last *coup*– the *coup de grâce*–by sending a million civilians to the firing squads at war-end.

"How could he have *not* won the war and destroyed Spain, allied to Hitler's Waffen-SS Troops and Mussolini's Black Shirt Brigades– two of the most evil, genocide-inflicting armies the world has ever known?" Doña Manola would later question her peers with profound grief and raving anger.

She had ample reasons to talk like that, having lost her husband to idiotic political ideologies that didn't coincide exactly with each other in a field of dozens of absurdly different ideologies, none worse than Franco's.

That Franco would rule Spain for another forty years with the same twisted mentality, she could never imagine or comprehend. Such insanity had no place in her mind. And yet many lived beyond her time to see it happen.

⁀෨

Tragedy had once again knocked on her door with her sister's parting. They had never been too close, but they were sisters nevertheless and memories of their sweet childhood together brought back beautiful feelings she had not felt in a long time, only to see them wither away in deep sorrow and pain. "She was the angel in our family, I was the spoiled brat," she told one of her close friends during the burial.

But now, locally, she had a new responsibility at hand–a second boy to raise. To be sure, Gaston looked a lot like her sister. What kind of a person would he ever become under her wing? Hard to say.

Walking along the shaded boulevard, past Rue Saint-Bernard, Doña Manola and Pierre approached a busy corner, where they stopped to buy some magazines and candies. Pierre had made a selection at a kiosk, waiting for his mom to pay, which she did using coins only.

It was a regular day. Vegetables and fruits from the morning-operated market had already been dispensed. Sidewalks stood wet and slippery after a light rain. A bit windy. The old Ville Rose district, spiced with stately pink-brick houses, rejoiced on its continuous historical gaiety. So did the friendly and efficient hotels on the Jean-Jaurès hills near the metro. As usual, they attracted a most fun group of tourists to watch, bouncing around their colorful bags ridiculously stuffed with city maps, potato chips, and cigarettes.

A tall raggedy vagabond, terribly unfed and ill with bloodshot eyes, meandered along without aim or reason, while three philosophy students from a local university argued the validity of a concept regarding their personal existence on this planet.

Girls, girls. Five of them–elegant, assertive, with irresistible faces–turned heads as they tapped along their jewelry-decorated high heels on those rain sprinkled sidewalks. Such was the day, right after noon, brooded over by a passing dark-robed priest, wearing a funny hat, but bluntly upstaged by two cute, fluffy-haired milk-white toy poodles strolling side by side in step along the boulevard...as if nothing else mattered.

"What did you get for your cousin?"

"Oh–a sports mag. And other small things."

He showed her the cover of the magazine with great excitement.

"A pole vaulter doing his big jump. You like that, huh?"

"Of course."

"That should keep Gaston entertained for a while," put in Doña Manola. "Dr. Purgon said he might be released in a few days. Except for the broken ribs, the bad dreams, and some headaches, he'd be okay. Almost."

"Which bed are you gonna give him at home?" asked Pierre. "Mine or the small one in the basement?"

"The small one. He's only eight, still a kid. He'll be fine."

⁓

In his hospital bed, Gaston read the sports magazine he'd started to browse while visited by his auntie and cousin, whose friendship he wasn't ready yet to welcome, let alone assimilate, in spite of the flurry of smiles and comforting words coming from their lips. Strangely enough, he couldn't make them out. Were they really who they claimed to be? Family? For all he knew, he'd never seen them before.

Both gone now, he tried to avoid, but not ignore, the large, painful, almost grotesque picture of the leaping pole vaulter splashed on the cover, which frightened him.

Most of his memory was back, unfortunately, because the bad stuff–car accident, himself thrown up in the air like a piece of junk, then falling down into the cold, murky, expansive lake—ravaged his mind.

Fighting his fears, he finally succumbed to quiet sleep.

Only to enter a nasty nightmare moments later.

⁓

Recurring several times during the night, the nightmare continued in similar fashion for several days, leaving Gaston confused and tired. In his last, he found himself hurled up in the air, higher, higher, higher…then sharply plunging down, freely and helpless, into a scary, immensely large body of olive-green water.

In desperation, he shouted, grabbing his face, "NON! NON! NE ME LAISSEZ PAS COULER AU FOND DU LAC! JE VOUS EN PRIE!" He violently shook his head side to side. "NON! NON! NON!" exposed to the cold, lonely, abrasive, frighteningly creepy bottomless abyss. "N-O-O-O-N-N-N-N-N-N!"

Above hovered Richard's soul.

GOOD AND BAD STRANGERS

A hospital doctor saluted Doña Manola Sandoval as she headed toward the left-wing corridor, entered the familiar room, and approached the bed where Gaston lay down quietly.

"My little boy...are you feeling better now?" she cheered. "It's not a good thing for an eight-year-old to be in bed. Not good at all. You should be in school with all your friends, learning, doing things."

Gaston just stared, a numb look in his face.

"You're coming with me today."

Gaston reacted with a faint smile, "...really...?"

"You bet. I have a nice house, a farm, in the outskirts of Alès, near Nîmes. It's in the Cévennes, a lovely village called Saint-Jean-du-Gard, surrounded by forests, mountains, rivers...warm people. Lots of horses, cows, goats, ducks, rabbits..."

"...rabbits...?"

She laughed. "Yes. All over. And if you like wild animals, they'll be there too. Deer, wild pigs, raccoons, foxes, even wolves." Noticing a bigger smile in the boy's lips, she said, "Your cousin will show you around."

"...cousin...?"

"Yes. Pierre."

Gaston remained quiet, impassive. Then his eyes blinked.

"Auntie...where's my mom? And my dad?"

"They're both in heaven. They're needed up there." Doña Manola spotted a sudden wetness in the kid's eyes. "They're okay. They're fine."

Gaston began to cry.

"I want them here. I need them too."

∾

In a street corner near the hospital, the young woman forming part of the medic team who'd slapped Gaston's face during his rescue from the lake, now without her uniform, dialed a number.

In the 31st century, precisely year 3081, Master Judge calmly sipped his coffee, seated next to the control panel in his cozy, elevated petit château overlooking the trial's unfolding stages.

He was also flipping the pages of a glossy sports magazine, splashed with a spectacular picture of a mid-air jumping pole vaulter on the June cover when a familiar faint signal from his ZCAP meter rang. *It's from 1955 France*, he quickly realized. Such was the z-communications technology of the period—sucking up, so to speak, calls from the far past as if they'd been dialed now and locally.

Clicking on "century and year magnification" for more details, he accepted and listened.

"Master?" a familiar voice said.

"Virginie?"

"*Oui*. Did not kill, not yet...ze boy is in ze ospital...recovering," said the agitated female voice with a very thick French accent.

"Not good! Try again and call me back. *Must be done!*"

He shut the conversation off.

"*Merde...*" said Virginie, hanging up.

Above hovered Richard's soul.

PART 2

SAINT-JEAN-DU-GARD
FRANCE, MARCH 1955

OLD FARM

Gaston had been out of the hospital for about a month now, recovering from his injuries.

He was staying at an old farm with close friends of Doña Manola's in the picturesque Cévennes village of Saint-Jean-du-Gard, about fourteen kilometers from Anduze (the Cévennes's gate) and twenty-eight from Alès (the Cévennes's capital), the Cévennes being a splendorous rugged mountainous area full of the stuff people all over the world are always fascinated about—historical villages, castles, hamlets, churches, and their connecting conflicts, wars, tales and legends.

Centuries ago it was the land of powerful kingdoms, fighting knights, troubadours, chivalry, and courtly love. Also, vile religious crusades, sacking, destruction, torture, and public burnings at the stake. Dark and reproachable medieval legacies.

A land otherwise graced with stunning forests, river boats, snow-capped peaks, wild horses, and locomotives of every style, size, and color.

Such was the place little Gaston landed on one beautiful spring day in 1955—a sort of Cévennes triangle, comprising the charming towns of Alès, Anduze, and Saint-Jean-du-Gard.

❧

Historically this triangle was viewed by their inhabitants as the chestnut-tree-based, mining-seated, silk-making, Camisards and Maquisards freedom-fighting center of southern France. A big deal.

Situated in the Languedoc-Roussillon region, precisely in the Gard department, they had painfully but heroically emerged from a very violent and bloody past of Protestant-choice-religion persecutions and Nazi occupation.

Doña Manola had convinced the Quinteros (Don Valerio, Doña Elvira, and their two sons Alfredo and Pablo) to absorb Gaston and Pierre into their farm livelihood, while she attended to her business elsewhere. She would, occasionally and briefly, reunite with them, depending on the circumstances.

"*No se preocupe, Doña Manola...le debemos nuestras vidas...y mas...*" (Don't worry, Doña Manola...we owe you our lives...and more...") had signified Don Valerio when Doña Manola had proposed to leave the kids with them.

Had Doña Manola not come to their rescue two years back in war-stricken Spain, they would've become dead meat for the vultures, like other family members before them, standing in the expeditious "opposition" firing-squad-execution line ordered by *Generalísimo* Franco. Opposition meant anti-Fascism, anti-corrupted Church, anti-absolute monarchy, and anti-Insurgency. In other words, virtuous pro-democracy sentiments anyone should be proud of. Not here. A junta had taken over the country after a bloody invasion, and a heinous, fascist Roman Catholic dictator had begun to rule.

"*Que Dios los bendigan...*" (May God bless you...") had replied Doña Manola, in Spanish, the only language Don Valerio could handle at this point in his life.

And that had sealed the issue.

༶

Preferring the company of other Spanish Civil War compatriot refugees who tended to populate the big and bustling cities of Perpignan and Toulouse, rather than this gorgeous tri-town enclave–where the beauty of sunrises and sunsets never ceased to amaze–Gaston's auntie was notoriously absent most of the time.

She missed out on swimming in the trout-streaked, sumptuous Gardon River, crossed over in so many places by ancient humpback cutwater bridges, serenaded by constant wing-sizzling cicadas and rare birds of exotic plumage only found in Languedoc.

She missed out on trudging through many and varied sun-warmed hiking trails that led to vision-fogged, hill-crested medieval sights of a long gone but not forgotten past. She missed out on listening to nocturnal owls and bats and daylight birds of prey, along lush pine, oak, fur, olive, and chestnut trees.

She missed out on admiring dense unspoiled forests on horseback dotted with craggy hills, hidden grottes, silver creeks, placid lakes, and breathtaking waterfalls of shining and lasting beauty.

She missed out on bumping into an occasional deer, rabbit, fox, wolf, or even wild boar roaming the community.

Not only did she miss out on all these magnificent things, including smelling the fragrant lavender aroma of the mountain-covered *garrigues* that bathed these lands, she failed to remember how fertile and gracious the peaceful vineyards and wheat fields had been all along and how rejoicing anyone could be among countless herds of grazing sheep, cattle, mouton, goat, and pig.

Nature was Queen, and she missed out on all that.

Including every opportunity to find, pick, and eat the sweetest chestnuts ever grown anywhere...without counting out the very Garden of Eden!

On a social level, Doña Manola missed out on being the local matriarch expected of her. She sorely failed to communicate personal feelings and love around her close friends and provide guidance to her growing son Pierre and deceased sister's son, Gaston. Beyond enrolling both of them to suitable public schools in the vicinity—*collège* (middle school) for Pierre and *école élémentaire* (elementary school) for Gaston—she didn't do much of substance, wisdom, or lasting value.

But that was her mystery. She simply didn't seem to care about raising kids. Her chosen profession of on-the-road meetings with mostly strangers to sell a cosmetic product or apply a face of makeup facilitated this kind of detachment. And such freedom she amply sought and cherished.

Life moved on. Like the wheels of the bicycle Pierre rolled on to school every day along a steep dirt track up the pine woods bordering the ruins of an ancient settlement, the decaying temple that followed, the two anchored aging river rafts splashed with bird poop he always noticed, and the recurrent flock of grazing sheep three quarters of the way that gave him pause to think about his current condition.

Yes, life moved on. Like the passing of Gaston's persistent mental mirages—whether here or there, day or night, past or present, or beyond his wildest imaginings—which greatly disturbed his senses and complicated his decisions, but nevertheless rolled on.

∽

The tingling fragrance of Saint-Jean-du-Gard's wild flowers in late March lingered in the air, enough to lure even the most skeptic *papillon* or dragonfly scouting the area. This was the day Gaston first noticed Juliette.

∽

As it turned out, the eight-year-old quite easily became part of a small group of youngsters playing in the neighborhood, Juliette and Pierre among them.

This particular morning's rushes of excitement, in the middle of the week, had combined to have Alfredo and his young brother Pablo join in. Their father owned the farm, soon to be partly managed by Alfredo, a charmer by excellence.

Warmly pleasant, twenty-one years old, with lots of dark long curls around his handsome face—that was him, Alfredo. Muscular body, no mustache or sideburns, and a friendly yet commanding baritone voice that drew respect.

A painter of nature and young beautiful girls as well as an accomplished accordion player, Alfredo appeared at times over protective of his beret-wearing brother Pablo, two years younger, thin built, tall, quiet, and passionate with his clarinet, which he played extremely well, to the point of never leaving the farm without it.

"Let's all go on this bicycle!" Alfredo declared, watching their excited stares. Already mounted on an old but sturdy one, he challenged all of them to climb up and ride with him along the old farm trail, which ran parallel to Route de Luc for a short stretch.

All on board now, the two-wheeler, slowly and laboriously, moved toward the woods by a dirt detour road dotted with manure. Only Pablo had declined the ride. His fertile mind had found expression in related matters that didn't require a lot of gymnastics.

Serenading the ensemble at close range with his clarinet, make-believe camera (using his folded beret), and artistic movements, he'd turned himself into a convincing brave and versatile *cinéma vérité* film-maker. "*Le cinéma français, c'est moi!*" he proclaimed playfully.

"Hey–we're picking up speed!" cheered Alfredo, pedaling faster and faster, his wild hair locks dancing in the air.

"Obstacles on the horizon!" warned Pierre loudly and eagerly. He stood perched over the front wheel, head bent down, his butt grotesquely stuffed onto a square metal grid basket, legs dangling free.

Seated on the front bar, shouted Juliette–a green-eyed twelve-year-old stage actress of rising fame in the south of France– "Yoo haaa! We're entering the shit zone! Bad timing!" She was gorgeous and funny, with her long golden tresses half-blocking Alfredo's view while at the same time back-tapping her cute ears.

"Dodge the pile! Pinch your nose!" roared Pierre, same age as Juliette and attending the same school, but conceited in grander scale. "Cowshit! Horseshit! Duckshit! All colors! Brown! Chestnut brown! Dark brown! Black!"

"Yellow green!" someone else on the bicycle yelled.

"Go faster, Alfredo or we're all gonna fall!" shouted Juliette. "You're losing the balance, jerk!"

"Doing my best–you fools!" yelled Alfredo. His muscular contour, covered with a sweaty T-shirt, appeared silhouetted against the faint light.

Gaston felt the rudely rolling and bumping motion underneath. He was bouncing on a leather-covered hard seat, barely one inch over the rear wheel, legs hanging. "Can't see a thing from here!" he bawled, full of joy. "Just don't make me fall on *the obstacles!*"

His younger age, by comparison, had no detrimental effect on him, except make himself surge with more curiosity and wonder than his friends and cousin. But there was also marks of sadness in his intelligent hazel eyes, having recently lost both his parents in that awful car crash Doña Manola had been so influential in trying to make him forget.

"The danger's over," Alfredo declared. "Soon we'll be swallowed by the forest...unless we do a U-turn."

"Hell no!" cried Pierre at the accompaniment of Pablo's clarinet music.

"Just kidding," said Alfredo, amused. "I know a short cut through the woods."

"Please take it," said Juliette, enjoying the feel of her provincial blonde mane blown by the breeze.

Pedaling on safe grounds, Alfredo whistled part of a song, then another. "Say, Gaston, you wanna go out sight-seeing and nature painting Saturday? Real early–like five o'clock in the morning?"

"Saturday? What's today?"

"Thursday," said Alfredo.

"Sure. If you can wake me up..."

"No problem. How about you Pierre?"

"I'll pass."

Pedaling faster, Pablo followed with his clarinet.

"I knew you would." Alfredo felt the caressing touch of Juliette's loose hair on his chin. He then pictured her naked on a lump of hay in the barn near him. "Juliette?"

"I can't. I'm performing Friday and Saturday night."

"Oh yeah," exclaimed Alfredo, "I almost forgot."

"I'll be tied up both afternoons...rehearing my lines...preparing for the trip to the city with my mom..."

"And you'll be returning late..." Alfredo's dark eyes glowed momentarily. "Do they need a good-looking, romantic actor in your play who's good with the accordion?"

Juliette answered quickly, "I'm afraid not. What kind of music?"

"Tarantellas...polkas...waltzes...Middle Ages songs..."

"Definitely not."

꩜

That very night Gaston dreamed about himself being in a peculiar place...called "Zoasis"...a small, round swimming pool...called "jacuzzi"...talking to someone who kept calling him "Richard."

"I'm not Richard..." he answered back in his dream, feeling very uncomfortable.

But things continued even in striking details.

A charming, robust, older man called "Master Judge" or simply "the judge" joined Richard in the Zoasis. Jumping into the jacuzzi, wild-eyed, he boasted, "Afraid of the water, rich man?"

"No. Just..." said Richard, cautiously. He was fidgeting with a handkerchief.

"Oh—c'mon. It's break time," quipped Master Judge.

"...gotta take a leak..."

"Hey, do it right here...in the water. Nobody will notice it." Master Judge pointed to a tray. "Grab a tuna fish sandwich..."

Richard complied, felt funny.

So did Gaston...in his dream....

Above hovered Richard's soul.

SPUNKY JULIETTE WOWS GASTON

"Yellow, yellow-green," said Gaston.

"Yeah," said Juliette.

"It's really cool, isn't it?"

"It's very cool."

Gaston could see an affinity of colors in both her vivid green eyes and the precious stone they both stared at as he kept his hand up close to Juliette's exquisitely chiseled face and lips.

She had just arrived on her bicycle carrying a tennis racquet. Both she'd dropped to the ground with a snap of her hand in her bratty rush to be with him.

Then the sparkling ring stole her attention.

∾

Returning from a successful publicity and promotional trip across parts of France, Juliette chose to keep this side of her life barely noticeable from Gaston's little world of daily trivial incidents, mostly related to the farm where he lived and roomed with his cousin Pierre. Deep inside, she was just a little girl...with little girl's needs.

Away from the farm and Saint-Jean-du-Gard, her hometown, however, she was a public figure.

She'd made front page news in the entertainment section of leading newspapers and magazines and had appeared in several radio programs as a special guest.

People mostly wanted to know if she planned to star in movies too, now that she was a stage star. She'd consistently answered, "Maybe. I already have some offers."

During her absence she'd famously turned thirteen somewhere in Nantes, close to Paris.

Both Gaston and Pierre had likewise celebrated birthdays, eleven days apart, but quietly at home. Each boy had received a small gift from Doña Manola, who made a point to drop by and give them company for three days, replacing thus a later visit set for their April-May school break.

"I love Saint-Jean-du-Gard, but my work and priorities are elsewhere. Sorry," she told them as she headed for her car.

"But, Mom...you said you were going to take us to the Train à Vapeur des Cévennes...and the Musée du Désert, which my teacher wants me to visit and write a paper on Camisard Chief Rolland," reminded Pierre, angrily.

"And the Bambouseraie de Prafrance...you know, this huge bamboo forest everybody's talking about...that you promised you would show us..." added Gaston eagerly.

"Next time, kids," Doña Manola said firmly, ending the talk, blowing kisses from inside her brand-new, shiny, black Peugeot 403, where she'd squeezed herself behind the steering wheel, ready to go.

Rumors had it that she was dating a divorced general from Pakistan...in Saint-Tropez.

෴

"I like it. What's it made of?" enthused Juliette, staring at the rare old ring, feeling some strands of her blonde hair caress the curvature of her neck.

She wore a pleated white tennis skirt and short-sleeved light-blue *jersey petit piqué* shirt—both tailored to her very special taste. Definitely more Parisian than Languedocian.

"I don't know," said Gaston, realizing she sported no pony-tail today.

"It's a green-yellowish color...kind of oily," Juliette said, pouting. "More green than yellow."

"And sparkles a lot, even at night," added Gaston with a jaunty little smile.

"It's real pretty." Her youthful eyes kept staring at the shining gemstone in stark fascination, while scratching the back of her right leg with the rubber sole of her left tennis shoe. One of those girlie things.

༓

Gaston had been painting for a couple hours before she'd shown up.

He'd established himself comfortably under the bright sun, which he revered, all setup with his little folding chair, mini table, canvas, and watercolors half way between the barn and the old structure that lodged the kitchen.

No one else around that particular afternoon–he pretty much looked like the star of his own show.

For a while, anyway.

He'd added two cows and a pig to his painting when Juliette made her cute tennis styled appearance.

Earlier, he'd been visited by a very intriguing ghostly lady, with fluffy white hair, known to be ninety-eight years old and crazy, living in the farm community–more like a mysterious wanderer than a grounded resident, whose real home, if any, no one knew for sure where it stood–but a charming, nameless person, nonetheless, whose preoccupation for "blue" went beyond description.

Unfortunately, Gaston's black cat didn't like her, and the moment she stepped in, he ran out. And didn't return for hours.

When he did, he carried a mouse in his mouth, as usual. His code of ethics forbade him from eating his prey, so instead, he tortured the mouse by forcing the little thing to play "hide and seek."

Gaston called his cat *Joueur* (player). Not exactly handsome, he managed to turn heads in his neighborhood among his kind when strutting down the block and bring bad luck among pedestrians when freakily cutting in front of their legs.

The ancient lady had arrived, like she often did, quietly, showing Gaston the usual words she'd written on a piece of paper, for she was deaf-mute:

"Follow me. Let's find it."

She meant, "Let's hunt in the woods, past the creek, for anything colored in blue."

And little Gaston followed her, as he often did, for twenty to thirty minutes until a "blue" discovery was made. The satisfaction of which for the poor lady couldn't possibly be described in words.

༝

"And it's set on gold," said Juliette.

As she admired the strange ring Gaston held up close to her face, she took his hand softly and guided it even closer to her eyes while relishing on the precious stone.

"Yeah gold..." said Gaston, unsure.

He was still holding his paint brush with the other hand, fresh from the last color stroke he'd attempted on the canvas. Some of his coloring tubes bulged out from one of his side pockets in his khaki shorts.

Juliette let go of his hand and stepped back a little, just brooding, while Gaston set the paint brush on the small table near them. Unconsciously, she also self-caressed her long, golden tresses in front of him, thrusting out her thick lips provocatively.

"Wait," she then said, rushing back to her bicycle.

This one stood about sixty yards away, where she'd left it, next to her tennis racquet.

"*My grandpa owns a jewelry store in town*," she shouted, so he could hear her, while rolling her bicycle up to a concrete wall near an old structure made of several decaying pillars. Still far from Gaston, she shouted, grabbing her tennis racquet in a lively manner, "*We should visit him...show him the ring.*"

"*What for*," shouted back Gaston. "*I mean...it's just a ring.*"

Juliette approached him again, holding her tennis racquet.

"How come you're wearing it? I don't see other boys wearing rings."

Gaston shrugged.

The ring had been on his finger longer than he could remember. He'd just been more aware of it since the car accident, about a year ago, since his stay in the hospital in Toulouse. Neither Doña Manola nor

Pierre had questioned him about it. But Juliette was now just doing that.

Flirtingly, she began to turn around and around, spiraling like a top, holding the racquet in various sexy ways, her long hair wildly wrapping around her face.

Gaston watched in awe how her skirt went up and down sinuously, at times high enough to reveal her soft light-blue panties.

"My uncle gave it to me before he died," he said, fighting his eyes. "He made me promise to never take it off my finger."

Suddenly, she stopped spiraling to listen.

"He said it'll bring me good luck." Gaston felt embarrassed saying this. "I actually dreamed this stuff. It's not real."

Juliette reacted oddly. "But your ring *is*. That's why you should let my grandpa see it. Some rings have legends, you know," she said, then pouted. Her pretty nose twitched a bit. "I'll talk to Grandpa tonight... see what he says..."

Again, she began to turn with her racquet like a ballerina, landing near the old pillars.

Gaston watched, enthralled.

She turned and stopped, and turned and stopped again, repeatedly, enjoying the circling and slapping motion of her loose long hair.

At one point, Gaston's photographic mind caught her holding the racquet in a peculiar way next to one pillar, mid-turn posture, her carmine-red plump lips pouting adorably, her long, golden tresses flowing over her fiery green eyes, a moment so fascinating he swore he'd never forget. Never!

"You play tennis?" asked Gaston then. "I don't recall seeing you with a tennis racquet before."

"I'm learning. I just started last week. It's fun."

"It looks like."

She laughed, enjoyed the way he stared at her with his enraptured hazel eyes.

"How old's your grandpa?" asked Gaston.

"Eighty-five. He's a strong man."

"I'm nine, by the way. How old are you?"

"Thirteen."

"My favorite number."

"I'm glad."

She bent down to grab a little yellow flower, but kept staring up at him sensually.

"What's his name?"

"My grandpa?"

"Yes."

"Marcel."

"What's you uncle's name?" she asked.

Gaston hesitated. "You mean George? The one in my dreams?"

"Yeah." Wind blew some blonde hair over her forehead. "So it's George." She smiled, revealing secret spots to her soft-sculptured face.

♋

Juliette played with her hair. "Have you dreamed other things lately?"

He looked down at the yellow flower she held in one hand, then at her gorgeous, seductive emerald-green eyes.

"Yeah...a future world..."

"Like what?"

"Weird stuff...like...huge stadiums crowded with noisy people... watching a spaceman fighting all kinds of–"

"Animals?"

"No, other people. One after another. One of them wearing a black cape, black gloves..."

"You do have strange dreams," she said with a pout.

Gaston hesitated. "I'm not sure they're dreams. They're too real."

"Interesting."

"There's also this person...very, very, very rich and–" Gaston stopped abruptly then grimaced. "I have to go, Juliette. I can hear my auntie calling me."

"Oh...she's back?"

"Yeah. I'll see you tomorrow."

"Take this flower with you," Juliette said, putting it in his hand, pouting. "Bye."

Above hovered Richard's soul.

ALFREDO THROWS A DARK SHADOW AROUND

Saturday morning. A constant tapping on the window woke Gaston up.

He forced his eyes open and saw a man's face through the window, then five erect fingers jangling the framed glass.

Trying to make sense of it, Gaston recognized Alfredo's naughty smile and the waving motion of a paint brush.

"Cock a doodle do! Cock a doodle doodle do!" a rooster announced the beginning of day.

Getting up at five o'clock in the morning wasn't Gaston's cup of tea, but today he would make an exception.

So would *Joueur*, his miffed cat.

Back to school, Monday, he thought. *Painting now? Why not!*

He hurried to the bathroom.

Outdoors painting held a mythical attraction to him, especially since the landscape was Saint-Jean-du-Gard. The more he thought about it, as he put his khaki shorts on and slipped a light blue T-shirt over it, the more he grew animated

Minutes before daybreak, they left the farm and rolled on.

Alfredo carried little Gaston on the front bar of his bicycle, the same place where Juliette had been two days before in her cheeriest moments with the young locals while gunning through the manure-spotted wood paths.

Their painting tools filled the backseat side pockets, over which rested a bunch of large and heavy items that made the ride painfully slow.

Content with himself, Alfredo whistled and pedaled like a little boy all the way to a place where the couple agreed to stop and camp out.

They unloaded their art tools near a river bank, enjoying the cool marsh greenery and surrounding foliage, finally under visible daylight.

While Alfredo set the heavier items on the ground, such as paint boxes, canvases, support wooden legs, and folded mini chairs, Gaston gathered the smaller pieces on a large white towel carefully spread over the rich grass next to coverings of sticks, shrubbery, and pine cones. Assorted art items, such as paint brushes, palettes, scrapers, sponges, sandpaper, penknives, water vessels, and gelatin soon filled the towel.

"Hey, let's do a little ritual here before the sun shows up over the hill," challenged Alfredo right off.

"A praying thing?"

"No..." smiled the artist, unfolding the two chairs and setting them side by side. "You black-paint my name on the back of your chair and I'll blue-paint yours on the back of my chair. And then we'll switch chairs. You like my idea?"

"Awesome."

ꙮ

Sitting side by side like movie directors, the back of their chairs bearing their important names, they watched the sun climb the sky to a point where they felt comfortable to begin their work.

"Need any help in mixing colors?" offered Alfredo, proud of his charming nature and painting skills.

"No, thanks...I can handle it myself..." The young boy was just as proud of his own nature and skills.

Perched on tall branches above their heads, a flock of sparrows chirped away their emotions. Dragonflies, armed with menacing wings and bulgy round eyes, zoomed by erratically. They wore vivid red-orange and blue-green colors.

"You like to paint horses, don't you?" Alfredo remarked, peeking at his canvas.

"I do...'

"It's an imagined white horse, I gather...I don't see any around here right now..."

"...it doesn't matter..." said Gaston.

Alfredo held one arm up in front of his face, pointing with his thumb to a tiny red-roofed house nested in the ragged relief of a distant mountain.

"See my thumb? See the little red house just above it? Well, that's the way I guide my eye to draw and paint...it gives me focus...it tells me about proportions...and it's real..." He patted the boy's shoulder. "You should try that too."

He showed Gaston his work in progress. "See my painting? It's all about thumbs."

"I like my white horse..." said Gaston, dismissively.

෫ා

They continued to work on their individual masterpieces.

About halfway through, Alfredo went back to his bicycle, feeling hungry. He dug for food inside the metal grid basket sitting on top of the front wheel and returned with ham sandwiches, cookies, and apple juice.

Clumsily, he dropped one of the cookies made with almond flour and honey on the ground–itself a natural mantle of twigs and dying leaves partially eaten up by ants, some of them still wandering aimlessly around. "Watch them how they go at it!" he shrieked, pointing a finger accusingly.

Searching for a safe spot on the towel, he sat down. "Good work. We've accomplished a lot so far," he said, shoving a slice of ham into his mouth.

Cookies and juice followed.

Past the yummy break, he sang along with Gaston some old but fun boy-scout melodies, while painting and thrilling at the occasional sight of a forest visitor, such as a long-eared fluffy-haired hare that nearly refused to leave and two soiled, rather thin, coyotes too young and shy to be harmful.

Alfredo also cracked a few jokes that brought some healthy laughter around. Mostly, he missed playing his accordion, which understandably he'd left at the farm, but didn't comment on that.

❦

"How do you like our neighbor Juliette?"

"She's fine, very beautiful."

"Have you seen her acting...on stage?"

"No."

"She's amazing," said Alfredo.

"I'm sure she is."

"Maybe *too* amazing."

Gaston drank some apple juice. "What do you mean?" he asked.

"She's heading for fame and fortune–big time. You understand that, kid?"

Gaston reflected, wondering. "Yeah..."

Alfredo lit a cigarette. "What I mean is...keep her as a friend only."

"She's my friend. We're friends, of course."

"Good." Alfredo inhaled and blew some smoke to one side of his face. "Just don't fall in love with her. I know you like her a lot, maybe too much."

Embarrassed, Gaston sipped some juice.

"What make you think that?"

"I've been watching you...and Juliette. I know it's easy to fall in love. She's so pretty...and talented...and bright."

"She certainly is."

Alfredo puffed on his cigarette, blew smoke out.

"What I mean is–and I tell you this because I like you–and don't want you to get hurt, you know, if your passion gets too heated up, too intense."

Gaston watched the smoke eddy through Alfredo's fingers, confused and sad.

"Because she's bound to leave town and go with showbiz people, sooner than you think, money-making people, fame-making people, you understand?"

"I think so."

Above hovered Richard's soul.

WATCHING JULIETTE PEDALING AWAY

Alfredo was playing the accordion, sitting on a bench by a bunch of chickens and ducks. Clad in his usual tight T-shirt, his bulging muscles seemed to blend with the music he at times also sang.

He saw Juliette pedaling into the farm, stopping, dismounting her bicycle, and reclining it against a tree. As usual, she looked adorable.

She waved a cutie hello to Alfredo, whose eyes were also on her, walking toward Gaston, her long, gorgeous golden tresses bouncing.

Gaston was done with his painting and his habitual hunt for blue colored objects with the old lady in the backwoods behind the creek. Seeing Juliette topped any excitement he'd felt today. Plus he'd not seen her in days.

"Did you bring the frog?" he quickly asked her.

"*Oui.*"

Surprise! The frog leaped off her cupped hands.

"Wow!" exclaimed Gaston. "He landed on the hay stack!" Swiftly moving after the tiny amphibian, he shouted to Juliette, "Hurry! Catch him!"

With agile steps, she grabbed the frog.

"It's a *she*," she corrected him, pouting. "A girl."

Innocently, he gazed at her bulgy young lips.

"How do you know?"

"I'm a girl. I should know, right?"

He nodded, now watching the frog settling on the back of her hand.

"Hello Adrienne," he said to the frog.

"Her name is Isabelle."

"Hello Isabelle."

Juliette caressed the frog's slim body with her lush lips, teasing Gaston with coquettish smiles.

"We're invited to Grandpa's house Monday night...my night of rest."

"He won't mind?"

"He wants to." She pouted. "He knows something about you already."

The frog jumped off and disappeared in the grass edging the barn.

"Let her run! She wants her freedom!" cried out Juliette. "I've got to go now."

She hurried to the tree where she'd left her bicycle. Mounting it, she pedaled off.

"Wait!" Gaston ran after her.

She kept going.

"Hey—maybe the three of us—you, me, and Pierre—could do some hiking tomorrow? Run through the wheat fields, chew some wheat on the way?"

"Sure..." She reduced her pedaling speed. "If Pierre's not reading another novel or practicing the clarinet with Pablo, he'll join us, like last time."

Gaston kept running, slightly behind her. "We could also play around the bonfire at sunset, sing old songs and listen to both Alfredo's and Pablo's music. Hey—that'll be fun!"

"I can't," lamented Juliette, increasing her speed. "Not at night. Remember—I have a theater commitment?"

"How much longer is that commitment?"

"About two months."

Running. "Then you'll be free to join us?"

Pedaling. "Yes...yes...yes."

Running. "I hear you're doing great on stage, performing. I mean, starring."

Pedaling. "Just talking lines."

Running. "You're famous, they tell me. All over France."

Pedaling. "Just in the south."

She extended one hand to him and caressed his face.

Pedaling. "You're famous too, in my book."

He finally halted, out of breath, watching her pedaling away, his heart beating like crazy.

Above hovered Richard's soul.

PART 3

CLASH #3—PLAYING GAY
(A TIME TRAVELED CLASH)
FRANCE, APRIL 1955

CASUAL CHAT IN THE ZOASIS

Bermuda Revelation Park, Zundo, June 3081

Halfway into small talk, Master Judge invited Richard to join him in the jacuzzi.

"...gotta take a leak…"

"Hey, do it right here...in the water. Nobody will notice it." The judge pointed to a tray. "Grab a tuna fish sandwich."

Richard complied, felt funny.

Master Judge spoke again, "Sorry, pal, I have *two* wins so far. That's two years added to your sentence–whatever your sentence turns out to be." He splashed some water around with his fingers, squeezing them like milking a cow. "Our next Clash is about playing gay characters."

Richard chewed on his bread, wondering.

"Like in a play production...on Broadway?"

"We don't have Broadway here in Zundo. But I know what you mean. I read a lot, all kinds of books—new and ancient," the judge said. "Anyway, our performance will be judged by the other judges."

He pointed to the Judges Box high above one of the Stadiums–the place where they were pleasantly seated hour after hour watching the trial's Clashes. "See them?"

He nodded, but his eyes bolted a mile higher to the sky, suddenly distracted by a descending gigantic silvery ball.

Above everybody's heads, the spinning Celestial Sphere came down to a few dozen feet showing the current Clash status:

JUST COMPLETED: CLASH #2—MOUNTAIN CLIMBING • OVERALL SCORE: JUDGES 2 DEFENDANT 0 • NEXT: CLASH #3—PLAYING GAY

"Are we going to mock gay people?" asked Richard, a bit uncomfortable.

"No. I love gay people. They're natural. Playing them is an honor, said Master Judge. "It won't be easy, though."

How ironical, reflected Richard. *They think I'm anti-gay and this is punishment for me.* His lips curled into a sardonic smile. *I hope they give me more Clashes like this one.*

LE CHÂTEAU DE VERSAILLES...IN PINK

Night had descended upon the crowd of spectators on this day of the trial. Powerful lights flooded the six Bisected Stadiums. People moved about on their seats with restless anticipation.

Master Judge was back in his cozy place inside the elevated Royal Den, dressed up again in his favorite gothic outfit. His black-gloved fingers touched a series of buttons on his control board. A small side screen to his left showed some data headed by the words "CLASH #3—PLAYING GAY," the punishment event keyed to begin.

"Yep yep yep..." he uttered to himself.

A replica of one of Louis XIV's luxurious rooms in the Château de Versailles appeared on a new platform as the old platform disappeared underground. True to French history, it was the least known of this absolute monarch's private rooms, having served him for only one weekend, still unnamed, before its demise as such and transformation into another more useful *chambre*.

Not shown in the system of platforms controlled by Master Judge were the *Salon de Vénus, de Diane, de Mars, de Mercure, d'Apollon, de l'Abondance*, and *d'Hercule*. Neither was, understandably, the mammoth and riveting to the eyes *Galerie des Glaces*.

Wrapped in his awesome black cape, the judge observed with delight the fruit of his creation.

His curious eyes drifted momentarily to the illuminated zhoenix shield, holding tons of coral reefs, multicolored sponges, and marine fish within its elastic domain. Sunk at the bottom of a moss-laden plateau, silhouetted a shipwreck, now populated by sleeping parrot fish—a sore sight for him that diluted his attention as fast as it had captured it.

Focus lights from different sources traversed a hidden colony of gobies, eels, and shrimp crawling around like underwater ghosts. What people saw in brevity from the Stadiums, quickly became food for memories as the lights dispersed and vanished.

Surprise! Master Judge and Richard suddenly entered the imperial room dressed in 18th century royal garments and wigs. They both removed their coats, which were taken away right out by a handsome valet, and continued inside.

Stately they accommodated themselves in the exquisitely furnished environment, ignoring a lone darkly hued cortez angelfish with yellow stripes drifting by.

The huge crowd applauded the presence of the two men-turned-actors, now ready to lay naked their vulnerabilities in their quest to win the Clash.

Silence then reigned for a tense moment.

Richard's eyes turned deceptively sweet above a childish smile that begged for attention. He was resting on a gilded chair, holding a fan, his head pulled back to catch a bit of the sunlight filtering through the garden window. "...years went by...me fooling around with incredibly gorgeous girls..." he said pompously, fanning his face.

Master Judge strolled by gracefully on his precious, rubies-embedded shoes, appraising the delicate frescoes and paintings adorning the high ceiling and elongated walls. "You mean gorgeous boys." he said.

"Oooops! How did I let my lips say such naughty things." Richard blushed, shyly covering his mouth.

Master Judge fell softly on a divan next to a marble bust of Emperor Julius Caesar. Crossing his legs, he said slowly, "It happens, it happens. We're sometimes slaves of our own idiosyncrasies."

Richard sighed, "Ohhhh...please, honey."

Putting the fan down on a *tabouret*, he stood up. His eyes veered toward a long, baroque-styled mirror extending beside him like a wall. It did wonders to his attention.

"Where was I?" he exclaimed. "Oh, yes. We played all sorts of crazy games."

He talked while adjusting his lace scarf and snug vest in front of the mirror, enjoying his extravagant looks and slender body.

Master Judge quietly watched him while seeping wine from a crystal glass.

Richard went on, "Things like...nude-o-tiptoe sailing, eleven-maids giraffe-chariot riding." His eyes turned vitreous. "Flame-du-kerosene-after-striking persecutions." He laughed. "They were so funny, so experimental."

"Very illuminating games," said the judge.

One hand to his hip, Richard admired his tight-fitting silk breeches and white stockings. "And so liberating. "I do have sexy calves, don't I?"

"Hummmm...." said Master Judge, detaching his lips from his wine glass.

Richard blinked stupidly and turned away from the mirror. "My gash—I had such a great time! And there were other games—even sillier."

"I'd bet there were."

৩৩

Richard ambled further along the royal room in the famous French Château, admiring a wall painting of Louis XIV. Set next to a Boulle cabinet heightened by tortoiseshell and brass inlay-work, the Sun King displayed a kind of opulence and grandeur hardly matched by any monarch in history. "*Très charmant*." Richard said, winking one eye.

He then stopped in front of a gold-made sensually tall, nude statue of a mythological Greek deity, quickly forgetting the King. Flauntingly, one hand caressing the sculpted neck, he said, "Yeah, I played lots of silly games in my heydays, games like windmills-upon-my-lance donkey hunting."

"*Don Quijote?*"

"Donkey hunting," corrected Richard. "But the same thing, really, if you get my drift..."

"*...de la Mancha...*" put in the judge wisely. "I do."

"Ha ha ha...other silly games like...eat-your-flute downhill rolling, pass-the-balls cherry-cocktail snipping." He laughed again. "I was nuts about this one—I tell you."

All this sounded so terribly wrong around and beyond the Astral Floor, Zundonians stood up jerking their clenched fists in total disgust. Reading from their ZCAP meter screen, they chanted in unison:

You're good for nothing octillionaire
You've come from the vanity fair
You pretend to be a teddy bear
You're headed for the electric chair

Demanding justice, many people began rioting in a greater scale. They shook the Park's outer metallic fences, the Promenade's armored rest-room's walls, and the main entrance hallway's trophies display board...breaking many trophies.

Loud shouts of hate and revenge overwhelmed the Stadiums. Empty bottles and cans flew around in protest.

Master Judge stood visibly revolted by the content of Richard's words in describing his wasted lifestyle and idiotic pass-times, but did nothing to stop the scene in progress for he was starring in it.

This dissonance of feelings, however, so different from what was expected of him in the current relaxed palatial setting, would cost him his act. At least that was what many people in the audience were betting on in the men's room during the break, in spite of the wild commotion against Richard.

Richard, on the other hand, oblivious of the whole world except his scene, just sighed in character. "Wasted, wasted...we were wasted out of our minds, me and my friends. I tell you—non-stop entertainment!" he said dramatically, picking his ear. "And so...these things, as you can imagine, occupied most of my evenings."

"I can imagine," said the judge.

⁶⌒⁹

Eyeballing passing schools of creole wrasse, grunts, and white-spotted file fish, Master Judge brooded over his own lack of enthusiasm. To his amazement, these waves of fish now flirted with the lustful Greek statue.

All around angered people shouted,

You're full of it, filthy man
You've insulted our intelligence
You're good at it, dirty man
You've stolen our confidence

Unaffected and in character, Richard lounged down on an armchair, also dressed with Boulle's baroque designs. This time, he revealed his gorgeous cuffs and epoch stone rings, both glittering over the mahogany veneer on beech with gilt bronze he rested on. "Fabulous parades of twilights and pre-dawns," he said. A touch of innocence stirred his face, his eyes fluttered. "Sweet, never-ending pleasures."

Master Judge closed his eyes. "Good grief..."

A bell rang, indicating the end of the Clash.

"Thank you," acknowledged a very short man with a big voice from the elevated Judges Box. Affectionately nicknamed Tall Midget by the news media, he was in fact the sharpest knife-throwing interrogator of the Astral Floor, formally known as Greed Judge.

❧

Moments later, a final, unanimous decision was reached.

"It's a win for the defendant," spoke up grandly the leader among the three remaining judges in the Box, not surprisingly Greed Judge himself.

On his feet, he waved a large yellow flag to the crowd, nicely captured by the ZCAP meters, ZSSE-55 funboxes, ZV sets, zell phones, and other communications devices. "RICHARD FLYNN. BEST ACTING PERFORMANCE" was written on it in huge red letters.

Only one-tenth of the crowd applauded, and applause died soon.

The sky-parked Celestial Sphere began to spin its way down to about twelve feet from the spectators' heads in the Stadiums to show the event's current status on its flashing panels:

JUST COMPLETED: CLASH #3—PLAYING GAY • OVERALL SCORE: JUDGES 2 DEFENDANT 1 • NEXT: CLASH #4— MONSTER TRUCK RACING

The Sphere then spun up once more to its sky high position one-hundred feet above the six Stadiums until needed again.

PART 4

THE BAGGAGE OF WAR, LOVE, FAME, AND FATE
FRANCE, MAY 1955

THE MUD MAN

"I call him Roberto. He's from Spain. The surviving fugitive Nazis want him badly for helping the *French Resistance* and clandestine operations in Europe against Hitler's and Mussolini's invading war tanks, planes, soldiers, and spies," said Gaston to Juliette and Pierre in a strangely mature tone. He was referring to *l'Homme de la Boue* (The Mud Man).

They had quite a morning so far the three of them...running, pushing and laughing across the large wheat field and beyond the olive groves and chestnut trees.

They wound up here by a ravine half way to Pont des Abarines–a major bridge over the river Gardon de Mialet. It stood graciously taller than any bridge in the region about four kilometers away from Saint-Jean-du-Gard if taking Avenue Abraham Mazel as a point of departure, which they did. So, hiking in the direction of Mialet, which also led to San Soubeyran and Grotte de Trabuc, higher up in the mountains, they penetrated this rough terrain so much loved by *l'Homme de la Boue* and championed by Gaston.

Neither his cousin nor Juliette could've imagined what sort of place lay there under the low-hanging branches of old but robust evergreen firs–the hideout where the young boy had agreed to show his friends his secret *Ruisseau de l'Exil d'Espagne* (Exile-from-Spain Creek)–an offshoot of Ruisseau de Rose de Camplausis, also lost in the dense shrubbery of time.

"Roberto was lucky to flee from the Spanish Civil War, flee from the Fascist and Nazi invaders, flee from the incendiary bombs and firing squad's bullets...after exposing his life in open battle trenches...in defense of his country's elected democratic government," continued

Gaston. His voice changed. "Not so his parents and sister. They were shot dead in cold blood in their own living room."

Doña Manola had trained Gaston to memorize and repeat these lines over and over almost daily without ever knowing about *Ruisseau de l'Exil d'Espagne* and *l'Homme de la Boue.* "You should never forget about your family's history and suffering."

Gaston and his father were French, no doubt, by birth and education and everything, and so was Doña Manola, by naturalization, like her late sister, but she'd inherited a heavy baggage of old Spanish culture and patriotic ardor, both turning to disenchantment and cold hatred at a level and speed never anticipated.

The sudden rise to power of Fascist General Franco and his clan of Catholic Inquisitors in the clashes of war had left a deep wound inside her heart, incapable of healing, it seemed. Testimony of this national betrayal and tragedy by these two double-faced conquerors, vile manipulators of politics and human lives, rested in her *Madrileño* husband—found dead on a rural dirt road with his severed balls stuffed inside his mouth and, like his young *Andaluz* friend, poet Federico García Lorca, his asshole shattered to pieces by a round of bullets.

"The more religious your bend, the more cruel your soul," she heard a fallen Republican comrade whisper in his dying breath. Heaps of parapets in the university's campus's barricades, where he, Doña Manola, and others fought back the invaders, had failed to protect him when he raised his head to shoot, and it was her moral instinct and crushing experience to keep holding his bleeding head in her arms while sharing his line of fire until a red cross ambulance showed up and took him away.

⤔

Although bitterly torn by these events, she forged ahead as best as she could, the iron axis inside her keeping her steady in her forward march to better days.

"Roberto later joined the underground *Resistance* in France to fight the same invaders...and almost got killed doing so...but persisted fighting until Victory Day on May 8, 1945...ten years ago today," ended his lines Gaston, improvising the last words.

"Well said, well said!" exclaimed Juliette. "I'm a fan of Roberto's!"

"If those runaway Nazis find him, I suppose they'll take him to Plaza de Toros, with hundreds others rounded up that day, with the Church's informers help, and paint the walls with their blood," put in Pierre, also trained by his mother to deliver lines of rage and revenge.

"Or send him to the death camps!" remarked Juliette, with a sullen pout.

"He's not alone," revealed Gaston, pointing to a dozen or more *Resistance* fighters appearing in various sizes and looks half hidden along the creek bank, all made of mud and baked by the sun. "Juan, David, Ivan," he said proudly. "Manuel, Pedro, Raúl..." on and on.

"Got to go!" barked Pierre in an odd tone. He'd been painfully holding his pee. Now he had to release it.

Scaling a little hill, he found a spot behind a leafy plant. It didn't matter if two morbid black crows watched him from the upper branches of a nearby pine tree.

Done with, he began to descend the hill.

"Feel better now?" Juliette had noticed his absence, guessed his distraction, from a distance.

"You watched me too?"

"Someone else was?" asked Juliette, puzzled.

"Never mind."

All three together again, Juliette leading the way, hiked up the area.

A vast, sun-sweetened prairie lay ahead, extending miles and miles due north and east.

They reached the edge of the forest, scaring off a pack of wobbly partridges.

Then they began the long march back to the farm, chewing grains of wheat fresh from the field and whistling popular cowboy songs they'd heard on the radio before like,

Oh! Susanna,
Oh don't you cry for me
For I come from Alabama
With my banjo on my knee

A rocky hill upon a ridge made them want to test their climbing skills. So Juliette again took the lead, followed by Gaston, followed by Pierre, who on second thought decided to scout the lower grounds instead.

Something about a huge boulder with a strange shape and texture that blocked his way made Gaston reflect in a hypnotic way. It seemed as though he'd seen this boulder before...in a dream...or something. Stopping to rest, he let his mind go...hoping to connect...to penetrate this dream again.

Apparently, he did.

Above hovered Richard's soul.

THE HUNTER IS HUNTED

Clusters of similarly looking chestnut trees confronted them upon the hills of Forêt Domaniale de la Vallée Borgne–today's selected field of action. A tactically placed arrow, built with tiny branches, signaled the hunters–Gaston and Pierre–to turn left.

They followed the arrow sign, the latest in a long and trying run of a multitude of signs through these Cévennes woods they'd left behind.

They wore cotton sweaters over their shirts as the temperature had predictably begun to drop, because of earlier forming veils of mist and fog under somberly drifting clouds. Mosquito bites and skin bruises crudely showed below their thighs for they sported only summer shorts, as usual.

As they searched deeper into the wet brush, past a canyon, they saw a paper note with the familiar handwriting stuffed into the crack of a rock.

Pierre grabbed it and read aloud:

"Gaston: Follow the narrow path to the right while counting to one-hundred twenty-five. Stop and look around for the remains of a dead fox. You will find your treasure eighty long steps past it. Pierre: Take the wide path to the left until you see a clearing. That may take you several minutes and a bunch of scary moments. Your treasure will be hiding behind an old, uprooted tree occupied by yellow-striped spiders."

Gaston cried out, "*Zut!* We're being challenged to split and take different routes. That could be dangerous!"

Pierre reacted, "Are you afraid?"

"No, just cautious."

Gaston turned to his right, Pierre to his left. Walking in opposite directions from each other, they began to penetrate deeper the spooky forest, guardedly feeling the chill of its daunting entrails.

‿

Gaston reached the awful site assigned to him after some difficulties. Parts of the dead animal were open and exposed to a sinister black bird feasting on them, while maggots, creamy in color, crawled around. After fifty long steps Gaston saw nothing but a large imposing chestnut tree standing like a general in front of him.

‿

Meantime Pierre approached the hollow trunk of an old, decaying beech tree. Yes, there were spider webs filling its cavity. Detestable, but not as bad as his just experienced episode of fleeing the ravaging attack of a wild boar. *Juliette! Juliette! I could strangle you!* he shouted in his mind, terrified.

‿

Gaston crouched down to pick up one particular broken branch, among others, of the commanding chestnut tree.

In its slender softness it still carried the flowering spiny fruit husks and attaching long green leaves, those edged with coarse, bristly teeth. Three glossy red-brown nuts awaited Gaston's stare and touch inside each husk.

‿

"Surprise!"

Gaston froze. Numbed from head to toe by Juliette's sudden presence, he dropped the chestnut fruit.

Out of the blue she'd appeared from behind the tree, lovelier than ever, her braids undone, golden hair loosened up to a sexual tease, the fire mostly in her eyes and sensual lips.

"You and me...alone in the woods."

"...indeed..."

She eagerly brought his body against hers, touched his face with tenderness, then kissed his lips fully. Passion ensnared them.

"I'm your secret treasure, Gaston."

"The best treasure on earth for me."

They kissed again.

She reached for her pocket.

"Here—a theater ticket to see me perform in Alès next week" Her sweet eyes blinked. "Tell Pierre that's your treasure—the ticket."

"Thanks."

She reached for another pocket. "And this is for you to keep," she said, handing him something softer to the touch, "all the time."

It was a snapshot of herself taken by her mom in the garden, not one of her autographed promotional photos. "Keep it in secrecy. I love you."

"I love you too."

Loud, urgent shouts from Pierre somewhere in the woods cut across the air, "*Where are you guys?! Gaston?! Juliette?!*"

The amorous couple remained quiet.

"*Gaston?! Juliette?!*"

The sound of approaching footsteps...cracking branches and twigs...also grew louder and closer.

Above hovered Richard's soul.

THÉÂTRE MUNICIPAL D'ALÈS

Occupying some of the best seats, Pablo, Pierre, and Gaston found themselves watching the play Juliette starred in: "Shattered Youth"–a powerful drama set in 1941 Nazi-occupied Nantes, based on the real story where forty-eight French communist suspects detained for unrelated reasons were indiscriminately held hostages, then executed, in reprisal for the gunning down of a German lieutenant-colonel by three Resistance activists.

Afterwards, comments from exiting people in the crowded hallways praised Juliette's portrayal of the daughter of one of the hostages as "absolutely riveting," "a tour de force," "chillingly poignant," and so on. Indeed, every act had ended with thunderous applause. Promoted on the printed program and through the news media outlets as Languedoc's most exciting teen star and one of France's best newcomers, she had once more lived to everybody's expectations.

Leaving Juliette with her mother, who would later drive her back home, Gaston and Pierre reunited with Pablo in the parking area, his old, open-roofed Citroën 2CV parked at his side.

"You guys ready?"

Pablo drove the two young boys back to the farm, joining them in their lively conversation inside. All three never stopped commenting on Juliette's great performance and the fact that they were lucky neighbors and close friends of hers.

Most affected was Gaston. Enchanted, proud, jumpy–it all showed on his expressive face, which also reflected some strong side effects. "She was really amazing–my girl, huh?" Bigger yet were his deep center effects, the wild beating of his heart and the rushing of hot blood through his veins. He was no Method actor, but all that and more seemed to want to explode inside out, just as Juliette had done on stage, as the old clunker rolled on Quai Jean Jaurès and turned right on Pont Vieux.

Like a high-class chauffeur, Pablo sat alone in the front, with distant stares to the rear view mirror and to some incoming cars looking more like sporadic fired missiles in the night. *His girl?* he mused, cynically. *My brother likes her too. Quite a lot.*

"Can you imagine?" he then said, in a rather somber voice, recalling moments from the play, "Hitler wanted 150 French hostages dead for this incident, not his usual 100 for every single killed Nazi."

"Too bad for him," snapped Pierre with a sneer. "He ended up with less than half his usual 100."

"He should've gotten zero–the son of a bitch!" uttered Pablo. "*He should've been the one to be shot dead to begin with–not the commander! The war would've ended sooner!*"

Moving on Faubourgh du Soleil, which became Avenue d'Anduze, he sped on toward Les Promelles.

◦◦

"Isn't that something?" said Pierre now with a touch of sadness. "Alès is losing its history. They're breaking every meaningful quarter it had from centuries past...downtown, by the temple, to give the city a face lift. Don't know if the temple itself will survive the demolition. Have you noticed the reshaping taking place?"

"I have," said Pablo, "but some of these old neighborhoods are so rundown...something must be done..." Of course, he was no fan of Protestant temples, having been raised as a staunch Roman Catholic.

"Juliette told me the other day about the noise, dust, and traffic mess she had to put up with crossing the area...to meet with her new producers," informed Gaston.

"New producers?" questioned Pierre.

"Yeah. Movie producers...early talks."

Pablo jumped in, "She's going to shoot a movie?"

Gaston revealed, "Her agent is negotiating a series of movies."

Pierre exploded, "That's fantastic! Imagine...a new Shirley Temple!"
"Different looks, though," said Pablo.
Soon they changed topics.

∽

At one point, Pierre, resting next to his cousin in the back seat, pulled something from his pocket. "Looks like we all got treasure tickets for the show," he cheered, showing his to Gaston.

"Not me. I had to pay for mine!" shot Pablo, spying on them in the rear view mirror.

Both Pierre and Gaston flashed big smiles in the dark, not without Pablo noticing it.

"You like blondes, don't you?" Pierre now teased his cousin with a barely audible whispery voice, poking his ribcage with his elbow to keep it kind of secret between the two of them.

"Just Juliette."

∽

Minutes later the Citroën gunned away on Route de Saint-Jean-du-Gard, past Anduze, deep into the Cévennes.

Above hovered Richard's soul.

LOVE AND JALOUSIE AT A TENDER AGE

Gaston stared at Juliette's snapshot amorously, under a mere candlelight.

He was lying down on his bed, holding the photo with one hand. A few tears rolled down his cheeks. He was remembering what Alfredo had told him about Juliette's rising fame and his ever diminishing reason and chances of being with her.

Lately, he'd noticed a certain coldness from Alfredo when bumping into him in the farm or sharing a little chat with Pierre and Pablo. He also seemed to appear too often, in his casual, charming ways whenever Juliette showed up with her bike. Of course, he was in his twenties, too old and inappropriate to court a thirteen-year-old girl like Juliette...but should he worry about this? Those thoughts vexed him. Love was a mystery, prone to enrich or break someone. Often he could see both Alfredo's and Pablo's eyes, in their individual manner, gazing at Juliette, or following her walk or movements, with a certain desire...a man's desire...more sexual than affectionate....

Gently, he slipped the photo under his pillow and blew off the flame.

Across the room Pierre was sound asleep in his bed.

Above hovered Richard's soul.

GASTON'S RING IS LINKED TO ANCIENT EGYPT, SAYS JULIETTE'S GRANDPA

The house Gaston had been invited to and was now stepping on hid under a huge boulder at one side of Route de Luc. Beyond a bend, it wound and disappeared from view deep into the vegetation sprawl, right after the Quintero's old farm where Gaston and Pierre lived.

Not seen from the road, an immense backyard–full of pathways that penetrated a private forest of juniper trees, wild flowers, and rocky slopes cloaked with thickets, sharp thorns, and hedgerows–filled a void that only Marcel Douvier, its owner, knew.

To the left near a creek cherry trees blossomed, to the right two Egyptian obelisks, forming part of a group of eroded limestone rocks, engaged the attention. Dry pieces of bark, twigs, and underbrush covered the soil. Further away behind the compound, perhaps a quarter of a kilometer, mountainous terrain studded with gigantic Mediterranean pines painted the landscape.

The mammoth boulder roof was held steady by potent lateral boulders as if purposely jutting from the floor. Essentially, the ensemble represented a natural engineering feat that prevented storms, hurricanes, mud slides, and external disasters (except maybe forest fires and earthquakes) from disturbing its inner living quarters. Those quarters embodied the exotic place where Juliette's grandpa lived.

Gaston jumped to the ground from the steeply rising boulder, after Juliette.

Soon they both made it inside through a tiny door laden with *garrigues*, their seductive mystic fragrance and nearly impassable texture conspiring to hide in perpetuity what Juliette unveiled with a simple touch of her hand.

❦

"Amazing...it's real and very old..." Juliette's grandpa was saying moments later, observing the peridot ring through a professional magnifying glass under a powerful light.

He stepped back a little, cleaned his spectacles with a handkerchief.

"It was owned by Bast," he said slowly, "the Lioness Goddess of Ancient Egypt."

"How do you know that?" asked Gaston, perplexed.

"It has the tiny, unmistakable coded mark of divinity...reserved for this goddess," he said, holding his breath, "Or the next-of-kin goddess."

"He knows *everything*–I told you!" exclaimed Juliette, pointing to the enormous bookshelf on one side of the living room filled with tons of books. "He holds a Doctorate of Philosophy in Anthropology and did post-doctoral work in Ancient Anthropology and Ancient Mysticism from–"

"Ancient Mythology," corrected Grandpa.

"–La Sorbonne."

"What's that?" asked Gaston.

"A short, popular name for the University of Paris," informed Juliette, pouting her way with related historical stuff she'd dug out from her grandpa's books recently. "Kind of cute, huh?" She giggled. "Named after its 13th century entry into the world of religion and higher learning." Her youthful eyes widened. "Collège de Sorbonne, founded by Robert de Sorbon."

"Okay, okay, my lovely Juliette," dismissed politely the distinguished old man, "but this is a most startling discovery."

"And he speaks Egyptian, Hebrew, Latin, Greek and Italian...in addition to–"

"–Enough, Juliette!" Monsieur Douvier cleaned his spectacles again and held the ring up in the air above his head with reverence. Then stared at the young boy paternally.

"This ring, my friend, is more powerful than an army of body guards. Wearing it will protect you from death for a thousand years."

Both Gaston and Juliette stood speechless, admiring the precious ring.

"I strongly suggest you don't tell anyone about it–just wear it."

He put it back on Gaston's finger.

"But...hardly anyone lives more than a hundred years, Grandpa."

"I'm not sure about that," said the very old man.

Above hovered Richard's soul.

SECOND ATTEMPT ON GASTON'S LIFE

A growing pain had begun to torture Gaston one sunny afternoon.

Within the hour he was crying and rolling on the ground with unbearable cramps in his stomach. High fever followed.

"My tummy hurts..."

His laments reached Don Valerio and Doña Elvira—the property's owners—who, in the absence of Doña Manola, immediately requested a local doctor to come to the farm.

"Ahhhh...ahhhh..." moaned Gaston.

∽

Bandages, syringes, small bottles of iodine, alcohol, and other first-aid supplies jerked to view from the physician's bag when he pulled it open on a side table.

Gently, but with words that sounded ominously dark, he questioned Gaston and Doña Elvira about what might have led to the problem or sickness.

Outside the room, Pablo and Alfredo tried to make sense of what had happened. Their neighbors gathered with them, expressing their concern and sorrow.

Gaston's temperature rose to about forty degrees Celsius.

Three school classmates, a teacher, and several farm workers who knew the boy well also appeared by the door, pacing back and forth. They all feared the worst.

Juliette was out of town, as usual performing on stage, unknowing, while Doña Manola kept herself invisible, leading her very private life elsewhere.

∽

"That explains everything," said the doctor moments later when Gaston revealed he'd eaten a forbidden fruit.

It turned out to be grapes, a bunch of them, sprayed with a strong, colorless, odorless pesticide.

Gaston had been wandering through clusters of vineyards in the farm, enticed by their luscious appearance and natural aroma. Something magnetic about their vines, the rich foliage they provided, and, for him, the freedom of just being there alone, undisturbed, with them.

Nobody, of course, had lectured him about the phylloxera and its crushing infestation on this land, in these very grapevines, only a few decades earlier. Nobody had cautioned him about why farmers took protecting their crops so seriously since the turn of the century. Chestnut groves, vineyards, even silkworms had been hit by devastating pests all along.

Recovering in bed the next day, Gaston could only flush with a queer mix of embarrassment, guilt, and joy when surrounded by his closest friends.

"...I guess I goofed...I should've known better..."

"You gave us a scare," said Juliette, now by his side.

Pierre kept staring down at his cousin's face in awe. "Your fever's gone now, they told me," he said with infantile eyes. "Maybe we can plan on a hiking trip tomorrow–what'd you say?"

"...funny guy–you..." half-laughed the sick boy.

"Never been to Grotte de la Cocalière, north of Saint Ambroix?" pushed further Pierre with excitement.

"One of these days we'll go together...but...thanks for caring and giving me company..."

Juliette winked one eye to Gaston, sort-of-privately. "Thank the *Lioness Goddess* too," she said.

"Gaston grimaced, "Who's *she?*" Then something clicked. "Oh... right."

"Never mind," said Juliette in her girlish way, flipping both her hands down dismissively. *Wasn't my grandpa's amazing revelation the other day in his house worth anything? How come you didn't jump at my saying it?* she pondered, staring at the ancient peridot ring he wore in one finger.

Gaston just kept staring at her, still numb by the medication.

Of course, you're sick today, unable to think straight, pondered further Juliette.

She can be so cute sometimes, even in silence, mused Gaston.

༄

In the outskirts of Alès, a car sped away, soon taking Pont Vieux to cross into Anduze. At the wheel, Virginie half-sang and hummed an old French song,

> **J'ai perdu le do de ma clarinette**
> **J'ai perdu le do de ma clarinette**
> **Ah! Si Papa il savait ça, tra la la**
> **Il me taperait sur les doigts, tra la la**

She parked and strode a clump of narrow, shaded alleys, filled with noisy kids, looking for an address she couldn't find.

Lost on Rue Cannau, she entered a winding cobblestone street, so narrow, spooky, and deceiving, it made her reconsider continuing on it at all. *Why in hell is it named Rue Droite (Straight Street), if it isn't!* she barked mentally.

Of course, she had no idea this particular word *"Droite"* wasn't even French. It was Cévenol...meaning "sloping"...

Frustration turned into anger.

Got to call Master Judge, too. If Gaston dies today, the local papers will have it tomorrow. I'll stay a couple of days in Anduze to make sure.

༄

At her first opportunity by a Protestant church, she dialed the number that she knew so well but feared the most. It was automatically analyzed, acted upon by the z-communications system of 31st -century Zundo, and rendered local.

In Zundo, Master Judge heard the musical notes of the French song "La Mer" come to life after a *"1955 France"* display on his ZCAP meter's lilac TT screen—an upgrade to the old, faint ringing and century and year magnification. "Hellooooo…" he drawled, making himself more interesting.

"*C'est mois, Virginie.*"

"*Bonjour.*"

"A doc-teur foi-leid my at-tempt…he's zill alive. Sor-ry."

Now he became flustered. More so because of the way she said it in her thick, guttural French accent.

"*Sorry?* How can you be if you didn't finish your job?!"

"I–"

"*Don't say anything!*" He coughed to clear his vocal cords of a sudden surge of phlegm. "I'll be expecting your next call very shortly. Make sure it's a triumphant call!"

The phone went dead.

"*Merde…merde…*" said Virginie. Above hovered Richard's soul.

PART 5

MIPHO REVISITS MONTMARTRE, FORMER FRANCE
ZUNDO, JUNE 3081

STRUTTING HER WAY THROUGH MEMORIES
OF BOHEMIAN PAINTERS

Thank the Lioness Goddess too? Mipho repeated in her head, wondering, a bit offended.

She repeated what Juliette had just said to a bedridden Gaston in a farmhouse in Saint-Jean-du-Gard, deep in the south of France. *What in hell is she thinking? Does she know about me?*

"The nerve!" she now voiced out, inadvertently. Then laughed to herself, realizing how harmless and insignificant the issue was.

"Is there a problem, *Mademoiselle...?*" said a man's voice.

Mipho veered her eyes to the gleaming white dome of Basilique du Sacré Coeur–the highest point in Paris–only a few blocks away from where she sat in Place du Tertre, sexily clad in green miniskirt and cross-legged to invite for a fleeting peek to her panties, surrounded by a bustling crowd of tourists and curious locals.

Strolling by with hot coffee cups in their hands, chatted the regular ones–artists, writers, intellectuals, occasional business VIPs, and possibly filmmakers–often revealing themselves and their current projects through bits of their enlightened conversations. Many artists remained hunched over their easels, either working or napping, among the chestnut trees in the crowded cobblestone square.

Mipho's long, blonde French braid fluttered gently in the mid-afternoon Saturday wind, blowing inland from the North Sea–a tiny distraction to the *fourth-millennium lost-generation-revival* painter who now sketched her face on a canvas under a bright colored sun umbrella.

Sandwiched between this and the next painter's setup stood a tiny wooden table with a drawer. It contained many of his painting tools and a half-empty pack of Gaulloises cigarettes.

"Please, do not hold your hair with your hand. Never mind the breeze," said the man's voice again.

"What part of my face are you working on now?"

"Your legs," teased the Bohemian painter, wearing a soft dark beret over messed-up silver white hair and Dali-like extravagant mustache.

෴

She had paid the painter three times the price he'd asked for, leaving his masterpiece on his table, to his utmost delightful surprise, and strutted her way off northeast, her swinging bag over one shoulder, to the remaining short stretch of Rue Norvins, where she turned south.

Following the Square Nadar curvature along the line of parked cars, she continued on Rue du Cardinal Dubois, headed for the two-hundred-five steps that would take her up to the elevated entrance of the famous Byzantine Basilique. Wisely, she wore her cushy soft leather Italian sneakers for the occasion, having left her suede high heel stiletto boots in her rented car near the Anvers metro station.

She reached a spot in her daring climb near the very top, already dotted with attention-seeking, mouth-kissing, jean-clad teenagers, spilling in every which way on the stair steps, where she simply turned around to enjoy the sweeping, breathtaking view of Paris. A ritual she did every other generation since the aftermath of the French Revolution. Except that this time one of the youths discreetly grabbed her ass, and for a change, she said nothing to him, letting it go, while continuing her sensuous walk into the church.

෴

More endless stair steps, bizarre narrow alleys, and vertigo-causing steep streets later, lined by arrays of ghostly lampposts twined with disheveled trees up and down the picturesque hill, she pushed her luck through waves of passing strangers of every race, creed, and culture, dressed in some of the most peculiar fashion styles she'd ever seen.

On a slippery sidewalk near Place Pigalle she had to fend off a bunch of aggressive Algerian hopefuls who tried to corner her against a wall. "You can't bang me—you fools!" she shouted, kicking three of them in the balls, and the next two in the shin—enough damage for the cops to take them away.

She visited Au Lapin Agile, cherishing old moments she'd had with Dante and Picasso up there long time ago, and stopped briefly at Montmartre Museum, a sweet place she and Utrillo had once shared candle lights with gusto on a winter's night many decades ago with bottles of cheap wine.

Along Rue des Abbesses she window-shopped for exotic jewelry, designer scarves, and fashion hats, trying scores of them on just for the fun of it. Stalls of colorful fabrics from the Orient likewise seemed to lure her attention away from the mingling crowd she also enjoyed.

She ate *crêpes* and apples. Never tired, she went on passing dozens of chic cafés, wine bars, and terraced restaurants, the last one graced with adorable lilac-hued little gardens...sparkling, it seemed, with the scent of humanity.

"*Merde!*" she suddenly uttered, checking the time. "*C'est tard. Je dois retourner a ma voiture!*"

And to the distant, cold grounds of metro station Anvers, she hastened.

PART 6

CLASH #2—MOUNTAIN CLIMBING (A TIME TRAVELED CLASH) FRANCE, EARLY JUNE 1955

THE ROOTS OF GREED

Bermuda Revelation Park, Zundo, June 3081

Fully equipped with climbing gloves, ropes, bolts, gears, anchors, and other tools, Richard and Master Judge were working their way up a very steep boulder the size of a four-story building.

"It's both competition and confession time!" shouted the powerful judge. "Watch your steps!"

His left foot dragged a few inches dangerously, but it quickly readjusted for balance.

Above, some twelve feet or so over the heads of the restless crowd, the Celestial Sphere already displayed the current Clash status:

JUST COMPLETED: CLASH #1— LOG FIGHTING • OVERALL SCORE: JUDGES 1 DEFENDANT 0 • NEXT: CLASH #2— MOUNTAIN CLIMBING

"So… basically…you started out your financial climb with 50 million already on the pot, right?" said Master Judge holding tight on his rope, remembering the defendant's previous *confess and fight* encounter, his first, on the floating log.

He'd advanced two body lengths ahead of Richard up the boulder, one shoulder hurting from that creepy, previous encounter over the black river. Wisely, he was now wearing a light climbing sack, with useful tools stuffed inside.

Richard moved faster now up the slippery rock wall, hanging by a set of cords.

"I was lucky," he said, then reconsidered. "Was I? My father dead by heart failure. My mother rendered blind by an unknown disease she caught at a county fair a year earlier—a disease that also killed her." He paused. "Both gone halfway through my elementary school."

His hands weakened but he managed to scramble a few inches.

"Sorry to hear that," said the judge.

Gasps erupted from the Stadiums. Feelings of sympathy seemed to go around the crowd. Some people remained strangely calm, others brought their hands up to their faces in various dramatic ways. At least three mutants were crying.

"So your uncle took care of you...from then on?" said Master Judge.

Seeing Richard almost catching up with him on the boulder, he threw a daring kick to his head, slightly scraping his skin.

"He did."

Richard, out of breath, moved up past the judge, with a show of dignity in his eyes. His badly injured left knee also from the previous Clash, seemed to drag behind uncooperatively, like the limp leg of a rag doll. But his voice sounded overly cocky when he continued to talk.

"...got rid of half-a-dozen financial advisers...seventy-two servants...eleven nurses...three vets..."

Pulling hard on one rope, he raised his right leg, feeling the heavy weight of his climbing sack on his back.

Master Judge showed surprise. "You did that?"

"Yeah..." said Richard. "Same day Uncle George asked me to sign all those papers—documents that would allow me to run my own life... my own affairs."

"Be your own boss."

"Exactly."

"At the tender age of *eleven*...I think you said before."

Richard felt the terrain rumble under his belly. He held on tight with his gloved hands without moving.

"Right."

"Good age to get started on your ambitions."

"Yeah."

Richard's eyes wandered to the judge's silly bald head. His cockiness returned when he spoke, "Hired a new team of business consultants...aids and the like...people attuned to the promises of tomorrow."

His fingernails inside his gloves were at work now against the boulder surface. It was a slippery moment that demanded a lot from him. He clenched his teeth as he continued talking, "...the procuring of real-gut's truths...the ultimate pursuit of riches..."

"Hummmm..." said the judge.

A fly kept buzzing around Master Judge's face. It stopped on his beard, chin area. He shook his head sideways in a frenzy, almost costing his balance.

This brought a smile to Richard's lips as he rested a moment.

Schools of French grunts and parrotfish paraded east of them by a protruding reef riddled with sea fans, gorgonians, and soft corals. They all graced this underwater part elastically controlled by the transparent zhoenix shield.

"Then it occurred to me that 50...50 million...was half the value of something. It sounded unfinished...halved..." Richard said. "So I devised a plan to bring this figure up to 100 million flat. I was amazed at the speed by which I conquered this caprice."

Master Judge regained new ground on the slick boulder surface.

"Doubling the loot, huh?"

Richard brushed some dust off his eyes and some dandruff off his right shoulder—always a nagging thing.

He clambered up a few inches, panted a little. "...the ease involved...." he said. "Once you have the tools and the skills–in my case, the millions and the power–you can accomplish anything you want."

Staring at the judge cynically, he burst into laughter.

"...say, be on top of the world..." he boasted, laughing even harder. "I think it took me roughly thirteen months to centennialize this figure...this early fortune. What a gas!"

Zundonians were not amused. They began to shout all kinds of ugly words, in both English and Undo-English, from the six Bisected Stadiums.

They also shouted collectively what they read on their individual ZCAP meters.

"DOWN THE FILTHY RICH! DOWN THE OCTILLIONAIRE!"

Hurriedly, while this went on, Master Judge reached the top of a salient on the crest of the boulder—the finish point—several feet higher than Richard's position.

He was a winner again.

Applause thundered around, mixed with outbursts of joy from the audience.

"LONG LIVE MASTER JUDGE! LONG LIVE THE CHAMPION!"

Clanking noises followed.

Above, the Celestial Sphere descended a few dozen feet onto the Astral Floor, around which the commotion raved. As it turned on its axis, the scrolling, red-flashing new trial status read:

JUST COMPLETED: CLASH #2—MOUNTAIN CLIMBING • OVERALL SCORE: JUDGES 2 DEFENDANT 0 • NEXT: CLASH #3—PLAYING GAY

The Sphere then ascended very quickly some two-hundred feet above the Stadiums, where it parked, slowly spinning like a top.

☙

Richard remained seated on the boulder for a while, head down. Things were not going well, he realized.

In this blurred confusion, his mind began to sail away...across time...

PART 7

A PALACE FULL OF RAGGED DOLLS AND HIGH SECRETS
ZUNDO, SUMMER-WINTER 3081

DR. UFAHH'S MOST UNLIKELY CONFIDANT

Summer 3081

Dr. Ufahh was alone with his gray cat in the ragged dolls room. A bunch of miniature objects spread on a small table beside them.

Holding a tiny round blue patch to the feline's eyes, he said, "See... Dancer? This wowzpin can make you time-conductive forever. Travel back and forth in time. Ain't it cool?"

The cat stared up at the blue patch, sitting quietly, one paw resting on a stuffed doll.

"It contains halfzun or doublezun. Can't tell. Unless you know its code number. Almost too small to see." He made a funny face. "You with me?"

Dancer just stared, immobile.

"Halfzun, like I told you yesterday, will cut in half whatever problems or suffering you have. Doublezun, on the other hand, will double them. That's really bad!"

He twisted his eyes slightly to get a reaction from his cat, but didn't succeed.

"Of course, you'll have halfzun, like I told you yesterday, when the time comes."

For a split second the cat's face became three faces when the scientist turned around to get another patch. Swiftly, each face's brain, independently, checked out the patches sitting on the side table, stealing information.

The scientist turned back to his cat, unaware, holding another tiny round thing in his fingertip.

"This yellow patch...endzpin... is meant to undo the halfzun or doublezun effect, if needed." He smiled. "In your case, Dancer, the halfzun effect. But it won't undo your time-conductive power.

Hey, that's great!" His eyes widened funnily. "Are you still with me, Dancer?"

The cat just glared at the talking lips.

"Maybe we can do it tomorrow—what'd you say?" Dr. Ufahh's expression changed abruptly. "Oooops..." he exclaimed. "Tomorrow's your birthday. I almost forgot!"

Now he cooled off a little, reflectively.

"We'll wait a few days...until you're ready. No problem." He rubbed his chin, staring at the cat. "I'll have to shave some hair off your forehead though. I'm sure you won't mind."

Dancer blinked.

∾

Some of the stuffed dolls lay on the floor the next time they met, messier than usual, but Dr. Ufahh didn't mind.

Picking one up and staring at her cute face for a brief moment, he crouched and squatted down next to his zaptop on the carpet.

His gray cat was facing him, a disheveled ragged doll under his paw.

"See, Dancer?...people like to complicate things," he told him casually. "There's really no past or future. Not even present!"

The cat stared at him with curious but quiet eyes.

"No linear or chronological passing of time," he added.

The cat remained quiet.

"No forward or backward, upward or downward, left or right lapsing of time—*only being somewhere and everywhere...always at the same time*—like mankind's visualization of God on earth—my own visualization, at least. You follow me, Dancer?"

The cat licked his whiskers.

"See?—we never left Ancient Egypt, Las Pampas, or Stalingrad. We're still there! And here in Zundo! You and me. Forever!"

Dancer blinked.

∾

"Your eyes look very curious today..." Dr. Ufahh said to his cat a few days later, reclined on a couch in the ragged dolls room. "You're asking me—*how did I ever become a scientist?*"

Dancer broke his gaze to lick his paw, sitting on the carpet next to a bunch of toys.

"I noticed, at a much younger age, that when I focused deeply on something...like a topic, a place, a person, an event...near or far, present or past, or not yet occurring or materialized...*fresh news on the media* about it or related to it popped out as if on cue...replaying, to similar degrees, my own thoughts or visions. You see, Dancer, with my mind... *engaged mind*, I should say...I was creating things to happen."

The cat brushed his whiskers with is paw, partially staring at Dr. Ufahh.

"I knew I had absolutely nailed this discovery when a very small event...with a person I had met a year before...made headlines in a local rural newspaper. The issue was so minor and so far away in another country, that there was no way—all odds against it—that a reporter, himself virtually unknown, would waste his time writing about it. You follow me, Dancer?"

The cat blinked.

"The thing is...I *had* remembered just a few days before...this old and far distant issue of absolute no importance to anyone but me...with a certain energy and passion...like stirring rich cream inside a coffee cup with a spoon." Dr. Ufahh paused, gazed at his cat's gray, fluffy hair, wishing he had this kind of hair himself.

Dancer stared back, with his head bent a little.

"And here's the big deal...one day I awoke fresh from a dream about Italo Calvino—one of my favorite writers from the 20th century—I don't know if it was really a dream or why he became a part of my thoughts that particular night...but..."

Dr. Ufahh coughed.

"...but...just like the things I told you I had discovered...about creating news with my own intense thoughts..." His eyes twitched oddly. "...I saw with my own eyes Mr. Calvino struggling with extremely volatile thoughts in the process of writing a novel...that...that...*C-R-A-C-K!!!*...he caused the earth to break and shake...and everything to crumble and fall apart...in Mexico City..." Dr. Ufahh stood up, emotionally transformed. "Dancer—*Italo Calvino caused the Mexican Earthquake of 1985 from Italy! And it killed him too!*"

The cat's eyes barely fluttered.

MASTER JUDGE'S BREAK-IN

Winter 3081

Late at night, while Dr. Ufahh entertained his cat in the "ragged dolls room" several doors down the hallway, Master Judge sneaked into his "hot research lab"—both unnamed for security reasons.

It was a bold move that could cost him his life if his boss ever found out.

He slipped through a set of zosmos-ray shower detectors, unhurt because of his preparation for the break-in, thus carrying in one of his pockets a zosmos-v neutralizing coin.

He pulled out his mini flashlight and illuminated a table full of scientific charts, graphics, maps, and old and torn notebooks, searching for a particular one. Finding it, he opened its rather ordinary beige cover, titled, in cursive English, "Confrontational Journeys."

He checked the table of contents and some words stuck to his mind, like *wowzpin technology*, *time manipulation*, and *Einstein's Special Theory of Relativity*. He then flipped through some pages, looking for specific research writing. Something in a paragraph grabbed his attention, particularly the underlined words in red ink: "The *time-conduction-causing blue wowzpin* patch allows a subject (animal, human being, mutant, etc.) to *pass through time*—not just today's time, but *ancient time* and *future time*...thousands of years before and after today."

He reflected a bit, went on reading, "*Time-conductive subjects* will be able to return to their starting point upon completion of their *punishment sentence*. Through *mental adaptation* and *assimilation* the *blue patch's substance* learns to understand a subject's goals and needs."

He paused and continued reading, picking up a different paragraph, "When placed on the *subject's forehead*, the *halfzun* or *doublezun* (*tailored substance* inside the *blue wowzpin* patch) will become absorbed by the *subject's brain*. During this trance, about two minutes, the subject must look straight into the *zobot's eyes without blinking*." Master Judge smiled for it read like fantasy, which he personally welcomed. "The *subject's head* will become progressively hot, reaching a *burning sensation*."

He continued to smile, enjoying his reading.

"Beyond that, the *blue wowzpin* patch, totally absorbed by the brain, will put a *mythical zpin* on the subject's journey to create either a *halved sentence*, if using *halfzun*, or a *doubled sentence*, if using *doublezun*. Both *duration* and *pain* will be either halved or doubled depending on the sentence. He stopped, repeating the word *doubled* several times in his head with a curious smirk added to his smiling lips. "Hummmm."

He swung the beam of his flashlight to a drawer, quickly finding a plastic box inside, labeled "Richard Flynn."

From it, he carefully extracted a blue wowzpin patch. "Wrong patch," he mumbled after reading its code.

Turning around, with the flashlight pointing to various scientific items of no importance to him on shelves and tables, he lit up a framed photo of Dr. Ufahh sitting on a counter. The famous scientist projected a friendly look.

"Hi pal," he saluted, theatrically. "Where the fuck do you keep the *blue doublezuns*?!" Noticing something, apparently, what he was looking for, he said, with a dismissive gesture, "Oh...never mind."

He extracted a blue patch from a small container, properly coded. It sat on a table studded with tiny silver, orange, and green bottles. "That's my baby," he mumbled happily, carrying it over to the "Richard Flynn" plastic box he'd seen before.

Now, with meticulous care, he switched the two blue patches, so the coded doublezun, not the coded halfzun, would stay inside.

He checked the time on the wall clock and hurried to the door. Just before exiting, he turned to Dr. Ufahh's framed photo, beaming it with his flashlight.

"Keep the secret, will you..." he then said, mockingly.

There were other secret things and special documents he wanted to spy on, but he knew Dr. Ufahh would be returning soon, and so he quickly disappeared into the night.

PART 8

SAINT-JEAN-DU-GARD
FRANCE, EARLY JUNE 1955

THIRD ATTEMPT ON GASTON'S LIFE

It'd been raining and thundering all day in Saint-Jean-du-Gard. Downtown itself looked pitiable.

Gaston left Musée des Vallées Cévenoles wearing a thick gray coat. He'd been researching in this 17th-century structure details about the "breeding of the silk-producing mulberry tree silkworm" for a homework assignment.

As he crossed the Grand Rue near La Mairie, a slick black Citroën sped up toward him with bad intentions.

To avoid being hit, Gaston jumped to his right, falling on a pond of water and mud near a brick wall. "What the fuck was *this* about?!" he shouted in anger.

Wrapped in mud, he tried to stand up, but someone pushed him deeper into it. "*Salopard!*" he yelled, getting out of the mud.

Crawling on his knees, he seized a foot, without looking up to check who it belonged to, and took a wild bite on the flesh he found. It was a freaky reaction from his part, something he'd done before when fighting bullies in school. And it always worked.

Screaming like a mad dog, his assailant let go of him and ran away under the rain. It must've hurt immensely for he vanished in the darkening sunset like a wailing ghost.

Gaston helped himself up and fled away in the opposite direction. Running on Rue du Maréchal de Thoiras, he continued on Avenue Abraham Mazel, always looking back in case he was being followed. He couldn't tell for the shadows of early night already engulfed the street, but he hurried to Route de Luc, out of breath, making it to the farm at last in a finish run he'd never forget.

❧

Sitting on a bench, Pablo played the clarinet.

Gaston wandered away from him to an area in the farm where wheat was being threshed by a huge machine that shook and rattled, near the barn. He needed space and time to think.

Neither Juliette nor Pierre had returned yet from school—the *collège* they shared in terms of buildings and resources, not classes and teachers. He was desperate to tell Juliette what had happened to him the night before, only two weeks after being bedridden sick with pesticide poisoning. Prone to bad luck? One could think so if his car accident half-a-year ago, where his parents died, could be added to the equation.

Gradually, his health was catching up. But he could've drowned in filthy mud only hours ago had he not been sharp and mean with his teeth.

He kept staring at the threshing vehicle, half-hypnotized by its rhythmical turning blades.

His mind slipped to a certain numbness...where big wheels and rattling noise came together...

"*Voilà!*" he seemed to hear in the vicinity.

ᢙᡃ

Gaston finally got to see Juliette the next day as she'd been unavailable riding a horse in the neighborhood's meadows and woods after school, two days in a row.

He wasted no time in telling her all about the incident, particularly how he'd been a brave boy by biting on the mysterious man's leg.

"Why would he attack you? You're only *nine* years old."

"I think I know why."

Gaston took out something small from his pocket. A piece of leather with a metallic emblem Juliette recognized right out.

"A swastika?"

"He dropped it on the ground during the fight."

"*Le salaud!*" she cursed, pouting. "One of these rotten Nazis still roaming around!" She took a deep breath. "Why you?"

Gaston sank into silence, then said, "It has to do with Spain, I'm sure...the war..."

"Sounds creepy."

"They want me dead...me...my family—what's left of it—my cat, anything that's not Fascist or Nazi or *Franquista*."

"You seem to know stuff that I don't know."

Indeed. And he began to tell her about it. Why he and his family were targeted. Why he lived in constant danger. Great danger.

"You should be very careful. Avoid being seen in public places... until things cool off."

"I'm not afraid."

"I know—but..."

"I hardly ever go to the city...downtown. I just went the other day because of this homework I'm supposed to turn in. I also had hoped to see you there...working on your homework. I wanted to see you. You're my friend. My best friend."

"Your *girlfriend*," she added, squarely, gazing at his bashful stare and nascent naughty smile. "That's sweet of you to say that...but...it's too dangerous. My god—you could be killed!"

She looked so beautiful saying it, her long blond hair framing her angelic face. On impulse, he kissed her on the mouth. Hot blood ran through his veins. His tongue found hers...and they locked into a long, passionate kiss.

⁊

Virginie dialed her contact number from the outskirts of town.

At the other end, in Zundo, the familiar voice of Master Judge answered, "Hello..."

Forgetful, he'd not set his usual "La Mer" or "The World We Knew" identifying songs on his ZCAP meter, so it took him a while to feel at ease regarding the caller. A tiny lilac screen revealed, among other details, it was coming from Café de la Paix, Alès, France, 1955.

"C'est moi, Virginie..."

His foreign spy in that zone, had something to report. She'd been secretly in contact with him for days now.

Unfortunately, she informed her hit man had failed to kill little Gaston outside Musée des Vallées Cévenoles in Saint-Jean-du-Gard. She'd try again another day.

"*What about the pesticide blast in the farm?!*" Master Judge shouted angrily.

"*Ze* almost *die*...but *eu docteur safe im*..."

"You failed me twice this time, Virginie!" shouted the powerful judge. "Dare not fail me again or I'll have one of my doctors inject cancer cells into your pancreas!"

She heard the disconnect sound of the line with fear.

Above hovered Richard's soul.

TORMENTED BY FALSE MEMORIES
AND NAUGHTY STORIES THAT MAY
ACTUALLY BE REAL

Doña Manola bumped into one of Gaston's elementary school teachers in the Pharmacie du Quartier during the weekend. They struck a casual conversation.

She'd been kind to visit Gaston at the farm, along with a few students, when he'd fallen terribly sick less than two weeks ago, a gesture Doña Manola was very appreciative of, particularly since she herself couldn't be there.

"How old did you say Gaston is?" asked the young, neatly dressed teacher, searching for a bottle of peroxide in one of the back shelves.

"Nine," said Doña Manola.

"Is he really?"

"Of course."

"Well, let me tell you—your nephew is mightily gifted—way superior to any student his age I've ever had."

"I hear you," said Doña Manola proudly, a brisk smile parting her lips.

"The way he thinks and talks...his choice of words when he speaks or writes."

Doña Manola nodded.

"His mature way of analyzing things," went on the teacher. "His knowledge of history and science."

"Yes, Madame Bertrand...he's very disciplined and curious about everything. I'm aware he's been collecting 19s...so far."

"If I could, I'd give him 20s—the highest by law, but never attainable, because nobody is perfect—and promote him to first or second year *collège* (middle School). That's where he belongs." Madame

Bertrand leaned closer to Doña Manola. "Were his parents...university educated?"

"Yes, they were. Both of them."

"I thought so."

"His father was a professor at the University of Toulouse." She paused to extract something from her handbag. "So was my late husband," she said proudly, showing her his photo, "at the University of Madrid–though, in Spain."

"I see....handsome man..."

"Loving too," she added.

"Well, I have to hurry, Mrs. Sandoval. I've got a lot of papers to mark tonight. A teacher's job is never done."

"Take care."

Doña Manola smiled, watching her go. It was a strange, deep, heart-felt smile that brought back pieces of the Spanish Civil War. His face in the photo, not the teacher's departing steps, mattered.

ಲ

Juliette was showing Gaston how to milk a goat the next day, which at first made him feel unease, then brought him big laughter, then appeasement.

"It's just messy," he told her. "Good thing the goat stays quiet, doesn't fight back."

"Hey, let's walk," exclaimed Juliette.

Soon they were strolling along a dirt road spotted with poop from cows and horses, away from the farm, moving toward the woods. Above, a spooky sky with darkening pudgy clouds smeared the view.

"You know, the other day I overhead your auntie talking to my mom...she said to my mom that we have something in common... *intelligence...*"

"Oh, that's nice to hear, since my auntie doesn't usually say much about me."

"She told my mom that *we're way superior* and *years more mature* than other kids our age–the way we think and talk...blah blah blah..."

"*Super honor* students?" He squinted, adding a haughty smile to his lips.

"At least," she said vainly, smiling bigger.

"Let's see..." he indulged, searching for examples. "Your talent as a *phenomenal* actress..."

"Oh–stop that." She laughed.

"I'm surprised and flattered to hear those things from Auntie Doña Manola. Maybe I should start liking her more." Gaston remained thoughtful, walking along slowly.

They wore simple blue denims and T-shirts, walked on dirty sneakers.

She pointed to a noisy woodpecker working on the middle part of a tall spruce. "Tell me more about those strange dreams that seem to invade your nights," she then said sprightly.

A pile of dark manure appeared on the road, forcing them to deflect their march.

"Oh...they only come now and then," said Gaston. "But they come strong." He laughed abruptly, avoiding another pile of manure. "I mean my dreams."

Juliette laughed too, then stared ahead at a group of grazing cows.

"You know, I'm also having reveries...daydreams...visions–I don't know what to call them–*memories of things that I know never existed* ..." revealed Gaston. "*False memories.*"

"That's fascinating."

"I thought you were going to say 'creepy'..."

"Both."

They were at close range to the cows. She cheerfully patted one of them on the back.

Juliette turned to Gaston. "How do you know these things never existed?"

Gaston reflected. "They all happened *before* I was eight...way before."

Juliette thrust out her lips innocently. "Are you trying to tell me you didn't exist *before* you were eight?"

Gaston patted the same cow. "No. Not really..."

"Ok," said Juliette, "You had a car crash suffered amnesia for a while, but things went back to normal. You started remembering things...your childhood...your friends..."

"Not the way they're coming back to me. I wasn't like that at all. I couldn't have been like that."

"Like what?"

Gaston pressed his mind. "For example, I see myself very young in these memories...like five or six...climbing a winding, steep, narrow road full of cobblestones...alone...in the outskirts of a big city...holding a toy gun that shoots arrows...."

Juliette laughed a bit.

"Then," continued Gaston, "a well-dressed businessman walks fast towards me, and just before he passes me, I shoot one arrow on his forehead, which gets stuck there...right above his eyes. Next thing I know, he's running after me, chasing me like a mad man..."

Now Juliette laughed out loud, finding it very amusing.

Gaston went on, "I get so scared, I begin to scream, repeatedly, 'MOM, MOM, THIS MAN'S GOING TO HIT ME!' And my running takes me to my school...where I find a place to hide...and the man, frustrated, finally leaves and walks away."

"Ok, so you *misbehaved*." She made a pout with her lips.

"I was bad."

She gave a corny smile.

"I used to play with dead cats...according to these strange memories..."

"Tell me about it."

Gaston bent down to pick up a tiny broken branch from a nearby birch.

"I used to go to a dirty little river, skipping school...where, for some reason, several dead cats lay there on one bank, amid stinking trash and old shoes. They had drowned, were fat and heavy...filled with water...miserable looking. And I, for some reason, found pleasure playing with them. I would pick one by one by the tail and swing them back and forth like a pendulum...slowly first, then faster...until

I would let go...aiming for the other side of the river. With luck some would make it, others would break apart in the air...and spill their guts into the river."

"That was awful, disgusting."

"One day my dad found me there...caught me red handed...by the river bank. He pulled me out by one ear...and gave me a huge spanking."

"I don't blame him, such a revolting scene."

"I told you...but in reality I don't believe this ever happened. It's like *something* or *someone* is forcing this ugly thing...this pack of filthy memories...on me..."

Juliette studied Gaston's truly hurting eyes with a certain calmness. She made a sad face and pushed out her lower lip.

"Don't worry. We all do crazy things sometimes."

Gaston shouted, "*But I didn't do those things! I swear!*"

Pierre and Gaston ventured into the woods one sunny morning. Soon they reached a stunning waterfall in the vicinity of Mialet, deep in the Bois de Malabouisse. This unspoiled, breathtaking terrain stood in the way of a rocky passage they needed to traverse.

Gaston freaked out when Pierre suggested they cross to the other side, stepping on a row of rocks, just where the water plunged some thirty feet into a small lake.

"I'm not going there!" he complained, staring at the tumbling rapids of the Gardon de Mialet river.

"Why not? It's kind of easy, really...big rocks, big protection."

"Don't you remember what happened to me in Toulouse a few years ago when we tried the waterfall shortcut to the public pool? The one that led to the large and popular recreational center...also used as a stage for the Tour de France?"

"No. What shortcut?"

"The one that wound through the forest...that ran over the half-dried, slimy, slippery waterfall up there?"

"I don't remember any waterfall in Toulouse."

"C'mon, cousin—try harder to remember."

"No, I don't remember."

"Remember, I slid down the edge? Face down first...mouth open...brushing my front teeth against the hard and slippery cement? Dragging my face all the way down to the bottom of the waterfall... scraping the slimy muck on the cement...my mouth full of blood? I was hurting a lot and crying...remember?"

"You must've dreamed it. I don't remember such a thing." A bit annoyed, Pierre stared at his cousin's mouth. "So your teeth must've cracked or something with the impact...and dragging...and everything, right?"

"Of course—look at my teeth," Gaston said confidently, parting his lips and showing them.

"Not a trace!"

"What? They're *damaged*—you know that!"

"They're as healthy as mine," said Pierre. "Take a look in the mirror."

He did. And Pierre was right.

"*Merde*!" cursed Gaston, apologetically. "I just had another encounter with false memories! It really sucks!" Remaining foolishly pensive, he added, "False memories—both ways—past and present!"

He'd been observing for the past few minutes, he realized, standing in the farm's old barn, Alfredo's crafted painting of a waterfall... in a strange way similar to the one seen in his mind. Obviously, he'd been tripping again, but this time with Pierre in it and his denial of it.

Weird, he mused.

Pierre wasn't even there with him in the old barn.

༄

Later on during the week Gaston got together with Pierre for real in their room. They engaged in small chat that led to larger conversation—the kind that made young boys, like themselves, all excited about. Girls stories.

"Do you remember that windmill we used to hang around with the gang? The underground maze of catwalks, so dangerous...bordering the grains being swallowed like quicksand...we stepped on..to reach our corner dungeon-like lair? You know...where this twelve-year-old little whore met with us...to have sex...one after another...standing in line? I was the youngest...four or five...but the bravest...and third in rank in our gang, you second, and...because all the boys were shit scared to be first in line...they put me first, which, of course, I accepted...but when the girl asked me to stick it, I couldn't get it hard... couldn't get it up...and she just laughed...and when the rest of the gang, yourself second in line, were done with...the three of us—the top leaders—invited her to the river bank outside the windmill...to continue fondling her, herself tied to a tree trunk, at her request, the three of us doing all kinds of dirty thinks to her naked body for a very long time? Remember, cousin?"

"I have no idea what the hell you're talking about...but it certainly sounds great."

"Remember the three of us...afterwards...licking and nibbling her naked body...like wolves...and she moaning like crazy...wanting more and more?"

"Again, no. But it's a real turn on to hear all that. Just make sure Juliette doesn't ever hear about it."

Gaston remained pensive like an idiot.

"She won't."

Above hovered Richard's soul.

PART 9

CLASH # 4—MONSTER TRUCK RACING
(A TIME TRAVELED CLASH)
FRANCE, MID JUNE 1955

BIG WHEELS AND SMALL POETRY

Bermuda Revelation Park, Zundo, June 3081
8:00 a.m.

People stood in line facing the six Bisected Stadiums, trying to rush in and take a seat.

"Day 3" of the most talked about trial of the millennium was just about to start.

Like everyone in the world, they couldn't wait to watch all the peculiar, capricious, and sickening things happening in the Zoliseum... the unfolding drama of high arrogance, greed, and pride perpetuated by the quickly vanishing power mongers of the past.

Behind closed doors, defendant Richard mentally prepared for his next punishment event–Clash #4 (Monster Truck Racing)–against consistent rival Master Judge.

The restless audience waited.

∽

"*Voilà!*"

The excited judge jumped into one of the trucks, gaining seat at the steering wheel. He invited Richard to do the same with the other truck.

Both trucks were enormous modified pickup big-wheelers with jacuzzi-size tires, popularly called monster trucks. They were parked side by side, taking center stage in a large field, separated by three regular trucks. Their engines were blasting and ready to go.

Both drivers had changed into country blue jeans, stripe cotton shirts, and leather boots before meeting in the field with a vigorous hand shake.

While waiting for the "go" signal, they turned on their monster zell phones and started a little chat, shouting over the engine idling noise.

"Two wins for me, one for you so far–agreed?!" shouted Master Judge proudly.

"Agreed!" shouted back Richard.

"Are you all set, Rich?!"

"I am!"

He extracted a handkerchief from one of his pockets and began to fidget with it, trying to calm some of his nerves down.

Above, some fifty feet over their heads, the Celestial Sphere spiraled downward. It stopped a few feet from the cheering crowd, displaying the trial current status:

JUST COMPLETED: CLASH #3— PLAYING GAY • OVERALL SCORE: JUDGES 2 DEFENDANT 1 • NEXT: CLASH #4— MONSTER TRUCK RACING

The Sphere spiraled up and away again to its base in the sky.

∽

Ready but pensive, Richard shouted, so he could be heard over the engine idling noise, "I was thinking...that...back then!"

"Back when?!" shouted the judge.

Playing with his mustache, the defendant shouted, "When I was rich and powerful!"

"Of course–back then!"

Master Judge brought the engine idling noise down and urged Richard to do the same, so they didn't have to shout when talking.

"I felt like a little poet...back then."

"Why not."

Richard's hands were still busy fussing with his handkerchief.

"Wanna hear one of my poems, judge?"

"Why not."

"Here it is–I call it 'Virgin of a One Kind'" Richard's face turned deeply inspired.

I don't mind opening two'shes
But when it comes to one'sh
I'd rather keep it'sh behind bushes

"Hummmm...just one poem?" said Master Judge, unimpressed.

A uniformed man holding a gun high in the air approached the two big trucks.

Both drivers revved their engines up with several deafening hums hums.

The man fired the gun.

Suddenly the two monster trucks took off at full speed, rolling over and smashing a series of parked cars in the raceway.

It was a short, fast race, which Master Judge won. Expectedly so, since his truck engine had more power and success history.

⁊

They both got out of their trucks. Walking side by side, they headed toward the exit area.

People in the surrounding Stadiums cheered and applauded fervidly in support of their great judge and leader, who could also be so sports-minded and cool.

Above, the Celestial Sphere began to move down again toward the cheering crowd, displaying the trial's latest status:

JUST COMPLETED: CLASH #4—MONSTER TRUCK RACING • OVERALL SCORE: JUDGES 3 DEFENDANT 1 • NEXT: CLASH #5—MUD WRESTLING

⁊

Richard had lost touch with the audience, didn't give a hoot what they were celebrating right now. It wasn't about his glory for sure.

Excitedly, he stopped on his walk and said to Master Judge, "I have this other one...MJ"

"Other what?"

"Poem."

"Oh, yeah..." came the delayed reply.

Passionately, Richard added, "It's tiny to suit me only, tiny to fit on a stamp."

He clapped his hands in applause, made bubbling noises with his mouth, and stuck out his tongue.

The judge pushed the exit door open for both of them. "What was that all about? You never give up, do you?" He closed the door behind him, stepped into the lobby after the defendant. He couldn't help noticing shiny flakes of something on Richard's shoulders. "Could that be hazardous to your health?" he casually asked the defendant.

"What?"

"Dandruff."

Richard twisted his neck as he turned his head to verify, saw the flakes.

"Yak! That fucking truck really shook the shit out of my head!"

"Looks like..."

A flurry of spadefish and tiger groupers crossed the area. Behind them bloomed a forest of black corals.

Richard brushed the flakes off his shoulders with one hand, then the other. Then, he said, "Where was I?"

"Something about a tiny poem..." reminded the judge.

"Right." Richard recollected his thoughts. "I almost bribed the Postmaster to have it printed on a special stamp commemorating 'avant-garde' literature."

"You don't say..."

Here it goes–I call it 'Rage'..." Richard said dryly.

Pits and pieces
Bits and bieces
Puck you poth!

A rude display of thumbs down and loud boos from the audience erupted everywhere.

"YOUR POETRY STINKS!" they yelled out.

Pop corn containers and chocolate bars, among other pieces of junk food, hurled up in the air, many reaching Richard's feet.

"JUST GO TO HELL NOW!"

PART 10

SAINT-JEAN-DU-GARD
FRANCE, MID JUNE 1955

A VERY OLD, DEAF-MUTE,
NUTS-ABOUT-BLUE-THINGS LADY

Someone quietly slipped a handwritten note in front of his eyes with shaky, furrowed fingers as Gaston sat in the courtyard sketching an elephant. Next to it, at the foot of an imagined hill, he'd sketched zebras grazing the brushland.

"Follow me. There's more blue to be found," read the note.

Laying down his charcoal pencil on the little table next to his canvas support legs, Gaston followed the old, deaf-mute woman.

She wore fluffy white hair over frail shoulders, clad, all the way to her toes, in a long floating garment made of pale-orange cotton. In mysterious shyness, often debatable, she walked rather fast, with a sharp sense of direction and alertness.

She had bright, intense black eyes that moved about briskly for any foolish reason, often assisted with the sudden turning of her head, to reveal the cutest smile one ever saw on so aged and sinister a person.

Her chimp-like fingers pointed the way.

Gaston trailed her every move, confident to reach a blue treasure at the end.

∽

Past the farm's early backwoods that led to a familiar tortuous creek if trespassing into Monsieur Douvier's property, which they did, a cluster of cherry trees and assorted pathways greeted them. Past these offerings, flourished a private forest of juniper trees already in the range of dense underbrush and wild flowers.

Further back, glimmered dark green vegetation and a bizarre formation of limestone rocks eroded into two small Egyptian obelisks. Around them dry strips of bark, clumps of weed, and a heap of damp grass teased the soil. Beyond, as far as the eye could see, only tall Mediterranean pines, climbing a hilly landscape, dressed the view, rich with evanescent mist and fog.

She went farther and longer than usual, searching for her precious treasure, Gaston politely walking behind her. Cicadas seemed to have a concert all around, with their unmistakable humming sound.

Somewhere, on a rocky outcrop rich with tufts of lavender, near a pine tree, she bent down ungracefully. Gaston saw her picking up something, which she immediately showed to him, making voiceless gestures. Suddenly she was dancing over a thicket of twigs, creating crackling sounds with the sole of her feet.

Indeed, she held in her gnarled hand a beautiful flower with tiny sky blue ruffled leaves. All excited, she wrote down on her little notebook, "Alpine Forget-Me-Not."

To which Gaston replied in kind, "Fantastic!" well prepared with his own little notebook and pencil.

༄

He remembered how efficient she'd been in other outings with him, always ending the excursion with a blue treasure—a flower, fruit, insect, stone, rock, or button (somehow it'd fallen from her own dress a previous day and resuscitated in a most precious way). Last time they'd shared the woods, she'd found a bundle of "Blue Fescue"—a rare type of blue grass. She wrote it down in a jiffy, all excited, and likewise turned herself into a jumping fool.

But she was no fool, Gaston would one day discover.

They always ended up sitting on a craggy rock facing the two obelisks, cheerfully gesturing and staring at the blue treasure.

If she could only talk, Gaston often pondered.

Above hovered Richard's soul.

EXCHANGING SECRETS WITH GASTON IS MORE THAN A WISH, BELIEVES GRANDPA

"Thanks for coming over..." greeted Monsieur Douvier.

"Hi Grandpa. Thanks for inviting us."

Gaston nodded and stepped in behind Juliette.

The old man offered them unsalted wheat crackers the moment they lounged comfortably on the master couch. He seemed all pumped up with energy. "I was so intrigued watching you the other day...sitting on that rock."

Gaston reacted oddly, "When? Where?"

He smiled broadly. "A couple of days ago, beyond the creek..."

"Oh...you mean me and..."

"Yes. Madame Rossi."

Juliette stared at both with curiosity.

"That's the place we always wind up every time she takes me out to the backwoods...to look for her thing." He smiled a bit saying that.

"What *thing*?" said the old man. He sat down on a cozy wooden chair near the fireplace, never keeping his eyes off him.

"...a blue thing..."

"Keep going, please."

"You know, she's obsessed with blue-colored things."

"I can see that."

Juliette intervened, "Grandpa, don't tell me you didn't know that. Everybody knows she's a blue-freak!"

"Sweetie, let Gaston continue, there's more to it."

Gaston exchanged glances with both of them, then said, "Well, she seems to be a very lonely old lady, cannot talk or hear, and for some reason likes to share her prize hunt with me. It's always a blue thing...like a blue flower or blue stone."

"Isn't that something?" said Juliette. "She's so cute and peaceful."

"She can see very clearly...and walks kind of fast for her age," said Gaston, admiringly, "...and she always finds something blue...at least the six or seven times we went out hunting together."

"And then she invites you to sit together on that rock? Always?"

"Yeah...to rest..."

"Interesting."

Gaston seemed a bit confused. He asked, "How come you saw us, Monsieur Douvier?"

"Oh...I just happened to be wandering by...and noticed you..." he said casually, hunching both shoulders.

Their chat drifted to other things. Soon they were laughing and munching on crackers and drinking apple juice.

"Why did you invite us, Grandpa? Something important?"

"Yes, yes...something..."

Both Juliette and Gaston fixed their attention on him. His small gray eyes moved erratically behind his spectacles with a certain fascination.

"I'd like to do something unusual with you Gaston. Something maybe historical."

"Sounds big and scary," Gaston said, sending a quick consulting glance to Juliette.

"What is it, Grandpa?"

"Let's exchange secrets."

"That's crazy," exclaimed Gaston.

"You tell me yours and I'll tell you mine."

Gaston lifted his torso up a little on the couch, both intrigued and worried.

"How do you know I have one?"

"Yes, Grandpa," shot Juliette. "How do you know?"

"The ring...remember?"

Gaston nodded.

"Last time you were here, I didn't tell you the whole story. Your ring isn't just *any* ancient ring. It's a mighty important ring...with a phenomenal history," said the old man, staring straight into Gaston's eyes. "I've done some research lately." His eyes jumped a little in their sockets. "Where did you get it from?"

"...I really don't know..."

"Don't be afraid to tell me, we're like family. No one outside this home's going to know, ever."

"I don't know how I got it. It's always been there in my finger."

"Grandpa–he lost his parents in a car accident last year. He doesn't remember much of his parents, his childhood, school."

"I'm sorry. I didn't know that."

"I should've told you, Grandpa."

"That's really tragic...and very sad."

"He's also having recurring dreams about...weird things...he told me." She turned to Gaston. "Right?"

He nodded.

"Like what?"

Gaston pulled a handkerchief out of his pocket, letting his fingers fondle with it, a habit that surged when feeling a bit nervous, like now. He took a deep breath and said, "Like...being much older...fighting another person in a huge, round place...a sort of stadium...surrounded by a huge, noisy crowd..."

"Hummmm. What else? Other dreams?"

He offered him more crackers.

"Yeah...being very, very, very rich...the same person I described before...fighting against this spooky-looking man wearing a black cape, black gloves..."

Monsieur Douvier looked totally engaged with his small, shiny gray eyes.

"*Wait!* The ring also came up in one of my dreams. Uncle George gave it to me. He said, 'Wear it, it'll give you good luck and protect you from the evils of night and sudden death.'" Gaston felt very embarrassed saying those things. "That was just a dream," he added, apologetically.

"A great secret, too." Monsieur Douvier said in a charming tone, watching the smile forming on Gaston's lips. "That explains certain things."

"Like what, Grandpa?"

"Sweetie, Gaston's ring goes back to Ancient Egypt...4000 BC."

"Are you serious, Grandpa?"

"Almost 6000 years ago...if you add our place in time..." said the charismatic old man.

"Wow, wow..." breathed out Gaston.

"Like I said last time you guys visited me, this ring used to belong to Bast, the Lioness Goddess, or her next of kin, like brother or sister."

"Are we getting into...Egyptian Mythology?" said Juliette. "Bast... daughter of Ra?"

"I'm afraid...yes."

"Awesome," said Gaston.

"It's a *peridot* ring...shiny green with hues of yellow...set in gold... meant to protect its wearer from sickness and death," explained the old archeologist.

"Amazing," declared Gaston.

Juliette's face was aglow with joy, so was Gaston's, but—

"How come? *Why me*? I mean...how can it be?"

"I'm not sure," said Monsieur Douvier, "but the most amazing thing is that our secrets are connected."

"*What?*" exclaimed both youths simultaneously.

"That would be very weird...if true..." remarked Gaston.

"Indeed," said his girlfriend.

They all sank into a relaxed pause, then Juliette, staring at her grandpa, reminded, "You never told us your secret, Grandpa."

Monsieur Douvier stood up, talked with his arms stretched out in bizarre but charming ways, "It's a long story. You'll have to come another day."

"Grandpa...are we going to leave now...without knowing about it?"

"Yeah...it's important that we know something...a speck..." added Gaston.

"I understand your concerns, but right now I have to get ready for a radio interview." Showing them the door, he added, "I promise you'll be totally pleased next time we meet." A cool breeze bathed their faces when he opened the door. "Tell you what, I'll be lecturing a group of archeologists in Montpellier Friday afternoon. There's a real cozy restaurant by the beach called Le Bateau Perdu. I'll be expecting you there at 7 p.m. Don't be late."

"Which beach?"

"Palavas."

They exited.

Route de Luc seemed deserted at this time of night. At least this stretch to the nearby Quintero's farm

"How are we going to get there? Palavas?" Gaston asked Juliette, hurrying his steps toward the farm next to her on the shoulder of the road.

"Pablo's car..."

"The beat-up Citroën?"

"Nothing better! I'll talk to Pablo."

"Look what I found!" exclaimed now Gaston, picking up a tennis ball from the ground as they went in past the gate.

"It's mine," cheered Juliette.

"Must be...'cause I don't play tennis. Neither does anyone in this farm. But you do."

She started bouncing it against the pavement

"Hey—move backward...more...more. 'll show you how to hit the ball. Just return it back to me the same way I hit it."

"With no racquets?"

"Pretend your hand is a racquet."

Gaston moved back a few steps.

"This is a forehand, okay?" She swung her right arm and hit the ball with a certain style.

Gaston saw it coming and missed.

She laughed.

"Your turn. Move back...more...more..."

He hit the ball once, toward her, after several misses.

Now she saw it coming and swung her arm gracefully.

∽

In his bed, late at night, he felt like a voyeur inside his mind... watching Juliette swing her arm and hit the ball gracefully...gracefully...gracefully...

Then his vision blurred and someone else—wearing a pointed beard, black cape and gloves—appeared...bouncing a ball against a cement floor. The ball seemed bigger and heavier than a regular tennis ball and the bearded person stood on a balcony.

Above hovered Richard's soul.

PART 11

FIRST BEHIND-CLOSED-DOORS MEETING BETWEEN DR. UFAHH AND MASTER JUDGE ZUNDO, JUNE 3081

THE MATURITY PUMPING FACTOR

Dr. Ufahh climbed to the Den where Master Judge worked alone in the wee hours of the night. It was an unexpected visit.

"How's Richard's 13th reincarnation going in France?" he asked the charismatic judge, who immediately felt intimidated but made the best of not showing it.

"Oh–fine. Gaston's right on target."

"Explain, please..."

"So far I've made him super intelligent...with a seventeen-year-old mind...at age nine, capable of having very mature discussions without losing his youthful traits." Master Judge clicked two links on a screen, closed a window, one finger pointing at special data. "I also matured his sexual abilities."

"A boy genius? A whiz kid?" said Dr. Ufahh, uncomfortably.

"Combined with early puberty," said Master Judge.

"Why make him so intelligent...and curious about sex?"

"To compress his life, move him faster to his next level of punishment–his next ordeal..."

"Hummmm....we'll have to talk about this some more...another time."

"No problem."

"Don't forget it's Richard's punishment, not Gaston's."

"Oh yes, I'm fully aware of that."

"Keep me up to date on what you're doing."

"I will."

PART 12

SANTA MONICA, CALIFORNIA
USA, WINTER 2958

UNCLE GEORGE TAKES MIPHO TO DINNER AND LEAVES WITH AN ANCIENT RING THAT SINGS HIP HOP MUSIC

Italian Restaurant

After a great cozy dinner that included minestrone soup, panzarotti (stuffed with mushrooms, tomato, spinach, mozzarella, and salted anchovies), fettuccine (flat thick noodles), and an almond pastry called Ciarduna Siciliana, they toasted with champagne, sealing thus a close friendships between the two.

"You put your life at risk for me," said Serene Lady (Mipho's name choice tonight), deeply grateful, her young, light-blue eyes (tonight) shooting little stars in his much older, brown eyes. "You almost got killed by this thug."

"Oh, this was nothing..."

His simple, unassuming dark corduroy jacket contrasted vividly with her trendy red dress, dangerously open to show perhaps too much of her voluptuous breasts.

Serene Lady sensuously caressed her short, *touché-au-soir* fashioned black hair and stared at Richard's uncle with a recharged expression. "Well, you're not exactly the type of person who'd say he has nothing to lose. You're *extremely* rich."

Uncle George replied, "Not me. My nephew." He laughed. "I'm just a modestly priced novelist, remember?" He scratched his chin. "I just manage Richard's wealth on the side...until he's old enough to take over his bank's accounts."

"You're funny—on the side?"

He smiled meekly.

"Anyway, I have a gift for you...as a token of my appreciation."

"I'm flattered."

"You've spent two weeks in a hospital, seriously injured. I can't imagine anyone doing so much for me...without even knowing me."

She placed the gift on the table for him to see.

"Oh, it's a ring...green-yellowish."

"Set in gold."

He picked it up, examined its shiny surface with excitement. "It's beautiful...soft...oily..."

"...transparent..." added Serene Lady.

"Yet it has this golden glow that never quits."

"Even in the dark," stressed the attractive lady.

Uncle George raised his eyes. "Must be very expensive, huh?" he said.

"Priceless."

"Where did you get it?" asked the seasoned man.

"It's a secret."

"I love secrets."

"Just wear it..." invited the beautiful young woman with the chic, short hairdo. "I'll bring you good luck...and more. As long as you wear it."

Uncle George slipped it on a finger of his left hand, looked a bit surprised.

"It fits me perfectly. Must have a fascinating history."

"It does," said Serene Lady, pouting her full, elastic red lips. "The ancient Pharaohs had their most precious gems mined from a small triangular island in the Red Sea...as far back in time as 3500 BC."

"Some enchanted island..."

"It went by different names through the ages...Serpent Isle, Emerald Island, Island of Topazos, Chitis, Ophiodes, Saint John's Island, Zabargad...you name it. Many legends, many interpretations."

"Serpent Isle?" Her gorgeous mysterious blue eyes had him doubly enchanted. He'd give anything to kiss her luscious lips right now.

"Yeah....It was infested with poisonous snakes in ancient times... really aggressive and vicious..." She talked as if she'd been there, knowing, expressive. "Until Ptolemy II Philadelphus, around 270 BC, had them destroyed by his soldiers...so miners in the island could work without fear."

Staring at the precious gem, Richard's uncle said, "So...is topaz the ring in my finger?"

Serene Lady sipped from her glass, flirtingly.

"No. They thought it was topaz—the whole world thought it was topaz—since it had plenty of yellow in it...and all yellow or yellow-like stones were considered to be topazes at that time...and for the next 4000 years."

"So what is it?" Again her eyes, her lips, took a toll of his imagination.

"Peridot," she said. "Named so by the French, only recently—around the 18th century."

"We're in the closing years of the 30th century, honey...so not so recently I would say...unless twelve centuries mean little to you..."

Serene Lady smiled.

"...little..."

Uncle George drank some champagne, relishing on her cute sense of humor.

"Truly fascinating story..."

"Except that this gem," she said, touching it with one finger, "is not exactly terrestrial...and I'm not exactly who I appear to be..."

"Oh...should I live forever in suspense?"

"If you wish."

A hip hop dancer sexily breaking, popping, and freezing her nude body in many creative ways appeared on an emerging stage near their table, stealing their full attention. "Meet you in the ghetto..." she rapped, rhythmically to the beat of music. "Meet you in the ghetto..."

PART 13

CLASH #8—RAPPING IN THE RAIN
(A TIME TRAVELED CLASH)
FRANCE, MID JUNE 1955

RICHARD GETS LOST IN THE BEATS OF HIP HOP AND RAP MUSIC

Bermuda Revelation Park, Zundo, June 3081

Master Judge's black gloved fingers were busy on the control panel setting up the rapping Clash. "Meet you in the ghetto..." he hum-sang to himself from his elevated Royal Den, his fingers typing important code words on a keyboard.

He ended the procedure staring, some thirty feet down, at the evolving product of his imagination materializing before the surrounding audience. Then he removed his gloves and gothic cape with a peculiar wickedness in his eyes, like a hot female strip tease dancer about to perform her magic act, his vainly salacious eyes still watching the reflection of his body adoringly in the tall mirror standing by one side of his control panel. Only that there was no *femme fatale* in it, just the crude, insolent, if not perverse, presence of an inner-city undefined rapper.

Wantonly, he caressed his bald head with one hand, waiting for mechanized special effects to take the crowd, whom he had so far distracted, to a higher level of euphoria.

This happened with the abrupt arrival of night and the rising of a new platform, replacing the old one, as the spreading mantel of darkness dissipated its tentacles across the Zoliseum. From virtually nowhere, a gang neighborhood, with all its spunky dynamics, mischievous adrenalin, and gory details jolted into view. The ghetto!

Someone turned the music on. Master Judge smiled copiously.

The Celestial Sphere began to descend from its crowning height above the six Stadiums to about a dozen feet flush with the cheering crowd below, announcing the trial's ongoing punishment event. Words flashed in red, scrolled to the right on its bottom panel:

JUST COMPLETED: CLASH #7—TENNIS MATCH • OVERALL SCORE: JUDGES 5 DEFENDANT 2 • NEXT: CLASH #8— RAPPING IN THE RAIN

∽

Under a street light, they both bounced from the shadows, wearing different styled baggy pants, oversized shirts, and stripe sneakers. They were, of course, Master Judge, the eccentric trial ruling judge, and Richard Flynn, the notorious super wealthy and hated defendant.

For a change, Master Judge looked wasted and silly, sporting a white bandanna.

Richard looked no less silly, brandishing a heavy silver chain on his naked chest, after tearing his shirt down to the ground, and four cheap satellite bracelets on each arm.

Suddenly a thunderclap cracked the sky, followed by furious rain, exactly as forecast by Master Judge's ZCAP meter twenty-two hours and seventeen minutes ago during the Detention Q&A Show.

∽

Plenty of umbrellas popped up all around, suspecting it would be for a short duration. Soon the gigantic, transparent, soft and pliable underwater wall would take care of the situation—no one doubted the zhoenix shield.

Spectators in the Bisected Stadiums automatically looked up to an awesome elastic veil, several miles long and many more wide, that majestically began to rise over their heads, shooting up to the tempestuous black and gray clouds in ensnaring fashion before it began to curve and settle down again in accommodating manner.

Technology had its way, countering in part the dreadful effect of partial living and sinking under the ocean, just as the intrepid population of the six Zoliseum's Stadiums were experiencing right now.

∽

Stormy weather or not, Richard responded valiantly to his present situation, succeeding in drawing the large crowd's attention to his crazy little world of robotic-like jerk and freeze moves. He pirouetted twice, braced by the deafening breaking sounds. Smacked silly into its entrails, he continued his confession, now on its third day, with growing zeal in spite of the falling rain.

"Meet me in the ghetto, *bitch...*" spewed the music from nearby loudspeakers in defiant urban-styled hatred-of-women lyrics, mixing its erotic hip-hop sounds with bad-ass East Coast funk.

Pinned to the back of his earlobes, drenched with streams of raindrops, were tiny hidden mikes, picking up and amplifying any vocals that he fervently produced. Over his naked chest, between nipples, vibrated the heavy silver chain he wore, now soaking wet.

He waited for the spoken lyrics that came in short, infrequent, repetitive, but insanely offensive batches—part disco, part jazz, part electro, part ballet, but mostly rap—to take a long absence so he could speak his own instead over the crying guitar sounds. "I did absolutely no work, except invest, for thirteen years before I went into deep-freeze sleep, man—you know what I'm saying?" he began, trying to rap and deejay like a real pro, but without conviction and soul for he was no inner-city black or latino dude.

"Thirteen—I like that number!" He wiggled his rear to the alluring scratching and breaking sounds. "Provided no benefit for mankind whatsoever, man," he went on rapping, jerking and locking his body. "I like it like that."

He twisted both legs and moved stiffly left and right like a robot. "Yet my real estate business multiplied nine times. *Neuf fois.*" Proud of his French, he flashed nine fingers from his hands. "You know what I'm saying?" He rolled his eyes. "I was suddenly a billionaire many times over! Seven billion, man! You know what I'm saying?"

"YOU FUCKING PRICK!" All around the Stadiums Zundonians showed their burning outrage by throwing shoes and umbrellas in the air.

"YOU'RE NOTHING BUT A SCUMBAG!"
They shook their raised fists while shouting despicable slurs.
"DROP DEAD! DROP DEAD MISERABLE JERK!"

৩৯

Meanwhile Master Judge wriggled his legs and hips to the rap music, delirious, frenzied, ignoring the angry shouts and splashing rain.

"You've got it, baby! Squeeze it, baby!" cried out the sex-infested lyrics from the speakers as they came and left and failed to come for a while, replaced by instrument sounds.

Without warning, he sprinted forward like a young gymnast and executed a somersault, landing on a perfect split. Up on his feet again, he brought both hands to his bandanna with abandon, simulating a sinful cabaret woman, his oddly seductive eyes directed to Richard's.

He also waited for a pure instrumental moment in the song to jump in with his own vocals. "You were suddenly rich many times over–hear me out, *ricachón*. But you were no better than trash, you know that, Mr. Flynn, hear me *yo'll*," he snubbed the defendant, also trying hard to rap and deejay his way, but failing to convince anyone but himself for like his rival rap dancer he made no reference to women as "*ho's*," carried no gun, didn't deal weed or pimped any chick, and couldn't tell where Compton was or had been even on a black city map!

Whatever. Zundonians applauded and cheered. He was their man— the ruling judge! And what a refreshing scene!

৩৯

Above, the deluge steadily fell over their heads, laps, and umbrellas, creating lots of sheets of rain blown by giant swats of wind. Overly slippery, the stone steps between the aisles caused some accidents among the unattended toddlers and preteens trying to cruise around.

More claps of thunder boomed across the sky, scary enough to divert people's attention back to the cranky clouds and the tall ever-stretching whipping trees below them.

But only briefly, for the mammoth zhoenix shield had finally absorbed the region's tempestuous mess, to everyone's relief, spectacularly turning it into myriads of docile flaring lights. They brightly dispersed like falling stars, none of them showering anymore the Bisected Stadiums, Astral Floor, and Promenade Corridor.

∽

Unaffected by Master Judge's attacking words, Richard continued his rap swaggering routine. All colored tattoos–pretentious and deprave–on his shirtless back revealed themselves under the street light.

Beads of sweat from his forehead, mixing with his already sopping headband, began to trickle down his nose and mouth. There was sexual fire in his eyes.

"Oh wow, wow, wow..." cheered a passing butterfly fish, horizontally stripped, showing off his tiny cute red tail. Aware of the chasing bigger fish that roamed the area, he quickly mixed with the white spaghetti fuss of staghorn coral and capillary sea fans six feet under.

"Again, I aimed for a 'ten' figure, man, which came to me in no time...and no effort. You know what I'm saying?"

The music scratched–backward, forward. Richard swiveled. "I was the absolute owner of ten billion dollars. Ain't that cool?"

He pulled a handkerchief from his pocket and started to fumble with it while spinning around like a top to the searing music.

"GET REAL, FAT OCTOPUS, YOU'RE HEADED FOR PIRANHA BAY!" More shouts of protest from the Stadiums pierced the air. Three human waves combined across the rows of seats to form the statement "WE HATE YOU SO MUCH WE WANT YOU DEAD!"

One flying umbrella landed on the stage, slightly hitting Richard on one ankle. But it wasn't serious. He just kept pivoting on his rubber sneakers, if anything, showing how great a dancer he was.

"Hear me out. No taxes, tariffs or impositions," he uttered while rapping. "No liabilities or attachments. I was voted 'The Greatest American Citizen of 2980' by tuxedo-clad folks of enormous wealth and clout. You know what I'm saying?"

"Of course," said a curious, slow-swimming seahorse surfacing a little to swallow some air, aware of mankind's corruption...the portion of the world above his head. "The fake rapper's known to have overslept ten decades of human history, tenderly cushioned in his deep-freeze coffin, right after getting this award."

"He was actually set to sleep another three decades...before the Zundonian authorities tore down his sleeping chamber and forced him out," remarked a jawless hagfish with his circular, horny, toothed sucking mouth.

Richard raised his chin with enormous pride. "Oh yes, I loved America—that great nation of ours...while still in existence. That was the year of continental famine...I remember. When food was scarce, even for the rich. Not me. I was a success."

Angry uproars erupted in the Stadiums again.

"SHOOT THE FUCKING FOOL DEAD WITH A RIFLE OR SOMETHING!" spectators shouted in unison, reading their words from their implanted ZCAP meters.

Master Judge stopped dancing momentarily, addressed the crowd with authority, "PLEASE! PLEASE! PLEASE!"

His clamorous voice filled the Zoliseum, cooled down the commotion. For a while.

"Yet 'ten'..." continued the rapping defendant, "on a scale from ten to one-hundred—with due respect to the lower scale I'd just conquered—is nothing but a beginning. You know what I'm saying?" He did a robotic jerk-lock combination. "Besides, I liked that number—thirteen—and it took me thirteen days to raise my wealth to thirteen billion."

"HANG HIM HIGH!"

"And thirteen weeks to raise it to thirteen quintillion..." He swaggered his hips. "I loved that system. The American system. It was so ridiculously unfair and stupid...but so good to me. Ha ha ha....You know what I'm saying?"

"BURN HIM ALIVE AT THE STAKE!"

Shoes, umbrellas, and cheap electronic gadgets flew in the air in violent protest.

"...and it took me thirteen months to raise my wealth to thirteen octillion."

"CUT HIS BALLS OFF TOO!"

They became hysterical, hurling unopened tea bottles and soda cans over adjacent rows.

"KILL HIM NOW!"

Master Judge intervened again.

"QUIET! QUIET! EVERYBODY SHUT UP!"

༄

When the dance ended moments later, it was clear to everyone that Richard had won the encounter...in spite of everything. Overall his hip hop moves had included Moonwalk, Glide, Soulja Boy, and Crip Walk routines, while Master Judge had struggled with the Sponge Bob without success and embarrassed himself doing the basic Harlem Shake. Knowing what was coming, Richard had been coached by The Zoice, a great dancer, who'd leaked the upcoming event to him for two billion dollars. Nice exchange and preparation!

Above, results scrolled and flashed red on the Celestial Sphere's bottom panel.

JUST COMPLETED: CLASH #8—RAPPING IN THE RAIN • OVERALL SCORE: JUDGES 5 DEFENDANT 3 • NEXT: CLASH #9-FISHING

Off the Bermuda Revelation Park area, the storm was very much alive, rain pouring hard and constant. Coastal ocean level had risen dangerously, turning the former Florida peninsula into a sort of aquarium, where fish, people, and amphibious animals mingled in a disorderly manner and not necessarily in good terms.

BOOK 3

THE THRUST OF PUNISHMENT

PART 1

THE LEGEND OF THE HORSE-RIDING KITES
FRANCE, LATE JUNE 1955

RETRACING SOME OF JULIETTE'S MEDIEVAL CATHAR ROOTS

"Your grandpa's really cool," said Gaston to Juliette, watching the cluster of tiny frogs swim in the little bay formed by the large stones.

They were both squatting by the bank of Ruisseau de la Vallée Obscure. This one would soon merge with Valat des Abrits to later enter the Gardon de Saint Jean at the gates of Peyroles—the charming neighboring town of scarcely fifty or fewer residents that had inspired them to visit today.

"He's full of secrets," said Juliette, one hand digging for a shapely blue-gray stone in the clear water. "Sometimes I get lucky and steal a couple of them from his fortress."

"What kind of secrets?"

"Middle Ages secrets, his ancestors...what happened to them."

"Good things? Bad things?"

"Bad. Horrible." Juliette pulled the stone out of the water gently, examined it for a while. "You don't want to know."

"Tell me...I'll keep it to myself. I swear."

She kissed the wet stone, then stared at him.

"Have you heard about the Cathars?"

"Nope."

Her face turned sober, reflective. Behind her shoulders dense-leaved firs stirred in the wind.

"They were a group of very religious, very peaceful people that came to this land, Languedoc, from the waves of early Christians that fled to Egypt and other coastal regions from Jerusalem after the Crucifixion, where they settled down for centuries and ended up in this welcoming land of ours around the 12th century."

"Cool."

"Languedoc was already populated with Arian Christians and Judeo-Christians among others."

"Something about this land, huh?" exclaimed Gaston.

"Freedom of religion...of ideas...for a while anyway."

"Good things," said Gaston.

"The Cathars had a different view from what the Roman Catholic Church preached and practiced. They called themselves 'the Good Christians'...because, among other things, they were very humble and pure...like Jesus Christ had been. Not greedy or manipulative, not selfish or arrogant, not abusive. They didn't pursue wealth, take bribes or steal lands from others. They didn't befriend rich people and noblemen and those in power to expect favors and gifts from them or live in luxury...like many Roman Catholic bishops did."

"Very contrasting mentalities."

"Languedoc suited the Cathars well. It was a striving, open-minded, peaceful, independent region in the deep south...our region...not willing to be attached to the north—you know, Paris and surrounding regions—where the King of France ruled and operated...because of huge economic, cultural, and religious differences."

"I can imagine," said Gaston.

"Both the fanatically religious King and his supporting Pope couldn't wait to grab Languedoc's territory and wealth and submit its people to the *exact* Roman Catholic religious dogmas and beliefs they both fiercely promoted. This greed and twisted thinking led to the Albigensian Crusade against the Cathars and other religious groups in Languedoc whose beliefs were *not* exactly in accord with the King's and the Pope's."

"What happened?"

"The Crusade turned into a huge massacre of peaceful citizens, a burning at the stake of hundreds of thousands of non-converts, the annihilation of an entire civilization—what we call today *genocide*."

"Wow."

"The Roman Catholic bishops themselves presided over and watched the genocide."

"Very sad."

Gaston reflected quietly, undisturbed by the persistent buzzing sound of cicadas in the vicinity.

"What have the Cathars got to do with your grandpa?"

"A lot. With me too, of course, by ancestry."

Gaston regarded her expressive eyes, the naughty pout forming in her lips.

"Grandpa raised me as a...far distant...modern Cathar. He made sure I understood I was as important a girl as any boy on earth. That this was not meant to be a boy's dominated world."

"I agree with that. But you don't have to be a Cathar to believe in that," said Gaston.

"I didn't really become a Cathar, I just picked up some of their beliefs and practices along the way. For example, I'm a vegetarian, non-violent, down-to-earth, and believe in reincarnation. You know that by now."

"Everything but *reincarnation*."

"Well, now you know."

He nodded, smiled.

"Do you believe in God?" asked now Gaston.

"Yes, but I reject organized church...indulgences, opulent temples, lavish decorations...and material wealth. I'm basically spiritual."

"What about Jesus Christ?"

"He was cool, not exactly *divine*, but a terrific guy."

"So...you think he was *mortal*...like everyone else?"

"Well yes. Just because a pagan Roman emperor named Constantine gathered three-hundred or so quarreling Christian bishops for several weeks in a particular place in the fourth century and decided *by vote* he should be *divine*, be called *Son of God*, and sit on the right hand side of God in Heaven...doesn't make him so. That's the way it was done."

Gaston remained speechless, astounded.

"Besides, he was in love with Mary Magdalene and had a kid with her...raised here in the south of France...after his Crucifixion..."

"Really?"

"Jesus got her pregnant before he died. Nothing wrong with that. But the Roman Church suppressed all available information through the centuries and twisted things around, including what's written in the Bible, to create a half-fictionalized, all-male, domineering Church. They voted Jesus up to the level of *divine* and Mary Magdalene down to the level of *prostitute*...among other things."

"How do you know all that?"

"Most of it from Grandpa. But it's not new knowledge. People have known that for centuries. People always find out...sooner or later."

"They don't teach this in school, of course, so besides your grandpa, who—"

"All the girls in our mission."

She laughed, made him smile oddly.

"What mission is that?"

"It's secret."

"Oh..."

"Yet legendary." She pouted.

Gaston scratched his head, pulled out his handkerchief, which provided his fingers with a needed softness.

"That's contradictory."

"Kind of..."

"What is it called?" His fingers fidgeted the soft material.

"The Legend of the Horse-Riding Kites."

"You're pulling my legs?"

"No, just the kites."

Gaston's eyes felt silly staring at her.

"Can you explain?"

She rose to leave...and did so with furtive steps.

"Another day, another time." she said simply.

Above hovered Richard's soul.

RETRACING SOME OF JULIETTE'S
18TH CENTURY PROTESTANT ROOTS

At age five, before she even showed any passion for stage acting, Juliette rode horses with great ease and skill. Now at thirteen, she felt motivated to train Gaston as well.

She didn't own a horse, but was always able to borrow one or two in a few hours' notice from Grandpa's circle of friends.

Occasionally, she'd ridden with another school girl her age, who also loved the outdoors, but preferred swimming competition and fencing to drama–the twisted, mentally exhaustive discipline Juliette engaged in (her friend's way of looking at it)–so the level of their friendship barely wobbled on the surface. Which was fine with Juliette.

Riding along with Gaston, on the other hand, even at this early stage of training, filled Juliette with joy. Likewise, the learning young boy, whom she totally adored, seemed to have a lot of fun. And his progress bordered on spectacular.

They'd been wandering in the woods of nearby Falguières, flanking a few stone-built houses roofed with brownish-orange baked earth, huddled together on a mount side. Terraced hills, chestnut trees, and green oaks dotted the area.

Then a steep horse trail, coiling up into awesome views of distant sierras and misty clouds deep in the Cévennes, welcomed them. Looking back for an instant, Juliette could glance at the little Col de Lamira up a peak they'd left behind some two kilometers earlier.

Further deep into St-Etienne-Vallée-Française, past Pont des Plans, Juliette approached Gaston with her restless horse.

"Do you realize we're riding on the land...actually, the hamlet... where the famous Camisard Chief Abraham Mazel was born and grew up?"

"Camisard?"

"Yeah...Cévennes-based Protestants fighting for religion freedom in their own land."

"Fighting? Against who?"

"The narrow-minded, cruel, and totalitarian papal and royal military forces from the north."

"Wow."

"Camisard derives from the type of shirt or *camise*—in Occitan language—these horse-riding mountain guerrilleros wore. It was a long, white shirt meant to be visible to one another at night while fighting the invading troops from the north."

"The usual thing—small people crushed by bullying giants," put in Gaston.

"Bullying and dogmatic," said Juliette. "Well, the Camisards...also called French Huguenots or Calvinists...finally erupted into violence after twenty years of unbearable chases, torture, and executions in their own Cévennes villages by those northern bastards."

"Who wouldn't..." put in Gaston.

"Those were barbaric *dragonnades*...following King Louis XIV's 1685 repeal of the Edict of Nantes. Such Edict, issued by his grandfather, King Henry IV, almost 90 years earlier, had given these religious peasants limited but welcomed freedom and peace in the Cévennes."

"Dragon—what?" asked Gaston.

"*Dragon-nades*—the frightening, sadistic manner these outsiders or *dragons* forced Protestants to convert to the Catholic faith. Their king— the Sun-King, Louis XIV—used the motto: *Un roi, une loi, une foi.* (One king, one law, one faith.)"

"So...*real* dragons."

"Also called *missionaries in boots*...but actually royal mounted terrorists...soldiers, clothed in red, authorized to be quartered in Protestant villages, hamlets, or homes, specifically the Camisards' scattered settlements in the Cévennes, with complete freedom to pillage, loot, beat, torture and rape...in their quest to *convert* people."

"Wow...wow...what a bunch of barbarians..."

Juliette stopped her horse in front of a large stone house partially covered by tall trees, dominating the hilltop hamlet from its perched position. Lateral stairs stuffed with scrubbing grass, led to the main door.

"Eventually the dragons destroyed everything, systematically..." she said somberly. "Not only the Protestants in this region, but all over France."

"Wow...another Jew or Cathar type of genocide...by the so-called servants of God?"

"Yep." She pointed to the old, but imposing two-story house. "Here's where Abraham Mazel spent his youth."

Gaston kept staring at the historical place with awe. "They also named a street in Saint-Jean-du-Gard after him, right?"

She nodded. "Next to our street..." She then blinked oddly. "By the way, in those days our town was called Saint-Jean-de-Gardonnenque."

"I like the present name better," said Gaston, redirecting his thoughts to Mazel. "So here...in Falguière...is where he went to school too?"

"Yep. Also where he had a *revelation* after a clandestine assembly in a grotte."

"Oh, what was that?"

"It had to do with the Abbé du Chaila—a so-called servant of God—who had taken upon himself the task of imprisoning and torturing Camisards in his home. Mazel had a vision from God urging him to prophesy and build a small army to free his agonizing friends.

"Sounds like Jeanne d'Arc's divine call," said Gaston, staring up at the elevated windows and chimney of Mazel's old home.

"One of his ablest combat men, also turned prophet, Esprit Séguier, led a surprise attack on the Abbé du Chaila on Pont de Monvert, resulting on the Abbé's death. This also became known as the starting point of the War of the Cévennes."

"A religious war..." said Gaston.

"Later referred to as the War of the Camisards...just at the turn of the 18th century."

"Not a bad looking house, *e?*" praised Gaston with a touch of Occitan, getting more curious.

"You see that lateral, bottom window?" she said, pointing and leading her horse there. "Right above the cave?"

"Yes," said Gaston, following with his horse.

"Well, this is the window he used to flee from the royal dragons that came to arrest him in 1705."

"You mean he jumped out through it? *That's high!*"

She nodded and laughed. "He feared nothing."

Gaston remained pensive.

"I'm amazed that you even remember the exact year he was arrested," he said.

"I have to, it's part of my education, plus I have access to my grandpa's private library...which is quite extensive and revealing...about this stuff."

Gaston nodded. "You know...I'm just learning too...without taking sides...because there's so much I don't know...and I'm also too young to judge history...although sometimes I follow my instincts..."

"You do...quite often..." She laughed.

"But to me everything boils down to freedom, freedom of choosing one own feelings and needs, one own ideas, one own religion or non-religion...something that was nearly impossible in those days." He stared at her smiling eyes, deeply green now. "Why were they going to arrest him?"

"He and his friends—all Camisard chiefs operating in fighting groups of fifty or less in different areas of the Cévennes—led many surprise attacks on the invading royal troops, killing some soldiers and important officials. Camisard heroes abounded. Freedom fighters like Pierre Laporte (nicknamed Rolland), Jean Cavalier, Pierre Séguier (Esprit), Jean Rampon, and Salomon Couderc—all targets of fervid persecutions."

She pushed some hair out of her face, grimacing to a sudden outburst of wind.

"Mazel managed a spectacular escape with other prisoners from the colossal Tour de Constance in Aigues-Mortes six months later–an almost impossible feat–but, like Rolland, died daringly in battle. Couderc was arrested and burned alive a year later, so was Séguier... like hundreds of other Camisards."

"Wow...like Jeanne d'Arc."

"Others were sent to the royal galleys–known to be a horrendous, hard-labor, slow-death punishment."

"Royal galleys?"

"Yes. War or merchant ships propelled by the rowing muscles of chained slaves. You know–hard and fast rowing while being flogged on the back by a barbarian master."

"Wow..."

"Actually, the Tour de Constance was also a hell-like place for condemned Camisards women, like Marie Durand...who spent thirty years locked up inside...completely forgotten by the prison warden."

"Terrible and sad."

"She had scratched the word *resister* on one wall with her fingernails to encourage resistance to the Catholic royal oppression."

"Wow."

"Three centuries earlier," said Juliette, "over forty Knights Templars were also dumped in this macabre dungeon that from the outside looked like a mighty, impregnable tower...a tower of terror..."

"Wow."

"From the resistance camp, only Cavalier lived a relatively longer life. A street is also named after him in Saint-Jean-du-Gard. He'd started fighting at seventeen in the South of France and ended up as lieutenant-governor of the isle of Jersey in London after bravely serving both the Camisards and the King of England. But Rolland is remembered as perhaps the most daring and popular of all. At least in France."

"Wow...wow...." gasped Gaston, with mixed feelings. "How many Camisards fought in the Cévennes?"

"Some two-thousand Camisards...against twenty-thousand Dragons..."

"That's a hell of a difference!"

"A hell. You said it!"

Above hovered Richard's soul.

FROM CHILDREN PROPHETS TO JULIETTE'S SACRED SCROLLS

"What about these prophets?" Gaston asked Juliette, edging a steep slope his horse might not appreciate. "I don't get it."

Juliette laughed.

"The more I tell you, the more you'll be surprised," she said with a funny pout not seen by Gaston. She tightened her hold on the reins. A slender path ahead, laden with large stones and thorny overhanging branches from a cliff-rooted tree, forced her to quicken her horse's pace away from danger.

"Just tell me about them...the prophets...." Gaston persisted after her, raising his voice.

"Because the King forbade regular temple gatherings for praying, singing, and conducting religious rituals, Protestants met in clandestine or secret assemblies," Juliette said, slowing down to catch up with Gaston's struggling pace.

"In the mountains?"

"Yes. These places more and more lacked adult preachers and prophets...since they were needed or killed in battle or executed elsewhere...at a quick rate..." said Juliette, pausing for breath.

"Terrible."

"Among those were François Vivent, Claude Brousson, and Elie Marion–the first two soon arrested and executed, the last one living in exile. Marion outlived most of her friends traveling through friendly Protestant countries in Europe, but fell ill and died in Italy." She met Gaston's attentive eyes, both horses now walking side by side. "So a new generation of young preachers and prophets emerged–children prophets mainly."

"*What?!*"

"A new phenomenon—the rise of children prophets—both girls and boys."

"*That's absurd!*" blasted Gaston.

"Not at all," said Juliette, pouting. "Camisards' children surfaced with positive prophesies."

"C'mon..."

"Divinely inspired, they said."

"They talked to those willing to listen in secret assemblies, gave hope to their fighting parents, made them feel stronger, determined... even invincible!"

"You believe *that*?" shot Gaston. "I mean it sounds good, but these were *kids*."

"Like us, Gaston. Do you feel inferior? Inadequate? Just because you're younger?"

"No. I feel very adequate," declared Gaston proudly with a naughty smile. "I really do."

She uttered with a pout, "I do too," and joined Gaston in sweet laughter, letting her horse take a small lead again, scouting more difficult terrain.

"How old and how intelligent were these kids?"

"Isabeau Vincent, a shepherdess in Dauphiné and one of the first and most popular prophetesses, was sixteen. But others were as young as five or six."

"*Are you kidding me?*" dismissed Gaston.

Juliette stopped her horse, turned to face him.

"They were truly illiterate, but they shared the claim that *they spoke in the voice of the Holy Spirit* during sleep...in clear French, which they didn't know, not in their Occitan language."

"C'mon...Juliette."

"And they practiced a form of *sudden collapsing* to the ground when showing their appeal to repentance, resistance, or attack...depending on the progress of the war...as if falling into a trance...weirdly shaking their limbs...uttering strange, ghostly sounds...and creating other theatrical displays that they said connected their physical experience with divine messages from above."

"That's spooky..."

"They actually derived all this from Brousson's earlier *remote desert* type of preaching and prophesying."

"Spooky..."

"Sounds familiar?"

"Not really," said Gaston defensively. Juliette could strike quick and hard on his most sensitive parts. At least he didn't turn his personal trances or reveries into religious ceremonies, claiming a contact with God. Although a contact with something or someone seemed possible. In fact, lately he'd been inundated with absolutely weird cinematic visions of two dancing idiots...imitating robots and voodoo sorcerers...surrounded by crazily shouting people...in a strange language...

ᖗ

Moving through a forest of pine and spruce, they were now climbing a very narrow, jagged, rock-strewn track that promised to widen and soften at its crest, but didn't. For hours the scenery had been misty at best and cold, their chat severely restricted by the harsh environment. Juliette's white horse led the way, advancing single file.

Turning her head to check on her boyfriend, she cheered, "You're doing great!"

Soon they reached the top of a mount where sat a half-hidden medieval fortress in ruins. Golden grasses covered this treeless area, way deep into the heart of the Cévennes.

Side by side again, they gazed straight down to the strange formation of a river, wild and turbulent, snaking through a green valley on the other side of the hill.

"A while ago we crossed the Ruisseau de la Cannonade without difficulty," remarked Juliette. "Granted, it was slim, shallow, and harmless...but I don't think we can cross this one now...it's just too brutal in this area."

"Must be the Gardon, huh?"

"The Gardon de Mialet...in this area..." informed Juliette.

Gaston remained thoughtful.

"Is it a good time now...for you to tell me about the legend of the kites?" he then asked with a little smile.

"The Legend of the *Horse-Riding* Kites," corrected Juliette, guiding her horse to a less rocky path.

Cautiously, they began to descend the steep slope, one horse after the other, heading for the valley.

Again, they halted the horses momentarily to enjoy the breathtaking view of chained mountains and dense evergreen forest of coniferous pines, spruces, and firs below a changing veil of burgeoning, furtive, cotton-soft clouds.

"Well?" reminded Gaston, still in limbo from his unanswered question.

Bringing her horse closer to Gaston's, Juliette said, in a low tone, "It may or may not be a good time." She remained pensive, relaxing her hold on the reins. "But I'll tell you some."

"You can tell me more...if you want," put in Gaston meekly. "I'll keep the secret."

"Well, thanks."

ೞ

The sound of swirling river waters echoed around, mixing with the sound of nearby singing cicadas. It rushed with force through a gorge below the hillside, exploding into small waterfalls.

"I have a bunch of things I can tell you, too..." challenged Gaston moments later, just in case, for she didn't seem to come out of her shell.

"I'm sure you do, but this is different. It's more about *them* than me."

"Who are *they*?"

Juliette squeezed both sides of her horse's body with her heels, getting it started walking. This encouraged Gaston to do the same.

Soon they moved side by side at a comfortable pace, enjoying the sight of a tiny village appearing in the distance, nestled down among green wooded hills covered with lush *garrigue*, this one stubbornly grabbing the hidden rocks with its bulk of dense shrubbery and shades of perfumed verdant claws.

Falguières, on the other hand, had progressively fallen behind and even vanished from view as they moved farther away into unspoiled territory.

"The Knights Templar, the Cathars, the Saracens, the Visigoths... the Carolingians, the Merovingians...Mary Magdalene...Jesus Christ... all of them and more," informed Juliette.

Gaston couldn't be more puzzled. "That's really heavy stuff."

"I read a lot."

"I know, you told me—your grandpa's library."

"That's right."

༄

They moved past an array of majestic elms, spotting a wild eagle circling overhead. Reaching the upper range of Cévennes slopes in this area, Juliette began to descend a hill signaling Gaston she was now heading back to Falguières. But rather than return the way they'd come, she took a more daring, different path, in direction of the Pont de Abarines.

Soon she guided her horse on the Rivière Gardon de Mialet itself, splashing its fresh, crystal clear waters with the impetuous horse's hooves.

Again, they crossed rocky lands covered with resilient *garrigue*, wild flowers, and mulberry trees leading to snaky creeks. Down a slope, they sighted a simple but picturesque stone church roofed with schist. It stood behind a cluster of old oaks animated with grazing goats.

"You can ask my grandpa about the details of this blood-soaking, power-chasing religious race, which has little to do with religion really, that has shaped and crushed France for the past two thousand years," said Juliette, sounding more like a serious school teacher than a fun-seeking thirteen-year-old.

"No, thanks."

"Or you can attend one of his popular lectures around the country, if you can make yourself look and act older...say, ten years older." Now she had touched his ego as well.

"No, thanks."

To their left, a herd of sheep quietly grazed the grassland.

"Cut the crop and tell me the story," then urged Gaston, half-laughing, patting his brown horse's mane. "I only recognize the names of Jesus and Mary in your list...and..."

"...and what?"

"...and...what in hell do they have to do with you and the Legend of the Horse-Riding Kites?"

She stared at him silently, both horses walking alongside.

"Once upon a time in the fourth century the super powerful Roman Catholic Church decided by a vote among three-hundred or so Christian bishops that Jesus Christ should be promoted to *divine*, not mortal anymore, not the marrying kind anymore, that people should call him Son of God and expect him to be seated next to God in Heaven all the time...stuff like that..."

"You told me *that* already last week, remember?" said Gaston, fidgeting with a handkerchief he'd pulled out of his pocket. "You also told me you learned all that from your Grandpa, remember?"

"The point is we have *proof* Jesus was romantically attached to Mary Magdalene, maybe not married but attached by love."

"Wow."

"We also have *proof* that his wife or lover, Mary Magdalene, was pregnant with his baby during the Crucifixion." She noticed a brisk widening in Gaston's eyes. "Nothing wrong with that, right?"

"Nothing wrong," uttered Gaston. "They're in love, they're consenting adults. What a great way to start a family!"

"Exactly. We have *proof* that afterwards Mary Magdalene raised the kid–a cute little girl–in the south of France...not too far from here."

"Wow. That's very cool."

Juliette's beautiful white horse snorted, jostled a little. She gently drew on the reins.

"What kind of proof you guys have? You keep saying *we*. Do you mean all the girls in your mission?" He felt funny saying that.

"Yep. We have two authentic ancient scrolls–one with a joint message of peace to the world from both Jesus and Mary before the Crucifixion from Palestine and the other with a single message of identification from Jesus' little girl after the Crucifixion from Marseille, France," revealed Juliette solemnly, staring at the wide prairie opening in front of them. "Let's take a gallop now!"

"*Wait!*" cried Gaston, watching her go off in her crazy, unexpected way. "*I want to hear more!*"

Above hovered Richard's soul.

THE BONFIRE OF REVELATIONS

Sitting cross-legged around a bonfire in the front grounds of the Quintero's farm, Juliette was getting warm, with a clear and relaxed mind, after a hard day's school work and other chores. A light breeze had started to caress her face. She watched the orange flames flickering, snapping, and puffing, quietly expecting Gaston's unavoidable two questions.

Sure enough, the first one came: "What's the joint message Jesus and Mary Magdalene put on the scroll?"

Juliette regarded Gaston's inquiring hazel eyes.

"I don't remember exactly. I can show you the scroll tomorrow."

"Can you just give me a few lines, a hint?"

"Well, something like..." She tried mentally, but nothing really came out. She expressed sadness by thrusting out her lower lip. "Sorry."

Looking around, she recognized every person sitting there in circle, enjoying the torching blaze. They all wore sweaters, either gray or brown, except Juliette who sported a green blouse and red scarf. French music from Pablo's clarinet and Alfredo's accordion mixed romantically with the soft evening wind as Pierre added logs to the flames.

"Take your time," Gaston said to Juliette.

"I rather not."

"Why not?"

"This is Jesus and Mary's stuff. I'm not a scroll."

"You're not *them*. Is that what you mean?"

"It wouldn't sound right...if I just said their message." she uttered with a pout.

Gaston remained silent, then said, "Will you show me the other scroll too...tomorrow? The one with—"

"Jesus and Mary's daughter's message?"

"Yes."

"I suppose I will." That took care of Gaston's not-yet-asked but answered second question. Impulsively, she moved her head to both sides, making her blonde ponytail bounce a little over the rim of her scarf.

"Good," he said, leaning and kissing her neck, just under her ear.

"But they're copies, not originals."

"I understand."

"Tiny copies."

He kept staring at her angelic face, her precious upturned red lips, now slightly parted, wondering.

"How did you get the scrolls? What are you planning to do with them?"

She squinted. "Why are your questions always so loaded?"

He laughed, stared at her smiling lips, feeling the warmth of the fire.

"We work in secrecy, you know."

This time, she leaned and smooched his forehead and cheek.

Driftwood burned freely in the flames, cracking now and then, arousing Gaston's curiosity.

"It all started in Château de Montségur," then said Juliette, opening up. "The historical Pyrenean fortress, where all ended for the Cathars. All except, their treasure."

"A *treasure*?"

"Yes. Actually, two—one material and one spiritual."

"Those Cathars—I thought they were humble, religious people." Gaston reached for his handkerchief inside his pocket. Began to fidget with it. "Weren't they?"

"They were," said Juliette. "They were also guardians of this double-value treasure—an ancient treasure so revealing and damaging to the Roman Catholic Church, it ultimately cost not only their lives but their total *extinction* as a thriving civilization."

"Wow."

"And also the extinction of another thriving civilization–the Knights Templar's–who were there to protect and continue the Cathars' legacy...regarding this treasure."

"You mean these two civilizations disappeared from the face of the earth? Why?"

"The Roman Catholic Church invented, or reinvented, a word many centuries ago, before the Cathars even existed, that classified any individual or groups of people *who were not totally in agreement with their religious beliefs* as unworthy of living on this planet, and therefore worthy of being burned alive at the stake," said Juliette. "And so the Cathars and the Knights Templar were wiped out from this world. But not before them putting up a big fight...that lasted many bloody decades."

"How grotesque and sad." Gaston wished he could've helped these people somehow. "What was that word Roman Catholics invented or reinvented?"

"*Heretic.*"

"Such an innocent-sounding word."

"Actually, they also invented something called *The Inquisition*, a secret group of really nasty people, like the Nazi *Gestapo*, who persecuted heretics, jailed them, tortured them, and made sure they died in the most horrible ways."

"And who invented the Roman Catholic Church?" Now Gaston was being either too funny or too naive.

Juliette laughed, even though she knew he was very serious.

"It invented *itself*–the papal system and all its sickening trappings, corruption, and arrogance." She paused. "So did the Kingdom of France...supremacy's conspirator...with all its fanfare, pageantry, and depravity...coronation after coronation." Her eyes lightened a bit. "At least it had the common sense to stop its nonsense along the way. But not the papal system. It's still there...ruling, pontificating, and frightening the Western world." She stared at the fire. "Of course, there are other frightening ruling systems in this world."

"Life's so complicated, so defective," said Gaston, also staring at the fire, "oppressed people being forced to live under such ignorance, brainwashing, and brutality."

"Two beautiful civilizations gone forever," stressed Juliette.

"It's hard to imagine this actually happened."

"It did."

Gaston rubbed his chin, thinking. "So the Cathars and Templars disappeared forever but the treasure stayed?"

"Yes."

"So..." said Gaston.

"So the hunt for the most coveted treasure on earth began in earnest," said Juliette.

"But I thought that was the Holy Grail Treasure?"

"It's the same one...many people say..."

Gaston fondled the soft piece of cloth he held in his hand in rhythm with the excited beats of his heart.

"So...where's the treasure now? Who has it?"

"Remember Montségur?"

"The château? The fortress?"

"Yes, yes. Well, according to the most reliable sources, dug up from my grandpa's books—because tons of stories have sprang out lately about this, and more keep appearing each year, some of them real crazy—a handful of Cathars escaped the siege with the treasure before they surrendered and were burned to death."

"Wait, wait, hold it there. There was a *siege* of the fortress?"

Gaston was now cuddled up to Juliette's shoulder, one hand caressing her silky, long pony tail as she talked.

"Yes. It lasted almost a year."

"Wow."

"Remarkable, considering the attackers numbered over ten-thousand Pope's and King's armies combined, knights and noblemen from the north of France and religious crusaders from all over Europe loyal to these rulers."

"Wow."

"The Pope promised these courageous invaders complete forgiveness of their sins, eternal salvation, and a great opportunity for stealing all these conquered peoples' properties," said Juliette.

"No kidding..."

Someone sitting opposite them around the fire–a chubby peasant full of wrinkles around his eyes, wearing a heavy mustache–played the guitar and sang the refrain of a quite popular old folk song:

Auprès de ma blonde, qu'il fait bon, fait bon, fait bon
Auprès de ma blonde, qu'il fait bon dormir

Hearing it made both Juliette and Gaston smile.

It seemed to fit their mood so perfectly, both snuggled against each other in the chill of night, luring all eyes around the bonfire to veer in their direction. For a brief moment they even tongue-kissed.

☙

"Of course, the château was known to be impregnable, unconquerable...looming like an otherworldly entity on top of a gigantic mountain...just like in a fairy tale...only real," went on Juliette.

"But the royal troops managed to reverse that...conquer the Cathars...and afterwards...burn them alive?" guessed Gaston.

"Yes. Happily so. Over two-hundred of them."

"*Happily so?*"

"Because Cathars believed this world, our world, was evil...material."

"I can see why."

"And the world they were transferring to was good...spiritual."

A long pause ensued, their stares lost in the aura of the burning logs facing them.

Gaston detached a little from Juliette's shoulder.

"So...how come some of the Cathars escaped?"

"They needed to protect the ancient treasure at all cost, couldn't allow these despicable, barbarian papal and royal soldiers to get their filthy hands on it," said Juliette.

"True."

"These bastards had already butchered some thirty-thousand peaceful villagers, including women and children, in Béziers."

"Wow."

"They had sacked other villages, slaughtered multitudes. They were vicious, power-seeking Crusaders without respect for anything but their own pathetic cause!"

She stared at the burning timber, hearing the pine needles crackling underneath as the hungry flames devoured the stack of logs.

Across the fire she could see Pierre and Alfredo hypnotically listening to Pablo's clarinet, its special rendering of Charles Trenet's "Douce France" under the present moonlight.

Collecting her thoughts, she continued, "So a handful of Cathars were able to smuggle out the treasure before the eminent surrender."

"And where did they go?"

"Some say the material treasure ended up in Rennes-le-Château and the spiritual treasure in Château de Quéribus—both in the vicinity of Château de Montségur."

"Château, château, château..."

Juliette smiled. "The Quéribus's spiritual treasure, we know, was split into four missions across Languedoc. One of them, our mission—for sure, I can tell you—has a definite direction...all mapped out and partly carried out."

"Oh, now we're going somewhere," exclaimed Gaston, with a smooch to his girlfriend's cheek.

It was a good moment too for Pierre. Somehow he'd joined Pablo's clarinet vocally.

> *Douce France*
> *Cher pays de mon enfance*
> *Bercée de tender insouciance*
> *Je t'ai gardé dans mon Coeur!*

~

"So your mission is one of four spiritual missions."

"Yeah."

"So how does this work? Your mission, your scrolls, your kites?"

Alfredo had started to put out the fire. People were leaving.

"Do you mind holding on to your questions until we meet again?"

"Juliette, Juliette..." grimaced Gaston, watching the sullen pout in her lips.

While he looked away for a second, checking on Alfredo's wrapping up of their cozy gathering, Juliette undid her pony tail, standing up, letting her hair flow lose. Her face changed gravely, staring deeper and farther with those enchanting green eyes. Her lips welled out. She was about to say something to Gaston...perhaps to the world...and finally did:

For eternal love and peace we preach
For spiritual abundance and harmony we live
For forgiveness and equality we teach

Dying embers mixed with smoke in the background.
Above hovered Richard's soul.

PART 2

CLASH #7—TENNIS MATCH
(A TIME TRAVELED CLASH)
FRANCE, LATE JUNE 1955

MASTER JUDGE'S SURPRISING DISCLOSURE

Bermuda Revelation Park, Zundo, June 3081

Four times in a row the dunking tank ball, borrowed from the previous Clash, bounced back to him. But this time, the fifth, it didn't go well because his long gothic cape got in the way. Not an easy thing to do from his Den, high above the Astral Floor.

Master Judge activated a small switch up in the controls panel, realizing he was still in the middle of a process. Obscenity Judge's pretty smile appeared on a lateral screen. "Your transfer back to me is complete," he spoke to the screen.

The smile faded away.

Turning to the defendant, he commanded, "You may continue now, Mr. Flynn."

"Where am I?" Richard was again confused, surrounded by pitch black darkness. "What am I supposed to do or say?"

His feet felt cold, wearing nothing but his jockey shorts, standing erect like a fool.

Master Judge, casually humming lyrics from a pop French song with his rich, intimidating voice, typed something on his keyboard and pressed a button.

Platforms moved below his royal post.

Above, detaching from the clouds, the huge Celestial Sphere began to descend. It settled a dozen inches over the crowd's heads in the Bisected Stadiums, spinning on its axis, announcing the new punishment Clash status of the trial:

JUST COMPLETED: CLASH #6—DUNKING TANK SPLASH • OVERALL SCORE: JUDGES 5 DEFENDANT 1 • NEXT: CLASH #7—TENNIS MATCH

Then it went up spinning faster some two-hundred feet above the six Stadiums, where it parked.

"Please, close your eyes, Mr. Flynn," commanded the charismatic judge, ready to flip a switch.

Some hydraulic sounds filled the air.

"You can open them anytime you wish now, Mr. Flynn."

Richard complied, not wasting a second.

Looking around him, he exclaimed, "Wow!"

He stood in the middle of a red clay tennis court, clad in classical white tennis clothes. Next to him stood Master Judge, also dressed in white tennis outfit.

"So fast?" cried out Richard.

The referee sat on an elevated wooden chair, dominating the court. "This match," he said to both players, in an elegant vocal display, "will consist of one set only, and the set will consist of one game only." Staring at Richard, he said, "You may toss the coin and begin to play." Cheers broke out all around the Bisected Stadiums. "Good luck gentlemen."

Richard got lucky with the toss. He chose to serve, his strongest asset as a player.

Looking up at the bright sun, Master Judge chose the side of the court which would blind Richard's eyes every time he attempted to serve.

Now they were both on their respective court side, properly positioned to start the game.

Richard prepared to serve, adjusting his position to the glowing sun. With a thoughtful stare, he tossed the ball high above his head and, just as the ball began to fall, coinciding with the highest reach of his stretched arm swing, smacked it real hard with his racquet. It was good.

Master Judge attempted to return the ball with a powerful forehand, but the ball hit the net and died there.

Next a fiery exchange of ground strokes dazzled the audience. With great skill Master Judge delivered two sharp cross-court shots and a killer down-the-line to even the score.

"YES!" congratulated himself the judge ferociously, shoving his right fist.

Across the court Richard pumped himself up his way, cursing, and throwing deadly stares at Master Judge, while pacing the service line. He held his racquet so close to his mouth, it appeared his teeth were actually clamped on the strings. Maybe they were.

Suddenly, he jerked his body, and his raging eyes exploded, "COM'ON!"

For some reason, he felt possessed, as if none of this behavior was his. Yet he couldn't change it. Alas, an illusion. It reminded him the amazing strength he once had at his dentist office when mistakenly overdosed with Xylocaine—a beastly reaction that not even five strong men, the size and toughness of Mike Tyson, could stop him from wrecking the place before he was forced away into an ambulance. Tyson was still hot in the year 3081. Mainly because ear-biting was hot.

He served, but missed the square corner on the opponent's side he was aiming at. Too long. His second serve was good.

They rallied like pros from behind the service line, until Richard executed a splendid drop shot that got Master Judge sprinting to the net like a mad man, trying to return it.

But all in vain.

Out of control, his legs split apart on the slippery red clay and *QUAAAAASH!* A miserable fall.

Richard stared at the ridiculous looking man, soaked in red clay, struggling to get up.

He prepared to serve again, announcing the score "30-15."

It was a kick serve that bounced real high with top spin on the opponent's side, but, amazingly, found a great arm and flair to return it just as fast as it came. Quite admirable from Master Judge's part.

The ball still in play, Richard hit it deep to one corner with his one-handed backhand, then smacked a winning overhead to the other corner when Master Judge attempted to lob him.

Now Richard was near victory. *40-15*, he pondered.

Tropical fish swam to his side.

He particularly liked the fairy basslets and the blackbar soldierfish better than the glasseye snappers, of which there were plenty of by the referee.

His attention drifted momentarily to a school of horse-eye jacks crossing the court some thirty feet above the red clay. Intriguing colonies of hanging sponges, sea fans, and gorgonians, he noticed, sheltered a family of garden eels and yellowtail snappers near the ZV cameras to his right.

"Then it occurred to me that 50...50 million...was half the value of something. It sounded unfinished...halved. So I devised a plan to bring this figure up to 100 million flat. I was amazed at the speed by which I conquered this caprice."

Brushing some clay off his shirt and shorts, Master Judge remarked, puzzled, "But you already said that!"

"I did?"

Master Judge raised one hand, asked for a time-out.

"Don't you remember our mountain climbing experience—Clash #2—a couple of days ago? Day 1 of the trial?"

Richard frowned.

"Oh—I'm sorry," apologized the judge, realizing something. "You haven't *even* spoken since OJ transferred you back to me..."

"I sure haven't." He slowly approached the net. "OJ?"

"Yeah, Obscenity Judge," said Master Judge.

"Oh—*the Asian girl*," exclaimed Richard, remembering.

Master Judge also walked to the net from the other side, provoking a face-to-face discussion. His mind seemed to choke on thoughts.

Suddenly, his face broke into a vigorous smile.

"I see what's happening," he proclaimed. "Accidentally, I have *re-wound* your speech on tape." He scratched his bald head. "You've been taped all along since the trial began...and *your tape*, not you, was coming on. I see my mistake now."

"Human error," put in Richard, meekly.

He swirled on his tennis shoes facing the service line to prepare for another serve.

"Beg your pardon?" Master Judge's voice came very strong, actually making Richard stop on his march and turn around to watch.

"I'm not a human! I'm a zobot!" shouted the judge.

"A *zobot?*" said Richard, wondering. "Then...zobot error."

"You got it!" shouted Master Judge, breaking into small laughter. "You thought I was human, huh? That's really funny. Heee heee heee..."

The crowd broke into mocking laughter too.

Taking advantage of the distraction, Richard served an ace and won the game, which was also the match.

At the net, they shook hands.

"You caught me off-guard...but that's okay. I'm still 5-2 ahead of you overall."

Richard glanced up at the scoreboard on the slowly spinning big Sphere above his head to confirm.

JUST COMPLETED: CLASH #7—TENNIS MATCH • OVERALL SCORE: JUDGES 5 DEFENDANT 2 • NEXT : CLASH #8— RAPPING IN THE RAIN

૭

Richard fidgeted with a handkerchief he'd pulled out of his shorts.

"...a *zobot*, huh?" he brooded over.

"Oh, I can become a real human being, if I want to," bragged the judge, approaching him. He directed his eyes to the audience in Stadium #5, searchingly, and pointed to someone sitting in the first row. "Isn't it true, Dr. Ufahh?"

Bathed with a spotlight, the famous scientist stood up and acknowledged with a nod of his head. He wore an exotic multicolored jacket that greatly reduced his old age.

"Change my donut into a mouse with big eyes, WB!" cried out a little voice from the audience, obviously a child's.

It was a typical, friendly request that only accentuated the reverence felt for a person loaded with knowledge and power. And kids loved to call him Walking Brain or simply WB, like now.

A flurry of similar requests and cheerful salutations floated around during this brief interval. He just smiled back to the callers, keeping it safe and simple.

"Let's have a round of applause for Zundo's greatest scientist—Dr. Ueh Ulah Ulevah Ufahh!" gloated Master Judge. Naming his full name, he reasoned, for sure would increase the spectacle of the moment—not exactly something the scientist desired, though.

It was the longest and strongest ovation ever for a high official since the Bermuda Revelation Park made its presence in the closing years of the 30th century.

PART 3

LA PETITE CAMARGUE
FRANCE, LATE JUNE 1955

TRYING TO CONNECT THE DOTS IN
PALAVAS-LES-FLOTS

Splashing cold ocean water on Juliette's face delighted Gaston to no end this early afternoon.

Pablo played his clarinet on the sand, lazily watching his friends having fun. Next to his tiny wooden chair, where he sat alone, lay a few magazines, two of them specializing in pop music.

He liked to keep a safe distance to anything that moved, people included, and he had no intentions to swim today, so he remained aloof, dressed in his chic big-city clothes.

Tentatively, he would later sneak out of this beach resort and drive his Citroën to downtown Montpellier, only six miles inland, where some night action might come handy.

Of course, he'd first drive Juliette and Gaston to Le Bateau Perdu on the quay after the swimming, so they could have dinner with Monsieur Douvier, as planned, after which he'd be free to get out of town. Juliette's grandpa would gladly drive them back to Alès. Done deal.

∾

For the next hour, the romantic couple played their silliness away in the salty, clear waters of Golfe d'Aigues-Mortes, recklessly riding the steep-breaking waves, crashing against each other in all sorts of crazy ways, and swimming without particular skills or aims. All the better! Horse-riding, Juliette on top of Gaston's shoulders, became their favorite pastime. Eventually, they ran back to their towels, where they stretched out on the sand next to a big rock.

Juliette lay down on her belly, accepting all the sunlight she could take, leaving only the area covered by her long, silky blonde hair, now wet, unexposed. She had a very nicely shaped body for her young age, plum rounded butts, and soft, lightly tanned back. In fact, her tiny orange-stripped bikini left little to Gaston's imagination.

While drying himself, still standing up, he continued to juicily observe his girlfriend's curves, marveling at her femininity. He himself looked pretty good for his age, he reckoned, slim frame and hard muscles—already turning other young girls' heads on the beach.

Flipping over, Juliette exposed her face and chest area to the sun. Gaston's curious eyes noticed a pair of nicely forming young breasts, barely covered by her skimpy bikini top.

"You know, lately I've been flooded with two kinds of weird dreams," he revealed, now making contact with her eyes. "Dreams about places and things I've never been a part of but Pierre swears I have...and dreams about places and things I know I've experienced but Pierre swears I never have."

"Use Pablo instead as referee," laughed Juliette.

She sat up straight on her towel and smiled apologetically realizing her comment had bruised his feelings.

Fifty feet away, Pablo couldn't hear. Plus he was practicing new sounds with his clarinet, his drowsy eyes nevertheless always on them.

Gaston tried to remain cool. Sitting down next to Juliette, he said, "They're not really dreams, they happen *anytime* during the day, like surreal visions, bearing strange messages...nothing natural."

"Hummmm..."

"For example, I had this terribly hurtful dream...or vision...recently," he began. "I was running with some three-hundred other students in the annual boarding school marathon in Hossegor, a sea village south of Bordeaux It was a race Pierre told me I was not supposed to be in because I was too young. He himself was running too. We were up in the mountains, steep mountains, full of pines, rocks, some snow. Somehow I'd managed to get in, and to everyone's surprise, I easily led the race from start to finish, proudly shouting my name to every teacher who clocked us at every stage of the race, beating everybody all the way to the top."

He paused dramatically. "Well, almost. Just four or five feet short of finishing the marathon, I was struck with a sharp pain under my ribs...that made me crouch and break into tears...as I watched every runner in the race run past me."

"A bummer–no question," said Juliette, screwing her lips into a bizarre pout. "But–"

"But what?" jumped Gaston, overexcited. "It was *intentional*, can't you see? *Something* or *someone* didn't want me to win!"

"God?"

"*No! Why would God ruin my day! There was no reason!*"

"Chill out, Gaston..."

"You know what? Pierre told me this event never happened. But I know it did. I'm *damn* sure it did."

"So...is he lying to you?"

"No, he isn't. I'm sure of that too."

"Well, I don't know what to say."

For a while no word was exchanged.

Noticing their silence, Pablo approached them casually. "How's everything going?" It was the catalyst they reluctantly needed to re-start their conversation. Soon they were back horse playing on the shore, tackling the waves, and kissing.

Pablo's clarinet played to the sunlight, to the balmy air, to the white sand. It also played to the fishing boats and yachts rimming the quay.

"Two ancient scroll messages, two kinds of treasures, three medieval castles, four spiritual missions, and the Legend of the Horse-Riding Kites," teased Gaston, now sitting next to Juliette on the sand, back to their base. "How does all this work?"

"You forgot the caves...or maybe I haven't mentioned them yet," teased back Juliette.

"Oh–excuse me."

Juliette became serious. "I wasn't able to find the ancient scrolls yesterday. My grandpa must have stored them in his safe. Sorry about that. I'll show them to you another day. But, for now, I'll tell you more about our mission since you—"

"I'm all ears."

"The Horse-Riding Kites mission was *one of four spiritual missions* planned on and created during the siege of Château de Montségur...so the four Cathars who smuggled out the spiritual treasure, before the surrender and burning, actually took with them these four missions," explained Juliette.

"To Château de Quéribis..." tried Gaston.

"Château de *Quéribus*..." corrected Juliette. "After spending some time in Grotte d'Usson, also in the vicinity."

"*There*'s the promised cave!" exclaimed Gaston.

"One of them."

"Actually, it was a castle," corrected herself Juliette. "My bad."

"Château d'Usson?"

"Right."

"So..." tried again Gaston. "This spiritual treasure from these four Cathars *re-appeared* in Château de Quéribus...split into *four spiritual missions*...the same year?"

"All we know is that the Château de Quéribus itself was under siege eleven years later, and that before this happened the Horse-Riding Kites mission had already began its journey northbound to Grotte de Calel...past Carcassonne."

"Cave—for sure?"

"Yes."

"Very cool," said Gaston. "And...the other missions?"

"I don't know. They moved differently through the centuries, followed other directions." Juliette paused. "I was chosen to focus on my mission only."

"*Centuries? Chosen?*"

"It's a commitment."

"What about your acting? The theater?"

"That comes second."

"You mean the Horse-Riding Kites mission comes *first?*"

"That's right."

"That's *horse shit*!" slammed Gaston, incredulous and very irritated. "That's *idiotic* and *addictive*!"

"Then let's not talk about it anymore—you *fool*!"

Above hovered Richard's soul.

FOURTH ATTEMPT ON GASTON'S LIFE

Pablo approached the unusually silent couple in the sand.

"Hey guys!–have you noticed you can rent bicycles or boats here–go off on a ride or sail along the quay?" he offered, sensing something was wrong with them.

"Or you can just join the strollers jamming the quayside street and visit some boutiques or cafes along the way."

He pointed to the crowded street with his clarinet. "I'd suggest the latter because we're running short of time. I'm sure you don't want to be late for dinner."

They agreed reluctantly, still angry at each other.

Soon they were lost in the array of walkers.

At an ice-cream stall they stopped to buy two cones loaded with vanilla, hers, and pistachio, his. Juliette was approached by a little boy of about five years of age as Gaston paid for the ice-creams.

The kid, barely reaching up to her tummy in height, also clad in a bathing suit, kept staring up at her with his mouth open and tongue hanging down. Next thing, and to their outmost surprise, he started licking one of her thighs.

"Watch out, kid!" Gaston shouted at him, kicking him away with his right leg.

The kid responded by returning to her thigh in a more demanding way, sticking his tongue out with a sick expression to his eyes, ready to lick again.

"Maybe he wants to lick my ice-cream," said Juliette, feeling sorry for the little boy. Bending down to his height, she offered it to him, expecting only one or two swaps of his little tongue. But to her surprise the boy yanked the whole cone out of her hand with a sharp jab and ran away with it.

"*Salaud*!" yelled Gaston, handing Juliette his cone ice-cream and running after him amid the hectic crowd. "I'll tell your dad so he can smack you hard, *petit voiyou!*"

Nearly caught, the little boy put the spilling cone on top of a cement fence facing the ocean, about two feet away from the nearest trash can.

Rapidly, Gaston grabbed what was left of the ice-cream, his hands full of it and dripping, his eyes traveling toward the disappearing kid in the multitude of beach strollers. "*Merde! Merde!*"

"Gaston!" a familiar voice called him from behind.

Swiftly, he turned around, watching Juliette end her trot behind him, laughing out loud, to his surprise.

A shot rang out.

"Did you hear that!?" exclaimed Juliette, worried.

"Yeah..."

Far away on the beach, people amassed by a mount of sand. Someone shouted in horror, "*Il est mort!*" (He's dead!) More desperate shouts followed. Soon a squad of police officers arrived, quickly scattering around with their guns drawn, staring in all directions.

The area where Gaston and Juliette stood, frozen in fear, had become a center of curious bystanders, growing in number by the minute.

"Let's get out of here!" Gaston said to Juliette.

༄

"Where's my ice-cream?"

"I ate it all—sorry," confessed Juliette with a little pout that turned into a sweet smile.

"How could you?" teased Gaston.

"It was melting too fast...but we can get another one."

"I really don't want any anymore."

So they ambled into town instead, meandering through a cluster of picturesque, tree-shaded, narrow streets, where alluring shops and boutiques lined the sidewalks.

"Are you thinking what I'm thinking?" said Juliette.

They were crossing a street, Gaston fighting off some of Juliette's blonde hair blown onto his face by a gust of wind.

"That the shot was meant for me?"

"Exactly."

"And the kid's odd behavior was part of the deal?"

"Exactly."

"It's just a thought," said Gaston, trying to forget.

"A shared thought," said Juliette.

❧

Window watching, they mingled with other beach strollers, some of them displaying sun burns. Lots of parents filled the sidewalks wearing funny hats and exotic summer shorts, their hands and shoulders loaded with cumbersome beach supplies.

"Look! Our boy is over there!" Gaston pointed to a street corner, way ahead of them.

"There's a lady with him...maybe his mom..." said Juliette.

"You know...she looks familiar to me," said Gaston, forcing his eyes to focus better. "I've seen this woman before."

By the time Gaston refocused, in the blink of Juliette's eyes, they both were gone.

It was a lost cause: too many people, too many unknowns.

They decided to forget about it.

The street alley they were on now took them back to the waterfront walk, where a sparkling white yacht could be seen darting by.

Gaston wanted to apologize so bad for his earlier stupidity when he'd insulted her and her obstinate drive to impose her religious mission over her acting career. He wanted to do it right away, but just couldn't get started. Likewise, Juliette, in silence, wanted him to accomplish the same. The feeling was mutual.

A small cage containing three gorgeous, playful kittens set on the flank of the promenade, provided the tools.

"Hey, let's watch!" burst out Juliette, all enchanted, pulling Gaston by the hand.

They joined a very excited crowd that had gathered around the cage, guarded by a sun-tanned lad much younger than Gaston. These little felines were not ordinary cats, they entertained beyond belief–leaping and charging against each other or deftly dodging their attacks with fascinating beauty and agility, sometimes pirouetting, somersaulting, and even creating unheard of wild acrobatics that were incredibly fun to watch.

Gaston and Juliette could not help but break into incessant and contagious laughter glued to the captivating kittens, totally oblivious of the outside world. So much, indeed, they themselves had become part of the show to other passers-by.

"Having fun?"

They both turned, recognizing the voice.

"We have to go now...sorry."

Pablo just added a friendly grimace.

◌◌

"I was thinking...if you like the ocean and the canals so much, we could come back another day. There's plenty to do here," informed Pablo, on their way back to the showers and changing rooms.

"Hey, that would be very cool," said Gaston, holding hands with Juliette, distracted by the scenic canal that crossed town.

"Have you heard of La Petite Camargue?"

They both shook their heads.

"It's only a few kilometers northeast from here, along the coast–or the canal, since they run parallel to each other." With his clarinet, Pablo pointed to a slowly cruising boat on the sumptuous canal. "I'd love to travel in one of those too."

"What about La Petite Camargue...what is it?" asked Gaston.

"It's an amazing place...lagoons...marshlands...full of pink flamingos, black fighting bulls, and wild white horses that look like unicorns."

"*Unicorns?*" both youngsters exclaimed in unison, stopping him on the march.

"Yeah. You guys could ride them next time."

"*Wow!*"

They made him promise next time would be soon. Very soon.

❧

Dutifully, Virginie dialed a number.

At the other end, in Zundo, the instrumental "La Mer" began to play on the ZCAP meter.

"Hello..." answered Master Judge, staring at the meter's flashing tiny lilac screen, revealing the call had crossed a millennium, precisely from Charcuterie Les Trois Maries, Palavas-les-Flots, France, 1955.

"C'est moi, Virginie."

"Bonjour."

As in previous occasions, she was embarrassed to report, in her heavy French accent that her team of spies had failed to kill Gaston. The bullet missed the boy by a hair.

"Remember what I told you last time you called...if you failed one more time?"

"Yes. Yu zaid yu'll giv me canzer."

"Good. Have a nice weekend."

Virginie twisted her lips as the phone line got disconnected.

Above hovered Richard's soul.

AN ANCIENT CAVE HIDING A SACRED RELIC IN GRANDPA'S OWN BACKYARD

"If I recall, we were talking about exchanging secrets last time we met," Monsieur Douvier addressed Gaston, who sat near Juliette. "You told me yours and I ran out of time to tell you mine."

Gaston nodded.

"Good memory, Grandpa."

They were enjoying the Palavas resort seafood cuisine offered by Le Bateau Perdu restaurant, only a few hundred meters from the sea on the azure Mediterranean shore where they'd swam with so much fun earlier in the morning.

The same area where they'd ventured into town barefooted, in their scanty bathing suits, past the beachfront ice-cream stands. Where they'd ambled, under shading trees, along canal-lined exotic boutiques, craft shops, and historic alleyways.

The same area where they'd been charmed to death by those three performing kittens on their way back to the waterfront promenade. And most interesting, the same area where a bullet most likely meant for Gaston had killed another person by mistake. So they'd truly been around on the Montpellier coast today.

Pablo had preferred adventuring into the big city with his old Citroën after dropping the young couple off at the restaurant, driving on Quai Paul Cunq. Downtown Montpellier was only minutes away.

Steering between stretches of sea and canals on a sand dune road, slightly pushed by Mistral winds, he'd decided to head for a jazz club he'd heard about in the area, but further toward the affluent suburbs. His clarinet lay on the passenger seat, just in case.

But he would stay there only a few minutes. His destination was a different one. In the same district, entertaining a special crowd too, but with contrasting aims.

∽

Pinching some baked sardines with his fork, Monsieur Douvier declared, "Long time ago...when I was quite young...I discovered something in my property. The rocky, brush area I hardly ever go to in the backyard...beyond the creek."

"What, Grandpa?"

Swallowing his sardines, the personable old man went on, "A cave."

"A cave?" repeated both youths, fascinated.

"I found it accidentally."

"How big?" asked Juliette.

"Quite big." He seized his bread, took a bite. "After clearing the entrance, I went inside and realized that it'd been occupied perhaps centuries ago. Paintings and messages on the walls by the Celts, the Visigoths, and other tribes."

"Awesome," exclaimed Gaston.

"Astounding," burst out Juliette.

She drank from her water glass and stared at Gaston, who probed his bowl of mussels. "Good?"

"Delicious."

The couple had agreed not to mention the shooting incident, neither to Pablo nor to Monsieur Douvier, unless definite evidence emerged in the news that Gaston was the target.

"Deep inside a corner," continued Monsieur Douvier, "covered with sediments of marlstone, sand, and clay, I found a blue box...small, rectangular...the size of a giant's shoebox." He ate a portion of his escargots. "Made of hard, durable material."

"Did you open it?" asked his granddaughter, pouting.

"Yes, slowly...painfully so...with a lot of struggle for it was stuck... stubborn and hard to detach." He dried his lips with the table cloth. "Reluctant to reveal its content."

"And?" said Juliette, bending forward, almost falling off the edge of her chair.

"It greeted me...sort of..." Monsieur Douvier's face turned strangely expressive. "How else could I see it?"

Juliette kept staring at him without chewing her food, which consisted of steamed Palavas eels and asparagus. "What greeted you, Grandpa?"

"An ancient relic."

"One of those religious objects?" tried Gaston, mesmerized.

"Yes. A bronze sculpted artwork...depicting three persons."

"Three? Who?"

Virtually suspended in air, Juliette held her breath.

"Jesus Christ...Mary Magdalene...and their baby," said the old man.

"Oh..." said Juliette.

"Wow..." said Gaston.

"Still in good condition...in spite of the many centuries it survived, buried and forgotten."

"Centuries?" gasped Gaston, incredulous. "How can you tell?"

"By its theme. It's a happy family gathering...by a fountain...in a garden...an artistic representation..."

"A piece of art," remarked Gaston.

"Based on the real thing," guessed Juliette, staring at her grandpa's approving eyes.

"How can you tell?" Gaston persisted.

"It's a first century made relic...by the famous sculptor Silvio Grasso, who also provided the boat."

"What boat?" asked Gaston.

"The boat in Alexandria, Egypt, that took Mary Magdalene and her loved ones to that beautiful place we call today Les Saintes Maries de la Mer...on La Petite Camargue coast, near Marseille."

"La Petite Camargue!" exclaimed Gaston. "Pablo mentioned it this morning. It's an awesome place!"

"Les Saintes Maries de la Mer!" that's exactly where Mary Magdalene landed in AD 40...pregnant with Jesus' baby," said Juliette.

Monsieur Douvier corrected, "Rather in AD 33...right after the Crucifixion..."

"So…they fled to Alexandria first?" asked Juliette, pouting.

"They had to."

"But Silvio Grasso sounds Roman, not Jew or Egyptian," remarked Gaston.

"He was a young Roman who defected. An unusual man with a big heart…who felt Mary Magdalene's pain and sorrow and knew he could help her escape."

"Must've been a harrowing experience," said Juliette.

Monsieur Douvier nodded. "But he had connections…camels waiting for them…a strong sailing boat ready to be boarded on a hidden shore."

"Wow…" exclaimed Gaston. "The two alone?"

"No, the whole entourage…the three Marys, Martha, Lazarus, Maximin, little Sarah, and others," said Monsieur Douvier. "Silvio, who became a Christian convert during the voyage, assisted Mary in delivering her baby three weeks after they landed in Les Saintes Maries de la Mer, not yet a village, just a shore…and reached Massalia."

"Massalia?" reacted Gaston.

"Yes, that's the way the Romans called Marseille in those days."

Monsieur Douvier put some bread in his mouth.

"Silvio delivered her baby? Jesus's baby?" Juliette was fascinated.

"Yes, he'd been a student of medicine before experimenting with art…and it went well." His eyes widened. "In fact, Mary named her baby girl *Sylvie* in his honor."

Gaston licked his fingers, drank some water. "How did they manage to get started here in our coast?" he asked, intrigued. "I mean…a foreign land to them."

"Silvio knew some Jews in Massalia and Narbo Martius–today's Narbonne–and Rhedae–today's Rennes-le-Château–who were glad to help, without drawing attention to themselves, since Romans also controlled these areas and Crucifixion news traveled fast," said Monsieur Douvier.

"Before splitting, Silvio made sure she was well received and taken care of by the Jewish community. He promised Mary he'd work on a special bronze sculpture dedicated to Jesus, Mary, and Sylvie–the three together–a holy gift to the world."

"I'm a little confused about something–why do you call the relic sometimes *relic* and sometimes *sculpture*? Aren't both the same thing?" Gaston asked Monsieur Douvier with a tinge of innocence to his eyes.

"No," replied Monsieur Douvier. "To be considered a *relic* , an object–that was part of, used or touched by, or very related to a saint or world revered person–must also be *venerated*, with proper documentation, by the Roman Catholic Church. Silvio's *sculpture*–the object I found in the cave—has not been venerated yet. It qualifies immensely to be venerated, of course, for it was touched by Mary Magdalene herself (now a sacred saint), who stands next to Jesus Christ (now a martyr and the Son of God himself, according to the Bible) and their daughter Sylvie...the sculpture itself created by an artist who not only knew the three of them, but also delivered little Sylvie."

"Wow..."

"So, although not yet venerated by the Church, because obviously it's still unknown to the world, its chances of one day being venerated is astronomically high...and so we can therefore safely among ourselves call it a relic, even a *sacred relic*."

"Wow..."

"But...on second thought...since what this sculpture or relic reveals is so unbelievably damaging to the Church–like shaking it from its very foundation–the chances that the Church will ever allow this to come to light is virtually zero. Not a chance. So it will never become a venerated relic...and we might as well fear for our own lives...if we ever try anything funny..."

"Wow...wow..."

A long, difficult pause followed.

"Who cares! Right?" exclaimed Juliette suddenly.

Monsieur Douvier laughed.

Then Juliette.

Then Gaston.

Above hovered Richard's soul.

ONLY 30 KILOMETERS TO
LES SAINTES MARIES DE LA MER

"Do you guys realize we're sitting here right now only *thirty kilometers* or so to Les Saintes Maries de la Mer?" announced Monsieur Douvier. He lifted his head with a certain vigor. "We could almost walk or swim up there!"

"Well, maybe you," laughed Juliette.

"I'll ride a white unicorn up there!" chanted Gaston.

"Yeah. Me too!" cheered Juliette, half-standing up.

They all chewed on their food for a moment.

Then Gaston asked Monsieur Douvier, "How do you know for sure it's them–Jesus, Mary, and Sylvie?"

The old man swallowed two escargots. "Because Silvio Grasso wrote their individual names *below each person* on the relic. It's obvious and unmistakable," he said slowly and clearly. "I'll show it to you at my first opportunity."

"Were they married?" asked Gaston again, one hand reaching for his handkerchief.

"Most likely." He sipped from his water glass. "I'm not really interested in marriage–I mean the institution of marriage. Companionship, yes. Having a baby, though, in those times, without marriage, was a very risky proposition."

Neither Gaston nor Juliette volunteered to comment.

"There was also a message from Jesus and Mary to the world," said Monsieur Douvier, with a tone that raised both Gaston's and Juliette's eyebrows.

"On the relic?" uttered Juliette, fervidly.

"Yes. Evidently, he knew, a day or two before being crucified, his baby with Mary was coming...and found a moment to jot down some

thoughts...which were slipped out of his cell to Mary by a secret fol-
lower during the night. Together with Mary's thoughts it became a
joint effort, on goatskin, for the world to know."

"What did it say?" asked Juliette, again holding her breath.

Monsieur Douvier searched his mind, then said, "Words of peace...
love...spirituality..." He paused. "...forgiveness...very deep thoughts..."
He vacillated a bit. "I couldn't weave these words the way they did.
Such a wonderful message." His face turned solemn. "One has to be a
prophet or a preacher to reach out, you know..."

"That sounds..." started saying Gaston, inspired.

"Beautiful..." added Juliette, raising her chin with eyes closed, producing the sweetest smile Gaston ever saw escaping her lips. "I think I
know how these words touch each other...touch the world..."

They sank into silence.

"But you know something?" Monsieur Douvier said, swiftly
catching their attention. "The blue box I told you about was mine. It
had been stolen from my attic years ago...and was I happy to find it
again!"

Perplexed, Juliette blinked twice. "If it was yours..." she said. "who
gave it to you? Or how did you happen to have it?"

Monsieur Douvier smiled blandly. "It's a long story." He stretched
his arms lazily, almost theatrically, like dismissing the question, but
actually revealing a growing tiredness.

"Yeah, who gave it to you?" Gaston insisted.

"Why do you still keep it in the cave?" Juliette asked, utterly
curious.

Monsieur Douvier showed both of them the palms of his hands
standing firm in front of his face like two towers. "Please...let me in-
hale for a minute." Watching their apologetic eyes, he composed himself. "No one but the old lady, Madame Rossi...and you guys...know
about it. She's approaching one-hundred years of age...fragile...deaf-
mute...lunatic...not expected to live much longer.

"The cave is a logical place to keep this treasure...better than my
attic. And it's terribly deceptive. For instance, you were sitting on it,
Gaston, the other day...without even knowing, huh."

"You mean...that rock beyond the creek...where me and Madame Rossi–?"

"Exactly. The cave's under the rock, camouflaged by the heavy brush and eroded layers of limestone. Its bizarrely shaped formations give way to subterranean life...with echoing flowing water...and–"

"Okay–we get it, Grandpa," interrupted Juliette. She thrust out her lips into a sulky pout. But...where in hell did you get this blue box that landed in your attic that this old quack stole and buried in this cave many years ago and now you don't want to repossess because it happens to be a good place to keep a treasure, Grandpa?"

"I knew you were going to hit me hard, sweetie," said Monsieur Douvier.

They all laughed, highly expectant, including the story teller himself.

"Let me surprise you bigger before we head back to Saint-Jean-du-Gard tonight. And promise me you won't ask me anything else regarding these matters while I'm driving. You'll have the full story next time we meet.

"It has to do with a young priest I knew long time ago, Abbé Bérenger Saunière, and his assigned village, Rennes-le-Château, in the foothills of the Pyrenees."

"We promise..." said jointly the young couple, seeing the surge of something intriguing to come.

"Is it a castle or a village...this Rennes-le-Chateau?" then asked Juliette, squinting one eye.

"Both, depending who you ask. It has enough in it to satisfy anyone," said Monsieur Douvier, wisely. "It used to be called Rhedae in Jesus time. Long before that, in its heydays, it was a striving city of thirty-thousand people. Now, almost forgotten, barely two-hundred or so live there. But let's focus for a moment on something no one's been aware of, not even me...until I did some meticulous research... and guess what?"

"What, Grandpa?"

"Well, you have to see the relic to realize what I discovered, what I meant when I said our secrets are connected." Monsieur Douvier ended his words staring intently at Gaston.

"You said that before, I remember," put in Gaston blandly, confused.

"How can this ancient relic be connected to Gaston and you, Grandpa?" jumped in Juliette.

"Simple. Mary Magdalene and Gaston are wearing the same ring."

"*WHAT!*" Exclaimed Gaston in half-horror.

"Microscopic evidence."

"*YOU'RE PULLING OUR LEGS, GRANDPA?!*"

"It's the same ring, absolutely, but in different times," explained Monsieur Douvier.

"Different *centuries!*" shot Juliette, twisting her lips.

"That's right."

Stupidly staring at each other, Gaston and Juliette could not, would not believe what had been revealed in this short but seemingly never ending minute.

"Let's hit the road now, kids!"

Marching toward Monsieur Douvier's regal French car—a sky-blue 1948 Delahaye 135MS Faget-Varnet Cabriolet—Gaston noticed two ducks making love on a nearby mud pond.

His fragile but fertile mind took it from there...

Above hovered Richard's soul.

PART 4

MIPHO'S DUBROVNIK, FORMER YUGOSLAVIA
ZUNDO, JUNE 3081

ALL GOOD—BUT WHO HELPED MARY MAGDALENE AND HER LOVED ONES MAKE IT HAPPEN IN FRANCE?

By a 13th Century-Built City Wall

Give me a break, Grandpa... thought Mipho, absorbing the old man's just spoken dialogue to both Juliette and Gaston in Palavas-les-Flots, former France, across a millennium or so. *Are you trying to unearth me? ...decode my existence?*

She opened her arms the widest she could in her newly acquired person, a lovely six-year-old spoiled brat from La Paz, Perú.

Pharaoh Richard Flynn is in deep trouble right now. Nothing I can do until he gives me a sign, she pondered, staring down at the exotic redness of unceasing rooftop tiles and ever-widening azure waters beyond.

What a sweeping view!

Her jet black, straight hair took a gust from the Jugo wind spanking the area. Precisely, the northern part of the gargantuan city wall where she bravely stood, feeling taller than the very tall stone wall that supported her, admiring the vast panorama, her back charming the steeply-rising Srd Mountain, between Fort Minceta and Fort Revelin.

I've climbed the Andean Mountains and crossed the Titikaka Lake several times...enjoying incredible sights, but this is awesome too...mighty awesome...in a different way...

Apart from the always-present historic architecture, both around and below the defensive city wall, there was plenty to see from above deep down the thriving, or sleeping, Old Town, depending where you looked and what time of day.

Puta!—look at these spooky, dark...endless steps...going down these narrow and sinister streets and alleys...all the way to and past this long, wide street crammed with walkers...

Later, she would find out she had just discovered, from her rising strategic position, the majestic Stradun promenade and its ghostly side streets making up the timeless and rewarding Old Dubrovnik.

Curiosity got the best of her at one point, focusing on a person in a distant tenement. *Mira!...desnuda y colgando sus pantaletas afuera de su ventana...* (Look!...naked and hanging her panties outside her window)

She could also see a girl chasing a cat, three boys kicking a soccer ball in an alley, a priest slowly climbing steep steps with a cane, and a young couple kissing behind a landing. *Ay Dios mio!...el tocándole sus nalgas...y ella disfrutándolo...* (Oh my God! ...he touching her ass-cheeks... and she enjoying it...)

Renewing her march on the elevated stone walkway, she laughed to the wind, happy to be covered with colorful shorts and jeans jacket over a nice lavender blouse. *Me naked? Nooooooo!*

She hurried a bit.

Okay, Monsieur Douvier, so you discovered that Mary Magdalene once wore and possibly owned my ring, she now reflected, dutifully. *You made the connection with Gaston's ring. That's interesting. But not genial.*

A flock of seagulls wandered overhead. Smiling, she followed their path in the sky with her eyes.

All you did was notice the ring on both fingers—Gaston's and Mary's...and realize they're the same ring...centuries apart, though.

She didn't say much mentally for a while, attracted by the stunning scenery around as she rounded the two kilometer elevated curtain wall walk, past Fort Bokar and the Convent of St. Claire...back to Pile Gate (west end) near the sea.

She could've exited, of course, via Ploce Gate (east end), and headed for Banje Beach, or the Old Port filled with pretty sail boats and luxury yachts.

Hummmm...I don't recall giving her my ring....My sister, Bast—who later became Mut, after the Greek invasion—maybe did. Climbing down to level ground and thinking, she reached the Big Onofrio Fountain opposite St. Savior Church, right at the western entrance to the Old Town.

She had a reason...they were both 'one'...or claimed to be 'one'...one embodied into the other...he he he....

Now she became fully aware she'd just started promenading on the polished cobblestones of Stradun, mingling with the crowd.

I've never shared rings or personalities with my sister or anyone. I've always been myself...well, except physical forms of myself...like now...

She smiled back to someone who'd smiled at her, past a little shop that sold postcards on the right corner of what appeared to be the beginning of an endless stone facade straight into the eastern recesses of the promenade.

I must give credit, though, to this handsome Roman artist...Silvio Grasso... who made that holy relic...dedicated to Jesus, Mary, and Sylvie...with such passion and precision one can even notice the inscription on Mary's ring...allegedly mine...

∽

All along, from the start of her journey today, she'd played tricks with bullies and adults who approached her asking for her parents, wondering why she would walk alone, herself so young and pretty. Then, bingo! She would smile and run to the nearest hiding place, like behind a door or a column or a food stand, and *voo doo voo*, she'd make herself disappear and reappear somewhere else, away from her attackers.

Of course Silvio was kind enough to provide the camels and the boat and his hands in delivering Mary Magdalene's little Sylvie...but who helped them cross the desert, cross the sea, and survive the new frontier from AD 33 till their deaths in Roman-occupied Gaul...today's coast of Languedoc in the south of France? Me, moi, yo, and myself—exceptional daughter of Ra!

Searching for stray cats, she now turned left on one of the up-climbing narrow streets, full of steep steps made of stones. The ones she'd spotted from the top of the curtain wall just one hour or so earlier. And to her amazement, she saw no trash or dirt on those stones. They were clean. "Quiri quiri quiri," she started calling out, wide-eyed and sharp at hearing. "Quiri quiri quiri."

It paid off. Three cats showed up.

She sat down on one step and caressed one cat after another full of joy.

Her long black hair mixed seamlessly with the only black cat she'd befriended among them. The other cats were white with gray or brown spots, but just as sweet and purring just as loud when she rubbed the area under their chins. *Good thing I'm wearing sneakers...looks like I'm headed for a very long, long walk...*

Minutes later, the cats gone, she pumped herself up, like Croatian tennis great Goran Ivanisevic, her own favorite, often did on grand slams, facing the big moment, "Dubrovnik, here I come!"

PART 5

CLASH #5—MUD WRESTLING
(A TIME TRAVELED CLASH)
FRANCE, LATE JUNE 1955

DEBATING RICHARD'S ALLEGED POETRY'S FILTH

Bermuda Revelation Park, Zundo, June 3081

Mud was on Master Judge's dirty mind this minute and the previous four. He'd just finished reading a graphic magazine filled with filthy sexual acts on a slimy pond frequented by ducks.

A pool of mud materialized on the Astral Floor when he flipped the main switch on the control panel after typing a bunch of instructions on his keyboard.

"Go bastards!" he boasted, cocky-eyed.

Timely enough, the big silver Sphere had descended all the way to its usual spot above everybody's head, spinning and flashing the current punishment Clash status:

> JUST COMPLETED: CLASH #4—MONSTER TRUCK RACING
> • OVERALL SCORE: JUDGES 3 DEFENDANT 1 • NEXT: CLASH
> #5—MUD WRESTLING

In a jiffy, it was gone, clearing the area for the combatants.

From either side of the newly formed stage entered the judge and the defendant, properly dressed for the Clash.

How was Master Judge able to change so quickly into this mud-specialty trimmed outfit from his gothic black cape, black gloves, and black pants trial tailored costume, no one knew. But there he was—flamboyant and ready for his tactical attack.

"CHEATER! CHEATER! NO HANDKERCHIEF ALLOWED!" yelled the crowd, noticing the object in the defendant's fingers—a dandruff duster.

"I'm afraid you'll have to get rid of it before we begin," uttered Master Judge.

"As soon as you get rid of your sun glasses," challenged Richard.

"Fair enough..."

In no time, past this compliance, they were at each other's throats in the warm, thick mud.

A zurbdog flew overhead giving the pilot a view of their individual red (the defendant's) and blue (the judge's) jump suits before they turned to mud color. Such details became also recorded on paper and tape.

Master Judge squeezed Richard's head with his right arm, pressing ever tighter. He would squash his brains, if he could. The man had so much disappointed him, even offended his intelligence, in their previous encounter, when he'd recited two of his most precious poems. Which turned out to be a pile of manure! "Ever tried substance?" he now asked him.

The defendant slipped away, discarding some of the mud stuck on his face.

"What do you mean? Substance abuse?" His hazel eyes lightened. "Yes, I have...of course..."

Master Judge tried to stand up, but his muddy butt didn't let him. He remained seated and sliding, looking up at the defendant.

"No, no, no. I didn't mean that! I meant meaningful poetry...larger poetry..."

Richard stayed back a little.

"Well, yes," he said happily. "Hear this one—

If you ever despair
Mail me your hand
I'll be glad to shake it
And even kiss it
What d'you think blackmail is for?

Without a hint, he attacked the judge ferociously, like a wild animal, hugging his chest with both arms, from behind. But his mud-covered arms little by little slipped out of it.

"Isn't this horribly short and dull?" questioned the judge, horrified at the quality of his poetry, but opting for diplomacy. "And—aren't you, Mr. Octillionaire, trying to bribe me somehow?" There was plenty of his ire in those spoken words.

"Not really–to both questions." Richard smiled, then kicked the judge in the groin.

Sea fans looking like stretched skeletal fingers from witches floated nearby, close enough for Richard to touch them. He could see a scuba diver scouting a chain of coral reefs, tropical fish, and other underwater creatures in the distance. Also a wall with deep fissures filled with sponges and ragged rocks housing a small octopus.

"Would you like to hear another one?"

Master Judge was in pain, crawling on his knees in the mud pit.

"Yes–but the last one!"

> **Ear banging**
> **That's it! I have no doubt**
> **When you write, I listen**
> **I mean, I hear**
> **My eyes don't see...**
> **Why should they?**
> **I'm not blind**
> **I'm just ear bland**
> **Please write, write, write**
> **Allow me to hear...a full melody's blast**

The judge got up. Swiftly, he charged onto Richard like a vicious bull, grabbing him by the neck.

"You surely know how to conjugate filth, eh?"

They both tripped down to the slimy floor.

"This is no filth, MJ. This is the way I see things."

Richard fought back the hand that tried to twist his neck in the pool of mud.

Master Judge turned on his back, making Richard's face sink fully and deeply into the mud. "No filth–eh?" he said cruelly.

Richard lifted up his soiled face and shook it vigorously side to side, seeing some of that slime fly around him. With mighty force, he detached from the judge.

"No filth," he said with conviction.

"Let's find out for sure. Let's consult the Obscenity Judge," proposed Master Judge.

But in a tricky way, he suddenly grabbed Richard's neck again with wrenching force, plying it like a hunk of metal, harder and harder, till the agonizing, choking sound of surrender from the defendant put an end to the fight.

The crowd went nuts in the six Stadiums. Standing up, they yelled, "BURY HIM! BURY HIM! BURY HIM!"

On its way down from the sky, slowly spinning, the big Sphere settled twelve feet above the spectators' heads, displaying the new trial status:

JUST COMPLETED: CLASH #5—MUD WRESTLING • OVERALL SCORE: JUDGES 4 DEFENDANT 1 • NEXT: CLASH #6—DUNKING TANK SPLASH

PART 6

LA PETITE CAMARGUE
FRANCE, JULY 1955

PABLO TEACHES GASTON REAL DEMOCRACY BEFORE HEADING FOR LES SAINTES MARIES DE LA MER

"Hi, I heard that you're the intellectual one around here..."

Pablo put down his clarinet to laugh, while hazily staring at Gaston and his bicycle from the log fence he sat on.

Gaston had just stopped by after pedaling around the farm community for a while. He missed Juliette, who'd just started rehearsing for a new play in Alès. And their planned trip to La Petite Camargue filled him with joy and blissful anticipation. But his pressing matter right now was to finish a school assignment regarding democracy.

"What are you up to, kid?"

Pablo was fresh from helping his brother Alfredo carry some bins of hay to one side of the farm after tending to the cattle and milking some goats.

"Do you know anything about tyrants? How do they affect a democratic government?" asked Gaston, pencil in hand.

Pablo rubbed one leg with his clarinet, as if scratching.

"School stuff?"

"Yeah..."

"A tyrant–usually a male–is a maniac with god-like delusions who rules a country with complete control, cruelty, deceit, and disregard for the constitution and the laws. He violates basic human rights everyday and doesn't give a damn what other leaders around the world think of him."

"He's bad."

"He's the rotten apple at the bottom of a barrel." Pablo collected more thoughts. "Very often a tyrant manages to steal and stash away, most likely to a Swiss bank, a big chunk of the country's wealth, and tries to stay in power for a lifetime, pretending he's democratic and good, protected by hundreds armed body guards, terror-causing secret police, and a humongous military force built to crush and conquer neighboring countries."

"He's evil."

"He's the scum of the world."

"How come he keeps on appearing in so many countries?" asked Gaston.

"Not in France—not since the end of the monarchy and the separation of state and church. Not in England since the monarchy became powerless—limited to cosmetic tasks and vanity endeavors—and the state and church also divorced for good. Not in the United States. Have you ever heard of a tyrant ruling America? No, never."

He rubbed his clarinet gently against his chest. "Tyrants can only emerge and succeed in countries with no democracy or very weak democracy...basically. Half-civilized countries with Middle Ages mentality. Some tyrants are so uncivilized they oppress their people down to Stone Age methods and practices, it seems." His reflective eyes seemed to search for space into which to lay his thoughts. "To have a democracy you must have a mature civilian government, not a military ruling establishment. A country's founding fathers' "Democratic Constitution" should never be changed, only amended, if necessary...and only by a careful, well-defined, and painstaking legislative process...allowed by such Constitution, not the whims of a tyrant or military junta, or the speculative mandate of a religious faith, which should have no place in government in the first place." A devout Catholic, Pablo said that with a grain of cynicism, remembering that Muslims had invaded and ruled Spain for 500 years—up to 1492, the year the Kingdom of Spain was formed, the Spanish Inquisition instituted, and Spain-sponsored Christopher Columbus' first voyage to the New World happened.

"Any king, supreme religious leader, president, prime minister, or ruler trying to *extend* his or her tenure in power by more than two successive terms—each one no more than 5 years or so–is suspect, if not guilty, of becoming a dictator or tyrant, no matter his or her excuse. Returning to power (after someone else's administration) to repeat such tenures makes anyone automatically a dictator or tyrant, and therefore shouldn't be allowed by the Constitution."

He paused, stirred by new thoughts. "Well, this would be ideal. But our world is still terribly old-fashioned and religion-driven and blindly capricious and many countries, like UK, Canada, Japan, Denmark, Monaco, Sweden, Belgium, Australia, Norway, the Netherlands, and others, as you probably know, insist in keeping their monarchies alive (as if the people they serve—correction!—the people they *look down on* and *manipulate* want or need that) by providing *limited* monarchies instead of *absolute* monarchies. They're constitutional monarchies, usually employing a parliamentary system of government headed by a prime minister. So the king and queen stay, if only to perform ceremonial duties, often involving silly and vain pageantry rituals."

He scratched one ear. "Absolute monarchies—where they *do* exist, in the form of revolving dynasties—can be as bad or worse than tyrannies and nearly as impossible to get rid of. It's a nation's total loss and tragedy to live under such oppressive, selfish, and abusive rule… where the common people are always forbidden to learn, let alone enjoy, the process of freedom."

Pablo enjoyed this moment, actually Gaston's undivided attention, as the boy usually steered away from deep conversation, unless Juliette started it being present with them. "Dictatorship and tyranny red flags are easy to spot in developing countries where greed for power, wealth, and possession are the only or ultimate reasons to govern. One thing is certain, as we speak, all countries in the world, except the few with strong democracies, have ongoing "would-be tyrants" plotting in secrecy to overthrow their governments. Such plotters may include their very active cabinet ministers, military generals, political party heads, and religious leaders."

"Wow…you surely know these things…" said Gaston, realizing the power of knowledge and the freedom to speak one's mind. "Our teacher, Ms. Leveque, mentioned three tyrants that almost destroyed the whole world–Hitler, Hirohito, and Stalin."

"She's right. There are others too that did a lot of damage…massacre entire villages…execute prominent intellectuals…just because they had different political opinions. Rulers like Mussolini, Franco, Salazar, Chiang Kia-Sek, and Kim Il Sung....ambitious to demolish, kill, torture, oppress, and seize absolute power...force a country into tyranny–the mother of all terrors and total corruption."

"*Assassin Franco!*" exploded Gaston.

"These tyrants or evil dictators," went on Pablo, ignoring the boy's emotions, "all fit the *delusional maniac scumbag* personality profile...and, sadly, there'll be new ones popping out and messing up our world... generation after generation...each time with more powerful weapons at their disposal...weapons of mass destruction."

"*That bastard Franco!*" tried Gaston again. "He's the one that executed my uncle and forced my auntie and half-a-million Spaniards out of Spain!"

"I know...we all suffered from him...and still do. The *cabron*'s still ruling Spain."

Gaston held his anger, remained silent, thinking.

"By the way," said Pablo, wishing to break up this grim discussion. "How's Juliette?"

"She's fine. Hanging out with her theater people...rehearsing..." His hand reached out for a handkerchief in his pocket. "A new production."

"I saw her briefly…this morning," stated Pablo. "From a distance."

"Riding her bicycle?"

"No. She was getting into Madame Clarice's car."

"Oh yeah–her mom always drives her to the theater...to Alès..."

"Madame Clarice's not her mom," said Pablo.

"What do you mean?"

He sensed he shouldn't have said that. Now it was too late.

"I thought you knew that."

"Knew what?"

Pablo's face turned somber.

"That...both her parents committed suicide..."

Gaston looked shocked.

"When?"

"When she was only three years old."

Gaston just stared at his face, his fingers fidgeting with a handkerchief he'd just pulled out of his pocket.

"Her grandpa raised her until she was about ten, then he paid a young woman he trusted, Madame Clarice Barré, herself a widow and childless, to continue raising her in her nearby farm...with instructions that Juliette be given all the freedom she wanted...in order to grow as an actress...a career she'd already started pursuing."

"Wow..."

"Madame Clarice knew Juliette's parents, knew baby Juliette, .so when tragedy struck, it all fit into place."

"Juliette never told me about it."

Pablo teased him. "You never asked, right?"

Gaston retreated into a sullen smile.

He returned the handkerchief to his pocket, staring at his bicycle, confused.

"I guess I should head back to my place...to finish my homework."

"Hey, you wanna play my clarinet?"

"No, not now, but thanks for everything."

He climbed on his two-wheeler and started out.

"Don't forget our trip to La Petite Camargue with Juliette this weekend."

"I won't."

Above hovered Richard's soul.

ACROSS MARSHY LAGOONS EMERGES PRINCESS JULIETTE OF OCCITANIA, SAYS TROUBADOUR PRETENDER GASTON OF ARAGON

Les Saintes Maries de la Mer

"I'll pick you up this afternoon at 4 p.m. sharp, same place. Don't worry about me and my clarinet. We'll be jamming like crazy with some friends in Coin-de-Mer Jazz in Aigues-Mortes. Beware of pesky mosquitoes and biting flies...also water snakes and birds of prey...they attack without warning," Pablo had said before driving away early in the morning.

Soon they could see why.

Cut in half by the Mediterranean-bound Petit Rhône river, between the historical towns of Aigues-Mortes and Les Saintes Maries de la Mer, La Petite Camargue extended all around in full mystery, like an exotic, unknown world rained down to exhaustion for hundreds of years by torrential river spills, thunder-clapping storms, and maddening sea tempests.

Such first impression—supported by what seemed to be the remains of a grand scale devastation, reflected in a surreal tapestry of swampy marshes, shallow saltwater lagoons, and desolate sand dunes—didn't last in Gaston's vulnerable mind. For sooner than expected he was exposed to the beauty of tall, swaying grasses, bamboo-like reeds, tamarisks, wild flowers, and the effortlessly gracious pink flamingos, not to say the wandering wild black bulls and white horses, among so many fauna and flora compositions.

Although he had told Juliette early on, "not exactly a land for lions and gorillas," deeply missing both wild animals, now he was sure, "elephants should love it here" and he just couldn't wait to watch them bathe freely and roll into those big pools of mud!

In the absence of such African ferocious beauties, two Camargue horses, acting as priceless replacements—all white like snow, long-maned and heavy-tailed—honored the landscape right now, walking side by side in a graceful, friendly pace, aware of being mounted by Juliette and Gaston, not the super skilled local herdsmen.

Each precious animal embodied a brand of muscular vigor, agility, and wisdom capable of wild feats only seen in regional festivals, such as those celebrated in May, July, and October each year, showing their prowess in local Arenas or helping reenact the legend-held landing of the Saints Maries and Saint Sarah on this coastal place. The latter drawing the largest pilgrimage of Gypsies in the world.

"They really look and feel like unicorns these Camargue white horses," remarked Juliette, holding the reins of her rented one in its gracious walk, her butt filling the saddle. "Good thing they're tamed now...easy to ride on."

She was clad in tight beige corduroy pants and light green spring jacket. Her black leader boots shone inside the stirrups.

"They say they used to be wild..." uttered Gaston, keeping pace with his girlfriend's. He wore a similar outfit, including riding hat, at her request.

She'd proposed they both look like twin sisters before leaving Saint-Jean-du-Gard this morning in the Citroën, Pablo driving. Gaston still believed she'd only teased him with the idea. Less so when she'd also procured his riding boots.

"They're wild and free like us...*yooo-hoooo!!!*" suddenly cheered Juliette with zest, leading the horse into a trot. "They roam these wet-lands without purpose or care...*yooo-peeee!!!*" She could feel strands of her long blonde hair whipping the back of her riding hat with the surging wind, making it rattle a little.

"I'm having all the fun in the world...*yooo-pee-o-yooo-pee-aaaa!!!*" chanted Gaston, catching up with her, contagiously overtaken too.

"And they're of Arab descent...from Saracen times. That's why they're shorter than regular French horses...*yooo-hoooo!!!*" cheered Juliette again, feeling sillier than ever. "Maybe I'll ask my grandpa to get me one. They're really cool."

"*Get two!*" shouted Gaston, visualizing both of them riding side by side in front of a fantasy castle, amid millions of lilac-hued flowers and jumping frogs.

Some obstacle on the road made the couple slow down their horses to a walking pace again. Turning to him, she gave that green-eyed *femme fatale* look that's supposed to melt men down to vapors. "Aren't you going to ask me about the Legend of the Horse-Riding Kites?"

Gaston appreciated what he saw instead—a more-dangerous-yet *fille fatale* look that challenges young boys to fight for a treasure. "I was just about to do so, My Lady. What else but surrender to the temptations of your mission, the sacrifices and endurance they entail?" he braved, chin up, noticing her full, carmine-red, mischievous pout.

"Shall I then begin to *raconter*–?

"Shoot!"

But she galloped away from him instead without warning at incredible speed on her pretty white horse.

"Juliette! Juliette!"

Having returned the rental horses to a farm near Les Saintes Maries de la Mer, they now trudged the spooky reed-covered land on foot, occasionally swayed by juniper trees, wild irises, and tamarisks.

"What do you make of what my grandpa said the other day...about your ring being the same Bast wore in 4000 BC?"

"The ancient Egyptian Goddess? That can't be true."

"The same Mary Magdalene wore in the first century...as shown in the relic Grandpa keeps in the cave...in his property?"

"Impossible."

"I wouldn't use such strong words. I don't recall Grandpa ever being wrong...scientifically."

"I'm not sure this is science."

They lapsed into silence, became more aware of their environment after sighting a beaver surfacing in the muddy water near them.

"So...your legendary mission reached Grotte de Calel, you said, past Carcassonne, heading north...from Château de Quéribus," probed Gaston, bringing back the old subject, with a surge of new energy, "Am I right, Lovely Princess Juliette of Never Forgotten Occitania?"

There was plenty of theatrics in the way he said it too, one hand placed to his chest amorously, evoking a 13th century chivalry-and-courtly-love touch.

"Yes, my Charming Ever Heroic Troubadour Pretender Gaston of Aragon," said she, turning to face him. "But who told you about Occitania, may I ask?"

"The books that I've read lately with burning passion, the songs that I've heard and made my own, Lovely Princess of these Wild and Mysterious Lagoons...now spreading before us," he said grandly, continuing his romantic offering.

"Now—you're mixing things up—you silly boy! There's no space for *wild and mysterious lagoons* in Occitania, but lush greenery in steep rising mountains filled with pines, castles, rocks, churches, and wolves—all mistaken for bewitching waterfalls!"

"*Mais qu'est-ce que tu me racontes,* silly girl? *Est-ce que tu a oublié tes racines?*"

⁂

They marched on in suspended silence, Gaston's mind buzzing with the elements of a singular, all-embracing question:

"Explain to me, Juliette, how this horse-kite-driven mission through timeless Languedoc...over centuries gone by...loaded with ancient secrets troubling even to the present world...works?

"Wait...*hush...*"

They had quietly approached a strip of sand bounded by lumps of underbrush, lavender, and glasswort, hoping to watch in close proximity the pink flamingos that feasted on small fish. Juliette had already planted her feet into the slushy floor, holding her leather boots with her hands—danger thus taking second place to vanity.

Softly stirred by Mistral winds, a large pond of salt water extended in front of them like a seductive mirage. Scores of long legged birds with bizarrely looking long necks and wide intense eyes strolled elegantly across the water.

For a gratifying long moment, the young romantic couple just stood there, half-crouched, half-breathing, observing these amazing birds. Other birds, like herons and ibises, in assorted shapes and colors, gave them company.

"...*shhhh*..." voiced Juliette with a cautious but sensuous pout. "...look at those...black headed...yellow legged...scarlet winged...purple necked creatures..."

"...some have slender billed gulls..." whispered Gaston, hearing the loud croaking of frogs behind him.

They moved out of the way in a hurry when Juliette spotted a large, brightly blue colored eel swimming close to their feet.

Above hovered Richard's soul.

THE REALITY OF JULIETTE'S 700-YEAR-OLD MISSION BLOWS GASTON'S MIND

"Juliette, how does your mission work? Tell me now, please..." asked Gaston again, always intrigued by her elusive behavior.

"Look up!" Juliette pointed to the top of a tall, slender tree, showing plenty of bare skin and hardly any leaves. "You see it?"

"See what?"

"The white stork...next to his nest!"

"I see it..."

Juliette was right. The big bird merited special attention. Sticking out from the fluffy ruff of white plumage that covered his head, neck, and body, Gaston could discern a straight pointed red bill apparently saluting them with a loud machine-gun-like rattle, making his black wing feathers dance in concert.

"Well done, pal!" saluted back the boy.

"Let's walk a bit. I need space to tell you these things," said Juliette.

In front of them lay a solitary patch of wet sand flanked by daisies, asphodels, and wild rosemary, which they quickly left behind. Near a pond filled with toads and tadpoles, she slowed to a stop, as if touched by the grace of reason. She stared sweetly into his curious, hazel eyes, the loose brown curls of hair teasing his ears.

"We learned how to build kites with long tails to specific measurements, using thin branches, simple paper, glue, and cloth. We made our kites roar with passion by design," she said importantly, marching on again.

A throbbing sound coming from the left where they stood made them turn their heads swiftly.

"Swans!" exclaimed Juliette.

Gaston's ears took a good fill of their palpitating wingbeats. "Oh... we scared them," he cried out, following their low-flying escape with his guilty eyes.

Juliette went on describing her mission, the intricate placement of scrolls on kites, "We inserted each one, tightly rolled, into a thin wooden tube the size of my pinkie, sealed at both ends. We placed the two tubes containing the secret scrolls carefully side by side on top of each kite." Proudly, she added, "That's how we were trained to do it."

"Wow...wow..." Gaston was amazed.

"The first loaded kite ever launched reached only a short distance on its way to Grotte de Calel, several hundred kilometers north of Château de Quéribus. Physical obstacles, bad weather, and sickness got in the way," she said, cautiously adding one detail after another.

She waved hello to a passing group of cowboy-looking horse riders, two of them carrying long poles. They wore wide-rimmed black hats and tight leather pants.

"Our written rules specify that only qualified thirteen-year-old horse-riding girls are to fly the kites from point to point, unless dictated by urgent circumstances. These points or destinations are assigned castles, caves, and village homes throughout Languedoc via an already established route," she explained methodically, surprising Gaston with her knowledge and seriousness.

"You're really something, Juliette!"

As she plodded next to Gaston, soothed by the constant sound of cicadas, her gaze drifted toward a mound of tall, waving grass, behind which loomed a bunch of low, whitewashed, windowless huts with thatched roofs. "They must belong to those herdsmen we've just passed," she said, then shifted her thoughts back to the details of her mission.

"Have you noticed," exclaimed Gaston. "All of them have a raised cross at one end of the roof."

"Yes, they do. Religion's everywhere in France...especially Roman Catholic."

She watched Gaston kick a small rock that lay there near the edge of the road with his boot, and continued delineate the tenets of her mission.

"Selected, trained monks with verifiable Cathar descent–by old documents or convincing oral testimony–are to dispatch and receive the horse-riding kites at each destination, thanking the heroic mounted girls finishing their rides," said Juliette, as if delivering well-rehearsed lines on stage, unabashed. "Cathar monks are also to welcome–at each destination or between destinations, if impeded by major accident or misfortune–the new, on-call mounted girls. Secret scrolls removed from the kites are to remain in each destination site as long as deemed safe–days, months, years, even centuries, if needed."

She threw Gaston a strange stare. "Watch the quicksand!"

Swiftly, Gaston dodged what seemed to be a simple pond filled with slimy water. Rather than test it, with a leaved branch or something, he marched on whistling.

"New scroll-loaded kites and fresh horses are to be available at each destination site within hours. Sooner if left stranded in a dangerous or questionable place between destinations," she said, firmly. "The overall journey is expected to last two dozen centuries or more. Such is the mission of the Horse-Riding Kites!"

"Wow...wow...wow..." Gaston was totally overwhelmed.

"Should we now spy on the wild black bulls?" she said with an edge to her voice, turning around. "I've seen some grazing in the vicinity."

"Wait! Wait!" he shouted after her, grabbing her by the hand. "That's immense!"

"It's a secret I should've never revealed...not even to you," said the young actress.

"Who else knows it?"

"Only my grandpa."

"I'll never tell anybody," said Gaston. "Never."

"Promise?"

"Promise."

They hugged tightly, then kissed.

"Did your mission ever reach Grotte de Calel?"

"Oh yeah...in 1275..."

"Are you *shitting* me?"

"Gaston, you shouldn't use these words! The dictionary is full of *clean* ones that do the job just as good or even better!"

"Are you kidding me?"

"Well said," approved Juliette. "No, I'm not kidding you."

"That's almost *seven* centuries ago!"

"I just explained to you a while ago that things can get very slow in our mission. But we always move forward... undeterred."

"I bet you do."

They renewed their march.

"It might surprise you to know that we've gone places since that difficult beginning. Places like Cordes-sur-Ciel, after a one-hundred-twenty-five-year rest in Grotte de Calel. Brousse-le-Château, after hiding for three-hundred-eighty years in Cordes-sur-Ciel."

"Hiding...the two scrolls?"

"Well, yes. I'm not made to live that long." She laughed, making him laugh too.

She pushed some hair out of her face, reacting to the breeze. "Our mission didn't feel it was safe to get our young girls out there riding horses. There were just too many incidents during that time reported in the press, and also by word of mouth, about Roman Catholic Inquisition agents doing secret searches in the region, specifically in this village. We were not about to let our young girls to be burned alive at the stake by those papal predators!"

"Amazing job!" said Gaston. "I bet you it was a big inspiration to Anne Frank during her hiding ordeal in Nazi-occupied Amsterdam." He could be so naive at times, lacking the scope, timing, and proportion of historical events.

"It might have...if she *knew* about our mission."

"Too bad it went bad for her. Secret informants were able to hunt her down in the end."

"We were luckier, in spite of the secret searches, and our girls finally rode off one day safely...to the next destination."

Gaston stopped to reflect, make sense out of everything. "So...this is hard to believe..."

"What is?"

"I'm trying to picture a millennium-long, horse-riding, kite-flying relay marathon...carried out by thirteen-year-old school girls...with an ancient-based mission so important the Roman Catholic Church might freak out and be broken forever?"

"Yeah. You've got it pretty much figured out," said Juliette, halting on her walk to applaud.

"Thanks," said Gaston oddly. "No offense, but this sounds like a real fairy tale."

"Any different than what you read in the Bible?" said Juliette.

"Well..."

Above hovered Richard's soul.

ON STANDBY ALERT FOR THE GALLOP
TO GROTTE DE TRABUC

Gaston remained thoughtful, staring at the watery land and naked dunes stretching ahead. "But I thought you were religious...Cathar-like," he said to Juliette, seeing a disconnect with what she stood for and the strict, deeply immersed nature of the Bible, which he, by contrast, coming from a different background, was at liberty to dismiss as a bunch of exaggerated and largely rooted on legends and fairy tales fabrication.

She renewed her march.

"Cathar-*derived* is a more appropriate word—here's where I depart from the mold. Cathar-like or Cathar-based is too confining, even though this religion is great for women."

"They're more accepted, right?"

"They're *totally* accepted and treated equally to men at every level...all the way to the top. No men's club superiority here. If Cathars had Popes, they would've had women Popes and in great numbers. There's no reason in the world why Roman Catholic Popes have excluded women from this post! Not only it's wrong, it's insulting and condescending!"

"I fully agree."

She retreated a bit to her core thoughts. "I've picked up a few things from Cathar philosophy, things I can believe in and practice in my personal life, but I'm not dead-dedicated or brainwashed silly like most religious people are. I see with clear eyes, clear mind."

"So why? Why this nearly impossible mission?"

Juliette slapped a bug clinging to her ear.

"Because it was unique in the history of mankind, in what it tried to accomplish. Perhaps the last opportunity to uncover the truth about what kind of relationship Jesus and Mary Magdalene had, whether a baby was born out of this relationship, whether Jesus was divine or mortal like the rest of us–a big deal."

Gaston kept nodding with his head, walking at her side, watching the profile of her precious face.

"What other places have these horse-mounted thirteen-year-old girls flown their kites to?" then asked Gaston, curious, imagining naughty things.

"Oh, La Couvertoirade–a former Knights Templar stronghold. The Grotte des Demoiselles, and the yet-to-be-nailed Grotte de Trabuc." She pouted.

"Trabuc? Sounds familiar."

"Yep. It's close to Saint-Jean-du-Gard. You probably heard Alfredo or Pablo mentioning it."

"Wow. The mission's moving in our direction. Close to our hometown," said Gaston in wonder.

Juliette caught the oddly rising smile in his lips.

"You mean *the horse riding girls*, right?"

"*You are* my horse riding girl."

"Oh thanks, horse riding boy."

They kissed, barely stopping on their walk.

"Funny, we're not even riding horses right now," said Gaston.

"We did for one hour, silly boy. Before we started spying on the wild birds," she said, teasing him. "You're actually getting good at it. Almost as good as the *gardians* we saw a while ago."

She was referring to the Camargue cowboys, spectacular horse riders known to manage the herds of wild horses and bulls in these wetlands. The same ones who lived in the windowless shacks or *cabanes* they'd also left behind.

"You just want a bigger kiss than the one I just gave you, huh, silly girl," said Gaston, showing off, removing both riding hats from their heads. Turning to face each other, they tenderly made it happen.

Over their shoulders, distant egrets and swallows dove into the salty lagoons. Eastbound flocks of wild ducks, inland, crowded a pond rich with small fish, frogs, and turtles.

Saying foolish things to their ears, now sitting on a fallen tree by the border of a pond, the couple relaxed lazily.

"In what way are you *personally* involved with the mission?"

Hat in hand, she remained serene momentarily. "My turn might be coming. It depends," she then said, filtering a bunch of thoughts. Her other hand started to caress strands of her long hair, delicately. "I'm in the monk's standby list to horse ride and fly the kite carrying the scrolls from any point after Grotte des Demoiselles to Grotte de Trabuc."

"Wow...unbelievable..."

Juliette crossed her legs, watching Gaston play with his handkerchief. It made her smile.

"My grandpa's in constant touch with the monk...and the latest news regarding the mission."

"Anything new happening?"

"News come every day...sometimes every few hours. I must be on alert all the time," she said calmly. "A girl named Danielle is already on the run...from Grotte des Demoiselles."

"Horse riding?"

"Yes. She's on her second day. But..."

"But what?"

"She's experienced some problems already..."

"Is she late?"

Juliette laughed.

"We've been on the road for over 700 years...so we get somewhere when we get somewhere. Whenever it happens. There's no delay, no timing, no hurry."

"That's cool, very cool."

Juliette checked her wrist watch.

"We'd better get going or we'll be late!"

They laughed hard and long.

But first, they immersed into a powerful embrace.

Not the best moment to bring a negative comment, but he felt he needed to. "I'm sorry about your parents...your real parents. Pablo told me about it a few days ago."

She pulled a bit away from his embrace, surprised, searching his eyes with hers. *The nerve of Pablo to spoil everything for me!* she thought angrily.

Before she could say anything, he spoke again, and it was the warmest, sweetest string of words she'd ever heard from him: "It won't change anything...I love you..."

As they were leaving, a flock of mean mosquitoes attacked them. Swiftly, they put on their hats and began to go crazy, wildly dancing around and slapping their bitten cheeks and foreheads and necks.

Ridiculously laughing and shouting obscenities, they fled the area, running in the direction that would take them back to Pablo.

Above hovered Richard's soul.

PART 7

SORTING OUT THINGS IN AND AROUND LA SORBONNE, PARIS FRANCE, JULY 1955

FROM EMINENT LECTURER
TO SMALL TOWN JEWELER

3 Months Later...

Université de Paris-Sorbonne

Marcel Douvier stared at the audience.

"Last question," he said.

Someone in a back row raised his hand.

"All this stuff you've been telling us, which sounds like high fantasy, but it's not, because it really happened, or we assume it did, comes mostly from *you* and *your private library*, right?"

"Right," answered Monsieur Douvier. "Ten years of university's brainwashing and my beloved collection of cherry picked naughty books." He paused to let the audience finish their sudden burst of laughter.

Detaching his frame a little from the podium, he said, "A great deal is also based on speculation, and we have to be highly skeptical... about what to accept and reject...what to believe..."

His small gray eyes danced briskly. "But remember, believing in something is just a personal choice—call it mental or spiritual, sane or insane, valid or invalid—nothing more. It certainly doesn't deserve a burning alive at the stake if it happens to be different than what someone else believes in. Should we shoot half of the world for not believing like I do that I'm handsome?"

He drank from his water glass, fielding more laughter with his teasing eyes behind his spectacles.

"We speculate when we don't have the facts...we exaggerate when we don't like the facts...and we lie when we don't care about the facts. This is called anarchy...exactly what we *shouldn't* be doing. Thank you."

Students, professors, and special guests started to head for the doors after a resounding applause that lasted over two minutes. This in spite of his insistence at the start of his lecture, his last, that he strongly preferred a quiet departure from the Sorbonne, meaning to everyone that it might render him too emotional.

It did.

Drying his eyes and spectacles with a handkerchief, Monsieur Douvier recognized two faces in the audience, what was left of it after the multitude had emptied the long curved rows of seats: his grand-daughter and Gaston.

"We loved your lecture!" Juliette exclaimed, squeezing herself into his chest for his big hug.

To both, he said, still a bit excited, "Thanks for being here. It's an adventure in itself finding the right building, the right hallway, and the right auditorium."

"Gaston was my guide," Juliette proclaimed, giving the young boy a look of extra importance.

Politely, Gaston shook hands with the distinguished old man. "As usual, we love your sense of humor."

"You never take me seriously—do you?"

Gaston smiled hugely. "I do...really."

"I'd like to walk a little, stretch my legs. Would you join me?"

"Of course," both said in unison.

Closing the door behind him, Gaston read the top lines of a flyer pinned to its wooden surface:

MARCEL DOUVIER
DOCTEUR EN PHILOSOPHIE
AUTEUR ET CONFÉRENCIER ÉMINENT
CENTRE INTERNATIONAL D'ETUDES D'HISTOIRE ANCIENNES,
D'ARCHÉOLOGIE MÉDIÉVALE ET DES LÉGENDES JUIVES

∾

"Grandpa, did you break your promise of *not* giving anymore lectures? I mean after five years of silence...working as an obscure local jeweler?"

"No. This is my very last...booked long time ago. I'm still alive." He looked to one side. "I didn't somersault back to the limelight and lure my critics, enemies, and sociopaths to do silly things against me...like shoot me." He laughed. "I think I've become irrelevant, news-unworthy."

He walked faster, exited the building ahead of Juliette and Gaston. "I had accepted the invitation to speak here about three months ago... only because it's my Alma Matter. The Sorbonne is responsible for making me who I am, what I've become...and I felt I owed them this favor. Starting tomorrow I'll go back to obscurity...to being just a simple small town jeweler." A little smile escaped his lips. "Nothing wrong with that."

They were now strolling down Rue Victor Cousin past Place de la Sorbonne, heading for Jardin du Luxembourg. So they turned right on Rue Soufflot and continued straight up past Place Edmond-Rostand, where Boulevard Saint-Michel meets Rue de Médicis, getting more and more casual with their chat, while peeking at the attractive windows of the many and varied shops, boutiques, and bookstores lining the streets. Droves of artists, writers, and musicians filled the sidewalks. Europeans, Asians, Africans, Arabs, Jews—a *mélange* of ethnicities and cultures.

They crossed to the gardens side of the square and penetrated the first geometric array of trees, flowers, paths, alleys, and statues. By now their chat had turned quite trivial and funny.

Precisely a terrific moment for Juliette to ask a difficult question. "Where did you get the blue box, Grandpa? You know, the one with the ancient relic?"

Monsieur Douvier had expected the question all along and fielded it this way, from a park bench where he sat down to rest, his old age catching up with him:

"Long time ago, when I was about thirty, I met a priest who'd been assigned to the parish of Rennes-le-Château...a tiny hilltop village near the Pyrenees...not too far from Château de Quéribus," he began slowly, inhaling with gusto the sweet aroma of garden flowers. "I think I told you something about it already...in Palavas..."

"Not much really," said his granddaughter, pouting.

"His name was Bérenger Saunière, in his mid forties, physically strong and passionate about his parish. He'd gotten very rich very quick without much of an explanation to the Church and his critics."

Both Juliette and Gaston joined Monsieur Douvier in the bench, intrigued.

"To make a long story, full of twists and spins and controversy, short, Abbé Saunière became a sort of fan of me and my work, showing up to a few of my lectures," he said. Looking at both side of his head and waiting for some approaching walkers to clear the area, he went on, keeping his voice low, "Saunière personally told me that he'd found a huge fortune...the coveted Cathar treasure...buried in his church."

Juliette guessed, "The material treasure...slipped out of Château de Montségur."

"Yes. Except for one ancient relic...so beautiful and finely crafted— by Silvio Grasso, one of the most admired Roman artists of the first century—"

Juliette interrupted, "—the same man who provided the camels and the boat and even delivered Mary Magdalene's baby...after landing in Marseille."

Gaston added, "Yeah, little Sylvie."

Monsieur Douvier exclaimed, dumbfounded, "Have I told you all these things? I swear, I cannot remember what I said last week anymore. How much I said...my age. It's kind of scary."

Juliette patted his shoulder, flashed her big brand of smile trying to comfort him, "Don't worry, Grandpa. Nobody's going to know about it. Only me and Gaston."

He looked at Gaston, who was also smiling. "How old are you, kid?"

"I'll be ten soon."

"A very bright, mature ten," praised Monsieur Douvier. Holding both kids' hands, he said, "You guys are fine people...I feel better already..."

Above hovered Richard's soul.

GRANDPA NAILS THE CATHAR TREASURE MYSTERY STARTED IN CHÂTEAU DE MONTSÉGUR

"What else did the priest tell you, Grandpa?"

"Oh...he told me that he'd used the material treasure...lots of gold, silver, and precious stones...to renovate the decaying St. Mary Magdalene church, which had been in existence for centuries...built by the Visigoths...later occupied or protected by the Cathars, then the Templars..."

"Wow..." gasped Gaston. "This Mary was so popular, I tell you..."

"You'd wish you'd met her, don't you..." teased Juliette.

"Of course."

"Now—let's put things into perspective," said Monsieur Douvier. "*La Madeleine* lived in the *first* century. Rennes-le-Château's church was dedicated to St. Mary Magdalene, to serve only the village's noblemen, in the *11th century*, on a Visigoth's Arian Christian structure dating from the *5th century*, then on a Carolingian's Christian superimposed structure dating from the *9th century*..."

"That's a mighty long time...since *La Madeleine* landed in Marseille..." uttered Gaston. "Looks like every invading tribe took over and rebuilt...imposing its own structure, religion, and rules on the church's site. And why not serve the entire village?"

"Hear this. Previously, there was another smaller church nearby called St. Pierre, serving Rennes-le-Château, formerly Rhedae, from the *8th* to *14th centuries*, when it was sacked. Little is known of its restructuring and rebuilding history, if any. Except that parts of it appear to be buried under an adjacent building. Afterwards, the large St. Mary Magdalene church became the defining and sole serving village church."

"Very confusing and mysterious past," said Juliette with a twisted pout.

Monsieur Douvier continued, "Apparently, the aging St. Mary Magdalene church was restored at least a couple of times several centuries before Abbé Saunière got around repairing and renovating it again late in the *19th century*."

"Wow. Almost twenty centuries since Mary Magdalene left the Holy Land...since the Crucifixion" said Gaston.

"Unreal..." said Juliette.

"That's right," said Monsieur Douvier. "But related to these mysterious events is the even more mysterious Cathar legacy...regarding an ancient treasure. Some call it the Cathar Treasure, others the Holy Grail Treasure. All I can tell you is what I know...and it's damn mystifying..."

❧

"Apparently, the Cathars were in possession of a mind-boggling treasure in the 12th century, which they were forced to surrender in the 13th century because of papal's and French royal troops' persecutions. It was the last phase of their total annihilation from this planet...and the surrender of all their lands, particularly this treasure," explained Monsieur Douvier.

"What was this treasure about?" asked Gaston.

"A material treasure—gold, silver, and precious stones—offered or stolen from *first century*'s Jerusalem or *other century*'s place...belonging to who knows who and why...and a spiritual treasure that in itself could destroy the Roman Catholic Church if divulged to the world."

"Wow...wow..." It all seemed to eco back from somewhere.

"Like I told you the other day, Gaston," said Juliette.

"Yeah...one material and one spiritual." No wonder.

The old man reflected on their level of knowledge, their advanced curiosity. Evidently, Juliette had been breaking her boyfriend quite significantly into her mission—more likely a good thing, considering his charming personality and good intentions. Plus the ancient ring's connection to—

"But please continue, Grandpa," pleaded Juliette. "You have more insight into this matter than we do."

"Yeah, continue," urged Gaston.

Monsieur Douvier smiled gently, staring at his intelligent granddaughter, then at the boy prodigy.

"The Cathars took the treasure to Château de Montségur as a last resort, hoping to find behind its mighty walls over the mountaintop a secure and final refuge," he continued. "But they were betrayed by some local climbers, who helped open a lateral gate...nearly a year after the siege began...and so a short time before their imminent surrender to the ten-thousand papal and royal troops camped out at the bottom of the mountain, they formulated a plan to smuggle the treasure out during the night."

"Wow..."

"Juliette can tell you all about it, if she hasn't done so yet, but my side of the story has to do with Rennes-le-Château, where a handful of Cathars managed to transfer the material treasure during the night, weeks before the stronghold's March 1244 surrender."

Monsieur Douvier sank into a long thoughtful pause, then went on, "The spiritual treasure has a spin of its own. In a way it's like a twin-brothers or twin-sisters legacy. Two unequal but related parts that cannot function well if apart from each other. So half of the spiritual treasure is a relic, sculpted by Silvio Grasso, with two ancient sacred messages...and the other half is two scrolls carrying the same ancient sacred messages..."

"One from Jesus and Mary Magdalene, and the other one from their six-year-old daughter Sylvie, a French girl," said Gaston joyfully.

"Excellent," congratulated Monsieur Douvier, exchanging sweet stares of approval with Juliette. "What's interesting is that for some reason the relic wound up in Rennes-le-Château...associated with the material treasure, while the two scrolls wound up in Château Quéribus... rightfully associated with the spiritual treasure. But the two—relic and scrolls—are meant to be together...and should."

"Thank you, Grandpa..."

"And the scrolls mission is only one of four spiritual missions launched from Château Quéribus after the Cathar surrender," added the distinguished archeologist.

"*Yeah—my mission!*" cried out Juliette.

"*The Legend of the Horse-Riding Kites!*" declared Gaston.

∾

It was Juliette's tormenting idea to apologize moments later for their lack of sensitivity in neglecting the fact that these great Cathars—over two-hundred of them—were immediately burned alive by the supervising Catholic bishops upon their peaceful surrender.

"How dreadful..." Gaston had a hard time imagining such tragedy. *Why didn't God intervene to stop it?* he mused.

∾

They had company. Behind their bench, pigeons and ducks flirted openly, hoping for a piece of bread or some nuts. All around, as far as their eyes could see, sprawled the gardens, traditionally groomed and impeccably laid out in French fashion, all trees—from orange, lime, apple, pear, chestnut, and pomegranate to plane, elm, palm, maple, and oleander—planted in patterns and giving refuge to all sorts of birds. Lovely flowerbeds of sages, dahlias, and roses crowned with terraces filled the green *parterre* of gravel and lawn.

The distraction of strolling people, especially kids and pets, in front of them acted as a sedative to any negative thought wandering to their minds.

Peculiar of funny little things, occurring for even a fleeting moment, proved to be a great catalyst to revitalizing the spirits or shutting down personal worries. Monsieur Douvier, for instance, laughed when a gust of wind blew a toddler girl's tiny skirt up as she caressed her poodle next to her mommy. Watching her embarrassed expression in that unexpected moment, gave him an immense blast of joy. And the effect was contagious for it stirred the same emotional outburst from Gaston and Juliette sitting at either side of him.

"I was thinking..." said Gaston within seconds. "If the treasure came from the first century...and the Cathars had it in the 12th century, who kept it between those unaccounted eleven centuries?" He turned to Juliette, who had remained silent. "Any idea?"

"No. My focus is in the spiritual mission of the two scrolls..."

"One can only speculate," said Monsieur Douvier. "Very little is known in these matters." He sighed. "Maybe one day someone will unearth something that will set a new industry in motion." Something clicked in his head. "One thing to consider in this respect is the Knights Templar. They had a healthy relationship with the Cathars. They shared cultures, visions, responsibilities, and secrets...before both civilizations were completely wiped out by these Roman Catholic warmongers."

∞

"What else did Abbé Saunière tell you, Grandpa?"

Monsieur Douvier's stare turned a little hazy. "Oh...I seem to have strayed away from a similar question you asked me a while back," he said slowly, "as if it was an open meadow...my usual bad habit." Aging did strange things to people, including him, but minimal in his case.

"It's okay, Grandpa."

"He told me that in addition to restoring St. Mary Magdalene church in 1887, he built a structure he called Tour Magdala to house his private library, another structure he called Villa Bethania to entertain notable guests (including myself, twice), and other smaller projects in Rennes-le-Château...with the money he got from the Cathars' material treasure."

He removed his spectacles, rubbed his eyes, and put them back on.

"He told me that he feared for his life...that the Roman Catholic Church wanted to take this relic away from him and kill him..."

"That's awful," said Gaston.

Monsieur Douvier scratched one ear.

"Saunière said that he made the mistake of blackmailing the Roman Catholic Church for a large sum of money in exchange for keeping quiet about what he knew about the Church. Specifically, what he knew from the ancient relic he kept...and its message—"

"That Jesus was mortal, not divine, like all of us..." interrupted Juliette.

"That Jesus and Mary Magdalene were lovers and had a baby girl together called Sylvie...born in Marseille..." provided Gaston.

"You guys talk like first-class journalists!" said Monsieur Douvier. The adulation was well-received. They both smiled.

"I told him that Jesus was probably growling in his grave or in Heaven watching the terrible distortion of his message to the world made by the Roman Catholic Church through the centuries after his death," added Monsieur Douvier forcefully.

He crossed his legs, seeking comfort.

"I really wanted to tell him more, in the spirit of freedom of speech I hold so dear in this 20th century. The search for truth. But I couldn't. His robust face and intense dark eyes scared me a bit."

Juliette pouted, jumped in, "What did you want to tell him, Grandpa?"

Monsieur Douvier remained momentarily pensive.

"I wanted to tell him how I felt about the Roman Catholic Church. How the mysterious succession of Popes and their armies of preachers had turned Christian religion through the years into a self-serving zillion dollar corporate enterprise...exempt of taxes...full of lies and deceit...driven by greed, arrogance, manipulation, abuse, immorality, and even high crime—a long shot from the original sandals-clad, pious, Jesus Christ once appeared in the world...with his immense love for humanity and personal sacrifices...the way his followers in Palestine used to know and revere him."

"I like sandals," remarked Gaston.

"By *high crime* I take it you mean the burning at the stake of all these people...elderly, women and children included...who practiced a different religion or a different interpretation of the same religion... right?" put in Juliette.

"At least."

Above hovered Richard's soul.

GUARDIAN OF THE MOST WANTED
ANCIENT RELIC ON EARTH

Monsieur Douvier stood up, took a glorious, deep breath, and gave out a loud shout to the tall trees surrounding him, feeling young again, "**RAAAAAAAAAAAAAAAAAAAAAAAAAAA!**"

"Let's walk some more," he then urged his small entourage. "Let's savor this park, let's relish another piece of Paris!"

"Great idea!" cheered Gaston, doing an improvised *Wizard of Oz* dancing routine next to them, which Juliette seconded with even greater charm.

"Don't forget Grandpa, we have to take the train back to Nimes, then continue with your car to Saint-Jean-du-Gard, before it gets dark," she then said tactfully.

"Oh, I'm aware of that."

Strolling ahead, they passed a gathering of elderly women wearing sun-shading hats or black berets, cigarettes dangling from their mouths. They played *boules*, their hubbies or lovers quietly watching. Gaston spotted the *théâtre des marionnettes* first and sat happily glued to the performers longer than Juliette and her grandpa, who in turn discovered the *carrousel* (oldest in Paris) sooner than the inspired boy. Twirling and picking up speed, belted to a wooden elephant, green eyes shimmering, a small stick in her right hand (meant to catch a ring the *carrousel* attendant held standing just outside the riding zone), the screaming blonde girl was eventually watched by Gaston, who joined Grandpa in the thrills and laughter of the moment. Rather small, modest, and limited in its offering, the classy merry-go-round turned out to be a perfect ride for *la princesse Juliette d'Occitaine!*

They reached the large, centered *bassin de huit côtés* with a jet of water in its middle and watched for a good moment children sailing toy boats on the water. Grandpa took particular interest in following the scene created by a lone barefooted infant who, crawling next to his older brother, succeeded in climbing to the top stone edge, just shy of dropping inside the pool, but overjoyed on just sticking one of his legs into it.

Those were quality moments Monsieur Douvier's tired eyes fondly focused on when little else mattered.

Encircling the large *bassin et le jet d'eau* in front of the Palais du Luxembourg spread a series of twenty marble sculptures representing *les reines de France et femmes illustres* (including Marie de Médicis, Blanche de Castille, Louise de Savoie, Marie Stuart, Sainte Bathilde, Jeanne d'Albret, Marguerite d'Anjou, Anne de Bretagne, and Marguerite de Provence, among them—those Monsieur Douvier chose to relate to his work and therefore comment accordingly) all selected by King Louis-Philippe, who reigned from 1830 to 1848. One hundred or so stone and bronze statues, monuments, and fountains signifying Greek mythological figures, animals, famous artists and writers (such as Beethoven, Baudelaire, Verlaine, and Georges Sand) were known to be scattered throughout the entire gardens. Unfortunately, having seen only a few of them, the other known factor to Grandpa was that they should be heading home soon.

಄

"With so much money coming from the Cathars' material treasure and the Pope's bribe, Saunière could've fled to Brazil or Mindanao or any distant land and start a huge empire out there," said Juliette, catching up again with their main discussion.

"Or he could've bought a thousand unicorns," said Gaston cheerfully.

They rounded the exquisite Palais du Luxembourg, built over three centuries ago for Reine Marie de Médicis, today housing the *Sénat français,* and took the Rue de Vaugirard off the park to tree-lined, shop-laden Boulevard Saint-Michel.

"Saunière told me that the money he'd stashed away had only raised his standard of living, his life style in Rennes-le-Château—but it didn't enrich him spiritually. He feared that if the Church got their hands on the relic, they'd destroy the truth forever, the only evidence available."

Crossing the street, with no one near them, he revealed with a whispering voice, "That's why he decided to give me the relic...in secrecy...so absolutely no one would know."

Gaston's oddly intrigued eyes met with Juliette's as they stepped on the sidewalk together with Grandpa and continued marching window-watching, and talking in the shade of the trees.

"He said he trusted me and was confident I would hide it in a safe place...at least for another thirty years."

"The cave...beyond the creek," guessed Gaston, smiling.

"Until the religious, social, and political climate of France changed," continued Monsieur Douvier.

Juliette jumped in, "I would say, of France *and the Western world.*"

ᢙ

They headed straight toward the Seine, the beginning of the Left Bank, cutting through throngs of ethnic people in this cultural milieu of ever-changing thinking–from traditional to avant-garde to alternative–the area known as *Quartier Latin*, properly spread out on this bank of the river.

Gaston asked, "Why *Latin*? Sounds very old, not current, considering what I see around me."

"Local students were forced to speak in *Latin* in the first centuries of the Sorbonne...founded as a *collège* of theology that became part of the Université de Paris...and gradually turned into a rebellious, political-minded international force. But the word *Latin* stuck with the people."

"How come Saunière trusted you, Grandpa? How well did he know you?"

Rather than stroll all the way to the Seine and beyond to Ile de La Cité, with the option of detouring to nearby Notre Dame, they turned right on Boulevard Saint-Germain, also bristling with elegant trees, stylish shops, and chic boutiques. Eventually, they would end up in

Gare D'Austerlitz, where they'd hop on a train bound for Nimes, in the south of France.

"He'd known me and my work for years."

Gaston's distracted eyes veered to the numerous cafés, restaurants, *créperies*, and bistros clogging the boulevard as they ambled by. There were bands of teenagers flashing their weird outfits and greasy hairs amid drifting clouds of Gauloises' cigarette smoke in front of certain *cinémas*, while trendy girls off their frequented fashion shops strutted their stuff among them without care.

"Saunière had attended some of my lectures in Toulouse, Montpellier, Lyon, and Paris...and had invited me to his villa in Rennes-le-Château twice...so, yes, he respected me and my work..." said Monsieur Douvier.

"Paris?" repeated Juliette.

"Yes. After my presentation in the Sorbonne that day, in the mid twenties, we strolled all the way to these gardens here from the Panthéon on Rue Soufflot, making a meditative stop at *la Fontaine Médicis*, a combative stop standing in front of *le marchand de masques* bronze statue in the vicinity, and a mesmerizing stop near Jean-Baptiste Carpeaux's sculpted 'four nude women supporting the globe' at *la Fontaine des Quatre Parties du Monde* (also known as *la Fontaine de l'Observatoire*) south of the Jardin Marco Polo. We had some hot chocolate with music playing in the background...coming from a gazebo... near a small café restaurant that featured both indoor and outdoor tables." He scratched his chin. "The same walk I took with you today I took with him many years ago, only it was colder and a bit hazy."

"So you hid the relic in your property's cave...in Saint-Jean-du-Gard?" said Juliette, back on focus, if that could be expected.

"No, in my attic," corrected Grandpa. "Temporarily. I needed time to think, to figure out what to do with it. So when Madame Rossi stole it and put it in the cave—way in the back of my property, where I hardly ever go—I realized, after a while, that this was an ideal place to keep it...given her very old age, frail health, and solitary way of living."

❧

"Were you kidding us, Grandpa, when you said last week that Gaston's ring is exactly the same one Mary Magdalene wears in the relic?"

"No. I have proof of it," he said confidently. "By the way, kids, if we have time we could stop at the Musée de Cluny right here on this side street...where they have an amazing display of six medieval tapestries of a lady and a unicorn–*La Dame à la Licorne.* Why are you laughing?" He halted.

Juliette explained: "We've already been there today. We saw it. It's pretty cool."

Gaston added, "Yeah, the lady and the unicorn...and the lion...and the monkey."

Perplexed, Monsieur Douvier said, squinting, "You saw it...before getting into the Sorbonne building?"

"Yes, Grandpa...before your lecture."

"We also walked around these really, really narrow, medieval cobbled streets...in the Rive Gauche, down Rue de la Huchette and Rue Saint Séverins. Very crowded...lots of weird people," said Gaston with glee.

"Especially, Rue du Chat-qui-Pêche...so narrow you can't turn a bicycle around on it..." expressed Juliette, adding colors to her vivid description with her hands and pouts.

"You just mentioned the narrowest street in Paris, sweetie," exclaimed Monsieur Douvier. "But how did you ever get there...without my permission? You know how dangerous this can be...for children your age? You were supposed to stay with Madame Duquesne."

"We also saw the Seine...by the Quai St. Michel," bragged Gaston proudly, "with this big, beautiful boat full of people...cruising..."

"We didn't like her. She acted like a...bitch..." said Juliette bravely. "So after she took us to La Madeleine and La Place de la Concorde by bus...and to Les Deux Magots in St. Germain-des-Prés by metro...we fled..."

"We waved hello to them..." said Gaston.

"To whom?" asked Grandpa.

"To the people on the boat..." burst out Gaston joyously.

Above hovered Richard's soul.

PART 8

CLASH #6—DUNKING TANK SPLASH
(A TIME TRAVELED CLASH)
FRANCE, JULY 1955

OBSCENITY JUDGE ANNOUNCES THE VERDICT ON THE FILTHY POETRY CHARGE

Bermuda Revelation Park, Zundo, June 3081

Richard waved one hand to the kids in the inflated banana boat as it passed near him for the sixth time.

This part of the festivity was crowded with a variety of air-pumped, fruit-shaped water vehicles piloted by groups of three or four youngsters that came alive when a switch was flipped from a control panel.

Dressed in his extravagant signature black cape and black gloves, Master Judge had minutes ago ended Obscenity Judge's ZCAP meter's call and created the environment needed for her to accept and test the defendant's alleged filthy poetry issue.

Their chat had been in Undo-English, not exactly the proper language for this type of techno babble. But one that Obscenity Judge cherished.

For his part, Richard had been wandering a little among several fun rides, watching peoples' thrills and dramas unfolding, the boat ride experience being the latest. Casually dressed in summer clothes, he ambled like a little lost boy, distracted and curious, feeding his mind and senses with whatever good thing came his way in this oddly exciting place.

Because he'd never really been exposed to such a fun ambiance in his childhood, in spite of his immense wealth, he valued the seductive playgrounds and merry-go-rounds and yummy candy stands that surrounded him more than anybody else. Oddly, he'd never walked in a country fair, where domestic animals were aplenty, where school kids and common folks shared similar fantasies, rubbing elbows and emotions, little things here and there, but so enjoyable in their mere simplicity and natural splendor.

Never missing a chance to flirt with the audience, Master Judge added another one of his good moments by mingling with the crowd near the attention-grabbing spot he'd set in motion for the Clash in his foolish outfit, while keeping an eye on both the defendant and the Obscenity Judge. Soon they would join forces, in quite unnerving and disparate ways.

⤫

Evidently, two dunking tanks stole everyone's attention in one crowded area as Obscenity Judge—a shapely and sexy Asian woman with full lips—climbed the few stairs to the top gate.

She squeezed herself into the narrow tank and onto her wooden platform, four feet above the water. For a fleeting moment, she stared down at the distracted defendant. "You too, Mr. Flynn—get your ass up here!" she shouted.

Richard complied.

He saw a small bright yellow dot up in the sky becoming bigger and brighter—the burning sun, actually. He also saw something big bright and round getting smaller up there in the sky, something spinning, with red-flashing scrolling words on its contour, still visible:

JUST COMPLETED: CLASH #5—MUD WRESTLING • OVERALL SCORE: JUDGES 4 DEFENDANT 1 • NEXT: CLASH #6—DUNKING TANK SPLASH

He read as it jetted away into the clouds.

Next thing he knew, he'd entered the tank and was sitting down beside the female judge, both his legs dangling in the air.

"It looks spooky...from here..." he told her, feeling a bit dizzy.

"I'm going to interrogate you, Mr. Flynn," said the pretty lady, coquettishly touching her long, silky black hair. "Is it all right with you?"

Richard eyes traveled to her thighs as she fixed a little her tight aqua-green miniskirt.

"Yes, it is...Ms—"

"You may call me OJ."

"Cool."

Two teenagers—a fat boy sporting braces and a pig-tailed brunette wearing glasses—began to throw heavy balls at both contiguous tanks, one of the youths hitting on target. Richard plunged into the water with a big splash.

Gargantuan laughs erupted everywhere in the surrounding Stadiums. They had been there all the time watching.

Obscenity Judge joined in the laughter, adding vitality to the Astral Floor's ongoing Clash.

"Now—your problem will be discussed openly...as we always do here in Zundo." She rubbed her forehead, making a sexy statement with her long, flowing hair. Then watched the defendant climb up the stairs again. "Let the Planet Undersea News take a quick poll on your obscenity case."

"You mean..." Richard said, perplexed, shaking some water off his hair and all the way down to the sole of his shoes, "the entire population of Zundo will vote on—?"

"—those wishing to do so," she interrupted. "I presume several billions of Zundonians." She watched him sneak a stare at her body as she cushioned a bit her butt on the wooden surface. "Which is better work than any dumb congress or parliament of the old days could've accomplished through dumb political debates and partisan gridlock."

Ball in hand, the fat boy struck the target, after one miss, making Obscenity Judge scramble down into the water, her uplifted skirt revealing panties and flesh.

She surfaced unhappily and wiped water off her eyes and nose. Her hair was now a wet mop.

Some laughter and whistles burst all around. Zundonians watched with mixed emotions how she struggled with her frustration, pulling herself out of the water.

Finally, she clambered her way up to her seat next to the defendant, the wet cloth accentuating her exquisite feminine curves. Jiggling some water off her hair, she looked at Richard. "Are you ready?"

"You mean they're going to vote *right now*?"

"They're going to press a button on the ZCAP meter each one has planted in the arm..."

"Simultaneously?"

"Within three minutes. No rush."

"I'll be damned..."

A local trumpet fish meandered by above their heads. Higher up passed a school of silversides.

On the other side of the zhoenix shield two reef sharks and a large barracuda cruised the warm sea waters, heading west to the Promenade drop-off.

The pig-tailed girl threw one ball right on target.

This time Richard plummeted into the water.

Again gigantic laughs and banging noises filled the air. "DROWN! DROWN! DROWN!" they also shouted.

The lady judge stared down at the disoriented defendant.

"Relax. I've already activated all meters on the planet with the question "**Is Richard Flynn's poetry filthy?**"

Richard climbed the stairs up again to the tune of incessant boos. Water leaked from his shirt and pants as he took a seat next to the gorgeous, also wet, judge.

On either side of them whitespotted file fish traversed elkhorn coral gardens and micro atolls, slightly pushed by the tides now hitting the system of islands.

A long whining sound, followed by an apple-green flashing light on a big screen above the Astral Floor, announced the result: "**NO.**"

"*Congratulations!* Your poetry is not filthy after all!" cheered the Asian woman.

Richard's face lit up brightly with joy. His hands were busy fumbling with a handkerchief someone gave him on his way up the stairs.

"Great! How fast!" he sighed. "I'm impressed."

He had ignored the audience's reaction in the Stadiums—the cheers and applause–which was anyway lame and hardly audible, in spite of its fair verdict–a sign of his minuscule, if not microscopic, popularity.

"Enough of that," commanded the Asian beauty. "I'll transfer you back to Master Judge now...so you can continue your confession...and await sentence on the other matter."

"What matter?"

"Degenerate greed–wealth greed!"

"Oh..."

"By the way, you've lost here—by falling *twice* into the water—and are down 1-5 overall in the Clashes. Sorry about that.

Richard looked up to the scoreboard on the big silver Sphere, already spinning above his head:

**JUST COMPLETED: CLASH #6—DUNKING TANK SPLASH •
OVERALL SCORE: JUDGES 5 DEFENDANT 1 • NEXT: CLASH
#7—TENNIS MATCH**

His vision turned murky, his face defeated in full recognition.

PART 9

TERRIBLE AND WONDERFUL MESSAGES TO PONDER ABOUT FRANCE, JULY 1955

LES ALLUMETTES' PRANK OR THREAT

Juliette's Home (same as her 2ⁿᵈ mother's or Madame Clarice Barré's)

Juliette rode her horse after school and returned home on her bicycle as usual, but the nagging feeling that she'd been spied on all along was not normal. Worse, a peculiar, folded handwritten note had arrived at her mail box, which, when unfolded, caused real panic.

Trembling fingers held the note, her spine shaken by a cold chill that swept through it from end to end, eventually bringing tears to her eyes.

> **Juliette,**
> **You're nothing but a witch. Think Jeanne d'Arc and her fate!**
> **Les Allumettes**

What to do! A prank?

Nervously, she ran out holding the note. Within minutes, she was pedaling at full speed, heading for Gaston's place less than a kilometer away. Daylight had turned somberly dark–not a good time for a young girl like her to ride a bicycle alone in such circumstances.

Short gusts of wind blew the delicate branches and leaves at both sides of the *chemin* as well as the long strands from her flowing hair. She was clad in simple summer shirt and blue jeans, having left her riding clothes in the stable area.

She reached the farm where Gaston lived and shoved her two-wheeler against the usual stone wall. Quickly, she knocked on the familiar old wooden door, up a bunch of dusty steps, expecting a quick response, as usual.

When Gaston pushed the door open, she threw herself in his arms, covering his face with the fluff of her disheveled blonde hair.

"Gaston, hold me tight!" Tears rolled down her cheeks.

"What happened!"

"I've become a target of hate mail!"

"What!?"

She explained, snuggled next to him on the steps.

∽

Next morning in school she felt insecure walking down the hallways, imagining all sorts of things.

Every stare from passing students and teachers seemed to reveal something—furtive glances, sneaky steps—all conspiring, yet none proving anything concrete.

She'd decided not to tell anyone, including her grandpa and second mother, not even the police, for the time being. Most likely, someone was playing a game, joking around, as morbid as it seemed. It couldn't be for real. Gaston had reluctantly agreed. They both would be on alert, ready to act, if things continued or escalated.

Could this be related to Gaston's attack in front of the Musée des Vallées Cévenoles in Saint-Jean-du-Gard a few months ago? Or the other attack in Palavas? she now pondered as she entered her classroom and headed for her chair. *He really had a history and a reason to be targeted. But she, none. She hardly socialized, kept her life simple. Except, her secret participation in the Legend of the Horse-Riding Kites.*

She reflected: *Across the room to her left sat a bully who'd given her a few headaches through the year, but nothing brutal or violent. The boy, tall and fat, bullied other students too. So, nothing specific against her. His ugly, round, devouring gray eyes were often on her legs when she sat down next to the Roman statues outside the building in the company of other girls. It had been her favorite spot during breaks, but now she would look elsewhere for a sitting place.*

Her eyes blinked repeatedly. *Bicycling, horse riding, stage acting, tennis classes,* she reviewed mentally, double-checking. *Plus, of course, her romantic thing with Gaston. And her close friends...Alfredo, Pablo, Doña Manola, Pierre, and Madame Rossi. People she trusted.*

Another problem that she'd kept to herself was a growing malaise, occasional vomiting bouts, general sickness...since she'd returned from Paris about a month ago.

She put a stop to her thoughts when the teacher began to talk, asking everyone to open the textbook and turn to a certain page. *Good grief,* Juliette suddenly muttered. *It's about Robespierre and his Reign of Terror...during the French Revolution!*

Above hovered Richard's soul.

EXHIBITIONISTS WITH REASONS

Cascade de Brion

She was giggling and running through the woods bordering Ruisseau de Brion–a wild creek of crystal clear waters, snaking down from Mont Brion further up the forest, creating a splendid waterfall on its path at one point. He was chasing her, at times bumping into casual rocks, also giggling.

Finally, Gaston caught up with Juliette, near a cluster of chestnut trees, where they threw themselves on the grass to rest.

Surrounding them loomed hundreds of Mediterranean trees, mostly pines and green oaks, defining the area with their strong aroma and vibrant beauty. Nothing mattered in this world except their brave acceptance of the present.

"Tell me about your previous girlfriends, Gaston..."

"I don't remember having any..."

"Come on...your school friends here in Saint-Jean-du-Gard...your previous friends in Toulouse..." said Juliette, laying flat on her stomach, her head with its cute ponytail resting sideways on the grass.

She was wearing a lovely light yellow summer dress, sensitive to the wind, and soft rubber shoes, perfectly suited for a non-horse-riding day.

"I hardly socialize, like you. Friends come and go. Nothing serious." He sat upright, staring up at the blue-gray spacious sky. Clad in summer shorts and a simple T-shirt, he had no ambition for dressing better or impressing anyone, except Juliette. "My focus is on learning, keeping my grades high."

She followed the furtively cruising clouds in their various shades of gray with her now-lightened green eyes, the glaring, potent sunlight filtering through them. Myriads of branches and leaves glittered in the approaching sunset.

"Come on, silly boy...tell me..."

"Actually, there's a girl who has popped up a few times in my dreams...my warped dreams or false memories."

"Tell me about her...in whichever environment you want."

Gaston crossed his arms behind his head for comfort.

"Last time she popped up we were together and alone in a place like this, but on top of a hill and no river."

"Keep going."

"I recall she was wearing a nice black skirt...was doing cartwheels in front of me...making sure her pink panties showed every time she rolled around."

"And your silly eyes just kept staring at her hot panties?" Lazily rolling next to him on the grass, she teasingly kicked his nearest leg. "Huh? Huh?"

"Well, yes...she was tempting me..."

"How old was she?"

"About your age, but dark long hair."

"Well, I can do a lot better than showing my panties to you," she said defiantly, rising to her feet.

Without hesitation, she stripped her clothes off in front of him, loosened her hair, and ran stark naked to the river.

Rising to his feet, Gaston kept following her every moves in disbelief until she plunged into the water by the *cascade*.

Gaston ran to the shore. "You're nuts! Absolutely nuts!" he shouted, watching her emerge topless and lovelier than ever.

"Come on, silly boy...show me your nuts!" she yelled from the water.

"I'll just go naked, like you. You'll figure out the rest!" he yelled back, getting totally undressed. "I'm in competition to match or beat your craziness—nothing else!"

"Welcome to my world!"

Above hovered Richard's soul.

THE MISSING LINE

A Week Later...
Juliette's Home

Slowly, Juliette lifted the top of the big, brown, elongated container that looked like an old pirate's treasure box. It squeaked a little and offered some resistance to the upward pull. Standing next to the teen actress, Gaston felt his fingers tremble a little, his vocal cords stiff inside his larynx.

The basement room was hot and spooky with a group of seemingly trashy and undefined items, some covered with spider webs.

"First time I've come here in a year or so..." whispered Juliette, acting more like an archeologist now.

"Where's Madame Clarice?" asked Gaston, remembering she owned the house and served as Juliette's second mother.

"She's out visiting her piano teacher." A silly pout detached her lips. "I encouraged her to do so...so we could have the evening for ourselves."

"Does she know about this? The Legend?"

"No. She lives her own life, independently. Has no desire to interfere with my private life, my acting career, *my obsessions!*" She laughed. "She's not nosy at all. I like her very much."

"Wow..." said Gaston.

She looked down at her pirate's box.

"My grandpa keeps everything in order in his house, ready for me to act upon when called to duty. This is just my own base. He keeps most of his affairs away from me. But we're connected, religiously, if we can put it this way, through the sacred messages found in the relic and the traveling scrolls, which we must indefatigably protect." She then touched the box warmly, possessively, as if it was a part of her own body. "I don't have 'little Resistance fighting men'...*guerrilleros*... like you do by the Ruisseau de l'Exil d'Espagne near Mialet...but our team of dedicated teen girls also operates in secrecy."

"Bless your soul," said Gaston, not knowing why but meaning it.

Digging deep inside a mess of old articles, Juliette pulled out what she'd been looking for. "Here!" It was a wooden matchbox, containing, when opened, something other than matches.

Gaston's excited eyes focused on the tiny tube she held in her hand, also made of wood, from which she extracted what appeared to be a rolled-up ancient scroll.

"Ancient paper?" guessed Gaston.

She laughed.

"Paper wouldn't last nearly two-thousand years." Grabbing his hand, she guided it to the material. "Touch it," she said, unrolling the scroll. "First-century *Vellum*...made of specially treated goat skin."

"Wow...that's really cool."

Still holding his hand, she began to read the ancient message from Jesus and Mary to the world:

> **For eternal love and peace we preach**
> **For spiritual abundance and harmony we live**
> **For forgiveness and equality we teach**
> **For our child's blessed arrival we give**
> **-Yahshua of Nazarene**
> **-Mary of Magdala**

"Awesome..." said Gaston, realizing more, "I have a feeling I've heard that before."

"You do. All but the last line," said Juliette. "From *me*."

"Yeah, now I remember. At the bonfire. When wrapping up our *soirée*." His eyes glittered, quickly envisioning the touching monologue she'd performed for him up there by the fire. "The actress in you."

She gave him a sweet smooch on his nose.

"So this is one of the two ancient scrolls that regularly fly with the kites in your mission," he guessed.

"Want to see the other one?"

"Can't wait to see it!"

Juliette extracted a second tiny tube from the matchbox.

Staring at the mesmerized young boy, ready to pull the rolled-up scroll out, she challenged him, "*You* do it now..."

He stared back at her, uncertain.

"Come on! Do it!" urged Juliette.

Slowly, very carefully, he began to pull.

"Read it now!" urged Juliette.

He read:

> **God bless you dad, Yahshua of Nazarene**
> **God bless your Crucifixion**
> **God bless you mom, Mary of Magdala**
> **God bless your Christian mission**
> **–Sylvie of Massalia**

"Don't faint now!" cried out Juliette, seeing the drastic pale look on his face. "Sit down..."

Gaston struggled for balance, his legs collapsing.

"...I feel funny..." he said from the ground.

"Take a deep breath...another..." she encouraged, also sliding herself down to the ground next to him.

She patted both his cheeks, blew air on his face.

"...I...I can't believe...I read it..." said Gaston, half-impaired vocally. Both his lungs and brain seemed to lack oxygen, momentum. "...sacred words...from...the beginning of time..."

"...the beginning of Christianity...." corrected Juliette.

"...words from Jesus and Mary's daughter..."

"...don't take it so hard...she was only six when she wrote it..."

"*Six?*" Something clicked. "Oh yeah...your grandpa mentioned it in Paris."

Juliette nodded and pouted.

Feeling slightly better, Gaston asked, "How did this ever find its way into a scroll?"

She shrugged.

"You know, I've been asking myself this question lately too. Now I think I know the answer."

"Tell me."

"Silvio Grasso–the famous Roman sculptor who defected and helped Mary Magdalene sail to Massalia–now Marseille–in AD 33," said Juliette.

"And deliver baby Sylvie," said Gaston.

"And sculpt the relic," said Juliette.

"You're right," shot Gaston with a surge of energy. "He worked from the notes Mary Magdalene gave him, according to what your grandpa said the other day."

"He also took care of Mary Magdalene in Massalia."

"Yeah..." said Gaston. "He introduced her to all his friends in the Jew communities of Massalia, Narbo, and Rhedae."

"Marseille, Narbonne, and Rennes-le-Château today," said Juliette, seeking clarity. "He also, I'm sure, helped Mary Magdalene raise her kid–Sylvie–who she named after him."

"So he..." began Gaston, thoughtfully.

"Yeah," put in quickly Juliette, "–he followed up on Sylvie's young life, Sylvie's growing up, Sylvie's going to school..."

"French school," signified Gaston with a smile.

"Yeah...and he suggested, along the way, she write something to the world...identifying herself and her famous parents," said Juliette. "This must have happened in complete secrecy and great understanding for she was at risk of being killed by the many Romans who hunted her...for the rumor of her being alive and well had already spread far and wide across the land."

"Being targeted...at age *six*?" questioned Gaston.

"Yeah. Orders were orders, from the Emperor, and he ruled this region of France in addition to Rome and all its colonies."

Gaston remained pensive, then asked, "Did Silvio ever sculpt a relic of little Sylvie?"

Juliette made a face, followed by a sullen pout, "I really don't know. Maybe we should ask my grandpa."

"We will," said Gaston strongly.

Something triggered new thoughts in his mind.

"So...what you showed me here a while ago in that matchbox are really *originals*, not copies, right?"

"Yes, I lied to you the other day...those are the originals Silvio Grasso put together on both the relic and the scrolls. My grandpa keeps the relic in his cave and I keep the scrolls here in my matchbox inside the pirate's treasure box. The world is too greedy and dangerous nowadays to expose originals to the mercy of unscrupulous thieves and criminals...such as those quartered in the Vatican!"

"If you say so..." said Gaston.

They both rose to their feet.

"How come you skipped the last line...when you improvised Jesus and Mary's message at the bonfire?" Gaston now asked, staring at Juliette's emerald-turned eyes.

She hesitated, then said, "I wasn't sure."

"Sure of what?"

"It applied to us...as well."

"To us?"

Gaston replayed Jesus and Mary's message's last line in his mind, trying to decipher what she meant, *For our child's blessed arrival we give.*

"*Are you? Am I? Are we?* " He jumped up and down in near disbelief full of joy.

"*Yes!*" she exploded.

"*It can't be! I'm not ten yet!*" cried out Gaston jubilant.

෩

"You're the only person I've done this with...so you must be the father of my upcoming child..."

"You're really pregnant?"

She nodded vigorously with felicity and tears. Touching her tummy, she said, "Sometimes I feel the baby move...inside."

"Wow...wow...wow...wow..."

This time his body reacted in concert with his emotions, and he embraced her passionately, also with tears in his eyes.

"I love you so much," he told her.

It was a gripping moment that persevered into the next hour, sunset approaching.

Hugging, kissing, whispering sweet things to each other, they finally detached. Then exited.

Outside, they strolled side by side on the dirt road that led to the forest, imagining the wildest things.

A nice breeze had begun to flutter some leaves around.

Under a chestnut tree, over a wide mantle of green grass, they cuddled up together moments later, happily watching a fully furred, big-eared rabbit watching them back from a distance...before they closed their eyes in the quiet of night.

Above hovered Richard's soul.

WHEN PHILOSOPHY PUTS
THE MIND IN OVERDRIVE

Old Farm

Lying down in bed late at night Gaston confronted an avalanche of thoughts, each one trying to upstage the others.

School year was ending, summer vacation around the corner. He'd gotten Juliette pregnant at age nine. She was thirteen, beautiful, adorable, warm, funny, and exciting.

At times he thought it must have been hard for her to grow up without the love and warmth of her parents...since age three...when they committed suicide.

It spooked him to realize that perhaps the biggest thing they had in common was a parentless childhood. Maybe this had something to do with their unusual maturity and superior intelligence, easily recognized by school teachers, classmates, and friends—his own, in particular, because of his very young age.

But why would Juliette's parents commit suicide? She never elaborated about it...and he never dared to ask.

Juliette was a rising star of the stage, potentially another Shirley Temple if she tackled the film industry as well. He and Juliette shared similar curiosities, ideas, hobbies, sports, feelings. Very compatible. But she had an ongoing career, he didn't. Was he supposed to choose a career now? Soon? Exactly what? Becoming a writer seemed the only logical thing. He'd never given it much thought. Maybe he should.

His auntie Doña Manola was forever absent. Did Pierre miss her? He never talked about her. Would Pierre become a writer too? Or a musician like Alfredo or Pablo? Or an actor like Juliette? Or a PhD in architecture or philosophy like Monsieur Douvier?

Tennis. Juliette played tennis now. But her mind was set on The Legend of the Horse-Riding Kites. Weird. His ring. Could it be connected to Mary Magdalene's? Eerie. Exactly the same ring? Insane.

He remained quietly stretched out on his bed, eyes still open, staring at the ceiling. All sorts of thoughts passed by...too fast and scattered. None sizable.

This one, he seized: *Juliette's snapshot.*

He pulled it out from under his pillow. Her picture. His eyes focused on Juliette's beauty and essence. *Warm and peaceful face...intelligent light green eyes...charming upturned nose...chiseled full lips...uplifting smile...lovely pouting...ivory smooth skin.* He touched her lips with one finger. *Long, soft, silky blonde hair...cute small ears.* He kissed the picture.

All this, however, took on a new meaning now that she was pregnant with his baby. It made her abundantly closer to him, as if both had come from the same mold and enjoyed the same roots. It seemed as if she was a part of him, not only spiritually, but physically.

Of course, only the baby was.

He shed no tears tonight looking at the photo. Juliette's career might shoot to the stars, as predicted by the news media, and he sincerely hoped so, but now nobody could take her away from him. One day she would be his wife. One day soon. Maybe after his tenth birthday!

With this train of thoughts, he fell asleep, still holding the photo.

Across the room Pierre dozed peacefully.

೧൦

Some two hours into his sleep, Gaston moved restlessly in his bed. His mind appeared to be struggling with something. He produced a few anxious vocal sounds, swiftly jerked his body sideways, as if avoiding a calamity. "WE'RE GOING TO DROWN! THE CURRENT'S PULLING US!" he shouted.

Above hovered Richard's soul.

PART 10

GASTON'S GOING *COUCOU*, SUSPECTS PIERRE FRANCE, JULY 1955

ECHOES OF DESPERATION

Juliette had just arrived on her bicycle after school. Sitting next to Gaston now on the sturdy log fence, she just smiled and kissed his nose.

"How's everything?" asked Gaston.

"Fine."

"The baby?"

"Kicking."

"Good to hear that..." He put one hand on her tummy gently, waited.

"I'm sure she's smiling inside..." she said, smiling.

"Like you now?"

"Like you, Gaston..."

"But she's a girl...you just said..." Gaston winked.

"What's wrong with a girl smiling like you?" she persisted.

They laughed.

"Any more hate mail?"

"No."

"Good."

"She could be a boy..." she said, pouting.

"I was thinking about that too..." said Gaston.

"*Hurry—touch now!*" she urged, grabbing his hand and making him feel the kick inside.

"Wow-wow!" he burst out, ecstatic.

"Has any thirteen-year-old horse-riding girl ever been attacked over the centuries?" Gaston munched on a chocolate bar she'd offered him.

"Yes. Forty-five have been seriously wounded...and seven killed."

"Wow..." He scratched his forehead. "Who tells you all these things?"

"My grandpa."

"Great source."

"The best."

His eyes veered to the barn area, where Pablo worked. He waved a hand to them in salute. They waved back.

"Have you had any more weird dreams lately?" she asked Gaston.

"*Reveries?*" Gaston nodded oddly, feeling a sudden overactive thickness in his head.

"*Daydreams? Visions? Trances? Peculiarities? Mental pictures? Hallucinations? Fancies? Head trips? Specters? Images? Delusions? Fantasies?*"

"Did you say all these things...right now?" he managed to ask, cutting through a mental storm or something.

"What things?" said Juliette.

"Never mind," said Gaston, struggling with his mind.

∾

"Are you okay?" asked Juliette, past the strange scene Gaston had created, where for no apparent reason his mind had gone *coucou*.

"...yes...I'm fine..."

She thrust out her lips.

"So...have you?" She was referring to her unanswered question minutes ago about whether he'd had more weird dreams lately.

Gaston was feeling better now, still sitting on the log fence next to her, but he'd lost his train of thoughts. Suddenly, his mind hit the right note. "...you mean...weird dreams?"

"Of course..."

"...yes...plenty..."

"Tell me about them..."

Above hovered Richard's soul.

PRESUMED FALSE MEMORIES ON THE RISE

Old Farm

"Tell me about them...those weird dreams..." repeated Juliette, seeing the delay in Gaston's reaction to her specific, clear, and friendly question.

Sitting beside him on the log fence, she could only speculate.

He shifted his balance by moving his legs a bit and adjusting his posture more upright next to her on the fence, sort of getting his act together after behaving so bizarrely for no reason at all.

"I had this dream or reverie about me being in a classroom somewhere in Toulouse...the teacher falling asleep...dropping his sleepy head on his desk.

"Without making noise, me and a group of daring students crawled out of the classroom on our knees...and left the school grounds. Outside, we walked to the river Garonne and rented canoes."

"How nice," said Juliette, smiling.

"Me and Adelle–Pierre's girlfriend then–shared one canoe...real narrow and tight. We paddled to the middle of the river, but suddenly we realized the current was getting too strong and fast...and our canoe just went wild with it like a flaky little toy. Me and Adelle panicked and started yelling...as the canoe passed under a big metallic bridge...out of control. We doubled our paddling efforts...paddling...shouting...asking for help...and we got lucky and finally made it to the shore...all wet and tired and scared..."

"I can imagine. How old were you then?"

"I was about six. So was she."

"Very young."

"So...we returned the rented canoes...all of us...and went back to our school...and crawled back to our seats in the classroom...to find our teacher..."

"Awake?"

"No. Still sleeping."

"Awesome!"

"Except that Pierre says that this event never happened!"

"When did you and Pierre talked about this?"

"Yesterday..."

"Oh...." Juliette remained pensive. Then she asked, "What about Adelle?"

"I don't know where she is now...and Pierre says he never knew her...so..."

"It's weird..."

Juliette sneaked a glance to Gaston's eyes, said, "Did you also have a girlfriend at that age?"

Gaston shrugged. "I don't remember..."

There was a long, odd pause.

"Any other dream or reverie?"

He shifted his weight on the log fence for more comfort.

"This one. Pierre, me, and the other kids in the neighborhood...we played a game that I usually—actually, always—won."

"*Heyyyyyy*–champ!" cheered Juliette.

Smiling, he continued, "It was really a stupid game...and dangerous like hell—now that I think about it."

"*Go get them!*" chanted Juliette, like a cheerleader.

"We just bunched out on one side of the sidewalk and ran across the street per turn whenever a car was about to pass. Whoever waited longer to cross before the car passed won. I always beat them. Never got hit by a car...although one time I crossed the street at the very last second...running really fast...and almost–"

"*Got hit!*"

"Yeah."

"That's bad! What a stupid game!"

"I told you..."

Juliette jumped down from the fence and turned to face him. "Terrible! How could you?!" Juliette's rising anger showed on her face, her eyes. "Trying to get killed?!"

"No! I knew I could do it! I was *that* good!"

"*You idiot!*" She shouted, walking away.

"*Wait!*" He shouted back. "*Pierre says it never happened!*"

She looked at him momentarily with a mean sulky pout, then continued walking away even faster without a word.

Gaston saw her pick up her bicycle and pedal off.

Above hovered Richard's soul.

PIERRE'S DENIAL OF GASTON'S REALITY
CONTINUES

At thirteen, Pierre's interests resided in subjects bordering on politics, social issues, and current events—not girls. The aftermath of the Spanish Civil War had left him and his mother very combative inside.

His father's death by execution for having done nothing but disagree with General Franco's political views of how Spain should grow as a nation had marked his mind forever. Deep inside he knew he would one day enter the political arena, emerge as a leader, and avenge his father. Sure girls would come along and satisfy his needs and curiosity, he reckoned, but they would only take a small part of his life.

Regarding his cousin, Gaston had impressed him a lot lately. He seemed so intellectually curious and analytical about just everything, plus he wrote extremely well for his young age and limited experience. Too bad he didn't share the political inclination he did—they could make a great pair together.

Well, Gaston now was busily pursuing the weaker sex. Worse, falling in love with Juliette. No question, a ravishing blonde with star potential as a film actress. Already a sensation in the theatrical world of Southern France. Languedoc's babe. Also a compelling debater with street smart on the side. All great. But distracting!

Where in the hierarchy of achievements would Gaston be ten years from now...at nineteen? Hard to say. Being determined, focused, and heading toward a specific goal was Pierre's unique forte. He knew exactly what he wanted in life and how to work for it. But his cousin? Well...

❧

They happened to be milking some goats side by side this Saturday morning in the farm, engaged in small chat, when Gaston, remembering a past experience with Pierre back in Toulouse, remarked, "Funny that...you could hold me so strongly going down the rope. Yet you're not exactly a muscle man...your biceps are just average...I would say..."

"What are you talking about?"

"The boarding school incident, remember? Getting into the girls' dorm ...through the roof...into the bathroom...using the rope, remember?"

Pierre stared at his cousin blankly. "No, I don't remember."

"Stop playing games!" shot Gaston, squeezing harder than necessary on the goat's nipple. "How can you forget–I was expelled from that school!"

"Gaston–we only went to non-boarding public schools and boys-only Roman Catholic schools," snapped Pierre, puzzled, but not entirely surprised.

His cousin had come up with weird stories like that before, strange incidents that had never happened...as far as he was concerned. Maybe he should see a psychiatrist, he even thought. He searched for the nipple with his distracted fingers and squeezed it, pouring some milk on the bucket that sat on the ground below the goat. "You're imagining thing."

"Hell no!" blasted Gaston.

"I don't know if you're losing your marbles or what, but–"

"But what?!" roared Gaston. "What about our gang days... in Toulouse? Rue Pharaon? Rue des 36 Ponts? La Garonne? La Garonnette?"

"What about them?"

"We both stood in a street corner at night...near the river...waiting for speeding big trucks loaded with merchandize to slow down so we could jump inside from the back...and steal stuff while riding in it. Stuff like *des grandes bouteilles de champagne*...and then jump out at another corner..." Gaston's face lit up. "Wasn't it fun? We did it almost every night."

Pierre afforded a little smile. "Stealing? Getting drunk...at that age? No. I wasn't part of it. Sorry."

"Pierre—*goddamned*—what about the neighborhood church!?" crackled Gaston, releasing the goat's nipple.

"What about it?"

"I was the youngest, but the smartest and bravest in the gang. That's why they assigned me the toughest tasks! Like breaking into the church's hall where they kept the donations box—I still remember—maroon, made of hard wood, with a slit on top, perched high on a wall—during the mass...and cracking the box open—"

"Stealing the church's donations?" Pierre also released his goat's nipple, enraged.

"All of it! Running off with the loot!"

"You're crazy, cousin!"

"I was the best at it!"

Pierre had no more to say. He just kept staring at his cousin with disdain.

"Good thing we moved out of town..." said Gaston slowly, now with little energy.

Pierre remained silent.

"Dad found out the hiding place where I stashed all my stolen goods...right on the entry way past the main door...in the building where we lived. If you knew about it, you only had to lift up the heavy, dirty wooden platform where everybody stepped on to go upstairs. It was like a cave...full of stuff..."

He gazed at Pierre's expressionless face, then went on, "Anyway, Dad took me to the police station and embarrassed me in front of the officer in charge...telling him what I had done and how bad a kid I was. I admitted guilt right there...and for the first time in my life...I realized I'd committed bad things...real bad...and deserved to be punished... and rehabilitated..."

Without talking to each other, they seized back the nipples and continued to squeeze.

Above hovered Richard's soul.

PART 11

MASTER JUDGE'S WICKED FUN BEGINS AFTER HOURS ZUNDO, JUNE 3081

TURNING A 9-YEAR-OLD INTO A MENTAL WRECK

Master Judge was alone at his controls in the Royal Den late at night. He studied a key moment in the latest taped video of Richard's 13th past life, real time. Something that had actually happened minutes ago.

In it, he pressed one button after another, moved levers left and right, augmented and decreased frequency ranges, typed things on his keyboard...moving from the 31st century to the 20th century...sort of experimenting with his most precious subject—9-year-old-Gaston behaving weirdly. Both Richard and Gaston appeared—not together, but combined–in one taped sequence. He knew he was taking a risk— basically breaking Dr. Ufahh's strict work rules.

"Reveries? Daydreams? Visions? Trances? Peculiarities? Mental pictures? Hallucinations?"

"Ha-ha-ha-ha-ha-ha..." laughed Master Judge.

"Fancies? Head trips? Specters? Images?"

"Ha-ha-ha-ha-ha-ha..."

"Delusions? Fantasies?"

"Ha-ha-ha-ha-ha-ha..."

PART 12

THE MISSING LINE LEGACY
FRANCE, JULY 1955

GASTON'S PERIDOT RING IS IDENTICAL TO MARY MAGDALENE'S ON GRANDPA'S ANCIENT RELIC

Monsieur Douvier's Property

"Come on in," invited the old distinguished man, showing Gaston and his granddaughter the backyard's entrance from inside the house. Like them, he wore dirty pants and a plain summer shirt.

By now the couple had cleared up their little grudge. Monsieur Douvier had just caught them kissing in the foyer when arriving, not minding it at all.

He led the couple deeper into the backyard, past the parked sky-blue Delahaye 135MS convertible, though a maze of pathways, benches, fountains, juniper trees, a creek, and a hilly area with weird-looking limestone rocks, split into two worn away small Egyptian obelisks, most of it covered with *garrigue* and wild flowers. "Looks familiar, Gaston?"

"Here...get closer...on your knees..." indicated Monsieur Douvier, flashing a light from a lamp typically used by miners.

He squeezed his slim body through a crack in the rock, hardly seen from where they stood, and disappeared from view with his lamp. Juliette followed, making faces, realizing how hard it was to imitate her grandpa's snaky movements to get in. So did Gaston, complaining a bit here and there, but making it deeper inside after them.

"Can you hear the underground *ruisseau*...running?" said Grandpa, cocking one ear with his hand.

"I can hear it," said Gaston.

"Me too," said Juliette with a curious pout. "How far deeper do we have to go?"

"Not much..."

They continued to penetrate what seemed to be a well-sculptured cave, with nicely chiseled walls, spacious tunnels, and solid limestone ceiling. Old rock residues mixed with muck and sediments of clay, sand, and marlstone filled the ground they stepped on at one end, Monsieur Douvier always leading the way.

Finally, he pointed to the blue box with his lamp. Half buried in the ground, he picked it up, crouching. Gaston and Juliette crouched around him. The floor was damp, slimy, and cold. He opened the box.

The ancient relic came to life before their eyes.

"Wow..."

"It's beautiful," exclaimed Juliette with adoring eyes.

"So well-crafted you can see every detail...every emotion in their faces," uttered Gaston, mesmerized.

"That's what Silvio Grasso was famous for—awesome minuscule detail work and virtuoso realism—unmatched in his time," said Mr. Douvier.

"How come he didn't sculpt a relic of six-year-old Sylvie...when she left her own message on the scroll for the world to know?" asked Gaston.

Juliette intervened, staring at her grandpa, "I showed Gaston the scroll a few days ago. He's up to date with almost everything."

"That explains—" Monsieur Douvier cut himself short. "Well, actually Silvio was about to start work on Sylvie's relic when he was found dead in his Languedoc villa. Rat poisoning, according to his sister. Months later his sister vanished from view...and to this date nobody's been able to connect the dots to complete the story."

"Bummer!" said Gaston. "History's so full of mystery!"

"Try religion and mythology, my friend," said Monsieur Douvier, a wry smile curling up his lips.

❧

Monsieur Douvier held the holy ancient relic higher up to the height of his chest for all eyes to feast on. "Look at Mary Magdalene's finger..." he then challenged proudly. He swiftly extracted a magnifying glass from his pocket and put it on top of the saint's finger, smiling.

"*The ring!*" the young couple exclaimed in unison.

"It really looks like mine!" burst out Gaston. "Identical!"

"It's yours!" cried out Juliette. "It really is!"

"You both said it...and you're both correct," confirmed the vastly educated and experienced old man. "One of these days we'll prove it in my lab...with the most advanced archeological tools available in Europe. We'll go the distance to leave no doubts."

"How did Silvio create such a masterpiece?" asked Juliette. "I mean...the ring, in particular, it's so tiny, yet–"

"–Look at these amazing details in the three faces–Jesus', Mary's, Sylvie's–" interjected Gaston, "Their eyes, lips, noses, chins...such realistic expressions. Even my ring is easy to identify in spite of its tiny size. And it's clearly mine."

"The fine strokes of Silvio's art on this holy relic were possible because of a secret Ancient Egyptian technique passed on to him by the great son of an Essenes high priest," informed Monsieur Douvier.

"Wow..."

"In addition, Silvio dipped his chisel in a special solution before he skillfully chipped away at the relic material...to give attention to minute detail for realism and authenticity and capture the spirit of his subjects."

"I'd love to see Silvio sculpturing his masterpiece," said Juliette.

"Yeah..." said Gaston. "I'd also love to watch how he painted these beautiful handwritten words at the bottom of the relic...comparing his words to mine 2000 years later...and–"

"–you should die in shame?" teased Juliette.

"At least," said the young excited boy.

They both laughed.

"He used a stylus made of metal, which he dipped in black ink..." said Monsieur Douvier.

Checking his wrist watch, he added, "Our time is up, kids. Let's close our treasure box now and put it back where it belongs," he told them, with a voice that echoed from wall to wall deep into the cave's entrails.

"But I want to read the message from Jesus and Mary's first!" blurted out Juliette.

"Okay. Read it for all of us, please."

Her eyes moved down past the facial and hip area of the holy family on the relic, where the message distinctly and clearly appeared.

She read calmly, with eloquence, both the actress in her and the person:

For eternal love and peace we preach
For spiritual abundance and harmony we live
For forgiveness and equality we teach
For our child's blessed arrival we give
-Yahshua of Nazarene
-Mary of Magdala

"Wow..." said Gaston, "so true...so fitting..."

"So timely..." added Juliette, exchanging glances with Gaston, Monsieur Douvier noticing it.

"Very well, shall we now wrap it up?"

And indeed they did. But not before Juliette whispering to Gaston, at her first opportunity on their way out, "For our child's blessed arrival we give..."

Above hovered Richard's soul.

SPREADING THE NEWS ABOUT JULIETTE'S AILMENT IS HARDER THAN DEALING WITH GASTON'S "BAD BOY" BEHAVIOR IN HIS DREAMS

Old Farm

"Hey, let's walk around. I need the exercise. The baby too." Juliette had just parked her bicycle in the usual area, past the farm's entry gate.

"How's he or she doing lately?"

"Fine...I think. I'm the one who's feeling weird sometimes...nauseated...vomiting..."

"When do you think we should tell your–."

"–Second Mom? Grandpa? Your family? The Quintero's?" She pouted.

"Well, yes...in that order maybe..."

Juliette stared at a nearby chestnut tree and the hills behind it. "Not yet...I still can hide my belly for a few more weeks. It's really very small. I need time to think."

"I also need time to think."

They rambled through a bunch of loose and noisy chickens, ducks, and pigs. Pablo had just fed them and they looked happy with themselves, save an occasional pursuit or fight.

"Any more strange dreams lately, big boy?"

He scratched the back of his head.

"Yes. Dreams about schools, different schools, but always Roman Catholic schools."

"Sounds good to me."

"Warning–I'm always a bad boy in those dreams or reveries."

"Why?"

"I have no idea."

"That's okay–I'm not that good myself."

"Yes you are!"

"You think so?"

"I'm positive, one hundred percent."

"Well, thanks, bad boy," she teased with a smooch to his cheek. "Let's sit down here." She'd picked a large stone step near the barn, just enough space for the two of them.

He smiled, said, "In my dreams my teachers are mean. They enjoy more punishing than teaching. They want students to feel sorry... guilty...miserable...for any little thing they've done. Then they enjoy watching them begging for mercy...expressing remorse...but mostly they love to see them hopelessly frightened...scared to death...falling apart in a sea of tears...and sometime pee or shit!"

"Well—that's a *strong* beginning!" burst out Juliette. "I can't wait for the rest!"

"It won't be pretty. You might not want to hear it."

"Shoot Gaston—I'm your *wife-to-be!*"

That made him real happy—she talking like that, with courage and firmness. She wasn't afraid of her current situation.

They kissed, Pablo watching from a distance.

"Where was I?"

"Mean teachers...Roman Catholic schools..."

"I wasn't a great student either. I often failed to finish my homework or do it at all...so the teacher, in this dream, called me up to his desk, asked me to face the whole class...and show the palm of my right hand...as if to shake hands with someone."

"Nice gesture..."

"Not really. Next thing he asked me to join all fingertips together, all pointing to the ceiling, while the whole class remains dead silent, watching.

Then, to my surprise, he pulls a long, heavy triangular ruler from behind his back and smacks the tip of my fingers with all his might. So painful the blow was to me, I automatically opened my hand...ready to cry...feeling miserable in front of all the students."

"*The bastard!*"

"Unfeeling, the teacher asked me to join my fingertips again... because my punishment that particular day demanded a second whack."

"*What?!*"

"I complied...but just when he was going to smack me again, after raising his ruler real high...I instinctively opened my hand...hoping for a less painful whack...which it was..."

"Good..."

"But this infuriated him like hell and shouted that because of this I would now get twice the number of whacks I was supposed to get, and that I'd better keep my fingertips together this time...or else expect double punishment again."

"*The son of a bitch!*" yelled Juliette, surprised at her own choice of words.

"I complied. I had no choice. After that I couldn't write well for a few days...my hand was in terrible pain...swollen...."

"It pains me so much...just to hear you, Gaston."

"I know...but it was only a dream..."

"Was it?" She pouted.

"Well, Pierre was not in my class...to confirm or deny it happened... so—"

"Deep inside, Gaston, do you think it happened? Not a dream or false memory—but a fact. A real incident."

He shrugged, took time to reply. "Hard to tell..."

"How old were you in this dream...or incident?"

"About six or seven."

She threw a fistful of corn grains she'd picked up while walking to a duck that sought their company.

"You know—I have a follow-up dream...that really makes it harder for me to believe it really happened...because...because I doubt very much I was that kind of a boy at that age..."

"Tell me about it...let me judge you."

"I'll tell you...but please spare the judging. I hate to be judged."

"Okay, master."

"One day I told three or four students who were my best friends, and actually sat close to each other in the classroom, to do something real foolish in retaliation for all the smacks our teacher had given us lately."

"Another foolish idea?"

"At that age most ideas are foolish, Juliette."

Sly-eyed, she said, "Maybe."

"So I told them I would annoy the teacher at one point in the class and make him actually walk to my seat with his triangular ruler in front of all students...then provoke him to hit me in the head with his ruler...at which point my other friends would also provoke him to hit them in the head as well."

"*What kind of a game is that!*" shouted Juliette. "*Are you totally crazy?!*"

"*Here's the thing!*" shouted Gaston, all excited. "Me and my friends had agreed to explode into uncontrollable laughter...one blow after another...no matter what...and just keep going until the teacher, seeing no results, would finally stop the beating and leave the class."

"*How stupid can you guys be—my God!*"

"*It worked! The whole class joined us! We created a riot! It was awesome!*"

"And the teacher?"

"He vanished forever!...in my dream..."

Above hovered Richard's soul.

FROM PAPA NOËL TO CITY STORKS TO THE ULTIMATE FANTASY MAN

Saint-Jean-du-Gard

"I didn't think he would actually buy it, but he did..." celebrated Juliette, referring to the white Camargue horse she was mounted on, one hand slightly pulling on the reins.

"I always wondered if he would...now I know he did," exclaimed Gaston happily, enjoying his own white Camargue horse. His body stood gracefully erect, above the saddle, both his eyes looking forward between the horse's ears.

They were returning from a short ride in the upper valley, deeper into the Cévennes, testing the horses that Monsieur Douvier had provided for them, as promised.

Juliette swung her right leg over her horse's back to dismount. "He's perfect for me!" she cheered.

"I like mine too," exclaimed Gaston, taking his feet out of the stirrups irons, preparing to step on the ground.

They led the two horses back to the stable, where someone was employed to take care of them, as well as other horses. Here Juliette often came to practice horse riding after school. The place, ran by monks, sported overnight stalls (complete with large, pipe-panel enclosed paddocks), an outdoor riding corral, and a gravel driveway entrance for horse trailers in addition to regular wood trails and an open grassy field.

Resting on a wooden bench by the gate, they began to chat.

"Good thing we're finally on vacation–no more teachers or books!"

"My school wasn't that bad," said Juliette casually.

"Neither was mine..."

"Small teaching?" teased the young actress.

"No. Simple. Too simple."

Juliette made the typical pout and grimace of "you're so conceited," then smiled to herself.

Gaston seemed entangled in peculiar thoughts.

"It's amazing how vulnerable to stories we are when growing up... we're told to blindly believe in certain things...only to learn on our own years later such things were lies...and that's supposed to be okay? I mean to be lied to?" he said, immersing into a subject that had always intrigued him ever since the disappearance of his childhood.

"What do you mean, *mon chéri*..." uttered Juliette, playing with the tip of her boots, which she rubbed against the gravel in front of them.

Gaston blinked. "I was so mad when somebody told me that Papa Noël didn't exist...that it was a fairy tale...that parents were the ones who brought toys to their children...never coming through the chimney. I wanted to kill that person for having the nerve to tell me that!"

"How old were you then?"

"Seven maybe..." Gaston's hazel eyes seemed darker now, flared up with intensity. "In the next few weeks I overheard little conversations about the same thing from other kids, older kids, gradually sinking me into terrible confusion...eventually leading me to believe I'd been lied to since childhood...that indeed there wasn't any Papa Noël...that there had never been one...and that there would never been one. Shocking revelation! Absolute hurt!"

"Yeah...I went through that too..."

"This hurt stayed with me for one or two years. It just lingered deep inside of me...like the sudden death of a loved one...unacceptable..."

Juliette sweetly patted his shoulder.

"Then, I was shocked by another one. Another revelation."

"You don't have to tell me...if you don't want to..." whispered Juliette in his ear, realizing how sensitive he was about these things.

"No. I will tell you." He pulled a handkerchief from his pocket, fidgeted a little with it. "I remember walking downhill to the Garonne River once...in this poor section of Toulouse where we lived...either Rue de 36 Ponts or Rue des Pharaons...hard to say because we often moved around to weird neighborhoods by the river...where kids my age had sex on the river bank."

"Well, well...naughty kids."

"Anyway...walking down the cobblestones, this kid friend of mine... classmate...told me that he'd recently learned that babies didn't come from city storks, but from inside a woman's body...specifically the crotch. It was so disgusting for me to hear that, I wanted to crush that person's head with a brick! Again, it took me months, maybe years, of total confusion and disbelief and hurt to realize I'd been lied to since childhood...that babies were not carried around by storks flying across town to expectant families. It was all a fantasy...a fairy tale...like the Papa Noël story..."

"I think I know what you're talking about," said Juliette with a corny little smile, reaching out for his hand and gently putting it on her tummy.

"Well, I'm almost ten years old now," defended himself Gaston with some pride.

"Almost?"

"Well, almost nine-and-a-half."

"Don't feel bad, I'm almost thirteen-and-a-half."

After a long pause, Gaston said, "So now I understand why many people around the world would feel so enraged and even would like to burn me at the stake, if they could, when I tell them the whole thing is a fairy tale...a fantasy. Our planet is not the center of the Universe. And nobody ever was born of a virgin, walked on water, performed miracles, rose from the dead, fed thousands with a few loaves of bread and two fish, became divine, and sat on the right hand side of God in Heaven as his authentic Son. And no priest can ever be able to drink a person's blood and eat his body during mass in Church. It's going to take a lot of time...past the shocking news, the incredible revelation, and the hurt...after so many years of believing in such fantasy...such fairy tale...to realize the truth."

"Are you saying that there's only God and period?"

"I guess so." Gaston remained thoughtful. "The world is full of story tellers, not reality tellers...possibly since the Stone Age."

"Sometimes you sound like you're much older—eighteen or nineteen."

"I'm kind of aware of that."

"Your point of view is very convincing...perhaps because you've been listening too much to what I've told you...about my own Cathar upbringing. But *there was* a man named Jesus of Nazarene and a woman he loved named Mary of Magdala and their cherished daughter named Sylvie of Massalia," said Juliette with confidence, even defiance. "They *did* exist!"

"I'm sure they did."

The shoreline where a pregnant Mary Magdalene landed in a boat washed ashore by the waves over 20 centuries ago, the soft sand of the beach where the tiny village of Les-Saintes-Maries-de-la-Mer stood, the white doves flying above—all that appeared in Gaston's mind as he walked back to his room later that evening. It felt good, peaceful, even warm.

Above hovered Richard's soul.

PART 13

CLASH #12—INK BEACH
(A TIME TRAVELED CLASH)
FRANCE, JULY 1955

A CONTEST BETWEEN RICHARD'S "PEN AND PAPER" AND MASTER JUDGE'S "TIRED VOICE"

Bermuda Revelation Park, Zundo, June 3081

A sunny beach appeared on a slowly rising Astral Floor platform. Blue ocean and clear sky filled the area as the platform vanished.

Beautiful young girls played volley ball in soft sand. Richard found himself sunbathing near them by a palm tree.

Master Judge's black gloves were at work on the control panel. His shiny bald head and pointed black beard marred the view, the doom in his eyes even more so.

Above, the spinning Celestial Sphere descended smoothly from its parked space in the sky to about a dozen feet over people's heads in the six Stadiums, red-flashing the current punishment Clash status:

JUST COMPLETED: CLASH #11—KNIFE THROWING • OVERALL SCORE: JUDGES 8 DEFENDANT 3 • NEXT: CLASH #12—INK BEACH

Turning faster now, the Sphere ascended majestically above the crowd and cleared the area.

All seated Zundonians sang in unison the lyrics displayed on their ZCAP meters–again insulting and condescending words, meant to break the defendant's spirit.

Impertinently wrapped in his black cape, Master Judge addressed the disoriented defendant from the Royal Den in the manner only a god would. That is, a god with a sore throat and a failing voice.

"We're going to continue our chat in this new environment...except that you will be *mute* and I will be *deaf*," said his whispery yet alluring voice through fluttering leaves, hypnotically inducing Richard to sit down in the soft, warm sand.

"So don't pretend to talk to me, because I'll pretend not to hear you."

Just then, he appeared floating on a tricolored bubble, clad on Bermuda shorts, wearing an eerie smile charged with malicious electricity.

With his pointed index finger, he popped the bubble open and landed next to the defendant.

The audience cheered, whistled, and threw things in the air.

"Pretend?" said Richard.

"Here's a pen and paper," whispered the eccentric judge. "I'll use my voice—well, what's left of it. As you can hear, I'm hoarse...swollen vocal cords..."

"Sorry about that..."

"Whoever runs out of gas first...loses."

"Gas?"

"*Ink* versus *voice*."

"Your voice sounds really bad right now. Are your vocal cords... metallic? Or...fleshy...like mine? I mean, you're a *zobot*."

"*Shut up mute-man! Can't hear you either!*" Master Judge shouted, exasperated, in spite of his ailing voice. "Start now!" he said in a slightly calmer manner.

A most awkward moment ensued.

Richard watched the judge acting strangely.

Master Judge pretended to play with the sand, lying down, sort of waiting for Richard's first input, which failed to come. So he took the initiative, said, huskily, "Do you realize now that it's over, Mr. Zilch?"

Richard tried to comment vocally, a bit nervous, but ended up jotting something down on the paper he was holding, following the judge's rules. He showed it to the judge.

"**What do you mean?**" it read.

Master Judge paid no attention.

Hoarsely, he continued, "...that heritage and history and myth have become extinct...that religion destroyed itself and vanished after proving itself wrong...after the *Handshake with God Day* debacle..."

Richard rushed to write down something, showed it to the judge, who again dismissed it.

Furious, Richard started jumping up and down in front of him, forcing him to react to his inked comments.

The judge finally grabbed the piece of paper and read, in a rush, **"Handshake with God Day? When? Where? What happened?"**

"Yes...handshake with our Creator...in the summer of 3000...Alice Springs, Australia..." he said huskily. "How could you miss it? You were about eighty-one years old, weren't you?"

He coughed a little.

"Over one-hundred million people from around the world gathered there to witness the event...or non-event...young and old, rich and poor, healthy and sick...people from all walks of life..."

Richard jotted down his comments, showed them to Master Judge, **"I was in deep-freeze sleep for ninety years already in 3000, set for a total of thirteen decades, but Zundo's rulers woke me up after only ten decades—too soon—for this 3081 trial..."**

"Busy, busy."

Richard wrote down, **"That's why I missed the handshake..."**

Master Judge remarked, after reading it, "Well, Mr. Zilch, 'you can't always have what you want'—quoting from a famous 20th-century rock song by Mike Jagger and his Rolling Stones band."

Richard just nodded.

"Anyway. God didn't show up...didn't shake hands with anybody. He let the world down."

"Sad, terrible," scribbled down Richard.

"...thousands of books have been written about it since that awful day...hundreds of movies had been released showing the religion fiasco..." said Master Judge, increasingly sore in his throat, "...three times as many songs had been cut expressing peoples' crushed feelings about God not being there when needed the most..." Master Judge paused to catch his breath. "...a heart breaking story for the world to bear..."

"Very painful indeed."

"How could he be there—many people said—if he didn't exist?" remarked the judge.

"**Good point**."

"...and then later...that same year...Zundo the Conspirator and his multiple armies of Zongdrolls took over the world...our new world... which they renamed Zundo."

Richard just nodded.

"Anyway...you must realize that we're no longer the way we used to be...that economic, social, and political systems have failed..." Master Judge said, struggling with his throaty and grating voice. "...that Capitalism, Islamism, Al-Qaedaism, Socialism, Communism, Fascism have been eradicated years ago..."

"**Hard to believe**," inked down Richard. As usual, he showed it to the judge.

Cynically, Master Judge tossed sand to his toes, watched how it dispersed slowly through them. Apparently, his vocal fatigue didn't deter him from acting oddly.

"...that America, Brazil, Canada, China, France," went on harshly the judge, mentioning nations alphabetically, "Germany, Great Britain, India, Israel, Japan, Mighty Arabia, Pakistan, Russia..." and all those powerful countries you used to know...have been effaced from the maps...while you were sleeping..."

"**Oh my...**" wrote down Richard.

Master Judge made circles in the soft sand with one finger. Very hoarsely, he said, "...that foreign affairs and world tension are no longer applicable to our society...that military power has been abolished..."

Richard scrabbled down, "**Incredible!**" and showed it to the judge. Then he added, with ink, "**What about Hitler's Nazism and the Perfect Race?**" before he showed it again to the judge, who happened to be playing with the sand.

In time, talking with difficulty, Master Judge replied, "...gone...before you even went to sleep...way before. How could you miss that?"

"**I never believed in that stuff**."

Master Judge read the defendant's comment.

"What stuff?"

"**You know...death camps**."

Angrily, the judge slammed, "You don't believe that genocide took place?" He coughed. "That more than six million Jews were exterminated by the Nazis?" He coughed again. "Where have you been Mr. Zilch all these years?"

Richard didn't write anything down, had nothing to say.

"And...have you forgotten we've already argued about that before? During our log fight...Clash #1? A Clash you miserably lost. Under a different last name—'Flynn,' I believe. Now you're rightly called 'Zilch.' What will it take you to come down to your senses? Shame on you! Dismissing him, the judge continued his sermon, as if he was reading from a book, "...that nuclear energy has been de-energized and restored to pre-Einstein times...that, in effect, it's a criminal offense to split the atom...or just disturb any Universe-given equilibrium..."

"Very profound."

Richard observed how the judge picked up a little shell from the sand and stared at it closely.

Huskily, Master Judge continued, "...that—well, to make it short—we're only responsible to Zundo...our one and only nation...our one and only world...our one and only system..."

Wild applause and cheers exploded across the Stadiums and surrounding areas. "LONG LIVE ZUNDO! ZUNDO IS GREAT! ZUNDO IS COSMOS'S SON!"

About half-a-million citizens rose to their feet shouting patriotic slogans in frenzied fervor. They waved their hands and jumped and tossed flowers in the air. It quickly grew into disorder, then chaos.

At which point Master Judge intervened, raising both his arms to the audience with brutal authority, from his sun-bathing, sand-warming position.

"PLEASE! PLEASE! PLEASE!" he commanded, hoarsely. "PLEASE LET THIS FUCKING TRIAL MOVE ON! ALLOW MR. ZILCH TO CONTINUE AND FINISH HIS CONFESSION. THANK YOU!"

"What about me?" displayed Richard his latest inked comment to the judge.

Master Judge simply let the latest sand he'd dug out with his fingers fall slowly and lazily over his bare stomach. "What about you?" he said, with a dash of malice, feeling a burning pain in his vocal cords.

Richard shifted his legs uneasily. **"I mean—am I a Zundonian?"** he wrote down and showed it to Master Judge.

Watching it on the Stadiums' multi-angular gigantic screens, the surrounding audience broke into laughter, mocking him. A battery of put down cries followed.

◦◦

A similar reaction occurred underwater.

"Aren't human beings pathetically funny up there?" remarked a passing mutton snapper to his parrotfish pal.

"A lot more than we are down here..." replied the parrotfish. "I'm just glad that they're sending this super rich dude away to *The Unknown*. I'd go mad or something if they'd send him down here.

"I'd commit suicide!" said the mutton snapper. "Can't stand greedy people!"

They swam between lush red and yellow sponges, gently drifting by like soft feathers over a terraced plateau, midway down to the dark abyss.

Neighboring formations of corals, rewarded with lots of sunlight, shone in rainbow hues of lilac, blue, and green, where spoiled angelfish sunbathed and prayed.

◦◦

"Seriously. Am I a Zundonian?" wrote again a frustrated Richard, hoping Master Judge would at last pay attention to his earnest plea.

"On probation...pending your X years of soul travel journey... pending the arm surgery..." answered the judge.

He dropped more sand over his legs, slowly, lazily.

"Will the surgery restore my freedom?"

Master Judge grabbed a small piece of dry wood and plodded it inchmeal through the sand.

"Maybe," he said in his failing, rasping voice.

"Will I be permitted to speak in Undo-English?"

The judge adopted a sitting position in the sand, smiled at some gorgeous passing girls.

"Maybe."

Richard rushed again with his pen. **"Will the surgery restore my freedom?"** He showed it to Master Judge, panting like a dog now. **"Will it?"** he added, desperately, holding the inked words to the judge's eyes.

Master Judge acknowledged the dramatic change in Richard's face, the deep anguish, as he lazily slipped more sand through his toes.

"No need to repeat yourself, man," he said, with a gruff, tired voice. "The surgery...if deserving...will make you one of us. It will free you...within our system..."

The defendant calmed down a little. He scratched one ear.

"However, you must understand that this blatant...incorrigible stubbornness of yours...with respect to your wealth–invisible wealth, for it just isn't there anymore–during those...notorious fifteen or so years...of your life–" he said very laboriously, pausing here and there to breath in, before Richard stopped him cold with one strong raised hand.

Master Judge watched the defendant jot down new words hurriedly.

"You mean the period I became active in business and multiplied my wealth?"

"Multiplied?" said the judge, narrowing his eyes and trying, but failing, to laugh. *"Zillionized!"* he nevertheless shouted.

He stared down, grabbed more sand with his playful fingers. "Mind you, I'm not counting the 13 decades–well, 10, since we had to stop you—the 10 decades you spent dozing away in the snow..." he said, coughing his way through.

Angrily, Richard wrote down his new remark.

"Sleeping in a deep-freeze coffin!"

Very hoarsely, "Whatever. Three punitive journey choices are available to you...our very competent Sentence Judge will let you know later on...and you will have to choose one of them...the one that will take you to *The Unknown*." He corrected himself. "Actually, all choices will take you there."

Richard watched how the judge lay down again, spread sand over his bare chest, unconcerned.

"Three punitive journeys? Now?"

"Yes..." said Master Judge. "Well, right after your next and last Clash of the trial...number 13...your time is almost up..."

"But" began to jot down Richard.

"It won't be an easy thing to do..." interrupted the judge with his rasping, fatigued voice. "...lots of humility...pain and hunger...will await you...lots of suffering and disgrace..."

Richard's face shrank, his eyes seemingly whining. Struggling with his deep feelings, he wrote, **"My God! What are you going to do to me? Am I..."** No more ink flowed from his pen. He forced his pen to write, but to no avail.

In desperation, he stared at Master Judge and tried to speak, when the judge intervened, himself not in good shape either, "...I'm afraid... you...lost..." he said in an awkward, terribly labored whisper. "...I still have...a voice..." His eyes blinked. "...but you ran o...ut...o..f... i..n... ....k...." No more voice flowed from his throat.

Dizzily, they both stared up at the big, spinning, slowly descending Sphere, which displayed the current Clash status to the very last second:

JUST COMPLETED: CLASH #12—INK BEACH • OVERALL SCORE: JUDGES 9 DEFENDANT 3 • NEXT: CLASH #13— POLE VAULTING

Cheers erupted everywhere. They all stood up, applauding, whistling, stamping their feet, and making all kinds of wild noises with bells, drums, and trumpets.

Women's leather bags, shoes, sunglasses, and cheap zell phones followed in all directions.

Stadium lights flashed in myriads of colors. Sounds from electric guitars blasted around.

While Zundonians celebrated, the huge silver Celestial Sphere ascended back to its sky-high position, turning like a top.

PART 14

A NEW CHAIN OF TWISTED EVENTS IN THE HORIZON FRANCE, JULY 1955

MORE TROUBLING MEMORIES—FALSE OR TRUE— SPOIL THE TRAIN À VAPEUR DES CÉVENNES' CHARMING RIDE

For a change, and taking advantage of the summer vacation, Juliette and Gaston found themselves riding together in this charming steam train from Anduze to Saint-Jean-du-Gard.

They were returning from a longer journey to sunny Alès, where she'd met with some film producers in a quaint office, near the old, historical section of town. Not invited in, Gaston had perused some glossy showbiz magazines in the lobby. Then he'd savored a big vanilla ice-cream outdoors with a few francs he'd fished in his pocket.

Nothing certain had come out of the meeting, and her agent wouldn't know with certainty if she'd struck a good deal with them until after perhaps several weeks. Too many details lingered in the air. So they got a ride from a friend to the train station at Anduze, where they'd boarded this fantasy-like brightly colored train in good spirits.

Past a very long tunnel that opened to a stately metallic bridge over the river Gardon d'Anduze, between Rocher de Saint Julien and Rocher de Payremale, the train moved on to La Bambouseraie–Europe's largest bamboo forest–just a couple of kilometers ahead. The complete trip to Saint-Jean-du-Gard was about 13 kilometers.

"No better way to enter the Cévennes than through these two cool brotherly mountains," remarked Juliette, sitting next to Gaston.

"May I touch your tummy?"

"You may...I think the baby is sleeping right now..."

"With these noisy wagons?"

Placing one hand on the special area, he waited for any sign of activity, which eventually translated into a tiny, hardly felt kick. But something. "Confirmed!" he exclaimed.

He then grabbed her hand warmly and they kissed.

"You know how they call these wagons?" said Juliette.

"No."

"*Boîtes de tonnerre.*" (Thunderous boxes)

He laughed.

"I actually like them. They remind me we're going somewhere."

The train made a stop at the Bambouseraie station, where they stretched their legs for a few minutes, shrouded in a strange world of bamboos and exotic Asian plants, then continued to the village of Générargues before entering the Tunnel de Prafrance.

"I'm curious about something..." said Juliette, pouting.

"What?"

"Were they real or false...those memories you told me you had the other day...about your school friends in Toulouse?"

"Which ones?"

"Memories you said totally crushed your faith in Papa Noël and baby-carrying city storks?"

"I'm not sure anymore."

"Well, you told me about them."

"I was younger than eight in those memories, before the car crash."

"Well, you're only nine now, so it wasn't that long ago."

Gaston remained pensive. "Anything appearing before the car crash becomes eerily suspect."

"But..." said Juliette.

"I faintly remember, whether true or false, we lived in a rundown neighborhood, lots of kids my age played in the street. We lived in the third floor of this ugly building. The toilet often would clog with shit."

"Bad word," objected Juliette.

"Then someone would call this special truck loaded with huge hoses looking like caterpillars, and slide them through the building hallway, and up the stairs to our apartment and deep into the living room, all the way to the toilet, where they turned on the machine that sucked out the shit."

"*Hugghh*—you don't have to be so graphic...and vulgar."

"Downstairs the building and outside in the street all the kids would be laughing, squeezing their noses, because of the stinking shit smell."

"*Gaston!*"

"And shouting out loud all together, *"Presser le nez, la pompe a merde est arrivé!"* (Pinch your nose, the shit pump has arrived!)

"Gaston—that's revolting! Stop it! Our baby's going to wake up!" she snapped, mostly with her fiercely stinging green eyes.

"I'm sorry. I got carried away."

"We're also missing the spectacular panorama at either side of the windows."

The train was now crossing the majestic eleven-arch Viaduc du Mescladou over the Gardon de Mialet and the Gardon de Saint-Jean—two large rivers which joined to form the powerful Gardon d'Anduze near the village of Corbés.

"By the way, Toulouse's beautiful—all over—I've been there several times," said Juliette. "So I don't know where you lived and went to school and hung out with your friends."

"I told you, by the river Garonne." He stared at her funnily. "School? Not pretty. Old and gray. Our uniform was black. Looked like a cheap kitchen apron." He laughed.

"Old and gray school?"

"Yes. Down by the river...where all kids hung out after classes doing all kinds of stuff."

"Like what?"

"Strange things...lots of sex...spread out over pissed-on shrubs...along the muddy riverbank." He searched his mind. "Over faded grass paths, behind coarse bushes, into the dark caves. Not a pretty sight. Not a safe place."

"I can imagine."

The train slowed down, then picked up speed again and rolled steadily at fifty km/hr for a while, cruising through more dazzling tunnels, viaducts, villages, and scenic places that neither one noticed.

"During morning school breaks, we entertained ourselves throwing rocks that sparked real big and bright against a very tall and imposing stone wall that somehow stood there as a centerpiece school structure. Lots of kids enjoyed that. And it was a regular past time not only permitted, but encouraged by the teachers.

"Alternatively, we often played a popular game with the pointed end of a big knife blade–a switchblade–that made each player self-poke parts of their fleshy body contour sequentially in ascending and descending order...head to toes..."

"Also encouraged by the teachers?" asked Juliette astounded.

"I really don't remember. We just played it. I know that."

"In your dream...or in your past?"

"I wish I knew."

"So...how do you play that...game?"

"Flipping the knife over with a quick jerk of your fingers while poking your flesh with the sharp blade tip...so the pointed end would somersault and stab-target the damp soil below."

"Weird..."

"Hitting key sensitive spots, up and down the contour of your body, you just keep going, poking, flipping the knife over, and stabbing the soil–without missing or you're out. Until you complete the cycle."

"What sensitive parts?"

"Chin, mouth, nose, eyelids, forehead, both ears...when ascending around and over the head."

"How reckless and useless," said Juliette.

"Tummy, thigh, knee, shin–"

"–*stop it!*" slammed Juliette.

"Very fast and without flaw. I'm sure the game has a name, but I don't–"

"–*stop talking about it!*" shouted Juliette, annoyed.

"Okay...okay..."

"I'm sorry, but pregnancy makes me edgy sometimes."

༄

Scarcely a few seconds went by when:

"*La vache!*" exclaimed Juliette, turning to the window. "We've already reached the Viaduc de Doucettes!"

"The trip's supposed to take forty-five minutes—we're not done yet," uttered Gaston.

"Was this a public school?" asked Juliette a moment later.

"I don't remember."

He watched the sweeping scenery for a brief moment, enhanced by the rattling train noise, feeling its shaking motion.

"Most of the time I was thrown into Roman Catholic schools by my parents, struggling to survive...in those stiff, scary religious places." His face turned oddly sad. "I remember trudging along the riverside with a group of boys my age one time, some boarding school outing we had, supervised by priests who also walked along with us."

"In Toulouse? Alès?"

"Wherever. I remember one young, tall priest forever hitting me on the calves real hard with a long green stick he'd pulled out of the river...yelling that I should move faster despite the fact that I'd told him I was dead tired and sore with blisters under my feet. Despite the fact that I begged him to please stop whacking me with the frigging stick. Despite the fact that he was leaving deep red cuts on my calves. All in vain!"

"This is painful—just to hear you."

"The point is, I don't know if I've dreamed or lived these things... whether they're true or not."

"Did you ever try to run away from these awful places...awful people?" Her lips pouted in a compassionate way.

"Yes, I did. Actually, a bunch of us—seriously hurt and bummed out—decided one morning to escape."

His mental eyes searched for images. "But after hours of trudging through rugged hills, endless valleys, and deserted beaches, we were suddenly attacked by a swarm of nasty mosquitoes."

"Where?"

"Oh...someplace...filled with sand dunes...near the ocean."

"You guys must've walked far away from school, huh?"

"Very far. And those mosquitoes drove us crazy–I mean, totally!"

He paused, smiled. "Thinking it would only get worse, we dragged ourselves back to *le pénitencier*–that's the way we called it–feeling like total losers, our swollen faces and necks full of mosquito bites. We arrived well past dinner time. Our punishment was so severe, we never tried it again!"

"Could your dreams or childhood or whatever get any worse, Gaston?" She obviously doubted.

"Oh yes. That's nothing. There's one incident that stands out, not the worst by any means, tough, but maybe you should never hear it."

The steam train entered the last stretch of the journey, having passed a rich goat landscape and the first visible skirting homes of Saint-Jean-du-Gard.

∿

They stepped down the train at *la Gare*, just as simple the place as its name, facing a pleasant wide, pink-red, two-story structure.

"Let's just walk home now..." invited Juliette, flushing a gorgeous smile. "It'll give you plenty of space and time to charm me, or scare me, with your latest *wacky dream*."

They took Avenue René Boudon and crossed the Pont Neuf, while staring to the left at the old Pont Vieux and down to the sumptuous river Gardon running between them. Reaching Avenue de la Resistance, they headed into downtown Saint-Jean-du-Gard, realizing neither one had said much about anything during this interval.

"Why are you so resistant to tell me about this dream?"

"Because it'll put me on the spot–whether true or false."

"I know a lot about you already." She pouted.

"Dream stuff."

"Maybe reality."

Juliette stopped on her march, near La Tour de l'Horloge in the Place du Marché.

"We'll sort it out later...tell me now."

Gaston saw a darker shade of green tinge her fiery eyes. He had no choice now.

"Okay," he said, walking slowly toward Le Château Saint-Jean on Rue Pasteur. "I was at this Roman Catholic school in Toulouse, where I'd done something terribly bad one day...so bad the school head priest requested an immediate formation of all students in front of the administration building."

She halted. "Terribly bad?"

"I really don't remember what it was. My dream didn't specify."

"Hummmm." She pouted.

They reached l'Hôtel de Ville in the Place de la Révolution.

He went on describing the priest. "He was a huge, mean-faced man with a big booming voice that scared everyone to death. His ears were small, but his round, fat lips looked like plump Mexican donuts out of the oven."

"Ha!" she echoed, amused.

"Clad in black cloth, he loudly, but politely, addressed the six-hundred or so students and ordered that the student who'd committed the despicable, unforgivable act, please step forward. Nobody did. Of course, I was the culprit. He called out again for the bad boy to volunteer in stepping forward...that he knew who that person was...and that it would be wise for him to do so...or else expect severe consequences."

"Gaston," she said, stopping on her walk again, and holding him steady with her eyes. "It's unfair of you not to tell me what you did wrong."

Ignoring her, he said, "*Harrowing consequences* were more appropriate words."

"I can imagine."

"I waited for one more and last warning, and finally stepped forward. Right there in front of him and the whole student body, I began to pee in my pants, feeling excruciatingly embarrassed. They all saw my pee becoming a lake and me standing in the middle of it with my head down, my shoulders hunched, and my heart broken."

"It must've been really bad what you did."

They crossed the Grand Rue.

He renewed his march on Rue du Maréchal de Thoiras, said with brisk intensity, "But that wasn't the end!"

Oh..."

"He then dismissed everyone, but me, and asked me to follow him to his office upstairs."

Gaston just stared at her, without blinking. "As he closed the door behind him, he suddenly grabbed me by the waist and violently threw me up in the air like a rag doll...so high I almost crushed my head against the ceiling."

"That's awful! A head priest...in a Catholic school?!"

"He threw me up repeatedly and savagely about ten times, each time shouting, *'You'll rot in hell, bad boy!'*"

They now continued walking on Avenue Abraham Mazel, heading toward Route de Luc.

"I can't believe that! He's insane! Evil!"

"He might not be real...that priest," Gaston said, dismissively. "He just appeared in my dream...a bad dream."

She pouted offensively. *"Nobody dreams like that!"*

"I possibly did."

"You don't give up, do you?"

She could punch him with her pout.

Above hovered Richard's soul.

JULIETTE'S SECOND SCARY
NOTE FROM LES ALLUMETTES

Juliette's Home

When Juliette walked back home after a nice ride on her Camargue horse in the nearby meadows, she found Madame Clarice holding a piece of paper in the porch with threatening handwritten words, her face pale and stressed out with anger and fear.

"What's wrong?'

She gave Juliette the written paper.

"Read this...it's sickening."

It was exactly the same frightening message she'd found at her door a few weeks ago:

Juliette,
You're nothing but a witch. Think Jeanne d'Arc and her fate!
Les Allumettes

She felt the same cold chill flash through her spine, but this time she contained the surge of tears.

Actually, there was something different. Under *Les Allumettes*, by itself, there was an encircled capital "A"–the "A" rather big and imposing.

"Don't worry, Mom, I'll talk to Grandpa."

"That's awful! We should inform the police!"

"It could be just a prank–teenagers from school, you know."

She was able to convince her to hold on a bit longer, a few days perhaps, to see if new information popped up. Neighbors might know something. Other students might come forward with details. No need to rush.

Certainly, Gaston would know sooner than anyone.

Above hovered Richard's soul.

NEZ FROID'S PUZZLING "A" MARK ON JULIETTE'S SCHOOL ESSAY

Old Farm

Juliette arrived, set her bicycle against the stone wall outside Gaston's door, as usual.

She entered the room carrying a dozen or so pages, all neatly written and marked up.

"What are you doing? School's over and you're messing around with old homework?" Gaston teased Juliette, baffled.

She gave him a serious stare.

"Here it is!" she said, pointing to a mark on the right margin.

"Your teacher gave you an 'A'? Not a '20'?"

"It's not a grade. And you know, nobody gets 'As' or '20s' in our schools—not even me!" She stared at him. "Neither you little genius!"

"I'm a 'straight-19' student!" bragged Gaston.

"Exactly. Not a 'straight-20' student."

"So what is it?" He closed the door to his room left open by Juliette, puzzled at her scholarly visit.

"This 'A' is Nez Froid's sort of signature for *Allumettes*."

"The bully's!?" exclaimed Gaston, worried. "How do you know?"

"They call themselves *Les Allumettes*—he and his buddies. They're bad!" She stared at his closet, his partly open chest of drawers, and the shaded hallway behind the portrait of James Joyce, by a French painter, leading to the bathroom, as making sure no one was hiding there, listening. "Really bad." She pouted.

"How do you know?" repeated Gaston.

"Some sick stories flooding around."

"Hummmm..."

"I remember several weeks ago I had this paper, this essay, open on my desk...in the classroom, during the morning break...and, I was out in the lavatory chatting with a friend...Monique...so when I came back I noticed he'd been sitting there reading my stuff."

"What kind of stuff?"

"Something I wrote in favor of Savonarola's bold stand against the rich and corrupt Catholic rulers of Florence, Italy, in the 15th century. You know, the eternal worship of luxury and pleasure by so-called servants of God...the extravagant ruling class." She pointed to it. "It's *here*." She read her literary piece to him, then mentioned George Eliot's *Romola* as her inspiration behind her writing.

"Who was Savon–?"

"Savonarola. Girolamo Savonarola. The famous Middle Ages Dominican monk who preached religious piety and upcoming doom in Florence...unless its people expelled the two-and-a-half-century old corrupt Medicis dynasty."

"Medicis?" Gaston's eyes widened. "The same ones who lived in that lavish castle we saw at Jardin du Luxembourg...in Paris?"

"Yes, the same ones. It was a very large family that yielded two French queens–including Marie de Medicis, whose Parisian palace we saw in the park you just mentioned–three popes, and several cardinals...among other titles. Many people viewed them as tyrants, yet with their wealth and influence they raised the level of culture in Florence to glorious heights. They became fervent patrons of the arts and nurtured giant talents like Michelangelo and Leonardo da Vinci."

"Did Savonatora succeed in his noble mission?"

She laughed. "Savonarola. Yes, for only a couple of years...following his rise to absolute ruler of this highly cultural city. A post that created many enemies for him and new problems for Florence with his stern religious demands and his so-called Bonfires of the Vanities."

"Bonfires of the Vanities? What's that?"

"The public burning of books, fashion clothes, artistic paintings, photographs, and anything he considered to be too open-minded, vulgar, edgy, or offensive to the city or the Church. In fact, anything that smelled of Medicis's liberal and progressive culture."

"Bummer," said Gaston.

"I wrote that too in my paper." Juliette took a deep breath. "But the people of Florence saw it in a much more serious way. Also the Church, who began to accuse him of preaching lies and inciting citizens to riots. Next thing, he was excommunicated, classified as heretic, and burned alive at the stake."

"Wow. Another one of those final solutions!" Gaston stared obliquely at her scholarly face. "Why are you telling me all this? This is Italian stuff, not French!"

"I used it in my essay. I purposely made a connection to French history and literature."

"I see a connection to your Cathar–I mean, the Cathar–issue."

"That's exactly why I got so interested." She pointed to the encircled capital "A" again on the right margin of her paper. *"Look!* He wrote it next to the words 'burned alive at the stake'–isn't that freaky!"

"'A' for *Allumettes...*" whispered Gaston. "Based on what you told me."

"And then the notes on my door...regarding Jeanne d'Arc's horrific destiny...and my own..."

They shared a grim stare.

She blinked twice tensely. "You saw him the other day...Nez Froid. Remember? Strolling down the street from the *crêperie*...with his buddies."

"Yeah. Tall and stout. Slimy-faced, show-off."

They remained momentarily silent.

"Maybe I should–" said Gaston.

"Don't!" uttered Juliette. "Not yet. We have to be sure...of his intentions. He's just a kid."

Above hovered Richard's soul.

PART 15

SUSPENDED IN PERMANENT TEENHOOD, THE 3Zs RULE ZUNDO BETTER THAN PREVIOUS LORDS, SAYS THE ZOICE
ZUNDO, JUNE 3081

ONCE UPON A TIME THE 3Zs WERE
VOTED LORDS OF ZUNDO

"It was clear to me after being ruled by a bunch of incompetent, arrogant, abusive, dysfunctional, and even scandalous Lords," said The Zoice to a CMM reporter in the far end of the Zoasis, "Zundonians would rebel and vote for something different and refreshing. Out of nowhere came these three lovely, intelligent, kind, and very capable teenagers—Z1, Z2, and Z3 (soon referred to as the 3Zs)—from three different regions, making news and gathering followers."

"I understand that Z1 was," said the reporter, "15 years old when voted Lord, red-headed, born Zoé in former France, has a degree in Philosophy from La Sorbonne…"

"Well…" said The Zoice, with a soft smile. "She's a Permanent Teenager—takes monthly shots of "PermaNentia-Z"…like Z2 and Z3. Not a secret. Most of this was published in the Planet Undersea News when campaigning for the Lordship."

The CMM reporter nodded. He checked his notes, said, "Z2, 'permanently 16' and brunette, born Zelia in former Brazil, holds a degree in Liberal Arts from the University of Sao Paulo and advanced studies in 30th Century European Literature from La Sorbonne."

"That's right."

"And Z3…" said the reporter, thinking. "Mixed Afro-American-Latino named Zana from former United States, 'permanently 17' and educated in the University of Atlantic Blue Holes and La Sorbonne with degrees in Third Millennium History and World Population Management. So all three met in La Sorbonne?"

"Yes. They became inseparable…attached by goals, visions, and love. Not a secret either—same gender love." The Zoice paused. "They also took the names Z1, Z2, and Z3."

A tiny smile escaped the reporter's lips. "So early on they forged visions for a better Zundo and put in place a simple but effective plan of changes that included ZCAP meter total allowance for education, recreation, artistic freedom, and health care for all. Also, a total ZHATEF commitment (under solemn oath) to the nation. ZHATEF, every citizen knew, stood for zero-greed, honesty, accountability, transparency, equality, and fairness. Zundonians loved what they saw and heard.

"Their campaign slogan *"Better to have three happy teen lesbians rule my world than two freaking dysfunctional straight parents ruin it!"* was a hit and the rest is history. In 3076 they were voted Lords of Zundo for a 10-year term, which still evolves today in non-surprising satisfaction, peace, and unity."

"Not bad," said The Zoice. "Off the records," he then whispered, hiding a little naughty smile while standing up to conclude the meeting. "I have a crush on Z2."

THE 3Zs GET AROUND REINSTATING "BASTILLE DAY" TO ITS GLORIOUS HISTORIC ORIGIN

Bermuda Revelation Park, June 14, 3081 4:00 p.m.

Crowds of Zundonians were standing in line in front of the six Bisected Stadiums, showing their numbered tickets to the gate officials. Dozens of parallel lines continued to form, all moving faster than the ones in the morning and the previous day.

In former France people celebrated Zastille Day today. Here in the offshore islands of former Florida they celebrated "Day 3" of the most talked about trial of the millennium. So far the trial thrived only on the Clashes or what could be considered the *hors d'oeuvres* or appetizers of Richard's soul travel journey to *The Unknown*.

In reality, the whole world stood in line today, figuratively, to watch all the peculiar, capricious, and sickening things happening in the Zoliseum.

It was said that a fit of rage and arrogance, possibly bipolar in nature, had made Zundo de Conspirator one day move Bastille Day to June 14, from its historic July 14, and rename it Zastille Day. Such despicable act, according to *Paris Match*, had raised Parisians blood pressure to extreme levels…with predicted immediate consequences. Luckily, Zundo's premature death by suicide prevented him from having his head cut off by the reinstated guillotine as hundreds of thousands shouting beret-clad protesters carrying torches, baguettes, and hardened steel pointed tools marched toward La Place de la Concorde.

The good news for former France today was that the 3Zs, by decree, declared Bastille Day fully restored to its glorious historic origin effective next year. This feat had not come by virtue of preference or sensationalism, however, but by a natural waiting process that preceded thousands of other equally important requested changes. Such was the integrity of the 3Zs, despite the assumed French bias because of Z1's place of birth and the leaning of The Zoice, as *chargé d'affaires*, toward its restitution.

Every conceivable communications and media device was hooked up to transmit the French breaking news simultaneously with the unfolding Day 3 event worldwide without interruption in English, Undo-English, and Peace English—the three universal languages. No longer an international language, French, like many other languages, was only spoken locally in its natal region.

No telling, however, how many days both events ("Richard's soul travel journey to *The Unknown*" and "the Parisian celebration for the reinstitution of July 14 – Bastille Day") would go on.

BOOK 4

THE ONSLAUGHT OF PUNISHMENT

PART 1

THE ENCHANTING CARCASSONNE FORTRESS' VERY OPINIONATED HORSE-CARRIAGE GUIDE FRANCE, JULY 1955

JULIETTE AND GASTON—
TRUE INVADERS OF LA CITÉ
DE CARCASSONNE, SAYS THE GUIDE

"How come your mission didn't use La Cité de Carcassonne as one of its hiding places?" exclaimed Gaston, staring at Juliette while taking the biggest breath ever from watching a truly wondrous place in his life.

"*Shhhh....*" voiced Juliette in alarm to her boyfriend, one finger up to her pouted lips in indication of *don't even begin to reveal anymore of this stuff to strangers–silly boy!* She even poked him on his rib with her elbow... to make sure.

"This got to be the most spectacular, amazing walled city in the universe!" went on Gaston, barely paying attention to her. "It's so huge...so large...so tall...so imposing...so out-of-this-world..."

"So enchanting..." burst out Juliette on her own.

"...so seductive...so ancient...so mysterious...so fairytale-like...wow... wow...wow...wow..." Slowly, he fished for his handkerchief deep in one of his khaki shorts side pockets.

"Take it easy, young boy," said Juliette, just as enthralled as her boyfriend, but a bit more composed. "We're on our way to invade it."

She wore a charming, garish red dress, barely reaching down to her knees. He was clad in screaming bright yellow from the waist up.

"There are only two entries..." said the old man seated in front of them, guiding the *calèche* (horse-drawn carriage) that wobbled on Pont Vieux over the Rivière de l'Aude toward Rues Trivalle and Nadaud, leaving behind the picturesque Ville Basse. He had more teeth than a face and when he spoke his shiny, round black eyes seemed to shrink and sizzle in their sockets. His pepper-gray strands of hair were covered with a cheap blue marine beret that fell slightly over his eyebrows in the front. His profile revealed an uncomfortably hooked nose and paper-thin lips. "Porte d'Aude–the gate by the river Aude on the western side, now facing us up on the mountain and quite steep to climb–and Porte Narbonnaise—the gate on the eastern side, heavily defended and considered the main entry."

"Which one should we take?" asked Gaston.

"Whichever you want," laughed the tour guide. "You're the invader."

"The main entry," decided Gaston, returning his handkerchief to his pocket after fidgeting with it.

"Good choice," said the guide, still half-laughing. "I was already headed that way."

He slightly pulled on the reins to allow the carriage to negotiate a space with another moving vehicle along the old stone bridge, this one separating the smaller but more modern city of Ville Basse they were now kissing goodbye and the historical, imposing, mountain-topped fortress of La Cité they planned to conquer.

"But it won't be easy to penetrate–a million arrows will be aimed at you from every conceivable slit in the 52 gigantic watchtowers the moment they see your face. You see–La Cité is formidably equipped and ready for any barbarian attack."

Juliette was cracking up, funnily staring at Gaston, who looked disoriented. "He called you a barbarian. That's big!" she teased, flirting with her golden ponytail. "Gaston the Barbarian! Ha ha ha!"

☙

It'd been a long day ever since they became passengers again in Pablo's old Citroën early in the morning heading toward Montpellier, then Beziers, then Narbonne along Golfe du Lion's coveted coast, then inland to Carcassonne, stopping only twice on the road to empty their bladders and grab a bite to eat–a beautiful 225 kilometer stretch of prime Langodocian sun, beaches, vineyards, and mountains.

The previous day Pablo had promised them a full day of unusual fun and spine-tingling adventures away from home if they accepted his invitation of giving him company on a trip to a fabulous place near the Spanish border.

"I hate to drive alone on long trips...but the catch is I won't reveal our destination until we get there. Deal?"

"Deal." Of course, they jumped at it with blind urgency–their first knock-out summer vacation offer!

Now as they rolled through the crenellated structure on the old drawbridge across the deep dry moat facing the twin colossal Narbonnaise Towers, they knew they were up for a memorable afternoon that could extend well into the night.

Already they imagined themselves being invited by the two most likely guiding patrons of La Cité, both represented by sculptural art at the entry gate–Virgin Mary, discreetly perched above it, and Dame Carcas, grounded in neo-Gothic style to its right side.

Foxy Pablo had parked the Citroën in the Ville Basse, the lower town of Carcassonne, and had, as usual, left the young couple on their own to scout and enjoy the area.

His casual promise of joining them later in the café-lined Place Marcou, deep inside La Cité, also referred to as the upper or fortified town, hung in the air. "I have an important *rendez-vous* with jazz musicians in a local club here in the Ville Basse," he told them, clarinet in hand. "Not too far from Place Carnot."

While the guide explained how Carcassonne was named after Dame Carcas, the rambling two-horse *calèche* turned to the left on *les lices*–the wide, flat, half grassy space between the two incredibly thick and long city walls, also referred to as "the curtain walls."

"According to a legend very solid among *Carcassonnais*, a princess in charge of the Saracen knights inside La Cité came up with a very smart idea that changed everything around."

"Like what?" said Gaston.

"Like stopping the great Emperor Charlemagne and his blood-thirsty troops from storming the food-starved fortress after a five-year siege."

"Wow," said Gaston. "When was that?"

"Late in the 8th century."

A long, tacky pause crept in, making Gaston and Juliette look at each other uneasily.

"Well? Aren't you going to tell us about Dame Carcas' bright idea?" finally asked Gaston, puzzled, realizing the guide had stopped narrating for good.

"No."

"Why?" asked Gaston, puzzled.

"It's your homework," the guide said, laughing. "You'll have to find out for yourselves."

"But..." hesitated Gaston.

"We're on vacation now..." added Juliette. "We're done with any type of homework...until September."

The guide tried to contain his laughter.

"Everybody knows this legend here, or variations from it, so it'll be rather easy for you to find out."

"You're not serious—are you?" dismissed Juliette, slit-eyed.

"I am."

"*Merde...le con...*" mumbled Gaston unhappily.

Above hovered Richard's soul.

GASTON MARVELS AT THE POWER OF TWO COINCIDING INDEPENDENT SOURCES– JULIETTE'S AND THE GUIDE'S

"Is it an expensive one or a cheap one I'm looking for?" Gaston asked Juliette from a distance, bent over the worn patches of grass and gravel.

The guide had stopped the *calèche* to give him a chance to find one of the bracelets she'd accidentally dropped on the ground playing with it.

"A cheap one," said Juliette, unapologetically.

Clusters of pedestrians strolled by, enjoying the spectacular architectural scenery around them. At least three other horse-drawn carriages with passengers could be seen approaching, only one of them going in the same direction.

The guide continued narrating, regardless, "These two massive protective stone walls, running parallel to each other encircling the fortress, were built centuries apart. Together with the colossal towers, turrets, barbicans, crenellated tops, and other parts of the rampart defensive system, they made La Cité totally inviolable and the most powerful fortress in Europe from the 13th century on."

"Totally inviolable?" Gaston heard the loaded words, which he repeated in his cool Saint-Jean-du-Gard flavored French accent, while searching for the bracelet on the ground.

"Totally inviolable," stressed the guide from the carriage in his even deeper Southern French accent, still holding traces of the old Occitan language, also known as *Provençal* or *langue d'Oc*.

"That's why it was nicknamed *la pucelle du Languedoc* (the virgin of Languedoc)" added the guide.

"Once a virgin, always a virgin?" threw in Gaston offhandedly, without thinking, distracted by his search.

"Not really..." burst out Juliette, laughing, joined by the guide, whose esophagus-deep laughter rang more like a choking experience.

"That's when the greedy and devious King of France annexed the fortified Cathar Cité to his Kingdom and built the outer or second wall that forever sealed its grounds."

"So it became a French citadel...no more Occitan..." rephrased a bit differently Juliette.

"Yes. Right after bloodily exterminating, in alliance with the equally greedy and deranged Pope, the entire religious Cathar civilization..." informed the guide.

"*Entire Cathar civilization?*" blurt out Gaston in shock, even though he could vividly remember Juliette's take on this issue with equal integrity a few days before. He'd found her bracelet and was on his way back to the parked horses and carriage.

"Yes," lamented the guide. "We call it now *genocide*...the deliberate and systematic destruction of a racial, religious, political, or cultural group. Mass scale criminal act conducted by human beings. Religious people annihilating religious people." His large ugly teeth partially showed as he went one after a pause. "You see, even atrocious crimes of the past...criminals thought they could get away with... returned ferociously in the future to haunt them."

"My girlfriend is a reincarnated Cathar," then said Gaston proudly.

"That's great!" uttered the guide, welcoming him back. "Where's she now?"

"Sitting behind you," said Juliette, pouting.

"Oh...oh..."

Pointing, Gaston directed their attention to a huge, silvery top-pointed, round structure–Tour de la Peyre–on the outer wall to their left, past Tour Saint Sernin on the inner wall to their right. It looked topless and more ancient than the other ones. "What a piece of art!" he exclaimed.

"Imposing, è!" said the guide, adding his Occitan touch.

"Awesome," said Juliette. "But I like the red top-pointed ones better. Like the Narbonnaise Towers we just saw."

"Stone towers in the citadel come in different shapes, sizes, and colors," informed the guide, "–square, round, horseshoe-shaped, cone-roofed, no roofed, gray, silver, and red–depending on the tribe that built them and the century they were built in. Many were restored to their original design, others enjoyed an approximation with added creative flair."

"An ageless stone city..." reflected deeply Gaston. "Right here...in front of us."

"Tournaments were held in this section, between the walls, all the way to Tour du Grand Brulas and Tour Mipadre...over there," said the guide.

"Where?" asked Juliette. She forced her eyes to see way ahead of her, like a kilometer or so, under the blaring sun, seeing only rows of undefined silhouetted medieval structures.

"Over there...not visible yet..." indicated the guide, one finger pointing. "They're facing each other across *les lices hautes* (the high lists)...behind the Grand Théâtre and the old Basilique Saint-Nazaire, which is about one-third of La Cité's total three kilometers of circum-venting ramparts."

Gaston exclaimed, "Yeah–I see the pointed top of the church in the distance." His hectic mind clicked. "*Three kilometers?* Wow!"

"As I was trying to say...spectacular knight jousting tournaments were held here along this field–and still are every year in August–with colorful medieval costumes, armors, shields, and long lances."

"You mean *next month!*" exploded Gaston, visualizing a dusty scene of fully-costumed fighting knights before him.

"Yes," said the guide, admiring Gaston's chic canary yellow shirt, which contrasted with the stronger yellow on his own trousers–a use-ful but lousy birthday gift from his grandmother, he thought. "Very soon."

"We'll have to come back to see it!" blurted out Juliette. "We're only here for one day!"

"*One day?*" laughed the guide. "You cannot possibly see everything in one day! It's too big and too interesting. You need a full week's time. Come back in August and I'll be glad to show you around."

"Well, thank you," said Juliette. "We'll do that."

"But you're going to miss the fabulous Bastille Day fireworks celebration...held on July 14...next week."

"*Merde!*" cried out Gaston, twisting his face.

"*Ah zut alors!*" yowled a likewise disappointed Juliette. She even angrily tapped the side of the waggling carriage onto which she leaned.

"You guys seem very let down," spoke softly the guide, turning his head to catch a glimpse at their misery. "The moment you make your way inside the inner wall through the big gate, after I'm done with you, and see the amazing things awaiting you, you'll forget everything else in the world! Believe me! It's magic!"

Above hovered Richard's soul.

MORE CONFIRMATION ABOUT THE SELF-PROCLAIMED MEDIEVAL RULERS OF THE WORLD'S MOST HIDEOUS DEEDS

"Are you allowed to talk like that about the King of France and the Pope?" Juliette asked the guide now, just out of curiosity. "I mean—the things you were saying before..."

"Why not! Both King Philip II and Pope Innocent III—and their lunatic successors—were arrogant criminals and big-time thieves of personal properties!"

"I know that, but—"

"They wiped out an entire region's population and they stole the whole Languedoc—La Cité included—and more!" shot the guide, raising his voice. He coughed. "Had they lived today, they would've been tried and sent to the guillotine! All of them!"

"I can imagine," said Juliette, noticing the massive façade of another outer wall tower nearby—the silver-pointed Tour de la Vade, with its striking sculpted decoration.

"Ughhhh—la guillotine," said Gaston, revolted, bringing one hand up to his throat like a cutting blade.

"Well, imagine the worst—" went on the guide. "To do the job, they assigned and *nurtured* Simon de Montfort—a military monster of the highest order from northern France, himself a baron with a despicable background."

"Crazy choice," said Gaston.

"This scumbag tricked, incarcerated, and assassinated La Cité's great hero—24-year-old Raymond-Roger Trencavel, Viscount of Carcassonne, Albi, and Beziers. By all standards, a brave vassal, kind man, impeccable citizen, and favorite son of Languedoc." He coughed again. "Simon de Montfort murdered Viscount Trencavel in his own château's dungeon tower."

"Very creepy," said Juliette.

"Which tower was that?" asked Gaston.

"The Tour Pinte–La Cité's tallest–overlooking the Cour d'Honneur, the Cour du Midi," said the guide, pausing to cough, "the Châtelet, the Barbacane du Château, the town's double curtain walls, and the bustling medieval life contained within these walls." He greeted someone wearing an eccentric 15th century costume.

"This tower also overlooks, from the other side, the Église Saint Gimer, the Canal du Midi, the Rivière de l'Aude, and the panoramic view of Ville Basse on the right bank of the river Aude...with its charming and extensive red-tiled roofs."

"Wow."

"So what happened with this wicked 'de Montfort'?" asked Juliette.

"He stole Trencavel's title, his fortress, and all his numerous estates! Anything he could get his hands on!" exploded the guide, with a passion and nerve now that greatly surprised the young couple.

"Thanks to the Pope's wholesale of indulgences to the northern Royal Crusaders–which divinely promised them a washing away of their sins, eternal life, and ownership of any conquered land if they only served the Crown in combat for 45 days–they all came ruthlessly crashing down on the Trencavel's...destroying everything...after three centuries of peaceful and thriving life under this dynasty!"

"So deceptive and twisted..." mumbled Gaston.

"Viscount Trencavel–widely known as a champion protector of Cathars–had negotiated in good faith a settlement whereby all occupants, including himself, his loving wife Agnes de Montpellier, and their two-year-old son and heir, would be allowed to leave the citadel totally naked but unharmed," added the guide.

"*Why naked?*" jumped in both Gaston and Juliette, perplexed.

"So everything they owned was left behind," said the inspired guide, showing his protruding upper teeth, some missing.

Watching both youths' astounded faces, he continued, "Remember that the fortress was inhabited by persecuted rich landlords, noblemen,

knights, damsels, troubadours, merchants, and traders from southern France...in addition to many Jews, Saracens, and the greatly admired, if not revered, Cathars, whose religion they either espoused or
tolerated."

He slowed his horses down a little with his reins. "So there was a
big loot to be taken...like priceless jewelry, expensive garments, gifts,
mirrors, paintings, sculptures, furniture, safes with lots of money and
precious stones, and other valuables....not to say the coveted ancient
Cathar treasure suspected to be hidden there."

"Cathar treasure?" put in Gaston, searching Juliette's eyes with
his. He remembered what she'd told him months ago at the romantic bonfire in Saint-Jean-du-Gard, confirmed by her grandpa's recent
chats with them. "Material and spiritual."

"Only material here," whispered Juliette to Gaston, but meaning a
whole lot more with her intense gaze now locked with his.

Wondering about their secretive whispers behind his back, the
guide went on, "De Montfort–known as the *Royal Knight of Terror,*
Crusading Wolf, and other feared names–had carried out the sacking
of Beziers a week earlier, slaughtering over twenty-thousand civilians,
including elderly, women and children, many of them even Christians
seeking refuge in the local Église de la Madeleine."

He paused for breath. "So atrocious was the butchery that when
the spiritual Crusade leader Abbé de Cîteaux, who gave the order to
massacre and burn the town, was asked how to distinguish the Cathars
from the Catholics, he quickly replied, '*Kill them all. God will know his
own!*'"

"Wow...wow..."

"Sick...sick..." spat Juliette.

"Later, his report of the attack to the Pope declared that this initial
campaign of death and destruction had been a complete success–*divine
vengeance raging marvelously! A miracle!*"

"Divine my butt!" exclaimed Juliette, making the guide swiftly
turn around to see her angry face and pout. "And...was the Christian
world supposed to revere this thug? Next in line to God, Jesus Christ,
and the Holy Spirit? *Damn!*"

"De Montfort stormed the near town of Bram in the next few months," continued the guide, "where he had a line of one-hundred Cathars forced to march toward the town of Cabaret—their eyes gouged out, their noses cropped, and their upper lips cut off—led by one Cathar left with a single eye." His voice faltered a little. "This, like every papal-approved act of terror in the Crusade, done for the glory of God and the honor of the Roman Catholic Church."

"Wow...wow...wow..."

"To tell you the truth, I don't know how politically correct or incorrect I'm allowed to be on my job..." he then said, lowering his voice and turning his head to face them. "All I know is I speak from my heart. This is still Cathar country so far as I am concerned—no matter how many centuries have passed since their demise. Certain things never die."

"I couldn't agree more," said Juliette with a big smile.

She was happy that the guide had volunteered to narrate everything in his own style and moods from the very beginning...after apologizing for his regular "taped narration" being out of order this particular day. It had happened before, twice in the winter last year, the guide explained. And he kind of preferred it this way, since he was a kind of talkative fellow.

"You should see her playing Jeanne d'Arc on stage," blurted out Gaston, making the guide again turn around to check her face in disbelief.

It was a little lie that gave truth to his own fantasy. Perhaps one day she'd play that role right here...in Carcassonne's finest or Languedoc's largest theatre...he sitting in the first row, watching. Right now he'd just added another worry to Juliette's without realizing it.

ꙮ

"How long has this fortress been in existence?" asked Gaston, hearing the echoes of horses' hooves blending with his voice.

"The very first peoples roaming this region were Iberians... around the 36th century BC. But things started getting hectic some 30 centuries later...around the 6th century BC...with the barbarian invasions...tribes such as the Celtics, Galls, Romans, Visigoths, Saracens, and Franks…which forced the latest locals to build defensive walls and structures…tribe after tribe, century after century…up to what in time became this incredibly huge and powerful *'forteresse de Carcassonne'* or simply *'La Cité'*… on this strategic rocky mountaintop"

"So…all this happened during the BC timeline?" said Gaston.

"No. Before and after…up to the Middle Ages. The rise of the Christian Church, after the Crucifixion, in 33 AD, and the formation of the Kingdom of France together with the deployment of Crusading armies against Muslims, Jews, and Cathars, among other groups, in the latter part of the first 13 centuries AD, complicated things for the flourishing Occitania-based fortress…to the point of being captured, pillaged, and absorbed by the conquering French crown based in Paris. Worth mentioning, the capture was done by an act of "despicable treachery" to the grace, fairness, and integrity of the beloved and reigning Trencavel Viscount."

The guide pulled on the reins, eyeing the towers and strollers ahead.

"You see, during the 11th-13th century lapse, the Counts and Viscounts of the Trencavel family owned and ruled most of Occitania—known as the Pays d'Oc—a thriving and prosperous time for all, attracting Cathars, Jews, and other good-hearted, peaceful religious sects declared evil by the Pope."

"That's when the Crusade against the Good Christians began," put in Juliette. "The Albigensian Crusade."

"*Exactement*," said the guide, impressed.

While the guide continued detailing the complex string of occupations from invading tribes to royal troops, Juliette fixed her ponytail with a rubber band and reached for candies inside her cute secret pocket in her red dress. Chewing one, she also perused in her casual manner the descriptive Pamphlet she'd gotten with the purchased tour tickets.

Meanwhile Gaston had fallen into a mental trance, or reverie, or not telling what, whereby he saw himself as a dignified mounted knight just off his tent…guiding his splendid white horse toward the gathering crowd in *les lists*…past Tour de la Peyre.

Clad in partial plate armor (topped with enclosed helmet) sandwiched between reinforced chain mail and surcoat fabrics, he artfully held a lance with one hand and a shield with the other, his eyes scanning the audience's first row for a particular face. A stunning lady's with fascinating green eyes.

His vision grew stronger, almost devouring in its seduction...

Above hovered Richard's soul.

.

UNDEFEATED KNIGHT GASTON LAGARDE "THE BARBARIAN" DEDICATES A JOUSTING ROUND TO JULIETTE DOUVIER, MYSTERIOUS DAUGHTER OF VISCOUNT OF SAINT-JEAN-DU-GARD, ANDUZE AND ALÈS

Knight Jousting Tournament

La Cité de Carcassonne, Pays d'Oc, Summer 1216

Riding his horse, Chevalier Gaston emerged from one of the many tents that lined the Carcassonne fortress' outer wall, headed for the grandstand in the pavilion, after being attended by his squire, grooms, and servants.

He proudly aimed his powerful white horse—a pure Camargue charger–whose ambling gait caused a gorgeous lady of the court with mysterious green eyes and her young demoiselles in the audience to gasp in admiration.

The noble animal wore a sturdy, head-fit, iron shield for protection against possible deadly lance blows. His body sported a long lilac-and-red decorative cloth featuring a golden three-headed lioness with blazing green eyes. Such imposing coat-of-arms, replicated on his surcoat, shield, and helmet, revealed the obvious aristocratic patronage Gaston was under and zealously fought for as "Gaston the Barbarian."

Gaston's charger snorted twice as he approached the crowded stand in the pavilion, slowly pacing to the spot where the mysterious lady sat. He slid the front of his helmet open to show his naked handsome face to her.

"*Gente Dame,*" he said, bowing, allowing his probing eyes to travel to her elegant pink velvet evening gown, displaying two rings of embroidered little unicorns in lavender near its bottom hem. "We both know my name and record of victories in battle and tournaments are already written in the pupil of your enchanting eyes, so I shall limit my salutation to the kiss I'm about to place in your heavenly hand, if you please extend it to me now."

She complied, lowering her chin delicately. But her avid emerald hued eyes stared at him steadily from under the sheer black hood that partly covered her hair, this one blonde, long, and as caressable as the soft sating tail of a flying kite.

Trembling with desire, she watched his virile lips courteously kissing the contour of her hand, covering without stopping in growing ardor the full length of her arm. Their eyes locked. "I'd love to dedicate this jousting round to you," he said without blinking. "May I ask you that you sponsor me with a simple gift from your kingdom? Rest assured, if you do, I shall be completely yours, forever in obedience to your wildest fantasies—however sweet, cold, or cruel. That's me–different, bold, determined, and passionate to obsession heights."

"Your wish is granted, Chevalier Gaston, if you don't mind my saying so," she said, with no delay and an adorable pout of her full lips. "I'm Juliette Douvier, daughter of Marcel Douvier, Viscount of Saint-Jean-du-Gard, Anduze and Alès."

He bowed again.

"Sitting behind me is Uncle George, Count of Palavas and Petite Camargue. And those thirteen lovely maidens surrounding me comprise my entourage." She blew a kiss to his face. "You may call me '*Princesse* Juliette' if you wish. Should my husband find out of this adventurous encounter," she added, in a whisperly coquettish voice, "all the better. It will teach him something about jealousy—a virtue, not a weakness, he has so far failed to display."

Gaston smiled appreciatively. "*Princesse* Juliette," he said, feeling a rush of hot blood through his veins. "There's no greater beauty and no kinder heart than yours in the whole Languedoc. No one in this land can possibly enjoy such intelligence, confidence, and imagination. And thirteen is my favorite number. I'm delighted to have met you."

"*Je vous en prie...*" she said humbly, lowering her eyes, "undefeated chevalier of Languedoc". Standing up, she wiggled her body a little, probing for balance on the uneven floor. Out of the blue, she fished for something under her gown with one hand–which required some twisting of her hips and thighs, and creative lifting of her legs–and pulled out what everybody understood to be her private silky azure panties.

Lewdly done, there was ample reason for commotion around. *"Mon Dieu!"* was heard spontaneously by many aristocrat ladies and noble spectators in the crowd. Others half-closed their eyes in shock or just gasped strange words, staring away.

Princesse Juliette smiled to herself. Capriciously, she then tied her panties to the tip of his lance, staring at him like a naughty school girl. *"Vas-y!"*

Gaston understood. She was as foolish as he was. A perfect match! With this in mind, he headed for the jousting arena in *les lists*, his horse in command of his charming ambling gait. About midpoint in the track, his adversary waited for him.

He was another charismatic champion. Known as "The Painter of Death," he rode a strong, fast, and agile Spanish Andalusian black destrier with ferocious eyes, expanded nostrils and pawing hoofs. Finely armored, like his master, and arrayed in handsome trappings, he surely looked impressive.

In symbolic chivalry gesture, both knights touched each other's shield and rode back to their respective starting points, facing each other from opposite ends of the fighting track.

All sorts of murmurs and whispers went through the impatiently waiting crowd in the pavilion. Impatience showed also in the adversary horses. They arched their necks, snorted, snapped their tails, and pawed the soil.

Proudly, Gaston took the lady's silk treasure from his lance and pinned it to a tiny hook on top of his barrel-shaped helmet—a bold move dearly appreciated by the seductive green-eyed lady in the main stand who now sat tight and half-remorseful with a frightened heart.

A trumpet sound echoed in the air.

By turn, each herald in the arena shouted a glorified introduction of each warrior's jousting victories over the years, followed by a poetic rendition from a popular troubadour.

Another trumpet sound cut through the air. *"Laissez-les aller, laissez-les aller!"* cried out the king of arms.

Suddenly both mounted knights charged at each other at full gallop with their tilted lances pointing, a dark-gray cloud of dirt created with the beating hoofs of their horses.

"T-H-H-U-U-N-N-N-K!" A crushing thud hurled one of the combatants up in the air. His punished body fell heavily on the ground–all bundled-up into a sad heap of himself.

The crowd gasped.

Gaston dismounted from his horse and approached the fallen knight. *"Mon dieu...* " he lamented in shock. The badly impacted helmet had detached from the warrior's head, revealing a horrendous sight: chunks of small broken skull bones, eyeballs, mutilated lips and nostrils as well as unidentifiable raw pieces of flesh soaked in blood spilled over the ground—an indication that Gaston's lance had gone through his face and head.

Worse, a confirmation that the knight had fought without head protection, intentionally leaving his helmet's visor open, just like Gaston had–a secret ritual of valor and honor they both had also agreed on before the joust, by courier's sealed missive, and carried through in this deadly combat.

Worst of all, Gaston soon realized the valiant, now vanquished, knight was none other than Alfredo Quintero, Pablo's older brother from the old farm–the gifted nature painter and skilled accordion player, the one with the handsome face and muscular prowess, who'd shown some personal amorous feelings toward a prohibitively too young Juliette in his peculiar way.

Contrary to "Gaston the Barbarian" and other knights in this jousting event, "The Painter of Death" had not dedicated his tilting round to any lady in the pavilion, although Gaston had seen his dark eyes through the open window of his helmet, assisted by suspicious turnings of his head, often traveling to the mysterious lady with green eyes—a motion that never went answered. Had he silently, in the sinister privacy of his mind, devoted himself completely to her? Died for her?

Truly sad for he'd been one of the most audacious and skilled knights in the land and a protégé of Queen Manola III Sandoval of the Kingdom of Aragon. Just last year he'd taken home in Montpelier the coveted 1215 Top Gallop Knight Grand Prix *trophée*.

Sword in hand, Gaston could do nothing but remain quiet beside the fallen knight, reflecting on the painful outcome, until two squires showed up to remove his body.

Trotting on his horse in front of the traumatized crowd moments later, Gaston raised his victorious arm to the mysterious lady, who, in spite of the awful incident, responded with a captivating smile. In his hand, secured with a firm grip, throbbed her kingdom's treasure, soft and azure blue and full of secrets…like all silky panties of private origins often do.

What would her next move be? A secret sealed missive?

Maybe not this week, but soon.

Above hovered Richard's soul.

PART. 2

A RICHARD-GASTON
INTER-MILLENNIUM CONNECTION
ZUNDO, JUNE 3081

RICHARD HAS 5 MINUTES TO EXIT HIS "GASTON THE BARBARIAN" REVERIE, SAYS THE ZOICE

Bermuda Revelation Park

Relaxing in the Zoasis' jacuzzi between two Clashes, Richard's mind traveled off into a strange land...as if in a trance or reverie...

Soon he was too deep into it to tell reality from some altered state of consciousness he'd fallen into...

...somewhere...a long field filled with tents, pacing horses, grooms, pages, squires, knights, heralds, troubadours...and a cheerful seated audience of medieval aristocrats and noblemen in a pavilion...between the ramparts of a colossal fortress. An early 13th century posted sign near a chemin laden with vacant horse-drawn carriages heralds a jousting event proclaimed by Queen Manola III Sandoval of the Kingdom of Aragon...

...the fortress appears to be the walled Cité de Carcassonne... where the jousting tournament is in progress now...

...I'm one of the mounted armored knights...never been defeated, they say. They call me "Gaston The Barbarian"...I wear partial plates, chain mail, surcoat, a triangular shield, a cylindrical helmet with a front window that can be easily closed...a lance and a sword...

...my white Camargue horse sports an amber gait that turns heads...a golden, sumptuous three-headed lioness coat-of-arms decorates his lilac-and-red fabric draped over his long body...it also decorates my surcoat, shield, and helmet...

...a beautiful, free-spirited, green-eyed blonde lady clothed in an elegant pink gown showing under a black hood has exchanged romantic glances with me...addressed me in magnificent ways, given me a piece of her kingdom's treasure for me to fight for...her current silk azure blue panties...which she now ties to my lance...before my tilting run...I have likewise promised her the sky, so to speak, my complete servitude to her (in Courtney Love's terms) if she favors me this way, which she had...in

return for my best arena's performance possible, which shall be, as usual, unhorsing
my adversary...at least...

A voice out of nowhere suddenly intervened:

"May I ask you that you do not waste trial time dwelling on un-necessary reveries?"

"What? What reveries?" said Richard.

"The one you're experiencing right now—you know, this medieval shit about knights jousting, courtly love, and chivalry."

"This is not a reverie. I'm in the middle of it...ready to combat and earn this gorgeous lady's treasure. But how do you know that?"

"Never mind. I'll give you five minutes to exit your reverie or else you'll lose extra points. Remember that you yourself are in a 31st century tournament right here right now."

Richard realized he was not entirely where he thought he was, actually sitting down with hot bubbling water up to his neck.

"How will I know my five minutes are up?" he asked.

"I'll ring you."

"You'll ring me? Where?"

"In your head, of course."

"Oh..."

"Remember, I'm The Zoice, your guiding voice."

"That's what I figured. Although for a moment I thought you were Mipho."

"Who's Mipho?"

"The Lioness Goddess."

Angry. "Cut the shit out! I don't have time to fool around now!"

"Okay, okay. Can you put me back in my reverie? Where I was... before you showed up?"

"Like I said—five minutes and counting!"

PART 3

GASTON DARES GOING FUTURISTIC
WITH JULIETTE
FRANCE, JULY 1955

LEAPING FROM A MEDIEVAL GENTE DAME'S SILK PANTIES TO A ZLONED COMBATANT JUDGED BY A BUBBLE-CARRYING ZOBOT

La Cité de Carcassonne

"Pop your eyes open, silly boy!"

Lovingly, she slapped Gaston's face again.

"...what?" coming out of a daze or something.

"What are you doing with your arm up? It looks funny."

"...I'm holding her panties..." said the bright boy, oddly coming to his senses.

"Whose panties?"

"The Viscount of Saint-Jean-du-Gard's daughter."

"Ha ha ha ha..." laughed out loud Juliette, sharing her laughter with the guide.

Gaston realized his situation, unhappily.

"I was in a trance...a reverie..." he apologized.

"You surely were."

"Weird stuff...awesome place...amazing people..."

She let him reveal himself more.

"It was so real...so clear...so touching..."

"What else?"

"So dangerous..."

"Looks like you'll have plenty to tell me next time. Not here."

"I wouldn't know how or where to begin."

"You'll find a way, honey."

"Where are we now?"

"Between the outer wall's flat-roofed Tour Cautières and the inner wall's silver-pointed Tour des Prisons...headed for Tour Saint Martin," informed the tour guide dutifully.

Another horse-drawn carriage moving in the opposite direction rolled past them with steady speed. They exchanged salutes.

"Could you stop the horses for a while?" Gaston said with urgency as they neared another tower. "I feel kind of sick in the stomach...going to throw up..."

"Are you *that* sick?" asked Juliette. "Maybe it'll go away."

"No..." he gasped. Then he shouted to the guide, "Please...stop the carriage!"

The guide complied, watching how the young boy dragged himself out with the young girl's help, and actually vomited.

Next, he watched, without joy, how the two trudged their way up on the hard soil toward the outer wall, where the Tour Cautières stood.

Clumps of other walkers dotted *les lices*. They also seemed to search the past of Carcassonne in these jousting grounds and tall towers between the two curtain walls—a stone-made historical and architectural foundation so much embellished on its surface to merit just a casual look. An engrossing one, for sure.

"I'm feeling better now..." Gaston just marched along the lower wall, Juliette at his side, for a moment. "Something I ate...before we started the tour..." He tried to laugh at himself. "I don't think is motion sickness."

"No," agreed Juliette, amused, pouting. "You were sleeping, then you woke up, then you threw up."

"I was dreaming...and doing well in my dream...or trance..."

"Right. You always seem to be in a different zone...when dreaming."

"Well, I've been hit with so many dreams or reveries lately–some of them right here in Carcassonne–that–"

"–I should know about...maybe?" interrupted Juliette, a bit offended.

Strands from her ponytail flapped her pretty face when a sudden breeze whirled by.

He laughed. "Yes."

"Are you getting dreams set in the future also?"

He nodded, watching a lovely pout surge in her mouth.

"Because so far you've told me lots of them set in the past, like in Toulouse, but–"

"–They're not really dreams," broke up Gaston. "Most of them appear in bright daylight...like reveries."

"I know...trances, imageries, revisited memories..."

"But false. Even though they're about me and people I know around me, they're false. Things that never happened."

"False memories." Juliette studied his eyes, the hazel texture in them. "What about your future encounters...the ones you've kept me uninformed about...also in bright daylight?"

"Yes, same thing."

"So why haven't you spent a minute yet telling me about them?"

"Because they're too crazy and you won't believe them."

"Give me examples."

"Stuff like...a gigantic circus atmosphere...somewhere..." Gaston's eyes and mind searched for images that had evaded him or had appeared only briefly recently, without clues about them.

"What do you usually see?" pressed Juliette.

She was now leaning on the edge of the wall next to him, her mounting boots crossed over each other, her thighs showing under her red dress.

"I see...a man they call Richard or "the Octidare"...they say he's very rich and powerful...sitting in a large glass room...surrounded by lots of people in huge stadiums shouting very bad words and insults...mostly booing him....He's always fighting another man they call Master Judge....He has a shinny bald head and a long pointed black beard...wears scary vampire clothes.... They both fight and talk a lot..."

"About what?"

"About money and politics and other things I'm not familiar with."

"In French?"

"No. Some foreign language...English...American English, I think."

"But you don't speak English..."

"I know, but I understand it…somehow…in my dreams."

"Strange…"

"I see a lion…female, I guess…with three heads…tearing apart a big tiger that was about to attack a person—that rich man again–in a street at night…somewhere in a place they call Bulgaria….His face is covered with blue paint…very thick paint…around his eyes and mouth….He wears a hood with bat ears….Lots of weird things happen…that I can't explain….They just happen…in front of me…like if I was watching a movie or something…."

"…very intriguing…"

"I see two men standing on logs that are floating on a river… a river filled with weird little creatures… .These two men…the same ones I told you before…are smacking each other with long poles and shouting real bad words….I see two gigantic trucks with gigantic wheels rolling over other cars like crazy and racing each other in a crowded place…lots of people cheering and screaming and throwing things in the air…and dancing like wild animals…"

"…unusual stuff…"

He took a deep breath.

"I see…this rich man again…they call Richard…reciting really bad poetry…with filthy and idiotic words… in front of this huge angry crowd…..I see a naked caveman crouching on a street…kind of deserted…somewhere in the future….I see a big, big, big ball coming down from the sky…and turning around…like the round plastic world we have in our classroom…full of flashing lights in all sorts of colors… passing words around like messages…I see an angry parrot shouting lots of bad words to a group of kids…making them run away scared… inside a place that resembles a huge transparent round cake with… with long worm-like hallways…full of weirdly dressed people playing games…with clinking and blinking machines…."

"…keep going…"

"I see big chunks of ground rising and falling…and turning into all kinds of scenes and situations…like in the movies…a very beautiful young girl about my age in pigtails…singing with a guitar to this huge crowd in those gigantic stadiums…a wild song they say she wrote…

with words that speak really bad of Richard…the very, very, very rich man….."

"…very nice…"

"I see someone being turned into two persons that look exactly the same…by an old man they call Walking Brain… looking like a sweet teddy bear or something…with very long arms…inside a strange-looking car going real fast…like flying….I see a man who says he's a zobot, not a real person…playing tennis….I see a man dressed like Dracula inside a violet bubble…floating around on a stage in front of this huge crowd….I see two male nurses…carrying first-aid kits trying to–"

"*–Hey there! We have to go now!*" interrupted the guide from the other side of *les lices*, bellowing his anger with reason. "*I can't sit here all day with my horses waiting for you, kids!*"

Gaston apologized, having completely forgotten about him. So did Juliette. "Give us another minute…my head's still turning a bit…"

"I bet you…"

They both saw the twisted smirk in his lips.

Juliette turned to Gaston, whispered with her own touch of Occitan, "Richard, *è?*"

"Yeah…that's the way they call him…in my dreams…"

"Do they come in some kind of order…structure?"

"What do you mean? You sound like a storyteller."

"I'm an *actress*, remember?"

He smiled, humbly. "How could I miss that one?"

"Never mind, *Chevalier des Rêves Tordus et Souvenirs Faux* (Knight of Twisted Dreams and False Memories)."

She gently fixed the collar of his shirt with one hand, noticing a tiny speck of vomit lodged there over the yellow fabric. "I read lots of scripts," she said, cleaning the speck of dirt with one finger. "Sometimes they contain dreams. Trust me, they always follow a structure, a chronological direction or timeline…true, fragmented but linear…with a beginning, middle, and end. You know, the way writers always write them, even though it's all crap."

He laughed–more at the funny pout swelling her lips than the substance of what she said–but the latter stayed longer in his mind.

"So...do they follow a standard structure...like a play, movie, or novel?"

"My dreams?" He rubbed his nose. "No. My dreams are weird and disjointed...uneven, scrappy, patchy. I don't think they follow any structure," he said seriously, but ending with a cynical twinkle in his eyes. "Should they?"

"Maybe not a linear structure," tried Juliette, "which is, like I said before, just a literary tool, a made-up thing to present the happening."

"A nicely boxed and wrapped program...a script," said Gaston, following her thoughts or so, "to facilitate narration and understanding."

"Exactly," said Juliette, realizing how mature in his thinking he'd grown lately.

"Well, no. My dreams or trances are more like non-linear happenings and unpredictable challenges. They just come and go without knocking on the door...disorderly and uninvited...often creating one hell of a commotion!"

"Hey! So maybe there's *something* there!" she cheered.

"Plenty, *mon cheri!*" chanted Gaston, agreeing.

Above hovered Richard's soul.

PART 4

SECOND BEHIND-CLOSED-DOORS MEETING BETWEEN DR. UFAHH AND MASTER JUDGE ZUNDO, JUNE 3081

DR. UFAHH'S EXPLOSIONS OF ANGER BRING BACK THE PUNISHMENT FOCUS OF JOURNEYING SUPER WEALTHY CONVICTS TO THE FOREFRONT WHILE ASSESSING GASTON'S STRANGE PROGRESS

Dr. Ufahh saw the need to visit his right-hand man again at his solitary post in the Royal Den above the Astral Floor.

He was not wearing his buggazis mind-reading contact lenses and had turned off his khorzos sound-debriefing earzotrons, both gestures to comply with a mutual agreement not to spy on each other in the Bermuda Revelation Park's premises.

"Master Judge—I've been viewing and reviewing some of the situations you've created for our super wealthy defendant, Richard, and I've seen things I should've *never* seen..." he told Master Judge in a tone that bordered on anger.

"What do you mean, WB?"

"Don't call me WB and don't even try to spell it for me!"

"But that's what everybody calls you around here, affectionately, short for Walking Brain."

"That's them, not you—*Master Shit*!"

"Why are you so upset?"

"You're going too far with your silly creativity and infantile wisdom. You've strayed away from your duties, giving Gaston—well, Richard's 13th past incarnation—too much leeway for fun instead of hard punishment. He's supposed to learn how it feels to be poor, to be just a regular guy, through suffering...pain..."

"I'm sorry. I got carried away."

"...misery...despair..."

"I understand."

"Capitalism insulted the world over a thousand years ago by creating the first few millionaires, little gods, extremely privileged ty-
coons…in certain parts of the world. Then it created the first round of
billionaires, bigger gods, super extremely privileged moguls."

"A sickness on the rise," agreed the judge, observing without joy
Dr. Ufahh's odds features—grossly broad koala-like forehead and terribly small, bunched-up black eyes—as he talked.

A few feet behind, past a cluster of azure vase sponges, two naughty yellow seahorses danced in aqua-green waters, purposely mocking
a passing school of spotted snake-eels headed for the New Assembly
Church of Corridorians.

Just a week ago it had been the reverse–several members of the
First Church of Half-Submerged Stadiums had ridiculed the warm
embrace (in fish terms) of two handsome gay male seahorses in plain
daylight. A small underwater religious war had thus begun.

Dr. Ufahh scratched one shoulder.

"While the common people remained common, these few mag-
nates rose in wealth, power, and fame *exponentially*….making the insult
to the world *exponentially bigger.*"

The brainy scientist paced the floor in front and around Master
Judge, his thick, metallic, almost offensive, Argentinian accent reso-
nating strangely, as if lecturing his students at the University of Atlantic
Blue Holes, an institution of higher learning he'd proudly founded two
decades ago.

"While these super gods enjoyed a lavish life style, the common
people suffered immensely and lived in misery or died in poverty…
completely ignored by the government, who on the other hand continued to praise, nurture, and celebrate these very few super wealthy
barons."

"Such an uneven system…"

"Uneven? *What a fucking stupid understatement!*"

"Well…I meant…"

"It's like comparing palm trees with garlic plants. Ridiculous!"
snarled the scientist. He looked away momentarily. "It never occurred
to these materialistic government brickheads that maybe they should

put *a cap* on how much loot these money-sucking scumbags could stash away in foreign banks?"

"Tax-free foreign banks," added the judge.

"You got that one right, *judgie*," he said with a snotty stare.

So over a thousand years later, what do we have? It runs parallel to the nuclear bombs—each decade more powerful and destructive weapons...to the point where we'll end up either blowing our planet to pieces by the 1% bad apples of the world or draining our world's money resources to zilch by the 1% super rich greedmongers of Wall Street Earth!"

"Neither one healthy," added the judge, meekly.

"Healthy? I'm talking about the end of the world—*you moron!*"

Master Judge just rubbed his bald head.

"So over a thousand years later," went on Dr. Ufahh. "What do we have? Sorry to repeat. Common people and super zillionaires! Struggling families to make ends meet on one side and unstoppable money-making human machines on the other side...with so much wealth and power that, for lack of proper space and security on earth, they're now scouting other planets to store their gargantuan fortunes! Talking about money addiction, nothing ever compares!"

"Dr. Ufahh, you forgot that we already put a stop to this when we took over the world, that in fact Richard, the richest person on earth, our current defendant, is now paying the price...going through soul travel punishment."

"Thanks for reminding me. Sometimes the side effects of despicable activities by these super greedy sons of bitches get to me. How could they have gotten away with it so easily? So smartly? For so long? It's beyond me!"

"Have no fear, Doc, they're all cruising through *The Unknown* now, most of them disappearing forever. Well, except Richard, who's still out there...in rehab...soul travel rehab."

"How much money did he have when we finally arrested him and put him on trial?"

"Over thirteen octillion."

"That's *insane!*"

Dr. Ufahh tapped one side of his head angrily as if getting sea water out of his ears.

"From scratch?"

"No. He inherited nearly fifty million when his parents died. He was still a kid."

"The lucky *bastard!*" shot the distinguished chairman of the Bermuda Revelation Park.

Master Judge nodded. "At the time of his arrest, he basically owned the world—major banks, financing institutions, health insurance companies, manufacturing and distribution industries, news media agencies, movie studios, radio and TV stations, commercial airlines, railroad systems, automobile corporations, oil conglomerates, sun energy factories, food processing facilities, research and development centers, and entertainment networks. He also exerted heavy influence on U.S. senators and congressmen, members of parliaments and secretaries of state in several countries, the United Nations, CIA, NATO, NASA, most of Wall Street, IMF, Hollywood, the Stock Exchange, and the Internet."

"That *idiotic guy* you've been mud-wrestling with?" Dr. Ufahh pulled out a handkerchief and blew his nose. "I watched it all on my ZCAP!"

"Yep," said Master Judge. "He had a history of going around those exclusive circles of political and economic moguls...collecting *signed pledges* of support for his own personal aggrandizement...in exchange for special favors..."

"That *pesky little bugger...?*"

"Yep..." said the judge. "He's no different from you and me—*one mouth* and *one asshole.*"

"And a *heart of steel* in between," said Dr. Ufahh.

"No real God, for sure!"

"Just acting like one," said Dr. Ufahh.

"Living life in big style and having a great time."

"Earning in a split second *a zillion times* more than what normal people make in a lifetime."

"Sickening," said Master Judge. He brushed the end of his pointed beard with one hand and blinked twice.

"But true."

"Thanks to Capitalism," said Dr. Ufahh.

"Or Free Enterprise–the way zillionaires call it, of course."

"To paraphrase 'The Beatles'–that iconic 20th century rock group we still play over here–*love's the only thing money can't buy*'..." slipped in the judge. "So true...so true..."

"Love?" asked Dr. Ufahh, strangely. "Is there *any* left in this world?"

◈

"Where's he now–that notorious octillionaire's reincarnated little twerp?"

"Gaston? Somewhere in Carcassonne, France," replied Master Judge. "Soon to be a father."

"A father?"

"Yes. With that child actress he hangs around...Juliette."

"Good. Make them suffer. Use your imagination." Dr. Ufahh took a deep breath, scratched an itchy spot under his chin. "I want you to focus on his *punishment*...relocate him to another country...expose him to more suffering...violent situations...horror...tragedy..." he said with increasing anger. "And please, please, stop making him *a lot smarter* than other kids his age! He sounds like a politician already...and he's only *nine*!"

"I will."

"And make the transition natural, organic. Don't force it!"

"Understood."

He started for the door, but turned around dangerously.

"By the way, I've noticed that there have been at least *three* attempts on his life already." His eyes were quietly set on the floor. "*He's not supposed to die, only suffer! If he goes, you go too! Am I clear now?!*" he then erupted like a volcano.

"Completely."

PART 5

TOWERS OF BEAUTY AND HORROR
FRANCE, JULY 1955

TROTTING THE NARROWEST AND DARKEST AREAS OF THE FORTRESS' COBBLESTONE PATHWAYS

Tour Saint Martin unlike other towers was embedded into the inner wall that encircled La Cité, a detail Gaston quickly noticed, as the lavish upper structure of the Basilique came into view from behind the wall.

The young couple had boarded the carriage that now wobbled in trotting mode toward Ville Basse. It seemed they were returning to this lower town, also called Bastide St. Louis, from a different angle, height, and gate, namely Porte de l'Aude. Only that the horses were climbing, not descending.

"We're moving now and for the next seven towers through the widest area of *les lices*," informed the guide with a loud, resonant voice.

"Great," burst out Gaston.

"Afterwards, we'll be entering the beginning of the narrowest and darkest area, which will stretch another bunch of towers to and past Château Comtal, where Viscount Trencavel and his family used to live."

"How narrow will it get?" asked Juliette with a worried pout.

"As narrow as to allow our carriage to go through."

"How dark?" asked Gaston, already uncomfortable.

"Very dark. In the narrowest part, in order to continue, we'll be forced to pass under the Tour de l'Évêque (the Bishop's tower)–a square tower."

"Oh how nice," exclaimed Gaston.

"Nice?" The guide exploded into a loud laughter that didn't sound human.

He fidgeted with his beret nervously, shook his head sideways, and, turning to face both youngsters, said, "You don't want to know why I'm acting so strangely–trust me." Pulling the reins in an awkward way, he signaled the horses to walk more cautiously from here on.

Juliette and Gaston kept staring at each other for the longest time. Above hovered Richard's soul.

SUDDENLY BOTH ALARMED AND FRIGHTENED

They reached La Cité's southernmost area, marked by the red-pointed Tour du Moulin du Midi.

Such beauty stood behind the Grand Théâtre, which faced the Basilique, and almost completed this section of the jousting grounds before it veered sharply to the right. It did so past Tour Mi Padre, along the same inner wall, and Tour du Grand Brulas, along the outer wall. Tour du Grand Brulas marked the turning point of *les lices*.

Straight ahead the road led to a post-Trencavel narrow, dark world of uncertainties, inquisitions, horrors, and deaths...deeper along the ramparts...starting with the western Porte d'Aude, which zigzagged down steeply, with its cobblestones, to Ville Basse, across Rivière d'Aude.

Stopping the horses, the guide excused himself for a few minutes by personally delivering a letter to a relative that lived there in a crossing alleyway. "Good that she was there to open the door," he explained upon returning and setting the horses trotting again. "This area used to be an eyesore around the 14th century...right after the royal troops left."

"How come they left?" asked Gaston.

"Here's the sad irony. After murdering everybody and conquering the fortress, they patrolled it for decades...until they got bored and abandoned it–just like that."

"Terrible," lamented Juliette.

"So the towers, buildings, and streets started to deteriorate and crack and poor people, like weavers and stone craftsmen, began to move in with their children, pets, and ducks, building their shackles and little stores along the disintegrating inner and outer walls...with stones and parts stolen from them. Not until the 19th century, did the

French government take on the job of renovating the whole citadel, which by then had become a pitiful, rundown, pot-holed, filthy rubbish pile," explained the guide with sorrowful hand gestures. "Two main streets in La Cité, you will see later, are named after Viollet-le-Duc, the architect, and Cros-Mayrevielle, the historian-journalist, responsible for the job."

∽

The guide nervously fidgeted a bit with his beret and scratched before tightening his hold on the reins of his cautiously pacing horses, as if having premonitions of something eerie and malevolent coming ahead, if not for him, for his passengers.

Only he knew why he felt this way.

"Aller!" he said to his horses.

The colossal outer and inner curtain walls for one thing had begun to get mysteriously ever closer to each other in this part of the ramparts, to the point of near suffocation. Shadowy contours of the moving carriage and silhouetted reflections of the guide traversing an aura of solemn quietude and isolation embraced them.

"I never get to enjoy this western front of the fortress," the guide then revealed with a strange thickness in his voice.

"Why's that?" asked Gaston, staring at his tense girlfriend.

"We're passing under Tour Carrée de l'Évêque right now...the only structure planted in the middle of the way. How arrogant and offensive!"

"Very odd..." said Juliette, staring up at the wicked vaulted stonework.

"And scary..." mumbled Gaston, feeling jittery inside.

"Intentionally so."

The rhythmical beat of the horses' hooves on the cobblestones, now slowing down, could be heard very clearly.

Too clearly for Gaston and Juliette.

Reappearing on the other side of the ghostly arched passageway, another sinister-looking stone tower of enormous size—perched on the inner wall, with a silvery pointed roof—stole their attention. "This is

Tour de l'Inquisition, also called Tour Ronde de l'Évêque. You might be too young to learn what it was used for, besides its obvious imposing surface appeal."

"Tell us!" rang their voices, without hesitation.

"Built by the French crown after Viscount Trencavel's death in the 13th century, it soon became the seat of the Inquisitor's court."

"Inquisitors?" Gaston wanted to know.

"Perverted, sadistic Roman Catholic interrogators—a frightening group of twisted-minded bishops, originally of the Dominican Order, selected by and serving the Pope—with God's love and approval, they claimed—to exterminate from the face of the planet Cathars, Templars, Jews, and any individual not practicing the Roman Catholic faith as prescribed by the Pope. Understandably, nothing more than a heinous strategy to achieve world domination, which they did, in the Middle Ages, and beyond, through intimidation, fear, torture, and murder."

"Wow...wow...wow..." mumbled Gaston.

"Incredibly sick..." said Juliette.

"They were in fact the creators and executers of mass-scale genocide...before Hitler even though about it," said the guide.

"How did this inhuman movement come about?" asked Juliette. This was a good time for her to compare notes with what she'd learned through her grandpa and the books in his private library.

"Not satisfied with their annihilation of innocent souls through the Albigensian Crusade and other created slaughters, the succeeding ruling Popes and reigning Kings of France used the Inquisition to hunt down, interrogate, accuse, torture and burn at the stake whatever Cathar, Templar, Jew, Atheist, or non-Christian was left in the world—the final solution." spoke up the guide. "Ironically, none of these *notorious achievements* ever appear in any Roman Catholic Bishop's *Curriculum Vitae* (résumé) when looking for a job. None!"

The carriage moved slowly, the horses' hooves banging crisply on the cobbled path.

"Periodic announcement from the papal office gave more and more freedoms to bishops and priests around the world to do whatever they wanted to eradicate these groups or individuals they spitefully classified as *hérétiques*..." went on the guide. He cleared his throat. "They used hypocrisy and blatant lies to get around the Catholic rules that forbade them from causing bloodshed, mutilation or death...as these types of torture and punishment, together with the burning at the stake, were supposed to be legally carried out only by the secular authorities. They routinely did those things anyway and continued to do so even more openly as the years went by," said the guide.

"For the glory of God?" Juliette used sarcasm to punctuate their wretched aberrations, already known to her.

One of the horses snorted as the carriage rode in front of the massive, ominous-looking Tour de l'Inquisition.

"So what did they do in this tower?" pressed Gaston again, staring up with awe at a mass of stone rising to the sky.

"Horrendous things. They tortured people using the most barbarous and painful methods known to mankind," said the guide.

"Wow."

"Of course, history revisionists and Catholic apologists never stop toning down everything to its minimum expression...even imply that the Church *acted mercifully in its cruelty*."

"Ha ha ha ha..." laughed Gaston, more from fear and anger than fun.

"As usual..." said Juliette.

"Iron tools of torture were heated in a huge furnace upstairs, after first sprinkling them with holy water. Non-recanting, non-repenting heresy suspects, or just accused persons—often without proof or reason—were beaten and forced into torture devices, machines, or chambers," expressed the guide gravely. "While black-hooded assistants burned their flesh with red-hot instruments, comfortably seated papal inquisitors observed their torment in utmost calmness." The guide coughed, continued, "These so-called servants of God were mainly bishops, who also acted as trial prosecutors, judges, jury, torturers, and even executioners. They skillfully manipulated their interrogation so as to always frighten, confuse, weaken, and finally break their subjects...to obtain written confessions."

"Wow...holy shit..."

No apology was necessary for the slipped vulgar word. The three of them felt deeply violated by the thrust of the message already.

"Such documents permitted them, among other things, to confiscate their properties and hunt down their family members and relatives, which they always did after torturing their victims to near death or death, in the *damnest* of places for the longest of times. Which in this tower meant 'being walled up'–chained to walls–between torture sessions, in windowless, airless, pitch black dungeons of decreasing size and increasing filth, including their own urine and excrement," narrated the guide.

"Disgusting..."

"Wow...wow..."

"Screams of agony could never be heard outside those thick walls, and food was limited to stale bread and fetid water, both causing slow but sure death. Such systematic, horrifying form of torture and walling worsened as the sufferers were periodically relocated deeper and deeper down the tower, one flight of steps after another, even after recanting and repenting, to the point where they preferred being burned alive at the stake than continuing living in this miserable condition."

"Could you make your horses walk a little faster out of here?" proposed Gaston, freaking out.

"Yeah–this is really creepy..." said Juliette, nervously shifting on her seat.

"Ha ha ha ha..." laughed the guide. "Tour de la Justice–the tower where the Bishops stored their wretched torture documents–is almost upon us!"

"Are you really serious...telling us all that *shit*?!" slammed Gaston with rising anger. "You're not pulling our legs, are you?"

The guide's laughter just got louder. "Monk justice? Ha ha ha ha! No justice–just monks!"

He laughed again.

"Consider this your second homework of the day. Am I making it all up to scare you? Or did it really happen? Find out for yourselves, kids! Ask questions around!"

"*Le connard...*(such a jerk)..." dismissed Gaston under his breath.

"*Aller, vite!*" the guide commanded both horses, sending them into a faster but steady trot along the narrow path between the two parallel massive walls.

Ahead, in their macabre path, loomed the fortified Château Comtal and the ancient northern towers of La Cité built by the Romans. Sweeping views of distant surrounding valleys and red-tiled roofs in half-hidden towns could be seen now and then over the shadowy walls when steep descents after sudden rises in their path occurred.

The horse-drawn carriage relaxed its pace in this northbound stretch of *les lices*, now called *lices basses*, amid a new round of watchtowers, headed for Porte Rodez. It crossed another noisy carriage moving in the opposite direction.

No one had talked for a while, including the guide.

Behind him, he could hear the wailing trail of a light snoring sound.

He took a quick look to check.

Predictably, they were both dozing off.

༄

He didn't wake them up until he'd completed the entire tour. Well, almost, until he'd reached Tour du Tresau, only a few minutes shy of Porte Narbonnaise–their starting point in the fortress.

"Wake up, guys, back there!"

No response.

"*Wake up, please!*"

Gaston rubbed his eyes, Juliette yawned.

"What happened? Did we fall asleep?"

"You did."

"Where are we now?" asked one of them.

"Near the end of your ride," informed the guide. "Back to where we began...in this fabled city of stone towers, knight playgrounds, dark passageways, and ancient legends. Enjoy now the bustling city street life of this medieval paradise on foot." Politely, he shook hands with both kids. "It was nice meeting you and showing you around."

"We enjoyed your company...and especially your insight into the history of this magnificent place," said Juliette, stepping down and out of the carriage.

"Mon plaisir..." saluted the guide, courteously lifting a little the front of his beret.

"Merci Monsieur..." said Gaston, throwing a gracious smile, following his girlfriend.

∾

Was this man for real?

The question would come up many times during their stay.

Above hovered Richard's soul.

A STRONG FEELING OF WALKING AMONG CATHAR GHOSTS, SINISTER CATHOLIC INQUISITORS, AND OTHER STRANGE MEDIEVAL FORTRESS LOCALS

Pedestrians jammed the cobblestone streets of *La Cité*.

"Nothing better than being surrounded by medieval life," cheered Gaston, relishing the colorful shops, cafés, restaurants, and myriads of little stores dotting the walled landscape.

He strolled on beside Juliette, shuffling his way through hordes of people.

"Nothing better than being here with you and our baby," chanted Juliette. "Baby girl or baby boy."

"How about medieval baby?" teased Juliette.

"With medieval eyes?"

"And medieval toes."

They both laughed at that.

"Heart, mind, and soul are more important," said Gaston, turning right on Rue du Petit Puits, past the square of the same name.

"Of these three, *the soul* reigns," said Juliette, beckoning Gaston to follow her inside a boutique stuffed with medieval souvenirs, stamps, postcards, and magazines.

Pushing their way through a bunch of school girls about Juliette's age crowding a section of the store, Gaston connected some dots in his mind. At his first chance, he asked Juliette, "I was thinking about your mission...the young girls."

"You always do," she teased him, staring at a nice piece of art recreating a Crusade attack on La Tour de la Porte Rouge near Château Comtal.

"No. I'm serious," said Gaston. "Why does your mission *only* ac-cept thirteen-year-old girls? I've been curious about this for a long time, but somehow I never got around to asking you."

"You probably have. But I never got around to answering you."

"That's more like it," said Gaston with a smile.

"The Cathars believed women should take leading roles in society, so when a group of thirteen-year-old, horse-riding, high school girls pro-posed over 700 years ago they should volunteer as a team to embark on a journey of service to the world, it caught the attention of a few Cathar *parfaits* and *parfaites*. Next thing they knew, they were on a very long mission to carry the torch of the greatest ancient secret on earth. The mission bore the name 'The Legend of the Horse-Riding Kites'...and it carried on."

"Wow..."

Gaston pondered. "Why kites?"

"Where would any king or pope searching for an ancient scroll on a galloping horse rider flying a kite *not* look?"

Gaston smiled. It made sense.

"In doing so," went on Juliette, "they established the youngest, female, cross-century, horse-riding, peace army ever attempted on this planet...and it's still moving forward 700 years later."

Gaston applauded.

"Had you been one of these young girls," Juliette proposed hypo-thetically, "had you joined?"

Gaston laughed. "Maybe."

"Chicken."

"Well...yes," said Gaston now, mainly to please her.

"That's better, my boy!"

She pulled him to a corner, where nobody could see them, and kissed the hell out of him.

Now—upon relaxing their tongues–they laughed hysterically.

∾

They were walking along Rue Raymond Roger Trencavel moments later, headed toward *La Poste*, she pirouetting a couple of times in her pretty red dress, he embracing her adoringly with his eyes.

"Don't you get the sense sometimes that Cathar ghosts are all over the place here. Good ghosts, happy ghosts…spiritually active, mingling with tourists," said Juliette casually.

She touched the fabric of a blue-royal velour medieval surcoat at the entrance of a Muslim store.

Turning to her enchanted boyfriend, she added, "For example, our own guide a while ago–didn't you get the feeling he might be a *returning* Cathar…from way back?"

"He surely was weird."

"I don't mean that." Juliette pouted. "His knowledge, his attitude, his confidence–he seems to be one of them. Well, except his rough manners and incendiary language."

"You mean he seems to be *reincarnated*?"

"Just a feeling…"

They stepped out of the store, blended again with the walking crowd.

"How about a *crêpe* with *café au lait*?" invited Gaston.

"Just *café*…without the *lait*…"

They entered a terraced Belgian restaurant with earthy ambiance that advertised special vegetarian dishes among others.

There were so many available tables around, it was hard to choose one. But they settled for a cozy place in a corner, a bit quieter than those tangled by brisk and noisy conversation, with soothing background medieval music.

"Hummmm," said Gaston. "Good thing I changed my mind about ordering."

On second thought, the young actress had asked for yummy food that didn't derive from animals and had no problems convincing Gaston to do the same.

He watched how she devoured her yolkless *crêpe*, while he ate his slowly.

"I didn't know you were so hungry."

On impulse, she rose from her chair.

"Where are you going?"

"To get some yolkless pastries too. You want some?"

"Sure."

As she sipped her *café* moments later, he recalled what Pablo had once told him about her deceased parents. She was only three when they left her. "Do you miss your parents?"

"Sometimes."

"I think you told me they both were...Cathars? Modern age Cathars?"

"Yes. Unlike me and my grandpa, they were completely dedicated Cathars.

Her mouth took a big bite on her vegetarian pastry.

"They believed our world is evil. So life after death has to be better—a lot better—so they took off one day, like a space rocket to the afterworld would. Simple."

Gaston finished his *crêpe* and brought his *café* cup to his mouth, thinking.

"What did they do for a living before they—".

"—They had a farm in Alès. My dad didn't get along well with my grandpa—his dad. Grandpa sent him to Lycée Jean-Baptiste Dumas, one of the finest and largest in Languedoc, hoping he'd develop a passion for science and archeology...like Grandpa...but he just graduated and took up farming instead." She sipped her *café*. "He married my mom...a Protestant Church leader from Anduze with a degree in European Literature, I think...well educated and bright...and the rest is history."

"You had *fantastic* parents then. Were they very much in love?"

"I hardly remember them. He wore heavy-framed glasses and she kept her long blonde hair high over her head tied up in a bun."

Gaston's lips broke into a smile.

"*Who* got you, then...into the 'Legend'?"

"My grandpa."

She pinched a steamed broccoli with her fork, mixed it with black bean sauce over brown rice—extra food she'd ordered together with the pastries. Then swallowed it.

"He's a very cool guy too...your grandpa."

"He is."

"Talking about Cathars, your family and you–what's the biggest attraction to their religion?"

"That there's no final day of judgment, no hell," for one thing, "so we're not going there, no matter what."

"I like that."

"We're all saved through God's grace. We just keep coming back through reincarnations...until we get it right."

"Sounds fair to me."

"We pray humbly and directly to God...from our home...without conditions, brainwashing or fear. We don't need consecrated church-es or spectacular cathedrals costing tons of money with phenomenal chorus that seems to have heavenly musical quality. All that is illusion, fantasy, unnecessary...so are the priests who pretend to act as interme-diaries between God and people on people's behalf, while getting rich on the side by selling indulgences...in exchange for cleansing of past sins and eternal salvation. Nonsense. Grand scale money robbery!"

"Poor people seem to go for those things..." remarked Gaston.

"That's why the Church preys on them...mostly their ignorance... lack of education...both rooted mainly in poverty...their fear of the unknown...of what evangelical teachings put in their minds through persisting and systematic indoctrination They're a major source of in-come for the Church."

"Looks like."

Juliette went on, "We believe worshipping images or kneeling down before idols or submitting to superstitious rituals, like eating simple bread and wine in mass believing it's actually Christ's body and blood...are ridiculous pagan practices from ancient times that ac-complish absolutely nothing since they're based on ignorance and lies. So we don't do that. We regard men and women as totally equal and deserving equal rights in all aspects of life."

"Wow....wow..." Gaston felt funny listening to her, almost unease. "You've already answered my second question as well–the one not yet posed," he said meekly.

"Which is?"

Gaston scratched his head.

"What was the thing that frustrated Cathars the most?"

"Greed and material gratification. Especially as indulged in by the arrogant and corrupt Roman Catholic bishops and the kings of Europe," said Juliette. "At least that's the thing that frustrates me the most. Even though, like I've told you before, I'm *not* a Cathar. Not even close. But you ought to know this—money in large quantities means little to me. People who seek and glut on fortunes are the worst kind to me."

"Millionaires?"

"Yes. They're the scumbags of the world!"

"Explain..."

"A life driven by personal greed for wealth, power, and superiority, if not domination—what human value does that have?"

"None that I can think of."

"What good does it do to a world plagued by rampant poverty, misery, and hardship?"

"Nothing."

"Zilch!" stressed the young actress. She stared hard in Gaston's eyes.

"Always remember that—*the pursuit of material wealth will only make you poorer in the next life,*" she said emphatically.

"And the pursuit of spiritual wealth," tried Gaston, "will make me *richer* in the next life?"

"*Spiritually.*"

"That's true only if you believe in reincarnation, right?"

"Well, what do you want to believe in? *Eternal damnation ringing in your ears at every step of your life...if you don't do well catholically?*"

Gaston laughed hard at that.

"Or *forever paradise won by 'endless purchased indulgences' in a place surrounded by wealthy bishops and papal renegades?*"

Gaston laughed harder and harder.

She looked around her shoulder with curious eyes, the next table, the window, the incoming customers by the counter, for once paying a little attention to the medieval sounds playing in the background.

Then, she said, "Hey, let's go. I want to drop a postcard at *La Poste*. It's for my agent. She's got to know where I am today."

She stood up.

"Wait!" she cried out. "The baby's kicking right now! Quick, put your hand in my tummy." As he did, she exclaimed, "You feel it?"

Gaston shouted, "He just gave me a big kick! Wow!"

Juliette shouted, "I think it's a she! She kicks hard!"

Gaston now put his ear against her belly, listening, all excited. It happened. The feeling was strange though…like the soft thud of the body of a playful little fish against an aquarium wall pressed against his ear. A bigger kick changed that. Now it felt like the stronger thump of a friendly roving manta against the bottom of the light boat where he sat fishing in a quiet bay. "*ooopa!*"

Two figures began to form in his mind, first blurred then clear, one calling the other Richard—his recurrent dream's mustached super wealthy man—the other the familiar bald-headed inquisitor clad in fishing outfit, not vampire clothes, this time. They chatted amicably aboard a boat…holding strings that stuck out of the water…like beams of sunlight….from a swimming fish's point of view…the yellow seahorse's, for example, who enjoyed observing the crazy world that evolved above the surface. For some reason Gaston felt the awkward sensation of being intimately related to Richard when he pulled a handkerchief from his pocket in the boat and began to finger fidget with it.

The amorous couple wasn't aware at least a dozen faces from this quaint place in La Cité had their eyes on them, wondering what in hell could they possibly be doing like that…in plain closeness…both without parents accompanying them, way under age, and apparently touching indecently in public.

No playful words from their part could ever mask their strange behavior, which wasn't, considering she was really pregnant and the young boy touching her was really the expectant baby's father.

Above hovered Richard's soul.

PART 6

CLASH #9—FISHING
(A TIME TRAVELED CLASH)
FRANCE, JULY 1955

FOREVER BRAGGING ABOUT HIS COLOSSAL WEALTH AND POWER WHILE PATHETICALLY HIDING HIS STINGINESS AND USELESSNESS TO THE WORLD

Bermuda Revelation Park

The silver Sphere parked gently over the audience's heads, announcing the trial's new punishment Clash status:

JUST COMPLETED: CLASH #8—RAPPING IN THE RAIN • OVERALL SCORE: JUDGES 5 DEFENDANT 3 • NEXT: CLASH #9-FISHING

Master Judge touched a button and a bay in a cluster of islands materialized. A fishing boat appeared on the wet sand, near a lavender jellyfish washed ashore by a tempest or a predator fish.

The judge motioned Richard to help him push the boat into the water.

Soon they were both rowing, seeking a good spot where to drop anchor.

"Were you big in donations, Mr. Flynn, in your heydays?"

Richard pulled on his fishing pole to see if there was a near-catch there, as nibbling persisted.

"I gave three-hundred grams away...to something called 'The Richard Flynn Online University of Mahwah Fellowship of Dentistry Foundation'...to help honorable students of tooth decay sciences attain their goals," he said proudly, breaking into sardonic laughter. "And prevent me from ever having to wear dentures–my God!"

His laughter became hysterical. "I felt tall, very tall–although I was short and chunky. I felt like a city, a big city–although I was only one citizen."

"Your donation–shamelessly less than a trillionth of thirteen octillion–is an infinitely small amount, ridiculously so, I might add, compared to the incredibly huge fortune you own."

Richard jumped in, "Well, I gave a bit more–one-hundred grams or so–with the condition they name one of their buildings after me, which they did."

"It's still a drop of salt water...from your Pacific Ocean reservoir."

He felt a tiny pull on his line.

"Did the notion of perhaps giving one million away to the poor ever escape you?"

"Never."

Richard wound the nylon string into the reel with a swift, rhythmically firm notion of his fingers, and hurled up the pole's end for another try. He also brushed off some dandruff from one of his shoulders.

Master Judge remained quiet, holding his fishing pole steady over the water.

"Did the slightest tinge of remorse–?"

"–Never."

Explosions of hostile boos from the Stadium's crowd to the defendant resonated all around.

Richard, ignoring them, looked up to a school of birds flying in "V" formation over the lake. It made him smile.

"They're really smart...these birds..."

Fluttering butterfly fish appeared in the exotic array of marine life below the boat, amid beautiful sponges and corals. Through cobwebby hanging sea fans and white algae glided three seasoned mantas.

Deeper in the teeming zone of fish life, a slithering green moray eel and two chomping checkered fish circled the moss-covered craggy rocks that also gave shelter to a peaceful family of shy and velvety conch fish.

Master Judge appeared busy, focused on the bay surface, where his line rested. "Did you ever realize," he said, scratching his bald head, "your fortune was plenty enough to supply the fundamental needs of your entire nation, excluding the rich?"

Richard steered his fishing pole to one side.

"Oh yes–I was aware of that."

"Did you enjoy knowing that?"

"Very much so. After all, I owned 90% of all U.S. businesses, including virtually all the manufacturing companies, nuclear facilities, publishing houses, news media agencies, TV channels, radio stations, telephone carriers, internet providers, entertainment companies..." He scratched one ear. "Movie studios, science centers, airports, railroads, hospitals, schools...you name it, virtually everything–the payoff of being an octillionaire."

The crowd in all Stadiums erupted in unison, "MONSTER! MONSTER! OCTOPUS MAN! HOW DARE YOU BE AN OCTILLIONAIRE!"

Master Judge waited for the gigantic commotion to die down before continuing his interrogation, mumbling obnoxious things to himself. His fishing pole suddenly bent and dipped into the water. He pulled hard on it. "I've got something there!" he exclaimed, watching the line cutting sharply toward and under the boat, where a forceful thump against its bottom made them both voice out a corny "*ooopa!*"

After some maneuvering, the judge took it out of the water.

Richard congratulated him. "So...you won this Clash, too...now?"

"I did. Six of them so far." Staring defiantly at Richard, he added, "Twice what you've got!"

Richard took a peek at the scoreboard to confirm.

JUST COMPLETED: CLASH #9—FISHING • OVERALL SCORE: JUDGES 6 DEFENDANT 3 • NEXT: CLASH #10-BOXING

His eyes followed for a moment the retrieving motion of the big, spinning, silver Sphere back to its sky-high parking spot.

Then he looked down at Master Judge's wobbling catch, some ordinary carp, his fingers fidgeting with a handkerchief. "...such a tiny fish you've got..." he told him.

"I'm baffled...it felt more like a manta..."

"...didn't it?"

PART 7

THE TOWERS' FRIGHTENING INSIDE REVELATIONS ONE TORTURE AT A TIME FRANCE, JULY 1955

JULIETTE IMPRESSES GASTON BY SOLVING THE TWO ANNOYING TASKS THE GUIDE HAS SURPRISINGLY ASSIGNED THEM

La Cité de Carcassonne

Juliette dropped the stamped postcard addressed to her agent into the postal slit after embellishing it with a few thoughtful lines and a creative sketch.

"She'll laugh when she sees my funny face hanging from the tallest tower!"

La Poste was mildly crowded, so they were out of the building rather quickly.

They continued walking on Rue du Comte Roger, very short in length, before they turned right on Rue Saint Louis, headed toward Basilique Saint-Nazaire. The same one they'd seen before from the jousting grounds in Porte Narbonnaise.

Again, curiosity took them to a bunch of seductive stores specializing in linen, jewelry, antiques, craft, leather, and art.

At a small bakery, Gaston bought *pâté de foie de canard*, which he joyfully spread on his hot crusty bread.

"Want some?"

"No. I'll pass," said Juliette with a sullen pout. "I don't eat meat or meat derived foods, but I'll have a glass of water."

"That's cool."

She watched him eat, standing by the door

Then they decided to move on, preferring the sights and sounds of the walking crowd over the cobblestones.

"Wasn't that interesting–the homework the guide gave us about Dame Carcas?" said Juliette at one point, laughing.

"Foolish."

Jubilantly somehow, she danced a little in front of him. "I'm in the mood for that. Let me ask someone, anyone...here in the street...about the legend of Dame Carcas."

"You may have to enter a library or tourism office to expect any assistance," he discouraged, annoyed and worried.

"No. *Right here, right now!*" insisted Juliette.

"*Who* are you going to ask—walkers? Store attendants? *What* are you going to ask?"

"Two questions. One–what did Dame Carcas do 1200 years ago to save La Cité from surrendering to Emperor Charlemagne's five-year siege?"

"Yeah–right."

"And two–how did it happen that Carcassonne was named after her?"

"Well, good luck, stubborn girl," mocked Gaston.

He watched her from a distance of about three dozen meters, shuffling himself behind her through packs of strollers without calling attention to himself.

Surprisingly, after stopping only five young individuals and two middle-aged couples, who didn't mind to pause to answer her questions, she waved Gaston to join her again, claiming victory.

"I got all my answers!" she cheered, jumping up and down, confusing the hectic strolling crowd around her. "You're talking to 'Journaliste Juliette Douvier' of pop magazine *L'Ecureuil Qui Rie* (The Laughing Squirrel)," she then announced soberly, improvising such a professional.

Gaston felt some relief. "No wonder Catharism is not exactly your calling," he teased her.

She gave him a dismissive pout, lifting her chin with pride.

"First answer," she said, renewing her walk beside Gaston along the picturesque street, flirtingly swaying her lovely body. "Realizing La Cité de Carcassonne got to the point where it had to surrender or starve to death after a five-year siege, Dame Carcas fed the last pig she found in the fortress with the last bag of wheat she found and pushed the fat pig over the edge of the tallest tower all the way down to Emperor Charlemagne's feet outside the massive curtain wall. The famous Frank warrior, who paced the ground impatiently out there by his white horse waiting for the eventual surrender with his formidable troops, saw the pig's belly crack open on impact and spill out its rich wheat content wastefully."

She halted momentarily to admire a *papagayo* perched on someone's shoulder in front of a store. "*Bonjour jeune fille blonde. J'adore ta robe rouge...et tes bottes en cuir marron...*" said the bird to Juliette with striking accuracy.

"Did you hear that?" burst out Gaston. "I can't believe it!"

"I can," said Juliette wisely. She whispered into his ear, "It's the guy who talked, not the Amazon parrot."

"Are you sure?"

She nodded yes repeatedly with her head.

Moving out of the area to a less crowded spot, she said, "Can I continue now, silly boy?"

"Of course, silly girl."

"Watching the wasted food in the pig's cracked belly, Charlemagne took it as a sign of overabundance, not deprivation, if La Cité could actually spare a pig like that. Frustrated, he ended the siege and took off with his troops."

"Wow. Fascinating."

"Second answer," said Juliette. "They named Carcassonne after Carcas because as the troops of Charlemagne were leaving, Dame Carcas started ringing the town bells in celebration, which was overheard by the departing troops. One of the soldiers said to another, 'Carcas sonne...' Meaning 'Carcas is ringing.' Somehow this simple comment reached the ears, minds, and hearts of an entire victorious population. So they named the city after her."

"Well done, well edited."

"Thank you."

"Carcas...Carcassonne," voiced Gaston, stressing both words. "It makes sense."

"Fact or fiction?" she raised the question.

Gaston added, "Now a legend."

He remained thoughtful. "Pretty clever idea. Very possible too." He welcomed a little breeze from the west—an offshoot of the territorial Cers wind—ruffling his ear-topped locks of brown hair. "It's not supernatural or out of this world like the religious stuff you're supposed to believe in."

"*Forced to believe in.* Remember? *Or else...*"

"Right."

Juliette laughed. "Good thing you don't live in the Middle Ages, *è?*"

"I'd be a piece of smelling charred flesh by now," he said, laughing too.

Above hovered Richard's soul.

FROM A THREE-HEADED LIONESS SAVIOR IN BULGARIA TO A MACABRE RING OF CATHOLIC BISHOPS IN CARCASSONNE'S DOUBLE-WALLED FORTRESS' TOWERS

"A three-headed lioness tearing apart a huge tiger...who chased a man in some dark street...somewhere in Bulgaria...?" Juliette giggled as she talked, revisiting one of Gaston's recent weird dreams. "That's really astonishing!"

Declaring herself tired, she'd settled for the nearest hot-meal joint, waiting to be served the Carcassonne's famous Cassoulet–a slow, covered cooked stew of white beans, partridge, confit, sausages, local vegetables and herbs.

"It wasn't a funny happening at all," said Gaston, watching how she made faces, teasing him. "I came out of it in panic, sweating and trembling."

"So it was a daytime reverie? A trance?"

"Yes, maybe." He stared momentarily at her intense green eyes, realizing how seductive they looked under certain lights, like the ones illuminating her face now. "I think I was walking, actually, when I saw it."

"Exactly what did you see?"

Gaston grabbed his handkerchief, indispensable as ever, from a pocket. His fingers messed with it as he said, "I really can't figure out what I saw, why it happened, and why I witnessed it."

"What about the terrifying moments...as you ran away from the tiger?" A sultry pout formed on her lips.

"It wasn't me! It was some man about three times my age, wearing a mustache and curly brown hair."

"And a lioness with three heads saved you?"

"That's what I saw when I turned around."

While Gaston fidgeted with his handkerchief, Juliette observed his evasive eyes. Obviously, he preferred not to dwell on this scary issue.

"I don't know what happened. I was attacked. I ran, saw the tiger, saw the three-headed lioness chasing us, and I arrived here safe and sound."

"But you just said it wasn't you."

He felt really stupid inside now and laughed at himself. "That's the thing—it couldn't be me," he finally said.

Laughing too, she said, "You're only nine and don't wear a mustache." She paused. "And where did you arrive?"

Gaston's fingers played with the soft cloth, squeezing it into a ball.

"Some vacant glass-walled room...with one piece of furniture...a brown-red wooden armchair..." He pushed the handkerchief back into his pocket. "Can we just not talk about it anymore?"

"What about the hood...the bat ears...and the thick blue paint around your eyes and mouth?" persisted the young actress.

"Your guess is as good as mine." He stood up. "I've got to take a leak..."

"Wait! How did you know he wore a mustache?" She watched him go, totally perplexed by his elusive nature.

ᏵᎥᏉ

The stew was delicious—the only dish with scrapes of meat Juliette occasionally accepted, but only because she'd trained her front teeth in recent months to filter its tiny chunks down to nearly nothing, rabbit-like, while lusciously sucking in the liquid soup with hardly any effort.

Sipping the light aromatic red wine from the house brought in by the friendly waitress, they delighted at their great view from the window. The picturesque winding road outside thrived with pockets of convivial people and pets from all walks of life.

"Amazing how tourists flock to this fortress," said Gaston, munching on his hot biscuit.

"*Medieval*—that's the keyword—medieval fortress," said Juliette.

"Medieval life, medieval streets," said Gaston.

"Medieval horror," added Juliette, doing a macabre-like dance with her eyes, something she'd rehearsed once on stage for a ghastly play.

"Stop that! You scare the hell out of me!" barked Gaston, then joining her in a giggling outburst.

"You never answered my question, Gaston," she said with a cute pout. "How did you know that mysterious man wore a mustache...if all you could see was thick blue paint around his eyes and mouth?"

"Because before he was attacked by the tiger, I saw fragments of him in my reverie, actually, picking his mustache, while walking down the street, as if itching or something from the paint."

"Why would he paint his face like that? I mean that's crazy."

Gaston laughed. "Aren't we all?"

Through the window, they could see throngs of tourists passing by, some carrying expensive photo cameras with all sorts of accessories, thriving on some kind of personal achievement, others just walking empty-handed, thrilling in the ambiance alone.

Appearing also were kids wearing plastic medieval armors and shields, bearing colorful emblems. They licked double-scooped ice creams with rapacious agility, while seniors with them, clad in bright-hued shorts and shirts or some sport-styled summer hats, trudged the slippery cobblestones, their frail feet and stiff backs one moment away from calamity.

Parading were also the unfailing vacation-starved teenagers in blue jeans and T-shirts, trying hard to validate themselves by grouping together. They hoped to indulge on smart talk, hoping or pretending to look interesting, while clowning around like dorks amid the plodding crowd.

Even monks of different orders, wearing cloaks and hoods in various shades of brown and black, cruised the populated street now and then as if seven centuries of meteoric changing history had not gone by.

A cinematographer and his crew stole everybody's attention when his camera focused on a mink-coated young girl, perhaps only a couple of years older than Juliette, with long red curls, and high hills, apparently their film's lead actress, drawing a growing crowd behind her.

Wearing the vacant stare of metropolitan chic ladies, she'd just started to climb the cobbled slope in grand style, only to trip miserably with one of her shoes. "*Oh...non!*" cried out Juliette, seeing what's coming, covering her face with both hands. More so because the young actress' fur coat snapped open, revealing her bare breasts afloat in her awkward fall.

"Wow...wow..." joined Gaston in amazement. "*Cinéma vérité parfait!*"

"Will you stop staring, child!" teased Juliette, realizing it was all scripted, not accidental.

"I'm not a child," protested Gaston, giggling. "She's really..."

"Really what?"

"Heavenly made," put in Gaston, as gently as he could.

"Heaven my butt!" snapped Juliette.

A brisk agitation of people blocked their view. Between the narrow space of a person's crooked hip and curved arm in front of them, all they could see was the passionate professional work of two long-haired assistants following the action in the street, cigarettes dangling from their mouths. Also, their constant struggle, shared with other crew members, to carry heavy portable equipment and loose coiling cables.

Gaston couldn't resist asking Juliette, "Is your agent a movie agent too?" He knew, of course, she was a stage actress. But...

"She's my first movie agent, negotiating my first movie role right now."

"Fantastic!"

"The shooting will start in September."

"Where?"

"Bordeaux."

"Oh...across the south of France," reasoned Gaston, "On the other shore."

"Yep. The Atlantic." She smiled. "Everything is sketchy so far. So she's asked me not to reveal anything to anybody yet, especially the press." She noticed the surge of insecurity in Gaston's paling hazel eyes. "Everything will be fine, honey–the shooting, you and me, our baby, everything." She pouted.

"But...your belly's going to grow big, like a balloon, during the shooting...and everybody's going to see it."

"It's perfect. I'm playing a *pregnant* thirteen-year-old."

Gaston laughed. He reached out for her hand, which he held warmly. Their eyes locked into a delicious gaze and they kissed fully, their hearts blending into one single thriving flame of fire.

∿

They were back on the cobbled street, mingling with the strolling crowd.

The bustle of life seemed infectious. Juliette elbowed her way in and out of shops that displayed anything from trendy blouses to books on hiking to tennis racquets to tarot cards to medieval wares. Gaston walked closely behind her, imagining all kinds of things.

They bumped into a group of young musicians settled in a hollow space, behind which a stunning silvery-blue array of medieval towers could be seen looming tall and grand. The real thing. A group of people gathered around them, more out of curiosity than sheer thrill for their musical talents.

Featured among them was a charming, courtly-love emissary-like troubadour from the 13th century, sporting a flowery hat, golden necklaces, long tunic, and pointed leather shoes. He performed with a medieval lute, providing alternate poetry between breaks.

"That's what we need today," Juliette said, applauding loudly after witnessing three of his special renditions.

"A mop-haired, cry-baby poet?" shot Gaston, with a tinge of jealousy.

"A romantic, gentle, well-mannered expressionist," replied Juliette, haughtily raising her chin.

Gaston rolled his eyes. "Just like me, huh?" he quipped, failing to gain her sympathy.

⌒♈

Songs and poems filled the air–a stone throw from the somber and peaceful Basilique Saint-Nazaire, tucked in Place Auguste Pierre Pont, next in Gaston and Juliette's path.

Such contrasts electrified Gaston's fertile mind, constantly hungry for uncharted territories. He now watched two black-robed Cathar *parfaits* crossing the street in solemn piety. They always walked in pairs. Next moment, he wasn't sure whether he'd seen them or not. Maybe just imagined. *I swear...* he pondered, uneasily.

For an instant, the opulent Romanesque-turned-Gothic Basilique presented itself in front of them, with its sinister, tall, narrow columns, huge north and south rose medallions, super crafted stained glass windows, and scary perched stone gargoyles.

"Did you hear those thunderous sounds?" exclaimed Gaston suddenly, pointing with a finger. "There's something big going on over there in the Grand Théâtre right now." He kept staring ahead to that spot, searchingly, puzzled.

"Orchestra music," said Juliette. "Apparently, they were resting when we came in, from the other side."

"In the horses-drawn carriage?" tried Gaston.

"Yeah, so quiet and serene," said Juliette. "Now it's all hell breaking lose!" She wrinkled her nose gawkily. "It's a classic concert–not for us!"

"They seem to stop and play, and stop again," remarked Gaston.

"They're just fine tuning the instruments for tonight's performance," clarified the actress. "Plus we don't want to be stuck there for another two or three hours. Pablo's going to be looking for us soon... in Place Marcou, remember?"

"Oh yeah..."

⌒♈

At their feet now towered the Basilique. Originally an Arian-Christian church of Visigoth construction in the 5th century, it became Catholic in the 11th.

French Pope Urban II, launcher of the First Crusade, was here in person in 1096 to bless the stones that would replace its old, modest structure with flamboyant walls and overindulgent architecture.

This happened during the tenure of Bernard Aton IV Trencavel, Viscount of Albi, Nîmes, and Beziers—one of the first rulers of the powerful Trencavel Dynasty and fierce protector of the popular and growing new religion known as Catharism.

Ironically, Italian Pope Innocent III, launcher of the Fourth and Fifth Crusades, in 1209 would begin their complete annihilation by also launching the barbarous and hated Albigensian Crusade—a crusade not against Islam to recapture Jerusalem, like the seven major crusades, but against itself or different colors of itself in the same land.

"You know," said Juliette. "Without myself being a hard-core Cathar and not exactly thrilled in seeing enormous display of wealth in houses of pray, particularly associated with organized religion's supremacy, I can only look at this church from distant steps, like now, with cautious eyes and great reluctance."

"Why's that?"

"Terror. Horror. Unspeakable suffering. Not only were Cathars interrogated and tortured right here behind these powerful doors by these despicable Inquisitors, but the Bishops who ruled this church got around burying Simon Montfort *right here* too!" blasted Juliette. "The so-called *Terror Montfort*–Pope Innocent III's *protégé*–reigned inside this place of prayer even in death for three years before his remains were transferred elsewhere!"

"Where?"

"Some monastery in the north of France."

"Where did you learn all this?"

"A while ago, at the leather shop, while you tried on those fancy medieval jackets."

"Yeah, I remember that," said Gaston. "But..."

"Well, I took the opportunity to question the shop lady about anything she might know or heard about the Inquisition here."

"And?"

"At first, she seemed ignorant of the subject or unwilling to get involved." She pouted.

"Like the other people we asked before...around here, *è?*" said Gaston, alluding to the apparent code of secrecy floating around Carcassonne.

"Yeah, but then, after gaining my trust, she began to tell me things."

"Terrific." Staring sideways uncomfortably, Gaston grabbed her hand. "Let's walk away from here while you talk. This place freaks me out!"

"It might be haunted too," added Juliette.

&

The shop lady, it turned out, owned the shop, was a long time resident of La Cité, and knew more stuff, good and bad, than she could safely put on paper or discuss openly with the news media.

Several generations of her family had lived and worked here before her. So their contribution to La Cité's historic, cultural, and economic heritage was enormous and lasting...considering that less than two-hundred people from perhaps three-thousand in medieval times only lived here now.

"You're good at making new friends," remarked Gaston, as they ambled on Rue du Four Saint Nazaire toward Porte D'Aude past Hôtel de La Cité—a former lustful palace for the Inquisition's supreme *Évêque.*

In those days, this powerful Bishop's silhouette could often be seen drifting through nocturnal shadows by the western rampart's Maison de l'Inquisition and Tour Carrée de l'Évêque.

The latter sat strategically on the narrowest space between the two massive ring walls of the citadel. Such passage was a short walk to the creepy Tour de l'Inquisition and Tour de la Justice—both principal centers of torture and exactly where Juliette and Gaston were headed for now, as they naively flanked Porte d'Aude and penetrated the quiet, dark, and narrow Rue du Four Saint Nazaire, indeed, tagged by those who knew better "the scariest street in the whole bloody compound!"

"No question—all the things the guide told us about these wicked towers and their sadistic occupants are true," Juliette said, forgetting Gaston was only a kid. Well, a *grown-up* kid, capable of harboring malicious and lasting dreams, even ghastly nightmares.

Gaston's precocity, on the other hand, she could safely add in thoughts, was actually enormous, some ten years ahead of his age, to the point of declaring him *mature* in her mind—an overlooked trait because of his tender age and physique. But *how deceiving this was!*

❧

"One of the most atrocious things ever done by these self-called 'servants-of-God Christian bishops,' the shop lady told me," went on Juliette, "was not burning Cathars, Jews, and Templars alive at a stake after first torturing them, but slowly *roasting* them to death over a small fire."

"Wow...wow...wow..."

Juliette halted to gather her thoughts. She also watched how Gaston covered his face with both hands in sheer revulsion.

"She told me that because one of her early ancestors in her family tree—Jacques de Molay, the last Grand Master of the Knights Templar— was executed this way in Paris. But to his 'after death' credit," she told me, "those responsible for his execution—Pope Clement V and King Philippe IV of France—also died within the year of his death."

"Why must Jacques de Molay get credit for that?"

"Because while he was being roasted, he cursed and challenged both of them to join him in trial before the Court of God within the year. His dying curse proved to be prophetic."

"Wow..."

"And we can imagine how God would've handled such thugs," she added with a big vengeful smile.

She renewed her march, adding a tiny coquettish gait, tapping the cobblestones with the hard sole of her boots.

"Is that a new purse you're wearing?" remarked Gaston, noticing its bouncing motion against her right hip.

"A handbag. I purchased it from her—the shop lady. You like it?"

"Very pretty. It blends with your red dress and boots."

"It's handmade, all leather."

"Medieval, perhaps?"

"Yes, yes." She pouted.

They laughed.

But their excitement was cut short by the sudden, sneaky appearance of something very familiar and massive and macabre.

"I can't believe this! Of all the many great towers crowning La Cité, we had to bump into *the forbidden ones!*" shouted Juliette in horror.

"*Tour de l'Inquisition!*" screamed Gaston.

"*And Tour de la Justice!*" yelled Juliette. "*Let's get out of here!*"

༄

Running north on Rue Porte d'Aude in the opposite direction, they reached Château Comtal, itself protected by a mighty set of private towers, a powerful drawbridge, and two large courtyards, which they only stealthily bordered on their way out of the area.

Turning right on Rue du Château, they quickly reached Place Marcou—their *rendez-vous* spot—by pure luck.

Here they settled for good. At least temporarily.

What they enjoyed, if such thing could be possible now, was a charming outdoors terrace table pertaining to one of the many tree-shaded restaurants lining the square.

They were not alone. Dozens of talkative tourists and local artists occupied the rest of the tables scattered all around them.

"But where's Pablo?"

Above hovered Richard's soul.

THE MUPITS ELBIB PAPERS

Enjoying the caress of a rising Cers breeze from the northwest, they considered visiting the opposite side of La Cité, where older towers stood since Roman times.

They aimed at keeping away as much as possible from the 13th-century built torture towers already familiar to them. After all, they were here only for fun...even though too many creepy things seemed to be pursuing them.

Pablo was supposed to join them here outdoors in this square, but no sign of him yet.

"Where the hell is he anyway?" barked Gaston every time Juliette mentioned him.

What they really wanted was to get going, explore the place a bit more, in spite of everything. Learn the good history, if there was any at all.

In the meantime, they tasted some fresh celery sticks and apple juice from a large pitcher kindly left on their table by the young waiter, with three accompanying glasses. The breeze blew with such increasing force, while they talked, the table cloth seemed to want to fly away at times.

"Do you think the baby's sleeping now?"

"I doubt, even though there's no movement at all inside my tummy." Juliette ran a smooth hand over the curvature of her stomach, showily. "There's just too much going on around here, in this mammoth fortress."

Turning her head, she scanned the latest arrivals passing through Porte Narbonnaise. Some continued on Rue Cros-Mayrevieille toward Château Comtal. Others took the Rue Saint Sernin, headed toward this square here where they sat now. They could've done that too, early on, when arriving in the *calèche*, but they would've missed everything they went through–good and bad!

Shaded by broad green leaves that partially fell over their heads, they seemed to hide from view in a cozy, romantic way. Other tables dotting the various cafés and restaurants were covered with bright-colored awnings. The lively hum and buzz of friendly chat could be heard all around.

Central to all, however, was the serene bust of Monsieur Théophile Marcou, topping a gracious little fountain in the balmy open air. Marcou was remembered as the mayor who gave running water to this town in 1871. A big feat!

The third glass sitting on their table was reserved for Pablo, when-ever he decided to show up. Although this could extend much longer since he'd never specified a time of arrival. Apparently, his jazz jam-ming sessions in downtown Ville Basse were just too good for him to let go. And his bragging about them early on upon their arrival only accentuated his enormous fascination for the *joi de vivre*.

Juliette checked her leather handbag, where she'd transferred her girly stuff, including some bills and coins left from her daily purchas-es. She still had plenty and knew it could go a long way, for both of them, for she'd learned in recent months how to share and restrain her spending to the absolute minimum.

As she casually stared at her pretty fair face, silky blonde hair, and fiery green eyes in a little mirror she kept there, another face, slightly familiar, registered in the mirror.

Surprised, she turned around.

"Hi," said the person approaching her, a woman. "I forgot to tell you about the *MUPITS Elbib Papers*..."

"*MUPITS?*" said Juliette.

"*Elbib?*" said Gaston.

"Yes. There's a secret pocket inside the leather bag you bought from me earlier today."

Juliette blinked. "Oh?"

She and Gaston exchanged intriguing glances.

"It usually takes time to be discovered."

Juliette smiled, said, "I haven't noticed it yet myself."

"Can I join you at the table for a while?"

"Sure. Be our guest."

"All our bags have this secret pocket."

"Great idea," said Gaston.

"Bigger idea than you think," said the woman, middle-aged, wearing pale brown clothes, dark long hair, and a cleft chin. "There are folded papers in it with written matter...in tiny print."

"Oh..." gasped Gaston.

"What does *MUPITS* mean?" asked Juliette.

"And *Elbib*?" asked Gaston.

"Elbib is Bible backwards," said the woman.

"Oh—right," said Gaston.

"The other one is something you'll have to read to understand," said the woman strangely.

"Creepy..." voiced Juliette.

"It is," said the woman.

"Wow..."

"Let me explain." She stared at Juliette. "I already told you something about the terrible things the medieval Inquisitors did here in La Cité when you popped up in my shop and inquired about them. Not unusual, others have approached me in similarly naive ways, and asked me the same hard questions."

She paused, pushed some hairs off her face.

"Clearly, we don't want it to go away."

Gaston shifted nervously on his seat. Juliette restrained the surge of a mild cough. But she did clear her throat a little.

"I imagine other stores here have experienced the same malaise. People's need to know, to uncover the virulent past." The woman's black eyes narrowed with chilling intensity. "Don't you think those enormous, mysterious, forbiddingly occupied towers talk...to those willing to listen?"

"Yeah, they seem to say something," put in Juliette.

"Something ugly and scary," added Gaston.

"Much more."

"Evil?" tried Juliette.

"Much more."

Gaston swallowed. Juliette held her breath.

"You see, history repeats itself, rather than learns from its past." The woman stared at both squarely. "My name's Martine, by the way."

"I'm Juliette."

"Gaston."

She smiled. "Brother and sister?"

"No. Very close friends," said Juliette.

"Extremely close," added Gaston showily.

"I get it," said Martine, smiling.

She bent forward a little, poured some apple juice on the empty glass, the one reserved for Pablo, and took a sip.

Neither Juliette nor Gaston found it necessary to say a word about it.

"Are you two...alone here? So young and–"

"–We're with Pablo," interrupted Juliette nervously. "Very adult." She let out a silly giggle, preparing to lie a little. "A relative."

"I see..."

"We're on our summer break from school," added Gaston with a glow in his eyes.

"How wonderful."

Martine's face turned somber again, then she said, "Getting back to the greater than evil thing–we must be constantly vigilant of its appearance. Sometimes it starts with a friendly hand, a warm voice, a sweet smile, an eloquent speech...all deceiving surface tricks...to little by little advance and gain our trust...only to later–once it's grown too big and powerful–show its true dreadful face."

She drank some apple juice.

"Other times it starts aggressively, with mania and cruelty, promising a rise in power and patriotic greatness. We recently experienced that with Hitler and his frightening SS units, the Gestapo secret police, and the whole Nazi army. Machines of terror!"

"You can say that," remarked Gaston.

"We also experienced that with Stalin and his horrifying totalitarian regime...his purges of generals, high ranked government officials, intellectuals, and people he personally didn't like...and similar butchery by other insane tyrants and dictators in certain parts of the world. But looking back to our history, it was medieval religious fervor, embodied in atrocious Catholic royal and papal military Crusades and Inquisition terror, that started all this horror, madness, misery, and... genocide."

She raised her glass and drank more apple juice.

"Christianity was given a chance to follow Christ's message of love and peace to make this a better world–and look what they did with it! They turned it into the most inhuman, fanatic, power-grabbing organization the planet has ever seen!"

She swallowed some saliva. "But they didn't have *enough* with the cruelty and destruction they caused in the 13th and 14th centuries, they were back at it in the 16th, 17th, and 18th centuries...teaming up with the usual succeeding Kings of France...all the way to the French Revolution, when finally a universal definition of human rights was declared in France. Such rights–natural, unalienable, and sacred–were drafted, signed, and proclaimed by some of the greatest statesmen of the time."

Her eyes intensified. "But mind you, hadn't the world gotten wiser and more educated and more resourceful, they would've done it again in the 20th and 21st centuries!"

"The Nazis got in their way," put in Gaston bravely.

"That too!" voiced the shop lady.

She finished her drink and stood up, releasing her intense stare from both youth's eyes.

"I have to go now, to pick up my daughter at school...but...I'd suggest very strongly that you take a look at the handbag's secret pocket and read what's there."

They both nodded.

"We cannot ever let the world forget what happened here in these towers. We cannot ever allow any individual or company or institution or organization to grow into gigantic proportions...unchecked–whatever their transparent intentions–personal, corporate, federal, royal, or religious. We cannot ever permit *horror history* to repeat itself!"

She gave them both a last look.

"My friends, spread the words!"

As she walked away from the table and disappeared into the hordes of pedestrians, Gaston released five "wows" in a row.

Freaked out, Juliette opened her leather bag and searched for the secret pocket.

"It's here!" she exclaimed.

"Open it!" urged Gaston.

She did and unfolded the printed papers, but was afraid to read past the sinister, underlined title.

Finally, she did:

Most Used Papal Inquisition Torture Solutions
(also known as The MUPITS Elbib Papers)

The Pulley Torture. Victims (men, women, or children) were stripped, their hands tied behind their backs, their wrists fastened to a long iron chain that wound over a pulley attached to the ceiling. Victims were then hoisted off the ground by the pulley, which caused their arms to twist back over their heads and crack with enormous pain, while overstretching their entire body. Stone weights of about a hundred pounds were then added to their legs to break their limbs' joints even more. To complete their excruciating pain and misery, if still conscious, their suspended wretched bodies were 'suddenly jerked down, then raised up' at intervals.

She paused, angrily pressed her lips together in disbelief.

At any moment, torturers, or Inquisitors themselves, would burn or cut off with special tools parts of a victim's face or body, with emphasis on the ears, nose, lips, and sexual organs. Often, they tore out the tongue or scooped out the eyes or inserted pointed tools under the fingernails to drive a victim crazy with screams and unbearable pain. Other special tools allowed them to compress the victim's fingers till the bones looked like pencils.

Juliette halted briefly, outraged.

Sometimes they poured molten lead or boiling liquid from iron containers into a victim's throat. Sadistically, they flogged, burned, pierced, overstretched, dislocated, disfigured, maimed, and mangled their bodies till they lost consciousness or died screaming. Although it was said that screams of agony could not be heard outside the thick walls of the towers, many walkers in the area along the years had sworn to the contrary in quite compelling and scary ways.

She stopped reading, trying to collect herself.

Gaston was totally incensed. "No no no no..." he gasped repeatedly, with deep sadness and rage, feeling a cold chill across his spine. "This is the most heinous, sickening thing I've ever heard."

Feeling likewise nauseated inside, Juliette took a long, deep breath.

Then she continued to read, her heart pounding faster and louder, afraid to encounter more of the same or worse, if that could be possible,

The Iron Pyramid Chair Torture. The victim was forced to sit on its pointed end for hours, while his or her feet were hammered into a wooden boot until the bones shattered and its core marrow spurted out.

"I don't think I can take it anymore..." said Gaston, weakly.

The Vice Torture. The victim's head was fitted into a vice and tightened until everything in it cracked and spouted out—teeth, bones, and staring eyes...

Unable to continue, Juliette stood up and walked away. Her face had paled dramatically and it was her turn to throw up.

"You okay?" Gaston patted her shoulders, unavoidably stepping on her vomit.

"It's just unbelievable...that men could be so cruel."

"Not just men...servants of God," reminded Gaston, cleaning up the dirt from his tennis shoe.

"Self-appointed servants," said Juliette. "Without any proof ever of God's approval or validation."

"Isn't that the way organized religion always operates?" put in Gaston.

Juliette nodded. "Unfailingly." She pouted.

"Something triggered Gaston's mind. "What if Martine's story is not true."

"What do you mean?"

"Often people write, even publish, lies. Propaganda, anything...to distort what really goes on...for personal or organizational purposes."

"Not this woman." Juliette gazed at his jumpy hazel eyes. "She's trustworthy. She's been hurt and *needs to repair her past. Needs the world to know about it so it doesn't happen again to others.*"

Juliette washed her mouth with a napkin.

She folded back the little piece of paper that had upset them so much and forced them to reconsider life's meaning at its deepest core. Returning it to the secret pocket, she sighed, "Let's move on again and try to enjoy our freedom."

"Yeah, freedom," cheered Gaston. "REAL FREEEEEEDOM!!!"

Above hovered Richard's soul.

PART 8

CLASH #10—BOXING
(A TIME TRAVELED CLASH)
FRANCE, JULY 1955

MASTER JUDGE HAMMERS RICHARD'S LAVISH LIFESTYLE AND MONEY-WASTING SYNDROME

Bermuda Revelation Park

Everybody looked at the big, silvery Celestial Sphere settling down on the usual spot above everybody's heads.

Spinning gently now, words scrolling and flashing, it announced the latest trial punishment Clash status,

JUST COMPLETED: CLASH #9—FISHING • OVERALL SCORE: JUDGES 6 DEFENDANT 3 • NEXT: CLASH #10-BOXING

Master Judge smiled. Clad in black cape, his index finger pressed a button, giving life to a boxing ring, similar to the ones used by experienced boxers.

In virtually no time, he made his way to the ring, wearing red shorts. The defendant stood there clad in blue shorts.

Things moved quickly.

Master Judge's first punch landed on Richard's abs, his second on Richard's crotch. The pain was unbearable. He nearly fainted. Only his blue shorts shone under the ring's bright lights.

"HAVE NO MERCY! KICK HIS BUTT!" shouted the audience in unison, watching the defendant collapse. Cheers and applause for the judge were wild and overwhelming.

Master Judge smiled gratefully at the riotous crowd.

He waited for Richard to get back on his feet, which didn't happen until the referee's count of eight. At which point, he scrambled up to a fragile standing position.

Lucky for him, Master Judge just danced around for a while, charming the audience with his tattooed glossy bald head. Likewise,

Richard danced, gloved fists protecting his chin, as he encircled the judge, seeking an opportunity to attack.

"How do you feel about the French society?" asked the tricky judge casually, covering his face and chin with his gloves.

"Oh—good question," Richard said, rotating and dribbling with his feet. "I love it."

Master Judge swung again, whacking Richard's upper lip and mustache with the back of his glove.

"Is that why you became the sole owner of all French-oriented ZV commercials worldwide...excluding France?"

He threw a quick jab to the defendant's left ear, half-hidden by his long locks of disorderly hair.

Richard let out a half-muffled "ouch". His head seemed to jerk inside out, beads of sweat dripping down his nose and cheeks.

The crowd roared.

"Exactly," answered Richard at last, quite annoyed at himself for failing to answer sooner. But ready to make up for it.

Another jab from the judge smacked Richard in the chin. It rendered him numb and stupid.

"TAKE HIM DOWN! DESTROY THE BASTARD!"

Master Judge asked Richard, ignoring his pitiful swollen face, "At a cost of?" He also pounded on Richard's chest, causing him to lose some balance.

"Sixty-five bees," replied Richard.

"DOWN THE FILTHY RICH!" raved the audience. "DOWN THE WASTED OCTIDARE!"

"Sixty-five billion?"

Richard charged, swiftly punching his pretentious opponent in the mouth. Blood spurted out between his lips, some of it dripping down his pointed black beard.

"Lipsticks...mouth washers...sperm-colored facial creams...malfunctioning teasing panties...pubic hair softeners..." said the defendant, turning around the injured judge with menacing eyes, "...male genital shaped products for women...double-bulge see-through fly-front slacks for men…slutted-up deep-sea miniskirts for cool young girls and–"

"–And *what could be next?*" challenged the judge cynically, his front teeth hurting. He also swung smartly against his adversary, but missed.

Richard chased Master Judge around the ring in a wide loop, searching for another opportunity. He could hear the crowd booing him like crazy. Smiling, he answered the judge, again with delay, "…special real-time erection mikes for female singers and gay comedians." He sneaked a creative blow to the judge's stomach and another one to his chest. Not enough to cause a dent. "That's in addition to the usual hair coloring products, *haute-cuisine* offerings, wines, and perfumes."

∽

Master Judge now asked, "How do you feel about the Russians?"

He dodged a punch, only to attack with a mighty jab of his own to Richard's chin.

The Stadiums crowd bellowed, watching the long-haired dude buckle. "CRUSH HIM! CRUSH HIM! BREAK HIM APART!"

"They're great people…" finally answered Richard, meaning of course the Russians, feeling dizzy.

"Why?"

"They made me one of them, for one thing." He then hammered the judge with three short, but hard, punches to the face. "They put me into orbit. They showed me the world from above."

Seeking another chance, Richard curled around his opponent, legs at work, eyes on his prey.

"The *starving* world?" interrupted Master Judge, politically hitting Richard where it mattered. The man was after all the richest person on earth ever.

"Whatever! Can't tell from above," blasted Richard angrily. His fist went wild, trashing the judge's nose real bad.

"What where you doing up there anyway?" asked Master Judge, incensed, shaking his head sideways to relief the pain.

"Joy riding…having fun," stated Richard.

"With the Russians?" exploded the judge.

He got even immediately with a heavy blow to Richard's left eye.

"RIGHT ON!" cheered the crowd.

"Why not?" the defendant said to Master Judge, dribbling, avoiding another hit to his eye. "They invited me into their spaceship."

"Nice gesture," noted the judge. "For free?"

Blood was dripping from Master Judge's nose from an earlier punch.

Richard laughed. "Well...almost...one-hundred trillion."

"One-hundred trillion just to see the world from above?"

"For a few hours."

The crowd erupted in anger, "YOU'RE AN UGLY SOB! YOU SHOULD DIE IN SPACE, MOTHER FUCKER!"

Master Judge used this distraction to hit him straight in his teeth, making him spit blood almost instantly.

"Even if it was for a few millenniums, can you ever justify this super gross caprice of yours? This immense vanity and utter selfishness...considering the rampant poverty, hunger, and misery affecting the world today?"

"I can't," said the mustached defendant.

"Do you realize now that...that it's all over...Mr. Octidare?"

A wild punch to his head made Richard dribble sluggishly. For a tiny fraction of time, he could only see things spinning and lights flashing. Strange things had happened to his head, his field of vision.

Erratically, he sensed the nearness of the judge.

"You called me...Octidare?" His breathing poured heavily. "Everybody's calling me Octidare. What's going on here?" He seemed delusional, eyes swollen, bleeding through his teeth. *"I'm an octillionaire—damn it!! The first one ever in the history of mankind!!"*

Master Judge approached him, said, "You are what we think you are! What we choose to call you!"

In a fit of rage, he cornered him with a series of jabs to his ribs, chest and neck, and one powerful blow to his forehead, sending him to the floor.

People screamed like crazy around the Astral Floor and into the hallways of the Alternative History Palace, throwing articles in the air in celebration. They were overwhelmed and hysterical with joy.

"JUST DROP DEAD MISERABLE MAN!"

The referee counted till ten.

❦

Meantime large schools of grunts, flamehawks, jacks, and copperbands visited the cavernous areas under the Stadiums and the Promenade Corridor, where vertical walls dripped with gorgonians and sponges of every shape and color. Out there, protected from currents and tides, many crabs, lobsters, and mollusks found refuge and solace.

A triple-eyed oddball coral fish, squeezing itself through tightly compressed chunks of algae fuss, came face to face with Richard in a wild surfacing stunt, just above the boxing ring, causing him to smile and sneeze.

❦

"DOWN THE OCTIDARE! DOWN THE USELESS RICH MAN!"

Richard lay there on the floor half unconscious.

❦

Master Judge spat on the defendant's face.

"What d'you expect–dare devil?!" he shouted. "We don't play around with money here like you do! We don't even earn money!"

On his knees now, Richard began to crawl away, humiliated.

"We earn allowances to goods, services, and freedom by authorization and validation only…through our arm-implanted ZCAP meter's readings! Which tell us how much useful energy to Zundo we've consumed and produced per any given time…to deserve such things!"

He stared down arrogantly at the defendant's wrecked face.

"*Useful energy to Zundo* are the key words!"

He spat again on Richard's face and his crushed body.

"No zillionaires or mega-waste here. No super gods." Suddenly he roared like a lion, and shouted, "YOU GOT THAT?!"

The audience went wild, creating a new song:

HOORAY! HURRAH!
MASTER JUDGE—OH GASH!
HOORAY! HURRAH!
YOU'VE WON ANOTHER CLASH!

Meantime, a crawling man tried to leave the scene, ignored, unnoticed.

Someone, however, caught the move. Alerted, he stepped forward to block his exit from the Astral Floor. Resting his heavy boot on Richard's shoulder, he belched, "The big silver Sphere's here already... above your head! You may want to check your score to know where you are in your punishment!"

Richard lifted his head to watch.

JUST COMPLETED: CLASH #10—BOXING • OVERALL SCORE:
JUDGES 7 DEFENDANT 3 • NEXT: CLASH #11—KNIFE
THROWING

෴

Master Judge wasn't finished yet. "Compose yourself and face the audience like a man!" he shouted, removing his weighty boot from the defendant's shoulder.

Richard complied.

"Now, repeat after me, loud and clear, 'useful energy consumption and production'!"

"Useful energy consumption and production!"

"Louder!" shouted the judge.

"USEFUL ENERGY CONSUMPTION AND PRODUCTION!"

"Useful to whom?" shouted the judge.

"USEFUL TO ZUNDO!"

"Not to you personally, but to—?!" shouted the judge.
"ZUNDO!"
"Again!"
"ZUNDO!"
"Again!"
"ZUNDO!"

BOOK 5

THE CULMINATION OF PUNISHMENT

PART 1

FLEEING VILLE BASSE'S SINISTER MONK COMMUNITY AND ANYTHING ATTACHED TO IT FRANCE, JULY 1955

A TIMEWORN HOUSE IDENTIFIED
WITH A TINY METALLIC PLAQUE

La Cité de Carcassonne

Past a *bonbon* shop on Rue Du Grand Puits, moments later, as they were just about to turn left on Rue Violet-Le-Duc, by the fabled big water well, Gaston noticed a person rushing through the crowd that bore great resemblance to Pablo. *It can't be him*, he thought. *He wears sandals, a dark blue cloak, and a hood over his head.*

Within seconds, he and Juliette hurried after him in disbelief.

The hooded head made its way into a warehouse on the street's stretch that faced the semicircular *barbacane* du Château Comtal and five of its nine defensive towers.

Wow...a fortress within a fortress, marveled Gaston, running past it, recalling the guide's version of its glorious and tragic history.

Out of breath, Juliette stopped by the beige-tinted building, where the cloaked and hooded figure had entered, ready to peek through the only window available there.

It was a bit too high for her to see inside. Fortunately, a loose brick, partially broken, left on the ground against the wall several meters away, called her attention. Swiftly, she carried it over to the area under the window, getting herself dirtier than she expected in the process, and mounted on it.

Standing on her toes, next to Gaston, who supported her with one outstretched arm to her back, she spied on the cloaked figure that moved around inside. It examined and picked up tools from a shelf, she noticed, stuffing many of them inside a robust dark leather bag. In the blink of an eye, the only moment the figure revealed its face, she confirmed her most feared belief.

No question, it's Pablo! The recognition made her bite her lips so sharply, it bled a little, some of it quickly spilling over her pretty red dress. *But why? What the hell is he up to in Carcassonne?*

"It's him!" she whispered loudly to Gaston, who raised his eyebrows in shock and almost relaxed his arm, causing her to sway off balance, without actually falling. "*Zut!*"

ᴄᴖ

It didn't take long for Pablo to leave the warehouse carrying his heavy bag and thread his way through crowds of people down to Rue de la Porte d'Aude, just before it became Rue du Four Saint-Nazaire. There he forged his way deeper into the sloping, winding, and obscure rampart passageways that led down to Ville Basse.

Whatever the risks, the young couple followed him down the road through Porte d'Aude, scrambling their way down the steep, twisting, Montée de la Porte d'Aude, leading to Église Saint Gimer at the bottom of the hill.

This perilous path, droned by rasping frog's and cicada's chants, overlooked the Trivalle district this side of the river. Across l'Aude and beyond extended the now illuminated Ville Basse and its pleasant, scattered but seen, taxi, bus, boat, train, and plane terminals.

"I can't believe this! Where's he going?" blasted Juliette, both furious and beaten inside.

"I have no idea...and I don't like it..." shot Gaston, feeling the weight of enveloping darkness over his shoulders.

They'd just come out of the torture towers zone, all freaked out, and somehow were thrown again into a field of eminent danger and mind-boggling uncertainties.

Time had passed them by in sinister ways from late afternoon to sunset to night, they knew, and faster than they could realize or describe, as the cloaked and hooded figure crossed the narrow, looping, cobbled street, a block past the church, with the slithering agility of a hungry panther.

The familiar figure slid along the shaded red-roofed homes of Rue Côte de la Cité, then glided left on Rue de la Barbacane, moving through the traffic of vehicles.

About fifty meters away, it turned left again to Rue Petite Côte de la Cité, another narrow, ghostly street lined with wall-to-wall Mediterranean styled houses, none taller than two stories. Nearby, sheltered in the trees, crickets hummed their retiring songs of the day.

Juliette saw the figure enter a small, timeworn house in a bleak area, below the mighty hilltop's silhouetted tower-studded fortress they'd left behind, looming in the background, now glistening fully in the nocturnal skyline.

A tiny metallic plaque affixed to one side of the front wall announced the titular of a certain profession or activity, which read:

Alberto Callado
RERTUTOR DEL RÉSIEHÉ

meaning nothing to Juliette and Gaston.

Somehow the door was left unlocked, and they pushed their way in like upscale thieves into a dilapidated museum of secret ancient archeological treasures.

Only that what lay ahead was so repugnant to see, even ghastly and inhuman, that it drastically wretched the sanctity of vision, let alone the sanity of mind.

Torture at its grossest form and highest level! Factory-produced horror!

⌒⌒

Pablo had removed the tools he'd gotten at the warehouse. They were all small but creepily pointed—all lined up on a wooden table as if ready for surgery.

"Oh my God!" cried out Juliette in panic, covering her mouth to muffle the sound of her voice.

Other cloaked and hooded monks waded in and out of the room, seemingly busy and driven. One of them held a red-hot probing or tearing instrument that he'd just pulled out of a burning furnace oc-cupying the far corner of an adjacent dungeon visible from this angle.

Two meters away from Pablo's table, lay on a rack, all stretched out, a fully undressed man, except for his underwear. His miserable, battered, near-starved appearance with protruding ribs and lacerated hip bones reminded Gaston of images of Jesus Christ he'd seen in Roman Catholic churches.

There was plenty of sadness in his tired grayish eyes and total ne-gation of speech as he was doubly gagged with a twisted piece of cloth that also ran around his head. His long strands of messy hair partially covered his face dotted with black spots of burned flesh, while pepper-gray chest hair fluffed up over what was left of his chopped off nipples.

Gaston's mind momentarily drifted away...to a boxing ring...fea-turing two bare-chested fighters throwing punches at each other's bodies...a tortured face receiving a jab...blood dripping...

Above hovered Richard's soul.

WITNESSING HUMANITY AT ITS LOWEST DEPTHS

Ville Basse

The tortured man curled his lips miserably.

The rack onto which his back lay with unbearable pain looked like a ladder, with rollers at both ends purposely set to keep his wrists and ankles tied.

Two black hooded figures standing at either side provided the tension that broke his eyes into tears and made his stomach growl. The dismembering pulls on his limbs by sticking iron rods into the rollers' holes caused him to howl in a half-suppressed manner like a wounded beast.

The whole torture setup rested on a sturdy stone frame about half Gaston's height.

Other tortured victims, in similar situations, were also visible from Gaston and Juliette's hiding spot, behind a partially erected stone wall.

A maze of cavernous cells, deeper and darker down a hallway, connected with stairs going at least a floor lower. Gaston saw a cloaked monk emerged from its depths holding more strange tools and containers. *How can such a small, ordinary house, the way it looks from the street, be so spacious and heinous inside?* he thought, gripped with the greatest fear he'd felt in his life. *How can human beings do such inhuman acts and get away with it?*

Like Gaston, Juliette stood there frozen in shock, asking herself impossible questions. Then she mused, *how can we now get out of here without being noticed? How are we going to get back to Saint-Jean-du-Gard tonight?*

Pablo approached the victim held on the rack near his table after pacing up and down the stretch surrounding his wretched body. He loosened the cloth stuck in his mouth and offered him his ranting eyes.

"For the last time—who else in your large family is a perverted heretic?!" he shouted with a frightening, mean voice unknown to either Juliette or Gaston.

"Give me names now or I'll hurt you beyond your imagination!"

The tortured man remained silent.

"I'll give you two options: gouge your eyes off your face or cut your tongue off," said Pablo dramatically now, without raising his voice.

"I'd rather go for your eyes...so you can have a tongue to talk later."

The man on the rack said nothing.

Pablo's sinister stare momentarily drifted toward the area where the young couple hid, as if responding to a certain faint noise. Apparently, only a nervous reaction to nothing.

Quietly, he reached for a tool on the table and motioned for assistance with a flick of his fingers.

Immediately the man on the rack was surrounded by three hooded monks who began to struggle with his jerking movements, the very last in his life.

"I can't watch this!" Juliette grabbed Gaston's arm. "Follow me!"

Luckily they stood at a safe distance and no monk wandered near them. Crouching down, holding their breaths, they slowly moved away on their knees toward the entry door, which fortunately was still unlocked.

In a rush, they slipped away through it, hearing a horrifying scream of agony behind them, and ran out at full speed back to Rue de la Barbacane.

"Where to now?" Gaston asked Juliette, panting, still running toward Côte de La Cité and the church.

"To Martine's house," she said, out of breath, in her running.

"Do you know where she lives?"

"Yes. She wrote her address on the back of my hand earlier...in her shop."

Slowing down, she read the address. "Don't stop!" she then shouted to Gaston. "We're going back to La Cité!"

"*What!*" gasped Gaston. "It's uphill now! In the dark!"

"*We'll manage!*"

Above hovered Richard's soul.

FETCHED BY GRANDPA VIA TWO GENDARMES AND OFF TO NÎMES BY PLANE

La Cité de Carcassonne

While exiting the torture house in the Trivalle district, Gaston had picked up from the floor a purple-tinted business card.

He'd seen Pablo accidentally drop it close enough to their hiding place before settling down with his tools near his table and his torture subject.

Printed on it, with professional flair, was the same information inscribed on the metallic sign outside the house.

Now, as they reached the illuminated streets of La Cité from the dark, steep, cobbled climb, he showed it to Juliette, who'd wandered under a lamppost to catch her breath.

She read aloud: *"Alberto Callado. Rertutor Del Résiehé."*

"Looks like Pablo Quintero has two names," remarked Gaston. "The rest sounds like Chinese to me," he added, puzzled. "Can you read that strange line again?"

"Rertutor Del Résiehé."

"Well, Chinese doesn't sound like that either," he admitted.

"It sounds, and looks like, misplaced Spanish or French to me," said Juliette with a thoughtful pout. "Whatever," she added, storing the card away in her leather bag's secret pocket. "You know,' she then said, in a reflective pause, "I don't want to worry you, but I think Pablo saw me for a split second…before he proceeded to butcher that poor man."

Gaston stared at her judiciously. "I doubt," he said. "Otherwise, he would've taken you prisoner and—"

"—Don't even let it cross your mind!" shot the young actress, annoyed. "Let's focus on finding the shop lady."

The walking crowd had declined considerably in size, in spite of the floodlit beauty of the surrounding towers replacing the daylight. They were now moving on Rue Cros-Mayrevielle, headed for Rue Agnés de Montpellier, where Martine lived. But two uniformed *gendarmes* stopped them cold.

"Are you Juliette Douvier and Gaston Lagarde?" asked one of the *gendarmes*.

"Yes, we are," said Juliette.

"Do you know Monsieur Marcel Douvier?" said the other *gendarme*.

"Yes. He's my grandpa."

The two *gendarmes* stared at each other with victorious smiles.

"We're taking both of you to the *Gendarmerie*," said the tallest one. Staring at Juliette, he added, "At your grandpa's request." His thin mustache curled briskly at both ends when he smiled, and Juliette's presence seemed to do wonders for his smile. "He's already there waiting for you."

"*What? Why? How?*" Juliette was astounded.

"We don't have the answers, but we're sure he'll be happy to give them to you," said the other uniformed man, also trying to impress the young girl with the pretty red dress.

Juliette kept staring at both police officers with puzzled eyes, but glad she and Gaston were at last in good company.

∽

The *petite voiture* that drove them reached the intersection of Avenue du Général Leclerc and Rue Paul Lacombe in the Trivalle district before it veered into a narrow alley and parked.

Gaston shook hands with Monsieur Douvier inside the building and watched the big, warm hug Juliette and her grandpa made afterwards in utter joy and relief.

In a rush, the old distinguished man asked for a taxi to pick them up and a moment of privacy with Juliette and Gaston.

"Juliette—something terrible happened this afternoon to the mission. Danielle was shot dead. One bullet to her head."

"Oh noooo...." gasped Juliette, genuinely hurt. For a while she stood immobile, her stare vacant, chin down, with nothing to say. "Then it's my turn...to continue..." she said, raising her chin, as if being reborn.

"Yes. We're heading to the airport immediately to catch the earliest plane to Nîmes," spoke up Monsieur Douvier.

"Wow..." said Gaston, with mixed emotions.

"Where did it happen?" asked Juliette, her heartbeats racing.

"Between Durfort-et-Saint-Martin-de-Sossenac and Tornac, about six or seven kilometers south of Anduze."

"How did you know we were here...in Carcassonne?"

"Alfredo told me. He knew about his brother's scheduled trip, and I figured the rest."

Juliette nodded.

"Where's Pablo?" asked Monsieur Douvier.

The young couple exchanged uncertain stares.

Juliette said, rushing to beat Gaston with her answer, "Downtown Ville Basse, jamming with a bunch of jazz musicians, he told us." She didn't feel like elaborating on the real things they'd seen and endured now because of this new, unexpected event that suddenly took priority. Soon she'd be riding her white Camargue horse with the kite toward the Grotte de Trabuc.

"We don't have time to loose, so he'll have to manage without you guys," said her grandpa.

"Great!" exclaimed Gaston with jumpy eyes. Juliette's curious pout, which he expressly noticed, made him realize very quickly his blunder, and he added, "I mean, he'll be okay"

The taxi arrived. Before boarding, Monsieur Douvier coached both youngsters to avoid talking about the issue at hand for security reasons.

The taxi sped away.

It crossed Pont Neuf in the first three minutes, allowing a sweeping view of the nightly lit Ville Basse.

Carcassonne Salvaza Airport operated well into the night and appeared less crowded than usual. So remarked the taxi driver as they arrived some ten minutes later and entered the flights departure area off Route de Montréal.

The plane took off.

§

"I know you're dead worried. Let's focus on the Legend of the Horse-Riding Kites now...my immediate and urgent participation... after this incident..." Juliette whispered to Gaston on the plane, halfway to Nîmes, sitting next to him. "We'll tackle Pablo and his torture clan later."

"But I won't see you anymore. Who knows for how long...if you're riding your horse day after day...through dangerous forests and rocky hills..." whispered back Gaston sadly, holding his tears.

"It's an honor for me to do that...for my mission's sisters...and for the world..."

"But you're pregnant...with our baby..."

"I'll be okay...so will our baby...all of us..."

"But..."

"Grandpa will tell you what to do...after I'm gone...follow his instructions..."

Juliette herself spent the rest of the flight listening to her grandpa's instructions, relocated next to him two rows in front of Gaston. It was crucial that she understood and followed every detail.

Monsieur Douvier had been in contact with the mission's Cathar lead monk for the latest news, and although his granddaughter had advance knowledge about how to proceed, there were specific issues related to the crime and transfer of ridership with minimum of conflicts with the local police and news media she had to master.

Gaston's mind also recreated the crime issue, sedated by the monotonous drumming of the plane's engine noise, before he dozed off. *Danielle...an innocent thirteen-year-old girl...was murdered only hours ago...riding a horse...and now Juliette's going to replace her? Before the murderer's caught? Not good! Not good at all!*

§

They continued the trip on Monsieur Douvier's car, the familiar sky-blue Delahaye 135MS Faget-Varnet Cabriolet. Both Juliette and Gaston fell asleep, which was actually an extension of the few hours sleep they got in the plane.

As they approached Maruéjols-lès-Gardon, Monsieur Douvier made his first attempt to wake his granddaughter up.

"Juliette...Juliette, we're almost here."

Her response was weak. She simply continued to sleep, which she needed badly.

The car stopped at a house known to Monsieur Douvier in this town.

He got out and knocked on the front door.

Moments later a curtain pulled to one side inside a window. The door opened.

"Marcel, what brings you to my home so early in the morning," said a white-haired, thick mustached man clad in his pajamas. Looking up to the sky, he mumbled, "The first threads of sunlight are still struggling to show up."

"I need a favor. Can you prepare breakfast for me, my granddaughter, and her boyfriend...while I get busy with something very important in my car? If you don't mind, we're all vegetarians and we're in a big hurry. Say hello to your wife, if she's awake."

"No problem."

"I'll explain at another time."

Above hovered Richard's soul.

PART 2

PHASE ONE OF JULIETTE'S TREACHEROUS JOURNEY TO GROTTE DE TRABUC FRANCE, JULY 1955

A TEAM'S WORK—GETTING JULIETTE, HORSE, AND KITE READY FOR THE HOLY GALLOP TO GROTTE DE TRABUC

Maruéjols-lès-Gardon

After a productive talk with the house owner, Monsieur Douvier returned to his car. This time he was successful in waking his granddaughter and Gaston up.

"Juliette, this is for real today. No rehearsals. You have only half an hour to build a kite that will make it all the way to Grotte de Trabuc."

His eyes were stern. "I have all the materials you'll need in the trunk of my car...including the two replacement scrolls and the tubes to contain them."

Juliette enthused, "I'll have it built in twenty-five minutes. Did you bring long and thin pieces of cloth to put together the tail? And a roll of string to raise and hold the kite up in the air?"

"Yeah. It's all in the car."

Monsieur Douvier opened the trunk and began to transfer items, assisted by a sleepy and yawning Gaston.

A distant voice said, "Breakfast's ready."

Monsieur Douvier dragged to the car a large, broken, wooden table he found near the water well on the yard, close enough to settle the food on, leaving this side of the car door's wide open for Juliette to continue her work.

In turn, Juliette negotiated her work with bites of toasted bread (spread with jam), hot *café noir*, *croissant*, steamed vegetables, and other tasty foods promised to be meatless and not derived from milk.

Eating faster, both Gaston and Grandpa watched with awe how a beautiful kite with a 'roaring' feature grew out of nothing while finishing their breakfast.

Monsieur Douvier drank some cranberry juice. Then, he addressed Juliette, "Before I left Saint-Jean-du-Gard last evening, I arranged for your Camargue horse to be waiting for you in Tornac this morning, about one kilometer off the crime scene, direction of Anduze, so you don't bump into unnecessary police questioning that would delay or hamper your mission."

"Great!" exclaimed the young girl. "I don't particularly like the *gendarmes.*"

"Neither do I," said Gaston, grabbing a banana.

"A dozen of our monks will be scattered around the area before police units and detectives even begin their investigation, searching for Danielle's horse and the stranded or damaged old kite, which might be several kilometers away by now. Hopefully, they'll find the old tubes containing the ancient scrolls."

Gaston listened judiciously, munching on his food, not realizing it was specifically veggie. Likewise, not informed about it, he wondered why no eggs, milk, sausages, ham, or chicken was served. "Kilometers? Shouldn't the horse stay or wander near Danielle's fallen body?" he questioned.

Juliette answered, staring at Gaston, "Our horses are trained to leave the area, trot away in those cases. Mine is."

"Your Camargue horse?"

"Yes. I trained him to do that. Never told you, but—"

"—That's very unfriendly for a horse to do!" uttered Gaston, disturbed.

"He's trained to recognize a living or dead body. Danielle is dead, sadly. So her horse noticed that and took off," explained Juliette. "We don't want the detectives to question the horse—sort of—and find out about our secret organization and mission. The world is not ready for this yet. We'll end up in jail or the madhouse." She pouted.

Silence.

"We must avoid the press. Reporters will be swarming the crime scene very shortly." said Monsieur Douvier.

"What about Danielle's body?" remarked Gaston. "Is she really... dead?"

"Very dead," said Monsieur Douvier, looking down at Juliette's finishing touches on the kite. "Our scouting monk, yesterday evening, found that out within the hour of the crime, before the first inspector arrived and his assistant took the required deceased body photographs...and the actual body was taken away to the morgue."

"Poor girl," said Gaston sadly. "I can imagine her grieving parents, brothers and sisters, school friends and classmates."

"Very distressful," said Monsieur Douvier.

"Who would do such a thing...and why?" Gaston tried to understand.

He'd learned so many rotten things about the 13th century, and yet there was still cruelty in the 20th century. In fact, he'd just witnessed torture of the vilest kind with Juliette in Carcassonne. His young mind raced in distress, thinking, *Cloaked and hooded Catholic men cutting, breaking, and mutilating other men's body parts. Burning their flesh...forcing them to convert to a religion they couldn't believe in...under agonizing muted screams and unbearable pain. How could these people represent what Jesus Christ stood for? How could the world be so blind in letting them be their spiritual leaders?*

"Fanatics, people with extreme ideas or beliefs, brainwashed people, said Monsieur Douvier, answering Gaston's question.

"I'm done!" Juliette stood up to stretch her legs. She walked in circles a bit, warming up her blood and muscles.

"Let's go," commanded Monsieur Douvier, waving a hand to his old friend and thanking him for everything.

"We should be there in fifteen-twenty minutes. Gaston and I will follow you with my car...all the way to Grotte de Trabuc...after you gallop away with your white horse."

"And the kite," added Gaston, winking at her.

Monsieur Douvier showed her a map and suggested Rue du Luxembourg through Anduze, then the bridge she needed to cross to the other side of town, where it met Route d'Alès at the traffic circle, and the singular, winding northbound road edging the river Gardon d'Anduze flowing at her side, which she already knew and had ridden on several times in the past.

Initially, she would also ride along the railroad track that split away to Saint-Jean-du-Gard with its many picturesque bridges, aqueducts, and tunnels, before hitting the small towns of Montsauve and Générargues—basically hamlets—near the wild greenery of Bambouseraie.

Then, the climb might get trickier and stickier deep in the forests of Mas Soubeyran, where the famous Camisard chief Pierre Laporte, nicknamed Rolland, was born.

The rest would be a single, difficult road up to the grotte, where an old, vintage monk would be ready to receive her.

Juliette's confidence had never been so strong. She was going to accomplish a feat of immense importance, only dreamed of until today. Finally, her turn to participate in the centuries-long Legend of the Horse-Riding Kites had arrived!

"I feel very sorry for what happened to Danielle," she told both her grandpa and her boyfriend as Monsieur Douvier turned the car engine on and sped away. "She was my mission sister, and a bright young girl. I only hope I can live up to the remaining of this stage's expectations, and guide the kite with the ancient scrolls to Grotte de Trabuc, as planned."

"Let's not forget that the killer's still at large, possibly in these woods," remarked Gaston, very uncomfortable with his girlfriend's boldness.

"We'll be right behind her with the car, all along at all times," put in Monsieur Douvier. "She'll have our protection plus our monks will be on alert."

"By the way, Gaston," exclaimed Juliette, flashing her intense green eyes. "While on the plane, Grandpa was able to break the code. You know, *decipher* the strange written message on Pablo's business card."

"Oh, what did it say?"

"TORTURER DE L'HÉRÉSIE"

"Wow! The bastard! Our very own friend," said Gaston.

"Not anymore!" said Juliette, pouting nastily.

"How did he ever get into this? What was the seduction about?" asked Gaston, bitterly astounded.

"Torture," said Monsieur Douvier from the steering wheel. "The joy of causing extreme physical pain to other human beings."

"Wow."

"But I'm going to put an end to this secret Carcassonne clan myself, as soon as Juliette's done with her ride to Grotte de Trabuc. In fact, I've already started a monk investigation on this matter."

"More monks?" remarked Gaston, worried.

"These are good monks," said Monsieur Douvier. "They work for me."

"Oh..."

A flock of black birds crossed the sky. It also brought back a sad image to the archeologist. "Speaking of strengthening our holly mission, I was planning to hire Madame Rossi as an assistant, except that she passed away yesterday. Natural causes...age 99."

"She *did?*" lamented Gaston. "Oh, she was my friend. I will miss her a lot."

"So will I."

Above hovered Richard's soul.

JULIETTE'S BOUNCING PONYTAIL AND ROARING KITE SWOOPING ABOVE A GALLOPING WHITE CAMARGUE HORSE DAZZLE A TOWN STILL HEALING FROM THE PAINS OF WARS

One Kilometer Away from the Crime Scene, Tornac

A monk stood still in the evanescent shadows of day-break outside the barber shop, which had not opened yet. It didn't matter, that was the encounter agreement–time and place–upon which Monsieur Douvier would meet the dark-robed cleric.

Tornac seemed virtually deserted at this quiet sunrise, so spotting any moving object would be rather easy, thought the veteran archeologist, slowly rolling his luxurious Delahaye between the two groups of lined houses. Less so, however, responding to a furtive gesture from a stationary object in this empty, surreal mist.

As was the case here now.

The agitated nostrils of a radiant white horse coming out of a shadow behind a brick wall, after a slight nod of the priest's hand, broke the monotony. In a preceding split second, he had recognized Monsieur Douvier.

"It's my horse! He's got my horse!" shouted Juliette, totally overjoyed, failing to respect her grandpa's rules, so necessary this particular moment.

"*Shsssss*…tone it down, Juliette…we don't want to attract attention," said Monsieur Douvier with a measured tone in his voice and infinite patience. "It's critical. Danielle's crime scene is only one kilometer south of here…toward Durfort."

"I'm sorry, Grandpa." She pouted guiltily.

"Any *gendarme* in sight, Gaston?"

"None that I can see, Monsieur."

They all got out the car, the engine idling.

"It didn't occur to me to bring jeans for your horse ride," apologized the savvy archeologist. "I'm afraid you'll have to continue with your pretty red dress, not exactly fit for your journey. But–"

"–Grandpa–I'll be fine! It's only fifteen kilometers or so to the grotte!"

"Give me a hug, sweetie," Monsieur Douvier felt his eyes turning moist. She was so adorable.

Gaston got her tender hug too. As they detached, she gazed into his saddened hazel eyes and said, "If anything happens to me, promise me you will continue the horse-riding mission to Grotte de Trabuc. The two ancient scrolls must get there no matter what."

"I promise."

He could feel the magnitude of her request through the power of her persuasive green eyes.

❦

Grandpa and Gaston just stood there, tense, and breathless, watching their most precious treasure move on to a new phase in her life.

❦

They both watched her running toward the white Camargue horse, proudly carrying her kite.

Assisted by the monk, she mounted the graceful animal and held the kite up above her head, gradually releasing more and more of the string. Then she tied it to the saddle so she could hold the reins for a while.

Awesome sight.

With the kite already roaring in the wind, she waved good bye and trotted away like a fairytale princess.

❦

Within the hour she'd left behind the historic village of La Madeleine at a steady gallop and entered the stretch of Chemin du

Plan des Molles at a trot, to the right, in the southern outskirts of Anduze, before continuing on Rue du Luxembourg at a faster pace.

Light early morning traffic helped the situation. Drivers of automobiles and bicycles watched the passing horse-riding, kite-teasing beauty with admiration, if not enchantment.

Walking kids cheered and ran after the roaring kite that flew low above Juliette's bouncing blonde ponytail. Many thought it was some new Disney promotional stunt. Others swore it was a religious apparition, an angel from Heaven visiting Anduze.

Some grown-ups appeared scandalized at what they saw under her pretty red dress when gusts of wind blew it up unmercifully, revealing her pink panties. And she laughed her way throughout blocks of townspeople waving their hands, mentally singing,

Sweet Anduze here I come
Flying a kite above my head
Legend mission comin' home
Riding a horse I know so well

At a safe distance behind, coasted Monsieur Douvier's sky-blue Delahaye convertible, with its two occupants watching and chatting. Despite their huge age and background difference, they got along just fine, for sure enjoying this moment.

"How come it took Danielle so long to ride from Grottes des Demoiselles to Tornac...on her way to Grotte de Trabuc?" asked Gaston casually.

"You're right. She spent weeks on the road, a journey that could've been made in a few days only, under normal conditions," said Monsieur Douvier. "But she encountered all sorts of problems."

"Like what?"

"Oh..." reflected the old man. "She started really bad...catching a virus infection somewhere in Laroque that sent her to a hospital in Granges, the next town. There she stood almost a week...incapacitated. Then our monks had to replace her horse and kite and everything... and the horse got sick too."

Juliette's horse was now approaching Vieux Pont past Rue du Plan de Brie, a short but important road stretch here.

Her roaring kite, pulling tightly from the end of the string she now snugly held with one hand, swooped down dangerously with a sudden shifting wind. Then it flew back up again twice as high as before in curious short dancing circles. It seemed to announce her audacious and jubilant entry into the Cévennes—something not seen perhaps since the latest religious wars of the previous centuries.

Nearby gushed the sumptuous river Gardon d'Anduze. Soon she would cross it too. She would do so unaware she'd been spied on all along by binoculars by the vicious Nazi-blooded clan of *Les Allumettes* from the clifftop of Mont Payremale.

Above hovered Richard's soul.

PART 3

UNIVERSITY OF ATLANTIC BLUE HOLES (UABH)
ZUNDO, JUNE 3081

A TALL SPEECH BY A MIDGET OF GREAT INFLUENTIAL POWERS

Main Auditorium, UABH

"Let me tell you about the pursuit of greed by a few privileged persons, popularly known as 'slimy scumbags'...because that's really what they are," said the very short man, often defined as "tall midget" by the press, to the flexible podium mike, wearing a black double breasted tuxedo suit, lilac long sleeve shirt, and white bow tie.

Strands of thick dark hair stuck from under his feathered Caribbean hat. In his mid forties, his large mouth, corrosive voice, and piercing blue eyes gave his speaking style a favored blend of confidence and fortitude.

"At the turn of the fourth millennium we'd reached the point in history where Capitalism no longer worked as first envisioned by its founding fathers over a thousand years ago. We'd allowed the creation of godlike figures having infinitely bigger wealth, possessions, and power than the common people...something terribly demeaning, wrong, and frightening," went on the man everyone knew as Greed Judge, or more specifically "the knife-throwing judge" at the mammoth Bermuda Revelation Park's Zoliseum.

His powerful eyes engulfed squarely the student crowd. Pouring some water from a large glass pitcher, he drank a little.

"We saw it coming, like a big comet thrusting to Earth at great speed, and we didn't do anything to divert it or stop it...centuries upon centuries. Just like Global Warming. When we finally tackled it, it was nearly too late! Maybe it still is!"

The large crowd sat in stunning silence.

"Just as we had to stop the alarming rise of infinitely destructive nuclear weapons, we had to stop the alarming rise of infinitely destructive rich zillionaires. When these extremes exist, life ceases to have meaning or purpose for the common people, who represent ninety-nine percent of the population," he said sternly.

"Such devastating unfairness and humiliating arrogance began to manifest itself in massive suicides–the ultimate protest sacrifice–not only here in the three Americas, but across Europe, Asia, and Australia!"

He stepped back a little to check his notes.

"At the rate it was going, a total population wipe-out within a year or two was projected. The end of an entire civilization in the planet... in the tradition of the dinosaurs, Aztecs, and Incas."

He banged the podium three times with his fist.

"That's when we took a stand! *Enough!*"

People applauded loudly and sustainably, left and right and as far as the last row in the auditorium. All Zundonians seemed truly moved and redeemed.

"Hordes of buffalo-mounted Zongdrolls led by our great Zundo the Conspirator rode the plains and meadows day and night at the end of the third millennium in search of answers. We established order, founded kingdoms, and renamed the world Zundo. Soon ZCAP meters began to appear everywhere...as Capitalistic endeavors disappeared. A new socioeconomic system devoid of monetary pressures was born!"

"LONG LIVE ZUNDO AND WHAT IT STANDS FOR!" yelled in unison rows of students from the far back. "LONG LIVE THE ZCAP METERS!"

All eyes suddenly aimed to the ceiling as two silvery gray-blue tiger sharks roamed the auditorium's second floor, seen through the transparent zhoenix shield. Aquarium-like, this floor teemed with marine life, tropical fish, and hanging cobwebs of corals.

Beneath the students' feet, seen through a similar layer of the shield, they could appreciate floating sea fans, sponges, gorgonians, and algae in their myriads of forms and colors.

Through them swam hundreds of newly created species of fish, many resembling little koalas. It was a sight to behold!

Three hundred feet west of them stood the stunning *blue hole* or newest natural wonder the university had befriended, so to speak, researched, and exploited to its very bones. Oceanographic degrees, therefore, were now commonplace and cherished by both the local community and Zundo at large.

Looking like a gigantic circular ocean pothole, from a passing zurbdog, dramatically weird things happened here...from the abrupt change of deep, dark-blue ocean waters (inner zone) to the light-blue shallow dissipated basin (outer zone)...never quite stopping the malicious rumor that this had become Dr. Ufahh's secret Alternative History Laboratory Waste Dump.

"Don't get me wrong–we didn't abandon Capitalism–the best workable system on the planet," the short man said, with haughty wisdom. "We'd attempted all kinds of stimulus packages, stiff regulations, and reforms, before the invention of the arm-implanted ZCAP meter...like putting a cap (say, seven million, for example, periodically adjustable to the cost of life) on maximum wealth allowed per person, with similar rules for companies and corporations (small or big), and redistribution to the poor and the needy of uncalled-for profits and extraordinary year-end bonuses among crooked CEOs trying to violate the law."

Greed Judge rubbed his chin. "But corruption robbed mankind of this opportunity. How low can you get when you learn that the top ten financial and banking institutions in the world are *too big to fail*? When you discover that they got *too big* in the first place because they played *too dirty*? Like, for example, selling worthless bonds disguised as high value investments and then placing bets on these investments predicted to fail? Sounds familiar?"

Audience reaction, vengefully agreeing with Greed Judge's assessment, made him pause momentarily in his speech. He lifted one of his very short arms to scratch the back of his head, thoughtfully. "Yes. Corruption trampled mankind. Unscrupulous swindlers of Ponzi schemes and other fraudulent programs that pocketed them zillions of dollars...while wiping out entire retirement savings from innocent shareholders–many of them close or best friends–reminded the world that human beings, particularly those wearing expensive dark business suits and shiny jewelry, can be worse with their intentions than a pack of hyenas stalking a fallen prey in the nether woods.

"Even democratic governments, largely run (under the table) by powerful zillionaires, we soon realized, were acting as anti-Robin Hood entities by bailing out (without jail punishment) these unscrupulous rich money players that collapsed the world economy, while making the masses of poor and low-income people instead pick up the debt tab.

"So cyclically, every ten years or so, these same *scumbags* responsible for collapsing the global funds and making everyone miserable repeated their crimes. A hopeless situation."

He looked at the ceiling, feigning an imploration to a higher being, getting in return the crude overstaging and water-cutting of a stealthily roaming tiger shark.

"So when the ZCAP meter came along, we knew we had hit the storm right in the eye...and at last a completely new and decent and non-addictive and totally efficient and safe system had been born. And indeed it has never failed us since."

He glanced at a weird-looking man to his right on the stage, separated from the audience by a partially drawn thick red curtain, who had approached him with a broad smile.

"And it is my joy and honor to welcome the very inventor of such a phenomenal device—my good friend and mentor, Dr. Ufahh."

A roaring applause and cheers that didn't seem to quit filled the auditorium.

Dr. Ufahh took the podium.

"Thank you...thank you..."

LISTENING TO ZCAP METER'S INVENTOR, ZOLISEUM'S CHAIRMAN, AND UABH'S FOUNDER–DR. UFAHH

Main Auditorium, UABH

"Thank you...thank you..."

Dr. Ufahh covered his mouth with his right fist, cleared his throat, and gathered some thoughts in his head, before he engaged the student audience.

Much to be desired in his looks, what quickly stole people's attention besides his koala-placid face was his twin chunk of fluffy blond hair crowning his otherwise bald head and his chimpanzee-long arms.

"I wish I had more time to spend with you this afternoon, especially since you're my favorite crowd..." he said warmly, pausing to allow cheers to resonate and die out, "but I'm in the middle of a *blue hole* project myself...intended to revolutionize the way we view and utilize the ocean, with a minimum of harm to our marine life and the underworld ecology."

For a *one-hundred-ten-year-old* who looked and felt only *sixty*, he broke all medical factual records and theories about aging, himself writing a new book on the matter. But being put together by stealing healthy parts from certain humans and animals in a privately owned surgery room did raise a lot of questions.

His use of a dozen strange, powerful drugs, supplied by questionable doctors, had almost gotten him in jail a few times, except that he retained the most able lawyers of the land. Lawyers, like all professionals, abided by the ZCAP meter rules.

"Let me tell you right off the bat that I have already succeeded in turning a blue hole into a tempest and this one into a major hurricane. Let me surprise you by telling you that I have succeeded also in sending this wildly spinning mass of thunder-clapping hell time-traveling to *The Unknown!*"

His paper-thin lips broke into a smile that was more eerie than congenial. But it blended, somehow, in strange, acceptable ways with the peaceful koala facial expression he normally wore.

"Which brings me to the issue of getting even with the new generation of unscrupulous convicted zillionaires appearing in our Zoliseum these days! Let me assure you, they are the very last generation to populate our shores! Kaput! Done! Fini! Terminado! There won't be any more generations of these *scumbags!*"

His large, funky, zapillon ears pricked a little, in response to split-second info signals from his camouflaged khorzos earzotrons, un-traceable by any type of high security intelligence.

"They gave us a good taste of who they are. What they're up to. What's cooking in their heads. And, let me tell you, it stinks. These *scumbags* only live to multiply their wealth. Which means to rape the world's funds...while leaving behind unspeakable poverty, suffering, and despair. That's what they're all about. Criminals of the highest order!"

His buggazis mind-scanning contact lenses were also at work. So were his zaigoo see-through object spectacles, for the moment tucked to his reversible Adolpho shorts.

"Interestingly, they always score zero on morality, zero on integrity, and zero on generosity. Such citizens have no place in our planet!"

His small, uneven black eyes glittered.

"And that's why, after making fools of themselves with the ZCAP meter, scoring the lowest readings ever attained here, they can only aspire to be sent away time-traveling to *The Unknown*."

Putting muscles on his voice, he raised one arm and banged the podium mike with his fist.

"But this time, having run. out of tolerance for their sickening greed, revolting arrogance, and deranged drive, I declare right here this minute on this podium that I will personally make riders of my time-traveling thunderstorms to hell any *scumbags* attempting to swell in wealth behind our backs and fool our system! *You hear me!? You'll rot in hell if you do!!"*

Breathing hard like a roaming prairie wolf, eyes fixed to the mesmerized audience, Dr. Ufahh said, more agitated than he'd ever been on guest-speaking tours, "I must leave now...so I will answer only a few questions."

He cleared his throat, pointed to a young blonde wearing a green scarf, among many students raising their hands. "Yes—you."

"I heard that many of these convicted septidares sent to *The Unknown* got rich by receiving absurdly gigantic year-end bonuses—in upwards of quintillion dollars—even when the companies they managed posted record losses."

"You heard well, unfortunately. This is the most recurrent question...everywhere I go," remarked Dr. Ufahh grandly. "These companies wrote 'employment rules for CEOs' that would allow these kinds of things in the first place, namely, *explosion of wealth from within for themselves*...regardless of length of employment, individual performance, company productivity, or external economic doom. They were *set to enrich themselves without effort or shame*, no matter what.

"And they did that in spite of the world economic collapse of 3013...when one-third of the globe population perished and my ZCAP meter invention finally took on as a universal life support tool. Such events marked the end of the antiquated monetary system worldwide and the beginning of Zundo's ZCAP-based society. Which also ended, I'm so glad to say, the *despicable fun ride of zillionaires*." He drank some water, flexed both legs.

"The timing was ominously right, considering the horrendous suffering, massive suicides, starvation, unemployment, and rampant infectious diseases like AIDS, cholera, tuberculosis, malaria, and others afflicting the globe in those infant years of our new millennium." He used a long pause to gather his thoughts. "Fortunately, we were able to stop all that and turn things around by punishing those evil greed mongers." Dr. Ufahh scratched his nose. "Not only money is useless now, it's illegal, as you all know, and those had-been die-hard zillionaires roaming the streets only live in fantasy today, because they have zero assets and zero bank accounts and zero chances of making any comeback ever!"

"How come they're still here and bragging about their wealth?" asked a law student, wearing a funny medallion over her bare breasts.

"They're doomed, standing in line, so to speak, to serve time in *The Unknown*. It's just a matter of rounding them up, putting them in the trucks, and dumping them into the zulag houses."

"How many are they?" said a squeaky voice from a back row.

"A few hundreds."

Checking the auditorium for a male contributor, he pointed to a young student of apparent Asian descent. "You."

"Are they coming back...from *The Unknown?*"

"Totally changed, if they do."

"If they do?"

"Yeah. Rarely so, though."

"Why?" asked a black male sporting a French beret.

"Their level of greed is extremely hard to eradicate."

Dr. Ufahh closed the meeting with a funny anecdote from his personal life.

Then he exited the auditorium signing autographs, now wearing his protective zaigoo spectacles. Obviously, he was well-liked and respected in spite of (or because of) his unsightly looks. But geniuses, like pretty girls, always got away with their shortcomings by playing the crowds. And he was not the exception.

All fine, except that he hadn't yet accomplished the "time-traveling thunderstorming feat" he'd just boasted about. "I'm working on it and I'll make it happen," he'd say to himself tonight in front of his bedroom mirror, like every previous night, before falling asleep, together with the reluctant admission, "Only God's smarter than me."

PART 4

LES ALLUMETTES
FRANCE, JULY 1955

SIZING UP JULIETTE'S TRIUMPHANT GALLOP THROUGH ANDUZE WITH BINOCULARS

Mont Peyremale, Anduze

From a cliff edge way on top of Mont Peyremale, facing the river Gardon d'Anduze, Anduze (the city), and Mont Saint-Julien behind it, a bunch of youngsters led by a thirteen-year-old bully of German descent nicknamed Nez Froid (Cold Nose) feasted on whatever activity happened on Vieux Pont, the town's old stone bridge.

Walkers (on two or more legs), drivers (on two or more wheels), and riders (on vehicles, bicycles, carriages, horses, or donkeys) crossed it regularly. So estimated Bouche Tordu (Twisted Mouth)—another fellow in the clan so nicknamed, who happened to be Nez Froid's older brother—from his precarious post on the craggy rocks.

He'd been there for the better part of an hour, checking out the physical mobility of people and domestic animals, as well as the moving objects related to them, sizing up with his binoculars the city's old and strange quarters, narrow and winding cobbled streets, little squares and parks, quaint buildings and houses, protestant and catholic churches, schools, community centers, river banks, and anything worth his time...to spot something or someone remarkable or bizarre... standing out among the myriads of photogenic warm roofs, peculiar scattered faces, and awesome fluidity of life. Basically, he searched for an excuse to raise hell with his buddies, having nothing else to do this hazy, uneventful summer morning.

But something unusual caught his eye.

"Hey—look down here! She looks familiar!"

Nez Froid grabbed the binoculars.

"I'll be damned—it's Juliette!"

All kinds of nasty thoughts crossed his mind.

The previous day the same gang of youngsters had been out in the wilderness around Le Vigan, hunting for rare birds, stags, red foxes, and beavers, ultimately finding themselves being hunted by a wild boar.

In previous days they'd been luckier fishing for brown trout, eel, and carp in the river Gardon de Saint-Jean with their parents. But old folk's presence always made them feel diminished and restless.

So staying away from them was a no-brainer.

"She's crossing the bridge on a white horse!" said his friend, sharing the binocular for a second.

"More than that—she's flying a kite at the same time!" exclaimed another teenager, passing the magnifying tool back to Nez Froid.

"That's her! She's half-crazy...free-spirited...and always looking for trouble!" he said, chewing hard and loud on a piece of gum he just stuck in his mouth. "I know you hate me passionately...never stare in my eyes during school breaks, even when I force myself on you to get your attention...but this time, baby, you're going to learn a couple of lessons from *Les Allumettes*."

Their clan name honored their secret ritual of burning to death any animal they managed to catch, still alive with wounds, during a hunt. So, to accomplish that, they always carried pocket-size match boxes.

"Where's she going, anyway?" said someone wearing a funny hat.

"With that tempting red dress—straight to me!" barked Nez Froid, clacking his wet gum with his teeth. Like his buddies he wore well-tailored and styled blue jeans and summer collar shirt.

"She's going straight to La Bambouseraie, I'd say..." shot Bouche Tordu with a little odd smirk.

"We'll see!"

Nez Froid swiveled on his sneakers.

Facing his entourage, he marked a threatening big capital "A" in the air with two crooked fingers.

"*Allez-allez-allez-allumettes*!!!" they all rallied in a tight circle, cheering their war cry in unison. "*Allez-allez-allez-allumettes*!!!"

"Boredom's over. Let's hit the road!" Nez Froid then shouted at the top of his lungs, almost maniacally, sprinting toward the parked Mercedes-Benz convertible, closely followed by his clan.

They ran like wild animals, one of them tripping with the twisted branches of an olive tree.

All around cicadas had a field day as well, singing their wings away.

༄

"Crank that fucking engine on, Bouche!" barked Nez Froid.

The engine roared.

"Let it settle a bit, Nez...before it explodes out of its bearings!" barked back his brother.

Ritually, they always lived in fantasy and used only their nicknames, even at home. More often, however, out of laziness, they just used only the first half of their nicknames.

"Hurry! She's already at least half-a-kilometer ahead of us!"

The 540K supercharger thundered away with a huge cloud of dirt, slamming the four occupants' heads against their side windows.

"We'll catch up with her in no time!" shouted Bouche Tordu with an eerie smile that craved for action.

By the time he'd finished his sentence and adjusted the rearview mirror, the German car had cut in front of two Renaults and a Volvo, speeding away toward Route de Générargues.

HIGH LEVEL NAZI PARENT'S DNA
TERROR ON THE LOOSE

Faubourg du Pont, Anduze

The flaming Mercedes-Benz convertible that Bouche Tordu steered toward Vieux Pont, in order to reach Faubourg du Pont on the other side of the river and continue north upstream toward Route de Générargues, had served the Third Reich officials during WWII and before. It had in fact been driven by top Nazi commandants, including Himmler, before it changed ownership a third time, the last one after the war.

Bruised and dented in several places, almost obliterated by a bomb that failed to explode near the combat trenches, and stolen for about three weeks in Berlin a few days shy of Hitler's bunker suicide, the German supercharger made it to Alsace, France, on a windy and rainy night.

A big truck meant to transport potatoes carried it to Dijon a week later, also in the night. Then, Bouche Tordu's dad drove it to Lyon, after a couple of beers, in plain daylight. Eventually, the Mercedes reached Nîmes and Saint-Jean-du-Gard, Southern France.

Classified as an eight-straight Mercedes-Benz 540K Cabriolet B and turning heads at every stop, it underwent some body work, painting, and chrome polishing in specialty shops known as automotive *coutouriers*, through friends and selective acquaintances. New red leather upholstery, sun visors, and fog light were added. Also, mechanical restoration and engine adjustments were made to the 540K 4-seater, which stood mostly indoors for months.

Its all-round servo-assisted independent suspension and brakes required some improvements and testing. So did its three forward speeds, full-throttle supercharger-accelerator engagement, and overdrive. Finally, it was ready for the road!

Except that nobody was supposed to see it.

It had the giant Nazi-by-association stigma—the unmistakable seal of infamy, disgrace, and shame. Lynching on the spot was still a possibility ten years after the war. People reacted in odd, violent, and unpredictable ways when facing danger or the unknown.

Nazism was an unknown matter to civilized people, even after its demise. Incomprehensible. Yet it grew from civilized people, to destroy civilized people, and finally to be destroyed by civilized people. A complete cycle. Unnecessary. Unwanted. Reproachable. Repulsive.

No matter how hard these youngsters' parents tried to stop them from getting the Mercedes out of their garage, they failed miserably.

The idea was to wait another decade, or perhaps two, until the public at large had forgotten about the Nazis and their menacing cars. Then those beauties, the very few left around, could be sold for extraordinary sums of money—several times their original cost!

Unfortunately for Nez Froid and Bouche Tordu's parents, reality was about to set in regarding their garage precious toy. Only ten years after the end of that bitter war they themselves still carried the baggage of having been Nazi leaders and could remember vividly their participation in many ugly and unspeakable acts against Jews and outspoken intellectuals of all stripes and races. So could any curious neighbor or professional acquaintance. Crucial to the family was maintaining a low-key life and avoiding the slightest of suspicion in any shape or form. But things didn't work out that way. Teenage blood, it seemed, had a mysterious component that revved a character's imagination and needs to heights too far off what was acceptable or understood by parent's. No exception here.

Three days in a row last week Bouche Tordu had driven the German supercharger in and out of the garage to adjacent neighborhoods, co-piloted by his reckless, bullying, even absurd younger brother Nez Froid.

Today it was the fourth time. A weird day.

PART 5

CLASH #11—KNIFE THROWING
(A TIME TRAVELED CLASH)
FRANCE, JULY 1955

OCTILLIONAIRE "RICHARD FLYNN" GETS PUNISHED AND RENAMED "RICHARD ZILCH" BY KNIFE THROWING GREED JUDGE FOR RAISING BOTH HIS GREED AND STINGINESS TO NEW LEVELS

Bermuda Revelation Park

"Would you like to see him now?" said Master Judge to Greed Judge over the ZCAP meter's speaker system. Parts of his red shirt still showed under his macabre black cape. "The Stadiums crowd is waiting."

He'd already pressed the button on his Den's control panel, made the next scene materialize, and seen his own intimidating figure (cute to him) several times in the previous moments on the wall mirror behind him.

"All *six* Stadiums?" asked Greed Judge, his curiosity soaring.

"All of them and all seats taken. We're blessed with one of the largest crowds ever seen here."

"Send him in."

"Oh...I want to congratulate you on your speaking tour."

"Thank you."

"You and Dr. Ufahh have made a fantastic impression." As he spoke, he removed the first of his gothic black gloves, and peeked one more time at the wall mirror, admiring his dark, pointed beard, glossy bald head (removable tattoo cleaned off today), and irresistible figure.

"Just being ourselves." said Greed Judge.

"I know what you mean," laughed Master Judge. "I do it all the time." He could hear laughter too at the other end of his wireless system. "Enjoy now *defendant Richard Flynn—former first-time-ever octillionaire and richest man on earth, soon to soul travel to The Unknown...*" he over-announced to Greed Judge in a teasing voice."

"*...as punishment for degenerate greed, a wasted lifestyle, and extreme danger to the world...*" continued the fragmented sentence now Greed Judge, breaking into code laughter. Of course, he'd simply repeated one of the trial's most mentioned lines, by now memorized by even the children of the Corridor's janitors.

Laughing too, Master Judge clicked off the "speaker" link and clicked on the "special moments" link on the viewfinder of his ZCAP meter's system. Then, setting up the "all angles close-up" for "Clash #11– Knife Throwing," he activated the *half-hour* link.

He loved to tape himself for he knew he would star in this Clash as he had in most of them, a reason to watch himself later, over and over.

"*Fuck! Fuck!*" he suddenly shouted to himself in utter disappointment, realizing the worst. "*I fucking miscalculated! It's Greed Judge, not me, who'll prosecute the defendant for the next half hour! Fuck me!*"

Turning his head, he acknowledged the Celestial Sphere's presence over the crowd's heads already, gently spinning with latest trial updates. Now, preparing to return to its sky-reserved parking spot, it announced the latest punishment Clash status:

JUST COMPLETED: CLASH #10—BOXING • OVERALL SCORE: JUDGES 7 DEFENDANT 3 • NEXT: CLASH #11—KNIFE THROWING

∽

For those watching above surface level, the night had already begun.

They could not see, however, the hidden ocean underworld scores of feet beneath their shoes and hundreds deeper down the abyss. They could not see the steeply and ruggedly textured wall that plunged to sea bottom, covered with delicate and colorful sponges, corals, and gorgonians among untold ledges, crevices, overhangs, and swim-throughs.

Down there, in depth and darkness, a manta ray was hit only minutes ago by one of Greed Judge's pointed toys during practice. The freaky accident, resulting from a poor shot of the toy's sharp blade cast by the judge, had traversed the slim fish's body, causing blood to ooze into the salty waters, before it squirmed weirdly a last time and died.

Sectional elastic shield contractions in the greater zhoenix underwater system for unrelated issues of the sea had compounded the problem.

Now dozens of acquaintances paid their respect to the fallen manta on a sullen sandy plateau surrounded by dense formations of sea whips, basket sponges, and plate corals. Among them two flounders, three seahorses, a frogfish, four lobsters, and a reef shark.

Above ground, oblivious of the underwater tragedy, many Zundonians, clad in sweaters, felt a certain chill as the various sea winds of the Caribbean touched their faces in oddly unkind ways and the coastal island temperature dropped at least five degrees Fahrenheit.

Everybody's eyes were now on a clockwise turning wheel with a diameter twice the size of the man strapped to it. He wore a flashy green jump suit.

The man was Richard.

"Yes, yes...I understand, honey. It was my fault...calm down please..." Talking to his ZCAP meter, a ragged-faced well-dressed midget, forty-five years of age, threw a sharp, kitchen-size knife to Richard's rotating body over thirty feet away for the sixth consecutive time. "Darling, can you call me later? I'm kind of busy now...yes, your French nightgown looks great on you...yes it does...talk to you later..."

He clicked the link off and apologized to Richard, whose tied body turned on the wheel.

Stadium lights flooded most of the Astral Floor's circular area, adding mystery and suspense, none of which interested Richard this very moment.

But he was exactly where destiny had placed him.

"They call me Greed Judge and I'm about to interrogate you, Mr. Flynn. Is it all right with you?"

"Yes, it is, Mr.–?"

The midget threw another sharp knife straight to Richard's face. It hit just above his right shoulder.

"Ahhhhhhhhh!" whined Richard.

"Greed Judge. I just told you!"

"I meant your real name."

"Never mind my real name, kid!"

The crowd applauded.

Richard stood briefly upside down on the turning wheel, his head brushing the floor.

Another midget's knife whistled by. It landed near Richard's hip, snipping a bit of his covering cloth.

"Ahhhhhhhhh!" cried out Richard.

The crowd cheered.

"Now your problem will be discussed openly, as we always do here in Zundo."

Greed Judge scratched his little fat nose, staring with cold indifference at the scared, speechless subject.

"Let me explain the rules of this Clash between you and me. If any of my nasty knives hits your flesh or strikes the outer red circular zone, I lose." He pointed to it with a long phosphorescent stick. "So I must aim and strike very close to you–the middle yellow zone–to win."

"That's insane!"

"Your remark is invalid. Sorry."

"But–"

"–Now, our records show that you–surely the stingiest person on this planet–has contributed a million times less than one tenth of a percent to Zundo. That's nearly less than zero."

He cleared his well-modulated, nice-ringing voice. "You also spent several decades frozen in deep sleep. Doing nothing. Yet your wealth rose to thirteen octillion dollars. Am I right, Mr. Flynn?"

"You are."

Greed Judge stared at the turning body, prepared to throw again. He aimed carefully with his sharp, pointed knife. "Can you imagine how many starving people could be fed with your money?" he said.

"I can." He rolled his eyes. "People keep asking me the same question—it's tiring."

Greed Judge's knife flew and landed between Richard's legs, under his crotch.

"Ahhhhhhhhh!" wept Richard.

The crowd roared. "HIGHER! HIGHER! HIT HIS BALLS!"

Richard tried in vain to free his hands and legs strapped to the turning wheel.

"Mind you," said the midget judge, "one octillion is one trillion times one trillion...and then one thousand times that! And you had *thirteen* of those!" He scratched his forehead. "Isn't this mind-boggling, Mr. Richard Flynn?"

Richard nodded while turning on the wheel.

"You're only one person—like you said earlier today, during Clash #9 (Fishing)—not a city. Not a country. Not a continent! Just *one goddamned asshole*!! Yet your wealth covered *the whole world* when we arrested you!!!"

"I agree. Judges keep reminding me of the same things, comparing me to the same—"

A flying knife chopped a mop of his hair off.

"Ahhhhhhhhh!" wailed Richard.

"LOWER! LOWER! HIT HIS FACE!" howled the audience.

Greed Judge looked momentarily concerned, then cheerful, realizing the blade point had not crossed the line. "*Yippee...no blood! I'm safe!*" he chanted.

Pacing around his marked area, nearly three dozen feet from the miserably turning and tortured defendant, he rubbed his chin and knitted his brows, obviously creating some sort of theater for himself.

"You know why, *scumbag*?" he then unleashed brutally.

"Why what?"

"Why your *single-assholed-personality's wealth* covered *the whole world* when we arrested you?"

"No."

"Because *the whole world* couldn't *fucking* understand why you became so *fucking* greedy and stingy!! Incomprehensible!! And why your *fucking* government, your *fucking* system of senators and congressmen, and supreme court judges, allowed this to happen!!"

He welcomed the thunder of applause from the six Bisected Stadiums with a bow of his head.

"Have you ever thought why people happen to have a life in this planet? Do you think it's to snatch as much money and possessions as you can to the point where you appear to others like a *goddamned* ZILLION MILES TALL TOWER OF GOLD…or to share a fair, decent, and common existence with others?

Richard sank into silence.

"Apparently, you've never considered those things," said the candid, philosophical midget. "Yet," he added, his intense blue eyes starkly focused on the defenseless defendant, "we have evidence that you had applied for a name change before we handcuffed you. Isn't that so, Mr. Flynn?"

Richard pretended not to hear.

"Let me help you out. Mr. Flynn, you had decided to call yourself 'Mr. Decil'…only because you contemplated to bring your wealth up *two notches*…in terms of zillions…to become a *decillionaire*. Am I right?"

"Yes sir."

"*The nerve!*" burst out the judge.

"CUT HIS HEAD OFF! SHOOT THE SOB!" raged the audience in unison.

"That's at least *a million times* what you already had. Isn't it true, Mr. Flynn? Or Mr. Would-be-Decil?"

"It is…"

Another knife zipped by. "Ahhhhhhhhh!" squalled Richard.

"With all due respect, Mr. Flynn, I'm going to rename you right here right now 'Mr. Zilch'…because you will have *none* of it! Ever!"

Turning to the crowd, he incited everyone, "Let's hear his new name!"

The crowd roared, "MR. ZILCH!"

"Again!" shouted the midget judge.

"MR. ZILCH!"

"Full name now!" shouted the midget.

"MR. RICHARD ZILCH!"
"Again!"
"MR. RICHARD ZILCH!"
"Again!"
"MR. RICHARD ZILCH!"

ZUNDO'S LEADING NEWSPAPER POSES TWO QUESTIONS TO ITS READERS CONCERNING RICHARD ZILCH'S SOUL TRAVEL JOURNEY AND PERSONAL PERIDOT RING

Bermuda Revelation Park

Greed Judge incited the audience to join him in applauding for the humiliating scene he'd subjected the *renamed* defendant in spotlighting his greed and stinginess.

It lasted a good two minutes.

He drank some water from a glass. "Let me show Zundonians what 'greed' looks like," he then declared grandly, turning to the defendant. "Please stand up, Mr. Richard Zilch."

"How?" said the defendant, helplessly turning on the wheel.

Greed Judge replied, "Say the word 'release' three times."

"Release, release, release."

To Richard's surprise, all straps holding him suddenly detached and the wheel stopped turning. He then removed his back from the wheel and walked a little in front of it, mainly to reset his nerves and muscles.

The midget judge announced, "Ladies and gentlemen...standing here before you is the embodiment of "greed." No other person in the planet has ever been so greedy...and so encouraged, so nurtured, and so rewarded for it by his own government–the former United States of America, the world's largest 'greed producer'–before it collapsed on its own greed-driven machinery!"

He took two steps to one side of the defendant. "And no other person in the planet will ever suffer the harsh consequences he's about to suffer today."

Cheers broke out everywhere. "BRAVO! BRAVO! PUNISH THE FILTHY RICH MAN NOW! SEND HIM TO THE LIONS!"

Greed Judge said to Richard, "You may return now to your wheel and your straps."

Richard complied. But in doing so, he mumbled, terrified, "Harsh consequences?" which went unheeded by Greed Judge.

The straps seized the defendant's limbs tight and secure again. The wheel started to turn again.

Pacing the floor back and forth, the midget judge declared, staring straight to the audience, "The moment for people's participation has arrived. Let the *Zundonian Undersea Evening News* take a quick poll on Mr. Zilch's case."

"Again?" complained Richard. "First it was Obscenity Judge who pestered me with that. Now you?" He breathed hard with anger. "And will you stop torturing me with these knives! I surrender. You win. Okay?"

Greed Judge threw another knife. It missed Richard's right leg by one-tenth of an inch.

"Ahhhhhhhhh!" writhed and wawled Richard on the turning wheel.

The crowd hoorayed, "GOOD SHOT MR. JUDGE, BAD LUCK MR. ZILCH!"

Pacing the floor on his chic blue suit, Greed Judge asked in a commanding voice, "Are you ready, Mr. Zilch?"

"For what?"

"For two major questions from the *Zundonian Undersea Evening News.*"

"Shoot."

"I meant are you ready *to hear* what all Zundonians in the land have to say about these questions?"

"No problem."

His tired eyes strayed to a school of parrotfish circling the area. He also found comfort with a friendly dolphin who gave him company for awhile.

"Last chance for all Zundonians across the land to activate the ZCAP meters. *Activate now!*" thundered Greed Judge. "First question: **Should Richard Zilch's degenerate greed be punishable by soul travel?**"

The answer came quickly from every corner of the Bermuda Revelation Park, social and sport centers, festivals, high schools, colleges, hospitals, stores, clubs, work places, residential homes, and every populated spot in Zundo.

"**YES**."

"Sorry," Greed Judge said to Richard.

The Stadium audience roared in unison, "FANTASTIC! BON VOYAGE TO HELL!"

"I guess I'm having a bad day today," expressed the defendant with a dimmed face. "Do you have to keep me all tied up to this turning wheel to hear that?"

"No, just repeat 'release' three times. You know that already, right?"

"Dumb me. I should've thought about it!"

"Never too late."

Richard released himself from the straps like he'd done before after repeating the magic words and wandered near the nicely clothed midget.

Depressed, he plodded to a nearby bench.

"*Do not sit down yet!*" shouted the judge.

Stepping forward, he said, stately, "I will pose the second question to the *Zundonian Undersea Evening News* first. Here it goes: **Should Richard Zilch be denied wearing his cute ring on his soul travel journey?**"

"**NO**," came the answer.

Very few people from the audience applauded. Some actually booed him.

"Congratulations, Mr. Zilch. You get to keep your little toy," said Greed Judge. "You may sit down now."

Richard complied with a little mixed smile hanging from his lips. "It's not all bad..." he mumbled.

"Hardly good either," discouraged the midget judge. "You're down 8-3 overall in the Clash score. Two more Clashes to go."

Richard lifted his chin to confirm as the big silvery Sphere had already descended with the current punishment Clash status:

JUST COMPLETED: CLASH #11—KNIFE THROWING • OVERALL SCORE: JUDGES 8 DEFENDANT 3 • NEXT: CLASH #12—INK BEACH

Greed Judge clicked something on his ZCAP meter, spoke a few words to someone into it. Facing Richard, he then said, "I will transfer you now back to Master Judge. Good luck."

PART 6

PHASE TWO OF JULIETTE'S TREACHEROUS JOURNEY TO GROTTE DE TRABUC FRANCE, JULY 1955

GREAT CONVERSATION IN GRANDPA'S SUMPTUOUS DELAHAYE BROKEN BY AN OVERTAKING SUPERCHARGER MERCEDES BENZ

Faubourg du Pont, Anduze

Juliette's beautiful white horse crossed Vieux Pont at moderate gallop to the other side of Anduze, saluting Route d'Alès at the traffic circle but taking the northbound Faubourg du Pont stretch instead. The young actress was now on her way to the Cévennes, through the well-known gate, passing between Mont Saint-Julien and Mont Peyremale on the left bank of the majestic river Gardon d'Anduze.

And doing so without difficulty.

Not too far behind glided the opulent Delahaye 135MS.

Its occupants had no idea of what had taken place a few hundred meters above their heads, on the rugged, rocky cliffs of Mont Peyremale.

Neither did they suspect a German car of fantastic appeal, dangerous power, and questionable history was trailing them and their beloved Juliette on this enjoyable mountain road by an ever smaller distance at a frightening speed.

"Then there was the La Baraque disaster—incessant rain storms that flooded and then swept this little village to pieces," went on Monsieur Douvier, steering his Delahaye convertible with gusto.

"Wow."

"Danielle had to take refuge in an elementary school, which unfortunately was run by a demented and unchecked administrator whose family practiced rituals of the occult and unexplainable phenomena."

"Incredible," said Gaston.

He scratched one ear, his eyes fixed on the road. "Against her wishes, she was taken into a secluded home...deep into a maze of strange narrow alleys, where the cult sacrificed her horse and burned her kite to ashes...leaving her in complete isolation with just dog food and water to survive on for three-and-a-half weeks."

Sparing a glance to Gaston, he said, "She was finally released by the local *gendarmes*, who also made sure she was medically attended to in town for another week. The kidnappers and administrator were all jailed pending what might become a lengthy trial. And the informer who saved her was rewarded with a kiss from Danielle and a monetary check from a concerned well-to-do town citizen."

"Wow."

Juliette's white Camargue horse now galloped northbound on Route de Générargues, flanked by the opulently flowing Gardon d'Anduze on her left side and the wild greenery on her right. Juliette's red dress flapped rhythmically to the wind, her pink panties at times showing underneath. The kite held steady some twenty-thirty meters above her bouncing blonde ponytail.

"Then the plane crash between Saint-Hippolyte-du-Fort and Durfort-et-Saint-Martin-de-Sossenac—that news-making accident that brought these two little villages together, while completely stopping the road traffic for two days in a row."

"What happened there?" asked Gaston.

"Two passengers in the plane were newlywed youngsters in their late teens—the girl from one village, the boy from the other village. She was a rising tennis star and a Protestant, he a soccer team captain and a Catholic. Hundreds of people attended the funeral, Danielle among them," said Monsieur Douvier.

"There were people from Lafont D'Alain, Cabriére, Fressac, Vergèle, Valensole, and Gouze on the Durfort side. And from Moliére, Jasse, Soulier, Laucire, and Bouzène on the Tornac side." Monsieur Douvier rubbed his forehead with one hand. "Paul Mauriat, who happened to be visiting some friends in the area, also attended the funeral."

"Paul Mauriat? The popular orchestra leader?"

"Yes."

"Funny...I used to see him all the time in Toulouse."

"You?"

"Yeah. Every time my parents took me to the theater to see a movie, he was there, conducting his orchestra...in the wide space between the big screen and the audience...before the movie started." Gaston shifted more comfortably on his seat. "He looked so proud and confident. Very entertaining."

Monsieur Douvier caught him issuing a little laughter. "You seem to be very amused, Gaston."

"Yeah. Because I don't really know whether it happened, I dreamed about it, or it's coming to me from the sky. Or it's just a false memory."

"Sounds very intriguing, my friend."

"But, regarding the movies, I always felt asleep during the first five minutes."

Now the old man laughed.

"Danielle had slowed down her speed by turning her horse's gallop into a regular trot and stopping at intervals to rest," he now said, continuing his own story.

"What about her kite?"

"Down, collapsed..."

"Tough."

"She just couldn't keep up with the swirling winds that afternoon."

"Very frustrating."

"Had she not done so, chances are she might have run straight into the falling plane, which nose-hit the ground and burst into flames right on the road...some two hundred meters in front of her."

"Wow."

He stared at Gaston. "Whatever, she was *the first* to drag one body out of the wreck and alert incoming drivers to contact the police. Help came in a hurry to drag the other bodies. A horrible scene."

"Wow."

"And then...a day later...someone shot her in the head while peacefully riding her horse and flying her kite. Apparently, a drive-by killer. It makes no sense," said Monsieur Douvier.

"Unbelievable."

Ahead Juliette's horse galloped at ease on Route de Générargues past the Viaduc de Gypières and later the Chemin de Comadel to the right.

Just then, shy of ending a large road curve fringed by a string of charming Mediterranean homes, a furiously speeding, chrome-embellished, bluish-gray mammoth car carrying a spare wheel over its teardrop-shaped front fender, overtook the peacefully moving Delahaye.

It did so with an almost ear-splitting devilish wailing howl that sent ice-cold chills to both talkative men's spines.

"*Le salaud!* (The bastard!)" spat Gaston. "*Il déconne avec ça bagnole!*" (He's going crazy with his car!)

"*It's a Mercedes-Benz 540K Supercharger!*" cried out Monsieur Douvier, utterly concerned.

"What about it?"

"One of the most powerful and menacing cars in the world, made in Germany. Was a favorite among top Nazi officials...Hitler, Göring, Himmler, Goebbels, Hühnlein..."

"That explains," reasoned Gaston. "Huge Nazi compatibility–car and men!"

"*The bloody bastards!*" cursed Monsieur Douvier.

"How does your car compare to that one? No doubt you own a pretty amazing car too!" said Gaston.

"Oh...mine can go just as fast–around 160km/h–if I want to. But we're talking about two different personalities, my friend."

"Oh...."

"Mean-spirited German idealism versus sumptuous French elegance. War versus peace."

"Good thing the war ended," reflected Gaston.

"Good thing Nazism ended," stressed the old man.

"Amen," they both said simultaneously.

                        ∽

"Will there ever be another Hitler?"

"Not from Germany," replied Monsieur Douvier sharply, with confidence, steering the Delahaye with great pride. "I think excesses and faults from both France and Germany have reconciled. Camaraderie, shared culture, and technology lie ahead. We need each other more than we're willing to admit."

"That car...really got my hair all over my body standing up," remarked Gaston, gently rubbing some of them with one hand.

"These were awfully young people, in the front and back seats. Nearly your age, Gaston," said Monsieur Douvier.

"I saw one of their faces in that split second," said Gaston. "It seemed to be possessed by malice and hate."

"I bet you their parents don't even know they're out there on the road scaring people around with this dangerous weapon."

"Somehow..." added Gaston, oddly, "that face looked familiar to me."

They were interrupted by a northbound passing train running parallel to the Delahaye at close range, but faster, on elevated rails for about two-hundred meters.

The road, sharply turning to the right in direction of Générargues, simply went under the elevated train track that headed for Corbès, Pagès, and Saint-Jean-du-Gard in a curved and opposite direction. It was the friendly Train à Vapeur des Cévennes that happened to be passing overhead, while also crossing over the Viaduc d'Amous. This also marked the beginning of the thirty-four hectare Bambouseraie—lush forest of tall bamboos and exotic Asian plants.

"Juliette and I took this train one day. It was a lot of fun," remarked Gaston briskly, pointing a finger at it. "It goes to Saint-Jean-du-Gard from Anduze...and back."

"I've taken it myself a hundred times," said Monsieur Douvier, looking up at it, watching its picturesque locomotion, listening to its gorgeous thunderous rattling.

"Wow. You travel a lot."

"I do. Here and all over the country."

They continued watching every passing wagon, listening to their soothing, rhythmical clattering as they vanished one by one in the lush verdant jungle ahead.

❧

Below, in sinusoidal fashion, the main road continued toward Montsauve and Générargues–their traveling options, rolling on the Delahaye. But the junction of three lanes here, two of them admitting people to the bamboo forest, had created enormous traffic.

Lines of cars, trying to get in, occupied both shoulders of each path, and walkers, many of them impatiently leaving their cars behind, also moved along in search of adventure. "Ruisseau l'Amous, dad," they could hear a kid voicing a choice, already familiar with his knowledge of the adjacent creek.

All fine, but, strangely enough, no sign of Juliette.

"Where's she now?" uttered Monsieur Douvier, alarmed.

"We lost her!" cried out Gaston, panicking.

"Maybe she took the other road to the left after the viaduct," said Monsieur Douvier.

"It's not a good road. She wouldn't do that."

"I know it will merge with our road again a bit later, after passing through Générargues," said Monsieur Douvier, "so we can either continue and catch it from that end, which is the Chemin de Picadenoux, or return and catch it from this end here, which is a road that appears to skirt the Bamboutique building, already in the bamboo forest."

They continued forward toward Générargues, but at twice the speed, hoping to spot her in the winding turns ahead, thinking she might have gone too fast without realizing it. But no, the looping road did not reveal any sign of her.

They were soon at the entrance of Chemin de Picadenoux, undecided, confused.

Time was the biggest factor!

"Maybe she's playing games, trying to lose us, just for the fun of it," opined Gaston now. "So maybe she's way ahead of us."

Agreeing, Monsieur Douvier forced the luxurious Delahaye to accelerate even more, skipping the Picadenoux entrance, and taking the elbow-like stretch near the water-splashing Gardon river instead. Then they gunned straight up northbound.

From a helicopter, they might have spotted Juliette already, possibly riding her white horse–a fleeting positive thought that crossed Monsieur Douvier's mind. Actually, from a chopper they could see right now the nearby Viaduc Mescladou, with its stunning eleven arches spanning the juncture of the two Gardon rivers–de Saint-Jean and de Mialet–to form the wider and stately Gardon d'Anduze, which they'd been following so far.

But continuing north this side of the mountain cliffs would mean following the Gardon de Mialet instead, toward Grotte de Trabuc. She couldn't be that far yet.

"I think we should come back!" said Monsieur Douvier after a while.

"*D'accord!*" said Gaston, tensely.

Something wasn't right.

Alarming things began to creep in Gaston's mind. He could see a line of pointed shiny blades, a dozen of them, flying in the air, one after another searching for a target, then striking to the sound of "Ahhhhhhhhh!"

He could see things turning around in an amusement park...a desperate face also turning around...a toddler throwing pointed things... crowds of people cheering....

Above hovered Richard's soul.

DESPERATELY ON JULIETTE'S TRACKS THROUGH THE PINE AND BAMBOO FORESTS

Chemin de Picadenoux, Sud, Montsauve

"Please, don't hurt my horse..." pleaded Juliette as she was brutally dragged into the Mercedes-Benz.

"Shut up–*bitch!*" shouted the young boy pointing the gun at the animal's head. "We don't care about your *fucking* horse. He's no use to us!"

"Let him go, Bouche," ordered Nez Froid.

Slowly, the animal trotted away.

Bouche Tordu put the Beretta M1934 back in his pocket.

In that hair-raising split-second, he couldn't tell he'd actually extended the inactive life of this 9mm semi-automatic twelve years, three months, seven hours and forty-six seconds since his father had last shot an unarmed Jew. But soon such scenario, without the details, did cross his mind.

Having no one used this pistol since WWII was an enormous incentive for him to use it today. Maybe he'd use it on this pretty girl before sunset. Hell, maybe sooner! Those thoughts flew through his mind as he got in the car ready to spin the wheels farther north to a more reclusive place.

"Stop around here...before the curve," commanded Nez Froid suddenly. "*Roule la voiture dans la forêt* (Roll the car into the forest)...to the right...and follow that hiking trail..."

Deeper into the forest they went.

The path–perhaps an old, forgotten Camisard passageway–smelled of fading skunk's release mixed with aging odor from crushed pine needles and dried lavender leaves. Stench that did nothing but spook out more the dense, clustered, and devious ambiance of this secluded track, already humped by clumps of gnarling roots, parched tall grass, and dregs of wild animal dung.

"Hardly manageable this bloody mess!" cried out Bouche Tordu, jerking the steering wheel sideways and around with desperation. Plus raving mad at his brother Nez Froid who kept torturing Juliette in the backseat with a mixture of sexual advances and historical reminders from WWII, the latter particularly annoying to him.

The other two teens in the car—Pieds Malin, seated in the front, and Trois Coudes, in the back—preferred to keep their involvement to a minimum, so they basically only watched and said silly things. Although the latter, fervidly aroused by the young girl's uncovered thighs next to him, wished he could take Nez Froid's place.

"You had to play her role, *bitch*? You had to insult our family?"

"I'm an actress...that's what we do on stage...no offense..."

"That great German commandant your *fucking* underground French rats killed was *my uncle*!" Their bodies jumped like rag dolls when the Mercedes hit a jutting rock beside a bed of mulberry bushes. "*My uncle*—you understand that?" His fingers forced themselves deep between her thighs, trying to separate them.

"Let go of me—you Nazi pig!"

"Our Führer wanted one hundred fifty of your French Resistance comrades to be shot for my uncle's assassination. You were lucky politics got in the way and only forty-eight of your kind were executed."

He pushed harder inside her thighs, fingering her panties now. "And you had the guts to bring that awful episode in German history to the French stage fourteen years later...by playing one of these filthy rats' daughters on stage?"

"It was just a role...among many that I played this year. I'm an actress." Her hand tried to block the way, but his thick fingers gained terrain.

"You told the press you were very proud to do "Shattered Youth"... to play this role, *fucking slut!*"

"Just the role...I wasn't there...I wasn't in Nantes when your uncle was shot...I had nothing to do with it...I didn't know the three Resistance fighters who actually did it either."

"You did, *little whore*...you probably worshipped them too!"

"I was only one year old."

The wheels banged against a bulging trunk.

"This *fucking* road's getting rougher every minute!" complained Bouche Tordu, putting muscles in his driving.

"Good thing you're thirteen now...and since you're an actress...and can play any role for fun...I'm going to give you a great role to play... right here in the Mercedes..." He unbuttoned his fly and forced her head down on his erected penis. "Imagine you're *une pute...une amazone* (a whore...a porn star). Suck my dick now." He was talking now like a Hollywood drama coach, mercilessly demanding. "Go for an academy award performance...use Method acting..."

"*Fuck you! Va te faire enculer, petit cretin!* (Go get fucked in the ass yourself, little prick!)"

She struggled out of his grabbing arms and kicked hard on his sheen. "*Salope!* (Bitch!)" he barked. His muscular hold rendered her powerless, incapacitated. He began to undress her, fiercely pulling and tearing at the material of her red dress.

"H-E-L-P! H-E-L-P! H-E-L-P!"

Nez Froid covered her mouth with one hand, worked on her panties with the other.

"*Tu va la sauter, Nez?* (Are you going to fuck her, Nez?)" Bouche Tordu said, alarmed, watching the commotion on the rearview mirror, but finally enjoying his young brother's assault.

"She fights me, but I know she wants me!"

"*Are* you? –*petit con*," persisted Bouche Tordu with his question.

"Just keep driving, Bouche. You'll be next!"

He rammed his thing inside and pounded her without mercy. Fully in control, he even bragged, half-laughing, "There's plenty of Juliette for everybody!"

And there was.

༄

After a while, they sort of camped out near a clearing, with even worse intentions in their minds. Except for Trois Coudes, who revealed some gay tendencies, they all raped her in bestial ways, without even realizing she was pregnant. By contrast, Pieds Malin, who first didn't want to, actually did it twice.

"*Dégénéré!* You will all rot in every reincarnation to come! I promise!"

"Reincarnation?" remarked Bouche Tordu. "Hey, that's better than hell!"

They all laughed, increasing her misery.

"Actually, we might be sent to hell. I don't think we deserve less... for what we're planning to do next," said Nez Froid coldly. Turning to Trois Coudes, he passed him the car keys. "Get the stuff from the trunk."

∾

"Nice place here," said Pieds Malin while waiting, pacing the leafy hard soil. "We're in the middle of nowhere. Away from civilization." He wandered to a thick, robust tree in the clearing, looking unlike the others for its lack of arterial branches and foliage. "Perfect."

Juliette was freaking out inside, much more than before. *These crazy boys are up to something heinous...*she thought.

She started screaming for help, but someone forced a piece of cloth into her mouth.

She vigorously shook her head to both sides and up and down, trying to reject the intrusion, but her mouth was suddenly clamped shut with a kind of strong tape that also hurt terribly. Now she could only scream with her eyes.

And she did for a while.

Next, she was rudely dragged to the barren, isolated tree, whereby hands from one of the boys wrapped her around it tightly like a transformer coil with a strong rope. Rough, corky, prickly bark plates scratched her delicate torso skin to no end. Suddenly, panic took hold of her. *I'm going to die here!*

All she could see was the glossy Mercedes-Benz's rear through the darkened, entrapping shrubbery surrounded by myriads of ghostly hanging plants, desolate brushwood, and discarded pine cones. Lots of them. Also, endless rows of tall coniferous trees. Such bleak tapestry tore her spirit apart.

Without warning, she received a punch in her face.

Then another one.

She noticed Pieds Malin's sadistic smile by her side. He, like the others, except Bouche Tordu, was in the school's soccer team. Now she remembered him well. A great player.

Nez Froid approached her with a tiny object in one hand and an eerie look in his eyes. "Here's a gift, a simple present for you, *little witch*, but first—"

He ordered all three clan members to throw dried branches and twigs at Juliette's feet, which they did in a rushed-up, disengaged manner, bringing a torrent of added anxiety and fear to Juliette. Not long ago she had refused his passes in school, now her life was about to end, she realized, unless...someone saved her.

"You look as good as any Cathar *parfaite*...as good as any Knights Templar lady...as good as the very glorious Jeanne d'Arc...and you will join them in the afterlife." Surprisingly, he'd done some significant comparative research. He snapped two commanding fingers to Pieds Malin. "*Versez l'essence*... (Pour the gasoline)."

They all stared at the singular wooden match Nez Froid had just lit.

Holding it steady, he sang:

Allumette, gentille allumette

Allumette, je te brûlerai

Then, stepping closer to Juliette, he dropped it into the heap of dry branches and shrubs. Flames rose quickly in a soft cloud of grey-blue sulfur and gasoline odor, turning to orange, with little crackling thumps of burning pine, fur, and oak.

Wild screams of horror resonated inside Juliette's head, her mouth gagged and taped shut.

Calmly staring at the human torch and plume of smoke, Nez Froid said, "*Adios muchacha bonita...*"

He swiftly gyrated on his sneakers. Facing his clan, he zealously painted an ominous big capital "A" in the air with two crooked fingers. *"Allez-allez-allez-allumettes!!!"* they all sang out loud in unison, pulled together and hunched in a tight circle. *"Allez-allez-allez-allumettes!!!"* they chanted out their war cry again over the muffled horrific screams of agony they knew exploded inside Juliette's throat and head behind them as hot-white flames enveloped her.

"Job's done. Let's hit the road!"

Madly, they sprinted toward the parked Mercedes-Benz convertible and drove off, first as slowly as the intricate foliage permitted, then at full speed when they reached Chemin de Picadenoux.

☙

The German 540K Supercharger gunned away southbound on this road unaware the French Delahaye 135MS carrying Monsieur Douvier and Gaston had just entered Chemin de Picadenoux from its northern end, also moving southbound, neither car visible from the other.

The 540K curved slightly to the left past large vegetable fields and some homes graced with swimming pools and lush greenery near the village of Montsauve at about the same time the luxury Delahaye spotted a lone running, disoriented white horse down the road.

☙

"Vite! Hurry! Cross Montsauve on your right and merge southbound with Route de Générargues at the traffic circle," Nez Froid ordered his older brother cleverly. This change of direction would certainly lose anyone chasing them.

In doing so, however, Bouche Tordu almost hit a crossing pedestrian.

"Alors, tu déconne? (Are you losing your marbles?)" exploded Nez Froid.

The Mercedes kept going until it approached the southern fringes of La Bambouseraie, sister forest to the pine forest they'd just ignited and left behind.

Then it slowed down to a stop at the triple intersection of roads and train track, where parked lines of cars, bikes, and strolling vacationers dotted the view. No other alternative!

Past this point, the high-speeding convertible reached Anduze in virtually no time.

Above hovered Richard's soul.

LES ALLUMETTES' "NEZ FROID" POPS UP ON GRANDPA AND GASTON'S CHAT WHILE URGENTLY SPEEDING THROUGH DANGEROUS WINDING MOUNTAIN ROADS

Chemin de Picadenoux, Nord, Montsauve

Gaston felt terrible inside. His Juliette was in peril. Suddenly the clear-cut realization of the worst dawned on him. *"That's him!"* he shouted to Monsieur Douvier. *"That's the guy!"*

"Who?"

"The face I saw in the Mercedes...in the front passenger seat!"

"Who's he?"

"A classmate of Juliette's...a bully who's been stalking her...scaring her to death lately..." He gave Monsieur Douvier a frightened look. "Hurry! Juliette's in trouble!"

"Which road?"

"Chemin de Picadenoux! I think she's somewhere out there!"

At his first chance, Monsieur Douvier made a U-turn. They'd already passed Ruisseau de la Baumelle and the little village of Luziers near the shores of Le Gardon de Mialet.

Soon the 135MS pushed its power and speed to the limits on this narrow and dangerous road.

"You guys should've told me about this stalker. Those things rarely have good endings. Did you contact the police?"

"No. We were planning to."

"Aie Aie Aie Aie!" cried out the old man.

"We were giving this guy–Nez Froid–that's his nickname–a chance to cool off, stop this stupid drive of his."

"What's his real name?"

"Günter Heissenbüttel," said Gaston. "He's a–"

"–Nazi!" accused the archeologist. "A *goddamned* Nazi!"

The Delahaye entered Chemin de Picadenoux at reduced speed after skidding on its side with Monsieur Douvier's foot on the brakes. It balanced to a near collision with a tree before it corrected itself and gunned forward.

"You said this teenager–Juliette's classmate–was scaring her to death? Why? How?"

"Not sure why. They're the same age, same teachers. He always tries to hit on her, but she keeps her distance since she doesn't like him."

"How does he scare her?"

"Leaving threatening notes by her door."

"What do these notes say?"

"*Look!*" Something made Gaston shout. "There's a white horse trotting toward us on this road...with no rider..."

"That's Juliette's horse!" said Monsieur Douvier in shock.

"Yes...oh no..." Gaston's heart started to beat faster.

"Something real bad happened to her," lamented the old man, driving slowly now to a near stop.

"He came out of the woods, somewhere up there...after the second curve," said Gaston emotionally, talking faster. "Stop the car, please."

Monsieur Douvier did. "No sign of anybody around here, and the trees keep blocking the sunlight...giving us just shadows," he remarked.

"Maybe I can calm down the horse. He knows me a bit."

He swung the Delahaye's door open and ran out toward the animal. Good thing no other cars drove by. The chemistry worked. The horse steadied his legs, recognizing the young boy. Gaston caressed his head and patted his long, white neck gently.

Monsieur Douvier joined him, leaving the car idling.

"We'll have to tie him to a tree while we look for Juliette. Let's hurry up!" said Gaston.

"Wait. Something's burning somewhere. Can you smell it?" said Monsieur Douvier, worried.

"Yeah..." Gaston sniffed the air and stared around. Smoke began to penetrate his nostrils. But he couldn't spot any fire in the row of small houses appearing in the distance near Montsauve, the nearest village.

"Definitely, there's a fire somewhere." Monsieur Douvier's eyes searched the woods for clues.

"*Up there!*" exclaimed Gaston. "I can see it...in the forest...toward Générargues."

A plume of dark smoke was rising some distance away in the woods.

Above hovered Richard's soul.

EXCRUCIATING NEWS OVERWHELMS FIREMEN, REPORTERS, GRANDPA AND GASTON

Chemin de Picadenoux, Nord, Montsauve

"WHOP WHOP WHOP…" A roaring prototype Alouette II helicopter cut over their heads like a giant hummingbird. Aware of the smoke, it scouted the forest, looking for its source and any possible endangered persons needing help.

"This old hiking trail here in the brush seems to go deep in the direction of the fire," cried Monsieur Douvier, blanking the overhead noisy disturbance. "Let's take it!"

"Hurry!" pressed Gaston, half-deafened by the chopper's rumbling engine and rotating blades.

They tied the white horse to a salient rocky outcrop near the trail. Without even looking back at the Delahaye, parked on the shoulder of the road between two lanky junior furs, they rushed into the woods.

Soon they were repelled by advancing flames and smoke. Several rabbits and a young deer almost collided with each other in front of them as they stampeded away.

Gaston started to cry, imagining the worst. If this bully and his friends had kidnapped Juliette, he thought, she would be in big trouble. Indeed, this could be the culmination of it all.

"We need to get a hold of the firemen! Maybe they're already on their way, like the chopper. This is too big for us to face!" shouted Monsieur Douvier, agitated. "Don't lose hopes, Gaston...she might not be in..." His trembling voice failed. "...in the fire..."

"It looks really bad to me..." sobbed Gaston, clearing branches from his eyes and wrestling the thick brush with his legs as he moved forward in blind desperation.

"They're near! The firemen! Can you hear their siren?"

"Yes," yelled Gaston, but he pushed his way deeper in, seeking empty spaces through the hot flames and nasty smoke to try to get to Juliette. Only that he couldn't anymore, and it was Juliette's grandpa who pulled him out of the imminent danger in time in spite of his vigorous objection. *"You will burn too if you don't back off–you crazy boy!"* Apparently, Monsieur Douvier had already seen too much.

Enveloped in fluttering flames, pines snapped and crackled as they fell one after another on the ground, releasing dark fumes. Ignited ambers flew around like soft snow, only vivid red in color.

"What else do you know about this...mental German boy?"

"He called Juliette a witch...promising she would end up like Jeanne d'Arc."

"Burned alive at the stake?" Mad as hell, Monsieur Douvier shouted, *"This could've been prevented! Damn it! Damn it!"*

A large branch, burning like a torch, tumbled down from a tall cedar, exploding in turn into tiny ardent shoots and needles. Some of them landed on Monsieur Douvier's shoulders.

Gaston helped him remove some of the blazing debris, while dodging another crashing tree engulfed in flames.

"It was Juliette's idea not to cry wolf...at least not too soon..." tried to explain Gaston, his eyes wet with tears, his heart beating so fast it hurt. "I respected her wishes..."

More sirens pierced the air.

"This is a post-war Nazi clan! A *goddamned* Nazi clan of teenagers!" shouted the old man, panting with rage. He thumped a knot of dried branches with his fist. "Not even teenagers–those are *grown-up toddlers! Immature fucking bastards!"*

Gaston remained silent, but hurting deeply inside. He dared not say anything that might upset Monsieur Douvier more than it already had.

"Do they have a name...these kids...this band of criminals?!"

Gaston's reply was muffled by the incoming commotion. A series of bellowing voices and clinking noises had broken out in the woods behind them. They were here now–the firemen–cutting messy shrubs and overhanging branches with special tools. They urged them both to get out of the way. They carried big and long water hoses, which they were about to operate.

"*Allez, allez...reculer!*" they shouted as they positioned themselves in strategic places amid clumps of wild brushes blocking the way, their protective helmets and colorful uniforms demanding respect.

Suddenly, a powerful gush of water exploded in the air, jetting out over wildly dancing flames in hues of red and orange. Clouds of surging smoke blackened the view. The smell alone made them cough and search for cover.

Could they help? He and Grandpa? They wanted so badly, but shouts from the brave fighting men, professionally driven, now in the middle of this hellish chaos, forced them to retreat and wait for new orders.

ᘒ

"...*Les Allumettes*..." answered Gaston at his first opportunity, avoiding the old man's angry eyes, torn as he was inside.

"That's how they call themselves?" said Monsieur Douvier, incredulous, through his clenched teeth from the less menacing side of a burning fir.

"They wrote that on their threatening notes…." put in Gaston blandly.

"Obviously, they're more than just grown-up toddlers, the *sons-of-biches*," slammed Grandpa. "Much more."

ᘒ

Within the hour, a police inspector accompanied by the chief fireman returned from the burning zone with a plastic bag containing pieces of a familiar red dress and handbag...mixed with ashes and dirt.

Juliette's brown leather boots, now a charred mess, filled a plastic box he also carried.

An assistant held up other identifying and incriminating items. Monsieur Douvier overheard the words "horrible crime" and "burned beyond recognition tied to a tree," but kept it to himself, for now.

No use in tearing Gaston's heart further. Although his was already wrecked.

Neither Monsieur Douvier nor Gaston could find proper words to express their mixed feelings, embodied in deep sadness and anger. Were they really part of this unfolding nightmarish, agonizing, inconceivable happening? Their weeping inner voices kept asking over and over again. They held each other for a while, as if they were father and son, their eyes red with tears and chagrin. Speechless, they made the embrace all-meaningful, all-encompassing, and lasting. They both loved this girl dearly, even passionately, in their very special ways.

They began to walk in short, broken steps, forcing their way back to the Delahaye and the horse. That took a very long, painful time.

Flashing red lights from fireman trucks, ambulances, and police cars occupied most of the area. News media reporters popped out from behind trees.

"Oh hell..." gasped a very tired old man, but grandpa no more. "What are we going to tell them?"

∞

The excruciating realization that Juliette wouldn't be around anymore bore an immense hole in Gaston's fragile heart. "This can't be true!" he kept mentally shouting to himself moments later, while starring blank-eyed at the serpentine road that led to Grandpa's property. "And the baby? Gone too? Why? Why?" Sitting next to him, with numb hands on the steering wheel of the plush Delahaye and eyes that hardly reacted to the traffic, Grandpa experienced similar loss of spirit, similar collapse.

Gaston spent the rest of the day remembering Juliette's adoring smile, fiery green eyes, pouting red lips, and soft round chin. Her golden upright ponytail or detached full mass of hair spilling down to her soft plum cheeks. The sound of her voice, especially when she said she loved him. Their intimate moments together, including love making. *What a love story!* he thought.

All this vanished to make space for a dark coating that simmered heavily in his head like street asphalt–an ominous, oppressive, black varnish that trampled his mind and devoured his consciousness.

So when Monsieur Douvier approached him again later in the evening in the living room with the warm advice that he should perhaps change climate and think about making new friends to try to fill the void of this tragic event, before it became a chronic torturing nightmare, he fervidly objected with a sharp "no way" answer. An answer he repeated several times, with more anger in his voice and more tears in his eyes than he could muster.

"I know you mean well...the best for me...but I just can't do that," said Gaston pitifully. "She's still with me...and I want to keep it that way...for as long as I can. For all my life I think..."

They both kept close to each other for a while, sharing their sorrow with little comforting words, feeling their agitated heartbeats punctuate the moment. He'd been invited to sleep over, considering what he was going through.

Especially, at his tender age.

Everything had looked so bright, so promising for all of them scarcely twenty-four hours ago...and now they all seemed to hang from the very helms of hell for no reason at all.

But there were encouraging words, from this old man, a powerhouse of knowledge and experience. A survivor himself of other tragedies and dreadful events. A specialist on matters of the soul.

"She'll come back...an even better person...in her new incarnation..." assured Monsieur Douvier with a nascent glowing smile, now pacing the living room next to his vibrant library system, where hundreds of hardcover and paperbacks, old and new, covering every archeological topic imaginable and many other subjects, filled bookshelf after bookshelf. "She's already on her way."

Gaston just stared at him, hoping it would be true.

In the ensuing moments his tears stopped falling and his cheeks felt dry. His mind also cleared and there was peace in his heart.

Raising his chin, he then declared solemnly, "I will complete her mission to the grotte...Grotte de Trabuc. I will ride her horse and fly her kite and make it happen!"

"Wow!" said Monsieur Douvier happily, using Gaston's language without realizing it. "Long live the *Legend of the Horse-Riding Kites!*"

They clicked glasses in the kitchen and drank Monsieur Douvier's vintage wine.

"*When?*" lingered the question both could readily answer.

"Tomorrow morning...eight o'clock!" said the archeologist.

Above hovered Richard's soul.

FALLING APART IN GRANDPA'S HOME WHILE SHOCKING LOCAL NEWS MAKES NATIONAL NEWS

Monsieur Douvier's Property

Things went well for a while.

Then melancholy descended upon Gaston again.

"You can stay here a week or two...even months...if you want to..." consoled Monsieur Douvier, while consoling himself since they shared the same grief.

"You're so kind...Monsieur Douvier...I really don't know what I'll do from here on...without Juliette..."

The old archeologist sat down on a sofa.

They'd just entered his large studio, where he usually read ancient documents and research papers. "I understand. I don't know myself how I'll face tomorrow...and every day...without Juliette. She had such a sprightful quality...made everyone feel good..."

He rubbed his face gently, with fingers that suffered from early arthritis. Watched how Gaston fidgeted with a handkerchief and fished for a chair to sit down near him.

"She was down-to-earth, unselfish, greedless...in spite of her rising fame as an actress...and very intelligent," said the old man.

"She was very funny too," said Gaston, breaking into an anemic smile.

"Oh yes...she really was."

The chat dragged on in this uncertain manner for a while until Mr. Douvier rose to his feet, explaining he had to go somewhere.

"I'll be back in a few hours. Feel free to turn the radio on and tune in to your favorite program or go to the kitchen to make yourself a sandwich or anything." As he exited through the front door, he said, "I have to contact my monks...keep them up to date."

"I'll be okay," said Gaston, watching him close the door.

Not really. He'll try to get some sleep, for sure.

∾

That was next to impossible, he soon found out.

Too many ominous things had happened lately.

Consumed by new thoughts, none good, he squeezed the blob of cloth he held in one hand as if strangling someone–*Nez Froid*, it dawned on him, *the Nazi clan leader.*

That scumbag will have to pay dearly with his life or something for his act of terror, he thought. *If I could I'd chase him down and do the same to him! Teach him a lesson! Make him feel what it's like to be helplessly tied up to a tree with fire on your legs and face!"* He realized he'd constructed the crime without even using the available evidence. Without exactly knowing how she died. Without consulting witnesses, if any. Although, he and Grandpa were the closest to being a witness as any...by a fraction of minutes, perhaps.

Hurt and confused, he wandered into the guest bedroom. He could see leaves from a nearby tree fluttering through a window with curtains drawn open. Vivid dark-green leaves...with so much good energy in them to give. Robust tree holding them. Such presence, resilient and sturdy, meant to be around for years and years. Oh...why not Juliette?

He lay down on the wide, comfortable bed, tummy up, feeling its smooth blanket and softly bouncing mattress. His own breath and respiration felt soft and bouncing now. But empty.

He switched positions, seeking to sink one of his cheeks into the blanket and relieve some painful pressure on his lower back. His eyes stared to the closet instead. A bit congested from earlier crying, he blew his nose with his handkerchief. This one, he put it away with a flip of his dazed wrist. *Such a punishing day!* he thought. *Why? Why?*

But Nez Froid wasn't alone, he remembered.

There were four people in the German Mercedes-Benz...a driver, Nez Froid, and two other teenagers sitting in the backseat. They did it together!

Les Allumettes!

꩜

Right now the most pressing thing is Juliette's mission. My promise to complete it.

Not an easy task. He kept shifting positions in bed as his thoughts grew deeper. *The last two girls trying to accomplish this were killed. Within the week. And those killers are still on the lose. Why would anyone want to kill me now? The ancient scrolls? Had someone leaked the secret? Were these two killings connected?*

Had Juliette really been burned alive...like Joanne d'Arc? By these Nazi hoodlums? He imagined Juliette wrapped in flames. Desperately screaming. Her hair and flesh burning.

Her body dying. Melting. Turning to ashes.

Inadvertently, he yelled out, "NOOOOOOOOOOOOOO!"

And grabbed his head like a crazy person in some mental ward having a paranoid schizophrenia attack.

He walked to the kitchen. Drank a glass of water. Monsieur Douvier had not returned yet. He noticed great paintings along the hallway, by Picasso and Renoir.

Back to his bedroom, he turned the radio on. Songs by Gilbert Bécaud, Édith Piaf, and Yves Montand came up.

A news break, then a few American hits by Frank Sinatra, Peggy Lee, Andy Russell, Vic Damone, and Perry Como.

He felt better, more relaxed, wondering if he would ever learn English and Spanish, like Russell, who'd just sang in both languages. Cool! But then three songs by Caterina Valente followed in French, Spanish, and English. The radio disc jockey mentioned that not only she sang beautifully in upwards of ten tongues, but actually spoke fluently in many of them. Super cool!

The next selection, after a few commercials, included Bing Crosby, Charles Aznavour, Rosemarie Clooney, Maurice Chevalier, Nat King

Cole, Sacha Distel, Eartha Kitt, and The Four Aces. By then Gaston was sound asleep.

"France's most beloved child actress...Juliette Douvier...only 13-years-old...died today..." broke a news report with last-minute details of the heinous crime.

Above hovered Richard's soul.

PART 7

THIRD BEHIND-CLOSED-DOORS MEETING BETWEEN DR. UFAHH AND MASTER JUDGE ZUNDO, JUNE 3081

DR. UFAHH'S TOLERANCE—FROM CASUALLY CONDONING ASSASSINATION MISSIONS TO CRUELLY PUNISHING BADLY FILTERED TIME TRAVELED INFO PARTICLES INTO A SUBJECT'S BRAIN

Alternative History Palace

"Punishment for octillionaires has to be harsh," said the Zoliseum's chair to Master Judge. "I'm sorry about the young boy's loss–his sweetheart. I didn't particularly approve of it…your methods. But the kid has to experience deep grief and pain somehow. Richard's journey to *The Unknown* cried for it. We're talking, of course, about 'the first and only octillionaire's journey, thanks God, transferred to Gaston…a thousand years down the road'..." The gifted scientist paused to reflect. "Richard's 13th reincarnated self and recipient of his punishment…in this kid's healthy but fragile body and mind'." Dr. Ufahh rubbed his chin. "This is one way to go about it. Again, not my choice. Yours."

"Thank you," said the judge, taking it as a compliment since the grouchy chairman, always hidden behind his peaceful koala face, hardly ever gave one. "Did I hear you say *thanks God…?*"

Dr. Ufahh laughed loudly and grossly, trying to hide the truth. "Must've been a wicked residue from one of those silly old movies that slipped into my vocal cords or something…from the previous millennium…I happened to watch last weekend while researching the end of Western Culture…ha ha ha ha…"

Master Judge joined the distinguished scientist laughing. It could help improve their shaky relationship.

"Can the boy on his own figure out what's going on?" Dr. Ufahh now asked Master Judge with suspicious eyes. He'd invited the Zoliseum's host and space travel director to his office in the Alternative History Palace to pin down a few things that didn't add up...in his mind.

"What do you mean?"

Dr. Ufahh paced the room, fully engaged in thoughts, holding a half-full glass of zodka. "Like...do we have a time travel and soul travel *conductivity leak* or something?" At last, he sat down, facing the judge's busy computer, a screen displaying rotating blocks of "journey" data in high activity mode.

"No TT or ST conductivity problem that I know of..." Master Judge caressed his bald head, watching the hardy scientist's fingers click links on his computer screen and examine tabulated data. "I don't follow you..."

"Somehow he's being bombarded with info from us here in the 31st century he's *not* supposed to know in the 20th century."

"You mean dreams? Reveries?"

Pillar corals in violet, yellow, and red colors showed through the large window, resembling ghostly fingers. A cruising long-tailed eagle ray stole the judge's attention. He marveled at his smooth, confident movement in the clear sea water. Spontaneous natural artistry in motion.

"Anything coming down from the future to the past should be organic...either singularly directed or scattered according to its own energy and rhythm..." said the scientist. "We stupidly organize or structure everything linearly, chronologically, to better understand it and assimilate it...but that's not the way things happen through time and space..."

Not wishing to be lectured on matters they had not totally agreed on in the past, Master Judge said, "Regarding Richard's exposure to unfiltered or unblocked info...as he penetrated and began to journey through *The Unknown*...yes, it's possible we cracked our own national security...with these recurrent leaks..."

"I call that *negligence*. You're supposed to be very focused on your work, MJ!" shot Dr. Ufahh.

The judge nodded without looking at his face.

"And you're still *fucking around* with what I told you *not to fuck around*...last time we met!"

"What...what do you mean?" reacted the judge, defensively. "I stopped calling you Walking Brain..."

"*You little piece of shit*—I told you not to call me that!" stormed the scientist.

"It just escaped me...sorry..." squeaked the judge.

"Second, I *fucking* told you to stop making Richard too bright. For cosmos' sake—he's only *nine*!"

"You mean *Gaston*."

"Yes. I meant the young boy in Richard's 13th past incarnation.

"I...I..."

"Third, I *bloody* asked you to transfer him to another location... another country..."

"*Former* country," corrected the judge timidly. "The way it used to be before Zundo came along."

"Yes. But *have you*?"

"I'm working on it."

"I'll give you another week to get all this done...or else!"

That could mean death—zobot death—for he knew he wasn't human.

"Why is it so difficult, *judgie*?"

DON'T FUCKING CALL ME JUDGIE! his mind raged inside. "I'm too consumed by Gaston's story. I don't want it to end," he actually said.

"You sentimental fool!—sometimes I wonder...what did I *fucking* miss in the design? Why did you come out like that? I swear—you're so pathetically incompetent," snarled Dr. Ufahh under his breath, trying to restrain himself, his eyes burning with fire.

"One week will do...sorry...sorry..."

"Out! Out of my office!"

PART 8

PHASE ONE OF GASTON'S TREACHEROUS JOURNEY TO GROTTE DE TRABUC FRANCE, JULY 1955

MONSIEUR DOUVIER ASSISTS GASTON IN LAUNCHING HIS HORSE-RIDING, KITE-FLYING JOURNEY

Monsieur Douvier's Property, Saint-Jean-du-Gard

Early in the morning Monsieur Douvier worked on the kite.

He'd learned how to make one by watching Juliette in several occasions, as she trained herself for that important day. Of course, his kite couldn't compare to the ones she made. It lacked presence, style, and that elusive quality called "magic."

It also took him three times longer to put it together.

His main problem was making it roar with the wind. It finally roared but more like a goat's roar than a lion's, so to speak.

When he tested it outside, the kite did a wrong dance. So he had to lengthen its tail by adding some of his old socks to it. Even a tie.

Little by little he saw the ensemble coming to life.

Then he inserted the two ancient scrolls in their respective little wooden tubes and fastened them in place on the kite, near the curved thin branch that made it roar.

While Gaston ate his breakfast, he saddled and bridled the white Camargue horse. Outdoors waited a cloaked monk and the light truck horse trailer he guarded. In time, he led the horse into the trailer, locked the door, and took up position at the steering wheel.

"Let's go..." Monsieur Douvier said to both Gaston and the monk. "The kite is in the trunk of my car."

"With the scrolls?"

"Yes."

The sky-blue Delahaye convertible led the way.

Leaving the Quartier de Luc in Saint-Jean-du-Gard, it turned right on Avenue Abraham Mazel and headed east toward Mialet only a few kilometers away.

Except for some road walkers seeking swimming spots on the shores of the river Gardon de Mialet near Pont des Abarines, nothing unusual occurred.

The Delahaye 135MS moved southbound parallel to the river, crossing Paussan and its two frontier ruisseaux—Roque Feuille and Montroucou—past Mialet. Behind followed at close range the monk and his loaded horse trailer.

They reached Luziers beyond Les Traves and La Rouquette, engaged in small chat, always alert of anything while flanking the Gardon, southbound on Route Mialet-Luzier.

"We're getting closer to the place," said Monsieur Douvier.

As in the previous situation, involving Danielle's road murder, he explained that they would try to fool the police and inspectors by continuing the mission about a kilometer past the scene of crime...so as to avoid any questioning or obstruction. The mission couldn't be jeopardized.

"Make sure your riding boots and jeans feel comfortable."

"They do."

"You've seen Juliette riding her horse and flying the kite at the same time before...so it shouldn't be an unknown to you, right?"

"Right."

"The horse has been fed and watered already...so that shouldn't be any concern to you."

"None."

"This horse, by the way, is Juliette's horse, the same one she rode yesterday, not the horse I gave you last month." He steered carefully, following a road curvature. "They're both good Camargue horses and look almost like twin horses, but I felt you should ride hers today, so your ending mission journey to Grotte de Trabuc is also hers."

"Thank you so much for making it possible. I also wanted to complete the mission riding Juliette's horse."

"The monk was very helpful in taking care of the horse issue. So now it will be your turn to make things happen!"

"I will, I will!"

Monsieur Douvier patted Gaston's shoulder affectionately.

"Where will the next mission stage be?" asked the young boy, "and who will continue it afterward?"

"Good questions," said Monsieur Douvier, slowing down his car. "One of our monks should be waiting for us in this area. Keep staring for a signaling hand."

He saw some homes grouped together to his left, denoting a hamlet, with a small bisecting road called Le Pradinas, and checked his rearview mirror to safely turn into it at his first chance. It took three more attempts and a lot of eyeing the cars going in the opposite direction to accomplish this. Just yesterday they had sped like crazy, northbound, on this coastal stretch searching for Juliette!

"We had a major monk meeting late last night," revealed the old archeologist, "in view of recent distressing events, as you know, and we decided by vote to make this Grotte de Trabuc *the one before the last* of the Legend's missions."

Monsieur Douvier stopped the car near the entry, allowing enough parking space behind his Delahaye to the horse trailer coming behind.

"After over 700 years of mission journeys, it dawned on us that we simply ran out of safe places where to camp out and operate. Too many freeway systems...too much commercialism associated with rural traveling and lodging," he said, his eyes probing the area. Facing them were old stone homes with vine-covered walls and slate roofs. One of them had shiny copper pots hanging from a rugged stone fence.

"Too many guided tours to remote mountains and rivers and grottes. Too many stories and curiosity about hidden medieval castles and fortresses. Too much spying from Big Brother."

"Too bad," said Gaston. He'd read George Orwell's *1984* early in the school year, around his birthday, and knew exactly what Grandpa meant.

"We're constantly being invaded by complex webs of bugging devices...compromising our privacy...offending our intimate world of living." His rearview mirror showed the monk's face and parts of the truck and horse trailer.

"It's really sad."

"It reminds me of what I've known for quite a long time now. That even some of the smallest particles in the universe...inside the atom... have an issue with being spied on by scientists."

Gaston coughed a little.

"So every time a scientist tries to measure them up and take data on their normal behavior with those powerful microscopes and sophisticated instruments, the particles *intentionally* change their behavior, acting abnormally, to confuse the scientist. They probably say, '*The nerve of this Peeping Tom watching us in our private moments! Fuck off!*'"

Gaston laughed, finding common ground with these particles.

"The irony is that by trying to make our country safer from dangerous foreigners or French citizens with organized criminal plans, our government takes away our private freedom. So good people like us with good intentions or missions cannot function anymore. And what are we after but the search for the truth? The noblest of all causes!" He stared out the window, left and right, searchingly. No sign of the scheduled monk.

"I heard someone say the other day that life is a—"

Hearing nothing, Monsieur Douvier asked, "What happened. You ran out of voice?"

"No. I don't think I can say the word to you."

"For God's sake, say it. Well, let me put it this way—what are you planning to be when you grow up? A dentist? A factory manager? A mechanic? A banker? A circus juggler?"

Gaston giggled.

"An engineer? An actor? A novelist? A professor? A senator?"

Gaston giggled louder, with little bursts of laughter. "I don't know yet. You talk funny."

"Those are real careers, real professions."

Monsieur Douvier laughed a little too.

"If you're more bent toward the last four—actor, novelist, professor, or senator—you should say the word you're afraid to say, because these people, these professionals, usually care more about what's going on in the country–social issues, political issues, things that matter. The big picture–good and bad. Above all the truth. Not what's easy or safe or convenient to say."

"I'm not afraid to say it–life is a *bitch*!"

"There! Bravo!" applauded Monsieur Douvier. "And it's true–life is very difficult...sometimes extremely so."

Their eyes met with a strange, even poignant intensity. Monsieur Douvier noticed Gaston's tears rolling down his cheeks. The fourth time this morning.

He himself had shed quite a few in his private moments.

Above hovered Richard's soul.

GASTON LEARNS UPLIFTING FACTS THROUGH SHOCKING TRUTHS ABOUT HIS OLDER SISTER ELISE AND AUSCHWITZ-BIRKENAU'S CREMATORIUM II

Route Mialet-Luzzier, Le Pradinas

While chatting and waiting for the monk, Monsieur Douvier instructed Gaston about key items to remember during his ride to Grotte de Trabuc and upon his arrival there, which shouldn't take more than ten-fifteen minutes.

The grotte almost touched Ruisseau de Montroucou up in one of the highest and densest crests of the mountains. Curiously enough, they had just passed a lower stretch of this creek a while ago, near Paussan, so the terrain might at least look a bit familiar to him when riding the horse to the grotte.

"How's your peridot ring doing?"

"Oh...it's always here, in my finger."

"Good. Very good. Don't lose it now!"

"I won't."

"Don't take it off...for any reason!"

"I won't."

The famous archeologist had told him and Juliette half a dozen secrets about this peridot ring, from Princess Mipho's time in Ancient Egypt to Mary Magdalene's days in Jerusalem to his own humble journey here in Saint-Jean-du-Gard, and so far he'd been right and precise. Well, in his personal, young mind's estimation.

Discovering along the way a futuristic "Richard connection" in one of his recurring day dreams or trances, only added to the mystery. But he was used to it, and he could trust Juliette's grandpa above anything.

Gaston remained pensive. Other thoughts crossed his mind.

"Do you think Nez Froid's parents are also Nazi criminals?" he then asked casually.

"All Nazis—dead or alive—are criminals." Monsieur Douvier scratched one ear. "They believe only one race should occupy this planet—their own—and make their urgent priority the extermination of any other race."

"In death camps?"

"Anywhere, but chiefly there."

"Why?"

"Efficiency. Factory-like mass production of gas-killed human beings. Well-organized and quickly-operated." He took a deep breath and said, "Genocide ...the Holocaust..."

"Wow."

Gaston felt a strange chill in his bones.

"Have you ever met anyone who escaped and survived a death camp?"

"Yes...myself..."

"*You?*" exclaimed Gaston, incredulous. "*You were in a death camp?*"

He nodded. "It's a very sad, long story...but let's not talk about this now."

"How long were you there?"

"A year...a year and a half."

"Wow." Gaston stared at the old man. "But you're not Jewish. Are you?"

"No. But I protected many Jews during the war. Kept them in hiding—right here in my house."

This man is a hero, Gaston pondered. *So was Juliette...and Danielle...and all those young girls in this mission who'd risked their lives for a cause.*

"Gaston, did you...?" Monsieur Douvier tried to ask him a question, but stopped short. "...um...I meant..." He realized the question could be too sudden, too harmful, if the boy had never been informed about a dark episode in his family history. "Oh...never mind..."

"You were going to ask me something?"

Now the old man had no choice. "Did you...were you ever told about Elise? Her courage?"

"Elise?"

"She was only seventeen...when..."

"When what?"

"When she died...in 1944..." Monsieur Douvier's eyes moistened a bit. "...in the camp...at Auschwitz..."

"Who was Elise?"

"Your sister..."

"*My sister?*" Gaston could hardly believe the old man. "How do you know all that?"

"I knew Elise. We were together at Auschwitz-Birkenau...for the same reason. Protecting Jews, helping them hide...escape."

"I didn't know I had a sister."

"She died before you were born."

"What did she look like?"

"A beautiful girl...a lot like you...bold....brave...smart..."

Gaston smiled, his eyes searching the old man's facial expressions for more clues.

"Your auntie Doña Manola and I had several conversations about the Holocaust...the death camps. Some of her close friends also died there. She confirmed many facts about Elise."

"Wow..."

Monsieur Douvier explained how he personally was able to escape one day with a group of Hungarians...several weeks after Elise and hundreds others were taken to the basement gas chamber of Crematorium II...at Birkenau. "It was horrible. Humanity's lowest point in my lifetime. Organized genocide. Millions of innocent people...beautiful human beings...mechanically exterminated based on one man's sick ideals—Hitler's. That incredibly wretched mind...who was able to brainwash an entire nation...Germany...into thinking like him."

Gaston felt cold chills again inside his entire body, remained silent. So did Monsieur Douvier, for a while.

But the memory of Juliette's sweet smile returned, even more pressing and moving than before. He loved her so deeply, so completely...she was his daily bliss, his graceful companion, his cheerful angel. *How can I live without Juliette now? She was my best friend...my wife-to-be...the mother of my soon-coming child!* he thought in anguish, smoothing his wet eyes with a handkerchief.

Just yesterday they'd chatted and laughed together...then hugged each other with so much joy and love before she mounted her beautiful white horse...and trotted away into the highlight of her dream mission. He stared at the passing cars on the road facing him without really seeing them, profoundly hurt inside. She'd looked so radiant and powerful, even princess-like. Only criminal bastards could've cut her life short and created such a tragedy!

"Something must have happened to the monk..." interrupted Monsieur Douvier. "I don't like it. He was supposed to be here...to scout the area...prepare the ground for your ride up this winding and steep road."

"All by himself?"

"No. He's got a few younger monks under his belt. It's a routine thing for them."

Gaston surprised him when he said, in a quite mature and strong voice, "I'm ready to mount that horse...with or without them! We cannot wait any longer! This is Juliette's mission and I must keep my word!"

"Your word?"

"Yes. I promised Juliette I would complete her mission to Grotte de Trabuc if anything happened to her!"

"Terrific! Let's get the horse out of the trailer and get out of here!" cheered the old man.

They both smiled at each other and stepped out of the car with a new vitality and purpose.

Above hovered Richard's soul.

LAST STRETCH TO GROTTE DE TRABUC

Le Pradinas-Mas Soubeyran

From his topless front seat at the steering wheel, Monsieur Douvier could see the white horse's trotting motion and hear the kite's roaring sound filtering down the string Gaston held with his right hand over echoing hoof beats. In spite of everything, it was a sight to behold.

Car and horse left Le Pradinas—windblown area where the river Gardon almost touched the road before they separated, only to re-approach each other again at the level of Luziers, further north.

Gaston had temporarily tied the kite string to the saddle to get the horse into a steady gallop. He'd also shortened the reins and lowered his hands, remembering Juliette's fast-riding tips.

He urged the horse on with his seat and legs, feeling his weight on his knees as he swiveled forward, keeping his nose down on the animal's neck.

His mane feels good on my face, he mused. *He must know Juliette's gone... and I'm just a substitute...a friend...*

Back to a trotting gait, his body rising up and down, he tried to focus more on the road and its flanks as he approached some homes and local people in Luziers, past Ruisseau de la Baumelle. He turned his head around to check on the sky-blue Delahaye, which rolled majestically behind him.

The Pont de la Rouquette and the Moulin de Bau—both to his left near the river Gardon de Mialet—and the hamlet of Mas Soubeyran to his right came into view little by little.

He proudly held the kite by its string again, struggling with the wind to keep it airborne and steady. Its roaring sound felt like sweet music to his young but sad ears.

Mas Soubeyran, the natal place of the famous chief Camisard Rolland, had its welcoming climbing road split into two roads. He took the one to his left, headed for the crest of the mountain. Somewhere up there, hidden from view, lay Grotte de Trabuc.

Above hovered Richard's soul.

PART 9

NO MORE ATTEMPTS ON GASTON'S LIFE FROM FRANCE-BASED VIRGINIE—JUST AN IMPLIED "AU REVOIR, YOU JUST KILLED ME" PHONE CALL TO MASTER JUDGE ZUNDO, JUNE 3081

VIRGINIE CONFIRMS TO MASTER JUDGE BY MILLENNIUM-DISTANT PHONE CALL SHE'S DYING OF PANCREATIC CANCER

Bermuda Revelation Park

Master Judge's ZCAP meter quivered with the distinctive, infectious sound of Bert Kaempfert's "The World We Knew." Had it played the French classic "La Mer" instead, he would've ignored it, as he'd been recently alerted of a security breach in the system by hackers from former China.

He accepted the incoming phone call from a hospital.

"Hellooo..." he answered in his usual fastidious drawl, reading the tiny lilac screen message: "Clinique Médicale Sainte-Madeleine, Avignon, France, 1955."

"*C'est mois, Virginie...*"

"*Bonjour...comment allez-vous?*"

"*Très mal...je creve…*"

"You're dying?"

"*Je suis...pres...que mor...te...*"

"That's bad all right..." He stared at a school of angelfish swimming by followed by snappers, east of the Promenade Corridor. "Almost dead from what?"

"...pan...cre...atic…can...cer..."

"Oh...that's really bad."

"I am sor...ry…" she barely voiced, "I… I…dis...ap...poin...ted you..."

Master Judge realized she was rapidly losing that heavy flavor to her throaty French accent he disliked so much. "*La paix soit avec vous...* (Peace be with you...)" he whispered, meaning the opposite.

PART 10

PHASE TWO OF GASTON'S TREACHEROUS JOURNEY TO GROTTE DE TRABUC FRANCE, JULY 1955

PABLO'S HEINOUS OBSESSION IN FINDING JULIETTE AND GASTON UNFORTUNATELY ALSO LEADS TO GRANDPA

Quartier de Luc, Saint-Jean-du-Gard

Pablo's old gray Citroën 2CV sped east-bound on Route de Luc.

It stopped at Juliette's home, where he received the incredibly grim news about Juliette's murder near La Bambouseraie in the Montsauve area. Madame Clarice Barré's eyes were red with tears, which she tried to contain with a handkerchief.

"Do you know where Gaston is?"

She negated with her head.

Next, Pablo drove to Juliette's grandpa's property nearby down the road, finding no sign of the old man there. The front door was locked.

Shit! Where's Monsieur Douvier! he mused.

Then, he walked next door to his own farm, finding more tears and handkerchiefs among his family members and relatives and helpers. The commotion was enormous.

"Where's Gaston?" he asked everyone, getting no precise answers, except from Alfredo–his older brother–who'd read the newspaper's headlines this morning and could hardly believe it or say a word.

"Route de Générargues...north," he finally let out with a trembling voice. "Past Chemin de Picadenoux."

"Oh...that's way over there," Pablo said, pointing to a distant place with his index finger. "On the other side of the river Gardon de Mialet."

Alfredo nodded, scratched his brawny chest. "A monk came by early this morning...asking questions. So did two inspectors from the *gendarmerie* later." His normal, strong voice had returned.

"What did the monk know?"

"He sort of hinted that they'd be near Luziers by now..."

"They?"

"Yeah...Juliette's grandpa and Gaston."

"Going where?"

"I don't know...Mialet...Grotte de Trabuc...somewhere..."

"Thanks!"

Within minutes, his Citroën whistled past Le Pont des Abarines, heading east for Mialet and Luziers. Driving by Mas Soubeyran–the last village before Grotte de Trabuc—he decided to turn left on a hunch they might be heading that way climbing to the crest of the mountain.

Adrenaline started pouring out from his adrenal medulla when he saw Monsieur Douvier's sky-blue Delahaye convertible rolling slowly uphill, the old man at the wheel alone.

He didn't know he was following Gaston, a horse rider now. He just saw a great opportunity to do something he'd been meaning to do long time ago.

In a rush, he parked his Citroën in the first half-acceptable place he could find, under a broad-leaved tree against the hill, bordering some old stone homes. Then he ran to the rolling convertible, grotesquely waving his hands to the old man, who upon seeing him stepped on the brakes.

"Hello...Mr. Douvier!"

"What's up?" said the old man cautiously, wondering what he was doing here. He could see dark malevolence in his eyes.

A shocking scene followed when Pablo vaulted over his car, falling next to him on the passenger's seat with a loaded pistol in his hand pointing at him.

"What is this all about?" complained Monsieur Douvier.

"Turn around and just keep driving...heading north to Mialet."

They rolled on Avenue Jacques Bernard through Mialet at slow speed before Pablo motioned him to take Pont des Camisards to the left."

A minute slipped by.

"There are two kinds of monks in this world," Pablo said. "Those who follow orders and those who create peace without them." His breath wheezed. "I had a pretty rough time with your heretic monks yesterday…and the day before. I don't know what you told them, but they tried to kill me."

"Their orders were only to investigate your doings…which are by no means peaceful."

"My doings?" He laughed. "Keep driving west on Paussanel. When the road splits, take the left side, forest-bound…away from Le Gardon de Mialet."

"You're so different from your brother and parents. They're good people."

He laughed louder.

"We know all about your filthy setup in Ville Basse…torture chambers…deaths by pointed tools…*Señor Alberto Callado* or *Monsieur Torturer de l'Hérésie*…"

"Please, slow down and park over there…by the chestnut tree," commanded Pablo.

The distinguished archeologist complied, feeling helpless, as Pablo hurried to tie his hands and legs, the pistol aiming at his chest.

"You've done your homework, Mr. Douvier…the problem is this will be your last…"

He pulled out and flicked open a switchblade knife from his oversized khaki pants, giving him the scare of his life.

"Don't panic…I'm not going to stab you…"

Next, he extracted a ripe tropical fruit from a pocket inside his pants, and cut it in half with obvious skill.

"I was going to let you taste this fresh avocado…before your departure—or transfer, shall I say, to your next reincarnation—but I just got hungry myself for it," he said, torturing him with his theatrical, malicious way of talking and staring. "So excuse me…"

Monsieur Douvier watched how he carefully removed the large, oval-shaped pit from its center and devoured the fleshy fruit, holding the pit up in the air with one hand.

"I will, however, let you have the avocado pit...if you want it..."

Monsieur Douvier shook his head negatively.

"You know, I'm actually very upset. My goal yesterday was to kill your granddaughter, Juliette, and her stupid boyfriend, Gaston—both *fucking* heretics, like yourself–but someone got to her first! I still have Gaston within my reach...today...after I'm done with you."

"You *bloody* monster!"

"Funny that you mentioned my older brother, Alfredo. He also had his eyes on Juliette...but sexually." Pablo's fingers played with the avocado pit, his face wore a lingering ice-cold texture. "He's a *pedophile*...a child molester...hungry for thirteen and under babes...and..." His eyes became very intense. "...You know...I'm so jealous about him taking over the farm...probably more jealous than he's of Gaston's scoring with Juliette...that...I've written a note I keep in my pocket...denouncing him as a pedophile...to give it to the police...maybe tomorrow..."

Pablo now held the shiny, dark-brown pit with the tip of his fingers, admiringly, a cynical smile escaping his lips. Then suddenly he smacked the old man's chest with such brutality with the other hand, it clamped his mouth wide open. A gruesome, painful "haaaaaaaa" came out. At which point, Pablo simply dropped the pit inside his mouth. *"Bon appetit!"* Watching him desperately coughing and jerking on his seat, he assisted his death by holding tight on his jaw.

Soon he was quiet and gone.

Above hovered Richard's soul.

GROTTE THE TRABUC'S WITHIN GASTON'S SIGHT

Near the Entrance to Grotte de Trabuc, Mas Soubeyran

Gaston turned his head again to check on the sky-blue Delahaye, but was surprised not to see it.

Where's Monsieur Douvier...Grandpa? his mind asked, astounded. *A flat tire? A car problem? A health problem? He's pretty old, but strong. Must be something else!*

He remembered a situation when he'd led a foot race all the way to a mountaintop in a large pine forest in Hossegor, southwest of France, at a very young age...seven or eight. Too young to qualify, yet forgiven...and accepted...competing against some three-hundred older students, his four-year-older cousin among them. He led the race all the way to the very top of the mountain. And when he was just about to cross the finish line—all alone and several minutes ahead of the nearest runner—something happened that stopped him cold...and made him not only lose the race but never cross the line.

It was a sharp, unbearable pain in his upper tummy, under his rib cage. So bad, it made him collapse in agony on the ground for as long as he could remember, perhaps a half-hour, tears spilling from his eyes. Strangely enough, he received no help whatsoever during his misery from any of the dozen or so Roman Catholic priests who supervised the event and stood at every stage of the race recording the leading runners' progress.

He even remembered sharing this story with Juliette a month or two ago.

And it was always one of those stories he couldn't tell for sure whether it really happened. He wasn't sure. It baffled his imagination.

It never happened! his cousin had argued angrily on several occasions. But, somehow, it felt too real to discard it. Dreams, trances, reveries, false images...false memories...all these seemed always to haunt him. Why?

So now he faced the same dilemma with Monsieur Douvier's incident.

But this time he'd go all the way and cross the finish line no matter what! He had to! A promise was a promise! And no promise was stronger than a promise to Juliette!

ᜆ

Anything wrong with Monsieur Douvier, he'd have to deal with after his arrival to the grotte. After the transfer of the kite and scrolls to the receiving monk, as agreed on.

So he continued the climb to Grotte de Trabuc...already within his field of vision...with Juliette's beloved white horse and the roaring sacred kite.

Above hovered Richard's soul.

HITCHHIKING, PABLO GETS PICKED UP BY LES ALLUMETTES, BUT GETS INTO DEEP TROUBLE ARGUING OVER THE HISTORIC "GUERNICA" ISSUE

Vallée du Gardon de Mialet, Pont des Camisards, Mialet

The powerful Mercedes-Benz threaded down the road aimlessly, approaching Mialet. Minutes earlier it had prodded through sun-scorched Saint-Jean-du-Gard and Aubignac, winding around like a hungry snake.

Inside, the four *Allumettes* seemed to carry more bad vibes than ever before. Trois Coudes, seated next to Pieds Malin in the back, was nagged by a dry cough–not unusual when pumping his malicious mind up in clear anticipation of danger–his own. Pieds Malin just tore the rim of his fingernails with his serrated teeth, his dark eyes set on the fast-passing forestland seen through the window. At the wheel, Bouche Tordu, a tad less wicked than his younger brother Nez Froid, who controlled the gang, now engaged in small, nasty talk to all from his front seat.

Early this morning, before going out to pick up their clan friends, the two brothers had an unusual encounter with their parents regarding the Mercedes-Benz. "No way you're going to drive the Supercharger today!" yelled their father, enraged at their recent outings without his permission. "You both are grounded...now and every day this week!"

Bouche Tordu gave him an ugly stare.

It didn't matter if the old balding man had been a top brass in the Nazi organization before and during the big world war that ended in 1945 with suicides and surrender scenes everywhere. It didn't matter if he heroically (Nazi's impression) managed to escape and rebuilt his life in post-war France, providing Nez Froid and Bouche Tordu all the schooling and essentials they needed to grow up and forge a future for themselves. It didn't matter if there was plenty of money in their bank accounts and secret connections to get by even in hard times. Nothing mattered to Bouche Tordu, the least of which was he being his father. And his brother's.

He just had enough of his temper, his restricting rules, and his lack of love for him and his brother in the first place. He could tolerate his mother who'd been pointedly unpleasant and supportive of her husband recently, but today neither parent was worth tolerating. Swiftly, he pulled his Beretta and fired a shot on each their heads.

Mom and dad fell to the floor, crashing their dead heads against the heavy marble tea table. Half-empty porcelain cups there took a splashing portion of dark-red blood before it spilled over the plush beige carpet floor below.

Frozen with surprise, Nez Froid said nothing. Nothing at all.

They left the house like they would any day, making no effort to hide the bodies, cover them with a blanked, or call the police. All they cared about was to meet with their clan friends and hit the road together.

⌒

Cruising the Aubignac-Mialet stretch for more hell-raising moments and nefarious thrills, the four delinquent-turned-criminal teenagers approached the Pont des Camisards on their Mercedes Supercharger.

Someone was hitchhiking near the historic stone bridge.

Plain clothed, he looked a few years older than anyone in the German car.

"Let's pick him up," suggested Nez Froid. "He looks interesting."

"Are you sure we want to do that?" said Bouche Tordu, reducing the speed. "He might complicate our journey."

They all laughed in the car.

"More than it already is?" put in Pieds Malin, chocking with his own laughter.

Bouche Tordu stepped on the brakes and pulled to the shoulder of the road. "Where are you headed?" he asked the stranger.

"Mas Soubeyran...just where the road to Grotte de Trabuc begins..."

"What's there for you?" asked Nez Froid.

"My car is parked out there."

"Your amazing Mercedes Supercharger?" teased Trois Coudes with a big sardonic smile, followed by a little burst of laughter.

Of course, rarely would anyone in these wild mountains drive such an expensive and unusual machine, especially a poor farmer like him.

Pablo didn't find the comment particularly amusing. But he needed the ride badly.

He produced an awkward smile, wrongly thinking the four convertible occupants were harmless school kids on their summer break trying to have some fun.

"No, a Citroën..." he simply said, bashfully.

"The big one?"

"No, the 2CV..." Meaning the cheapest.

They all roared with laughter.

"Jump in," invited Bouche Tordu. "We'll drive you up there."

Pablo complied, squeezing his slim frame between Pieds Malin and Trois Coudes in the back seat.

"Don't mind our screwed up personalities...we kind of like you actually..."

"What's your name?" asked Nez Froid.

"Pablo."

"Oh...Spanish...or Spanish-blooded..." cheered Pieds Malin.

He nodded.

"*Señor Pablo...como está usted?*" teased Trois Coudes.

They introduced themselves, using their nicknames, as usual, while Bouche Tordu jerked the car forward.

"Are you guys from here...too?" asked Pablo now.

"Well...partly..." said Pieds Malin, holding on his urge to reveal more.

Nez Froid turned and faced Pablo from his front seat, sizing him up. "Are you in exile from the Spanish Civil War?" he asked.

That hit Pablo straight in the spine. It couldn't have been more direct and impertinent.

"Sort of..."

"How long now?" asked Nez Froid.

"About seven years."

"My dad was there too...in Spain," said Nez Froid proudly. "Our dad..." he added, pointing at Bouche Tordu.

"Oh really?" said Pablo. "Republican? Nationalist?"

"Neither one...Condor Legion."

Pablo froze.

Of course, if they rode on such a blazing, head-turning German car, chances were their parents or relatives were former WWII Nazi officials, which he highly suspected. But Spanish Civil War Nazi Condor Legion pilots? That was hard to swallow.

No doubt, they must have participated in the atrocious bombing of Guernica—the razing to the ground of this peaceful ancient Basque city near the northern border with France.

Such bombing had caused a world outcry and made Picasso paint that symbolic artistic masterpiece that truly touched humanity's conscience. Such grand scale terror, such carnage and human suffering was all there shown on his canvas, reminding all nations that such barbarism had no place in a civilized world. Particularly when the motivation behind it was "just a testing of Nazi's latest weapons (with General Franco's nod)".

An entire charming and friendly city, the spiritual capital of the Basque people, totally destroyed and burned to the ground with its citizens in a matter of a few hours. WWII would see a lot of these weapons in action, especially London's skies.

They fucked up Spain...my beautiful country...these foreign Nazi desgraciados (bastards)... Pablo's insulted mind began to race furiously. *...just when Spain was beginning to enjoy democracy after the elections. Without the Condor Legion's help Franco might have never won the war and become the wretched dictator he is today!*

He couldn't care less if Franco was as staunch a Roman Catholic as he was, Spanish national pride came first, and he was going to show these little *mocosos del diablo* (devil brats) who they were dealing with.

"Condor Legion?" repeated Pablo, allowing the German teenager to reveal more. "So...your dad was a pilot?"

"Oh yeah," said Bouche Tordu, skirting the Pont de Paussan and gaining speed. "German Luftwaffe Air Force. Third Squadron. Junker Ju 52 bomber."

"Any military target or mission that you remember your dad telling you about?"

He searched his memory, then said, "Guernica...in April 1937."

"Guernica?" Pablo's blood started to burn inside his veins. He knew it all along.

"Yeah...somewhere north...by the Bay of Biscay. My dad kept telling us all these years at dinner time...just about every week...how he took off from Burgos, the base, and tore through the skies with his triple-engine Ju 52...loaded with 250Kg bombs and lots of 1Kg incendiaries...and dropped these fuckers all over the town...in formation with other Ju 52s...for total carpet cleanup..."

Nez Froid added, in his annoying manner, "What a show—buildings exploding in bright-red-orange flames...surviving souls and wounded civilians running along the streets like crazy in all directions trying to escape the inferno...and then the poor bastards being strafed cold by Messerschmitt Bf 109 and Heinker He 51 fighters from the Lutzow Squadron..."

"Your dad is really cool..." cheered Pieds Malin.

"*Was* cool" corrected Nez Froid, offended.

"Of course," said Trois Coudes. "You shot him dead this morning."

"My brother Bouche Tordu did..." corrected Nez Froid. "He also shot our mother dead."

"Whatever..." said Trois Coudes.

"SHUT UP! SHUT UP! SHUT UP! MOTHER FUCKING IDIOTS!" Pablo suddenly exploded, pistol in hand, waving the barrel at everyone. "YOU GUYS ARE SO FUCKING SICK I FEEL LIKE THROWING UP!"

"Take it easy, man..." said Bouche Tordu cautiously.

"Yeah...we're just talking bull..." said his brother Nez. "Nonsense and lies...just having fun..."

While Pablo's lethal eyes were on Nez Froid's apologetic lips, unable to cover the full range of the exchange, Trois Coudes' right hand seized, without a hint of movement, a heavy boot (the one he'd removed a while ago) bunched behind his right leg in the back seat.

"We're just kids...meaning no harm to you..." said Pieds Malin, stealing a fraction of his attention to his left, on the back seat. Enough for the boot, now violently swinging, to crash against his skull.

∾

When Pablo opened his eyes, a half hour later, he found himself helplessly tied up with a rope all around his waist and chest, both his arms starkly immobile and pinned to his chest. A swastika-stamped leather belt, full of iron spikes, coarsely grabbed the contour of his bleeding head, and there was something terrifyingly lumpy and hard stuffed inside his mouth, this one also clamped shut with wires. *Fuck me!* he cried out hysterically in his mind. *Is this the avocado I had in my pocket? The second one?* He'd already murdered Juliette's grandpa early on today with the seed of the first one, he remembered. *Oh God, help me! This is the entire fruit, not the seed! Help me God!!!*

Too late.

Two strong juvenile hands began to push the pulpy fruit deeper inside his throat, while two others held Pablo's head steady, as the Supercharger roared up the road like a wild animal.

UPON CROSSING THE FINISH LINE TO GROTTE DE TRABUC, GASTON'S WARMLY RECEIVED BY THE ASSIGNED MONKS AND GLORIOUSLY USHERED INSIDE, UNAWARE GRANDPA'S BODY LIES HALF EATEN BY WOLVES IN THE FOREST

Grotte de Trabuc, Mas Soubeyran

Mounted on Juliette's white horse and pulled to a certain extent by the roaring kite, Gaston finally made it to the Grotte de Trabuc up the steep road.

He was welcomed by a group of cheering monks clad in long green robes and sandals under a terrific blue sky. They applauded his courageous yet painful arrival to the site.

One of them assisted Gaston dismount from the horse, while another one guided the horse to a special area beyond the tall pine trees facing the left side of the building. A third seasoned monk, with a flair for diplomacy, took care of the kite.

"We're honored to have you among us. Enjoy your stay," spoke up the head monk.

"Thank you so much. This is Juliette's victorious mission... with a little help from me."

"We understand..."

"Please, follow us."

Apparently, public scheduled hours for this day had been suspended. Gaston could see no other persons around. The wide space facing the entry, presumably used as parking for visitors, stood strangely deserted—a fact he quickly noticed before being ushered inside like a king.

"This way..."

Facing three sun-bathed rows of stone steps, he proceeded through a stately half-open glass door—the whole structure, single-story, peaceful and neatly maintained, couldn't be more pleasant and friendly.

Gaston crossed a cute but spacious area that wisely combined souvenir shop and café services, with three simple tables of various shapes and sizes in two shades of green and white. He followed the monks along a lateral path pinned against a wall that started with a series of steps. From here he could see the local artworks for sale he'd just left behind in the doubly functional large room officially called *Hall d'accueil*.

A platform with railed fence led to a passageway at the corner-end, flanked by a gigantic Green Lagoon-like creature reaching to the ceiling, previewing, perhaps, what was coming inside.

Above, hanging low from the ceiling, an orange sign said "*DÉPART des visites*" painted in white. Three standard encircled symbols, under it, showed what was prohibited from the public inside the grotte.

The head monk dispersed the other monks at one point. Carrying the kite on his walk, he began to show Gaston their fantastic, naturally formed, underground world.

Prominently stood *Le Passage des Cent Mille Soldats* (The Passage of Hundred Thousand Soldiers)—tiny stalagmites not more than 10 cm each, mysteriously standing in formation, still without scientific explanation.

Then the spectacular emerald-green *Lac de Minuit* (Midnight Lake) followed by the amazing turquoise waterfalls, the subterranean rivers, and the spooky tunnels.

Huge cavernous cathedral-like chambers stunned the view. They contained aging crystals that changed colors every few meters with the changing presence of oxides in them.

Gaston was enthralled, letting out a series of half-muffled "wows' on his path.

Approaching a quiet corner, washed by a stream of clear water and shielded by a small rocky outcrop, the head monk thanked him again.

At issue was the historical importance of the Legend of the Horse-Riding Kites, which they began to discuss sitting side by side on a cozy flat stone bench.

"Is Monsieur Douvier ill today?"

"No," said Gaston, "but–"

"–I was also expecting him today," expressed the head monk. "He left late last night. We had a long meeting."

With great pain Gaston explained what had transcribed in the last hour or so, his fear that Juliette's grandpa might be in grave danger too, and that in fact he was hoping their meeting would end soon so he could look for him. The sooner the better.

The monk wasn't sure what he could tell the young boy, and vice versa.

"How old are you?"

"Nine...almost nine-and-a-half..."

"That's wonderful!"

"I should go then..."

"Be careful, my son."

"I will."

The monk bent his torso a little to touch a half-concealed button under the rock outcrop. In doing so, he tripped a bit clumsily, causing one of his sandals to go loose. "Sorry..." he said, fitting it back to his foot.

Gaston smiled, then he stood up to go.

"Wait," the monk urged. "One of our brothers will take you back to the exit door. Your horse must be impatient by now."

"It's Juliette's horse...her beloved Camargue horse."

"I'm sure he is," the monk said, lowering his stare. "I'm very sorry about what happened to her. Those criminals will be caught and punished, I'm sure."

Waiting for the other monk, they touched on a subject dear to the grotte community. "All sorts of tribes and wild animals have inhabited this cave complex since ancient times...even Marco Polo mentioned it in his *Book of Marvels*..."

"Wow..."

"The Camisards...the Maquisards...all kinds of freedom fighters... used it...even bandits made this place their home in recent times."

A younger monk approached the area.

He'd been delayed by an unusual event, so cruel, sad, and urgent, he had great difficulty in relaying it to them: "Monsieur Douvier has been found dead near Mialet. The police dragged his partly-eaten body from a pack of wolves...in the forest...by the road to the Pont des Camisards..."

"Ohhhh...." gasped the head monk in horror. "Gracious God. How could this have happened?" As he began to pray, he realized Gaston had fainted by his side.

"He was murdered before the wolves got to him," went on the young monk.

"How? By whom?"

"The police found an avocado seed stuck in his throat. He was asphyxiated...no suspects yet..."

Above hovered Richard's soul.

GASTON RECOVERS FROM A FAINTING SPELL CAUSED BY MORE SHOCKING NEWS AND LEAVES THE GROTTE TO HUNT DOWN THE KILLERS SUSPECTED TO BE LES ALLUMETTES

Grotte de Trabuc, Mas Soubeyran

Gaston was taken to a special, isolated place in the grotte through a damp, spidery tunnel, near a bizarre cluster of rocks called *Tas de Pierres de l'Espoir* (Rock Piles of Hope), where in a short time he was revived and soft-talked into reality about the tragedy.

A glass of fresh water, a few pats on the shoulder, and a sort of battle cry for action got him back to his feet and on Juliette's white horse before he could assimilate everything.

He waved goodbye and trotted down the steep, inclement mountainous *chemin*, already soaked in sweat from sun exposure, to a point bordering living quarters at its base. These were old stone houses with terracotta roofs, bunched together in the hamlet style of the Cévennes—a sight he remembered from his earlier arrival.

He now steered the horse to his right, away from Mas Soubeyran, on the merging main road near La Rouquette and Le Moulin de Bau, letting an incoming Renault pass, headed toward Mialet.

A quick choice: either he would continue on La Bonté or cross Pont de Paussan, threading through Le Traves past Le Gardon de Mialet. He settled for the first.

Galloping on La Bonté for a while, he slowed down to a trot when homes of interest appeared at both sides of the road, hoping to spot a German car, then decided for a tranquil pacing gait, feeling the soft swaying of his saddle and the pulsing beats of the animal's hooves. While crossing Mialet, vile images of Nez Froid and the *Allumettes* crammed his mind.

They could be now watching him from behind a house or a wall... ready to ambush him...or they could be driving around the back roads and alleys...planning another crime. These kids had no scruples. They had killed his pregnant Juliette and most likely, although not proven, killed her grandpa too. And who knows who else!

But "death by asphyxiation with an avocado seed rammed deep in the throat," as told by the monks, didn't seem to be a killing technique used by the Nazis. This was more elaborate and sadistic than a quick and cold gunshot, more psychological and personal.

But neither was burning someone to death tied to a forest tree. Two persons, actually. Mother and child. That was medieval horror *par excellence* as perpetually committed by the ruling Roman Catholic bishops.

Well, he didn't know enough about the wretched Nazi mentality. Which organized group was worse—them or the bishops? What he knew was that the latter had tried to rule the world by raping its innocence with unspeakable lies and crimes over centuries of manipulations while the former had tried to do the same by way of pre-announced cold and direct crimes only over a mere decade. If there was hell, they surely would meet there.

Could he now be after two or more criminals in his avenging mission? Catholic fundamentalists? Nazi ideologists? Deranged psychopaths? Or a wicked mixture of the three? If his auntie showed up today, she would be in stark shock seeing all the things that had transpired in her absence. Had she been here all along, providing guidance and support to Pierre and Gaston, perhaps none of these things would've happened. Those things often escape parents' and aunts' imagination. Parents' and aunts' hearts.

Doña Manola had been good at taking care of herself. She'd done a lot in her life, for herself and others, but this time she has failed Pierre as a mother and Gaston as an aunt.

A bunch of other thoughts crossed his mind as he galloped the horse toward Saint-Jean-du-Gard, some ten kilometers from where the *Allumettes* might be wandering around, by foot or by car–who knows!

If he didn't find them there, he'd go to Anduze and even farther to Alès.

He wasn't aware of the latest news that sporadically popped up on the radio. Other murders had been reported by these deranged teenagers, including Nez Froid and Bouche Tordu's own parents early this morning.

"Apparently, their crime spree began this week with two thirteen-year-old lovely girls from our region, one of them, our very own child phenom of the national stage, Juliette Douvier," broadcast a local radio station. "Also...maybe related...a slain monk in his twenties and an illustrious archeologist in his mid-eighties. Police units and inspectors are currently on these criminals' tracks."

West of Aubignac, he approached the long and tall Pont des Abarines, the one so familiar to him and Juliette for having often frog-hunted and sun-bathed in the nude in its vicinities, specifically the river Gardon de Mialet's crystal waters. Often, they had also come here to paint, fish, swim, picnic, and photograph birds. A total road attraction. Now it all felt so strange, so devastating...riding on Juliette's white Camargue horse...searching for Juliette's killers.

Above hovered Richard's soul.

AN IMMINENT COLLISION OVER PONT DES ABARINES ENDS THE SICKENING RUN OF THE PERPETRATORS

Pont des Abarines, Vallée du Gardon de Mialet

A local architectural marvel and historic place, the Pont des Abarines stood right in front of Gaston and his mounted white horse.

He approached it at a cautiously reduced trot, somehow knowing it was the proper moment to cross it.

The bridge's weathered stony surface and lateral railed fences shone obliquely in various shades of gray, silver, and brown. Thirty meters below, the river Gardon de Mialet, with its sprawled boulders and agitated waters, ran effortlessly in search of space, power, and abundance. Occasionally, a floating trunk, pushed by its stealthy current, could be seen.

Not today. Its surface was barren and quiet, but lush in its capacity for responding to any provocation.

Not that they would face another barbarian army of arrogant and twisted-minded barons from the north sent by the Crown of France, with the usual nod from the Pope, but that a similarly sick entity had already emerged in the horizon coming straight at them from the other side.

The fucking Mercedes-Benz 540K Supercharger and Les Allumettes—there you are, miserable exterminators of innocent lives! pondered Gaston in silence, containing his explosive rage, lightly tugging at the reins to keep the pace.

The wild, roaring machine, aware of the danger, upped its speed in full recognition of the calamity it might cause.

A collision was imminent about midway on the bridge, unless either party pulled to one side. Gaston and the horse wouldn't. The Mercedes finally screeched to a stop inches from them.

Bouche Tordu got out with his pistol drawn, leaving the engine idling and the door open. He aimed at the horse, but the animal's front legs were wildly up and kicking. Bang! Bang! Bouche's face sank into its own cracking bones on impact, brains above it hemorrhaging, blood spurting out through both ears.

He was dead before hitting the ground. His brother, Nez Froid, held him in his arms momentarily enraged like a choleric gorilla, then pushed his limp body into the backseat of the Mercedes. He was pointing Bouche's pistol to Gaston, when another blow from the horse broke his shoulder blade.

With painful effort, he rolled himself into the driver's seat and cranked the car out of the way. Then he tried to roar it into infernal speed, but lost control.

The heavy 540K Supercharger hit the bridge protective fence with such force it spun on itself into the air, somersaulting dramatically over the bridge edge and going straight down onto the large boulders sticking out of the water. The fall was spectacular and harsh. A flock of black crows flew off the area in concert with the crashing sound of punishing metals and human bones.

Scattered brain parts and a curious smashed avocado with human teeth clung to it were visible from the top of the bridge. They landed over twisted debris, intertwined with rising grayish vaporous clouds, spewing nasty smelling fragments of life and dust. At least, that was what Gaston thought he saw when bending over the fence. The river accepted their profuse blood and it was the end for all of them.

Headed for the morgue in Saint-Jean-du-Gard—after removal of their bodies from the crushed Mercedes-Benz convertible—were heretic torturer Pablo Quintero (a.k.a. Alberto Callado), Juliette's bully classmate Nez Froid, his gun-trigger-happy brother Bouche Tordu, and wicked clan members Pieds Malin and Trois Coudes.

"Five more fatalities related to the so-called *Les Allumettes* teen clan that has recently terrorized our peaceful community were pulled out of the river Gardon de Mialet today after the luxurious Mercedes-Benz that carried them tipped over the historical Pont des Abarines midway between Saint-Jean-du-Gard and Mialet," reported the radio in a special bulletin. "Elaborate and vigorous police investigation is currently underway."

After detailing some of the aspects of the tragedy, the newscaster touched briefly on the history of the famous bridge itself, explaining that it had been designed by François Bataille and built by Charles Autajon in 1900. Contrary to other news media reports, Gustave Eiffel, responsible for building Paris' celebrated La Tour Eiffel, never touched this bridge, except for his early proposal, soon abandoned, to build it in metallic pieces.

ॐ

Nothing could be more painful, more excruciating than suffering the loss of the most loved person in one's life. Nothing could be more tragic than knowing that this loss was actually two loved persons—mother and baby. Could it be lesser the pain if the baby was only a conceived baby? Not yet completely formed? Not yet out of the womb? Such was Gaston's dilemma.

Horridly, he could see Juliette and the baby together screaming and burning in flames, melting, and turning to ashes. He could see their disappearance. Both losses harrowing reminders of a never materialized, never consumed parenthood, with or without marriage.

Now, at age nine, Gaston realized life had to go on, without her. It was hard, very hard, but he would make it somehow. That was his challenge. There was no other way.

Above hovered Richard's soul.

AT LAST ANCIENT RELIC AND SCROLLS UNITE IN PEACE IN GRANDPA'S OWN BACKYARD'S CAVE

Grotte de Trabuc, Mas Soubeyran

Gaston returned to Grotte de Trabuc riding at full gallop the first stretch of the road, then just trotting the rest.

The monks were not surprised for they also knew his reason. A difficult one. The day before he was murdered, Monsieur Douvier told Gaston, with great chagrin, Juliette's murder marked the end of the 700-year-old mission…the end of The Legend of the Horse-Riding Kites. There was no point in continuing it. The world had changed too much, with webs of highways and great roads for speeding cars built everywhere.

Southern France, in particular the Languedoc, was no longer the land of horse-riding knights and chivalry, where hidden castles and hamlets and caves could lure people to carry incredible missions and fulfill realities approaching fantasies. There were no places to hide anymore, no secret roads through mountains and rivers and lakes to follow. Pine forests were open to everybody. No reason anymore to fly kites on horses across the meadows and plains.

Monsieur Douvier told the monks the same sad story. For now, he'd take the responsibility of keeping the two scrolls in his property, unless anyone objected. No one did. They didn't know, and he'd never told anyone, except his granddaughter and her boyfriend Gaston, that an ancient relic with the same message from Jesus and Mary Magdalene to the world already hid in his property.

Monsieur Douvier's last words on this matter to everyone sounded like a premonition of what was going to happen to him.

So when Gaston returned to Grotte de Trabuc, it was all clear to the monks that he was here for the scrolls. Ritually, they were already set with a new kite built by the oldest monk, the kite loaded with the two scrolls…ready to be flown in the air on a galloping horse a last time.

"I don't think *Les Allumettes* will bother us anymore. They all went down the tall bridge, we heard on the radio, including a fellow named Pablo we ourselves were investigating," said the head monk, with a happy little smile.

"I know," said Gaston, also with a little smile.

Waving goodbye, he began to climb down the hill, aiming Juliette's white Camargue horse on, holding the string tied to the roaring kite above his head. He knew now that this ride from Grotte de Trabuc to the place he'd just decided on would be the mission's very final destination.

To avoid being stopped and questioned by the police, he took another, longer road to Saint-Jean-du-Gard, galloping at Juliette's usual pace and arriving safely without any incidents.

First, he guided the horse to what used to be Juliette's home, which was also Madame Clarice Barré's home, her second mother's, hoping to find the gentle woman there. Upon opening the front door, and exchanging warm salutes with her, he explained he needed to pick up something his girlfriend kept in her room.

Without revealing Juliette's secret, he managed to spend a few private moments there in Juliette's room, enough time for him to trade the *two original scrolls* she kept hiding there in the pirate's treasure box for the *two copies* he kept in his pocket. The copies were the same ones he'd removed from the kite before knocking on Madame Clarice's door.

Back on the horse, he now headed for Monsieur Douvier's property in the neighborhood.

He found the gate to the backyard unlocked, and seeing no one, he continued ahead using a side path. The horse stayed outside, tied to a wooden column. Soon he was inside the cave—a place perfectly hidden and completely unknown to the world. Of the four persons who knew it—Monsieur Douvier, Madame Rossi, Juliette Douvier, and

Gaston Lagarde–only Gaston, himself, remained alive to keep the secret.

Carefully, he placed the two scrolls next to the relic in the blue box, covering the box with some sandy soil mixed with marl and clay. Now the ancient treasure (original scrolls and relic) had found its final resting place. Facing it with awe and respect and heaving a sigh of relief, he pondered, *extended mission completed.*

Above hovered Richard's soul.

PART 11

A CROWDED GATHERING IN ALICE SPRINGS, AUSTRALIA, MORE THAN TWO HUNDRED TIMES "WOODSTOCK" TO WITNESS NOTHING, RECALLS DR. UFAHH ZUNDO, JUNE 3081

INVITED BY DR. UFAHH ON HIS MEGAYACHT, LOVELY SENTENCE JUDGE LEARNS HER BOSS HAD ATTENDED MANY DECADES AGO THE "HANDSHAKE WITH GOD DAY" EVENT

North of Boca Raton, Former Florida

Flying at low altitude, Dr. Ufahh's chauffeur driven ziderot arrived to a secluded lavish marina north of Boca Raton from the Alternative History Palace, where he kept his two-story 110-foot megayacht Zangio.

"Thanks for coming," he told Sentence Judge moments later.

The black, curvaceous judge smiled.

"My pleasure."

She wore a trendy bikini, topless and scarce in material for its remaining part, leaving little to the imagination. Her shoulder-length soft black hair enhanced the model-like figure she possessed, although she knew Dr. Ufahh cherished her more for her mind than her body.

"Very impressive boat you have."

"A gift from the 3Zs."

"Oh..."

Both the stately cruiser and their conversation picked up speed, heading south toward Miami Beach. A nice breeze kept the scientist's Adolpho shorts fluttering. She comfortably leaned against a railing, unaware some crew members watched them from the upper deck, Mipho among them, going by another name.

Early chat led to something intriguing. "I didn't know you were in Alice Springs...for the Fourth Millennium Handshake with God Day."

"Oh yeah...I was there."

Sentence Judge furrowed her brows. "Wait a minute...that was in 3000...81 years ago." Her face looked puzzled.

"That's right..." He kept a little corny smile going.

"But you don't look that old."

"That's right."

She narrowed her eyes.

"So...what's going on?"

The megayacht sped nicely over the flapping waves. Standing in the sun deck, near a pool and a saloon that could be accessed by a curved staircase, they had a sweeping view of the blue ocean.

"Technically, I'm really much older than you think."

"So...you've invented something to keep you young?"

"Younger."

"One more invention in your arsenal?"

His thin lips parted with a big conceited smile.

"Couldn't help...doing it."

She kept staring at his face—eyes, ears, nose...the weird ensemble... with its missing wrinkles and other aging spots—the yellowish little oasis of brush growing on top of his bald head. "Are you over 100?"

He nodded affirmatively with his head.

"My God...your body is also firm...strong...and those arms are really..."

"Long?"

She smiled.

He teased her, "You never said handsome...attractive..."

It was true, of course. And now she felt funny, unable to continue.

"Don't worry," he said gamely. "I couldn't care less about beauty... my own. I just want to live a very long time, be around."

She kissed his left cheek, then his right.

"You're amazing to me."

OVER 100 MILLION BELIEVERS CROWDED ALICE SPRINGS AND SURROUNDING CITIES, REVEALS DR. UFAHH

Boca Raton-Miami Beach Coast, Former Florida

The stunning 110-foot megayacht headed south toward Miami Beach along the Atlantic coast at a speed of only 20 knots, using its very capable 900 hp engine. Dolphins could be seen swimming nearby in their playful, friendly way.

Shortly, they returned to the Handshake with God topic.

"It was an incredible day. People had been traveling from all over the world by plane or boat and 'swarming the place like bees'–to quote an airborne Sydney ZV reporter."

"No restrictions?"

"None. All human beings who wanted the witness the event–believers and non-believers–were allowed to come in...with just a passport, no visa or other security regulations. 'Making the whole continent of Australia tremble and sink a little with those 100 million ledheads'–to quote a respected Irish novelist, friend of mine based in Paris, concerned with sanitary conditions, contagious diseases, pollution, and other health and environmental issues."

"Such a humongous concentration of people..."

"The Adelaide-Brisbane-Darwin triangle was totally congested."

"I can imagine."

"The Northern Territory became a huge promenade of walkers... and Alice Springs...well, with its satellite cities...Engawala, Wallace Rockhole, Titjikala, Areyonga, Haasts Bluff, Papunya, Laramba...a parking lot of sitting butts."

"Incredible."

"I mean...even farther...Mutitjulu, Nyirripi, and Wutunugurra... were taken up."

"Where were you...in this mess? You seem to know Australia very well."

He laughed warmly. "I know this part like the palm of my hands. I had some projects developed out there in the deserts. I love the land and its people. It's really the closest you can get to God."

She gave him a teasing smile. "Not long ago you said to me over the phone that 'soul traveling' was the closest you could get to God, remember?"

He nodded.

"Alice Springs *here* on Earth, soul travel *out there* in the Cosmos."

Sentence Judge watched his inspired koala-like face, expressive black eyes. "Where did you camp out in Alice Springs?"

"Oh...I never made it that close...impossible...too crowded...massive pedestrian traffic. Wheels were not allowed for a radius of over 300 miles. Paralyzed people on wheels yes, but not ground-moving or flying vehicles of any kind. Awesome atmosphere." He saluted a flock of white birds passing over their heads. "I took the northbound A87 road, seeing lots of marchers from Coober Pedy on...and that was about two weeks before the Big Day. I joined them...walking...walking...arriving to Mintabie...where I got new desert shoes..."

"Any blisters? Sunburn?" She laughed.

"Oh yeah...plenty...and thirsty like hell!" He laughed too. "Anyway, I stopped somewhere between Imanpa and Wallace Rockhole...off the Stuart Highway...near the Henbury Meteorite Craters. People were saying God would appear farther north...on top of one of the high points in the East MacDonnell Ranges...where a rather humble, loved, local pastor had been chosen to shake God's hand at exactly 5 p.m. Australia time. But as you know, it didn't happen."

"Such a historical moment."

"It was both exciting and creepy to mingle with so many strangers...and finally settling for a single spot for hours...waiting and waiting and waiting..."

"About how old were you then?"

He stared up at her beautiful young face.

"I was twenty-nine."

"A *believer?*"

"Yes. Then and now...in spite of everything." He dropped his stare, smiled. "How else can you explain the marvelous details of our intimate little chat here...and the perfect ways everything works all around us and out there in the greater Universe? It's just mind-boggling, isn't it?"

She remained reflective, sharing his passion.

"In spite of everything?"

"In spite of God not showing up here," he said.

"Not shaking hands with anyone?"

"It would've been nice of him to appear here...simply and plainly...without mystery or conditions...for once in the history of human kind...to validate himself...give us hope...make us feel good and relaxed..." he said.

"Give us a reason to believe...have faith..."

"Foster good will...peace..." said Dr. Ufahh.

"Stop all religious wars..."

"It was a great opportunity for him to show up. We were 100 million human beings...rich and poor, young and old, men and women and children, gay people, healthy people, sick people, homeless, outlaws, mutants, ex-convicts, everybody...expecting him to appear at the scheduled *5 p.m. local time*...that amazing day of *June 20th, 3000*...after more than three millenniums of waiting..."

The distinguished scientist paused, his reflective eyes deeply affected. "Our hands stood there all stretched out...our hearts beating like crazy...and he missed the appointment...didn't show up..." he said, with somber, sad eyes.

"He let everybody down..." put in the young Zoliseum judge.

"It was heart-breaking...and hard for everyone to return home... empty-handed...neglected...sort of abandoned...even betrayed..." added Dr. Ufahh.

Sentence Judge felt the deep pain, remained silent.

"...but..." Dr. Ufahh struggled to continue. "I still believed in him... in God..."

FEARING TO BE DENOUNCED AS A "CATHOLIC BELIEVER" (HERESY IN REVERSE), DR. UFAHH BEGS FOR CLEMENCY WITH HIS DECEIVING KOALA FACE–BUT WILL HE EVER STOP YEARNING FOR RICHARD'S IMMENSE FORTUNE?

Near Miami Beach, Former Florida

They ate chicken sandwiches, drank cranberry juice, relaxing some more. They were now lounging by the pool side, the powerful megaboat magnificently cutting through the warm Atlantic coastal waters.

"Your secret is a very big one," Sentence Judge told him, surprising him a little.

"Which one?" Dr. Ufahh asked.

"Religion."

"Oh..." He dismissed the thought of it with an arrogant flip of his hand. "That's just personal."

"But it's against Zundo's principles and regulations...which you, yourself, helped write into the Constitution."

"I know..." he said, dismissively, again, staring down at the clear and serene pool water.

She stood up momentarily to stare at a barracuda cutting through gentle ocean waves at one side of the boat, stately commanding her territory amid other drifting fish. Her stare returned to him. "Religion is dead in our society...even extinct...yet you seem to cling to it in secrecy. And in everybody's eyes you're the least likely to do that. You're regarded as anti-religion...atheist..."

"I know..." he said, barely moving his lips. Raising his chin, he strangely asked, "Are you a believer?"

She was caught by surprise, but it didn't matter. Her feelings were well cemented. "No. Why should I be...considering all the suffering and injustice going on in the world? Considering the perpetual inequalities and abuses between men and women and between the rich and the poor. Considering all these preventable atrocities and genocide by ruling tyrants...preventable world wars and natural calamities that kill millions of innocent people decade after decade...century after century..."

She paused.

"Considering all these things and more, I cannot bring myself to believe in a god that watches over the world and takes care of our problems...when he doesn't even have the decency to say hello to us." She blew a sudden jet of air from her lungs to her nose with force in anger. It made her breasts bounce in plain view. "No, I cannot believe that a god is protecting us in any way. I wish it would be true, but fairy tales are not true. And all we have is fairy tales."

"Are you going to denounce me for believing in God?"

"No. Why would I ever do that? I'm not an informer."

For a moment, they stared into each other eyes as if a hair of distrust had been awaken between them.

"You could be an Inquisitor in reverse...a heretic idolater carrying a concealed torch to set Catholics on fire...and I could lose my job and my life right here...because of your accusations," he said defensively, "...under your ruler's watch."

"Trust me. None of this will ever happen. And no one but our 3Zs, yourself, and Master Judge is ruling me." She smiled. "What else is becoming extinct?"

He smiled back, hardly amused. "Money...after first being outlawed..." he uttered. "So we won't have octillionaires anymore...not even multi-millionaires. That's gone...history...like everything else."

"Well said. We don't need phony, self-made gods or demigods... we're moving into an era of reason and truth, not fantasy."

Dr. Ufahh had begun to worry like never before in his life. What was this shapely, topless, intelligent, young black girl up to?

PART 12

DISCORD BETWEEN THE SUB-LORDS OF ZUNDO ONLY MAKES MIPHO WISER AS RICHARD'S RELOCATION TO VENEZUELA BECOMES A REALITY ZUNDO, JUNE 3081

A MATTER OF MANIPULATING THE 3Zs OR PLAYING WITH FIRE, THINKS MIPHO

Bermuda Revelation Park

While atrocious crimes struck the towns marked by the trail of the Legend of the Horse-Riding Kites mission leading to Grotte de Trabuc in the Cévennes and other Languedoc areas in 1955 France, serious problems developed in the far future, precisely 3081, all countries now combined into a solid one, named Zundo, ruled by the 3Zs.

The two evil science mongers and sub-rulers of Zundo who created the punishing maze of nightmarish events across time and space for their greed-driven defendants, revealed their own weakness against them and themselves. Gaston had become their latest obsession.

Battling their own wrangling, they only succeeded in agreeing to relocate him (the boy in Richard's 13th past life) to a new land and turning point—Venezuela, 1955 tyranny. This South American country was on the verge of a bloody student revolution. All ZCAP meter's history search returns pointed to "volatile events" and "extreme violence" in late December 1957, spilling to January of the following year. Such were the tenets of this new ordeal or punishment escalation for school-bound Gaston.

But first, a meeting with the 3Zs had to take place. Using his selfish and sneaky skills, Dr. Ufahh managed to make himself *only* available to the meeting. Master Judge, he explained to them, was presently too busy with a tedious and urgent task that left him no time to do other things.

Of course, in his personal aim to one day acquire, through creative legal recourses and illegal manipulations, the better part of Richard's wealth, he would make sure his long term plan rolled on smoothly. He would ensure his potential culpability in any wrongdoing, if suspected at all, was promptly erased and no first-degree criminal act from his part ever hit the newspapers. For one thing, the 3Zs, the only ones *not* interested in Richard's immense fortune—luckily, the very Lords of Zundo–had proven themselves to be uncannily smart, methodic, and expeditious in dealing with subversive and criminal elements. *There* his challenge!

∾

Regarding Master Judge, he had vicious plans too. He was no fool. In fact, he was already ahead of the game concerning Richard's second phase of punishment in Venezuela. To accomplish his mission, he had to know every detail of the relocation process, like timing, place of appearance, Gaston's frame of mind, expected local encounters, and Gaston's first 24 hours of action. He needed to hire a cold-blooded, intelligent hit-man. Someone familiar with the geography and culture of this explosive South American nation.

He would get that man. Right now he'd try to talk to Z2, as soon as he was done with this tedious task Walking Brain had given him. Z2 was more approachable and casual than her two partners, Z1 and Z3, and she had sided with him a couple of times before for different problems. Her candor might bring some lights on Gaston's initial relocation status in Venezuela. The details he needed.

But, again, overall, he had to carry his plans without Walking Brain's knowledge. A slip could cost him his life! He knew Walking Brain too well to even raise any suspicion. Indeed, he had to be extra careful and, whenever possible—scratch that—*always* call him by his name, Dr. Ufahh, instead of his nick name! The day would come when money possession would be legal again and owning uppers of sextillion dollars, from Richard's immense wealth, with Richard (and Gaston) out of the way, would make him very happy!

∾

Meantime Dr. Ufahh met with the 3Zs in the Pink House–the recently painted and renamed White House in honor of these out-of-the-closet lesbian teenager rulers–and over coffee and crackers they nailed the place where the young boy would appear. *Exactly* inside a PamAm flight, from Montreal, Canada, to Caracas, Venezuela. His seat in this flight–within fifteen minutes of take-off–30,000 feet above sea level, en route to Aeropuerto Internacional de Maiquetia–would be 3rd class.

❧

Likewise, Master Judge scored points with 16-year-old Z2, from former Brazil. Rarely using her native name, she smiled when the bald-headed judge with pointed beard called her Zelia. But she made it clear to him to always address her as Z2 from this moment on. No intimacy allowed. However, she did provide him with geographical, social, and political background information of Venezuela, including maps of key cities he will certainly need to keep an eye on Gaston. Additionally, she offered him secret tips regarding the "Venezuelan character" in both metropolitan districts and rural areas.

Later in his Den, checking his facial looks and scornful smile in the wall mirror, he remarked, "Hummmm. A student revolution is about to explode out there. That should kill him!" Turning to a large poster of the 3Zs pinned to another wall, he cheered, "Thank you Z2." Of course, Z2 didn't know anything about Master Judge's personal plans and criminal intentions and would've never handed him this information.

❧

What neither Dr. Ufahh nor Master Judge knew, however, was that another factor existed that came into play, capable of derailing any and all their combined plans.

Such factor was Mipho—known to be well-rounded and intelligent as well as resourceful, creative, and skilled at using all sorts of manipulations to get what she wanted. She was currently on a mission to protect defendant octillionaire Richard Flynn (a.k.a. Richard Zilch)—the world's richest man and (to her mind) Ancient Egypt's latest Pharaoh.

Mipho—appearing under various names in many forms and styles, from ferocious three-headed lioness to Red Sea merchant ship crew member to Bermuda Revelation Park sky-anchored fuel station attendant to sexy femme fatale strutting her stuff in medieval circles and modern Montmartre's steep hills to six-year-old spoiled Peruvian girl to megayacht upper deck spy on a Miami Beach cruising trip to just a fly hovering over a Vatican's plush toilet—was quite apt at gathering intelligence from any part of the world on any given day.

Recently, she'd made it possible for Richard/Gaston to wear her own ancient peridot ring, once also worn with piety by Mary Magdalene in southern France and other religion-driven lands.

For now, she would go along with both Dr. Ufahh's and Master Judge's plan of relocating her renamed Pharaoh, Richard Zilch, to "Little Venice"—the way Christopher Columbus's fellow Italian navigator Amerigo Vespucci first began to call Venezuela when he saw the natives around Lake Maracaibo living in huts sustained by pillars in the water.

Oh well, there was plenty to be done by all concerned in the near and far future.

PART 13

GASTON'S LAST MOMENTS IN FRANCE (JULY 1955) AND FIRST MOMENTS IN VENEZUELA (JULY 1955) MINUTES APART

HAUNTING MEMORIES OF JULIETTE

Monsieur Douvier's Property, Saint-Jean-du-Gard

Juliette's white horse waited outside the gate.

Gaston mounted it again after exiting the cave, with no particular place to go, only a great desire to leave town and gallop away as far as his strength would allow.

Crossing the usual sprawl of cultivated vineyards, lavender flowers, and olive groves, boy and horse dashed away into the humbling sunset. In the farthest reaches of wind-blown grasslands, Gaston's mind swirled with remembrances of his beloved Juliette.

He could see her dancing...turning around ever faster like a top, then slower, holding a tennis racquet...her pleated white tennis skirt swooping up and down in a sinusoidal manner, revealing her delicate light blue panties...feline green eyes and carmine red lips partly hidden by the wild wrapping mass of silk golden hair around her face and neck. It all came down to a near stop when a photographic moment disclosed a fiery sexiness about everything he saw...plus the oddly angular way she grabbed her racquet...in front of the old pillared stone structure that guarded, like a devoted sentinel, the room he shared with Pierre.

The moment cleared and Juliette reappeared, this time near Grandpa, a cloaked monk, and her white Camargue horse. She hugged him tighter and longer than she ever had before and said without blinking, "If anything happens to me...promise me you will continue the horse-riding mission to Grotte de Trabuc..."

His immediate voiced promise, later fulfilled by actions, also whirled in his mind.

Fading lights of day blended now with rhythmic sounds of echoing horse's hooves. Gaston felt a strange pull...and he no longer was there...or anywhere near...

Above hovered Richard's soul.

BRAVING A NEW WORLD

Maiquetia, Caribbean Sea, Venezuela

The nine-year-old boy in the plane, the only one emerging from a mind-blowing past, knew no Spanish, had no friends, and felt no joy in arriving at Maiquetia.

Sitting next to him was a very attractive young girl about his age with a nice tan color to her face, big brown eyes, and thick cherry-red lips. Lots of black curls covered her round face.

She introduced herself as Zarita with awkward gestures of her hands, exaggerating the pronunciation of her words with her lips, having quickly realized they had a language barrier.

Her great effort to make him feel at ease impressed him. Now he knew there was something in this girl for him to explore.

Their friendship soared. By the time the plane landed, he could compose four types of simple sentences in Spanish with the dozen words or so he had learned.

Zarita's mother picked her up at the airport with an old van. No sweat, he already had her home address written on his forearm.

Things would pick up again for him. He would be strong and as clever and enduring as ever before. Besides, he would soon reunite with cousin Pierre and solidify his friendship with his new gal–well, *muchacha*–from *los médanos de Coro*, Venezuela!

Casually, he scratched his nose, feeling the presence of his ring on his finger.

A familiar sweet voice soothed his mind as he headed for the baggage pickup area, "...tell me more, Gaston, please...about these scary reveries you're having lately...about this mustached tycoon who looks so much like you and even claims to be you...fighting other humans... in those futuristic gigantic stadiums filled with roaring crowds... "

Gaston kept walking, realizing Juliette had not left him at all. Her memories would be with him, drifting in and out of his consciousness, competing against this new girl he'd just met or any girl he might meet along the way...on his journey to who knows where and why.

Above hovered Richard's soul.

THE END